序 言

　　大學愈來愈多，台灣勢必和美國一樣，未來沒有研究所畢業，很難找到好的工作。現在考研究所的人日益增加，競爭愈來愈激烈，準備研究所最好的方法，就是讀考古題，教授出來出去，都是大同小異。

　　「研究所英文試題詳解」這本書，已經出版多年，每年都有新的試題。研究所的試題太珍貴了，實在捨不得刪去，所以不得不分爲兩冊，每一冊都將近 1000 頁，厚度已經快到書的極限。要考上研究所，就必須把所有的考古題全部都讀完，各校試題的難易度相同，這些資料就等於是考研究所的範圍。

　　根據統計，歷屆研究所英文試題重複出現的機率很大，如80年台大的克漏字第一篇，在87年淡江大學的閱讀測驗第一篇出現，83年中正大學的閱讀測驗 "Alcoholism" 一文，在85年彰化師大及86年交大又重複出現，因此，從歷屆考古題中去發掘各研究所出題來源、命題趨勢，以及常考題型，使準備的範圍縮小，才能集中力量，一舉成功！

　　很多讀者問我們，爲什麼書出得那麼慢？因爲有些原來試題中錯誤的地方，我們一定要更正，每份試題，我們都要有詳細的解答，不馬馬虎虎，是「學習出版公司」一貫的原則。

　　本書另附「研究所最新考情資訊」與「研究所英文準備要點」，包括「文法重點整理」、「翻譯拿分要訣」、「閱讀解題妙招」、「作文拿分技巧」等，囊括所有必考的重心，幫助你在最短的時間內，做最完善的準備。本書編輯和全體工作人員本著審慎的原則和誠摯的態度，以期對研究所考生提供最佳的服務，若有任何疏漏之處，敬請各方先進不吝指教。

編者　謹識

目　錄

CONTENTS

CONTENTS

CONTENTS

CONTENTS

各校系研究所應考科目一覽表

學校	所	別	考　試　科　目
台 大	財務金融	EMBA	分析能力，管理實務，英文
		乙組	經濟分析，商用統計學，財務管理，英文
		丙組	應考：英文，微積分 選考：統計學，經濟學原理，工程數學（含微分方程、線性代數）（三擇一）
		丁組	經濟學原理，商用統計學，財務管理，英文
	國際企業	EMBA	分析能力，管理實務，英文
		乙組	微積分，經濟學，英文
		丁組	應考：微積分，英文 選考：工程數學（含微分方程、線性代數），統計學，經濟學（三擇一）
	會　計	EMBA	分析能力，管理實務，英文
		乙組	應考：中級會計學，成本及管理會計學，國文，英文 選考：審計學，統計學（二擇一）
	資訊管理	乙組	資訊科學（含資料結構、演算法），統計學，資訊科技（含資料庫、網路），資訊管理，英文
		丙組	資訊管理，系統分析，英文
	商　學	MBA	分析能力，管理實務，英文
		乙組	經濟學，統計學，英文
		丙組	經濟學，應用微積分，英文
	工業工程	甲組	應考：英文 選考：統計學，數學（線性代數、離散數學）（二擇一） 選考：資料結構，資訊科技（二擇一）
		乙組	應考：英文 選考：統計學，數學（二擇一） 選考：經濟學，計算機概論（二擇一）
		丙組	應考：英文 選考：作業研究，工程數學，統計學（三擇一） 選考：機械製造，生產管理，電子學（三擇一）
政 大	資訊管理	丙組	應考：國文，英文，管理資訊系統，計算機概論 選考：管理學，系統實務（二擇一）
	金　融		英文，統計學，經濟學，財務管理，微積分

學校	所	別	考　　試　　科　　目
政 大	風險管理 與　保　險	法律	會計學，英文，民法，保險法
		管理	應考：統計學，英文，保險學 選考：會計學，經濟學（二擇一）
		精算 科學	微積分，英文，統計學，數理統計學
	統　　計		國文，英文，統計學，數理統計學
	資訊科學		應考：英文，計算機概論，計算機系統 選考：計算機數學（一）（含離散數學及機率）， 　　　計算機數學（二）（含離散數學及線性代 　　　數）
	企業管理	甲組	應考：英文，經濟學 選考：統計學，會計學，管理學（三擇一）
		乙組	英文，經濟學，微積分
		丙組	英文，經濟學，管理實務個案
	財務管理		應考：英文，經濟學 選考：財務管理，統計學，微積分，會計學（四 　　　擇一）
	國際貿易	國經組 財管組 企管組	應考：英文，經濟學 選考：統計學，數學（微積分、線性代數）（二 　　　擇一）
		經貿 法組	英文，經濟學，商事法及民法
	資訊與圖書館		應考：國文，英文，電子計算機概論 選考：西洋文學概論，中國文學史，資訊儲存與 　　　檢索、中國通史，法學緒論、社會學，教 　　　育心理學、經濟學（五擇一） 選考：圖書資訊學，檔案學（二擇一）
	財　　政		應考：英文，財政學，經濟學 選考：會計學，微積分，統計學（三擇一）
	會　　計		國文，英文，會計學，成本與管理會計學，審計 學
	資訊管理	甲組	應考：國文，英文，管理資訊系統，計算機概論 選考：作業研究，會計學，統計學，經濟學（四 　　　擇一）
		乙組	應考：國文，英文，微積分，計算機概論 選考：離散數學，資料結構與演算法（二擇一）

學校	所	別	考　試　科　目
師大	資訊教育	資訊教育	計算機概論（含資料結構），數學（機率與統計），教育專業科目（含電腦輔助教學、教育心理學與資訊教育概論），國文，英文
		資訊科學	計算機概論（含資料結構），數學（線性代數與離散數學），教育專門科目（含作業系統、演算法與計算機結構），國文，英文
	資訊工程		數學基礎（含線性代數、離散數學），計算機系統（含計算機結構、作業系統），軟體基礎（含資料結構、演算法），國文，英文
中興	企業管理		國文，英文，管理學，經濟學
交大	資訊管理	甲組	計算機概論，資料結構與網際網路概論，英文
		乙組	英文，資訊管理概論，網際網路概論
	科技管理	甲組	應考：國文，英文，微積分 選考：計算機概論，經濟學（二擇一） 選考：物理，管理學，會計學（三擇一）
		乙組	應考：國文，英文，統計學 選考：計算機概論，經濟學（二擇一） 選考：物理，管理學，會計學（三擇一）
	經營管理	甲組	應考：國文，英文，微積分 選考：普通物理學，普通化學，生物學，心理學（四擇一）
		乙組	應考：經濟學，國文，英文 選考：會計學，社會學，商事法，統計學（四擇一）
中央	產業經濟	甲組	英文，統計學，微積分，經濟學原理
		乙組	英文，統計學，個體經濟學，總體經濟學
	企業管理		應考：英文，經濟學 選考：經濟學，管理學，統計學，會計學，微積分（五擇一）
成大	企業管理	戊組	應考：英文，統計學或微積分 選考：經濟學，計算機概論（二擇一） 選考：物理，化學，管理學（三擇一）
		己組	應考：英文，管理學，統計學 選考：醫務管理，心理學（二擇一）
	國際企業		應考：英文，經濟學，管理學 選考：統計學，微積分（二擇一）
	資訊管理	甲組	計算機概論，管理資訊系統，統計學，英文
		乙組	計算機概論，管理學，英文，管理資訊系統

學校	所 別		考　試　科　目
成大	工業管理科學	甲組	統計學，微積分，經濟學，英文
		乙組	統計學，管理學，經濟學，英文
	企業管理	乙組	應考：英文，經濟學，管理學 選考：會計學，行銷管理，企業政策（三擇一）
		丙組	英文，經濟學，管理學，統計學
		丁組	英文，經濟學，管理學，微積分
中正	企業管理	甲組	應考：管理學，英文 選考：經濟學，會計學，統計學（三擇一）
		乙組	應考：管理學，英文 選考：微積分，計算機概論（二擇一）
		丙組	應考：管理學，英文 選考：商事法，心理學（二擇一）
	會計	甲組	中級會計學，成本及管理會計學，商學英文
		乙組	初級會計學，管理資訊系統，商學英文
	資訊管理	甲組	應考：計算機概論，管理資訊系統，英文 選考：統計學，管理科學（二擇一）
		乙組	應考：計算機概論，資料結構，英文 選考：離散數學，資料庫（二擇一）
中山	人力資源管理		管理學，英文
高師大	資訊教育	A組	國文，英文，計算機概論，資訊教育專業科目
		B組	國文，英文，計算機概論，資訊科學專業科目
	數學	A組	分析（包括高等微積分及複變數函數），代數，微積分與線性代數，國文，英文
		B組	分析（包括高等微積分及複變數函數），代數，普通數學與數學教材教法，國文，英文
東吳	商用數學		應考：國文，英文，經濟學 選考：微積分，統計學（二擇一）
	經濟		國文，英文，總體經濟學，個體經濟學，統計學
	資訊科學		應考：計算機概論，國文，英文 選考：計算機系統，資訊管理（二擇一） 選考：離散數學，統計學（二擇一）
	數學		應考：國文，英文，高等微積分，線性代數 選考：微分方程，機率論，代數學（三擇一）
	企業管理	A組	應考：統計學，管理學，國文，英文 選考：經濟學，會計學（二擇一）

學校	所	別	考　　試　　科　　目
東 吳	企業管理	B組	應考：國文，英文，經濟學 選考：統計學，理則學，微積分（三擇一） 選考：管理學，商事法，組織行為，計算機概論，社會學（五擇一）
		C組	管理學，管理實務分析，當前經濟問題分析，國文，英文
	國際貿易	國際貿易金融	應考：國文，英文，經濟學，統計學 選考：國際貿易理論，貨幣銀行學，財務管理（三擇一）
		國際企業	國文，英文，經濟學，統計學，企業管理
	會　　計		國文，英文，財務會計學，成本及管理會計學，審計學
輔 大	金　　融		應考：國文，英文，經濟學 選考：會計學，統計學，電子計算機概論，微積分，財務管理（五擇二）
	經　　濟		國文，英文，個體經濟學，總體經濟學，統計學
	管　　理	甲組	應考：國文，英文，經濟學 選考：會計學，統計學，企業管理（三擇二）
		乙組	應考：國文，英文，經濟學 選考：微積分，管理學，計算機概論（三擇二）
		丙組	國文，英文，經濟學，企業個案分析，企業管理
	應用統計		應考：國文，英文 選考：統計學，微積分（二擇一） 選考：回歸分析，經濟學，計算機概論（三擇一）
	資訊管理	甲組	國文，英文，計算機概論，微積分，資料結構
		乙組	國文，英文，計算機概論，統計學，管理資訊系統
文 化	國際企業		應考：國文，英文，企業管理，經濟學 選考：會計學，統計學，微積分（三擇一）
	會　　計		國文，英文，會計學，成本與管理會計，審計學
	資訊管理		應考：國文，英文，計算機概論，資訊管理 選考：離散數學，統計學（二擇一）
	經　　濟		國文，英文，個體經濟學，總體經濟學，統計學
銘 傳	財務金融		應考：英文，經濟學，統計學 選考：財務管理，貨幣銀行學，微積分，計算機概論，會計學（五擇一）

學校	所　　　別		考　　試　　科　　目
銘傳	國際企業		應考：經濟學，統計學，英文 選考：會計學，管理學（二擇一）
	資訊管理		應考：計算機概論，管理學，英文 選考：資料結構，管理資訊系統（二擇一） 選考：微積分，統計學，離散數學（三擇一）
	傳播管理	甲組	傳播理論，當代傳播問題，英文
		乙組	經濟學，管理學，英文
東海	企業管理	甲組	應考：經濟學，統計學，英文 選考：企業管理，會計學（二擇一）
		乙組	應考：經濟學，微積分，英文 選考：企業管理，計算機概論（二擇一）
		丙組	審計學，財務會計，管理會計，英文
	工業工程	甲組	應考：國文，英文 選考：統計學，計算機概論，作業研究，線性代數與微積分（四擇二）
		乙組	應考：國文，英文 選考：統計學，計算機概論，經濟學，線性代數與微積分（四擇二）
	統　　計	甲組	線性代數與微積分，數理統計，統計學方法，英文
		乙組	微積分，統計學方法，英文
	資訊科學		計算機概論，離散數學，本國語文與英文
彰師大	會　　計		會計學，管理會計，審計學，英文，國文
	資訊管理		計算機概論，統計，資訊管理，英文
	人力資源管理		管理學，心理學，經濟學，英文
嘉義大	管　　理	甲組	經濟學，管理學，英文
		乙組	管理概論，個案分析，英文
		丙組	管理概論，個案分析，英文
	資訊工程		計算機概論，數學（含離散數學及資料結構），英文
南師	資訊教育	教學	國文，英文，計算機概論，資訊教學專業科目，數學（含機率、統計）
		科學	國文，英文，計算機既論，資訊教學專業科目，數學（含線性代數、離散數學）
屏科大	企業管理		國文，英文，統計學，管理學與經濟分析
	資訊管理	甲組	國文，英文，計算機概論，資料結構
		乙組	國文，英文，資訊管理導論，統計學
	工業工程		國文，英文，生產管理，統計學

學校	所	別	考　試　科　目
長	企業管理	科技與作業管理	應考：國文，英文，統計學 選考：經濟學，線性代數，微積分（三擇一）
		財務管理	應考：國文，英文，經濟學 選考：財務管理，統計學，會計學，微積分（四擇一）
		一般管理	應考：國文，英文，經濟學 選考：管理學，統計學，會計學，微積分（四擇一）
庚	資訊管理		應考：國文，英文，計算機概論 選考：統計學，離散數學，電腦網路，資料庫系統，管理資訊系統（五擇一）
	資訊工程		國文，英文，計算機數學（含線性代數、離散數學），計算機系統（含計算機結構、作業系統），軟體設計（含資料結構、演算法）
長榮管院	經營管理	甲組	應考：國文，英文，企業管理（含企業概論、管理學） 選考：微積分，統計學，作業研究（三擇一） 選考：會計學，計算機概論，經濟學（三擇一）
		乙組	應考：國文，英文 選考：管理資訊系統，資料庫管理，作業系統（三擇一） 選考：統計學，離散數學（二擇一）
淡	資訊工程	A組	國文，英文，數學，計算機概論（含資料結構、程式語言結構），計算機組織與系統
		B組	國文，英文，數學，計算機概論（含資料結構、程式語言結構），邏輯導論與機率論
	管理科學	A組	應考：英文，統計學，微積分 選考：經濟學，作業系統（二擇一）
		B組	應考：英文，統計學，管理學 選考：經濟學，會計學（二擇一）
江	國際貿易	A組	應考：國文，英文，經濟學，統計學 選考：管理學，財務管理，行銷學（三擇一）
		B組	國文，英文，個體經濟學，總體經濟學，統計學
	資訊與圖書館		國文，英文，圖書館學與資訊科學概論，參考資源與服務，圖書分類編目
	資訊管理	A組	國文，英文，資訊管理導論，統計學，資訊概論
		B組	國文，英文，離散數學導論，資科結構，資訊概論與程式設計

學校	所	別	考　試　科　目
淡 江	產業經濟	A組	應考：英文，個體經濟學，總體經濟學 選考：微積分，產業經濟學，計量經濟學（三擇一）
		B組	英文，個體經濟學，總體經濟學，統計學
	經　濟		英文，個體經濟學，總體經濟學，統計學
	運輸管理	A組	應考：國文，英文，運輸工程 選考：計算機概論，力學，數學（三擇二）
		B組	應考：國文，英文，運輸工程，統計學 選考：經濟學，作業系統，數學（三擇一）
逢 甲	企業管理		應考：英文，統計學，管理學 選考：會計學，經濟學，微積分，計算機概論（四擇一）
	財務金融		英文，財務管理，經濟分析，統計學
	保　險		應考：國文，英文，保險學，經濟學 選考：統計學，會計學，保險法（三擇一）
	會計財稅	甲組	英文，國文，會計學，租稅法，成本及管理會計
		乙組	英文，國文，會計學，財政學，經濟學
	經　濟		英文，個體經濟學，總體經濟學，統計學
	工業工程		應考：英文 選考：計算機概論，機率與統計學，作業系統，線性代數（四擇一） 選考：生產管理，人因工程，工程經濟，品質管理（四擇一）
	應用數學		英文，線性代數，微積分
	資訊工程		應考：國文，英文，計算機概論，基礎數學 選考：計算機結構學，系統程式（二擇一）
	統計與精算	統計	英文，微積分，統計學
		精算	應考：英文，微積分，統計學 選考：經濟學，機率論（二擇一）
	交通工程與管理		應考：英文，統計學或工程力學 選考：經濟學，計算機概論（二擇一） 選考：運輸工程，數學（二擇一）
大 同	事業經營	甲組	經濟學，國文，英文 選考：會計學、統計學，經營概論、微積分，經營概論、統計學（三擇一）
		乙組	經濟學，經營概論與個案分析，英文
	資訊工程	乙組	國文，英文
	應用數學		高等微積分，線性代數，英文

學校	所	別	考　試　科　目
大同	資訊經營		應考：計算機概論，英文 選考：資料結構與演算法，管理資訊系統（二擇一） 選考：統計學，管理科學（二擇一）
世新	行政管理		國文，英文，行政學
	資訊管理		應考：英文，電子計算機概論 選考：管理學，管理資訊系統，統計學（三擇一）
	經　濟		英文，個體經濟學，總體經濟學，統計學
	資訊傳播		國文，專業英文，資訊傳播學概論
元智	資訊傳播	網路傳播	英文，資訊網路應用，傳播理論
		數位媒體設計	英文，資訊網路應用，視覺分析
暨南	國際企業		應考：英文 選考：統計學，微積分，經濟學（三擇一）
	經　濟		總體經濟學，個體經濟學，統計學，英文
朝陽	企業管理		應考：經濟學，專業英文，統計學、微積分（二擇一） 選考：企業管理，會計學（二擇一）
	保險金融管理		保險學，專業英文，經濟學、統計學、會計學（三擇一）
義守	資訊管理	管理	計算機概論，機率與統計學，英文
		資訊	應考：計算機概論，英文 選考：計算機數學，微積分（二擇一）
	管　理		應考：管理應用英文 選考：微積分，經濟學，統計學，計算機概論，微積分（五擇一）
	資訊工程		英文，線性代數與離散數學，計算機概論
靜宜	資訊管理	甲組	計算機概論，英文，系統程式，離散數學
		乙組	計算機概論，英文，管理資訊系統，管理數學

94年各校研究所新增系所及科目變動一覽表

(一) 公立大學

學 校		考 試 科 目
政治大學	變更	企業管理學系、財務管理研究所
警察大學	變更	甄試：刑事警察所、犯罪防治所、消防科學所 一般：行政警察所 、刑事警察所、犯罪防治所、消防科學所、水上警察所、行政管理所、外事警察所、 公共安全所
台灣大學	新增	臺灣文學研究班、 法醫學所、資訊網路與多媒體所 科際整合法律學所
	變更	電子研究所奈米電子組 、 醫學院醫學檢驗暨生物技術學系、生物資源暨農學院動物科學技術學系
清華大學	變更	工業工程與工業管理系碩士班系
台北大學	變更	會計學系、犯罪學所
嘉義大學	新增	資訊管理學系
	變更	農學研究所碩士班、園藝學系碩士班、動物科學系碩士班、農業生物技術研究碩士班、運輸與物流工程研究碩士班、光電暨固態電子研究所碩士班、外國語言學系碩士班、應用化學系碩士班、休閒事業管理研究所碩士班
交通大學	新增	分子科學所
	變更	外國文學與語言學所、資訊科學與工程研究所碩士班、網路工程所碩士班、多媒體工程所碩士班、電機資訊學院聯合招生

(二) 私立大學

學 校		考 試 科 目
東海大學	新增	財務金融學系碩士班
玄奘大學	新增	外國語文所、教育人力資源與發展所
逢甲大學	新增	環境工程與科學學系博士班、科技管理研究所碩士班 在職專班： 保險學系、航太與系統工程學系
	變更	**資訊電機工程碩士在職專班：** 「資訊工程組」、「電機與自動控制組」、「電子與通訊組」 **經營管理碩士在職專班：** 「經營管理組」、「高階管理組」

中國醫藥大 學	變更	中國醫學所、中國藥學所、藥物化學所、醫務管理學所、環境醫學所、藥學系碩士班、醫學研究所臨床醫學組、醫學研究所基礎醫學組、中西醫結合所、營養所、職業安全與衛生學系碩士班
華梵大學		碩士在職專班「資通安全組」

(三) 師範大學

學　校	考　試　科　目	
台中師範學院	新增	體育學系碩士班、音樂教育學系碩士班、教育測驗統計所博士班
	變更	早期療育所、社會科教育學系碩士班、特殊教育與輔助科技所、語文教育學系碩士班、美勞教育學系碩士班、諮商與教育心理所
彰化師範大 學	新增	統計資訊研究所碩士班
花蓮師範學院	變更	多元文化教育所

(四) 科技大學

學　校	考　試　科　目	
高科大	新增	系統與控制工程所、科技法律研究所
	變更	營建工程系、系統與控制工程所、風險管理與保險系、運籌管理系、資訊管理系、財務管理系、企業管理所、應用日語系在職專班：運籌管理系
嘉南藥理科技大學	變更	碩士在職專班及碩士班、生物科技系
北科大	變更	冷凍空調工程系碩士班、自動化科技所、電機工程系碩士班、電腦與通訊所、資訊工程系碩士、光電工程系碩士班、土木與防災所、環境規劃與管理所、材料及資源工程系碩士班、化學工程所、生物科技所、工業工程與管理系碩士班、技術及職業教育所
台科大	變更	碩士班甄試：高分子工程系、化學工程系、電機工程系、企業管理系、資訊管理系、財務金融研究所 博士班甄試：化學工程系、電機工程系 碩博士在職專班：電機工程系

國立師範大學九十學年度
碩士班研究生入學考試英文試題

I. Vocabulary: 20%

Choose the most appropriate word according to the given context.

1. After years of _____, the unfortunate woman was forced to live in poverty.
   (A) deficiency　　　　　　(B) affluence
   (C) possession　　　　　 (D) mortality

2. As an architect, John Nelson witnesses the overall process, from the birth of an idea to paperwork, the making of a model, and _____ the erection of a concrete house.
   (A) eternally　　　　　　(B) exclusively
   (C) ecologically　　　　 (D) eventually

3. In addition to having a stressful life, people living in modern society have to be patient and _____ when they deal with those around them.
   (A) skillful　　　　　　 (B) amateur
   (C) incompetent　　　　　(D) stunned

4. It really is more accurate to think of accumulation of knowledge to be a _____ of East and West.
   (A) paradigm　　　　　　 (B) manufacture
   (C) synthesis　　　　　　(D) compound

5. It seems that both the official and the non-official recordings of the social reformer's contributions have either been forgotten or _____.
   (A) perceived　　　　　　(B) uttered
   (C) overlooked　　　　　 (D) rewarded

6. Ms. Lin always tells her students that it's not
   _____ to ask questions in class. At least,
   they know what they don't know and they are not
   doing anything wrong.
   (A) shameful   (B) refined
   (C) immortal   (D) upright

7. My boyfriend and I had frequent quarrels over our
   dates because I was often late. I then struggled
   between an attempt to _____ the relationship
   and do what I wanted to do.
   (A) assert   (B) maintain
   (C) demolish   (D) suspect

8. The principle is that if a person gets in trouble
   due to his ideals instead of his own moral
   _____ , I will help him. Hence, no matter
   whether someone is a 'big potatoe' or a nameless
   hero, I went to help.
   (A) assets   (B) residual
   (C) merits   (D) flaws

9. Users of Linux are _____ Internet service
   providers, software developers, universities and,
   now, large corporations.
   (A) drastically   (B) elegantly
   (C) primarily   (D) urgently

10. With his own clinic opened, the dentist was able to
    _____ the number of patients instead of being
    forced to see as many as 200 in half a day.
    (A) confine   (B) limit
    (C) defy   (D) restrain

II. Cloze: 20%

Tropical forests are located in some 70 countries, but about 80 percent are in Bolivia, Brazil, Colombia, Gabon, Indonesia, Malaysia, Peru, Venezuela, and Zaire. The rain forests ___(1)___ nearly half of all the plants, animals, and insects in the world. Notes the World Wildlife Fund, "More species of fish live in the Amazon River than in the entire Atlantic Ocean."

Tropical plants produce chocolate, nuts, fruits, gums, coffee, waxes, wood and wood products, rubber and petroleum substitutes, and ingredients ___(2)___ toothpaste, pesticides, fibers, and dyes.

In addition, several medical wonders of the twentieth century have come from plants found only in rain forests. These plants have been used to treat high blood pressure, cancer, and Parkinson's disease. A tiny flower from the rain forest in Madagascar, ___(3)___, is key to a drug that has been successfully used to treat leukemia. And rain forests may hold the answer to ___(4)___ for several types of cancer. A study of the Costa Rican rain forest found that 15 percent of the plants studied had potential as anti-cancer agents.

"We are destroying the biological heritage that developed ___(5)___ billions of years and doing it in a matter of a few human generations," says Paul Ehrlich of Stanford University. "Our descendants, if any, will be very much the poorer for it."

1. (A) live with   (B) are home to
   (C) need to have   (D) do not grow

2. (A) made of   (B) known as
   (C) living on   (D) found in

3. (A) as a result   (B) at least
   (C) for example   (D) in other words

4. (A) treatment   (B) destruction
   (C) termination   (D) danger

5. (A) on   (B) at
   (C) over   (D) with

As scholars and citizens of the world understand more of the interrelationships of cultures, we gain an appreciation of the evolution of civilization as a cross-fertilization of many cultures over the few thousand years of recorded history. I am intrigued by the process of sharing information and discovery among societies, ___(6)___ they are separated by distance, language and value systems.

Information in the form of invention and discovery is often shared (or incorporated) ___(7)___ the nature of the perceived value to others. Marco Polo's travels to China in the 13th century offered Western society a look at undiscovered (to them) goods and ideas. Ideas and inventions often were added to the "native" culture ___(8)___ notice of the origin. One of the greatest secrets of history is the immense contribution of Chinese society to the Western world. Equally interesting is the failure of some discoveries in China to cross over to Western civilization, or even to survive into modern times. For example, a smallpox vaccination ___(9)___ in

China in the 10th century, and then 800 years later in the West. However, the practice of modern diagnostic medicine was not widespread in China in more modern times. The mechanical clock was invented in China in the 8th century, ＿＿＿(10)＿＿＿ independently in Europe in 1310. When the Chinese imperial court was shown a mechanical clock by Jesuit missionaries in the 17th century, the scholars were awestruck.

6. (A) often　　　　　　　(B) however
   (C) although　　　　　　(D) more

7. (A) for the sake of　　(B) as far as
   (C) in case of　　　　　(D) due to

8. (A) so much　　　　　　(B) with little
   (C) for few　　　　　　(D) as none

9. (A) had used　　　　　　(B) was using
   (C) was used　　　　　　(D) used

10. (A) and then　　　　　　(B) for sure
    (C) later on　　　　　　(D) at last

III. Matching: 20%

Choose the most appropriate word for each of the blanks below.

Flowers are sunny, positive, and full of vitality. The sight, the smell, and the touch of them delight me so ＿＿＿(1)＿＿＿. When I look at how flowers blossom and ＿＿＿(2)＿＿, I can see and feel how time goes by, how everything changes. I consider myself pretty lucky to be able to combine my interests with my work, and to do my job in such an ＿＿＿(3)＿＿ environment.

I believe everyone is endowed with talents in a certain field. As for me, I am very ___(4)___ with numbers, but I have always had a keen sense of how flowers can be arranged to look their best. Therefore, when I graduated from the horticulture department of a vocational school, I decided to ___(5)___ a career that utilized my abilities. I really didn't know what ___(6)___ I could do. But it took me ten years to accumulate enough experience, confidence, and investment ___(7)___ to start up my own business.

I opened this flower shop last March, and pay a monthly ___(8)___ of NT$50,000. After one year in operation, I was ___(9)___ able to make ends meet, and began to reap investment returns. Nonetheless, it's ___(10)___ that I'll make big money by operating such a small shop. But I didn't expect anything else when I decided to engage in this business.

A. capital　　B. calculate　C. unlikely　D. rent
E. pursue　　F. awkward　　G. far　　　H. holistically
I. agreeable　J. bonus　　　K. else　　　L. wither
M. much　　　N. abrupt　　　O. finally

IV. Reading Comprehension: 20%

When my father spoke to me, he always began the conversation with "Have I told you yet today how much I adore you?" The expression of love was **reciprocated** and, in his later years, as his life began to visibly ebb, we grew even closer...if that were possible.

At 82 he was ready to die, and I was ready to let him go so that his suffering would end. We laughed and cried and held hands and told each other of our love and agreed that it was time. I said, "Dad, after you've gone I want a sign from you that you're fine." He laughed at the absurdity of **that**; Dad didn't believe in reincarnation. I wasn't positive I did either, but I had had many experiences that convinced me I could get some signal "from the other side."

My father and I were so deeply connected I felt his heart attack in my chest at the moment he died. Later I mourned that the hospital, in their sterile wisdom, had not let me hold his hand as he had slipped away.

Day after day I prayed to hear from him, but nothing happened. Night after night I asked for a dream before I fell asleep. And yet four long months passed and I heard and felt nothing but grief at his loss. Mother had died five years before of Alzheimer's, and, though I had grown daughters of my own, I felt like a lost child.

One day, while I was lying on a massage table in a dark quiet room waiting for my appointment, a wave of longing for my father swept over me. I began to wonder if I had been too demanding in asking for a sign from him. **I noted that my mind was in a hyper-acute state**. I experienced an unfamiliar clarity in which I could have added long columns of figures in my head. I checked to make sure I was awake and not dreaming, and I saw that I was as far removed from a dreamy state as one could possibly be. Each thought I had was like a drop of water disturbing a still pond, and I marveled at the peacefulness of each passing moment. Then I thought, "I've been trying to control the messages from the other side; I will stop that now."

Suddenly my mother's face appeared — my mother, as she had been before Alzheimer's disease had stripped her of her mind, her humanity and 50 pounds. Her magnificent silver hair crowned her sweet face. She was so real and so close I felt I could reach out and touch her. She looked as she had a dozen years ago, before the wasting away had begun. I even smelled the fragrance of Joy, her favorite perfume. She seemed to be waiting and did not speak. I wondered how it could happen that I was thinking of my father and my mother appeared, and I felt a little guilty that I had not asked for her as well.

I said, "Oh, Mother, I'm so sorry that you had to suffer with that horrible disease."

She tipped her head slightly to one side, as though to acknowledge what I had said about her suffering. Then she smiled — a beautiful smile — and said very distinctly, "But all I remember is love." And she disappeared.

I began to shiver in a room suddenly gone cold, and I knew in my bones that the love we give and receive is all that matters and all that is remembered. Suffering disappears; love remains.

Her words are the most important I have ever heard, and that moment is forever engraved on my heart.

I have not yet seen or heard from my father, but I have no doubt that someday, when I least expect it, he will appear and say, "Have I told you yet today that I love you?"

1. Which of the following phrases defines the word "**reciprocate**" in paragraph 1?
   (A) To share the feelings and behave the same way.
   (B) To turn down the invitation and refuse to show up.
   (C) To become closer to each other.
   (D) To become more responsible.

2. In paragraph 2, what does "**that**" refer to?
   (A) The thought of a dead person becoming alive.
   (B) The thought that a dead person could be fine.
   (C) The idea of receiving messages from the dead.
   (D) The idea that one can be positive about death.

3. Which of the following sentences is closest in meaning to the sentence "**I noticed that my mind was in a hyper-acute state.**" in paragraph 5?
   (A) I realized that I was half-asleep.
   (B) I found myself flying high in the air.
   (C) I thought I was in a dreamy state.
   (D) I knew that I was wide-awake.

4. In paragraph 6, why did the author mention his mother's favorite perfume, Joy?
   (A) To show that he felt his mother's presence.
   (B) To convince the readers that he liked his mother very much.
   (C) To prove that he had good memories of his mother.
   (D) To indicate that he felt guilty for not asking for his mother.

5. What is the main idea of this article?
  (A) Receiving a message from one's parents after they are dead could be very meaningful.
  (B) The love we give and receive is what is remembered and remains after everything goes away.
  (C) People will come back to you after they die if you always think about them.
  (D) If you ask anybody for a sign "from the other side," you will never get it.

The Dalai Lama and Vice President Annette Hsiou-lien Lu, both reviled by the Chinese government, which accuses them of promoting separatism, shared the stage yesterday and appealed for peace and understanding from Beijing. On the second day of a 10-day visit to Taiwan, the Tibetan spiritual leader, accused by Beijing of visiting the island to collaborate with "Taiwan independence forces," led the first of a series of public sermons to the faithful.

Asked by a listener if he would be willing to spread the Dharma, or Buddhist law, in officially atheist China, the Dalai Lama said it would first require some enlightenment on Beijing's part. "Everywhere, if there are some people who are really eager to learn from the Dharma, then it is our duty and responsibility to explain," the Nobel Peace Prize laureate said. "So in the future, of course, when the sort of political situation — or I think the way of thinking in the minds of the government of the People's Republic of China — becomes more open, more realistic, then of course everything will be easy."

While the Dalai Lama has said he was on a purely spiritual journey, China's state-run Xinhua news agency said his meeting with members of the ruling DPP government showed a political agenda. "The Dalai Lama's second Taiwan trip will certainly be a political visit for collaborating with Taiwan independence forces to separate Taiwan from the motherland," Xinhua said. "With such a political backdrop, how could the Dalai Lama's trip be a pure 'religious tour'?"

Lu, whom China has branded "scum of the nation" for describing Taiwan and China as "close neighbors but distant relatives," thanked the Dalai Lama for braving China's disapproval and showing concern for Taiwan. "Tibetan compatriots have faced all kinds of oppression from the Chinese Communist Party, but he still has the heart and compassion to come to Taiwan, because he knows we have many difficulties as well," she said in an address ahead of an interfaith prayer meeting attended by the Dalai Lama. "Don't forget, 90 nautical miles away, on the coast of the Chinese mainland, 300 missiles have already been deployed, and 50 more will be added every year," she said. "With so many religious leaders here, we hope to use Buddhist compassion to pray that all people with power will be humble, work hard, love the people, be peaceful and treat all life with kindness," Lu said.

Aside from Lu's appearance, the meeting's focus was more spiritual than political. Followers held hands in prayer or waved Tibet's snow lion flag as the exiled spiritual leader addressed them from a five-tier stage decorated with a large tapestry of the Buddha. Sitting on a throne with his legs crossed, the Dalai Lama told the crowd in a packed stadium that real happiness comes from "a sense of satisfaction in the heart," not from physical comfort.

The Dalai Lama fled his Himalayan homeland after a failed 1959 uprising against Chinese rule. More than 120,000 refugees followed him to India, where his government-in-exile is based in the northern city of Dharamsala.

6. What is the main idea of paragraph 3?
   (A) The purpose of the Dalai Lama's second trip to Taiwan was to cooperate with Taiwan independence group.
   (B) Xinhua news agency claimed that the Dalai Lama wanted to separate Taiwan from the motherland.
   (C) The Dalai Lama's main purpose of the trip to Taiwan was to visit the ruling party, the DPP.
   (D) The Chinese government believed that the Dalai Lama visited Taiwan for a political reason.

7. According to this article, why was the Vice President of Taiwan, Annette Lu, considered "scum of the nation" by China?
   (A) Because she thanked the Dalai Lama for showing his concern for Taiwan.
   (B) Because she considered China as a neighbor rather than a family member.
   (C) Because she wanted to use Buddhist compassion to bring peace to China.
   (D) Because she criticized China for deploying missiles everywhere.

8. Which of the following statements about the Dalai
   Lama is true?
   (A) He and over 120,000 of his followers fled to
       India in the late 1950s.
   (B) He visited Taiwan two times in the same year
       and stayed 10 days each trip.
   (C) His trips to Taiwan were considered as more
       political than religious by all.
   (D) He was eager to enlighten Beijing regardless of
       what China thinks about him.

9. According to this article, on what condition will
   the Dalai Lama be willing to spread the Buddhist
   doctrine in China?
   (A) When China agrees to let Tibet become
       independent.
   (B) When Taiwan and China are united under one
       government.
   (C) When the political situation in China becomes
       more open and more realistic.
   (D) When Xinhua news agency stops criticizing him
       for making spiritual journeys.

10. What would be a good title for this article?
    (A) The Dalai Lama and Vice President Lu.
    (B) The Dalai Lama and His Journey to Taiwan.
    (C) The Dalai Lama and His Relationship with China.
    (D) The Dalai Lama and His Followers.

IV. Writing: 20%

   Read the following news report and write a passage
   of no more than 150 words to express your opinions.

   Acting on a letter of complaint, Tainan prosecutors
carried out a search of student dorms at Cheng-kung
University in Tainan on April 11, during which they
confiscated 14 computers.

　　　　While some maintain that any unauthorized download is illegal, some hold that the students' acts could be exempted on the ground of "fair use." The Copyright Law prohibits unauthorized "reproduction" of literary works, sound recordings, photographs and computer programs. In theory, one could be held liable under the law for simply downloading or printing material from the Web without authorization. However, the law allows exemptions under the circumstances of "fair use," which include the use of copyrighted materials for educational purposes, in the judicial process, or for personal non-profit use.

國立師範大學九十年度
碩士班研究生入學考試英文試題詳解

I. 字彙：20 ％

1. (**A**)　(A) ***deficiency*** 〔 dɪˈfɪʃənsɪ 〕 *n.* 缺乏；不足
　　　(B) affluence 〔 ˈæfluəns 〕 *n.* 富裕
　　　(C) possession 〔 pəˈzɛʃən 〕 *n.* 擁有；財產
　　　(D) mortality 〔 mɔrˈtælətɪ 〕 *n.* 難逃一死；死亡人數
　　　be forced to 被迫

2. (**D**)　(A) eternally 〔 ɪˈtɜnəlɪ 〕 *adv.* 永恆地
　　　(B) exclusively 〔 ɪkˈsklusɪvlɪ 〕 *adv.* 排外地；僅限於
　　　(C) ecologically 〔 ˌɛkəˈlɑdʒɪkl̩ɪ 〕 *adv.* 在生態學方面
　　　(D) ***eventually*** 〔 ɪˈvɛntʃuəlɪ 〕 *adv.* 最後；終於
　　　architect 〔 ˈɑrkəˌtɛkt 〕 *n.* 建築師
　　　witness 〔 ˈwɪtnɪs 〕 *v.* 目擊
　　　overall 〔 ˈovɚˌɔl 〕 *adj.* 全部的
　　　paperwork 〔 ˈpepɚˌwɜk 〕 *n.* 設計工作
　　　mode 〔 mod 〕 *n.* 樣式
　　　erection 〔 ɪˈrɛkʃən 〕 *n.* 建造；豎立
　　　concrete 〔 ˈkɑnkrit 〕 *adj.* 混凝土的

3. (**A**)　(A) ***skilful*** 〔 ˈskɪlfəl 〕 *adj.* 巧妙的；熟練的
　　　(B) amateur 〔 ˈæməˌtʃur 〕 *adj.* 業餘的
　　　(C) incompetent 〔 ɪnˈkɑmpətənt 〕 *adj.* 無能力的
　　　(D) stunned 〔 stʌnd 〕 *adj.* 吃驚的
　　　stressful 〔 ˈstrɛsfəl 〕 *adj.* 緊張的；壓力大的
　　　deal with 與～交往

4. (**C**) (A) paradigm〔'pærə,daɪm〕*n.* 範例

(B) manufacture〔,mænjə'fæktʃə〕*v.* 製造

(C) ***synthesis***〔'sɪnθəsɪs〕*n.* 結合體；合成

(D) compound〔'kɑmpaʊnd〕*n.* 混合物

　　accurate〔'ækjərɪt〕*adj.* 準確的

　　accumulation〔ə,kjumjə'leʃən〕*n.* 累積

5. (**C**) (A) perceive〔pə'siv〕*v.* 察覺

(B) utter〔'ʌtə〕*v.* 說

(C) ***overlook***〔,ovə'luk〕*v.* 忽略

(D) reward〔rɪ'wɔrd〕*v.* 報酬

　　recording〔rɪ'kɔrdɪŋ〕*n.* 記錄

　　reformer〔rɪ'fɔrmə〕*n.* 改革者

　　contribution〔,kɑntrə'bjuʃən〕*n.* 貢獻

6. (**A**) (A) ***shameful***〔'ʃemfəl〕*adj.* 可恥的

(B) refined〔rɪ'faɪnd〕*adj.* 精製的；高尚的

(C) immortal〔ɪ'mɔrtl̩〕*adj.* 不朽的

(D) upright〔'ʌp,raɪt〕*adj.* 正直的

　　illegal〔ɪ'ligl̩〕*adj.* 非法的

7. (**C**) (A) assert〔ə'sɝt〕*v.* 聲稱；斷言

(B) maintain〔men'ten〕*v.* 維持

(C) ***demolish***〔dɪ'mɑlɪʃ〕*v.* 破壞；撤銷

(D) suspect〔sə'spɛkt〕*v.* 懷疑

　　quarrel〔'kwɔrəl〕*n.* 爭吵　　date〔det〕*n.* 約會

　　struggle〔'strʌgl̩〕*v.* 掙扎

　　attempt〔ə'tɛmpt〕*n.* 企圖；嘗試

8. (**D**) (A) assets〔'æsɛts〕*n. pl.* 資產；財產
   (B) residual〔rɪ'zɪdʒʊəl〕*n.* 剩餘
   (C) merit〔'mɛrɪt〕*n.* 優點
   (D) ***flaw***〔flɔ〕*n.* 瑕疵
      principle〔'prɪnsəpḷ〕*n.* 原則
      moral〔'mɔrəl〕*adj.* 道德的
      big potato 大人物   ***nameless hero*** 無名英雄

9. (**C**) (A) drastically〔'dræstɪkḷɪ〕*adv.* 大大地；徹底地
   (B) elegantly〔'ɛləgəntlɪ〕*adv.* 高雅地
   (C) ***primarily***〔'praɪ,mɛrəlɪ〕*adv.* 主要地
   (D) urgently〔'ɝdʒəntlɪ〕*adv.* 迫切地
      software〔'sɔft,wɛr〕*n.* 軟體
      corporation〔,kɔrpə'reʃən〕*n.* 公司

10. (**B**) (A) confine〔kən'faɪn〕*v.* 使侷限
    (B) ***limit***〔'lɪmɪt〕*v.* 限制；限定
    (C) defy〔dɪ'faɪ〕*v.* 公然反抗
    (D) restrain〔rɪ'stren〕*v.* 抑制
       clinic〔'klɪnɪk〕*n.* 診所   dentist〔'dɛntɪs〕*n.* 牙醫

II. 克漏字：20 %

【譯文】

　　熱帶森林遍布約七十個國家，而約有百分之八十的林地，是位於玻利維亞、巴西、哥倫比亞、加澎、印尼、馬來西亞、祕魯、委內瑞拉，以及薩伊。熱帶森林是全世界約一半的動植物及昆蟲的棲息地。世界野生動植物基金會指出：「住在亞馬遜河裏的魚類，比整個大西洋還多。」

熱帶植物能製成巧克力、堅果、水果、口香糖、咖啡、蠟、木頭和木製品，橡膠、石油替代物，以及牙膏、殺蟲劑、纖維和染料中的原料。

此外，二十世紀有一些醫學的奇蹟，都是來自雨林中的植物。這些植物已被用來治療高血壓、癌症，以及帕金森氏症。例如，在馬達加斯加所發現的小花，就是某種藥物的主要成份，而這種藥能成功地治療血癌。雨林可能可以提供治療好幾種癌症的方法。一項針對哥斯大黎加的雨林所做的研究發現，其所研究的植物中，有百分之十五，可能可以培養出抗癌藥劑。

「我們人類大約只用了幾個世代的時間，就破壞了數十億年來所形成的生物遺產，」史丹佛大學的保羅‧伊林區說，「我們的子孫，如果他們真的存在的話，將會因而變得非常不幸。」

【註】

tropical〔'trɑpɪkl̩〕*adj.* 熱帶的　　***be located in*** 位於
some〔sʌm〕*adv.* 大約　　***rain forest*** 雨林
note〔not〕*v.* 提到　　wildlife〔'waɪld'laɪf〕*n.* 野生動植物
species〔'spiʃɪz〕*n.* 種　　gum〔gʌm〕*n.* 口香糖 (= *chewing gum*)
wax〔wæks〕*n.* 蠟　　petroleum〔pə'trolɪəm〕*n.* 石油
substitute〔'sʌbstə,tjut〕*n.* 替代物
ingredient〔ɪn'gridɪnt〕*n.* 成份；原料
toothpaste〔'tuθ,pest〕*n.* 牙膏
pesticide〔'pɛstɪ,saɪd〕*n.* 殺蟲劑
fiber〔'faɪbɚ〕*n.* 纖維　　dye〔daɪ〕*n.* 染料
Parkinson's disease 帕金森氏症　　tiny〔'taɪnɪ〕*adj.* 微小的
key〔ki〕*n.* 關鍵　　leukemia〔lu'kimɪə〕*n.* 白血病；血癌
potential〔pə'tɛnʃəl〕*n.* 可能性　　agent〔'edʒənt〕*n.* 劑
heritage〔'hɛrətɪdʒ〕*n.* 遺產　　***in a matter of*** 大約
descendent〔dɪ'sɛndənt〕*n.* 子孫　　poor〔pur〕*adj.* 不幸的

1. **(B)** 依句意,選 (B) *be home to*「是~的棲息地」。

2. **(D)** 這些原料是可以「在」牙膏、殺蟲劑、纖維和染料「中被找到」,故選 (D) *found in*。而 (A) be made of「由~製成」,(B) be known as「被稱為」,(C) living on「以~維生」,則不合句意。

3. **(C)** (A) as a result　因此
    (B) at least　至少
    (C) *for example*　例如
    (D) in other words　換句話說

4. **(A)** (A) *treatment*〔ˋtritmənt〕 *n.* 治療
    (B) destruction〔dɪˋstrʌkʃən〕 *n.* 破壞
    (C) termination〔ˌtɝməˋneʃən〕 *n.* 終結

5. **(C)** 表「在~期間」,介系詞用 *over*,選 (C)。

【譯文】

　　隨著全球的學者與民眾更了解文化間相互依存的關係後,我們就能體認到有歷史記載的幾千年來,人類文明是如何因為相互間的交流而進步。雖然各個文明社會中相隔甚遠,語言與價值觀亦不相同,但他們之間仍有資訊與新發現共享的現象,這個過程令我非常感興趣。

　　以發明與新發現為形式的資訊,通常會相互分享(或合作),而這樣做是由其他人察覺到了這個資訊本身是非常有價值的。馬可波羅十三世紀到中國的遊歷,提供了西方世界一個可以觀察到前所未見(對他們而言)的貨品與觀念的機會。觀念與發明通常都會被融入「當地

的」文化中，至於出處爲何是不太有人注意的。歷史上最大的祕密之
一，是中國文明對西方文明的巨大貢獻。同樣讓人感興趣的是，中國
的一些發明，無法傳達到西方世界，或甚至還無法保留到現代。例如，
中國在第十世紀的時候，就有天花疫苗接種了，而西方卻直到八百年
後才出現。然而，中國現代化的醫藥診療，即使在晚近仍沒有廣泛實
施。中國在第八世紀就發明了機械鐘，而歐洲在西元一三一〇年時才
自己發明出來。而當耶穌會傳教士在十七世紀的中國宮廷展示機械鐘
時，所有的文人學者卻都肅然起敬。

【註】

interrelationship〔͵ɪntərɪ'leʃənʃɪp〕 *n.* 相互關連；相互的依存關係

appreciation〔ə͵priʃɪ'eʃən〕 *n.* 了解

evolution〔͵ɛvə'luʃən〕 *n.* 演進

civilization〔͵sɪvələ'zeʃən〕 *n.* 文明

cross-fertilization〔'krɔs͵fɝtḷə'zeʃən〕 *n.* （思想、文化、技術等）進
   行交流而相互得益；相互影響

intrigue〔ɪn'trig〕 *v.* 激發好奇心；使感興趣

incorporate〔ɪn'kɔrpə͵ret〕 *v.* 合併　　perceive〔pɚ'siv〕 *v.* 察覺

travels〔'trævḷz〕 *n. pl.* 遊記　　origin〔'ɔrədʒɪn〕 *n.* 起源

immense〔ɪ'mɛns〕 *adj.* 巨大的

smallpox〔'smɔl͵pɑks〕 *n.* 天花

vaccination〔͵væksn̩'eʃən〕 *n.* 疫苗接種

practice〔'præktɪs〕 *n.*（醫生的）業務；工作

diagnostic〔͵daɪəg'nɑstɪk〕 *adj.* 診斷的

mechanical〔mə'kænɪkḷ〕 *adj.* 機械的

imperial〔ɪm'pɪrɪəl〕 *adj.* 帝國的　　court〔kort〕 *n.* 宮廷

Jesuit〔'dʒɛʒuɪt, -zjuɪt〕 *n.* 耶穌會的信徒

missionary〔'mɪʃən͵ɛrɪ〕 *n.* 傳教士

awestruck〔'ɔ͵strʌk〕 *adj.* 畏懼的；肅然起敬的

6. (**B**)　依句意，選 (B) *although*「雖然」。

7. (**D**)　依句意，選 (D) *due to*「由於」。而 (A) 為了～緣故，(C) 如果，
皆不合句意。

8. (**B**)　依句意，「不太」注意起源，選 (B) *with little*。

9. (**C**)　依句意為過去式的被動語態，故選 (C) *was used*。

10. (**A**)　原句是由…, and then it was invented
independently…簡化而來。而 (C) 須改為 and later on
才能選。

III. 配合題：20 ％

【譯文】

　　花朵是快活、積極向上，而且神采奕奕的。花的模樣、香味與觸
感，都讓我非常快樂。當我看到花朵如何綻放與枯萎，我彷彿看到時
間如何流逝，萬物如何幻化。我認為我非常的幸運，能將我的興趣與
工作結合在一起，而且還能在這樣賞心悅目的環境中工作。

　　我相信天生我才必有用。以我自己為例，對於數字我是非常的遲
鈍，但對於如何排列，才能讓花朵展現它最美的一面，這方面我卻非
常的敏銳。因此，自從我從職業學校的園藝系畢業以後，就決定要從
事能讓我發揮所長的職業。除此之外，我真的不知道我還能做什麼其
他的工作。但這卻花了我十年的時間，以累積足夠的經驗與自信，還
有一筆足夠的資金，開創我自己的事業。

　　去年三月，我開了這家花店，每月付五萬元的租金。開業一年之
後，我漸漸能夠收支平衡，而且開始回本。儘管要靠經營這間小店賺
大錢是不太可能的，但是當我決定要做這一行時，就已別無所求了。

【答案】

1. (**M**)　　2. (**L**)　　3. (**I**)　　4. (**F**)　　5. (**E**)

6. (**K**)　　7. (**A**)　　8. (**D**)　　9. (**O**)　　10. (**C**)

【註】

positive〔'pɑzətɪv〕adj. 積極的；正面的

vitality〔vaɪ'tælətɪ〕n. 活力　　blossom〔'blɑsəm〕v. 開花

wither〔'wɪðɚ〕v. 凋謝　　**go by**（時間）過去

agreeable〔ə'griəbḷ〕adj. 令人愉快的

be endowed with 天生具有　　field〔fild〕n. 領域

keen〔kin〕adj. 敏銳的　　horticulture〔'hɔrtɪˌkʌltʃɚ〕n. 園藝

vocational school 職業學校　　utilize〔'jutḷˌaɪz〕v. 利用

accumulate〔ə'kjumjəˌlet〕v. 累積　　capital〔'kæpətḷ〕n. 資金

start up a business 開店；成立公司

monthly〔'mɛnθlɪ〕adj. 每月的　　rent〔rɛnt〕n. 租金

operation〔ˌɑpə'reʃən〕n. 經營

make ends meet 使收支相抵

reap〔rip〕v. 獲得　　returns〔rɪ'tɜnz〕n. pl. 利潤

nonetheless〔ˌnʌnðə'lɛs〕adv. 雖然如此；但是

engage in 從事

IV. 閱讀測驗：20%

【譯文】

　　當我父親跟我說話的時候，他總是以這句話當開場白：「我今天跟你說過有多愛你了嗎？」這種愛的表達是互相的，而在他晚年，身體日漸衰弱時，我們變得更加親密…如果還有可能的話。

　　當他八十二歲時，已行將就木，而且我已有心理準備，要讓他就此往生，以停止他的痛苦。我們又哭又笑，握著彼此的手，訴說對彼此的愛，而且都同意大限已至。我說：「老爸，你往生之後，一定要讓我知道你過得很好」。他認為這樣的想法太過荒謬，而大笑不已；他並不相信所謂的投胎轉世。我也不是很確信，但我之前有很多經驗，讓我相信我能從「另一個世界」得到一些訊息。

　　我與父親之間的關係是如此的密切，所以當他心臟病發作而死亡時，我的胸口甚至可以感受得到。後來，院方的食古不化令我十分惋惜，他們不願讓我在他過世的一剎那，握著他的手。

　　我日日祈禱能得到父親的消息，但卻什麼也沒發生。我夜夜在入睡前祈求能夢到父親。但漫長的四個月過去了，除了失去他的悲痛外，我仍然聽不到也感受不到任何東西。母親在五年前因為阿滋海默症而過世，雖然當時我的女兒都已經長大成人了，我還是覺得自己像個迷失的小孩。

　　有一天，當我躺在安靜而黑暗的房間裡的按摩床上，等候預約時間時，一陣對父親的渴望情緒突然在我心中湧現。我開始懷疑，是不是因為我實在太想知道父親的情況才會如此。我注意到我的精神是完全處於高度敏銳的狀態。我當時頭腦清晰程度是前所未有的，要我用心算算出一長串的數字加總，也沒有問題。我確信我是清醒的，而不是在作夢，而且我也知道，自己絕不可能是在夢境中。每一個思緒對我而言，就好像是一滴滴在平靜無紋的小池塘的水滴一樣，而我也驚嘆，在每個流逝的時刻都是如此的安詳。之後我就心想：「我已經試著控制來自另一個世界的訊息了；我應該適可而止了。」

　　突然間，我母親的臉龐出現了——是我母親受到阿滋海默症折磨她心靈、人性與瘦了五十磅前的臉孔。她那美麗的銀髮，如皇冠般覆蓋在她甜美的臉龐上。她是如此的真實與接近，我甚至認為只要我伸出手，就可以碰觸到她。她看來就像十幾年前，還沒開始消瘦前一樣。我甚至可以聞到「愉悅」的香味，那是她最喜歡的香水。她似乎在等待什麼，而默然不語。我在想怎麼會在我想念我父親的時候，是我母親出現呢？而且我還為沒有對她有相同的渴求，而感到些許的愧疚。

我說：「喔，媽媽，我對妳必須受到如此可怕的病痛折磨，感到非常的遺憾。」

她將頭稍微地偏向一邊，好像承認我對她的痛苦所說的話一樣。之後她笑了一下，那是個非常美麗的微笑，接著非常清楚地說：「但是我只記得愛而已。」然後就消失了。

她突然變冷的房間裏，我開始發抖，我深深地知道，最重要的是我們互相分享的愛。痛苦會消失，但愛卻可以永遠留存。

她的話是我聽過最重要的話，而那一刻也永遠銘記在我心中。

我到現在還是沒看過或聽到我父親的消息，但我確信有一天，當我比較不想他的時候，他自然就會出現了，而且會跟我說：「我今天跟你說過我有多愛你了嗎？」

【答案】

1. (**A**)　　2. (**C**)　　3. (**D**)　　4. (**A**)　　5. (**B**)

【註】

expression〔ɪkˋsprɛʃən〕n. 表達
reciprocate〔rɪˋsɪprə‚ket〕v. 報答；互惠
visibly〔ˋvɪzəblɪ〕adv. 看得見地；明顯地
ebb〔ɛb〕v. 衰退　　suffering〔ˋsʌfərɪŋ〕n. 痛苦
sign〔saɪn〕n. 信號　　absurdity〔əbˋsɝdətɪ〕n. 荒謬

reincarnation〔͵riɪnkɑr'neʃən〕*n.* 再投胎；轉世

positive〔'pɑzətɪv〕*adj.* 確定的　　signal〔'sɪgnḷ〕*n.* 信號

heart attack 心臟病發作　　chest〔tʃɛst〕*n.* 胸部

mourn〔morn〕*v.* 感到惋惜

sterile〔'stɛrəl〕*adj.* (思想或講話) 缺乏新意的

slip away 去世　　*hear from* 得到某人的消息

pray〔pre〕*v.* 祈禱　　grief〔grif〕*n.* 悲傷

Alzheimer's〔'ɑlts͵haɪmɚz〕*n.* 阿滋海默症

grow〔gro〕*v.* 罹患　　massage〔mə'sɑʒ〕*n.* 按摩

wave〔wev〕*n.* (情緒的) 突發；高漲

longing〔'lɔŋɪŋ〕*n.* 渴望　　sweep〔swip〕*v.* 橫掃；掠過

demanding〔dɪ'mændɪŋ〕*adj.* 苛求的

hyper-〔'haɪpɚ〕過度的　　acute〔ə'kjut〕*adj.* 敏銳的

clarity〔'klærətɪ〕*n.* 清晰　　column〔'kɑləm〕*n.* 列

figure〔'fɪgjɚ〕*n.* 數字　　remove〔rɪ'muv〕*v.* 移開

dreamy〔'drimɪ〕*adj.* 似夢的　　still〔stɪl〕*adj.* 靜止的

pond〔pɑnd〕*n.* 池塘　　marvel〔'mɑrvḷ〕*v.* 感到驚訝 < *at* >

passing〔'pæsɪŋ〕*adj.* 瞬間的　　strip〔stɪp〕*v.* 剝奪 < *of* >

humanity〔hju'mænətɪ〕*n.* 人性

magnificent〔mæg'nɪfəsənt〕*adj.* 華麗的；極美的

crown〔kraun〕*v.* 為…加冕　　*reach out* 伸出 (手臂)

waste away 消瘦　　fragrance〔'fregrəns〕*n.* 香味

tip〔tɪp〕*v.* 傾斜　　acknowledge〔ək'nɑlɪdʒ〕*v.* 承認

shiver〔'ʃɪvɚ〕*v.* 發抖　　engrave〔ɪn'grev〕*v.* 銘記

turn down 拒絕　　*show up* 出現

wide-awake〔'waɪdə͵wek〕*adj.* 十分清醒的

presence〔'prɛzṇs〕*n.* 存在；在場

【譯文】

達賴喇嘛與副總統呂秀蓮兩人，都曾被中國政府大加韃伐，控訴他們鼓吹獨立，而昨日兩人同台，呼籲北京應有和平與相互理解的善意。這位西藏精神領袖的此次訪台，被北京指為與「台灣分離勢力」掛勾之旅，在此次十天訪台行程中的第二天，他開始了一連串為信徒舉行佈道大會的第一場典禮。

當聽眾問他，是否願意在官方意識型態上，為無神論的中國弘揚藏傳秘宗或佛法時，達賴喇嘛回答說，首先必須要北京方面有些許受到啓蒙的跡象才行。「不論在任何地方，如果有人真的想要修習藏傳秘宗，我們都有責任為他闡明教義。」這位諾貝爾和平獎得主說。「當然以後只要中華人民共和國的政治情勢，或我認為政府當局的想法變得更加開明、更加實際時，任何事情當然都會變得比較容易。」

當達賴喇嘛說，此次訪台純粹只是精神之旅的同時，中國官方的新華社卻報導，這次他與執政的民進黨員會面，顯示了一種政治訊息。「達賴喇嘛第二次訪台，毫無疑問是個為了與台獨勢力掛勾，以分離祖國的政治性訪問。」新華社說。「在這樣的政治背景下，達賴喇嘛訪台，怎麼可能單純只是『宗教之旅』？」

呂秀蓮，因為曾經形容中國與台灣的關係為「遠親近鄰」，而被中國扣上「國家的人渣」的帽子，十分感謝達賴喇嘛敢勇於對抗中國對他的否定，並表達對台灣的關心。她在一場達賴出席的跨宗教的祈禱大會上致詞時說：「西藏同胞面臨了中國共產黨各種層面的打壓，但他仍有心且深具慈悲地來台灣訪問，因為他知道我們也有很多相同的困難」。「我們別忘了，在九十海浬外的中國大陸沿海，有三百枚飛彈已經部署完成，而且每年還會增加五十枚。」她接著說：「有這麼多宗教領袖群聚於此，我希望我們能用佛教的慈悲為懷，祈禱所有權力的人都能謙遜、努力做事、愛護人民、追求和平，並且能以仁心對待所有的生命。」

　　除了呂秀蓮的出現外，這次大會的焦點著重於心靈層面，而非政治層面。當這位被放逐的精神領袖，從鋪著佛陀畫像的刺繡毛毯的五階舞台上走下為信徒佈道時，信徒們都合手祈禱，或揮舞著西藏雪獅旗。達賴喇嘛盤腿坐在寶座上，對著擠滿整個體育館的信眾說，真正的快樂來自於「心靈的滿足感」而非物質的享受。

　　達賴喇嘛在一九五九年反抗中國統治的起義行動失敗後，從喜馬拉雅山的故鄉逃亡。有超過十二萬名流亡者，跟隨他到位於印度北方達蘭沙拉城的流亡政府。

【答案】

6. (**D**)　　7. (**B**)　　8. (**A**)　　9. (**C**)　　10. (**B**)

【註】

revile〔rɪ'vaɪl〕*v.* 辱罵　　accuse〔ə'kjuz〕*v.* 指控 < *of* >

promote〔prə'mot〕*v.* 提倡

separatism〔'sɛpərə,tɪzm̩〕*n.* 分離主義

appeal〔ə'pil〕*v.* 呼籲 < *for* >　　Tibetan〔tɪ'bɛtən〕*adj.* 西藏的

collaborate〔kə'læbə,ret〕*v.* 合作；通敵 < *with* >

a series of 一連串的　　sermon〔'sɝmən〕*n.* 佈道

the faithful 信徒　　spread〔sprɛd〕*v.* 傳播

Dharma〔'dɑrmə〕*n.* 藏傳密宗　　Buddhist〔'budɪst〕*adj.* 佛教的

officially〔ə'fɪʃəlɪ〕*adv.* 官方地　　atheist〔'eθɪɪst〕*n.* 無神論者

enlightenment〔ɪn'laɪtmənt〕*n.* 啓蒙

on one's part 就某人而言　　laureate〔'lɔrɪɪt〕*n.* 得獎者

purely〔'pjurlɪ〕*adv.* 純粹地；完全

state-run〔'stet,rʌn〕*adj.* 國營的

news agency 新聞通訊社　　ruling〔'rulɪŋ〕*adj.* 執政的

agenda〔əˈdʒɛndə〕n. 議程；討論事項

backdrop〔ˈbækˌdrɑp〕n. 背景　　brand〔brænd〕v. 加…污名於

scum〔skʌm〕n. 渣滓；人渣　　brave〔brev〕v. 敢於冒犯

compatriot〔kəmˈpetrɪət〕n. 同胞

oppression〔əˈprɛʃən〕n. 壓迫

compassion〔kəmˈpæʃən〕n. 憐憫；同情

interfaith〔ˈɪntɚˈfeθ〕adj. 不同宗教間的

prayer〔ˈpreɚ〕n. 祈求；禱告　　nautical〔ˈnɔtəkl̩〕adj. 海上的

missile〔ˈmɪsl̩〕n. 飛彈　　deploy〔dɪˈplɔɪ〕v. 部署

humble〔ˈhʌmbl̩〕adj. 謙遜的　　*aside from*　除了…之外

follower〔ˈfɑləwɚ〕n. 教徒　　exile〔ˈɛgzaɪl〕v. 放逐

address〔əˈdrɛs〕v. 向～發表演說

tier〔tɪr〕n.（階梯式座位的）一排；一層

tapestry〔ˈtæpɪstrɪ〕n. 刺繡毛毯

Buddha〔ˈbʊdə〕n. 佛陀　　throne〔θron〕n. 寶座

packed〔pækt〕adj. 塞得滿滿的；擁擠的

stadium〔ˈstedɪəm〕n. 體育場　　fleed〔flid〕v. 逃走；逃離

Himalayan〔hɪˈmɑljən〕adj. 喜馬拉雅山脈的

homeland〔ˈhomˌlænd〕n. 祖國；家鄉

uprising〔ˈʌpˌraɪzɪŋ〕n. 起義；叛亂

refugee〔ˌrɛfjʊˈdʒi〕n. 難民；流亡者

base〔bes〕v. 以～為基地　　sue〔su〕v. 控告

enlighten〔ɪnˈlaɪtn̩〕v. 啟發　　cooperate〔koˈɑpəˌret〕v. 合作

claim〔klem〕v. 聲稱　　motherland〔ˈmʌðɚˌlænd〕n. 祖國

ruling party　執政黨　　doctrine〔ˈdɑktrɪn〕n. 教義

Tibet〔tɪˈbɛt〕n. 西藏

IV. 寫作：20 %

Copyright Law and the Internet

The recent incident at Cheng-kung University, in which 14 computers were seized because students were suspected of illegally downloading information, shows that the public must become better informed of copyright issues where the Internet is concerned. This is a confusing issue because it is permissable to download information or print material in some cases, but not in others. In my opinion, most people are not aware of the laws governing copyrighted material, especially on the Internet.

Perhaps those students at Cheng-kung were unfairly profiting from the Internet, but it is more likely that they were unaware that what they were doing was wrong. We often hear that the Internet is full of free information, and many websites offer free services to subscribers. This may give people the impression that everything on the Internet is free when, in fact, it is not. I believe that the best solution to the problem is to educate the public about their rights and responsibilities when using the Internet. In this way, the problem can be avoided in the future.

國立政治大學九十學年度
碩士班研究生入學考試英文試題

I. Vocabulary: 30%

In each of the following 15 sentences there is a blank where a word is left out. Choose the answer that best completes the sentence and write its corresponding letter on the answer sheet.

1. Despite the worldwide economic downturn, many small companies here did well enough to _____ the recession.
   (A) weather
   (B) wither
   (C) withdraw
   (D) whittle

2. I consider it reasonable that the law _____ every car must have seat belts for the driver and every passenger.
   (A) articulates
   (B) stipulates
   (C) manipulates
   (D) circulates

3. According to some analysts, the recent interest rate rises have _____ new problems for the government.
   (A) stressed
   (B) snorted
   (C) startled
   (D) sparked

4. The government decided to _____ those foreign workers because they had no visas.
   (A) repatriate
   (B) retrieve
   (C) reiterate
   (D) recline

5. One of the president's advisors is a well-known shipping _____. He owns more than 100 container ships.
   (A) mandate
   (B) magnet
   (C) magnate
   (D) maggot

6. The new administration faces almost _____ difficulties in its attempt to unite its country's people.
   (A) insurgent   (B) immortal
   (C) incredulous   (D) insurmountable

7. The new managing director has reorganized the company a bit, but nothing has _____ changed.
   (A) reluctantly   (B) arguably
   (C) forcibly   (D) fundamentally

8. Apparently what she did was wrong, but I don't think it _____ quite such severe punishment.
   (A) sprinkled   (B) guaranteed
   (C) warranted   (D) commanded

9. Most participants agreed that the richer countries of the world should take _____ action to help the poorer countries.
   (A) concerted   (B) conceived
   (C) convicted   (D) convinced

10. The teacher was found guilty of being _____ in allowing the children to swim in dangerous water.
    (A) ingenious   (B) negligent
    (C) vigilant   (D) congenial

11. He has spent the past three months in the US, _____ for medical treatment, but in actual fact to avoid prosecution.
    (A) permanently   (B) vehemently
    (C) ostensibly   (D) inquisitively

12. The uniformed soldier looked _____ among the group of civilians.
    (A) conspicuous   (B) prospective
    (C) flammable   (D) authentic

13. Don't you think it immoral to declare racial
    _____ against ethnic minorities?
    (A) campaign   (B) antipathy
    (C) sanction   (D) embargo

14. In order to repair barns, build fences, grow crops, and
    care for animals, a farmer must indeed be _____.
    (A) versatile   (B) elusive
    (C) lucrative   (D) divergent

15. The quality of university teaching may be _____
    if the government increases the number of students
    without providing additional funding.
    (A) fabricated   (B) integrated
    (C) jeopardized   (D) outstayed

II. Grammar: 20%

   For each sentence, identify the one underlined part
   that is grammatically incorrect, and write its
   corresponding letter on the answer sheet.

1. <u>On</u> my break, I came out <u>behind</u> the counter and <u>passed</u>
   A   B   the time</u> with two men <u>who ran</u> a shoeshine stand in a
   C   D
   dark corner of the corridor.

2. Freedom of speech is the lifeblood of <u>the democratic</u>
                                          A
   <u>system</u>, and <u>especially is</u> important for minorities
   B
   because <u>often it is</u> their only vehicle for <u>rallying</u>
   C
   <u>support</u> for the redress of their grievances.
   D

3. People <u>who are secure</u> enough to develop an enduring,
           A

mutual, affectionate <u>relationship with</u> another
                       B

person <u>have accomplished</u> an <u>extraordinary</u> difficult
          C   D

psychological task.

4. In recent years, the elitist view <u>which</u> only "high
                             A

art" is <u>worthy of study</u> has been challenged, <u>since</u>
        B   C

all cultural productions, <u>high or low</u>, reveal the
                          D

social meanings of our world.

5. If credibility replaces reality <u>as</u> the decisive test
                           A

of truth-telling, political leaders <u>need not be</u>
                                 B

<u>troubled</u> very much with reality <u>provides</u> that their
                            C

performances consistently <u>generate</u> a sense of
                         D

verisimilitude.

6. The cost of living has <u>skyrocketed</u>, unemployment has
                     A

gone up, <u>going to college</u> doesn't guarantee you can
             B

get a good job, and many young people are underachievers

who <u>loaf around</u> the house until <u>well passing</u> their
       C   D

college years.

7. The blurring of cultural styles occurs in <u>everyday</u>
                               A

<u>life</u> to a <u>great</u> extent than anyone can imagine and
        B

<u>causes</u> a sensational conflict <u>between</u> people of
    C   D

different backgrounds.

8. The sale and domestic production of semiautomatic assault weapons <u>must be stopped</u>; these <u>killing machines</u>
A   B
clearly <u>have no</u> legitimate sporting purpose, <u>since</u>
C   D
the president recognized when he permanently banned their importation.

9. Men are <u>airing</u> their frustration with the <u>limited</u>
A   B
rules they face today, compared with the multiple options that women seem <u>to have won</u>, so they are
C
groping to redefine themselves <u>on their own terms</u>.
D

10. The prospects of <u>women's</u> professional team sports
A
don't look bright, and the reasons for the lack of financial support have gone beyond simple <u>economics</u>
B
and <u>have entered</u> the realm of <u>rooted-deeply</u> sexual
C   D
bias and homophobia.

III. 30%

Reading Comprehension: Each reading passage is followed by five questions. Choose the best answer to each question, and write its corresponding letter on the answer sheet. 20%

Passage 1

Many educators now see the transformation of history into social studies as the root of what's wrong. Social studies began in the 1930s as an effort to make

the subject more "relevant." Paul Hanna, its original
champion, wrote that children were failing to "face the
realities of this world in which we live — they escape,
they retreat to a romantic realm of yesterday." Social
studies developed fully in the 1960s and 1970s, when
such romantic stories and legends were frequently
replaced in the lower grades by studying family and
neighborhood life. In higher grades, social studies came
to mean an interdisciplinary approach that threw history
into an academic stew with psychology, anthropology,
ethnic studies, civics, and other subjects.

The results have been discouraging. The "romantic
realm" Hanna denigrated turns out to have a narrative
thrust and natural appeal far more memorable than soupy
sociology. "Kids like history because it's the story
of real people," says Elaine Reed of the Ohio-based
Bradley Commission, which helps states reform their
history programs.

As a practical matter in elementary school,
there's just not enough time in the day to make history
separate from civics, community issues and similar
topics, but the aim should be for history and geography
to play a larger role in the mix. And from junior
high on, it makes more sense to define the subject as
history. Otherwise schools are providing "escape
hatches for uninterested students to satisfy their
diploma requirements." When psychology or anthropology
or even driver's education classes count as social
studies, it's no wonder so many students don't know
anything about the Civil War.

1. According to the passage, which of the following is true?
   (A) Students like social studies more than history.
   (B) Social studies became popular three or four decades ago.
   (C) History is a major subject in high school.
   (D) Children are not fond of true stories.

2. Which of the following is NOT mentioned in the passage?
   (A) The history of different ethnic groups should be taught.
   (B) History programs are changing.
   (C) A lot of students are not familiar with the Civil War.
   (D) Ethnic studies are included in the interdisciplinary programs.

3. Why was Paul Hanna regarded as a champion in this passage?
   (A) He defeated other educators.
   (B) He knew history has a natural appeal.
   (C) He disagreed with the interdisciplinary approach.
   (D) He fought against the romantic realm.

4. In the last paragraph, the phrase "escape hatches" means _____
   (A) the teacher does not have enough time to discuss community issues.
   (B) history and social studies are practical.
   (C) history is neglected in social studies.
   (D) Students can avoid studying history by taking other social studies courses.

5. The author believes that ───────
   (A) students do not have enough knowledge of history.
   (B) the geography program should be changed.
   (C) history should be a separate subject in elementary school.
   (D) social studies is more important than history.

Passage 2

The world oceans make up a vast desert, desperately short of nutrients and with living things spread most thinly through them. This is the shocking message of our inquiry into the blueness of the sea. Our generation has been treated to tales about the sea as the last frontier. No journalist seems to be able to write on the subject of feeding the hungry without mentioning farming the oceans, as if they were some great untapped source of food for people. But they are not. The oceans are deserts with little more food in them than we are taking out already.

The reason for this appalling unproductiveness of the sea is the scarcity of chemical fertiliser. On land, fertilising nutrients can sometimes be in short supply too, though wild vegetation usually manages to hoard and recycle the stuff to meet its needs. As a result, unless there is no water, or it is winter and too cold, the production of land plants is limited by shortage of the raw material carbon dioxide. In the sea, plants get their carbon in solution as bicarbonate, and usually they get more than they can use. And the reason the tiny sea plants cannot work up to their carbon limit is that they first run out of chemical fertilizers such as iron, phosphate, or nitrate.

But nature herself has made some patches of the sea fertile, for this is where we go fishing — the North Sea, the Newfoundland Banks, the waters off Peru — and it seems strange that some patches in this fluid thing, the sea, can be fertile, because the waters that support the fisheries are continuously replaced. Where there are shallow banks or island arcs, the moving currents of the deep sea are forced to the surface, so that the water flows up from below. A similar thing can happen when two deep currents meet head-on so that water is forced upward, leading to some of the celebrated "upwellings." In all these places of banks and upwellings, life is provided with a vertical, slowmoving conveyor belt of water that brings endless supplies of fresh nutrients from the depths.

6. Which of the following is mentioned in the passage?
   (A) The waters off Peru are chemically different.
   (B) People may not have enough fertilising nutrients.
   (C) Chemical fertilisers determine productivity
   (D) The hungry can obtain food in different ways.

7. According to the passage, which of the following is true?
   (A) Sea plants do not have enough bicarbonate.
   (B) Fertilisers are good for fisheries.
   (C) The deep sea has fewer nutrients than shallow waters.
   (D) The ocean is not a place of unlimited wealth.

8. Wild vegetation _____
   (A) survives in cold winter.
   (B) can store fertilizers.
   (C) is often unproductive.
   (D) grows better in the sea.

9. How does constant water replacement fertilize the sea?
   (A) The deep sea currents move up.
   (B) The deep sea currents move down.
   (C) The shallow sea currents move up.
   (D) The shallow sea currents move down.

10. People tend to believe that _____.
    (A) journalists write about the sea
    (B) the sea will keep provide more and more food.
    (C) farming the sea will destroy the environment
    (D) the last frontier lacks living things

Cloze Test: The following passage has 5 blanks. For each blank there are four possible answers. Choose the best answer and write its corresponding letter on the answer sheet. 10%

English has 1,120 different ways of spelling its 40 phonemes, the ___(11)___ required to pronounce all its words, ___(12)___, Italian needs only 33 combinations of letters to spell out its 25 phonemes. ___(13)___, reading Italian takes a lot less effort, and that's probably why the reported rate of dyslexia in Italy is barely half that in the U.S., where about 15% of the population is affected to varying degrees. ___(14)___, Americans spend more than $1 billion a year to help their kids cope with dyslexia. Many Italian dyslexics, ___(15)___, aren't even aware they have a problem — and would notice it only if given a battery of psychological tests.

11. (A) voices   (B) accents
    (C) sounds   (D) utterances

12. (A) Of course   (B) By contrast
    (C) Moreover   (D) In addition

13. (A) As a result   (B) By and large
    (C) In the meantime   (D) Nonetheless

14. (A) Based on comparison (B) According to figures
    (C) With this in mind   (D) On the contrary

15. (A) on the other hand   (B) in other words
    (C) apart from that   (D) under this condition

IV. Translate the following sentences into English: 20%

 1. 更具意義的事實是，植物不可能在水庫沿岸自行繁衍。

 2. 他發覺自己對家庭的牽絆比他想逃避責任的欲望更強烈。

 3. 在觀看表演時談話顯然是非常不好的行為，但是許多人非常大聲地竊竊私語，卻以為沒人會聽得到。

 4. 令人吃驚的是，時至今日，很多人仍不知道什麼會構成性騷擾，也不知道他們所引起的苦惱與憤怒。

國立政治大學九十年度
碩士班研究生入學考試英文試題詳解

I. 字彙：30 ％

1. (**A**)　(A) **weather**〔'wɛðɚ〕v. 平安度過（困境）
　　　　 (B) wither〔'wɪðɚ〕v. 枯萎
　　　　 (C) withdraw〔wɪð'drɔ〕v. 撤回
　　　　 (D) whittle〔'hwɪtḷ〕v. 削減
　　　　　 downturn〔'daʊntɜn〕n.（經濟）衰退
　　　　　 recession〔rɪ'sɛʃən〕n. 經濟蕭條

2. (**B**)　(A) articulate〔ɑr'tɪkjəˌlet〕v. 清楚地表達
　　　　 (B) **stipulate**〔'stɪpjəˌlet〕v. 規定
　　　　 (C) manipulate〔mə'nɪpjəˌlet〕v. 操作
　　　　 (D) circulate〔'sɜkjəˌlet〕v. 循環
　　　　　 seat belt 安全帶

3. (**D**)　(A) stress〔strɛs〕v. 施壓；強調
　　　　 (B) snort〔snɔrt〕v. 哼著鼻子說
　　　　 (C) startle〔'stɑrtḷ〕v. 使驚訝
　　　　 (D) **spark**〔spɑrk〕v. 導致
　　　　　 analyst〔'ænḷɪst〕n. 分析者
　　　　　 interest rate 利率

4. (**A**)　(A) **repatriate**〔ri'petrɪˌet〕v. 遣返
　　　　 (B) retrieve〔rɪ'triv〕v. 取回；恢復
　　　　 (C) reiterate〔ri'ɪtəˌret〕v. 不斷重述
　　　　 (D) recline〔rɪ'klaɪn〕v. 往後靠
　　　　　 visa〔'vizə〕n. 簽證

5. (**C**) (A) mandate〔ˋmændet〕*n.* 命令

(B) magnet〔ˋmægnɪt〕*n.* 磁鐵

(C) ***magnate***〔ˋmægnet〕*n.* 鉅子

(D) maggot〔ˋmægət〕*n.* 蛆

advisor〔ədˋvaɪzɚ〕*n.* 顧問　　***container ship*** 貨櫃船

6. (**D**) (A) insurgent〔ɪnˋsɝdʒənt〕*adj.* 反叛的

(B) immortal〔ɪˋmɔrtḷ〕*adj.* 不朽的

(C) incredulous〔ɪnˋkrɛdʒələs〕*adj.* 不相信的

(D) ***insurmountable***〔͵ɪnsɝˋmauntəbḷ〕*adj.* 無法克服的

administration〔əd͵mɪnəˋstreʃən〕*n.* 政府

unite〔juˋnaɪt〕*v.* 使團結

7. (**D**) (A) reluctantly〔rɪˋlʌktəntlɪ〕*adv.* 不情願地

(B) arguably〔ˋɑrgjuəblɪ〕*adv.* 可辯論地

(C) forcibly〔ˋforsəblɪ〕*adv.* 有力地；強制地

(D) ***fundamentally***〔͵fʌndəˋmɛntḷɪ〕*adv.* 基本上；本質上

managing director 總經理

reorganize〔riˋɔrgə͵naɪz〕*v.* 組織再造

8. (**C**) (A) sprinkle〔ˋsprɪŋkḷ〕*v.* 灑

(B) guarantee〔͵gærənˋti〕*v.* 保證

(C) ***warrant***〔ˋwɔrənt〕*v.* 使有正當理由；成為～的根據

(D) command〔kəˋmænd〕*v.* 命令；指揮

severe〔səˋvɪr〕*adj.* 嚴厲的

9. (**A**) (A) ***concerted***〔kənˋsɝtɪd〕*adj.* 一致的

(B) conceive〔kənˋsiv〕*v.* 認為

(C) convicted〔kənˋvɪktɪd〕*adj.* 被定罪的

(D) convinced〔kənˋvɪnst〕*adj.* 確信的

participant〔pɑrˋtɪsəpənt〕*n.* 參與者

take action 採取行動

10. (**B**) (A) ingenious〔ɪn'dʒinjəs〕*adj.* 靈巧的
        (B) ***negligent***〔'nɛglədʒənt〕*adj.* 疏忽的
        (C) vigilant〔'vɪdʒələnt〕*adj.* 有警覺的
        (D) congenial〔kən'dʒinjəl〕*adj.* 意氣相投的
        guilty〔'gɪltɪ〕*adj.* 有罪的

11. (**C**) (A) permanently〔'pɝmənəntlɪ〕*adv.* 永久地
        (B) vehemently〔'viəməntlɪ〕*adv.* 狂暴地
        (C) ***ostensibly***〔ɑs'tɛnsəblɪ〕*adv.* 表面上地
        (D) inquisitively〔ɪn'kwɪzətɪvlɪ〕*adv.* 好奇地
        medical treatment 醫療
        prosecution〔ˌprɑsɪ'kjuʃən〕*n.* 起訴

12. (**A**) (A) ***conspicuous***〔kən'spɪkjuəs〕*adj.* 引人注目的
        (B) prospective〔prə'spɛktɪv〕*adj.* 有希望的
        (C) flammable〔'flæməbl̩〕*adj.* 易燃的
        (D) authentic〔ɔ'θɛntɪk〕*adj.* 眞正的
        uniform〔'junəˌfɔrm〕*v.* 穿上制服
        civilian〔sə'vɪljən〕*n.* 平民

13. (**B**) (A) campaign〔kæm'pen〕*n.* 競選活動
        (B) ***antipathy***〔æn'tɪpəθɪ〕*n.* 反感
        (C) sanction〔'sæŋkʃən〕*n.* 制裁
        (D) embargo〔ɪm'bɑrgo〕*n.* 禁運
        racial〔'reʃəl〕*adj.* 種族的
        ethnic〔'ɛθnɪk〕*adj.* 民族的
        minority〔maɪ'nɔrətɪ〕*n.* 少數
        ethnic minorities 少數民族

14. (**A**) (A) *versatile*〔ˋvɝsətḷ〕*adj.* 多才多藝的
    (B) elusive〔ɪˋlusɪv〕*adj.* 巧妙地逃避的；難以捉摸的
    (C) lucrative〔ˋlukrətɪv〕*adj.* 有利益的
    (D) divergent〔dəˋvɝdʒənt〕*adj.* 分歧的
      barn〔bɑrn〕*n.* 穀倉   fence〔fɛns〕*n.* 籬笆

15. (**C**) (A) fabricate〔ˋfæbrɪ͵ket〕*v.* 製造
    (B) integrate〔ˋɪntə͵gret〕*v.* 整合
    (C) *jeopardize*〔ˋdʒɛpəd͵aɪz〕*v.* 危害
    (D) outstay〔aʊtˋste〕*v.* 久留
      additional〔əˋdɪʃənḷ〕*adj.* 額外的
      fund〔fʌnd〕*v.* 提供資金

II. 文法：20%

1. (**B**) *behind* → *from behind*
    break〔brek〕*n.* 休息   counter〔ˋkaʊntɚ〕*n.* 櫃台
    run〔rʌn〕*v.* 經營   *shoeshine stand* 擦鞋攤
    corridor〔ˋkɔrədɚ〕*n.* 走廊

2. (**B**) *especially is* → *is especially*
    lifeblood〔ˋlaɪf͵blʌd〕*n.* 命脈
    democratic〔͵dɛməˋkrætɪk〕*adj.* 民主的
    vehicle〔ˋvi(h)ɪkḷ〕*n.* 媒介   rally〔ˋrælɪ〕*v.* 集合
    redress〔rɪˋdrɛs〕*n.* 補救；賠償
    grievance〔ˋgrivəns〕*n.* 抱怨；委屈

3. (**D**) *extraordinary* → *extraordinarily*
    secure〔sɪˋkjʊr〕*adj.* 有自信的；有安全感的
    enduring〔ɪnˋdjʊrɪŋ〕*adj.* 持久的
    mutual〔ˋmjutʃʊəl〕*adj.* 互相的
    affectionate〔əˋfɛkʃənɪt〕*adj.* 深情的

4. (**A**) *which* → ***that***　　that 引導名詞子句，做 view 的同位語。
　　view〔vju〕*n.* 看法
　　elitist〔ɪ'litɪst〕*n.* 精英主義者　***be worthy of*** 值得

5. (**C**) *provides* → ***provided***　　***provided that*** 如果 (= *if*)
　　credibility〔,krɛdə'bɪlətɪ〕*n.* 信任
　　decisive〔dɪ'saɪsɪv〕*adj.* 決定性的
　　consistently〔kən'sɪstəntlɪ〕*adv.* 一致地
　　verisimilitude〔,vɛrəsə'mɪlə,tjud〕*n.* 逼眞

6. (**D**) *well passing* → ***well past***
　　skyrocket〔'skaɪ,rɑkɪt〕*v.* 使猛然上漲
　　unemployment〔,ʌnɪm'plɔɪmənt〕*n.* 失業
　　underachiever〔,ʌndəə'tʃivə〕*n.* 成績未達理想的學生
　　loaf around 遊蕩

7. (**B**) *great* → ***greater***
　　blur〔blɝ〕*v.* 變模糊
　　extent〔ɪk'stɛnt〕*n.* 程度；範圍
　　sensational〔sɛn'seʃənḷ〕*adj.* 轟動的
　　conflict〔'kɑnflɪkt〕*n.* 衝突

8. (**D**) *since* → ***as***
　　domestic〔də'mɛstɪk〕*adj.* 國內的
　　semiautomatic〔,sɛmɪɔtə'mætɪk〕*adj.* 半自動的
　　assault〔ə'sɔlt〕*n.* 攻擊
　　legitimate〔lɪ'dʒɪtəmɪt〕*adj.* 合法的
　　ban〔bæn〕*v.* 禁止
　　importation〔,ɪmpor'teʃən〕*n.* 輸入

9. (**B**) *limited → limiting*
  air〔ɛr〕*v.* 公開發表 frustration〔'frʌstreʃən〕*n.* 挫折
  multiple〔'mʌtəpḷ〕*adj.* 多重的 grope〔grop〕*v.* 摸索
  redefine〔,ridɪ'faɪn〕*v.* 重新下定義
  on one's own terms 以某人所希望的條件

10. (**D**) *rooted deeply → deep-rooted* 或 *deeply-rooted*
  prospect〔'prɑspɛkt〕*n.* 展望
  team sport 團隊運動
  financial〔faɪ'nænʃəl〕*adj.* 財務的
  realm〔rɛlm〕*n.* 領域
  deep-rooted〔'dip'rutɪd〕*adj.* 根深蒂固的(= *deeply-rooted*)
  bias〔'baɪəs〕*n.* 偏見
  homophobia〔,hɑmə'fobɪə〕*n.* 對同性戀的恐懼

III. 閱讀測驗：30 %

【譯文】

  很多教育者認為，歷史科演變成社會課程，是某種錯誤的根源。社會課程起源於一九三○年代，當初是努力讓此學科更具實際價值。最初的積極倡導者保羅‧漢那曾寫道，兒童無法「面對我們所生活的現實——他們會逃避，退縮到昔日的浪漫的境界中。」社會課程在一九六○及七○年代發展得最為成熟。當時，低年級的學童，常以家庭及鄰里生活的研究，代替羅曼史及傳奇故事；對於較高年級的學童，社群研究意味著一種跨學科研究的方法，也就是將歷史學丟到學術的大雜燴中，裡頭有心理學、人類學、民族研究、公民，以及其他的學科。

  結果卻頗令人氣餒。漢那貶低為「浪漫的夢境」，結果卻證明，比故作多情的社會學還偏重記憶，且淪為要點的敘述與天真的訴求。替各州改革歷史課程，設立於俄亥俄的不雷德雷委員會的艾倫瑞德說：「小孩喜歡歷史，是因為那是真人真事。」

　　小學的實際狀況是，一天的課程中，並沒有足夠的時間將歷史科與公民、社區議題，及其他類似的主題分開，但至少應將目標設定為，讓歷史地理在學科混合中的比重增加。而且從國中開始，就將科目定義為歷史科，這樣會比較合理。否則現在校方就會提供「沒興趣的學生緊急逃生門，以達到取得文憑的標準。」當心理學或人類學，甚至駕駛教育課程都算作社會課程時，也難怪很多學生對南北戰爭一無所知了。

【答案】

1. (**B**)　　2. (**A**)　　3. (**D**)　　4. (**D**)　　5. (**A**)

【註】

see ~ as 把～視為…

transformation〔,trænsfɚˋmeʃən〕*n.* 轉化

social studies 社會課程　　root〔rut〕*n.* 根源

relevant〔ˋrɛləvənt〕*adj.* 有相關的

champion〔ˋtʃæmpɪən〕*n.* 擁護者　　retreat〔rɪˋtrit〕*v.* 退卻

realm〔rɛlm〕*n.* 王國；夢境　　flower〔ˋflauɚ〕*v.* 興盛

interdisciplinary〔,ɪntɚˋdɪsəplɪn,ɛrɪ〕*adj.* 各學科間的

stew〔ˋstju〕*n.* 大雜燴

anthropology〔,ænθrəˋpɑlədʒɪ〕*n.* 人類學

civics〔ˋsɪvɪks〕*n.* 公民學　　denigrate〔ˋdɛnə,gret〕*v.* 毀謗

narrative〔næˋrətɪv〕*adj.* 敘事的　　thrust〔θrʌst〕*n.* 要旨

soupy〔ˋsupɪ〕*adj.* 矯情的　　sociology〔,soʃɪˋɑlədʒɪ〕*n.* 社會學

escape hatch 緊急逃生門

diploma〔dɪˋplomə〕*n.* 學位；畢業證書　　*count as* 視為

no wonder 難怪　　*Civil War* （美國）南北戰爭

【譯文】

　　全球的海洋是個遼闊的荒漠，極度地缺乏養份，且分布於其中的生物極端地稀少。我們調查藍色大海，而得到如此令人震驚的訊息。我們這一代一直被灌輸著，海洋是最後的未完全開發的領域。似乎從來沒有記者在寫到有關餵飽飢餓人口時，能不提到海洋養殖的，就好像這是能供給人類食物來源的某個處女地一般。但實際上卻不是如此。海洋這樣的荒漠，還能讓人類再榨取的食物已相當有限了。

　　海洋如此地缺乏生產力是令人非常驚訝的，原因是海洋缺乏化學肥料。在陸地上，有時養份的供給可能也會出現短缺，但通常野生植物能設法將養分儲藏及再利用，以供其需求。因此，除非沒有水，或多天太冷，陸生植物的生產力是受其原料，即二氧化碳的缺乏所限制。在海洋中，植物從溶解物碳酸氧鹽中取得碳，而且通常不虞匱乏。而小型海生植物卻無法充分利用這些碳，原因是，在那之前，其所需的化學肥料，如鐵、磷肥、或硝酸鹽類化肥，就已經先用光了。

　　但海洋本身還是有些養分充足的地帶，也就是人類捕魚的地方——如北海、紐芬蘭沙洲漁場及祕魯外海——但似乎很奇怪的是，海洋這樣的流體，竟會有些地帶養分充足，而形成漁場的卻是會水不斷地流動及替換的。在有淺洲或島弧的地方，其深海中流動的洋流會被迫流往海面，造成海水從海底向上流動。當兩股深海海流正面交會時，海水往上竄流，也會造成類似的結果，形成著名的「湧升流」。所有有沙洲與湧升流的地帶，皆有從海底緩慢流動的水流傳送帶，能將深海無窮的新鮮養分送往海面，以供給生物所需。

【答案】

　　6. (**C**)　　7. (**D**)　　8. (**B**)　　9. (**A**)　　10. (**B**)

【註】

make up 組成　　desperately〔ˋdɛsp(ə)rɪtlɪ〕adv. 絕望地
be short of 缺乏　　nutrient〔ˋn(j)utrɪənt〕n. 養分
living thing 生物　　inquiry〔ɪnˋkwaɪrɪ〕n. 調查
frontier〔frʌnˋtɪr〕n.（探索的）新領域；未完全開發的領域
untapped〔ʌnˋtæpt〕adj. 未開發的
take out 取得　　appalling〔əˋpɔlɪŋ〕adj. 令人震驚的
scarcity〔ˋskɛrsətɪ〕n. 稀少　　fertilizer〔ˋfɝtl͵aɪzɚ〕n. 肥料
wild vegetation 野生植物　　hoard〔hɔrd〕v. 儲藏
carbon dioxide 二氧化碳　　solution〔səˋluʃən〕n. 溶解狀態
bicarbonate〔baɪˋbɑrbənɪt〕n. 碳酸氫鹽
work up 發展　　phosphate〔ˋfɑsfet〕n. 磷肥
nitrate〔ˋnaɪtret〕n. 硝酸鹽類化肥　　patch〔pætʃ〕n. 地帶
fertile〔ˋfɝtl〕adj. 肥沃的　　fishery〔ˋfɪʃərɪ〕n. 漁場
shallow bank 淺灘　　*island arc* 島弧
current〔ˋkɝənt〕n. 洋流　　head-on〔ˋhɛdˋɑn〕adv. 正面地
lead to 導致　　celebrated〔ˋsɛlə͵bretɪd〕adj. 著名的
upwelling〔ʌpˋwelɪŋ〕n. 湧升流　　conveyor〔kənˋveɚ〕n. 輸送帶

克漏字：10%

【譯文】

　　英文的四十個音素中，其拼法上有一千一百二十種不同的方式，而且每個字都必須發音，相對而言，在義大利文中，只需三十三種字母的組合，即可拼出所有的音素。因此，閱讀義大利文較不費力，這大概就是為什麼義大利經報導的閱讀障礙百分比，幾乎不到美國一半的原因了。在美國，大約有百分之十五的人，有不同程度的閱讀障礙。根據數據顯示，美國每年大約花超過十億美元，以幫助孩童克服閱讀障礙。而另一方面，很多在義大利有閱讀障礙的人，甚至不知道自己有這方面的問題——要經過一整套的心理學測試後，才會注意到。

【註】

　phoneme〔ˈfonim〕n.【語】音素
　dyslexia〔dɪsˈlɛksɪə〕n. 閱讀障礙
　barely〔ˈbɛrlɪ〕adv. 幾乎不
　to varying degrees 在不同程度上　　**cope with** 應付；克服
　battery〔ˈbæt(ə)rɪ〕n. 一組；一整套

11. (**C**)　(A) voice〔vɔɪs〕n. 聲音；噪子
　　　　　　(B) accent〔ˈæksɛnt〕n. 口音
　　　　　　(C) **sound**〔saʊnd〕n. 音
　　　　　　(D) utterance〔ˈʌt(ə)rəns〕n. 發言；語調

12. (**B**)　**by contrast** 相對而言

13. (**A**)　(A) **as a result** 因此
　　　　　　(B) by and large 大體而言
　　　　　　(C) in the meantime 同時
　　　　　　(D) nonetheless〔ˌnʌnðəˈlɛs〕adv. 仍然

14. (**B**)　(A) based on comparison 根據比較
　　　　　　(B) **according to figures** 根據數字
　　　　　　(C) with this in mind 將這件事牢記在心
　　　　　　(D) on the contrary 相反地

15. (**A**)　(A) **on the other hand** 另一方面
　　　　　　(B) in other words 換言之
　　　　　　(C) apart from that 除了那個之外
　　　　　　(D) under this condition 在這個條件下

IV. 中譯英：20 %

1. A more significant fact is that plants cannot grow by themselves near banks of dams.

2. He feels his attachment to family is stronger than his desire to avoid the responsibilities.

3. Conversing when watching a performance is obviously very improper behavior; however, many people chat openly and think others cannot hear them.

4. Surprisingly, many people nowadays still have no idea what leads to sexual harassment, and neither do they know the problems or the anger their actions might give rise to.

國立交通大學九十學年度
碩士班研究生入學考試英文試題

I. Vocabulary(Part I): For each item, choose the word that is synonymous with the underlined word in the sentence. 14%

1. Many young couples tend to believe that divorce is a contemporary <u>panacea</u> for all matrimonial ills.
   (A) pain   (B) remedy
   (C) skill   (D) desire

2. Wells and Company is about to <u>incorporate with</u> National Steel.
   (A) join with   (B) come up with
   (C) in with   (D) negotiate with

3. This department is the best place to study, <u>given</u> my interest in finance and marketing.
   (A) despite   (B) if
   (C) considering   (D) although

4. The passage in the book was <u>emended</u> before printing.
   (A) proofread   (B) inserted
   (C) removed   (D) corrected

5. The vice president has expressed her recent <u>espousal</u> of feminism.
   (A) interest   (B) support
   (C) comment   (D) objection

6. The <u>onus</u> of bringing up six children was on the father.
   (A) obligation   (B) happiness
   (C) achievement   (D) philosophy

7. If diplomats are <u>accredited</u> to a country, they are officially sent there and accepted as representatives of their own country.
    (A) allocated   (B) accustomed
    (C) nominated   (D) appointed

II. Vocabulary (part II): Choose the most appropriate word for each blank in the passages or the sentences. 16%

    Do people really want to ___(8)___ their lives? They may not want to live longer if the additional years are spent in poor health. As people age, their senses such as sight and hearing ___(9)___ and their general health becomes worse. However, people can take action to ___(10)___ good health. For example, they can take exercise and eat a sensible ___(11)___.

  8. (A) increase   (B) aggregate
     (C) extend   (D) improve

  9. (A) deteriorate   (B) decline
     (C) reduce   (D) decrease

10. (A) increase   (B) become
     (C) promote   (D) facilitate

11. (A) food   (B) dining   (C) diet   (D) meal

    There are several important factors related to the process of aging. One of these is the influence of the body's genes. It ___(12)___ that aging may be largely controlled by a relatively small number of genes. There has been a ___(13)___ interest in this topic. Some researchers ___(14)___ that if the secret of genes can be ___(15)___, the human lifespan can be prolonged.

12. (A) appears   (B) reports
    (C) confirms   (D) explains

13. (A) much   (B) better
    (C) more   (D) growing

14. (A) hold   (B) research
    (C) denote   (D) hesitate

15. (A) realized   (B) unraveled
    (C) opened   (D) refined

III. Grammar: 30%

16. Flying costs much more money ＿＿＿＿＿ other forms of transportation.
    (A) than do most   (B) most than do
    (C) than most do   (D) do than most

17. With blossoms that retain their freshness for some time, amaranths have ＿＿＿＿＿ of immortality.
    (A) long been symbols   (B) been long symbols
    (C) symbols been long   (D) long symbols been

18. Nearly 3,000 alkaloids have been recorded, ＿＿＿＿＿ are of plant origin.
    (A) most of which   (B) in which
    (C) which most   (D) all

19. Ozone, a dangerous pollutant in smog, can cause damage to ＿＿＿＿＿ it touches.
    (A) which   (B) what
    (C) that   (D) them

20. The first ascent to the summit of Aconcagua, the highest peak in the western hemisphere and now an extinct volcano, ＿＿＿＿＿ in 1897.
    (A) was made   (B) made
    (C) making   (D) being made

21. The greater the surface of the ski that is in contact
_____ ground, the easier it is to control.
(A) with
(B) the
(C) with the
(D) X

22. It is prohibited by law to carry aboard the plane
anything that might prove _____ to flight safety.
(A) dangerous
(B) with danger
(C) dangerously
(D) having danger

23. The gas _____ is used primarily for home heating.
(A) the western states being produced
(B) producing in the western states
(C) produced in the western states
(D) the western states producing

24. Plants obtain atmospheric CO_2 required for
photosynthesis by diffusion through open leaf stomata.
While _____ is taking place, water in the leaf
parenchyma tissues evaporates into the sub-stomatal
cavities and diffuses through the open stomata into
the atmosphere.
(A) it
(B) this
(C) what
(D) those

25. If such a merger _____, the company would have
been saved from bankruptcy.
(A) have been proposed
(B) had been proposed
(C) was proposed
(D) is proposed

26. By extracting the lead 204 from the rock sample,
_____.
(A) the rock's age can be determined
(B) the rock can be determined its age
(C) the geochemist can let the rock's age determine
(D) the geochemist can determine the age of the rock

27. One of the studies _____ such a phenomenon.
    (A) indicate   (B) indicates
    (C) is indicated   (D) are indicated

28. The chemical is heated at the second stage,
    _____.
    (A) as shows in Fig. 1   (B) as Fig, 1 show
    (C) as Fig. 1 showing   (D) as shown in Fig. 1

29. The experiment has _____ before next Tuesday.
    (A) to be finished   (B) to finish
    (C) finish   (D) finishing

30. The report is well written; the student _____ a
    lot of time collecting data.
    (A) must spend   (B) must have spent
    (C) will spend   (D) will have spent

IV. Reading Comprehension: 40%

Military awards have long been considered symbolic of royalty, and thus when the United States was a young nation just finished with revolution and eager to distance itself from anything tasting of monarchy, there was strong sentiment against military decoration. For a century, from the end of the Revolutionary War until the Civil War, the United States awarded no military honors. The institution of the Medal of Honor in 1861 was a source of great discussion and concern. From the Civil War until World War I, the Medal of Honor was the only military award given by the United States government and today it is awarded only in the most extreme cases of heroism. Although the United States is still somewhat wary of granting military awards, several awards have been instituted since World War I.

31. The tone of the passage is
    (A) angered.　　　　　　　(B) humorous.
    (C) outraged.　　　　　　(D) informational.

32. The author's purpose in this passage is to
    (A) describe the history of military awards from the Revolutionary War to the Civil War.
    (B) demonstrate an effect of the attitude toward royalty.
    (C) give an opinion of military awards.
    (D) outline various historical symbols of royalty.

33. This passage would probably be assigned reading in a course in
    (A) military science.　　　(B) sociology.
    (C) American history.　　　(D) interior decoration.

At the end of the 20th century, the world is changing in important ways. Until recently, nations acted independently. Each country did its business and tried to solve its problems alone. But now, the economy is worldwide and communications technologies have connected people all over the globe. Many problems are global, too, and can no longer be solved by individual nations.

Environmental destruction is one of these problems. As the world's population has grown and technology has developed, the environment has suffered. Some nations have begun to try to stop pollution and environmental destruction. But the environment is global—the atmosphere, the ocean, and many forms of life are all connected. Thus, the solutions require global thinking.

The problem of ocean pollution is a good example. All the oceans of the world are connected. Pollution does not stay where it begins. It spreads out from every river and every harbor and affects bodies of water everywhere.

For centuries, people have used the oceans as a dumping place. Many cities take tons of garbage out to sea and dump it there. The quantity of garbage that ends up in the water is incredible. Five million plastic containers are thrown into the world's oceans every day! Aside from plastics, many other dangerous substances are dumped in oceans. These include human waste and chemicals used in agriculture. And every year, oil tankers accidentally spill millions of gallons of oil into the sea.

Some people believe that the oceans are so large that chemicals and waste will disappear. However, many things, such as chemicals and plastics, stay in the water and create problems. They eventually float to shore and are eaten by tiny sea creatures. Then the large animals that eat the tiny creatures are poisoned and die. Harbors and coasts around the world have become unsafe for humans and animals. The world's fish population is rapidly shrinking.

34. This passage is about
    (A) air pollution.
    (B) recycling.
    (C) global thinking.

35. You may infer from this passage that in the past
    (A) problems were more local.
    (B) nations were more interested in the environment.
    (C) individual nations did not have as many problems.

36. Until now, most nations followed the principle that
    (A) all countries should share their problems.
    (B) each nation should take care of its own problems.
    (C) what happens in one country affects other countries in the world.

37. According to this passage, many environmental problems
    (A) are caused by global thinking.
    (B) are caused by old ways of thinking.
    (C) lead to globalization.

38. The solution to ocean pollution requires global thinking because
    (A) no one cares about the ocean.
    (B) the oceans are so large.
    (C) all the world's oceans are connected.

39. In the second paragraph, the phrase "these problems" refers to
    (A) the problems individual nations have.
    (B) the global problems.
    (C) the economic problems.

40. In the last line, the word "shrinking" means
    (A) increasing.
    (B) decreasing.
    (C) expanding.

　　Transmigration of souls, sometimes called metempsychosis, is based on the idea that a soul may pass out of one body and reside in another, human or animal, or in an inanimate object. The idea appears in various forms in tribal cultures in many parts of the world. The notion was familiar in ancient Greece, and was adopted in a philosophical form by Plato. The

belief gained some currency in Gnostic and <u>occult</u> forms
of Christianity and Judaism and was introduced into
Renaissance thought by the recovery of the Hermetic
books.

The most fully articulated doctrine of transmigration
is found in Hinduism. Central to the conception of human
destiny after death was the belief that human beings are
born and die many times. Souls are regarded as <u>emanations</u>
of the divine spirit. Each soul passes from one body to
another in a continuous cycle of births and deaths, its
condition in each existence being determined by its
actions in previous births. <u>Thus</u>, transmigration is
closely interwoven with the concept of karma, which
involves the inevitable working out, for good or ill, of
all action in a future existence. The whole experience
of life, whether of happiness or sorrow, is a just reward
for deeds, good or bad, done in earlier existences. The
cycle of karma and transmigration may extend through
innumerable lives; the ultimate goal is the re-absorption
of the soul into the ocean of divinity whence <u>it</u> came.
This union occurs when the individual realizes the truth
about the soul and the Absolute (Brahman) and the soul
becomes one with Brahman.

The idea of transmigration has been propagated in
the Western world by movements such as theosophy and by
the more recent <u>increase</u> of Oriental religious cults.
Most of these Westernized versions appear to lack the
intellectual rigor and philosophical content of the
classical Hindu doctrine.

41. The subject of the passage is
    (A) the belief in a regression to past lives by souls in search of perfection.
    (B) the belief in the transcendence of physical aspiration.
    (C) the belief in the soul's quest for oneness with the Absolute.
    (D) the belief in the proliferation of Oriental cults.

42. In paragraph one, the word "occult" could best be replaced by
    (A) shallow.
    (B) rural.
    (C) arcane.
    (D) urbane.

43. From the first paragraph, it can be inferred
    (A) transmigration of souls is not in the mainstream of Judeo-Christian philosophy.
    (B) an inanimate object can not have a soul.
    (C) Plato may have first postulated the idea of transmigration of souls.
    (D) metempsychosis is a mental disorder characterized by fervent beliefs in specious concepts.

44. Which of the following is closest in meaning to the word "emanations" in paragraph two?
    (A) Issue.
    (B) Propagation
    (C) Mutation.
    (D) Emaciation.

45. What does the word "thus" in paragraph 2 allude to?
    (A) Souls are regarded as emanations of the divine spirit.
    (B) Each soul passes from one body to another in a continuous cycle of births and deaths.
    (C) ...its condition in each existence being determined by its actions in precious births.
    (D) ...which involves the inevitable working out, for good or ill, of all action in a future existence.

46. According to the passage,
    (A) the Hindus believe that souls move ever closer to ultimate perfection with each successive life.
    (B) the idea of transmigration has its roots in the philosophy of Plato.
    (C) Hinduism is based on the belief that each soul came from and seeks to return to ocean of divinity.
    (D) the idea of transmigration has its roots in the Renaissance.

47. In paragraph 2, the word "it" refers to
    (A) ocean.   (B) goal.
    (C) divinity.   (D) soul.

48. According to the author's explanation of karma,
    (A) if one does bad deeds, his soul will never enter the ocean of divinity.
    (B) doing a bad deed in this life will make a person worse off in the next life.
    (C) human beings never die.
    (D) If one leads a happy life, he will become one with Brahman.

49. According to the passage, the concept of the transmigration of souls is viewed by its adherents as
    (A) a proof of doctrines of predestination.
    (B) a side-branch of the doctrine of free will.
    (C) their concept of the soul's destiny.
    (D) the pathway to Valhalla.

50. In paragraph 3, the word "increase" could best be replaced by
    (A) proliferation.
    (B) diffusion.
    (C) section.
    (D) absorption.

國立交通大學九十年度
碩士班研究生入學考試英文試題詳解

I. 字彙：14%

1. **(B)** panacea〔ˌpænəˈsiə〕*n.* 萬靈丹
   (B) **remedy**〔ˈrɛmədɪ〕*n.* 治療法
   contemporary〔kənˈtɛmpəˌrɛrɪ〕*adj.* 當代的
   matrimonial〔ˌmætrəˈmonɪəl〕*adj.* 婚姻的
   ill〔ɪl〕*n.* 問題

2. **(A)** incorporate〔ɪnˈkɔrpəˌret〕*v.* 合併 < *with* >
   (A) **join with** 合併
   (B) come up with 想出
   (C) in with 把～放進裡面；～撤回
   (D) negotiate with 與～磋商

3. **(C)** given〔ˈgɪvən〕*prep.* 就～而言
   (A) despite〔dɪˈspaɪt〕*prep.* 儘管
   (C) **considering**〔kənˈsɪd(ə)rɪŋ〕*prep.* 關於；就～而言

4. **(D)** emend〔ɪˈmɛnd〕*v.* 修訂
   (A) proofread〔ˈprufˌrid〕*v.* 校對
   (B) insert〔ɪnˈsɝt〕*v.* 插入
   (C) remove〔rɪˈmuv〕*v.* 除去
   (D) **correct**〔kəˈrɛkt〕*v.* 改正

5. **(B)** espousal〔ɪsˈpaʊzḷ〕*n.* 信奉；支持
   (B) **support**〔səˈport〕*n.* 支持；擁護
   (C) comment〔ˈkɑmɛnt〕*n.* 評論
   (D) objection〔əbˈdʒɛkʃən〕*n.* 反對
   feminism〔ˈfɛmənɪzəm〕*n.* 女性主義

6. (**A**) onus〔ˋonəs〕*n.* 責任；負擔
　　(A) *obligation*〔͵ɑbləˋgeʃən〕*n.* 義務；責任
　　(C) achievement〔əˋtʃivmənt〕*n.* 成就
　　　　bring up 撫養

7. (**D**) accredit〔əˋkrɛdɪt〕*v.* 任命 < *to* >
　　(A) allocate〔ˋælə͵ket〕*v.* 分派
　　(B) accustom〔əˋkʌstəm〕*v.* 使習慣於
　　(C) nominate〔ˋnɑmə͵net〕*v.* 提名
　　(D) *appoint*〔əˋpɔɪnt〕*v.* 任命；指派
　　　　diplomat〔ˋdɪpləmæt〕*n.* 外交官

Ⅱ. 克漏字：16%

【譯文】

　　人類真的想延長壽命嗎？如果年歲增長，健康狀況不佳的話，也許就不會想活久一點了。當人類年老的時候，感官能力，如視覺與聽覺，就會減退，而且整體的健康會變差。但是，人們還是可以為促進健康而採取行動。例如，可以做運動與慎選食物。

【註】

age〔edʒ〕*v.* 變老　　sense〔sɛns〕*n.* 感官
sight〔saɪt〕*n.* 視覺　　sensible〔ˋsɛnsəbḷ〕*adj.* 明智的

8. (**C**) (B) aggregate〔ˋægrɪ͵get〕*v.* 合計
　　(C) *extend*〔ɪkˋstɛnd〕*v.* 延長

9. (**A**) (A) *deteriorate*〔dɪˋtɪrɪə͵ret〕*v.* 降低品質；惡化
　　(B) decline〔dɪˋklaɪn〕*v.* 衰退；拒絕

10. (**C**) (C) *promote*〔prəˋmot〕*v.* 促進
　　(D) facilitate〔fəˋsɪlə͵tet〕*v.* 使便利

11. (**C**)　(B)　dining〔'daɪnɪŋ〕*n.* 吃飯

　　　　　(C)　*diet*〔'daɪət〕*n.* 飲食

　　　　　(D)　meal〔mil〕*n.* 一餐

【譯文】

　　有幾個與老化有關的重要因素。其中之一是身體基因的影響。老化似乎主要是由比較少數的基因所控制。大家對這個課題的興趣與日俱增。有些研究人員認為，只要能解開基因謎，就能延長人類的壽命。

【註】

be related to 與～有關　　gene〔dʒin〕*n.* 基因

lifespan〔'laɪfspæn〕*n.* 壽命　　prolong〔prə'lɔŋ〕*v.* 延長

12. (**A**)　*It appears that～* 似乎～

　　　　　(C)　confirm〔kən'fɝm〕*v.* 證實

13. (**D**)　*growing*〔'groɪŋ〕*adj.* 愈來愈多的

14. (**A**)　*hold*〔hold〕*v.* 持有（見解）

　　　　　(C)　denote〔dɪ'not〕*v.* 為～的象徵

15. (**B**)　*unravel*〔ʌn'rævl̩〕*v.* 闡明；解開（奧秘）

　　　　　(D)　refine〔rɪ'faɪn〕*v.* 提煉

Ⅲ. 文法：30%

16. (**A**)　...than do most other forms of transportation

　　　　　= ...than most other forms of transportation do

17. (**A**)　have long been symbols of 表「長久以來，一直是～的
　　　　象徵」。
　　　　blossom〔ˈblɑsəm〕*n.* 花
　　　　amaranth〔ˈæmə͵rænθ〕*n.* 莧菜；不朽花
　　　　immortality〔͵ɪmɔrˈtælətɪ〕*n.* 不朽

18. (**A**)　空格須填一關代，且依句意，選 (A) *most of which*。
　　　　alkaloid〔ˈælkə͵lɔɪd〕*n.* 生物鹼
　　　　origin〔ˈɔrədʒɪn〕*n.* 來源

19. (**B**)　what = the things which
　　　　ozone〔ˈozon〕*n.* 臭氧　　　pollutant〔pəˈlutənt〕*n.* 污染物
　　　　smog〔smɑg〕*n.* 煙霧（常見於大城市的煙、氣和霧的混合物）

20. (**A**)　主詞為 ascent，空格須填一動詞，且依句意為被動，故選
　　　　(A) *was made*。
　　　　ascent〔əˈsɛnt〕*n.* 攀登　　　summit〔ˈsʌmɪt〕*n.* 峰頂
　　　　hemisphere〔ˈhɛməs͵fɪr〕*n.* 半球
　　　　extinct volcano 死火山

21. (**C**)　*be in contact with the ground* 與地面接觸

22. (**A**)　prohibit〔proˈhɪbɪt〕*v.* 禁止
　　　　aboard〔əˈbord〕*adv.* 在飛機上

23. (**C**)　本句是由 The gas which is produced in the west
　　　　states... 省略關代與 be 動詞轉化而來。
　　　　primarily〔ˈpraɪ͵mɛrəlɪ〕*adv.* 主要地

24. (**B**)　依句意，選 (B) this「這種情況」。
　　　atmospheric〔ˌætməsˈfɛrɪk〕*adj.* 大氣中的
　　　photosynthesis〔ˌfotəˈsɪnθəsɪs〕*n.* 光合作用
　　　diffusion〔dɪˈfjuʒən〕*n.* 散佈
　　　stoma〔ˈstomə〕*n.*（植物的）氣孔（複數為 stomata）
　　　parenchyma *n.* 薄壁組織
　　　tissue〔ˈtɪʃʊ〕*n.* 組織
　　　evaporate〔ɪˈvæpəˌret〕*v.* 蒸發
　　　stomatal〔ˈstaʊmətl̩〕*adj.* 有氣孔的
　　　cavity〔ˈkævətɪ〕*n.* 凹洞

25. (**B**)　依句意，為與過去事實相反的假設，故 If 子句用「過去完成式」，選 (B)。
　　　merger〔ˈmɝdʒɚ〕*n.* 合併
　　　bankruptcy〔ˈbæŋkrəptsɪ〕*n.* 破產

26. (**D**)　Extracting…sample, 為分詞構句，故前後主詞應相同，且依句意，選 (D)。
　　　extract〔ɪkˈstrækt〕*v.* 萃取
　　　geochemist〔ˈdʒɪoˈkɛməstrɪ〕*n.* 地球化學家

27. (**B**)　主詞為 one，故用單數動詞，且依句意為主動，選 (B)。
　　　indicate〔ˈɪndəˌket〕*v.* 顯示
　　　phenomenon〔fəˈnaməˌnan〕*n.* 現象

28. (**D**)　*as shown in Fig*. *1* 表「正如圖一所示」。
　　　stage〔stedʒ〕*n.* 階段

29. (**A**)　依句意為被動語態，故選 (A) *has to be finished*「必須被完成」。

30. (**B**)　must + have + p.p.「當時一定~」，表對過去事實肯定的推測。

Ⅳ. 閱讀測驗：40%

【譯文】

　　長久以來，軍事獎章一直被視爲王權的象徵，因此美國剛完成獨立革命，還是個很年輕的國家，急切地想遠離一切有王權意味的事物之際，對於軍事勳章就有種強烈的反彈情緒。從獨立戰爭到南北戰爭，整整一個世紀，美國從未表彰過軍事殊榮。一八六一年制定的榮譽勳章，就引起了很大的討論與關注。從南北戰爭到第一次世界大戰，榮譽勳章是美國政府唯一授與的軍事獎章，現今，只有非常顯赫的英勇事蹟，才會被授與榮譽勳章。雖然美國對於頒發軍事獎章仍有點小心翼翼，但自從第一次世界大戰後，也已經制定了好幾個獎章。

【答案】

　31. **(D)**　　32. **(B)**　　33. **(C)**

【註】

royalty〔'rɔɪəltɪ〕*n.* 王權　　monarchy〔'mɑnəkɪ〕*n.* 君主政體
sentiment〔'sɛntəmənt〕*n.* 情緒
decoration〔ˌdɛkə'reʃən〕*n.* 勳章
institution〔ˌɪnstə'tjuʃən〕*n.* 制定
Revolutionary War 獨立戰爭　　***Civil War*** 南北戰爭
Medal of Honor 榮譽勳章（美國國會授與軍人的最高戰功章）
heroism〔'hɛroˌɪzəm〕*n.* 英勇的行爲
somewhat〔'sʌmˌhwɑt〕*adv.* 有點；稍微
wary〔'wɛrɪ〕*adj.* 謹愼的＜*of*＞　　institute〔'ɪnstəˌtjut〕*v.* 制定

【譯文】

　　二十世紀末，世界正經歷重大的改變。不久之前，各國還是各自爲政，每個國家處理自己的事情，也試圖獨力解決問題。但現今經濟已經全球化，通訊科技也將全人類連結在一起，很多問題已經是全球性的，單一國家已無法解決這些問題了。

　　生態環境的破壞是問題之一。當人口不斷增加,科技不斷發展,生態環境就一直遭受破壞。有些國家已開始試著停止污染與破壞環境。但生態環境是全球性的,大氣、海洋,與多數生命型態都是相互連結的。因此,要找出解決之道,必須要有全球性的思考。

　　海洋污染的問題是個很好的例子。世界上所有的海洋都連在一起。污染並不侷限於污染源頭。污染會從每個河流與港口擴散出去,再影響到各地的水域。

　　幾個世紀以來,人類一直將海洋當作丟棄廢棄物的場所。很多城市把數以噸計的垃圾丟到海裏。最後留在水裏的垃圾數量是很驚人的。全球每天有五百萬個塑膠容器被丟到海水裏!除了塑膠以外,還有其他危險物質也被丟到海裏,其中包含人類廢棄物與農業用化學藥品,而且每年還會發生油輪外洩數百萬噸原油到海水中的意外事件。

　　有人相信,海洋是如此的廣大,因此化學製品與廢棄物終究會消失。但是,有很多物體,如化學製品與塑膠,則會持續地留在水裏,而且還會製造一些問題。它們最後會漂流到岸邊,被海中的微生物吃掉。大型動物再吃掉這些微生物,就會中毒而死亡。全世界所有的港口與海岸,對於人類與動物而言,已經愈來愈不安全了。全球的魚群數量正在急劇萎縮中。

┌─────────────────────────────────
【答案】

34.(**C**)　　35.(**A**)　　36.(**B**)　　37.(**B**)　　38.(**C**)
39.(**B**)　　40.(**B**)
└─────────────────────────────────

【註】

aside from 除了~之外　　waste〔west〕*n.* 廢棄物
oil tanker 油輪　　shrink〔ʃrɪŋk〕*v.* 縮小

【譯文】

靈魂的輪迴，有時稱爲轉世，是建立在靈魂能逸出軀殼，進駐另一個人體、動物或無生命體中這樣的觀念之上。這觀念在世界很多地方的族群文化中都有跡可循。這種想法在古希臘是很普遍的，而且也被柏拉圖擷取而成一種哲學形式。此信仰在諾斯替教、基督教與猶太教的神秘哲學類別中廣爲流傳，也經由煉金術書籍的再度風行，而傳入文藝復興時期的思想之中。

最爲完整且清楚的輪迴教義存在於印度教之中。人類死後命運的核心概念，是基於對於人類會生死很多次的信仰之上。靈魂被視爲聖靈的發散物。每個靈魂從一個軀殼到另一個軀殼，是在一個連續無間斷的生死循環之中進行的，而每世的存在狀態，則取決於前世的表現。因此輪迴與因果報應的概念是緊緊結合在一起的，也就是無論行爲好壞，都無法避免會影響到來世。整個人生歷程，不論快樂或悲傷，都只是前世善業或惡業的報應。因果報應與轉世的循環，會一直延長到無數世，終極目標是能再融合回到來時的無限神性。合而爲一只發生在個人了悟靈魂與絕對（婆羅門）的眞義，此時靈魂就會與婆羅門合爲一體。

輪迴的觀念，因爲證道學與晚近東方教派的興起，而在西方世界廣爲流傳。而大部分這些西化的版本，似乎都缺乏智識上的嚴謹態度與經典印度教義的哲學內涵。

【答案】

41.（**C**）	42.（**C**）	43.（**A**）	44.（**A**）	45.（**C**）
46.（**C**）	47.（**D**）	48.（**B**）	49.（**C**）	50.（**A**）

【註】

transmigration〔ˌtrænsmaɪˈgreʃən〕n.（死後靈魂的）輪迴；轉生

metempsychosis〔ˌmɛtəmsaɪˈkosɪs〕n.（死後靈魂的）輪迴；轉生

reside〔rɪˈzaɪd〕v. 存在＜in＞

inanimate〔ɪnˈænəmɪt〕adj. 無生命的　　tribal〔ˈtraɪbḷ〕adj. 部落的

notion〔ˈnoʃən〕n. 想法　　currency〔ˈkɝnsɪ〕n. 流傳

Gnostic〔ˈnastɪk〕n. adj. 諾斯替教徒（的）

occult〔əˈkʌlt〕adj. 神秘的　　form〔fɔrm〕n. 類型

Christianity〔ˌkrɪstʃɪˈænətɪ〕n. 基督教

Judaism〔ˈdʒudɪˌɪzəm〕n. 猶太教

Renaissance〔ˌrɛnəˈsans〕n. 文藝復興

Hermetic〔hɝˈmɛtɪk〕adj. 煉金術的

articulate〔arˈtɪkjəˌlet〕v. 清楚地表達

doctrine〔ˈdaktrɪn〕n. 學說；教義

Hinduism〔ˈhɪnduˌɪzəm〕n. 印度教　　divinity〔dəˈvɪnətɪ〕n. 神性

emanation〔ˌɛməˈneʃən〕n. 發散物

interweave〔ˌɪntɚˈwiv〕v. 交織；混雜＜with＞

karma〔ˈkarmə〕n. 因果報應　　***work out*** 努力達成

deed〔did〕n. 業報　　re-absorption〔ˌriəbˈsɔrpʃən〕n. 再融合

whence〔ʰwɛns〕adv. 從那個地方

Brahman〔ˈbramən〕n. 婆羅門

propagate〔ˈprapəˌget〕v. 傳播；宣傳

theosophy〔θiˈasəfɪ〕n. 證道學（尤指近代襲用佛教或婆羅門教教義的
信仰）　　Oriental〔ˌorɪˈɛntḷ〕adj. 東方的

cult〔kʌlt〕n. 教派　　Westernized〔ˈwɛstɚˌnaɪzd〕adj. 西化的

intellectual〔ˌɪntḷˈɛktʃʊəl〕adj. 智識的　　rigor〔ˈrɪgɚ〕n. 嚴謹

regression〔rɪˈgrɛʃən〕n. 倒退　　aspiration〔ˌæspəˈreʃən〕n. 渴望

quest〔kwɛst〕n.（長期的）探尋　　oneness〔ˈwʌnnɪs〕n. 同一性

proliferation〔proˌlɪfəˈreʃən〕n. 激增

arcane〔arˈken〕adj. 神秘的

mainstream〔ˈmenˌstrim〕n.（思想、行為的）主流

postulate〔ˈpastʃəˌlet〕v. 假設　　fervent〔ˈfɝvənt〕adj. 狂熱的

specious〔'spiʃəs〕*adj.* 似是而非的　　issue〔'ɪʃu〕*n.* 發出
propagation〔ˌprɑpə'geʃən〕*n.* 宣傳
mutation〔mju'teʃən〕*n.* 突變
emancipation〔ɪˌmænsə'peʃən〕*n.* 解放　　***allude to*** 暗指
successive〔sək'sɛsɪv〕*adj.* 連續的
adherent〔əd'hɪrənt〕*n.* 信徒；擁護者
predestination〔prɪˌdɛstə'neʃən〕*n.* 得救預定論（認為按照上帝的意
　志，人死後有的上天堂，有的入地獄的一種信仰）
free will 自由意志　　pathway〔'pæθˌwe〕*n.* 通路
Valhalla〔væl'hælə〕*n.*（北歐神話）英靈殿（奧丁神的宮殿，陣亡英
　雄的亡魂安於此殿）

國立成功大學九十學年度
碩士班研究生入學考試英文試題(二)

I. Select the word following each selection, which best
   completes the meaning of the statement as a whole. 30%

1. Compulsory education was instituted for the purpose
   of preventing _____ young children, and
   guaranteeing them a minimum of education.
   (A) prison   (B) ignorance
   (C) abuse   (D) exploitation

2. Any person who is in _____ while awaiting
   trial is considered innocent until he has been
   proven guilty.
   (A) custody   (B) jeopardy
   (C) suspicion   (D) probation

3. Although there is reason to expect an improvement
   in business conditions, at least a seasonal rise
   would be necessary to show that the _____ of
   the slump has been passed.
   (A) nadir   (B) majority
   (C) minority   (D) economics

4. Attendance at museums and galleries increases
   by leaps and bounds, new exhibition facilities
   _____ and possession of works of art become
   a badge of cultural honor.
   (A) proliferate   (B) simulate
   (C) coagulate   (D) conglomerate

5. Even as many of them _____ their pledges of
   support, their actions belie their words.
   (A) conform   (B) reiterate
   (C) remand   (D) decline

6. There has been an almost _____ fear of
   inflation, which has been especially terrifying
   to people who live exclusively on a fixed income.
   (A) neurotic   (B) sadistic
   (C) concomitant   (D) puerile

7. Automobile tire tracks found at the scene of a
   crime constitute an important link in the chain of
   _____ evidence.
   (A) moral   (B) culpable
   (C) physical   (D) intangible

8. When the first white men came to America, they
   found vast amounts of _____ resources of
   tremendous value.
   (A) variable   (B) developed
   (C) monetary   (D) natural

9. Milk is a suspension of nourishing materials in
   water, which _____ about 86 percent of the
   total weight.
   (A) constitutes   (B) cohesive
   (C) infers   (D) contrives

10. Repetition of words and ideas can confuse as well as
    emphasize a point, and may make your speech _____.
    (A) redundant   (B) concise
    (C) alliterate   (D) apathetic

11. Just as I got down to work, my friends _____ —
    to visit me.
    (A) identified   (B) solidified
    (C) decided   (D) rectified

12. Many diseases formerly considered _____ are
    now treated successfully.
    (A) incurable   (B) curable
    (C) rectifiable   (D) retrogressive

13. The newspaper _____ that seven persons had been drowned.
    (A) requested
    (B) spelled
    (C) reported
    (D) unfortunately

14. Not every individual offered _____ opinion during the discussions, but many opposing viewpoints came to light later.
    (A) no
    (B) their
    (C) whose
    (D) his

15. The man said that if he had received such a letter, he would have _____ it into the wastepaper basket.
    (A) threw
    (B) throwing
    (C) throw
    (D) thrown

II. Translate the following passages into English: 20%

1. 如果想要小孩愛電腦，可以花時間、精力來設計一流的軟體，讓他們產生興趣，或讓電腦滑鼠長得像卡通人物。10%

2. 竹子在中美洲國家溫暖的氣候中極易栽培，是一種可以無限再生的資源。10%

III. Translate the following passages into Chinese: 20%

1. Western critics routinely greet the new films from Taiwan with raves and awards. Such films, however, find a more muted reception at home. 10%

2. Many of you come to my management seminar as optimistic, creative, clear-thinking individuals. 10%

IV. Essay writing: 30%

Write an essay of about 200 words to support or oppose one of the following statements:

a. Human life should be preserved at all costs.
b. Terminally ill patients must consider their families.
c. In some instances, shortening or ending human life is acceptable.

國立成功大學九十年度
碩士班研究生入學考試英文試題（二）詳解

I. 字彙：30%

1. (**D**) (A) prison〔'prɪzn̩〕*n.* 監獄
     (B) ignorance〔'ɪgnərəns〕*n.* 無知
     (C) abuse〔ə'bjus〕*n.* 虐待
     (D) *exploitation*〔,ɛksplɔɪ'teʃən〕*n.* 剝削
        compulsory〔kəm'pʌlsərɪ〕*adj.* 義務的
        institute〔'ɪnstə,tjut〕*v.* 制定
        guarantee〔,gærən'ti〕*v.* 保證
        minimum〔'mɪnəməm〕*n.* 最小量；最低限度

2. (**A**) (A) *custody*〔'kʌstədɪ〕*n.* 拘留　　*in custody* 在拘留中
     (B) jeopardy〔'dʒɛpədɪ〕*n.* 危險
     (C) suspicion〔sə'spɪʃən〕*n.* 懷疑
     (D) probation〔pro'beʃən〕*n.* 緩刑
        await〔ə'wet〕*v.* 等待　　trial〔traɪl〕*n.* 審判
        innocent〔'ɪnəsn̩t〕*adj.* 無罪的

3. (**A**) (A) *nadir*〔'nedɚ〕*n.* 最低點
     (B) majority〔mə'dʒɔrətɪ〕*n.* 大多數
     (C) minority〔maɪ'nɔrətɪ〕*n.* 少數
     (D) economics〔,ikə'nɑmɪks〕*n.* 經濟學
        slump〔slʌmp〕*n.* 不景氣

4. (**A**) (A) *proliferate*〔prə'lɪfə,ret〕*v.* 激增
     (B) simulate〔'sɪmjə,let〕*v.* 模擬
     (C) coagulate〔ko'ægjə,let〕*v.* 使凝結
     (D) conglomerate〔kən'glɑmərɪt〕*v.* 使凝固
        gallery〔'gælərɪ〕*n.* 畫廊
        by leaps and bounds 急速地
        possession〔pə'zɛʃən〕*n.* 擁有　　badge〔bædʒ〕*n.* 象徵

5. (**B**) (A) conform〔kənˋfɔrm〕*v.* 遵循
(B) ***reiterate***〔riˋɪtəˏret〕*v.* 重覆
(C) remand〔rɪˋmænd〕*v.* 遣返
(D) decline〔dɪˋklaɪn〕*v.* 衰退；拒絕
　pledge〔plɛdʒ〕*n.* 誓言
　belie〔bɪˋlaɪ〕*v.* 違背

6. (**A**) (A) ***neurotic***〔njʊˋrɑtɪk〕*adj.* 神經過敏的；非常焦慮的
(B) sadistic〔sæˋdɪstɪk〕*adj.* 虐待狂的
(C) concomitant〔kɑnˋkɑmətənt〕*adj.* 附帶的；伴隨的
(D) puerile〔ˋpjuəˏrɪl〕*adj.* 孩子氣的
　inflation〔ɪnˋfleʃən〕*n.* 通貨膨脹
　exclusively〔ɪkˋsklusɪvlɪ〕*adv.* 僅僅
　unearned〔ʌnˋɝnd〕*adj.* 不勞而獲的
　income〔ˋɪnˏkʌm〕*n.* 收入

7. (**C**) (A) moral〔ˋmɔrəl〕*adj.* 道德的
(B) culpable〔ˋkʌlpəbl̩〕*adj.* 有罪的
(C) ***physical***〔ˋfɪzɪkl̩〕*adj.* 實物的
(D) intangible〔ɪnˋtændʒəbl̩〕*adj.* 無形的
　tire〔taɪr〕*n.* 輪胎　　track〔træk〕*n.* 痕跡
　scene〔sin〕*n.* 現場
　constitute〔ˋkɑnstəˏtjut〕*v.* 構成
　link〔lɪŋk〕*n.* 環節　　chain〔tʃen〕*n.* 一連串

8. (**D**) (A) variable〔ˋvɛrɪəbl̩〕*adj.* 多變的　*n.* 變數
(B) developed〔dɪˋvɛləpt〕*adj.* 已開發的
(C) monetary〔ˋmʌnəˏtɛrɪ〕*adj.* 貨幣的
(D) ***natural***〔ˋnætʃərəl〕*adj.* 自然的
　natural resources 天然資源
　vast〔væst〕*adj.* 龐大的
　tremendous〔trɪˋmɛndəs〕*adj.* 巨大的

9. (**A**)　(A) ***constitute*** 〔 'kɑnstə,tjut 〕 *v.* 構成
　　　　(B) cohesive 〔 ko'hisɪv 〕 *adj.* 有附著力的
　　　　(C) infer 〔 ɪn'fɝ 〕 *v.* 推論
　　　　(D) contrive 〔 kən'traɪv 〕 *v.* 設計；策劃
　　　　　suspension 〔 sə'spɛnʃən 〕 *n.* 懸浮物
　　　　　nourishing 〔 'nɝɪʃɪŋ 〕 *adj.* 有營養的

10. (**A**)　(A) ***redundant*** 〔 rɪ'dʌndənt 〕 *adj.* 多餘的；重複的
　　　　(B) concise 〔 kən'saɪs 〕 *adj.* 簡明的
　　　　(C) alliterate 〔 ə'lɪtə,ret 〕 *adj.* 押頭韻的
　　　　(D) apathetic 〔 ,æpə'θɛtɪk 〕 *adj.* 冷淡的
　　　　　repetition 〔 ,rɛpɪ'tɪʃən 〕 *n.* 重複
　　　　　emphasize 〔 'ɛmfə,saɪz 〕 *v.* 強調

11. (**C**)　(A) identify 〔 aɪ'dɛntə,faɪ 〕 *v.* 辨認
　　　　(B) solidify 〔 sə'lɪdə,faɪ 〕 *v.* 使團結
　　　　(C) ***decide*** 〔 dɪ'saɪd 〕 *v.* 決定
　　　　(D) rectify 〔 'rɛktə,faɪ 〕 *v.* 整頓；矯正
　　　　　get down to 靜下心來（工作）

12. (**A**)　(A) ***incurable*** 〔 ɪn'kjurəbl̩ 〕 *adj.* 無法治癒的
　　　　(B) curable 〔 'kjurəbl̩ 〕 *adj.* 可痊癒的
　　　　(C) rectifiable 〔 'rɛktə,faɪəbl̩ 〕 *adj.* 可矯正的
　　　　(D) retrogressive 〔 ,rɛtrə'grɛsɪv 〕 *adj.* 退化的
　　　　　formerly 〔 'fɔrməlɪ 〕 *adv.* 以前

13. (**C**)　(A) request 〔 rɪ'kwɛst 〕 *v.* 要求
　　　　(B) spell 〔 spɛl 〕 *v.* 拼字
　　　　(C) ***report*** 〔 rɪ'port 〕 *v.* 報導
　　　　(D) unfortunately 〔 ʌn'fɔrtʃənɪtlɪ 〕 *adv.* 不幸地
　　　　　drown 〔 draun 〕 *v.* 使淹死

14.（ **D** ） every individual「每個人」的代名詞是 he，所有格是 his。

opposing〔ə'pozɪŋ〕*adj.* 反對的

viewpoint〔'vju,pɔɪnt〕*n.* 觀點

come to light 顯露出來

15.（ **D** ） would have + p.p.「當時早就…」，爲與過去事實相反的假
設語氣。

wastepaper〔'west,pepɚ〕*n.* 廢紙

wastepaper basket 廢紙簍（ = *wastebasket* ）

II. 中翻英：20%

1. If you want children to love computers, you can spend time
and energy devising first-class software to interest them, or
make the mouse look like cartoon characters.

2. It's easy to cultivate bamboo, which is a replenishable
resource, in Central American countries due to the
warm climate.

III. 英翻中：20%

1. 西方的評論家常以高度好評或頒獎的方式，歡迎台灣的新電影。
但這些電影在國內卻乏人問津。

critic〔'krɪtɪk〕*n.* 評論家

routinely〔ru'tinlɪ〕*adv.* 例行地；慣常地

greet〔grit〕*v.* 歡迎　　rave〔rev〕*n.* 激賞

award〔ə'wɔrd〕*n.* 獎

muted〔'mjutɪd〕*adj.* 輕聲的；淡漠的

reception〔rɪ'sɛpʃən〕*n.* 歡迎；風評

at home 在國內

2 你們這些參加我的管理學研討會的人，很多都是樂觀、有創造
力，而且思路清晰的人。
　　seminar〔ˈsɛməˌnɑr〕*n.* 研討會
　　optimistic〔ˌɑptəˈmɪstɪk〕*adj.* 樂觀的

IV. 短文寫作：30%

Human Life

　　With the advance of medical knowledge and
technology, it is now possible to prolong life, even in
cases of very serious disease or injury. However, we
must consider the question of whether this is always
the best course of action. In some cases, the patient
may be in great pain or be leading a life without
meaning. Some would say that human life should be
preserved at all costs, but I disagree with this position.
I believe that shortening or ending human life is
acceptable in some instances for the following reasons.

　　First of all, an ill or injured person may not wish
to prolong his life if he is in pain and has no hope for
recovery. He may be looking forward to death as release
from his suffering, and I believe that individuals have
the right to make this choice. In addition, a terminally
ill person or one who is "brain dead" — a patient
whose organs are still functioning, but who has no brain
activity — may be a terrible emotional and financial
burden on their families. Both the patient and the family
may wish to shorten life in order to ease this burden.

Whether or not to end or shorten a life is not an easy decision to make, especially when the person involved is incapable of speaking for himself. However it is an option to consider when prolonging life only causes more pain. It should be an informed decision, made with the participation of all concerned, including the terminally ill patient, his family, and his doctor.

國立中央警察大學九十學年度
碩士班研究生入學考試英文試題

I. Fill in the blanks.
（填空 25%，除第 12 題佔 3 分外，其餘每題均爲 2 分。）

Directions: Questions 1-12 consist of 12 short talks between two persons. On your answer sheet write down the English word that would <u>best</u> fit the blank in each talk.

1. Officer   : I have failed the exam twice in the past two years. I have been under great stress lately.

   Colleague : Relax. Don't worry. Believe me—you can _____ it this time.

2. Judge   : Did you _____ the suspect his rights?
   Officer : Yes, I did.

3. Officer 1 : The commander of a SWAT team in California is visiting Taiwan tomorrow. Do you know what SWAT stands for?

   Officer 2 : Of course. It stands for Special Weapons and _____.

4. Son   : Daddy, will you be able to have supper with us tonight?
   Father : I wish I could. We have to crack _____ on a drug-trafficking ring this week.

5. Foreigner : How _____ is the chance of getting my car back?

   Officer   : I can't tell, but we'll do our best to find it.

6. Officer : How tall is the robber?
   Victim : About 5 _____ 6 (5'6'').

7. Shoplifter : Will I be put _____ bars?
   Officer : It depends.

8. Officer : How long do you plan to stay in Taiwan?
   Victim : I'll be here until August. I am willing
   to _____ in court, if summoned.

9. Foreigner : Some of my foreign friends told me officers
   here offer good service.
   Officer : Thank you for the _____. It is our
   duty and pleasure to help.

10. Motorist : Why are you ticketing me?
    Officer : Because you violated _____ 53 of the
    Highway Traffic Code—running a red light.

11. Caller : Operator, I'd like to make a _____
    call to Taiwan. The area code is 02 and
    the local number 23338888. My name is
    John Lin.
    Operator : Hold on a sec. I'll see whether they will
    accept the charges.

12. Secretary : _____ some reason, I just can't find
    my keys.
    Colleague : Aren't they right there in the keyhole?

II. Reading comprehension. (閱讀測驗 25%)

Directions: In this section, you will be given 2 kinds
of reading material followed by questions about the
meaning of the material. You are to choose the <u>one best</u>
answer to each question. Then, on your answer sheet,
write down the letter of the answer you have chosen —
(A), (B), (C), (D),or (E).

Questions 13-17 (15%) refer to the following passage:

Deciding to become a law enforcement officer is an exciting career choice, but becoming a manager in law enforcement is even more challenging. It is an opportunity to develop personally and responsibility to develop others. You can become a successful law enforcement manager in many ways.

Prepare and develop yourself for promotion. Study, attend training programs, take correspondence courses, read trade journals, attend academic courses, use the public library and the law enforcement agency's library and listen to contemporaries. Be ready when opportunity arises.

Support your manager. An old adage advises: "If you want your manager's job, praise and support him or her because soon that person will move up the ladder. Be derogatory to your manager and he or she will be there forever." Complaining, continually finding fault, being negative or non-supportive—all are fast tracks to organizational oblivion. You may accomplish a short-term goal, but in the long run you will destroy your career. Be supportive; if you criticize, make it constructive criticism. Be positive. Praise the good things that happen.

Select an advisor or mentor. There are people within or outside the police organization who can assist and counsel you. Advisors can point you in the right direction. They can be a sounding board.

13. Which one of the following is not a law enforcement officer?
    (A) surgeon   (B) sergeant   (C) FBI agent
    (D) inspector   (E) prosecutor

14. The word "adage" means
    (A) a wise saying.
    (B) a humorous phrase.
    (C) a warning.
    (D) a suggestion.
    (E) an abstract.

15. In this passage, "move up the ladder" means
    (A) go mountain climbing.
    (B) get promoted.
    (C) climb up the ladder with difficulty.
    (D) step down.
    (E) move to another office.

16. According to the author, your supervisor "will be there forever" if you
    (A) flatter him.
    (B) give him warning.
    (C) offer him constructive suggestions.
    (D) criticize or libel him.
    (E) don't give him a ladder.

17. According to this passage, which of the following statements is NOT true?
    (A) You should take correspondence or academic courses.
    (B) You should make best use of the library's resources.
    (C) You should have a mentor who can help and guide you.
    (D) You should go to the pub and listen to contemporary music.
    (E) You should offer constructive opinions if you really want to criticize.

Questions 18-22 (10%) refer to the following Taiwan-issued English magazine index:

Cover story	3-15
Editorial	16
National News	17-30
Economy and Business	31-37
Asia	38-40
World News	41-49
Sports	50-53
Travel	54-56
Cinema	57-60

18. Which of the following pages would most likely contain a story about the production of Li An's movie *Crouching Tiger, Hidden Dragon*?
    (A) 16   (B) 57   (C) 41
    (D) 50   (E) 54

19. On which of the pages of the magazine would one probably find a list of the current trading prices of stocks?
    (A) 50-53   (B) 31-37   (C) 54-56
    (D) 3-15   (E) 41-49

20. Which of the following would most likely contain a report about the 18-year-old juvenile who was just engaged to a 51-year-old woman in Taiwan?
    (A) 31   (B) 60   (C) 17
    (D) 50   (E) 41

21. On which of the pages would one probably find a report about juvenile delinquency in the Philippines?
    (A) 17-30   (B) 16   (C) 31-37
    (D) 57-60   (E) 38-40

22. In which section would one find a statement of
opinion by the publishers of the magazine?
(A) Sports　　　(B) Cover Story
(C) Economy and Business
(D) Cinema　　　(E) Editorial

III. Vocabulary & Phrases（中譯英 10%，每題 1 分）

1. 犯罪現場　　　6. 無期徒刑
2. 偽造證件　　　7. 巡邏勤務
3. 警察事業　　　8. 警民關係
4. 交通管制　　　9. 目標管理
5. 非法移民　　 10. 縱火嫌犯

IV. Translation（英譯中 40%，每題 10 分）

1. Law enforcement administrators know that they should
plan for future events or assignments. Depending on
their organizations' assets and primary jurisdiction,
these situations could range from a civil disturbance
to a terrorist's threat to activate a weapon of mass
destruction. However, administrators often perceive
planning as tedious and formidable. They feel that no
matter how hard they plan or how much they plan, the
plan never works the way they designed it. Fortunately,
administrators can overcome this negative perception
by following some basic planning procedures.

2. Law enforcement is springing into action to fight
Internet crime. Federal agencies have set the tone,
with the FBI, U.S. Secret Service, and the U.S.
Customs Service heading the Internet crime-fighting
initiative. Many state and local agencies are joining
in by implementing Internet programs and giving

their personnel online law enforcement training.
However, the true effort comes from agencies that
have dedicated resources to maintaining online
crime-fighting units. They have acknowledged that
law enforcement must enter the 21st century as an
online force.

3. In order for the police to develop a true community
policing culture, training must become more effective
in both form and substance. Some police scholars have
asserted that traditional police training, course
titles, and content were designed to reflect the
peculiarities of the police subcultures in which they
were administered. Training remains an effective and
necessary tool that administrators can use to help
officers make the change to a more community-minded
and crime prevention culture.

4. While on patrol late one evening, police officer Cheng
of Taoyuan County received a call about a possible
suicide. Officer Cheng located the distraught female
at a local park. She was sitting in her vehicle with
the doors locked. She had a can of white gas in one
hand and a cigarette lighter in the other and stated
that she was going to set herself on fire. Officer
Cheng immediately smashed the driver's side window
with his flashlight and took the woman into custody.
She was transported to a local hospital as was Officer
Cheng, who received injuries to his right hand from
the broken glass. Officer Cheng's quick response
thwarted the suicide attempt.

國立中央警察大學九十年度
碩士班研究生入學考試英文試題詳解

I. 填空：25%

1. *make*

警員：前兩年的兩次考試我都沒有過。最近我壓力很大。

同事：輕鬆點。不用擔心。相信我，這次你一定會成功的。

make it 成功；辦到

2. *tell*

法官：你有告訴嫌犯他應有的權利嗎？

警員：是的。我有告訴他。

suspect〔ˋsʌspɛkt〕*n.* 嫌犯　　right〔raɪt〕*n.* 權利

3. *technologies*

警員一：加州斯威特小組主管將在明天訪台。你知道斯威特代表
　　　　什麼意思嗎？

警員二：當然特殊武器與科技。

commander〔kəˋmændɚ〕*n.* 主管　　***stand for*** 代表

weapon〔ˋwɛpən〕*n.* 武器

4. *down*

兒子：爸爸，你今晚會回家跟我們一起吃飯嗎？

父親：我也很想。可是我們這星期都要去掃蕩販毒集團。

crack down on 掃蕩；取締

drug-trafficking〔ˋdrʌgˋtræfɪkɪŋ〕*n.* 毒品交易；販毒

ring〔rɪŋ〕*n.* 集團；幫派

5. **much**

外國人：我車子找回來的機會有多<u>大</u>？

警員　：我也不知道，但我們會盡力去找的。

tell〔tɛl〕*v.* 知道

6. **feet**

警員　：搶匪有多高？

受害者：大約五<u>呎</u>六（5'6''）。

7. **behind**

順手牽羊者：我會不會<u>坐牢</u>？

警　　員：看情形。

shoplifter〔'ʃɑpˌlɪftə〕*n.* 順手牽羊者

behind bars 坐牢　　　**It depends.** 看情形。

8. **witness**

警　員：你打算在台灣待多久？

受害者：待到八月。如果傳喚我的話，我願意在法庭<u>上</u><u>作證</u>。

victim〔'vɪktɪm〕*n.* 受害者

willing〔'wɪlɪŋ〕*adj.* 願意的　　witness〔'wɪtnɪs〕*v.* 作證

court〔kort〕*n.* 法庭　　　summon〔'sʌmən〕*v.* 傳喚

9. **praise**

外國人：我一些外國朋友告訴我，這裡的警察提供人民很好的
　　　　服務很好。

警　員：謝謝您的<u>誇獎</u>。這是我們的本分，我們也很樂意助人。

10. **article**

機車騎士：你爲什麼開我罰單？

警　　員：因爲你違反道路交通管理條例第五十三<u>條</u>：闖紅燈。

ticket〔'tɪkɪt〕*v.* 開罰單　　violate〔'vaɪəˌlet〕*v.* 違反

article〔'ɑrtɪkl̩〕*n.* 條款　　　code〔kod〕*n.* 法規

11. *collect*

　　來電者：接線生，我想打一通對方付費電話到台灣。區域號碼是
　　　　　　02，電話號碼是23338888。我叫林約翰。

　　接線生：請稍待，我先確認對方是否願意負擔這筆費用。

　　collect call 對方付費電話　　charge〔tʃɑrdʒ〕*n.* 費用

12. *For*

　　秘書：因為某種緣故，我一直找不到鑰匙。

　　同事：鑰匙不就插在鑰匙孔上嗎？

　　colleague〔ˊkɑlig〕*n.* 同事　　keyhole〔ˊki͵hol〕*n.* 鑰匙孔

II. 閱讀測驗：25%

【譯文】

　　　　立志成為一位執法人員，是一種令人興奮的生涯規劃，但是要成為一個執法的主管，則更具挑戰性。這是個既能自我發展，而且還必須負責幫助他人發展的一種機會。有很多方法可以讓你成為一位成功的執法主管。

　　　　隨時充實自我，以把握升遷的機會。讀書、參加訓練課程、函授課程、閱讀商業期刊、上學術性的課程、利用公共圖書館與執法機構的圖書館，以及傾聽同期的人提供的意見。當機會來臨時，必須要有充足的準備。

　　　　支持你的上司。有一句古老的諺語是這樣說的：「若你也想成為主管，就讚美或支持你的主管，因為他很快就會升上去了。若是你讓上司揹黑鍋，他就會永遠留在原來的職位。」抱怨、不停地挑毛病、反對或不願支持——這些都是在組織中被忽視的最快途徑。也許你會達成短期的目標，但最後一定會毀掉你的事業。要支持你的上司；就算要批評，也必須有建設性。態度要積極。對於好事要不吝於讚美。

慎選良師益友。在警界內外，都有可以幫助你，或給你適當建議的人。好的建議者可以指引你正確的方向，他們能夠分享你的想法，並給你意見。

【答案】

13. (**A**)　　14. (**A**)　　15. (**B**)　　16. (**D**)　　17. (**D**)

【註】

enforcement〔 ɪn'forsmənt 〕*n.* 執行

challenging〔 'tʃælɪndʒɪŋ 〕*adj.* 有挑戰性的

promotion〔 prə'moʃən 〕*n.* 升遷

correspondence course 函授課程　　journal〔 'dʒɝnḷ 〕*n.* 期刊

academic〔 ͵ækə'dɛmɪk 〕*adj.* 學術的

agency〔 'edʒənsɪ 〕*n.* (政府) 機構

contemporary〔 kən'tɛmpə͵rɛrɪ 〕*n.* 同時期的人

arise〔 ə'raɪz 〕*v.* 發生　　adage〔 'ædɪdʒ 〕*n.* 諺語

ladder〔 'lædɚ 〕*n.* (成功的) 晉身階梯

move up the ladder 升遷

derogatory〔 dɪ'rɑgə͵torɪ 〕*adj.* 貶低的　　*find fault* 挑剔

negative〔 'nɛgətɪv 〕*adj.* 否定的　　track〔 træk 〕*n.* 途徑

oblivion〔 ə'blɪvɪən 〕*n.* 被遺忘　　*in the long run* 到最後

constructive〔 kən'strʌktɪv 〕*adj.* 有建設性的

positive〔 'pɑzətɪv 〕*adj.* 積極的

advisor〔 əd'vaɪzɚ 〕*n.* 顧問　　mentor〔 'mɛntɚ 〕*n.* 良師益友

counsel〔 'kaʊnsḷ 〕*v.* (給某人) 忠告

sounding board 諮詢人　　surgeon〔 'sɝdʒən 〕*n.* 外科醫生

sergeant〔 'sɑrdʒənt 〕*n.* 警官　　agent〔 'edʒənt 〕*n.* 幹員

inspector〔 ɪn'spɛktɚ 〕*n.* 督察員

prosecutor〔 'prɑsɪ͵kjutɚ 〕*n.* 檢察官

abstract〔 'æbstrækt 〕*n.* 摘要　　*step down* 離職

supervisor〔 ͵supɚ'vaɪzɚ 〕*n.* 主管　　libel〔 'laɪbḷ 〕*v.* 毀謗

參考下列一本台灣發行的英文雜誌的索引：

封面故事	3-15
社論	16
國內新聞	17-30
經濟與商業	31-37
亞洲	38-40
世界新聞	41-49
體育	50-53
旅遊	54-56
電影	57-60

【答案】

18. (**B**)　　19. (**B**)　　20. (**C**)　　21. (**E**)　　22. (**E**)

【註】

issue〔'ɪʃjʊ〕v. 發行　　index〔'ɪndɛks〕n. 索引

editorial〔ˌɛdə'tɔrɪəl〕n. 社論

economy〔ɪ'kɑnəmɪ〕n. 經濟

cinema〔'sɪnəmə〕n. 電影　　crouch〔kraʊtʃ〕v. 蹲伏

current〔'kɝənt〕adj. 目前的　　**trading price** 交易價格

stock〔stɑk〕n. 股票　　juvenile〔'dʒuvəˌnaɪl〕n. 青少年

engaged〔ɪn'gedʒd〕adj. 訂婚的 < to >

juvenile delinquency 青少年犯罪

section〔'sɛkʃən〕n. 部分

publisher〔'pʌblɪʃɚ〕n. 發行人

Ⅲ. 字彙與片語（中譯英）：10%

1. crime scene

2. forgery of identification
   forgery〔'fɔrdʒərɪ〕*n.* 偽造　　certificate〔sə'tɪfəkɪt〕*n.* 證件

3. police career

4. traffic control

5. illegal aliens / illegal immigrants
   alien〔'eljən〕*n.* 外國人
   immigrant〔'ɪməgrənt〕*n.*（來自他國的）移民

6. life sentence / life imprisonment
   sentence〔'sɛntəns〕*n.* 徒刑
   imprisonment〔ɪm'prɪzn̩mənt〕*n.* 監禁

7. patrol duties
   patrol〔pə'trol〕*n.* 巡邏

8. police-community relations

9. goal-oriented management
   oriented〔'orɪˌɛntɪd〕*adj.* 重視~的

10. arson suspect / suspect of arson
    arson〔'ɑrsn̩〕*n.* 縱火罪　　suspect〔'sʌspɛkt〕*n.* 嫌疑犯

Ⅳ. 翻譯（英譯中）：40%

1. 執法機關的行政官員都知道，他們應該為將來可能發生的事件或任務有所規劃。根據其組織的資源及主要的權限，其範圍可以從違反公眾秩序到恐怖份子發動大規模武裝破壞的威脅。然而，行政官員通常覺得計畫的過程十分冗長繁瑣，令人生畏。他們認為不論自己多努力規劃，或計畫得多麼周詳，執行效果都會大打折扣。幸運的是，行政官員還可以藉由遵循基本的規劃程序，克服這種負面的想法。

【註】

administrator〔əd'mɪnə,stretɚ〕*n.* 行政官員
assets〔'æsɛts〕*n. pl.* 資產
primary〔'praɪ,mɛrɪ〕*adj.* 首要的
jurisdiction〔,dʒʊrɪs'dɪkʃən〕*n.* 權限
civil〔'sɪvḷ〕*adj.* 公民的　　　terrorist〔'tɛrərɪst〕*n.* 恐怖份子
activate〔'æktə,vet〕*v.* 發動　　　perceive〔pɚ'siv〕*v.* 察覺
tedious〔'tidɪəs〕*adj.* 冗長乏味的
formidable〔'fɔrmɪdəbḷ〕*adj.* 可怕的
perception〔pɚ'sɛpʃən〕*n.* 看法
procedure〔prə'sidʒɚ〕*n.* 程序

2. 執法機關開始針對網路犯罪採取打擊的行動。聯邦政府機構決定了
   大方向，其中包括聯邦調查局、美國情報局，與帶頭打擊網路犯罪
   的美國海關。很多州立或地方的機構也以安裝網路程式，與安排員
   工參加網路執法課程的訓練，來加入此項行動。但是，真的有實際
   效果的，還是那些擁有能持續進行打擊網路犯罪專門資源的單位。
   他們知道，執法單位必須具有在網路方面的執法力量，以跨入二十
   一世紀。

【註】

spring into 突然熱心於某工作
federal〔'fɛdərəl〕*adj.* 聯邦的　　***set the tone*** 決定基本方針
initiative〔ɪ'nɪʃətɪv〕*n.* 主動的行動
implement〔'ɪmpləmənt〕*v.* 安裝
personnel〔,pɝsṇ'ɛl〕*n.* 人員
online〔'ɑn,laɪn〕*adj.* 線上的；網路上的
dedicated〔'dɛdə,ketɪd〕*adj.* 熱忱的；專用的
acknowledge〔ək'nɑlɪdʒ〕*v.* 承認

3. 爲了使警察能夠成功地發展出警務人員共同的文化，所以必須在形式上與實質上，讓訓練課程更有實效。有些警察學學者聲稱，傳統的警察訓練、課程名稱，與內容的設計，都反映了警察這個被管制的團體其次文化的特質。訓練仍是一種有效而且必要的工具，行政官員可用它來幫助警官改變，以發展出更具團隊精神與防範犯罪的文化。

【註】

substance〔ˋsʌbstəns〕n. 實質　　assert〔əˋsɝt〕v. 聲稱
title〔ˋtaɪtḷ〕n. 名稱
peculiarity〔pɪ͵kjulɪˋærətɪ〕n. 特質
subculture〔ˋsʌb͵kʌltʃɚ〕n. 次文化
administer〔ədˋmɪnəstɚ〕v. 執行；管理

4. 一位桃園縣的陳姓警員，在傍晚巡邏時，接到一通疑似企圖自殺的電話。陳姓警員找到在當地的一座公園，一名心煩意亂的女子。她坐在車門鎖死的車內。她一手拿著瓦斯罐，一手拿著打火機，揚言要點火自焚。陳姓警員馬上用手電筒打破駕駛座的車窗，逮捕這名女子。她被帶到當地一家醫院，而陳姓警員的右手也因爲碎玻璃而受傷。陳姓警員機警的反應，阻止了一場企圖自殺的事件。

【註】

on patrol 巡邏　　distraught〔dɪˋstrɔt〕*adj.* 心煩意亂的
locate〔loˋket〕v. 找出～的位置　　smash〔smæʃ〕v. 打碎
custody〔ˋkʌstədɪ〕n. 拘留　　*take sb. into custody* 逮捕某人
thwart〔θwɔrt〕v. 阻止

私立輔仁大學九十學年度
碩士班研究生入學考試英文試題

I. Choose the best answers to make the following sentences complete.

1. Although it hasn't rained for a long time the newspapers say there will be _____ water for the summer.
   (A) sufficient
   (B) efficient
   (C) affluent
   (D) fluent

2. An undersea communication cable linking North America and Asia broke last week, _____ millions of Internet users in Taiwan.
   (A) affected
   (B) affecting
   (C) effected
   (D) effecting

3. After studying English intensively for several years, Helen became _____.
   (A) capable
   (B) activated
   (C) diligent
   (D) proficient

4. Elderly people seem to have neither the chance nor the _____ to get plugged in.
   (A) indication
   (B) declination
   (C) inclination
   (D) declamation

5. We don't know whether the _____ weather extremes we've been having lately are normal changes in the planets atmospheric systems or not.
   (A) billiard
   (B) bizarre
   (C) blizzard
   (D) billet

6. The annual duck-watching event at the Huachiang bird sanctuary aims to foster conservation consciousness and to provide an educational _____ for the public.
   (A) venture
   (B) avenue
   (C) avenge
   (D) venue

7. Too much TV watching tends to cause children to be passive _____ who can only respond to action, but not initiate it.
   (A) visitors
   (B) spectators
   (C) inspectors
   (D) detectors

8. The major theme of our discussion is focused on the necessary steps that Taiwan has to take in order to _____ in the knowledge-based economy era.
   (A) thrive
   (B) thresh
   (C) thrill
   (D) thrust

II. Complete the following two dialogues with the given expressions.

   (A) I really had a good time!
   (B) What's the matter?
   (C) It was pretty spicy, though.
   (D) Can I help you?
   (E) How about the food?
   (F) Can't you get it fixed?
   (G) Thank you very much.

1.

Julia : You look worried, Sam. ___(9)___

Sam : My computer's broken down. I have no idea what's wrong with it.

Julia : ___(10)___

Sam : Of course, eventually. But I have a paper due tomorrow.

2.

Peter : How was you trip to Mexico?

Lucy : Fascinating. ___(11)___

Peter : Did you have any culture shock?

Lucy : Not really. I wasn't there long enough for that.

Peter : ___(12)___

Lucy : That was no problem. ___(13)___

III. Structure and Word Usage

___(14)___ that you are strong enough ___(15)___ regular visits to your family doctor? Although you try hard to stay in shape ___(16)___ always do trimming exercises, ___(17)___ had better ___(18)___ your doctor often and ___(19)___ about your physical condition.

14. (A) Do you convince   (B) Are you convinced
    (C) Are you convince   (D) Will you convince

15. (A) but needs to pay   (B) but need pay
    (C) and needn't pay   (D) don't need

16. (A) so that (B) and   (C) to   (D) but

17. (A) and however, you   (B) but you
    (C) you   (D) and still

18. (A) contact   (B) contacted
    (C) contact with   (D) keep contact

19. (A) get informed   (B) is informed
    (C) informed   (D) inform

You may ___(20)___ the *Wild Lives* monthly magazine, enjoy reading each issue ___(21)___ to your residence, and ___(22)___ in a white-washed bungalow in the sprawling bush country and driving a ___(23)___ vehicle roaring down a bumpy track in ___(24)___ wilds, ___(25)___ herds of oryx.

20. (A) subscribe　　　　　(B) too subscribe
　　(C) be subscribe　　　 (D) subscribe to

21. (A) deliver　　　　　　(B) delivering
　　(C) delivered　　　　　(D) be delivered

22. (A) imaging living　　(B) imagine yourself living
　　(C) imagining yourself to live
　　(D) image to live

23. (A) four-wheeled　　　 (B) four-wheels
　　(C) four of wheel　　　(D) four-wheeling

24. (A) game-hunting　　　 (B) hunting of game
　　(C) hunted game　　　　(D) game-hunted

25. (A) be scattered　　　 (B) scattered
　　(C) scatter　　　　　　(D) scattering

IV. In the following passage, some of the words have been
　　left out. First, read through the entire passage to
　　understand what it is about. Then, choose the word
　　which best fits in each blank from the choices
　　offered after the passage.

Life on Smooth Shores

Most people think of a beach as being a great waste
of sand, devoid of life and suitable only for sunbathing
or the construction of sand castles. Of course, the
naturalist knows this is not true. All you have to do is
watch the host of sandpipers, plovers and other birds
feeding fussily along the shoreline—they, like the
naturalist, know that beneath the sand is whole different
world of creatures.

No sensible organism would live on top of the
____(26)____, being dried and blistered by the sun and wind
____(27)____ low tide and then rolled about like a marble
____(28)____ the tide comes in. You have to investigate

beneath ___(29)___ sand if you want to find the creatures
of ___(30)___ smooth shores, for it is here that you will
___(31)___ the many different kinds of burrowers and
buriers and ___(32)___. On the face of it, the sand of a
___(33)___ beach does not look a very attractive habitat,
but ___(34)___ does have certain advantages. One of the
reasons that ___(35)___ an abundance of life can be found
here is ___(36)___ rather interesting fact that sand as an
environment is ___(37)___ constant. A few inches below the
surface, conditions are ___(39)___ much the same whether
the tide is in or ___(39)___, or whether it is warm or cold,
or sunny ___(40)___ raining. A film of water surrounds
each sand grain, ___(41)___ this water acts as a sort of
cement, sticking ___(42)___ grains together so that up to
the high tide ___(43)___ the sand is always moist. The
temperature remains fairly ___(44)___ all through the
year, and the salinity of the ___(45)___ in the sand is
unchanged even if there are ___(46)___ winter storms and
rain.

Here, in this world beneath ___(47)___ sand, you find
the hunters and the hunted exactly ___(48)___ you do in
other communities. However, at first glance ___(49)___ may
not readily appreciate what the hunted creatures feed
___(50)___. In the darkness under all this sand how can the
usual base of the food web—green plants—exist? The
answer is, of course, that they cannot, and the food for
shore creatures is "imported" by the tides. Some
sand-dwellers filter the incoming sea water through their
bodies and extract food in the shape of suspended
plankton and minute bits of detritus. Large particles
brought in by the tide fall to the bottom and provide
sustenance for the creatures that creep along the

submerged surface of the sand. Organic matter also gets mixed up in the sand itself, like a sort of soup, and you find that burrowing creatures eat the sand to extract the debris and its associated bacteria in much the same way that an earthworm eats soil.

26. (A) shoreline   (B) sand
    (C) water   (D) ground

27. (A) on   (B) when   (C) at   (D) in

28. (A) when   (B) by   (C) from   (D) if

29. (A) ocean   (B) dry   (C) under   (D) the

30. (A) some   (B) living   (C) the   (D) beach

31. (A) notice   (B) find   (C) investigate (D) study

32. (A) tube-dwellers   (B) beach fish
    (C) hunters   (D) plankton

33. (A) organic   (B) rocky   (C) ocean   (D) smooth

34. (A) it   (B) one   (C) water   (D) beach

35. (A) it   (B) so   (C) such   (D) many

36. (A) the   (B) this   (C) a   (D) one

37. (A) much   (B) frankly
    (C) biologically   (D) surprisingly

38. (A) so   (B) very   (C) quite   (D) that

39. (A) up   (B) low   (C) high   (D) out

40. (A) or   (B) not   (C) but   (D) and

41. (A) maybe   (B) then   (C) moreover   (D) and

42. (A) cement   (B) the   (C) sandy   (D) many

43. (A) way   (B) land   (C) standard   (D) mark

44. (A) warm　　　　　　　　(B) fluctuating
　　(C) constant　　　　　　(D) hot

45. (A) life　　(B) water　　(C) animals　　(D) salt

46. (A) serious　(B) many　　(C) heavy　　(D) strong

47. (A) much　　(B) the　　(C) some　　(D) grainy

48. (A) where　(B) what　　(C) when　　(D) as

49. (A) you　　(B) one　　(C) we　　(D) they

50. (A) for　　(B) on　　(C) them　　(D) of

私立輔仁大學九十年度
碩士班研究生入學考試英文試題詳解

I. 字彙：16%

1. (**A**) (A) ***sufficient*** 〔 səˋfɪʃənt 〕 *adj.* 足夠的
   (B) efficient 〔 əˋfɪʃənt 〕 *adj.* 有效率的
   (C) affluent 〔 ˋæfluənt 〕 *adj.* 富裕的
   (D) fluent 〔 ˋfluənt 〕 *adj.* 流利的

2. (**B**) (B) ***affect*** 〔 əˋfɛkt 〕 *v.* 影響
   （which affected 簡化爲分詞片語 affecting⋯ ）
   (C) effect 〔 əˋfɛkt 〕 *v.* 引起；產生
   cable 〔 ˋkebḷ 〕 *n.* 電纜

3. (**D**) (A) capable 〔 ˋkepəbḷ 〕 *adj.* 有～的能力 < *of* >
   (B) activated 〔 ˋæktə,vetɪd 〕 *adj.* 活性化的
   (C) diligent 〔 ˋdɪlədʒənt 〕 *adj.* 勤勉的
   (D) ***proficient*** 〔 prəˋfɪʃənt 〕 *adj.* 精通的
   intensively 〔 ɪnˋtɛnsɪvlɪ 〕 *adv.* 密集地

4. (**C**) (A) indication 〔 ,ɪndəˋkeʃən 〕 *n.* 跡象；指標
   (B) declination 〔 ,dɛkləˋneʃən 〕 *n.* 指南針磁針的偏角
   (C) ***inclination*** 〔 ,ɪnkləˋneʃən 〕 *n.* 傾向
   (D) declamation 〔 ,dɛkləˋmeʃən 〕 *n.* 慷慨激昂的演說
   get plugged in 跟上時代；接受新知

5.（**B**）(A)　billiard〔'bɪljəd〕*adj.* 撞球用的
　　　　(B)　***bizarre***〔bɪ'zɑr〕*adj.* 怪異的
　　　　(C)　blizzard〔'blɪzəd〕*n.* 暴風雪
　　　　(D)　billet〔'bɪlɪt〕*n.*（軍隊的）營舍（通常是民房）
　　　　　　extreme〔ɪk'trim〕*n.* 極端
　　　　　　atmospheric〔,ætməs'fɛrɪk〕*adj.* 大氣的

6.（**B**）(A)　venture〔'vɛntʃə〕*n.* 冒險
　　　　(B)　***avenue***〔'ævə,nju〕*n.* 途徑
　　　　(C)　avenge〔ə'vɛndʒ〕*v.* 復仇
　　　　(D)　venue〔'vɛnju〕*n.* 舉辦地點
　　　　　　annual〔'ænjuəl〕*adj.* 一年一度的
　　　　　　sanctuary〔'sæŋktʃu,ɛrɪ〕*n.* 保護區
　　　　　　foster〔'fɔstə〕*v.* 培養
　　　　　　conservation〔,kɑnsə'veʃən〕*n.* 保護
　　　　　　consciousness〔'kɑnʃəsnɪs〕*n.* 意識

7.（**B**）(B)　***spectator***〔spɛk'tetə〕*n.* 觀眾
　　　　(C)　inspector〔ɪn'spɛktə〕*n.* 檢查員
　　　　(D)　detector〔dɪ'tɛktə〕*n.* 探測器
　　　　　　tend to 傾向於　　initiate〔ɪ'nɪʃɪ,et〕*v.* 創始

8.（**A**）(A)　***thrive***〔θraɪv〕*v.* 繁榮
　　　　(B)　thresh〔θrɛʃ〕*v.* 打穀
　　　　(C)　thrill〔θrɪl〕*v.* 使興奮
　　　　(D)　thrust〔θrʌst〕*v.* 用力刺
　　　　　　theme〔θim〕*n.* 主題
　　　　　　era〔'ɪrə〕*n.* 紀元；時代

II. 完成下列對話：10%

(A) 我真的玩得很高興！　　(B) 怎麼了？
(C) 不過它非常的辣。　　　(D) 我可以幫你嗎？
(E) 食物怎麼樣？　　　　　(F) 你不能把它修好嗎？
(G) 非常謝謝你。

1. 茱麗亞：山姆，你好像很擔心。<u>怎麼了？</u>
　　　　　　　　　　　　　　　　　9

　山　姆：我的電腦壞了。也不知道是什麼問題。

　茱麗亞：<u>你不能把它修好嗎？</u>
　　　　　　　　　10

　山　姆：當然可以，最後一定會修好的。可是我明天有一份報
　　　　　告要交。

【答案】

9. (**B**)　　　　　　10. (**F**)

【註】

break down 故障　　eventually〔ɪ'vɛntʃʊəlɪ〕*adv.* 最後
due〔dju〕*adj.* 到期的

2. 彼得：妳去墨西哥旅行怎麼樣？
　露西：太棒了。<u>我真的玩得很高興！</u>
　　　　　　　　　　　　　　　11

　彼得：妳有沒有什麼文化衝擊？
　露西：還好，我在那邊待得沒那麼久。

　彼得：<u>食物怎麼樣？</u>
　　　　　　12

　露西：沒什麼問題。<u>不過非常的辣。</u>
　　　　　　　　　　　　　13

【答案】

　　11. (**A**)　　　12. (**E**)　　　13. (**C**)

【註】

fascinating〔ˈfæsnˌetɪŋ〕*adj.* 迷人的；很棒的

culture shock 文化衝擊（與不同的文化或新的生活環境接觸時所受到的衝擊）

spicy〔ˈspaɪsɪ〕*adj.* 辣的

Ⅲ. 結構與字詞運用：24%

【譯文】

　　你是不是相信自己已經夠強壯，不需要定期去看你的家庭醫師？雖然你非常努力地想保持身體健康，而且總是勤做塑身操，但最好還是要經常與醫師保持聯絡，而且要知道和你身體狀況有關的資訊。

【註】

regular〔ˈrɛgjələ〕*adj.* 定期的　　visit〔ˈvɪzɪt〕*n.* 就診

stay in shape 保持身體健康　　*trimming exercise* 塑身操

14. (**B**) *be convinced that* 相信

15. (**C**) 兩個動詞之間須有連接詞，且語意並無轉折，故選 (C) *and needn't pay*。need 在此為助動詞。

16. (**B**) 以句意，選 (B) *and*「而且」。

17. (**C**) 本句已有連接詞 Although，不需要另一個連接詞，故選 (C) *you*。

18.(**A**) *contact sb.* 與某人保持聯繫 (= *keep contact with sb.*)

19.(**A**) *get informed about* 得知關於～的消息

【譯文】

　　你可以訂閱「野生動物」月刊，享受寄到府上的每一期刊物，然後想像自己生活在灌木叢生的鄉間，住在漆成白色的小平房裏，開著四輪傳動車，在崎嶇的狩獵野地小徑呼嘯而過，將成群的羚羊驅散。

【註】

issue〔ˋɪʃjʊ〕*n.* (雜誌) 一期　　residence〔ˋrɛzədəns〕*n.* 住所
white-washed〔ˋhwaɪt͵waʃt〕*adj.* 漆成白色的
bungalow〔ˋbʌŋgə͵lo〕*n.* 小平房　　sprawl〔sprɔl〕*v.* 蔓延
roar〔ror〕*v.* 呼嘯　　bumpy〔ˋbʌmpɪ〕*adj.* 崎嶇的
roar〔ror〕*v.* 乘坐著轟響著疾馳的車
track〔træk〕*n.* 小徑　　wilds〔waɪldz〕*n.pl.* 荒野
herd〔hɝd〕*n.* 獸群　　oryx〔ˋorɪks〕*n.* 羚羊

20.(**D**) *subscribe to*～ 訂閱～

21.(**C**) 本句是由…which is delivered…簡化而來。

22.(**B**) 依句意，「想像自己正住在漆成白色的小平房中」，選 (B)。

23.(**A**) four-wheeled〔ˋfor͵hwild〕*adj.* 四輪驅動的

24.(**A**) game-hunting〔ˋgem͵hʌntɪŋ〕*adj.* 狩獵的

25.(**D**) 兩個動詞之間無連接詞，第二個動詞須用現在分詞，故選 (D)。
　　　　scatter〔ˋskætɚ〕*v.* 驅散

IV. 填字：50%

【譯文】

平靜潮間帶中的生物

　　大部分的人想到海灘，就會把它想成是一大片荒蕪的沙，沒有生物，只適合做日光浴跟築沙堡。當然，自然學家知道這並不是事實。你只須觀看成群的磯鷸、雎鳩以及其他鳥類，煞有介事地正沿著海岸線覓食，就跟自然學家一樣，牠們知道在沙灘底下是個完全不同的生物世界。

　　聰明的生物是不會住在沙灘的表面，因為在退潮時，沙灘會因為風吹日曬而乾枯，然後在漲潮時，又會像大理石一樣被海浪所拍打。因此，如果你想要在平靜的潮間帶中找到生物的話，你一定要探究沙灘的下層，因為在底下，你會發現很多不同種類的穴居物、藏在地下的生物，以及管穴居住生物。表面上看來，平坦的沙灘似乎不是個吸引人的住所，但卻真的有某些好處。沙灘的環境，有著令人訝異的恆久不變性，這是個相當有趣的事實，也是此處能發現如此豐富生物的理由之一。在沙漠表面以下幾吋的地方，不論是漲潮或退潮，不論冷暖、晴雨，環境都非常的一致。每顆砂粒都有薄薄的水層包著，水的作用就像水泥一樣，將很多沙粒黏附在一起，因此到高潮標的沙灘，這裏永遠都是潮濕的。終年保持一定的恆溫，沙灘中的水分鹽度，即使冬天有強烈的暴風雨，也不會有所改變。

　　在沙灘底下，你會發現就像其他群體一樣，有獵捕者也有獵物。然而，你可能難以一眼就看出，被獵捕的生物是靠什麼維生的。在所有沙灘的黑暗下層，食物鏈的慣常基礎 —— 綠色植物 —— 要如何生存呢？當然答案就是無法生存，是故潮間帶生物的食物是靠潮汐「進口」的。一些住在沙灘的生物，會以牠們的身體過濾湧進的海水，再從蜉蝣生物及細小的碎石中萃取食物。潮汐所帶來的較大微粒會掉落到底層，就提供養分給那些沿著被淹沒的沙灘表層爬行的生物。有機物也是沙灘的一部分，就像一種湯一樣，因而你會發現，藏在洞穴中的生物會跟蚯蚓一樣，靠吃泥土而從中萃取碎屑與碎屑上的細菌。

【答案】

26. (**B**)	27. (**C**)	28. (**A**)	29. (**D**)	30. (**C**)
31. (**B**)	32. (**A**)	33. (**D**)	34. (**A**)	35. (**C**)
36. (**A**)	37. (**D**)	38. (**B**)	39. (**D**)	40. (**A**)
41. (**D**)	42. (**B**)	43. (**D**)	44. (**C**)	45. (**B**)
46. (**D**)	47. (**B**)	48. (**D**)	49. (**A**)	50. (**B**)

【註】

smooth〔smuð〕*adj.* 平靜的；平坦的

shore〔ʃor〕*n.* 潮間帶　　waste〔west〕*n.* 荒地

be devoid of 缺乏　　sunbathe〔'sʌn,beð〕*v.* 作日光浴

naturalist〔'nætʃərəlɪst〕*n.* 自然學家　　host〔host〕*n.* 大量

sandpiper〔'sænd,paɪpə〕*n.* 磯鷸　　plover〔'plʌvə〕*n.* 雎鳩

fussily〔'fʌsəlɪ〕*adv.* 煞有介事地；小題大作地

shoreline〔'ʃorlaɪn〕*n.* 海岸線

creature〔'kritʃə〕*n.* 生物

organism〔'ɔrgən,ɪzəm〕*n.* 有機體

blister〔'blɪstə〕*v.* 猛烈日曬　　***low tide*** 退潮的時候

roll〔rol〕*v.* 海浪拍打　　marble〔'mɑrbl̩〕*n.* 大理石

burrower〔'bɝoə〕*n.* 穴居者

burier〔'bɛrɪə〕*n.* 將自己藏在地下的生物

habitat〔'hæbə,tæt〕*n.* 居住處

abundance〔ə'bʌndəns〕*n.* 充足　　film〔fɪlm〕*n.* 薄膜

grain〔gren〕*n.* 粒子　　cement〔sɪ'mɛnt〕*n.* 水泥

moist〔mɔɪst〕*adj.* 潮濕的

salinity〔sə'lɪnətɪ〕*n.* 鹽分；鹽度

filter〔'fɪltə〕*v.* 過濾　　extract〔ɪk'strækt〕*v.* 萃取；提取

in the shape of 以～型態

plankton〔'plæŋktən〕*n.* 浮蝣生物

minute〔maɪˈnjut〕*adj.* 微小的

detritus〔dɪˈtraɪtəs〕*n.* 碎石　　particle〔ˈpɑrtɪkḷ〕*n.* 微粒

sustenance〔ˈsʌstənəns〕*n.* 食物　　creep〔krip〕*v.* 爬行

submerged〔səbˈmɝdʒd〕*adj.* 淹沒的

organic〔ɔrˈgænɪk〕*adj.* 有機物的　　matter〔ˈmætɚ〕*n.* 物質

debris〔dəˈbri〕*n.* 碎屑

bacterium〔bækˈtɪrɪəm〕*n.* 細菌（複數為 bacteria）

earthworm〔ˈɝθ,wɝm〕*n.* 蚯蚓

心得筆記欄

國立台灣大學八十九學年度
碩士班研究生入學考試英文試題

Choose the Best answer for each question. To indicate your choice, blacken the appropriate space on your computer card for each question.

Example : It was Joan's first visit to the country, and
everything was fresh and ＿＿＿＿＿＿ to her.
(A) dull　　　　　(B) quickly
(C) new　　　　　(D) excite

Answer : A　B　C　D

Vocabulary : Part ── Sentence Completion
Instruction : Choose the answer that best completes the sentence.

1. In college, students learn to ＿＿＿＿＿＿ from specific facts to larger situations.
   (A) harmonize　　　　(B) randomize
   (C) neutralize　　　　(D) generalize

2. The girl did not want to take sides in the argument between her two friends, but her ＿＿＿＿＿＿ only made them both angry at her.
   (A) improbability　　(B) impartiality
   (C) impatience　　　(D) immorality

3. The student ＿＿＿＿＿＿ through her locker looking for her chemistry assignment.
   (A) rummaged　　　(B) discarded
   (C) stormed　　　　(D) careened

4. Even though he managed to _____ through the interview, he didn't think he had a very good shot at getting the job.
   (A) bear   (B) argue
   (C) muddle   (D) doze

5. Don't bother yourself with such _____ details; the professor will only test you on the main ideas of the chapter.
   (A) trifling   (B) lagging
   (C) threatening   (D) compromising

Vocabulary : Part II — Vocabulary in Context
Instruction : Choose the answer that best reflects the meaning of the capitalized word in each sentence as used in that particular context.

6. Macy's is committed to customer service. If we can be of further help, please feel FREE to call on us at any time.
   (A) released   (B) comfortable
   (C) perceptible   (D) frank

7. The purpose of the telescope is to gather light that has been EMITTED by distant sources.
   (A) created   (B) rescued
   (C) discharged   (D) escaped

8. Geometrical ideas correspond to more or less exact objects in nature, and these last are undoubtedly the EXCLUSIVE cause of the genesis of those ideas.
   (A) excluding   (B) sole
   (C) regular   (D) necessary

9. The neighborhood of Porto Praya, viewed from the
   sea, wears a desolate aspect. The volcanic fires of
   a past age, and the scorching heat of the tropical
   sun, have in most places RENDERED the soil unfit
   for vegetation.
   (A) helped   (B) made
   (C) followed   (D) planted

10. Pursuing this line of inquiry, I found that in Arab
    thought I had no rights whatsoever by virtue of
    occupying a given spot; neither my place nor my
    body was INVIOLATE.
    (A) sacred   (B) unused
    (C) touched   (D) departed

11. The view arose of information as an active agent,
    something that does not just sit there passively,
    but INFORMS the material world, much as the messages
    of the genes instruct the machinery of the cell to
    build an organism.
    (A) admonishes   (B) attempts
    (C) affirms   (D) advises

Vocabulary : Part III — Analogies
Instruction : In each of the questions below you will
find a related pair of words or phrases, followed by
four more pairs of words or phrases. Choose the pair
that most closely mirrors the relationship expressed in
the original pair.

Example : SMILE: HAPPINESS:
           (A) boredom: apathy   (B) cook: food
           (C) comedy: laughter (D) scowl: anger
Answer   : D

12. CHAIR: FURNITURE:
    (A) album: offering   (B) vaccine: polio
    (C) fine: penalty   (D) present: allowance

13. NECESSARY: INDISPENSABLE:
    (A) corrupt: delighted
    (B) genuine: distorted
    (C) placid: fractious
    (D) mysterious: bizarre

14. DEFENSELESS: SECURITY:
    (A) jubilant: foundation
    (B) inferior: service
    (C) backward: personality
    (D) incapable: skill

15. INTELLIGENT: DUMB:
    (A) scattered: concentrated
    (B) frightened: suspicious
    (C) elderly: envious
    (D) creative: unbelievable

II. Cloze Test
    Instruction: Choose the best answer to fill in the blank.

  Throughout history, humans have been forming relationships with other animals. ____(16)____ of these relationships have been mutually beneficial, ____(17)____ many have served human needs or wants ____(18)____ the animals involved. It is important that we ____(19)____ humans recognize these relationships and ____(20)____ they affect both animals and us. ____(21)____ we understand that we, as humans, are also animals and share many common characteristics ____(22)____ other members of the animal kingdom, we will be ____(23)____ sensitive to the rights of animals and will ____(24)____ be capable of making more responsible decisions ____(25)____ our personal relationships with animals.

16. (A) Much　　　　　　　　　(B) All
    (C) Less　　　　　　　　　(D) Few

17. (A) and　　　　　　　　　　(B) because
    (C) but　　　　　　　　　　(D) since

18. (A) in case of　　　　　　　(B) at the expense of
    (C) for the sake of　　　　(D) in stead of

19. (A) for　　　　　　　　　　(B) like
    (C) such　　　　　　　　　(D) as

20. (A) how　　　　　　　　　　(B) what
    (C) when　　　　　　　　　(D) which

21. (A) Since　　　　　　　　　(B) If
    (C) That　　　　　　　　　(D) Whether

22. (A) with　　　　　　　　　　(B) by
    (C) for　　　　　　　　　　(D) on

23. (A) much　　　　　　　　　(B) less
    (C) fewer　　　　　　　　(D) more

24. (A) automatically　　　　　(B) consequently
    (C) reluctantly　　　　　　(D) purposely

25. (A) are concerned　　　　　(B) concerned
    (C) concerning　　　　　　(D) are concerning

III. Reading Comprehension
    Instruction: Read each of the following passages and choose the best answer to each question.

    Learning to play a musical instrument — keyboard, piano, flute, guitar — is a long-term project. You should get a good teacher, one whom you respect and like. You should plan to practice every day for at least a year before you see any real progress, and

several years before you play well. You should be
patient; like everything else that's worthwhile,
success will not come easy. If you do all this and you
still sound terrible, well, maybe you just weren't
born with a musical gene!

26. What is the topic of this passage?
    (A) a musical gene
    (B) a long-term project
    (C) learning to play a musical instrument
    (D) how to become a successful guitar player

   Public distance (12 feet and farther) is well
outside the range for close involvement with another
person. It is impractical for interpersonal communication.
We are limited to what we can see and hear at that
distance; topics for conversation are relatively
impersonal and formal; and most of the communication
that occurs is in the public-speaking style with
subjects planned in advance and limited opportunities
for feedback.

27. What is the topic of the passage?
    (A) public distance
    (B) topics for conversation
    (C) formal communication
    (D) the importance of nonverbal communication

28. Which of the following is not mentioned as a feature
    of "public distance"?
    (A) Most conversation that occurs is in a public-
        speaking style.
    (B) The topics involved are often impersonal and
        formal.
    (C) It's a common practice between good friends.
    (D) It's impractical for interpersonal communication.

The absence of instincts in people leads to a variety of behavior that is not observed in other animals. Whereas a cornered rat always exhibits the same automatic and predictable aggressive reaction, a "cornered" human being may not necessarily act the same way. Imagine a young boy, say 6 or 7 years old, walking in the woods one day who happens upon a bear cub. He does not know yet that it is dangerous to be near the young of wild animals. When the boy sees how playful the cub is, he begins to run and play with it. Shortly, the mother bear returns and finds this fellow cavorting with her cub. The adult bear, instinctively perceiving a threat to her young, automatically reacts. She growls and makes other noises indicating her intent to attack and chases the boy through the woods into a small box canyon. The boy, like the proverbial rat, finds himself "cornered" and must turn to face his enemy. What will he do?

29. This reading is primarily concerned with
    (A) the proverbial rat.
    (B) a mother's love for her young cub.
    (C) the instinctive behavior of a boy.
    (D) the unpredictability of human behavior.

30. The writer relies on which of the following to explain his ideas to the reader?
    (A) Statistics.
    (B) Examples.
    (C) Experiments.
    (D) Personal experiences.

Students who start or return to college after the age of twenty-five often take a reading/study course to brush up on their efficiency. These reentry students have had experience in the world of work and family, they bring this knowledge to their course work, and they know exactly what they want from college. They use their time well because their busy lives force them to; family, exercise, study, and jobs must be carefully balanced if they want to succeed. Students who are middle-aged and older often study harder and get better grades, for personal satisfaction but also, perhaps, because of a sense of competition with their younger classmates.

31. This passage is primarily concerned with
    (A) older (reentry) students.
    (B) types of students in college.
    (C) competition among students.
    (D) how to balance school work with family life.

32. Which of the following is not mentioned as a factor in the older "reentry" students' better performance at college?
    (A) Reentry students are smarter.
    (B) Reentry students know what they want.
    (C) Reentry students simply work harder.
    (D) Older students are highly motivated.

Effective listening means listening with a third ear. By this I mean trying to listen for the meanings behind the words and not just to the words alone. The way words are spoken — loud, soft, fast, slow, strong, hesitating — is very important. There are messages buried in all the clues that surround words. If a mother says, "Come in now," in a soft, gentle voice, it may mean the kids have a few more minutes. If she says, "Come in NOW," there is no question about the meaning of the command. To listen effectively we have to pay attention to facial expressions and eye contact, gestures and body movement, as well as to the quality of the other person's voice, vocabulary, rhythm, rate and tone. Listening with our third ear helps us to understand the whole message.

33. What is the topic of the passage?
   (A) cues in words
   (B) listening techniques
   (C) body language
   (D) effective speaking

34. An effective listener uses all of the following to increase his/her understanding of the message EXCEPT
   (A) the ears of the speaker.
   (B) vocabulary used by the speaker.
   (C) the facial expressions of the speaker.
   (D) the voice quality of the speaker.

The Bill of Rights is an inexhaustible source of potential conflicts over rights. Clearly, the Constitiution meant to guarantee the right to a fair trial as well as a free press. But a trial may not be fair if press coverage inflames public opinion so much that an impartial jury cannot be found. In one famous criminal trial an Ohio physician, Sam Sheppard, was accused of the murder of his wife. The extent of press coverage rivaled that of a military campaign, and little of it sympathized with Dr. Sheppard. Found guilty and sent to the state prison, Sheppard appealed his conviction to the Supreme Court. He argued that press coverage had interfered with his ability to get a fair trial. The Supreme Court agreed, claiming that the press had created a virtual "Roman circus," and reversed Sheppard's conviction.

35. The reading is mainly concerned with
    (A) the Bill of Rights.
    (B) a Roman circus.
    (C) the Sheppard murder case.
    (D) an impartial murder trial.

36. The reason that the author mentions Sheppard's trial is to show
    (A) that Sam Sheppard was a cold-blooded murderer
    (B) that Sam Sheppard did not have a fair trial.
    (C) how a virtual "Roman circus" was created during the Sheppard trail
    (D) how extensive press coverage can sometimes interfere with civil rights

　　The current high divorce rate in the United States does not mean, as common sense would suggest, that the institution of marriage is very unpopular. On the contrary, people seem to love marriage too much, as suggested by several pieces of evidence. First, our society has the highest rate of marriage in the industrial world despite having the highest rate of divorce. Second, within the United States, most of the southeastern, southwestern, and western states have higher divorce rates than the national average but also have higher marriage rates. And third, the majority of those who are divorced eventually remarry. Why don't they behave like Mark Twain's cat, who after having been burned by a hot stove would not go near any stove? Apparently, divorce in U.S. society does not represent a rejection of marriage but only of a specific partner.

37. This passage is mainly about
    (A) rejection of marriage.
    (B) acceptance of marriage.
    (C) high divorce rates.
    (D) Mark Twain's cat.

38. Which of the following statements is NOT true?
    (A) The Americans have the highest divorce rate in the industrial world.
    (B) The institution of marriage in the United State is not very popular.
    (C) Most Americans who are divorced will eventually get married again.
    (D) Most of the western states have higher divorce rates than the national average.

    It was a medieval custom to swaddle infants during their first year. Swaddling involved wrapping the infant in cloth bandages with arms and legs pressed closely to the body. Parents feared that infants might scratch their eyes and distort their tender limbs by bending them improperly. Swaddling also kept them from touching their genitals and from crawling "like a beast." However, De Mause, a historian who has studied concepts of childhood and child-rearing practices of the past, has found evidence that the main purpose of swaddling was for the adults' convenience. Swaddled infants tend to be quiet and passive. They sleep more, their heart rate slows, and they cry less. Swaddled infants might have been laid for hours "behind a hot oven, or hung on pegs on the wall," and leading-strings were sometimes used to "puppet" the infant around for the amusement of adults.

39. What is the topic of the passage?
    (A) De Mause, the historian
    (B) swaddling infants
    (C) medieval customs
    (D) child-rearing practices of the past

40. In the passage, the word "swaddle" means
    (A) to crawl like a beast.
    (B) to hang something on a wall.
    (C) to put a baby behind a hot oven.
    (D) to wrap a baby tightly in many coverings.

   "We've got a form of brainwashing going on in our country," Morrie sighed. "Do you know how they brainwash people? They repeat something over and over. And that's what we do in this country. Owning things is good. More money is good. More property is good. More commercialism is good. More is good. More is good. We repeat it and have it repeated to us over and over again until nobody bothers to think otherwise. The average person is so fogged up by all this, he or she has no perspective on what's really important anymore."

   "There's a big confusion in this country over what we want versus what we need," Morrie went on. "You need food. You want a chocolate sundae. You have to be honest with yourself. You don't need the latest sports car, you don't need the biggest house. The truth is you don't get satisfaction from those things. You know what really gives you satisfaction?"

   "What?"

"Offering others what you have to give." Morrie looked out the window of his study. "Remember what I said about finding a meaningful life? I wrote it down, but now I can recite it. Devote yourself to loving others. Devote yourself to your community around you. Devote yourself to creating something that gives you purpose and meaning."

He grinned. "You notice there's nothing in there about a salary."

I jotted some of the things Morrie was saying on a yellow pad. I did this mostly because I didn't want him to see my eyes, to know what I was thinking, that I had been for much of my life since graduation, pursuing these very things that he had been railing against — bigger toys, a nicer house. Because I worked among rich and famous athletes, I convinced myself that my needs were realistic, my greed inconsequential compared to theirs.

This was a smokescreen. Morrie made that obvious.

41. Why does Morrie feel that most people are confused?
    (A) Because they haven't graduated from college.
    (B) Because they watch too many commercials.
    (C) Because they don't understand what's important in life.
    (D) Because the weather is foggy so they can't see where they're going.

42. Refer back to Morrie's sentence. "You notice there's nothing in there about a salary." What is in there referring to?
    (A) his local community   (B) his current job
    (C) his study window   (D) his life philosophy

43. Which of the following is something that Morrie would consider a want and not a need?
    (A) clean drinking water
    (B) designer clothes
    (C) sanitary food
    (D) adequate shelter

44. In this passage, Morrie is most likely _____.
    (A) giving a sermon in a church
    (B) talking with a friend
    (C) lecturing to a large audience
    (D) giving a political speech

45. The author of this passage feels _____ his past behavior.
    (A) proud of
    (B) modest about
    (C) presumptuous about
    (D) embarrassed by

"Good heavens," muttered the guard to himself, as the wiry, dark-haired man entered the carriage. There's something just plain undignified, if not downright suspicious, about a man wearing a pajama top under a sports jacket, especially when the jacket hasn't been cleaned since it left the shop, observed the guard, as he moved down the carriage checking tickets.

It would no doubt have come as quite a shock had the guard known that the "suspicious-looking" man in the rumpled sports jacket, nervously twisting and bending his second-class ticket to Cambridge, was one of the prime contributors to the Allies' recent victory over Germany, a man unknown to the general public but regarded as brilliant in scientific circles.

Alan Turing had done his war service at Bletchley
Park, a rural estate midway between Cambridge and Oxford,
working as a code-breaker. When it became known, early
on in the war, that the German military was sending
coded orders to its forces using a machine termed the
Enigma, a handful of mathematicians, led by Turing,
analyzed methods of using intercepted messages and
various searching techniques to pin down the workings
of the Enigma machine. These scientists developed
strategies that eventually led to their being able to
decipher messages as if they were receiving the
uncoded text directly from the German High Command.
By the end of the war, Turing had enough daily contact
with electronic machinery and its uses for uncovering
patterns in data to begin to think seriously about
building a computing machine that could actually
duplicate — if not exceed — the thought process of the
human mind. And it was this very notion that occupied
his mind that afternoon on the way from Manchester to
downtown Cambridge.

46. The characters in the above passage are riding
　　_____.
　　(A) in a prison bus
　　(B) on a train
　　(C) in a police car
　　(D) on an airplane

47. The "suspicious looking" man is all of the
　　following EXCEPT _____.
　　(A) thin　　　　　　　　　(B) neat
　　(C) smart　　　　　　　　(D) fidgety

48. Turing is going from _____.
    (A) Oxford to Cambridge
    (B) Cambridge to Manchester
    (C) Manchester to Cambridge
    (D) Bletchley Park to Oxford

49. By the end of the war, Turing had already _____.
    (A) built a computing machine
    (B) defeated the Allies
    (C) used a machine called the Enigma
    (D) helped break the Germans' codes

50. From the above passage, we can infer that Turing
    is _____.
    (A) an eccentric genius
    (B) the man who invented personal computers
    (C) a notorious Englishman
    (D) a war criminal

國立台灣大學八十九年度
碩士班研究生入學考試英文試題詳解

I. 字彙：30%

Part I

1. (**D**)　(A)　harmonize〔ˈhɑrməˌnaɪz〕*v.* 使和諧
　　　　(B)　randomize〔ˈrændəmˌaɪz〕*v.* 隨意挑選；隨機化
　　　　(C)　neutralize〔ˈnjutrəlˌaɪz〕*v.* 使中和
　　　　(D)　*generalize*〔ˈdʒɛnərəlˌaɪz〕*v.* 歸納
　　　　　specific〔spɪˈsɪfɪk〕*adj.* 特定的

2. (**B**)　(A)　improbability〔ɪmˌprɑbəˈbɪlətɪ〕*n.* 不可能
　　　　(B)　*impartiality*〔ˌɪmpɑrˈʃælətɪ〕*n.* 不偏不倚；公正
　　　　(C)　impatience〔ɪmˈpeʃəns〕*n.* 無耐性
　　　　(D)　immorality〔ˌɪməˈrælətɪ〕*n.* 不道德
　　　　　take sides 偏袒　　argument〔ˈɑrgjəmənt〕*n.* 爭論

3. (**A**)　(A)　*rummage*〔ˈrʌmɪdʒ〕*v.* 翻找
　　　　(B)　discard〔dɪsˈkɑrd〕*v.* 丟棄
　　　　(C)　storm〔stɔrm〕*v.*（天氣）起風暴；颳大風
　　　　(D)　careen〔kəˈrin〕*v.*（將船）傾側
　　　　　locker〔ˈlɑkɚ〕*n.* 置物櫃

4. (**C**)　(A)　bear〔bɛr〕*v.* 忍受
　　　　(B)　argue〔ˈɑrgju〕*v.* 爭論
　　　　(C)　*muddle through* 混過去；胡亂應付過去
　　　　(D)　doze〔doz〕*v.* 打瞌睡
　　　　　shot〔ʃɑt〕*n.* 嘗試　　*have a shot at* 嘗試

5. (**A**)　(A) ***trifling*** 〔 ˈtraɪflɪŋ 〕 *adj.* 微不足道的

　　　　 (B) **lagging** 〔 ˈlægɪŋ 〕 *adj.* 緩慢的

　　　　 (C) **threatening** 〔 ˈθrɛtn̩ɪŋ 〕 *adj.* 威脅的

　　　　 (D) **compromising** 〔 ˈkɑmprəˌmaɪzɪŋ 〕 *adj.* 損害（名譽等）的

　　　　 bother 〔 ˈbɑðɚ 〕 *v.* 使苦惱　　detail 〔 ˈditel 〕 *n.* 細節

　　　　 chapter 〔 ˈtʃæptɚ 〕 *n.* 章節

Part II

6. (**B**)　free 〔 fri 〕 *adj.* 自在的

　　　　 (A) **released** 〔 rɪˈlist 〕 *adj.* 釋放的

　　　　 (B) ***comfortable*** 〔 ˈkʌmfətəbl̩ 〕 *adj.* 輕鬆自在的

　　　　 (C) **perceptible** 〔 pɚˈsɛptəbl̩ 〕 *adj.* 可感覺到的

　　　　 (D) **frank** 〔 fræŋk 〕 *adj.* 坦白的

　　　　 be committed to 專心致力於

　　　　 call on 拜訪（某人）

7. (**C**)　emit 〔 ɪˈmɪt 〕 *v.* 發射

　　　　 (A) **create** 〔 krɪˈet 〕 *v.* 創造

　　　　 (B) **rescue** 〔 ˈrɛskju 〕 *v.* 拯救

　　　　 (C) ***discharge*** 〔 dɪsˈtʃɑrdʒ 〕 *v.* 發射；放出

　　　　 (D) **escape** 〔 əˈskep 〕 *v.* 逃走

　　　　 purpose 〔 ˈpɝpəs 〕 *n.* 用途

　　　　 telescope 〔 ˈtɛləˌskop 〕 *n.* 望遠鏡

　　　　 distant 〔 ˈdɪstənt 〕 *adj.* 遙遠的

　　　　 source 〔 sors 〕 *n.* 來源

8. (**B**)　exclusive〔ɪkˈsklusɪv〕*adj.* 唯一的
　　(A)　excluding〔ɪkˈskludɪŋ〕*prep.* 除～之外
　　(B)　*sole*〔sol〕*adj.* 單一的
　　(C)　regular〔ˈrɛgjəlɚ〕*adj.* 定期的
　　　　geometrical〔ˌdʒiəˈmɛtrɪkl̩〕*adj.* 幾何的
　　　　correspond to 符合；一致
　　　　more or less 或多或少；幾乎
　　　　undoubtedly〔ʌnˈdautɪdlɪ〕*adv.* 無疑地
　　　　genesis〔ˈdʒɛnəsɪs〕*n.* 起源

9. (**B**)　render〔ˈrɛndɚ〕*v.* 使成為
　　(B)　*make*〔mek〕*v.* 使
　　　　wear〔wɛr〕*v.* 帶有　　aspect〔ˈæspɛkt〕*n.* 外觀
　　　　desolate〔ˈdɛsl̩ɪt〕*adj.* 荒涼的
　　　　volcanic〔vɑlˈkænɪk〕*adj.* 火山的
　　　　scorching〔ˈskɔrtʃɪŋ〕*adj.* 灼熱的
　　　　unfit〔ʌnˈfɪt〕*adj.* 不適宜的
　　　　vegetation〔ˌvɛdʒəˈteʃən〕*n.* 植物

10. (**A**)　inviolate〔ɪnˈvaɪəlɪt〕*adj.* 不受侵犯的
　　(A)　*sacred*〔ˈsekrɪd〕*adj.* 神聖不可侵犯的
　　(B)　unused〔ʌnˈjuzd〕*adj.* 不用的；閒置的
　　(C)　touched〔tʌtʃt〕*adj.* 感動的
　　(D)　departed〔dɪˈpɑrtɪd〕*adj.* 過去的；死去的
　　　　pursue〔pɚˈsu〕*v.* 繼續　　inquiry〔ɪnˈkwaɪrɪ〕*n.* 調查
　　　　whatsoever〔ˌhwɑtsoˈɛvɚ〕*adv.* 無論如何
　　　　be virtue of 憑藉；由於　　occupy〔ˈɑkjəˌpaɪ〕*v.* 佔有
　　　　given〔ˈgɪvən〕*adj.* 特定的

11. (**D**) inform〔ɪnˈfɔrm〕v. 通知
   - (A) admonish〔ədˈmɑnɪʃ〕v. 告誡
   - (B) attempt〔əˈtɛmpt〕v. 試圖
   - (C) affirm〔əˈfɜm〕v. 肯定
   - (D) **advise**〔ədˈvaɪz〕v. 通知
        arise〔əˈraɪz〕v. 由…產生　　agent〔ˈedʒənt〕n. 作用者
        gene〔dʒin〕n. 基因
        instruct〔ɪnˈstrʌkt〕v. 教導；命令
        machinery〔məˈʃinərɪ〕n. 組織
        organism〔ˈɔrgənˌɪzəm〕n. 有機體；生物

Part Ⅲ

12. (**C**)
   - (A) album〔ˈælbəm〕n. 相簿；專輯唱片
        offering〔ˈɔfərɪŋ〕n. 提供；贈品
   - (B) vaccine〔ˈvæksin〕n. 疫苗
        polio〔ˈpolɪo〕n. 小兒麻痺症
   - (C) **fine**〔faɪn〕n. 罰款
        penalty〔ˈpɛnḷtɪ〕n. 處罰；刑罰
   - (D) present〔ˈprɛzṇt〕n. 禮物
        allowance〔əˈlaʊəns〕n. 津貼；零用錢

13. (**D**)
   - (A) corrupt〔kəˈrʌpt〕adj. 腐敗的
        delighted〔dɪˈlaɪtɪd〕adj. 高興的
   - (B) genuine〔ˈdʒɛnjuɪn〕adj. 眞正的
        distorted〔dɪsˈtɔrtɪd〕adj. 扭曲的
   - (C) placid〔ˈplæsɪd〕adj. 溫順的
        fractious〔ˈfrækʃəs〕adj. 易怒的
   - (D) **mysterious**〔mɪsˈtɪrɪəs〕adj. 神祕的
        bizarre〔bɪˈzɑr〕adj. 奇異的；古怪的
        indispensable〔ˌɪndɪˈspɛnsəbḷ〕adj. 不可或缺的

14. (**D**)　(A)　jubilant〔ˋdʒublənt〕*adj.* 歡呼的
　　　　　　　foundation〔faunˋdeʃən〕*n.* 建立；基礎
　　　　　　(B)　inferior〔ɪnˋfɪrɪɚ〕*adj.* 較差的
　　　　　　　service〔ˋsɝvɪs〕*n.* 服務
　　　　　　(C)　backward〔ˋbækwɚd〕*adj.* 向後的
　　　　　　　personality〔͵pɝsnˋælətɪ〕*n.* 個性
　　　　　　(D)　*incapable*〔ɪnˋkepəbḷ〕*n.* 不能勝任的
　　　　　　　skill〔skɪl〕*n.* 技能
　　　　　　　defenseless〔dɪˋfɛnslɪs〕*adj.* 無防備的
　　　　　　　security〔sɪˋkjurətɪ〕*n.* 安全

15. (**A**)　(A)　*scattered*〔ˋskætɚd〕*adj.* 分散的
　　　　　　　concentrated〔ˋkɑnsṇ͵tretɪd〕*adj.* 集中的
　　　　　　(B)　frightened〔ˋfraɪtṇd〕*adj.* 害怕的
　　　　　　　suspicious〔səˋspɪʃəs〕*adj.* 懷疑的；可能的
　　　　　　(C)　elderly〔ˋɛldɚlɪ〕*adj.* 年長的
　　　　　　　envious〔ˋɛnvɪəs〕*adj.* 嫉妒的
　　　　　　(D)　creative〔krɪˋetɪv〕*adj.* 有創造力的
　　　　　　　unbelievable〔͵ʌnbɪˋlivəbḷ〕*adj.* 難以相信的
　　　　　　　intelligent〔ɪnˋtɛlədʒənt〕*adj.* 聰明的
　　　　　　　dumb〔dʌm〕*adj.* 笨的

Ⅱ. 克漏字：20%

【譯文】

　　　有史以來，人類就一直和其他動物建立關係。這些關係當中，極少部分是雙方互惠的，有許多關係滿足了人類的需要或是需求，卻犧牲了相關的動物。身為人類，很重要的一點是，我們應該認清這些關係，以及這些關係如何影響動物和人類。如果我們了解到，人類本身也是動物，並且和動物界的其他成員有許多共同的特徵，我們將對動物應享的權利更敏感，因而能夠做出關於人和動物之間的關係，更負責任的決定。

【註】

　　throughout〔θru'aut〕*prep.* 遍及
　　relationship〔rɪ'lessn,ʃɪp〕*n.* 關係
　　mutually〔'mjutʃʊəlɪ〕*adv.* 互相地
　　beneficial〔,bɛnə'fɪʃəl〕*adj.* 有益的
　　involved〔ɪn'vɑlvd〕*adj.* 有關的；牽涉在內的
　　recognize〔'rɛkəg,naɪz〕*v.* 認識到；明白
　　characteristic〔,kærɪktə'rɪstɪk〕*n.* 特徵
　　kingdom〔'kɪŋdəm〕*n.*【生物】界
　　sensitive〔'sɛnsətɪv〕*adj.* 敏感的 < *to* >

16.(**D**)　依句意，「極少的」關係，選 (D) *Few*。

17.(**A**)　前後句意並無轉折，且無必然的因果關係，故選 (A) *and*。

18.(**B**)　*at the expense of*~　以~代價

19.(**D**)　我們「身為」人類，選 (D) *as*。

20.(**A**)　依句意，這些關係是「如何」影響我們和動物選 (A) *how*。

21.(**B**)　依句意，選 (B) *If*「如果」。

22.(**A**)　*share sth. with*~　與~共有某物

23.(**D**)　依句意，我們將會對動物應享的權利「更」敏感，為肯定比較，選 (B) *more*。

24.(**B**)　(A) automatically〔,ɔtə'mætɪkḷɪ〕*adv.* 自動地
　　　　(B) *consequently*〔'kɑnsə,kwɛntlɪ〕*adv.* 因此
　　　　(C) reluctantly〔rɪ'lʌktəntlɪ〕*adv.* 勉強地
　　　　(D) purposely〔'pɝpəslɪ〕*adv.* 故意地

25. (**C**)　concerned〔kən'sɝnd〕*adj.* 關心的；擔心的
　　　　 concerning〔kən'sɝnɪŋ〕*prep.* 關於

Ⅲ. 閱讀測驗：50％

【譯文】

　　學習彈奏樂器——鍵盤樂器、鋼琴、長笛、吉他——是一項長期的計畫。你應該找個好老師，一個你尊敬而且喜歡的老師。你應該計畫每天練習，而且至少持續一年，才能看見實質的進步，要演奏得好，則須練習好幾年。你應該有耐心；就像做其他每件值得去做的事情一樣，成功不會輕易到手。如果你全部照做了，但仍然演奏得不好聽，好吧，或許你天生就沒有音樂細胞！

【答案】

26. (**C**)

【註】

musical instrument 樂器
keyboard〔'ki,bord〕*n.*（樂器的）鍵盤　　　flute〔flut〕*n.* 長笛
progress〔'prɑgrɛs〕*n.* 進步；進展　　　gene〔dʒin〕*n.* 基因

【譯文】

　　人際距離（十二英尺以上）遠超過與人密切接觸的範圍。它無益於人與人之間的溝通。我們受限於在那樣的距離裡所能看到和聽到的部分；談論的話題相當不牽涉個人感情而且正式；而且大部分的對話，也是用演說的形式來呈現，有事先計畫好的主題，以及獲得反饋的機會也有限。

【答案】

27. (**A**)　　　　28. (**C**)

【註】

range〔rendʒ〕*n.* 範圍　　involvement〔ɪnˈvɑlvmənt〕*n.* 關連

impractical〔ɪmˈpræktɪk!〕*adj.* 不切實際的

interpersonal〔ˌɪntɚˈpɜsən!〕*adj.* 人與人之間的

relatively〔ˈrɛlətɪvlɪ〕*adv.* 相對地；相當地

impersonal〔ɪmˈpɜsn!〕*adj.* 不牽涉個人感情的；無人情味的

public-speaking〔ˈpʌblɪk ˈspikɪŋ〕*adj.* 公開演說的

in advance 事先　　feedback〔ˈfidˌbæk〕*n.* 反饋；反應

nonverbal〔ˌnɑnˈvɜb!〕*adj.* 非言語的　'　feature〔ˈfitʃɚ〕*n.* 特色

practice〔ˈpræktɪs〕*n.* 慣例

【譯文】

　　人類本能的喪失，會導致各種在其他動物身上看不到的行為。一隻被逼入困境的老鼠，始終會表現出欲做攻擊的反應，那是本能反應而且是可預期的反應。但是被逼入困境的人，就未必會做出像老鼠那樣的反應。想像一個大概六、七歲的小男孩，有一天他走在森林裡，遇到一隻小熊。他還不知道接近野生動物的幼獸是危險的。當他看到小熊愛玩的樣子，他開始跟小熊跑來跑去、玩在一塊。不久之後，母熊回來了，發現這小男孩和她的小熊正在嬉戲。這隻母熊本能地察覺到她的小熊受到威脅，就本能地做出反應。她大聲咆哮，發出其他的吼聲，表現出要攻擊的意圖，她追著小男孩跑，穿越森林，跑到一個沒有退路的峽谷。這個小男孩，就像眾所周知的老鼠，發現自己被逼入死角，必須轉身面對他的敵人。他會怎麼辦？

【答案】

29.（**D**）　　　　　30.（**B**）

【註】

absence〔ˈæbsn̩s〕*n.* 缺乏　　instinct〔ˈɪnstɪŋkt〕*n.* 本能
lead to 導致　　***a variety of*** 各式各樣的；各種的
observe〔əbˈzɝv〕*v.* 看到；注意到
whereas〔hwɛrˈæz〕*conj.* 但是
cornered〔ˈkɔrnəd〕*adj.* 逼入困境的　　exhibit〔ɪgˈzɪbɪt〕*v.* 表現
automatic〔ˌɔtəˈmætɪk〕*adj.* 本能自發的
predictable〔prɪˈdɪktəbl̩〕*adj.* 可預測的
aggressive〔əˈgrɛsɪv〕*adj.* 有攻擊性的
not necessarily 未必　　***happen upon*** 偶然遇到（= *happen on*）
cub〔kʌb〕*n.* 幼獸　　young〔jʌŋ〕*n.* 幼小動物
playful〔ˈplefəl〕*adj.* 愛玩的　　cavort〔kəˈvɔrt〕*v.* 嬉戲
instinctively〔ɪnˈstɪŋktɪvlɪ〕*adv.* 本能地
perceive〔pɚˈsiv〕*v.* 察覺
threat〔θrɛt〕*n.* 威脅；構成威脅的人、事、物
automatically〔ˌɔtəˈmætɪklɪ〕*adv.* 本能自發地
growl〔graʊl〕*v.* 咆哮　　indicate〔ˈɪndəˌket〕*v.* 表示
intent〔ɪnˈtɛnt〕*n.* 意圖　　box〔bɑks〕*n.* 困境
canyon〔ˈkænjən〕*n.* 峽谷
proverbial〔prəˈvɝbɪəl〕*adj.* 眾所周知的

【譯文】

　　二十五歲之後才進入，或再回到大學就讀的學生，通常修閱讀/學習課程，以重溫他們的效率。這些再進入校園的學生，已有工作經驗和家庭，他們把這樣的知識融入他們的課程中，而且他們也清楚地知道，自己要從大學得到什麼。他們善於利用時間，因為他們忙碌的生活迫使他們如此；如果他們想要成功，家庭、運動、學業和工作之間，一定要謹慎地取得平衡。中年或比較老的學生，經常較用功念書，成績也較好，這是因為為了追求個人的滿足感，也或許是因為從較年輕的同學身上，感受到競爭的壓力。

【答案】

31. (**A**)　　　　32. (**A**)

【註】

brush up on 復習　　efficiency〔əˋfɪʃənsɪ, ɪ-〕*n.* 效率
reentry〔riˋɛntrɪ〕*n.* 再進入　　highly〔ˋhaɪlɪ〕*adv.* 非常地
motivated〔ˋmotəˏvetɪd〕*adj.* 有動機的

【譯文】

　　有效的聆聽指的是以第三隻耳朵聆聽。我這樣講的意思是指，試著花心思去聽出弦外之意，而不是只聽出字面上的意思。言語表達的方式——大聲、輕柔、快速、緩慢、強烈、猶豫——都是很重要的。言語各方面的線索都隱藏著訊息。如果有個母親用溫和的聲音說：「現在進來吧」，可能表示小孩子可以再晚幾分鐘。如果她說：「**現在**進來」，毫無疑問地，這是個命令的意思。要有效地聆聽，我們必須注意臉部表情、目光的接觸、手勢，和肢體動作，還有對方聲音、用字、節奏、速度，和聲調的特性。以第三隻耳朵聆聽，能幫助我們了解全部的訊息。

┌【答案】────────────────
│　　33. **(B)**　　　　34. **(A)**
└────────────────────────

【註】

effective〔əˋfɛktɪv〕*adj.* 有效的　　***listen for*** 凝神傾聽
hesitating〔ˋhɛzəˏtetɪŋ〕*adj.* 猶豫的；支支吾吾的
bury〔ˋbɛrɪ〕*v.* 隱藏　　command〔kəˋmænd〕*n.* 命令
facial expression 臉部表情
effectively〔əˋfɛktɪvlɪ〕*adv.* 有效地　　***as well as*** 以及
quality〔ˋkwɑlətɪ〕*n.* 特性　　rhythm〔ˋrɪðəm〕*n.* 節奏
rate〔ret〕*n.* 速度　　tone〔ton〕*n.* 語調　　cue〔kju〕*n.* 線索

【譯文】

　　人權法案本身就是有可能發生關於權利方面，種種衝突的來源。很顯然地，憲法的用意是確保公平審判以及新聞自由的權利。但是如果新聞報導過份煽動輿論，導致沒有公正的評審團的話，就可能會造成審判不公。有個著名的刑事審理案件，一位俄亥俄州的內科醫生，山姆‧薛伯德，被控謀殺他太太。媒體報導的程度不亞於報導一場軍事戰役，而且極少部分是同情薛伯德醫生的。結果他被判有罪，進入州立監獄服刑，薛伯德向最高法院提出上訴。他宣稱，新聞報導已經妨礙他獲得公平審判的資格。最高法院同意他的論點，認為媒體已經造成了虛擬的「古羅馬競技場」，因而撤銷對於薛伯德的判決。

【答案】

35. (**C**)　　　　　36. (**D**)

【註】

Bill of Rights 人權法案（美國憲法的第一條修正案，1791 年通過）
inexhaustible〔͵ɪnɪg'zɔstəbl̩〕*adj.* 用不完的；無窮盡的
potential〔pə'tɛnʃəl〕*adj.* 可能的
Constitution〔͵kɑnstə'tjuʃən〕*n.* 美國憲法
guarantee〔͵gærən'ti〕*v.* 保證　　fair〔fɛr〕*adj.* 公平的
trial〔'traɪəl〕*n.* 審判　　press〔prɛs〕*n.* 新聞界
coverage〔'kʌvərɪdʒ〕*n.* 報導　　inflame〔ɪn'flem〕*v.* 煽動（情緒）
public opinion 輿論　　impartial〔ɪm'pɑrʃəl〕*adj.* 公正的
jury〔'dʒʊrɪ〕*n.* 陪審團　　rival〔'raɪvl̩〕*v.* 與～匹敵；比得上
campaign〔kæm'pen〕*n.* 戰役
sympathize〔'sɪmpə͵θaɪz〕*v.* 同情＜*with*＞
appeal〔ə'pil〕*v.* （提出）上訴
conviction〔kən'vɪkʃən〕*n.* 宣判；定罪
Supreme Court 最高法院　　interfere〔͵ɪntɚ'fɪr〕*v.* 妨礙＜*with*＞
ability〔ə'bɪlətɪ〕*n.* （法律上的）資格；能力
virtual〔'vɝtʃʊəl〕*adj.* 虛擬的
circus〔'sɝkəs〕*n.* （古羅馬的）圓形競技場
reverse〔rɪ'vɝs〕*v.* 推翻；撤銷

【譯文】

　　現在美國的高離婚率，並不像一般人所想的，婚姻制度已經很不受歡迎了。相反地，有好幾個證據顯示出人們似乎是太喜歡結婚了。首先，雖然我們社會有最高的離婚率，但在所有的工業化國家中，我們的結婚率最高。其次，在美國境內，東南部、西南部，和西部大部份的州，都有比全國平均更高的離婚率，但結婚率也較高。第三，大多數離婚的人最後會再婚。為什麼他們不表現得像馬克吐溫（書中）的貓，牠被熱爐燙傷後，就再也不靠近任何爐子了呢？很顯然地，美國社會的離婚率並不代表拒絕婚姻，而只是拒絕一個特定的伴侶。

【答案】

37. (**C**)　　　　　38. (**B**)

【註】

current〔ˈkɝənt〕*adj.* 目前的　　***divorce rate*** 離婚率
common sense 常識　　institution〔ˌɪnstəˈtjuʃən〕*n.* 制度
on the contrary 相反地　　majority〔məˈdʒɔrətɪ〕*n.* 多數
eventually〔ɪˈvɛntʃuəlɪ〕*adv.* 最後　　stove〔stov〕*n.* 爐子
rejection〔rɪˈdʒɛkʃən〕*n.* 拒絕

【譯文】

　　在中世紀有個習俗，就是在嬰兒出生後的第一年，用長布條包裹嬰兒。包裹嬰兒需要用布條把小孩包住，讓他的手臂和腿緊貼住身體。父母害怕嬰兒可能會抓傷眼睛，或因為不當的扭曲，而扭傷他們脆弱的四肢。用長布條包裹嬰兒，也讓他們避免碰觸自己的外生殖器，或「像野獸一樣」地爬行。但是，一位研究歷史中童年概念和育兒習慣的歷史學家，迪莫斯，已經發現證據，指出用長布條包裹嬰兒的主要目的，是為了大人的方便。被包住的嬰兒較容易安靜，而且較被動。他們睡得比較久，心跳緩慢，而且比較少哭。被包住的嬰兒可能會被放在「熱爐後面，或掛在牆上的掛鉤」好幾個鐘頭，而且有時候，大人為了好玩，會用引導幼兒走路的繩索「牽引」嬰兒，像是操縱木偶一般。

【答案】

　　39. **(B)**　　　　　　40. **(D)**

【註】

medieval〔͵midi'ivḷ〕*adj.* 中世紀的

swaddle〔'swɑdḷ〕*v.* 用長布條包裹嬰兒

bandage〔'bændɪdʒ〕*n.* 繃帶　　scratch〔skrætʃ〕*v.* 抓傷

distort〔dɪs'tɔrt〕*v.* 扭曲；使變形　　tender〔'tɛndɚ〕*adj.* 脆弱的

limb〔lɪm〕*n.* 四肢　　improperly〔ɪm'prɑpɚlɪ〕*adv.* 不適當地

keep *sb.* ***from V-ing*** 使某人無法～

genitals〔'dʒɛnətəlz〕*n. pl.* 外生殖器　　crawl〔krɔl〕*v.* 爬

beast〔bist〕*n.* 野獸　　passive〔'pæsɪv〕*adj.* 被動的

oven〔'ʌvən〕*n.* 烤爐；烤箱　　peg〔pɛg〕*n.* 短釘

leading-strings〔'lidɪŋ strɪŋz〕*n. pl.* 引導幼兒走路的繩索

puppet〔'pʌpɪt〕*n.* 木偶

amusement〔ə'mjuzmənt〕*n.* 樂趣；開心

covering〔'kʌvərɪŋ〕*n.* 覆蓋物

【譯文】

　　「我們的國家正在進行一種洗腦的活動，」莫里嘆氣說道。「你知道他們如何洗腦人民嗎？他們一再地重覆某件事情。那就是我們國家發生的情況。擁有東西是好的。有更多錢很好。有更多財產很好。更利益導向很好。*多就是好。多就是好。*。我們反覆灌輸這想法。而且對我們自己不斷地重覆，直到沒有人費心去有不一樣的想法。一般人都被這樣的想法所蒙蔽，所以就不再清楚地知道什麼才是真正重要的。」

　　「在這個國家，人們分不清楚什麼是我們想要的，什麼是我們所需要的，」莫里繼續說。「你需要食物。你想要巧克力聖代。你必須對自己誠實。你不需要最新的跑車，你不需要最大的房子。事實上，你不會從這些事物得到滿足。你知道真正會帶給你滿足的東西是什麼嗎？」

　　「什麼？」

　　「給別人你所能付出的東西。」莫里從書房的窗戶望出去。「記得我曾說過，要尋找一個有意義的人生？我寫下來過，但是我現在能夠把它背出來。努力去愛別人。把自己奉獻給周圍的人。致力於創造能給你目標和意義的事物。」

　　他咧著嘴笑。「你會發現有這樣的人生觀，薪水就不重要了。」

　　我把一些莫里說的話草草記在便條紙上。我這麼做主要是因為我不想讓他看到我的眼睛，知道我在想什麼，自從畢業後，我人生的大部份是追求這些他一直強烈不滿的東西——比較大的玩具，比較好的房子。因為我跟有錢而且有名的運動員一起工作，我使自己相信，我的需求是合乎實際的，我的貪婪和他們比起來是微不足道的。

　　這是個煙幕。莫里清楚地說明了這一點。

【答案】

　　41. **(C)**　　42. **(D)**　　43. **(B)**　　44. **(B)**　　45. **(D)**

【註】

brainwashing〔'bren,waʃɪŋ〕*n.* 洗腦
property〔'prɑpətɪ〕*n.* 財產
commercialism〔kə'mɝʃəlɪ,zəm〕*n.* 商業主義；利潤第一的想法
fog〔fɑg〕*v.* 使迷惘＜*up*＞
perspective〔pə'spɛktɪv〕*n.* 正確的看法
versus〔'vɝsəs〕*prep.* 與～相對　　sundae〔'sʌndɪ〕*n.* 聖代
devote* *oneself* *to 致力於　・jot〔dʒɑt〕*v.* 匆匆記下

pad〔 pæd 〕*n.* 便條紙本　　　rail〔 rel 〕*v.* 對～強烈不滿 *< against >*
realistic〔 ˌriə'lɪstɪk 〕*adj.* 現實的；實際的
inconsequential〔 ˌɪnkɑnsə'kwɛnʃəl 〕*adj.* 微不足道的
smokescreen〔 'smokˌskrin 〕*n.* (掩蓋眞相的)煙幕
foggy〔 'fɑgɪ 〕*adj.* 有霧的
designer〔 dɪ'zaɪnɚ 〕*adj.* 由專門設計師設計的
sanitary〔 'sænəˌtɛrɪ 〕*adj.* 衛生的
adequate〔 'ædəkwɪt 〕*adj.* 足夠的；充分的
sermon〔 's3mən 〕*n.* 講道　　　lecture〔 'lɛktʃɚ 〕*v.* 演講
modest〔 'mɑdɪst 〕*adj.* 謙虛的
presumptuous〔 prɪ'zʌmptʃuəs 〕*adj.* 自以爲是的

【譯文】

　　「天啊」，列車長喃喃自語，當那名精瘦結實的黑髮的男子走進車廂時。把睡衣穿在運動夾克裡的男子，尤其是夾克從買來後就沒洗過，看來是有幾分平淡粗俗的味道，不算是完全會讓人起疑心，列車長在車廂上走動，檢查車票時，仔細地打量他。

　　無疑地，列車長會大爲震驚，如果他知道這名穿著皺巴巴的夾克，「看來可疑」、緊張兮兮地折著他前往劍橋的二等票的男子，是最近同盟國戰勝德國的主要貢獻者之一，一般大衆並不認識，但在科學界被認爲是個聰明絕頂的人。

　　艾倫‧圖靈在位於劍橋和牛津的鄉野間布雷奇利營區當兵，他專門負責破解密碼。戰爭初期，聽說德軍用一台名爲「謎」的機器，發送經密碼處理的命令給他們的部隊，而有少數幾個數學家，由圖靈接任總指揮，利用截取到的情報，和各種不同的搜尋技術來進行分析，了解「謎」的運作方式。這些科學家研發出策略，終於能夠破解情報，就像是直接從德國最高指揮部收到未經密碼處理的文件。戰爭結束時，圖靈每天接觸電子機器，利用它來破解資料的模式，他對此非常熟悉，所以他開始認眞思考建造一個電算機器，能夠比得上——如果無法勝過——人類心智的思考過程。就在那天下午，他要從曼徹斯特到劍橋市中心的路上，這個想法正在他的心中盤據著。

【答案】

46. **(B)**　47. **(B)**　48. **(C)**　49. **(D)**　50. **(A)**

【註】

Good heavens! 天哪！　　guard〔gɑrd〕n. (火車的) 列車長

mutter〔ˈmʌtɚ〕v. 低聲地說　　*mutter to oneself* 喃喃自語

wiry〔ˈwaɪrɪ〕adj. 瘦而結實的　　carriage〔ˈkærɪdʒ〕n. 火車車廂

plain〔plen〕adj. 樸素的

undignified〔ʌnˈdɪgnəˌfaɪd〕adj. 有損尊嚴的

downright〔ˈdaʊnˌraɪt〕adv. 完全地

pajama〔pəˈdʒæmə〕adj. 睡衣的　　top〔tɑp〕n. 上衣

rumple〔ˈrʌmpl̩〕v. 把…弄皺

contributor〔kənˈtrɪbjətɚ〕n. 貢獻者 < to >

Allies〔əˈlaɪz〕n. pl. (第二次世界大戰之) 同盟國

brilliant〔ˈbrɪljənt〕adj. 卓越的　　circle〔ˈsɝkl̩〕n. ～界

rural〔ˈrʊrəl〕adj. 鄉村的　　estate〔əˈstet〕n. 大片私有土地

midway〔ˈmɪdˈwe〕adv. 位於中間　　code〔kod〕n. 密碼

early on 早先；在初期　　term〔tɝm〕v. 把～稱為

enigma〔ɪˈnɪgmə〕n. 謎　　handful〔ˈhændˌful〕n. 少數 < of >

intercept〔ˌɪntɚˈsɛpt〕v. 攔截　　*pin down* 確定；證實

working〔ˈwɝkɪŋ〕n. 活動；運轉

decipher〔dɪˈsaɪfɚ〕v. 破解 (密碼、謎等)

high command (一國或各盟國部隊的) 最高指揮部

uncover〔ʌnˈkʌvɚ〕v. 揭露；發現

duplicate〔ˈdjupləˌket〕v. 複製；比得上

exceed〔ɪkˈsid〕v. 超過；勝過　　notion〔ˈnoʃən〕n. 想法

fidgety〔ˈfɪdʒɪtɪ〕adj. 煩躁的　　eccentric〔ɪkˈsɛntrɪk〕adj. 古怪的

國立政治大學八十九學年度
碩士班研究生入學考試英文試題

I. Vocabulary: 30%

Choose the meaning that best fits the word, and then write its corresponding letter A,B,C, or D on your answer sheet.

1. derogatory
   (A) a lot of   (B) helpful
   (C) tending to belittle   (D) talkative

2. euphemism
   (A) a wise saying
   (B) a saying
   (C) elegance
   (D) a less distasteful description of something

3. intimidate
   (A) to scare   (B) to lean
   (C) to insult   (D) to make unfriendly

4. discreet
   (A) fearful   (B) friendly
   (C) careful   (D) evil

5. unanimous
   (A) moody and changeable
   (B) complete agreement
   (C) regretful
   (D) lacking control

6. trite
   (A) worn out by constant use (B) humorous
   (C) tense   (D) mysterious

7. disdain
   (A) a disagreement   (B) side effect
   (C) to regard as unworthy   (D) effigy

8. haughty
   (A) hostile   (B) disagreeable
   (C) spoke well of   (D) arrogant

9. allot
   (A) to make a distribution of
   (B) to donate
   (C) to allege   (D) to sell a lot

10. liability
    (A) gift   (B) legal
    (C) debt   (D) liberal

11. stagnant
    (A) moving   (B) lacking movement
    (C) healthful
    (D) flowing like running water

12. inquisitive
    (A) strive   (B) prying
    (C) quiz   (D) squander

13. terse
    (A) concise   (B) frank
    (C) superfluous   (D) relentless

14. amnesty
    (A) short   (B) yield
    (C) muse   (D) a pardon

15. overt
    (A) relating to   (B) closed
    (C) secret   (D) open

II. Structure: 20%

Choose the word, phrase, or clause that best completes
the sentence, and then write its corresponding letter
A,B,C, or D on your answer sheet.

1. _____ legally into codeine and morphine, the
   poppy provides us with a drug unsurpassed in treating
   extreme pain.
   (A) When it is processing   (B) By processing
   (C) Processed   (D) Processing

2. Linda was reviewing her project, _____ over a
   pile of chemistry notes.
   (A) her head slightly bent
   (B) her head was slightly bent
   (C) her head being slightly bent
   (D) her head slightly bending

3. _____ racing in the special Olympics, wheelchair
   athletes also raced in the 1992 Olympics in Barcelona.
   (A) With   (B) During
   (C) Despite   (D) In addition to

4. _____ began as the tinkering of two hackers in
   a suburban garage became the Apple Computer Company.
   (A) What   (B) Whichever
   (C) Whether   (D) This

5. After making the final choices, _____ to the
   new Nobel laureates.
   (A) the committee members have sent telegrams
   (B) the committee members send telegrams
   (C) telegrams are sent
   (D) telegrams send

6. You _____ him. He died before you were born.
   (A) hadn't seen   (B) didn't have seen
   (C) couldn't see   (D) couldn't have seen

7. Christopher Columbus, _____ voyages made him
   the most famous seafarer in history, did not train
   as a sailor but as a weaver in his family wool
   business.
   (A) his   (B) whose
   (C) in which   (D) however

8. "_____," said the reporter.
   (A) Limping away from the huddle, the sympathetic
       crowd cheered the injured quarterback
   (B) Limping away from the huddle, the quarterback
       was cheered by the sympathetic crowd
   (C) The injured quarterback limped away from the
       huddle, the crowd cheered him
   (D) Limping away from the crowd, the injured crowd
       was cheering the quarterback

9. _____ is an American territory.
   (A) Puerto Rico which is an island
   (B) Puerto Rico that is an island
   (C) Puerto Rico, that is an island,
   (D) Puerto Rico, which is an island,

10. Michael is _____.
    (A) so good student that it is easy for him to get
        100 on all his tests
    (B) so good a student it is easy for him to do
        well on all his tests
    (C) such a good student that he gets 100 on all
        his tests
    (D) such good student that it is easy for him to
        do well in all his tests

III. Reading Comprehension: 30%

In this section you will find three reading passages
followed by questions about the meaning of the
material. Choose the best answer to each question,
and then write its corresponding letter A,B,C, or D
on your answer sheet.

Passage 1

It is ironic that, if we consider the hazards to man
from food, many people would say that the most serious
hazards are food additives. In reality they are the least
of our problems. Microbiological hazards, resulting in
food poisoning, are a far more serious threat each year.
Not only is food poisoning a more serious problem than
food additives, but it is also significantly more serious
than environmental contamination of the food supply.

Many of those who complain about food additives
do not realize that antioxidant preservatives (food
additives) may be responsible for the decline in the
nation's incidence of stomach cancer. Even honey, which
is one of the staples of health food, has been shown to
contain small quantities of a cancer-causing agent
derived from pollen.

We seem to jump from fad to fad, convinced that there is an elixir of life which will guarantee perpetual youth, sexual vigor, and freedom from obesity. Millions are spent each year in this futile effort. It should be noted that man has shown his adaptability and ability to live healthfully in any part of the world and to thrive on a wide variety of diets. Because no single food provides all of the known nutrients, it is advisable that we select a variety of foods, and that doesn't mean fifty-seven varieties of snack crackers. Many in this country do not necessarily eat intelligently, but, among the countries of the world, we do have a unique opportunity to eat healthfully.

1. Which of the following is considered the most serious threat to our health in this article?
   (A) Environmental contamination.
   (B) Food supply.
   (C) Food additives.
   (D) Food poisoning.

2. What do the first and second paragraphs mainly discuss?
   (A) Food additives hazard.
   (B) Microbiological hazard.
   (C) Food poisoning hazard.
   (D) Health food hazard.

3. According to the author, which statement below is true about honey?
   (A) It may help prevent stomach cancer.
   (B) It may be contaminated by its supply.
   (C) It may be responsible for some incidence of cancer.
   (D) It may be derived from pollen.

4. What can replace <u>fad</u> in the context of this article?

(A) vogue   (B) myth

(C) heresy   (D) fable

5. What does the author believe?

(A) No one in this country eats intelligently.

(B) There is no wonder food that will guarantee longevity.

(C) We should eat more natural foods.

(D) There might be some organic food that prevents obesity.

Passage 2

Some children do not like school. So what else is new? But in Japan that familiar aversion has reached alarming proportions. About 50,000 unhappy youngsters a year (out of a total school-age population of 20 million) suffer what Japanese behavioral experts call school phobia. School phobia is distinguished from other common childhood and adolescent psychological emotional disorders by the patient's reaction to, and fear of, the idea of going to school. Typically, it begins with fever, sweating, migraine headaches, and diarrhea; it often progresses to complete physical inertia, depression, and even autism.

A doctor on a house call found a thirteen-year-old Tokyo boy who had not been to school in more than a year. He lived in a darkened room, receiving his food through a slot under the door and lashing out violently at his parents if they came too close. Once the boy was placed in a psychiatric ward for treatment, he again became an open, seemingly healthy youngster. When he was sent home, however, his symptoms returned, and he was never able to go back to school.

School phobia can be cured, usually with tranquilizers and psychotherapy. Rehabilitation takes about two years. Yet victims who are put in clinics or mental wards often prefer to stay there. Their day is filled with activities like knitting, painting, music, free time, and sports.

Nurses, who outnumber the students two to one, try to create a familiar environment in which the children can feel that they are taking a certain amount of responsibility for their lives and can find some sense of self-worth. Psychiatrists and counselors meet with the children once a week to talk about their problems and feelings.

The causes of school phobia are not precisely known. In a few severe cases brain disorders have been diagnosed. A more common factor may be the stereotypically overprotective Japanese mother who, some psychiatrists say, leaves her children ill-prepared to face the real world. Many researchers point to the unrelenting pressures to succeed faced by both children and adults in Japan, where stress-related disorders of all sorts are common. In addition, the Japanese educational system is one of the world's most rigid, suppressing a child's individual creative and analytical development in favor of obedience and rote memorization. Says Dr. Hitoshi Ishikawa, head of the department of psychosomatic medicine at Tokyo University, "The problem won't be cured until Japanese society as a whole is cured of its deep-seated social ills."

6. What is <u>not</u> a typical symptom of school phobia?
   (A) migraine   (B) diarrhea
   (C) nausea   (D) autism

7. What obvious symptom of school phobia does the
   thirteen-year-old Tokyo boy have?
   (A) autism   (B) migraine
   (C) depression   (D) violence

8. Which statement below is <u>not</u> the reason why the
   victims often prefer to stay in clinics or mental
   wards?
   (A) They have many activities to do there.
   (B) They receive tranquilizers.
   (C) Psychiatrists and counselors help them with
       regular visits.
   (D) Nurses create a pleasant environment and offer
       attentive care to them.

9. What is <u>not</u> mentioned by the author as a cause of
   Japanese school phobia?
   (A) Japanese educational system.
   (B) Japanese society.
   (C) Japanese technology.
   (D) Overprotective Japanese mothers.

10. What might be the main cause of Japanese school
    phobia?
    (A) Japanese school phobia might be an illness of
        the brain caused by a virus, which has been
        evidenced by medical research.
    (B) The inexperienced mothers who neglect their
        children's education might be the main reason
        for their children's school phobia.
    (C) The Japanese education in favor of obedience
        and discipline might get the blame for the
        children's fear of attending school.
    (D) Some physical disorders and some impact from the
        Japanese conventions might lead to school phobia.

Passage 3

The Environmental Protection Agency [EPA] recently warned that unless action is taken to halt ozone depletion, "the United States can expect 40 million additional skin cancer cases and 800,000 deaths among people alive today and those born during the next 88 years." The EPA's warning was based on the assumption that worldwide production of CFCs would grow at 25 percent a year. Some estimates show they're already growing faster than that.

Ultraviolet radiation is also a major cause of cataracts, a clouding of the lens of the eye that causes blurred vision and eventual blindness. The EPA estimates that unchecked ozone depletion would bring this affliction to anywhere from 555,000 to 2.8 million Americans born before 2075. Like mild forms of skin cancer, cataracts can be treated with relatively simple surgery. Needed medical services would be available to residents of the developed world, albeit with an increasing cost to national resources. But a lack of medical treatment in less-developed countries would leave an escalating percentage of the world's <u>burgeoning</u> population at far greater risk of going blind or dying from skin cancer. The bulk of this neglected population would be the poor who live closer to the Equator and who now contribute least to ozone destruction.

There is yet another danger to humans from increased exposure to ultraviolet radiation. Too strong a dose can lower the body's ability to resist such attacking organisms as infectious diseases and tumors. Some medical experts worry that excess exposure will undermine the inoculation programs that have controlled diseases that once caused epidemics. Instead of protecting people from a disease, an inoculation could inflict the disease on those whose immune system has been damaged by excessive exposure to ultraviolet radiation.

11. According to EPA findings, what is <u>not</u> true?
   (A) Action to halt ozone depletion is well under way.
   (B) The worldwide production of CFCs is apt to grow faster than we think.
   (C) Skin cancer is closely related to the production of CFCs.
   (D) The ozone layer will determine the death toll from skin cancer in the future.

12. What is true about cataracts?
   (A) This disease is caused by the production of CFCs.
   (B) This disease is a condition of the eye in which the inner shape of the eye is changed.
   (C) This disease cannot be treated with an operation.
   (D) This disease may cause blurred vision or even blindness.

13. Which word can replace <u>burgeoning</u> in the context?
   (A) rising
   (B) extinguishing
   (C) aging
   (D) existing

14. Which statement below can be inferred from the article?
   (A) The developed countries lack medical treatment for cataracts.
   (B) The medical services for cataracts is funded by the government in less-developed countries.
   (C) Most of the people who are more vulnerable to skin cancer and cataracts live closer to the Equator.
   (D) The people who are most responsible for the ozone problem live closer to the Equator.

15. In addition to skin cancer and cataracts, how else may ozone depletion affect us?
   (A) It may strengthen our body's ability to resist disease.
   (B) It may make our inoculation programs ineffective.
   (C) It may rebuild our immune system.
   (D) It may give rise to a lack of food supply.

IV. Translate the following sentences into English. 20%

1. 三位前總統候選人的兩岸政策都很相似，他們都主張中華民國是個主權獨立的國家。

2. 科學家發現，有氧運動可藉著增進腦部血液流量延緩老化過程。

3. 股票到現在為止已連跌三天。政府應採取因應措施以穩定股市。

4. 台灣在 1999 年平均每人所得為美金 13248 元，大約是中國（中共）的 17 倍。

國立政治大學八十九學年度
碩士班研究生入學考試英文試題詳解

I. 字彙：30 ％

1. (**C**) derogatory〔dɪˋrɑɡəˏtorɪ〕*adj.* 貶低的
   (C) belittle〔bɪˋlɪtl̩〕*v.* 輕視；貶低
   (D) talkative〔ˋtɔkətɪv〕*adj.* 饒舌的

2. (**D**) euphemism〔ˋjufəmɪzəm〕*n.* 婉轉的言辭
   (A) saying〔ˋseɪŋ〕*n.* 諺語
   (C) elegance〔ˋɛləgəns〕*n.* 高雅
   (D) distasteful〔dɪsˋtestfəl〕*adj.* 討厭的；令人不愉快的

3. (**A**) intimidate〔ɪnˋtɪməˏdet〕*v.* 使害怕；恐嚇
   (A) *scare*〔skɛr〕*v.* 使害怕
   (B) lean〔lin〕*v.* 倚靠

4. (**C**) discreet〔dɪˋskrit〕*adj.* 謹慎的
   (A) fearful〔ˋfɪrfəl〕*adj.* 可怕的

5. (**B**) unanimous〔juˋnænəməs〕*adj.* 一致同意的
   (A) moody〔ˋmudɪ〕*adj.* 易怒的
   (C) regretful〔rɪˋgrɛtfəl〕*adj.* 後悔的
   (D) lack〔læk〕*v.* 缺乏

6. (**A**) trite〔traɪt〕*adj.* 陳腐的
   (A) *worn out* 過時的；陳腐的
   (C) tense〔tɛns〕*adj.* 緊張的

7. (**C**) disdain〔dɪs'den〕v. 輕視
    (B) side effect 副作用
    (D) effigy〔'ɛfədʒɪ〕n. 偶像；肖像

8. (**D**) haughty〔'hɔtɪ〕adj. 自大的；高傲的
    (A) hostile〔'hɑstɪl〕adj. 有敵意的
    (C) speak well of 稱讚
    (D) *arrogant*〔'ærəgənt〕adj. 自大的

9. (**A**) allot〔ə'lɑt〕v. 分配；指派
    (A) *distribution*〔,dɪstrə'bjuʃən〕n. 分配
    (B) donate〔'donet〕v. 捐贈
    (C) allege〔ə'lɛdʒ〕v. 斷言；宣稱

10. (**C**) liability〔,laɪə'bɪlətɪ〕n. 債務
    (A) gift〔gɪft〕n. 禮物；天賦
    (C) *debt*〔dɛt〕n. 債務
    (D) liberal〔'lɪbərəl〕adj. 自由的

11. (**B**) stagnant〔'stægnənt〕adj. 停滯的
    (D) running water 流水

12. (**B**) inquisitive〔ɪn'kwɪzətɪv〕adj. 想問的；好追究的
    (A) strive〔straɪv〕v. 努力
    (B) *prying*〔'praɪɪŋ〕adj. 愛打聽的
    (C) quiz〔kwɪz〕v. 測驗
    (D) squander〔'skwɑndɚ〕v. 浪費；揮霍

13. (**A**) terse〔tɜs〕adj. 簡潔的
    (A) *concise*〔kən'saɪs〕adj. 簡明的
    (B) frank〔fræŋk〕adj. 坦白的
    (C) superfluous〔su'pɝfluəs〕adj. 多餘的；浪費的
    (D) relentless〔rɪ'lɛntlɪs〕adj. 無情的；殘酷的

14. (**D**)　amesty〔ˋæm͵nɛstɪ〕*n.* 特赦
　　　(B)　yield〔jild〕*v.* 出產；屈服
　　　(C)　muse〔mjuz〕*v.* 沈思
　　　(D)　*pardon*〔ˋpɑrdn̩〕*n.* 特赦；原諒

15. (**D**)　overt〔oˋvɝt〕*adj.* 公然的
　　　(A)　relate to 有關

II. 結構：20 ％

1. (**C**)　Processed legally…是由 Because it is processed legally…轉化而來。

　　　process〔ˋprɑsɛs〕*v.* 加工；處理
　　　legally〔ˋliglɪ〕*adv.* 合法地
　　　codeine〔ˋkodɪ͵in〕*n.* 可待因（採自鴉片的鎮痛止咳劑）
　　　morphine〔ˋmɔrfin〕*n.* 嗎啡
　　　poppy〔ˋpɑpɪ〕*n.* 罌粟
　　　unsurpassed〔͵ʌnsəˋpæst〕*adj.* 卓越的
　　　extreme〔ɪkˋstrim〕*adj.* 極度的

2. (**A**)　… , her head slightly bent over…是由 , and her head was slightly bent over…轉化而來。

　　　review〔rɪˋvju〕*v.* 再檢查
　　　bend〔bɛnd〕*v.* 使彎曲
　　　pile〔paɪl〕*n.* 堆

3. (**D**)　依句意，選 (D) *In addition to*「除了~之外」。

　　　race〔res〕*v.* 參加競賽
　　　wheelchair〔ˋhwilˋtʃɛr〕*n.* 輪椅
　　　athlete〔ˋæθlit〕*n.* 運動員

4. (**A**) What began as…表「原本是…」，在句中，what 引導名
詞子句，做動詞 became 的主詞。

tinker〔 ˈtɪŋkɚ〕v. 實驗性地玩弄機器零件
hacker〔 ˈhækɚ〕n. 駭客（非法入侵電腦網路的人）
suburban〔 səˈbɝbən〕adj. 郊外的

5. (**B**) 依句意為現在簡單式，且做決定的是「人」而非「電報」，
故選 (B)。

committee〔 kəˈmɪtɪ〕n. 委員會
telegram〔 ˈtɛləˌgræm〕n. 電報
laureate〔 ˈlɔrɪɪt〕n. 得獎者

6. (**D**) couldn't have + p.p.表「當時不可能～」。

7. (**B**) whose 引導形容詞子句，修飾先行詞 Christopher
Columbus。

voyage〔 ˈvɔɪɪdʒ〕n. 航行
seafarer〔 ˈsiˌfɛrɚ〕n. 航海家
weaver〔 ˈwivɚ〕n. 編織者；織工

8. (**B**) Limping away from…是由 When he limped away
from…轉化而來。

limp〔 lɪmp〕v. 一瘸一拐地走
huddle〔 ˈhʌdl̩〕n.（美式足球）隊員賽前在爭球線後面
    舉行的指示聽取會
quarterback〔 ˈkwɔrtɚˌbæk〕n. 四分衛
cheer〔 tʃɪr〕v. 向～歡呼
sympathetic〔 ˌsɪmpəˈθɛtɪk〕adj. 有同情心的

9. (**D**)　which 引導補述用法的形容詞子句，修飾先行詞 Puerto
　　Rico。而 (C) 關代 that 之前，不可有逗點，故不合。
　　territory 〔 'tɛrə,torɪ 〕 *n.* 領土

10. (**C**)　such a good student that… 是非常好的學生，所以…
　　　= so good a student that…

III. 閱讀測驗：30 %

【譯文】

　　很諷刺的是，當我們考量食物對人體健康的危害時，很多人都會
說，最危險的是食品添加物。事實上，食品添加物算是最微不足道的
問題。每一年造成食物中毒的微生物學方面的危險，才是更加嚴重的
威脅。食物中毒不僅比食品添加物還要嚴重，也顯然比在食物來源所
遭受的環境污染更嚴重。

　　許多抱怨食品添加物的人並不知道，抗氧化劑之類的防腐劑（也
是食品添加物），可能是全國人民胃癌罹患率下降的原因。即使是一
般熟知的，像蜂蜜這樣的健康食品，也發現含有少量來自於花粉的致
癌物質。

　　我們似乎不斷地追逐不同的流行，相信有長生不老藥，能永保青
春、性能力，並且免於肥胖。每一年我們都花了好幾百萬元，來做這
種無謂的努力。我們必須注意的是，人類有其適應力，能夠在世界上
任何地方，靠各式各樣的飲食成功地生存下去。因為沒有單一的食品，
能提供我們所知道的各種營養成份，我們必須很明智地選擇吃各式各
樣的食物，但那並不表示，要吃五十七種不同種類的餅乾零食。國內
有許多人並不一定會聰明地選擇食物，但相較於世界各國，我們的確
擁有能吃得更健康，這種獨一無二的機會。

【答案】

1. **(D)** 2. **(C)** 3. **(C)** 4. **(B)** 5. **(B)**

【註】

ironic〔aɪˋrɑnɪk〕*adj.* 諷刺的 hazard〔ˋhæzəd〕*n.* 危險
additive〔ˋædətɪv〕*n.* 添加劑 ***in reality*** 事實上
microbiological〔͵maɪkrobaɪəˋlɑdʒɪk!〕*adj.* 微生物學的
food poisoning 食物中毒
significantly〔sɪgˋnɪfəkəntlɪ〕*adv.* 值得注意地
contamination〔kən͵tæməˋneʃən〕*n.* 污染
antioxidant〔͵æntɪˋɑksədənt〕*n.* 抗氧化劑
preservative〔prɪˋzɝvətɪv〕*n.* 防腐劑
be responsible for 是～的原因
incidence〔ˋɪnsədn̩s〕*n.* 發生（率）
staple〔ˋstep!〕*n.* 主要產品 agent〔ˋedʒənt〕*n.* 媒介
be derived from 源自於 pollen〔ˋpɑlən〕*n.* 花粉
jump〔dʒʌmp〕*v.* 突然轉換 fad〔fæd〕*n.* 一時的流行
be convinced that 相信 elixir〔ɪˋlɪksɚ〕*n.* 長生不老藥
guarantee〔͵gærənˋti〕*v.* 保證
perpetual〔pɚˋpɛtʃuəl〕*adj.* 永久的 vigor〔ˋvɪgɚ〕*n.* 活力
freedom〔ˋfridəm〕*n.* 免除 obesity〔əˋbisətɪ〕*n.* 肥胖
futile〔ˋfjut!〕*adj.* 無效的 note〔not〕*v.* 注意
adaptability〔ə͵dæptəˋbɪlətɪ〕*n.* 適應性
thrive〔θraɪv〕*v.* 成功 < *on* >
nutrient〔ˋnjutrɪənt〕*n.* 營養物；養份
advisable〔ədˋvaɪzəb!〕*adj.* 明智的 variety〔vəˋraɪətɪ〕*n.* 種類
snack〔snæk〕*n.* 點心 cracker〔ˋkrækɚ〕*n.* 薄脆餅乾
unique〔juˋnik〕*adj.* 獨特的；唯一的
context〔ˋkɑntɛkst〕*n.* 上下文 vogue〔vog〕*n.* 流行；風尚
myth〔mɪθ〕*n.* 神話 heresy〔ˋhɛrəsɪ〕*n.* 異教；異端邪說
fable〔ˋfeb!〕*n.* 寓言

【譯文】

　　有些小孩不愛上學。那又有什麼稀奇的呢？但是在日本，這種為人們所熟悉的厭惡上學的比例，已高達令人擔憂的程度。一年大約有五萬名不愉快的小孩（學齡兒童總數為二千萬），罹患日本的行為專家所謂的上學恐懼症。上學恐懼症特別的是，患者對要上學的反應及恐懼，使這種病症與其他常見的兒童與青少年的心理疾病大不相同。通常，一開始會發燒、流汗、偏頭痛，以及拉肚子；進而發展成身體行動呆滯，沮喪，甚至會產生自閉症。

　　一位出診的醫生發現，東京有位十三歲的小孩，已經有一年多沒去上學。他住在陰暗的房間裏，從門下面的細縫獲得食物，如果父母太接近，他就會粗暴地破口大罵。一當這個男孩被送進精神病房接受治療時，他又變成一個很坦率，看起來很健康的年輕人。當他被送回家時，症狀又復發了，然後他就再也無法重返校園。

　　上學恐懼症是可以治好的，通常需要鎮靜劑及心理治療。需要兩年的時間，才能康復。然而這一類被安置在診所或精神病房的患者，通常會比較喜歡待在那裏。因為在那裏的日子，充滿了活動，像是編織、繪畫、音樂、空閒時間，以及運動。

　　護士的人數比學生多，通常是二比一，他們會設法營造一個熟悉的環境，設法讓孩子們負起生活中的某些責任，並找回一些自尊心。精神病醫師和輔導人員，會一週和孩子們見一次面，談談他們的問題和感覺。

　　上學恐懼症的病因，目前尚無法明確地知道。在一些嚴重的病例中，曾診斷出有腦部方面的疾病。有些精神病醫師說，更常見的原因，是傳統上過度保護子女的日本母親，讓孩子沒有做好面對現實世界的準備。許多研究人員指出，日本的兒童與成人，都必須面對一定要成功的無情壓力，所以在日本，各種和壓力有關的疾病都十分常見。此

外，日本的教育系統是全世界最嚴格的系統之一，會壓抑孩子個人的
創造及分析能力的發展，提倡服從及反覆的背誦記憶。東京大學身心
醫學部門的主管 Ishikawa 博士指出，「除非能治好日本社會根深蒂固
的疾病，否則這種病將無法治得好。」

【答案】

6. (**C**)　　7. (**D**)　　8. (**B**)　　9. (**C**)　　10. (**C**)

【註】

aversion〔ə'vɝʃən〕n. 厭惡
alarming〔ə'lɑrmɪŋ〕adj. 令人擔憂的
proportion〔prə'porʃən〕n. 比例
youngster〔'jʌŋstɚ〕n. 小孩　　phobia〔'fobɪə〕n. 恐懼症
be distinguished from 有別於
adolescent〔͵ædḷ'ɛsn̩t〕adj. 青春期的　n. 青少年
disorder〔dɪs'ɔrdɚ〕n. 疾病　　typically〔'tɪpɪkḷɪ〕adv. 典型地
fever〔'fivɚ〕n. 發燒　　sweat〔swɛt〕v. 流汗
migraine〔'maɪgren〕n. 偏頭痛　　diarrhea〔͵daɪə'riə〕n. 拉肚子
progress〔prə'grɛs〕v. 提高；前進
inertia〔ɪn'ɝʃə〕n. 不活潑；惰性
autism〔'ɔtɪzəm〕n. 自閉症　　**house call** 出診
darkened〔'dɑrknd〕adj. 黑暗的　　slot〔slɑt〕n. 細長的孔
lash〔læʃ〕n. 猛擊；斥責　　violently〔'vaɪələntlɪ〕adv. 粗暴地
psychiatric〔͵saɪkɪ'ætrɪk〕adj. 精神病的
ward〔wɔrd〕n. 病房　　symptom〔'sɪmptəm〕n. 症狀
tranquilizer〔'træŋkwɪ͵laɪzɚ〕n. 鎮定劑
psychotherapy〔͵saɪko'θɛrəpɪ〕n. 心理療法；精神療法
rehabilitation〔͵rihə͵bɪlə'teʃən〕n. 復健
clinic〔'klɪnɪk〕n. 診所　　knit〔nɪt〕v. 編織

outnumber〔aʊt'nʌmbɚ〕v. 數量上勝過

self-worth〔'sɛlf'wɝθ〕n. 自尊（心）

psychiatrist〔saɪ'kaɪətrɪst〕n. 精神病醫師

counselor〔'kaʊnsəlɚ〕n. 輔導員

precisely〔prɪ'saɪslɪ〕adv. 正確地

severe〔sə'vɪr〕adj. 嚴重的

stereotypically〔ˌstɛrɪo'tɪpɪkl̩ɪ〕adv. 刻板地；老套地

diagnose〔'daɪəgnoz〕v. 診斷

unrelenting〔ˌʌnrɪ'lɛntɪŋ〕adj. 無情的

sort〔sɔrt〕n. 種類　　supress〔sə'prɛs〕v. 壓制；壓抑

rigid〔'rɪdʒɪd〕adj. 嚴格的　　*in favor of* 贊成；支持

rote〔rot〕n. 機械性的背誦；反覆

memorization〔ˌmɛməraɪ'zeʃən〕n. 記憶

head〔hɛd〕n. 首長

psychosomatic〔ˌsaɪkoso'mætɪk〕adj. 身心相關的

as a whole 整體而言

deep-seated〔'dip͵sitɪd〕adj. 根深蒂固的

nausea〔'nɔzɪə〕n. 反胃

attentive〔ə'tɛntɪv〕adj. 注意的；體貼的

virus〔'vaɪrəs〕n. 病毒　　evidence〔'ɛvədəns〕v. 證明

impact〔'ɪmpækt〕n. 影響

【譯文】

　　環保署最近提出警告，除非我們採取行動，阻止臭氧層的枯竭，否則可預料的是，美國將會增加四千萬個皮膚癌的病例，並在現今人類，以及接下來八十八年內出生的人當中，造成八十萬人死亡。環保署的警告，是基於氟氯烷類以每年百分之二十五的成長率來計算。有些估算的數據顯示，氟氯烷類增加的速度已變得愈來愈快。

　　紫外線的輻射也是造成白內障的主要原因，這種病會使眼球的水晶體出現雲狀花紋，造成視線的模糊，終致失明。環保署估計，未加抑制的臭氧層的枯竭，將會使各地的人罹患這種病，使得 2075 年前出生的美國人，從原本的五十五萬五千名病患，增加到二百八十萬。就像較輕微的皮膚癌一樣，白內障可以用較簡單的手術治好。先進國家擁有必要的醫療服務，儘管全國必須付出愈來愈多的資源成本。但是在這個人口日益增加的世界中，那些缺乏醫療設備的未開發國家，將會有愈來愈多的人，有失明或是死於皮膚癌的危險。這一群不被重視的人，大多數是住在靠近赤道地區，較貧窮的人，而他們則是現在對臭氧層破壞力最小的一群人。

　　然而，人類接觸紫外線的機會愈來愈多，還可能有另一種危險。照射紫外線的份量如果太多，將會減低人類對像是傳染病和腫瘤，這種對人體具有傷害的有機體。有些醫學專家擔心，過度照射紫外線，會破壞預防接種的計劃，這樣的計劃，曾用來控制會引起傳染的疾病。預防接種不是要保護人們不生病，而是讓因過度照射紫外線，而免疫系統受損的人，罹患這種病。

【答案】

11. **(A)**　　12. **(D)**　　13. **(A)**　　14. **(C)**　　15. **(B)**

【註】

halt〔hɔlt〕*v.* 使停止　　ozone〔'ozon〕*n.* 臭氧
depletion〔dɪ'pliʃən〕*n.* 耗盡
assumption〔ə'sʌmpʃən〕*n.* 假定
CFCs 氟氯烷類（如冷媒，有破壞臭氧層的作用）
estimate〔'ɛstə,met〕*n.* 估計數
ultraviolet radiation 紫外線的輻射
cataract〔'kætə,rækt〕*n.* 白內障

clouding〔ˈklaʊdɪŋ〕*n.* 雲狀花紋

lens〔lɛnz〕*n.*（眼球的）水晶體

blurred〔blɝd〕*adj.* 模糊不清的

unchecked〔ʌnˈtʃɛkt〕*adj.* 未受抑制的；未經檢查的

affliction〔əˈflɪkʃən〕*n.* 苦惱；折磨

mild〔maɪld〕*adj.* 溫和的　　resident〔ˈrɛzədənt〕*n.* 居民

albeit〔ɔlˈbiɪt〕*conj.* 雖然

escalating〔ˈɛskəˌletɪŋ〕*adj.* 擴大的；增強的

burgeoning〔ˈbɝdʒənɪŋ〕*adj.* 急速成長的

bulk〔bʌlk〕*n.* 大多數

the Equator 赤道　　**contribute to** 促成

exposure〔ɪkˈspoʒɚ〕*n.* 暴露；接觸＜*to*＞

dose〔dos〕*n.* 一次份量

organism〔ˈɔrgənˌɪzəm〕*n.* 生物；有機體

infectious〔ɪnˈfɛkʃəs〕*adj.* 傳染性的

tumor〔ˈtjumɚ〕*n.* 腫瘤　　excess〔ɪkˈsɛs〕*n.* 過量

undermine〔ˌʌndɚˈmaɪn〕*v.* 暗中破壞；逐漸損害

inoculation〔ɪnˌɑkjəˈleʃən〕*n.* 預防接種

epidemic〔ˌɛpɪˈdɛmɪk〕*n.* 傳染病

inflict〔ɪnˈflɪkt〕*v.* 使遭受　　immune〔ɪˈmjun〕*n.* 免疫

death toll 死亡人數　　fund〔fʌnd〕*v.* 提供資金

be vulnerable to 易受～傷害　　**give rise to** 造成

IV. 翻譯：中譯英：20％

1. The cross-strait policies of the three presidential candidates in the last election were very similar. All of them advocated that the R.O.C. was a sovereign country.

2. Scientists found that aerobics could delay the process of aging by means of increasing the flow of blood to the brain.

3. So far the stock market has been falling for three days. The government should take measures to stabilize the stock market.

4. In 1999, the average income in Taiwan was 13,248 US dollars, which was about 17 times the average income in mainland China.

國立清華大學八十九學年度
碩士班研究生入學考試英文試題
（語言學研究所）

I. 摘要寫作：細讀下列二篇短文，然後利用所規定的英文字數各寫一段
　摘要分別概述它們的主要內容。請勿直接抄襲短文中的句子。並請在
　你的摘要後面註明所用到的確實英文字數。　30%

1-1 請爲下列短文寫一段英文摘要（字數要少於 30 個英文單字，含標
　　點符號）。（本小題 15 分）

　　Vijaya Krishnan of the University of Alberta studied
the contraceptive practices of Canadian women. He used
data from the Canadian Fertility Survey, a study of
5315 married or cohabiting women between 18 and 49.
Krishnan found that women who already have two sons
are significantly more likely to be using contraception
than those with two daughters and no sons. More than
half of the women using contraception in Canada choose
to be sterilized. This suggests that these women have
made a definite decision not to have any more children.
On the other hand, couples postpone the use of effective
contraception until their family is the size and
composition they desire.

　　If, as Krishnan believes, this phenomenon for sons
has survived even in a highly developed country such
as Canada, then it would appear to be not just a
consequence of the stage of development of a society
but an inherent preference. He surmises that if
techniques for determining a fetus's sex become widely

available and more efficient, then this phenomenon
could eventually lead to an imbalance between the sexes
which would almost certainly have considerable social
consequences. (187 words)

1-2 請為下列短文寫一段英文摘要（字數要少於 50 個英文單字，含標點
符號）。（本小題 15 分）

Some moths emit ultrasonic noises when they hear
the squeaks that bats use to locate insects at night, and
this lessens their risk of being caught. One possibility
zoologists have considered is that the moths startle the
bats with these noises, or even jam their echolocation
system. But now researchers in Canada have come up with
another explanation. Dorothy Dunning and her colleagues
at York University in Ontario studied several Canadian
species of moths from the family Arctiidae. These moths
react to bats' ultrasonic squeaks by emitting ultrasonic
clicks.

First, the researchers confirmed that the moths
really do taste unpleasant by presenting dishes with
a selection of moths on them to captive brown bats
(Eptesicus Fuscus). In all, they offered the bats 466
moths, of which 163 were arctiids and 303 not. The bats
killed 281 of the control moths (93 per cent) and ate
all but 7, but they killed only 87 of the arctiids
(53 per cent) and left 19 of them uneaten. Clearly, they
did not like the arctiids.

Next, the biologists noted how many moths of various
families were caught by red bats (Lasiurus borealis) as
they hunted the insects around streetlights. By counting

the moths caught in ultraviolet traps the researchers measured the proportion of each family in the population as a whole, and from this they calculated that the red bats caught a significantly smaller proportion of arctiids than if they had been catching moths at random.

Dunning and her colleagues then 'muted' some of the arctiids by puncturing the tympanae they use to make their clicks. When they tossed the moths into the air in the path of foraging bats they found that the bats caught only 9 per cent of the moths which clicked, but more than 80 per cent of the muted ones, about half of which they later dropped.

Finally, the researchers checked the responses made by free-flying moths to artificial bat squeaks. They found that while 484 of 534 non-arctiid moths (92 per cent) tried to escape by diving, looping or turning, only 27 of 147 arctiids (18 per cent) bothered to do this. (355 words)

II. 英文作文：請依照下列題目及相關建議，用英文寫出一篇約 250 字的短文。20%

Topic　　　　: The Importance of Religious Education in Taiwan.
Suggestions : Your essay is required to include the following points.
(1) Definition of religious education.
(2) Desirability of religious education at home.
(3) Importance of religious education in school.
(4) Conclusion

國立清華大學八十九年度
碩士班研究生入學考試英文試題詳解

I. 摘要寫作：30%

1-1. A Canadian study shows that couples are more likely to use contraception if they have sons rather than daughters. This preference for sons may lead to an imbalance between the sexes.

1-2. Unlike other moths, the arctiid moth emits ultrasonic clicks in response to the squeaks of bats. This variety of moth tastes unpleasant to bats. Therefore, the bats do not catch moths that click. Likewise, the arctiid does not make an effort to avoid the bats.

II. 寫作：20%

Religion in Taiwan

Taiwan has a long and interesting religious history. However, as in many countries, it does not satisfy the needs of everyone. The fact that thousands of people flocked to hear the Dalai Lama speak in Taiwan tells us several things about the religious life and needs of the Taiwanese people.

First of all, the Dalai Lama's visit illustrates that Taiwanese have an open attitude toward religion. They are not afraid to hear new ideas and appreciate the beliefs of others. Their lack of dogmatism in religious matters is a very differing beliefs. However, the fact that so many people were eager to hear what the Dalai Lama had to say about empowerment indicates that something may be lacking in their current system of beliefs. Perhaps so many people turned out for the Dalai Lama because they are unsatisfied with the answers they have gotten from society and religion. It is also possible that many people feel alienated from the religious system in Taiwan or do not understand it fully.

In these modern times, society presents us with many challenges. As people strive to succeed in such a competitive environment, many ignore their spiritual lives. They become disconnected from tradition and traditional beliefs that can support them in times of trouble. In my opinion, the eagerness of the people to hear the Dalai Lama demonstrates that they feel a certain amount of insecurity. They are searching for answers that modern society is unable to provide them.

國立交通大學八十九學年度
碩士班研究生入學考試英文試題

I. Transitions: 20%

Choose the letter of the correct answer.

_____(1)_____ a referee's immediate judgment is correct, he's still got to face the resentment that continues long after a game. _____(2)_____ that resentment takes on overtones of hostility. _____(3)_____, Umpire Larry Barnett's 1975 World Series ruling brought him a threatening letter stating that if he did not pay for a $10,000 bet loss, the sender would "put a .38-caliber bullet in your head." _____(4)_____, as one official states, "An umpire is really in trouble — not when he makes poor calls — _____(5)_____ when his decisions bring happy mail and smiles."

_____(6)_____, a profession has its boundaries. Let us take, _____(7)_____, the profession of professing. There can only be as many professors in any town _____(8)_____ teaching positions available, but _____(9)_____ the local college graduates more professors than there are teaching jobs, then some of these young scholars will not be able to acquire tenure. _____(10)_____, they will have to move elsewhere or change fields in order to make a living.

1. (A) Then　　　　(B) Even when　　(C) Until now

2. (A) Sometimes　　(B) However　　(C) Similarly

3. (A) For example　(B) On the other hand
   (C) Similarly

4. (A) Consequently　(B) However　　(C) Earlier

5. (A) but　　　　　(B) if　　　　(C) unless

6. (A) Earlier　　　(B) Meanwhile　(C) Similarly

7. (A) for example　(B) on the other hand
   (C) thus

8. (A) to fill the number of
   (B) because of the number of
   (C) as there are

9. (A) if　　　　　(B) although　　(C) because

10. (A) Therefore　　(B) Likewise　　(C) Yet

II. Only *one* of the three sentences is joined and
punctuated correctly. Choose the letter of that
sentence. 6%

11. (A) Mr. Smith will retire next month, we are having
       a party for him.
    (B) Mr. Smith will retire next month; and we are
       having a party for him.
    (C) Mr. Smith will retire next month, and we are
       having a party for him.

12. (A) They finally finished the work, but they still
       had to clean the room.
    (B) They finally finished the work; but they still
       had to clean the room.
    (C) They finally finished the work, however they
       still had to clean the room.

13. (A) The young couple had an outdoor wedding; but
    unfortunately they did not anticipate rain.
    (B) The young couple had an outdoor wedding, but
    unfortunately they did not anticipate rain.
    (C) The young couple had an outdoor wedding,
    unfortunately they did not anticipate rain.

III. Only one of the three sentences is grammatically
     incorrect. Choose the letter of that sentence. 10%

14. (A) Troubled by a lack of steady income, a job was
    felt by Mary to be more important than college.
    (B) Because Mary was troubled by a lack of steady
    income, she felt a job was more important than
    college.
    (C) Troubled by a lack of steady income, Mary felt
    a job was more important than college.

15. (A) One of the unsual features of Copenhagen are
    Tivoli, an amusement park right in the middle
    of the busy city.
    (B) One of the unusual features of Copenhagen is
    Tivoli, an amusement park right in the middle
    of the busy city.
    (C) Tivoli, an amusement park right in the middle
    of the busy city, is one of the unusual
    features of Copenhagen.

16. (A) Education is free and compulsory; however,
    children in remote areas is often unable to get
    to school because of the snow.
    (B) Education is free and compulsory; however,
    children in remote areas are often unable to
    get to school because of the snow.
    (C) Education is free and compulsory, but children
    in remote areas are often unable to get to
    school because of the snow.

17. (A) We don't know who will be coming from the
       employment agency.
    (B) We don't know whom will be coming from the
       employment agency.
    (C) We don't know the person who will be coming
       from the employment agency.

18. (A) Picketing outside the school board office, the
       students protested the increased tuition.
    (B) Picketing outside the school board office,
       increased tuition was being protested by the
       students.
    (C) Students picketed outside the school board
       office; they protested the increased tuition.

IV. Choose the letter which best represents the most
    logical order of the instructions on *how to replace
    a blown fuse.* 6%

19. (A) D-E-A-C-B   (B) C-B-D-A-E
    (C) C-A-E-B-D   (D) E-B-D-A-C

A. Then locate the bad fuse. A blown fuse will have
   either (1) a scorched window or (2) a clear window
   with a broken metal strip inside. (A discolored
   window indicates that the fuse was blown by a short
   circuit; a broken metal strip indicates that the
   circuits were overloaded.)

B. Then screw in the spare fuse by turning it clockwise,
   just as you would screw in a light bulb. Make sure
   the spare fuse has the same capacity as the old one.
   In other words, you shouldn't replace a 20-ampere
   fuse with a 15-ampere fuse.

C. First, open the door of the fuse box and flip the main switch to the "off" position so that there is no electrical power running through the circuits. Also make sure you are standing on a dry floor.

D. Only when you have completed these steps can you flip the main switch back to the "on" position.

E. After you have located the blown fuse, remove it by turning it counterclockwise.

V. Certain sentences in the following paragraph are irrelevant (無關主題). Choose the letter that best represents all the irrelevant sentences. 8%

20. (A) (1)(5)(7)(9)   (B) (2)(4)(6)(8)
    (C) (3)(9)(15)(20)   (D) (2)(13)(14)(15)

(1) Although most of my friends disagree with me totally, I think it is better for an unmarried girl to live at home with her parents for the first two years of college. (2) Of course, maybe it is better for a girl that age to be married, but there are many people who don't approve of young marriage. (3) College differs in a number of ways (from high school) that take getting used to without living alone for the first time. (4) Even living with a roommate is a lot different from living with your family. (5) Some of the reasons that make it better are financial. (6) Whether you are supporting yourself or your parents are supporting you, it costs much less to live at home. (7) Maybe you are working and paying your family board, but you almost

certainly pay less at home than you would on your own, and, therefore, have to work fewer hours. (8) So right there, you have a saving in money and time. (9) And don't underrate that saving in time. (10) Assuming that you want to be successful in college, time is your most precious commodity. (11) While you are still a resident member of the family, your mother probably throws in your clothes with the rest of the household's when she's doing the laundry and cooks for you as, for everyone else. (12) Suppose you do help out; there's a big difference between that and doing everything for yourself. (13) Some men only learn after a divorce how much their wives did for them. (14) Women who are "only housekeepers" work longer hours and perhaps undergo as much stress as their unappreciative husbands. (15) Stress, I think, is the result of responsibilities. (16) When you are new at college, you have plenty of responsibilities directly related to college. (17) You really don't need the obligations of an independent adult in addition. (18) Most of my friends relish the freedom they feel when living on their own. (19) For myself, living with my parents gives me the freedom to have enough fun but still control myself enough to do well in college. (20) Of course, it depends on what kind of parents you have. If they are very strict or still consider you their "little girl," things might be very different.

VI. Choose the letter of the correct topic sentence for the following paragraphs. 10%

21. (A) Pheromones have an important function among
    honey bees in regulating the reproductive cycle
    of the colony and marking the target when a
    worker stings an intruder.
    (B) An extraordinary complexity of behavior patterns
    sustains insect societies, although there is
    no intelligence, at least in the way that this
    concept is applied to humans.
    (C) Pheromones have a wide range of functions in
    the insect world, perhaps about as many as there
    are activities that require some sort of
    communication.

_____(topic sentence)_____. Pheromones are secretions
whose odors convey certain messages to or incite
certain behaviors in other organisms. They are important
in the formation of swarms of migratory locusts, for
example, and are seen as sex attractants. The female
gypsy moth has about 0.01ml glyphure, which under good
conditions would be potent enough to excite more than a
billion males. The uses of pheromones are not learned,
however; pheromones are automatically released and
automatically responded to. Experimenters have proved
this by manipulating situations artificially. Among
ants, a certain pheromone indicates that the ant is alive,
and another indicates its death. When experimenters
smeared living ants with this death pheromone, ants
were repeated carted off to the refuse pile by others
in the colony.

22. (A) The studies of the German naturalist von Frisch
       (1955) did much to extend our understanding of
       the behavior and communicative abilities of
       bees and their colonies.
   (B) The studies of the German naturalist von Frisch
       (1955) show that bees convey the location and
       direction of food discoveries to other bees in
       a series of movements resembling a dance.
   (C) The German naturalist von Frisch (1955) proved
       that if bees are restricted to horizontal
       surface and deprived of sunlight, they are
       unable to communicate the direction of their
       food discoveries.

_____(topic sentence)_____. Von Frisch constructed a hive
with glass walls, which permitted him to observe the
behavior of the bee tenants when they returned from
foodseeking flights. When the source of nectar was
close — say, within a hundred feet or so — the finder
bee would perform a "dance" consisting of circular
movements. To indicate longer distances, the bee would
run in a straight line while moving its abdomen rapidly
from side to side. For distances in excess of two hundred
yards, the number of turns made by the bee would
decrease. A run followed by only two turns, for
example, might indicate that the food source was
several miles away.

VII. Choose the most appropriate word for each of the
     blanks in the following passages. 22%

A. Passage I: ROC Government's Policies After the 921
   Earthquake. 10%

A special committee will be set up to ____(23)____ the use of quake disaster funds so as not to cause confusion and complaints among either the quake victims or donors. The establishment of this special committee will ____(24)____ that the public's money is used in a fair and ____(25)____ way. The government also announced a 5-year ____(26)____ for the rebuilding, and the ____(27)____ plan is divided into three stages.

23. (A) garner   (B) coordinate
    (C) ensure   (D) limit

24. (A) ensure   (B) assign
    (C) regulate   (D) identify

25. (A) powerful   (B) peaceful
    (C) efficient   (D) thoughtful

26. (A) shelters   (B) deadline
    (C) timetable   (D) slot

27. (A) relief   (B) reconstruction
    (C) prefabricate   (D) eminent

B. Passage II: Amid the Dangers: Opportunity 12%

Taiwan's presidential election is a triumph for Chen Shui-bian and his party, the DPP. The anxieties aroused by the shift from Kuomintang to DPP rule should be rapidly ____(28)____. In fact, Taiwan's successful and peaceful transfer of power ____(29)____ great praise and support worldwide. On the other hand, Beijing fears the DPP will accelerate Taiwan's drift from the mainland. Thus, China's leaders have warned Taiwan that a declaration of independence would ____(30)____ an attack. A mainland assault against Taiwan would inevitably draw

in the United States. Even limited Chinese military
action — such as seizure of Taiwanese ships in the
strait — would ____(31)____ some sort of American
assistance to Taiwan. Tokyo and Washington have
responsibilities as well. They should neither pressure
Taiwan to enter into negotiation with Beijing nor so
____(32)____ Taipei that it feels no need to do so. The
urge for dialogue must come from within. At the same
time, the United States and Japan must continue to
maintain a security architecture in the western Pacific
that enables China and Taiwan to expand their contacts
without ____(33)____ the security of either.

28. (A) unveiled   (B) alleviated
    (C) adopted   (D) revised

29. (A) embraces   (B) secures
    (C) merits   (D) declaim

30. (A) provide   (B) commit
    (C) trigger   (D) pledge

31. (A) spark   (B) clarify
    (C) prolong   (D) deploy

32. (A) discourage   (B) irritate
    (C) interrupt   (D) indulge

33. (A) intercepting   (B) eroding
    (C) jeopardizing   (D) preventing

VIII. Reading comprehension.

(Passage) Both exports to and imports from mainland
China during 1999 hit record highs of US$21.236 billion
and US$4.522 billion, respectively, according to

statistics published by the Board of Foreign Trade. Exports to mainland China rose significantly due to a combination of internal and external factors.

PRC authorities announced a series of measures to boost PRC exports, creating greater demand for industrial materials and goods imported from Taiwan.

The international market has also picked up since mid-1999, leading to higher demand for exports from the mainland, which in turn boosted demand for industrial goods imported form Taiwan.

Taiwan's exports to the mainland include machinery, electronic devices and equipment, plastics, steel, and synthetic fibers. Exports of these products took up a 75.8 percent share of Taiwan's total exports to the PRC.

Imports from mainland China rose due to greater demand for raw materials produced there and it took up 4.1 percent of Taiwan's total imports during 1999.

According to the PRC customs office, Taiwan's market share dropped slightly by 0.1 percentage point despite the growth in PRC imports from Taiwan. The shrinkage was mainly due to the expansion in the market shares of other countries. Malaysia, Australia and Japan increased their market share in the mainland market.

Decide which one of the following inferences or statements is false. 10%

34. (A) Bilateral trade between the ROC and PRC in 1999 reached US$25,758 billion.
    (B) The international market was more active in the latter half year of 1999.
    (C) Because of the growing PRC imports from other Asian countries, Taiwan's market share in the PRC showed a slight shrinking.
    (D) The PRC's demand for ROC goods was reduced because of increased PRC exports to international market.

IX. Graph study: 8%

Decide which *one* of the following statements, drawn from the graph, is incorrect.

35. (A) The increase in sales volume from 1992 to 1995 was about the same as that from 1998 to 2001.
    (B) The market drop from 1995 to 1996 was about the same as that from 1997 to 1998.
    (C) The sales volume in 1999 was substantially higher than that in 1995.
    (D) The sales volume in 2002 is projected to be twice that in 1998.

國立交通大學八十九年度
碩士班研究生入學考試英文試題詳解

I. 轉承語：20%

　　即使裁判當下的判決無誤，賽後很長一段時間，他還是要面對別人不滿的情緒。有時候，不滿的情緒隱含著些許敵意。舉例來說，一九七五年世界盃，裁判賴瑞・巴耐特的判決，導致他收到一封恐嚇信，威脅他如果不賠償他一萬元賭金的損失，寄信人就會「送一顆點三八的子彈到他的腦袋瓜。」然而，就如同一位官員所說的：「裁判眞的有麻煩，不是因爲他作出的判決不好，而是因爲他的判決，而收到滿意的信件和笑容。」

　　同樣地，每個行業都有其限制。就拿教授爲例，任何城鎮的教職名額有多少，就只能有那麼多的教授，但如果當地的大學培養的教授，其數量多於教職數量，那麼這些年輕的學者當中，就有些人無法獲得終身職。因此，爲了謀生，他們必須搬到別的地方，或是轉換工作領域。

【答案】

1. (**B**)　　2. (**A**)　　3. (**A**)　　4. (**B**)　　5. (**A**)

6. (**C**)　　7. (**A**)　　8. (**C**)　　9. (**A**)　　10. (**A**)

【註】

referee〔͵rɛfəˋri〕*n.* 裁判（員）

resentment〔rıˋzɛntmənt〕*n.* 憤慨；怨恨　　*take on* 具有

overtone〔ˋovɚ͵ton〕*n.* 弦外之音　　hostility〔hasˋtılətı〕*n.* 敵意

umpire〔ˋʌmpaır〕*n.* 裁判（員）　　ruling〔ˋrulıŋ〕*n.* 裁決

state〔stet〕*v.* 聲明　　bet〔bɛt〕*n.* 賭金

caliber〔ˋkæləbɚ〕*n.*（子彈的）直徑

call〔kɔl〕*n.*（運動、比賽中）裁判員的判決

boundary〔ˋbaundərı〕*n.* 界線；範圍

profess〔prəˋfɛs〕*v.*（以教授身份）教授

tenure〔ˋtɛnjɚ〕*n.*（大學教授等的）終身任職權

II. 選出正確的句子：6%

11. (**C**) (A), → , **and** 或 ;
　　　　　(B) ; **and** → , **and** 或 ;

12. (**A**) (B) ; **but** → , **but** 或 ;
　　　　　(C), **however** → ; **however**, 或 . **However**,

13. (**B**) (A) ; **but** → , **but** 或 ;
　　　　　(C), → , **but** 或 ;
　　　　　anticipate〔æn'tɪsə,pet〕v. 預料

III. 選出錯誤的句子：10%

14. (**A**) *Troubled* → *Because Mary was troubled*
　　　　　steady〔'stɛdɪ〕adj. 穩定的

15. (**A**) *are* → *is*
　　　　　feature〔'fitʃə〕n. 特色
　　　　　Copenhagen〔,kopən'hegən〕n. 哥本哈根（丹麥首都）
　　　　　amusement park 遊樂園

16. (**A**) *is* → *are*
　　　　　compulsory〔kəm'pʌlsərɪ〕adj. 義務的
　　　　　remote〔rɪ'mot〕adj. 偏僻的

17. (**B**) *whom* → *who*
　　　　　employment agency 職業介紹所

18. (**B**) picket〔'pɪkɪt〕v. 派遣罷工糾察員
　　　　　board〔bord〕n. 董事會　　tuition〔tju'ɪʃən〕n. 學費

IV. 重組：6%

19. (**A**) 首先，將保險絲盒的蓋子打開，而且要將總開關「關掉」，
確保所有電路都沒有電了。也必須確定你所站的地板是乾燥
的。然後找出壞掉的保險絲。燒掉的保險絲會有 (1) 燒焦的
檢視窗，或 (2) 乾淨的檢視窗中有燒斷的金屬線。（變色的
檢視窗代表保險絲因為短路而燒斷；而斷掉的金屬絲代表
保險絲因為電量過大而燒斷。）找到燒掉的保險絲後，就
逆時鐘方向旋轉後將它移除。然後將備用的保險絲依順時鐘
方向旋入，就好像在裝電燈泡一樣。要確定備用的保險絲容
量跟舊的一樣。換句話說，你不能用十五安培的保險絲換二
十安培的保險絲。確定所有的步驟都已完成後，才能將開關
打「開」。

locate〔loˊket〕*v.* 找出　　fuse〔fjuz〕*n.* 保險絲
scorched〔skɔrtʃɪd〕*adj.* 燒焦的
window〔ˊwɪndo〕*n.* 檢視窗　　strip〔strɪp〕*n.* 條；帶
discolor〔dɪsˊkʌlɚ〕*v.* 使變色
blow〔blo〕*v.*（保險絲等）燒斷　　***short circuit*** 短路
circuit〔ˊsɝkɪt〕*n.* 電路　　overload〔ˊovɚ lod〕*v.* 負荷過多
screw〔skru〕*v.*（用螺釘等）將…旋緊或固定
capacity〔kəˊpæsətɪ〕*n.* 容量
ampere〔ˊæmpɪr〕*n.* 安培　　flip〔flɪp〕*v.* 以手指輕彈
counterclockwise〔ˌkaʊntɚˊklɑkˌwaɪz〕*adv.* 反時鐘方向地
　（↔ *clockwise*）

V. 選出不相關的句子：8%

20. (**D**)　儘管我大多數的朋友都不贊成，我還是認為對一個未婚的女孩子而言，大學的前兩年還是跟父母住在一起比較好。大學與「高中」相比，有很多方面都不一樣，這些不一樣的地方在於，要漸漸地習慣跟別人一起生活。即使跟室友住在一起，也與跟家人住在一起相當地不同。其中有些理由是，就財務上而言，與父母住在一起會比較寬裕。不論是自食其力或靠父母供養，住在家中都會比較節省。也許你必須工作支付家中的伙食費，但幾乎可以確定的是，住在家裡會比一個人住還省錢，因此，打工時數可以少一點。所以，住在家裡可以存錢且節省時間。而且別低估了所節省的時間。如果你想要在大學生活有所收獲，時間就是你最寶貴的資產。當你還住在家裡，你母親要洗衣服的時候，也許也會把你的衣服拿來一起洗，或著也會幫你一起準備餐點。假設你真的有幫忙作家務，那也與你自己一個人住時，樣樣必須自己張羅，有很大的不同。當你是大學新生時，大學裡已經有很多必須要做的事。你實在不需要再額外負擔一些成人的義務。我很多朋友都因為自立更生，而感受到自由的解放。就我而言，跟父母住在一起讓我有足夠的自由去玩樂，也讓我有足夠的控制力去完成大學學業。當然，這取決於你擁有什麼樣的父母。如果他們非常的嚴格，或還是把你當作「小女孩」的話，那情況可能就會大不相同了。

board〔bord〕*n.* 膳食費
underrate〔ˌʌndəˈret〕*v.* 低估
assuming (***that***) 假定
commodity〔kəˈmɑdətɪ〕*n.* 商品；有價值的東西
help out 幫助；出力
obligation〔ˌɑbləˈgeʃən〕*n.* 義務
relish〔ˈrɛlɪʃ〕*v.* 享受

VI. 選出主題句：10%

21. (**C**) <u>在昆蟲的世界裡，費洛蒙的功能非常廣泛，也許就像他們所</u>
<u>進行活動一樣多，而這些活動都需要某種溝通的方式。</u>費洛
蒙是一種分泌物，它的氣味能傳達特定訊息，或刺激其他生
物的行為。舉例來說，它們對於一群蝗蟲的遷移型態非常重
要，而且也被視為一種性激素。雌性的靫欒蛾會散發零點零
一的公撮的 glyphure，在良好的狀況下，會刺激上百萬隻
的雄性。費洛蒙的使用並非後天學習而來的，而是自然散發
與自然反應的。實驗人員曾經在人為操作的狀況下證明這項
推論。在螞蟻群中，有某種費洛蒙表示螞蟻是活的，而有另
一種是表示螞蟻是死的。當研究人員將它塗抹在活的螞蟻身
上時，其他的螞蟻群就不停地將這些被塗過的螞蟻搬到廢棄
堆中。

pheromone〔ˈfɛrəˌmon〕*n.* 費洛蒙

secretion〔sɪˈkriʃən〕*n.* 分泌物　　odor〔ˈodɚ〕*n.* 氣味

convey〔kənˈve〕*v.* 傳達　　incite〔ɪnˈsaɪt〕*v.* 刺激

organism〔ˈɔrgənˌɪzəm〕*n.* 生物；有機體

swarm〔swɔrm〕*n.*（昆蟲等的）群

migratory〔ˈmaɪgrəˌtori〕*adj.* 遷移的

locust〔ˈlokəst〕*n.* 蝗蟲

attractant〔əˈtræktənt〕*n.* 引誘劑

gypsy moth 靫欒蛾　　potent〔ˈpotn̩t〕*adj.* 強有力的

manipulate〔məˈnɪpjəˌlet〕*v.* 處理；操縱

artificially〔ˌɑrtəˈfɪʃəlɪ〕*adv.* 人工地

smear〔smɪr〕*v.* 塗抹　　cart〔kɑrt〕*v.* 強行帶走

refuse〔ˈrɛfjus〕*n.* 廢物　　pile〔paɪl〕*n.* 堆

colony〔ˈkɑlənɪ〕*n.* 群體

22. (**B**)　德國自然學家文·佛利雪在一九五五年，展示了蜜蜂如何用
　　　一種類似舞蹈的連續動作，傳達食物的地點與方向給其他蜜
　　　蜂。文·佛利雪建造了一個有玻璃圍牆的蜂窩，讓他能夠觀
　　　察覓食歸來的蜜蜂。當花蜜的源頭在附近時，例如大約在一
　　　百英呎以內，發現的蜜蜂就會跳一種繞圈圈的「舞蹈」。為
　　　了要表示在更遠的距離，蜜蜂會直線地飛行，同時快速地翻
　　　轉腹部。當距離超過兩百碼時，蜜蜂旋轉的次數會減少。舉
　　　個例子，當飛行中，旋轉的次數只有兩次時，也許就意味著
　　　食物的來源在好幾英哩外。

　　　naturalist〔ˈnætʃərəlɪst〕*n.* 自然學家（尤指在戶外研究動植
　　　物者）　　　convey〔kənˈve〕*v.* 傳達
　　　a series of 一連串的　　hive〔haɪv〕*n.* 蜂巢
　　　tenant〔ˈtɛnənt〕*n.* 居住者　　nectar〔ˈnɛktɚ〕*n.* 花蜜
　　　consist of 包含　　circular〔ˈsɝkjələ〕*adj.* 圓形的
　　　abdomen〔ˈæbdəmən〕*n.* 腹部　　***in excess of*** 超過

VII. 克漏字：22%

A. 短文一：中華民國九二一震災後的政策：10%

【譯文】

　　　將成立一個特別委員會，以協調震災款項的使用，如此才不至於讓
受災戶與捐款者產生疑惑與埋怨。特別委員會的成立，將確保公眾的捐
款能公正而有效地利用。政府也宣布，將以五年的時間進行重建工作，
而此重建計畫將分三階段進行。

【註】

set up 成立　　fund〔fʌnd〕*n.* 基金；專款
donor〔ˈdonɚ〕*n.* 捐贈者

23. (**B**) 　(A) garner〔'gɑrnə〕*v.* 儲存
　　　　　(B) ***coordinate***〔ko'ɔrdn̩,et〕*v.* 協調

24. (**A**) 　(A) ***ensure***〔ɪn'ʃʊr〕*v.* 確保
　　　　　(B) assign〔ə'saɪn〕*v.* 指派
　　　　　(C) regulate〔'rɛgjə,let〕*v.* 規定
　　　　　(D) identify〔aɪ'dɛntə,faɪ〕*v.* 辨識

25. (**C**) 　(B) peaceful〔'pisfəl〕*adj.* 和平的
　　　　　(C) ***efficient***〔ɪ'fɪʃnt〕*adj.* 有效率的
　　　　　(D) thoughtful〔'θɔtfəl〕*adj.* 體貼的

26. (**C**) 　(A) shelter〔'ʃɛltə〕*n.* 庇護；避難所
　　　　　(B) deadline〔'dɛd,laɪn〕*n.* 截止期限
　　　　　(C) ***timetable***〔'taɪm,tebl̩〕*n.* 時間表
　　　　　(D) slot〔slɑt〕*n.* 投幣孔

27. (**B**) 　(A) relief〔rɪ'lif〕*n.* 救濟；補助
　　　　　(B) ***reconstruction***〔,rikən'strʌkʃən〕*n.* 重建
　　　　　(C) prefabricate〔pri'fæbrə,ket〕*v.* 預先製造組合配件
　　　　　(D) eminent〔'ɛmənənt〕*adj.* 卓越的

B. 短文二：危機就是轉機：12%

【譯文】

　　台灣總統大選由陳水扁與他所代表的民進黨取得勝利。政權由國民黨轉移至民進黨所引起的不安，應該會迅速地趨於緩和。事實上，台灣政權轉換過程的成功與和平，值得世界各國的讚賞與支持。但另一方面，北京當局卻害怕，民進黨政府會加速台灣與中國大陸的分離趨勢。因此，中國領導當局警告，台灣若宣佈獨立將會引發戰爭。大陸對台灣的攻擊，將不可避免地將美國捲入。即使中國僅發動有限的軍事行動——如在台灣海峽實行海運封鎖——都會引起美國對台灣某種程度的支持。

東京與華盛頓都有責任要如此。他們既不應該強迫台灣與北京談判，也不會縱容台灣，讓台灣覺得不需要談判。同時，美國與日本必須繼續維持西太平洋的安全架構，如此才能讓中國與台灣擴大交流，而不會危害到彼此的安全。

【註】

amid〔ə'mɪd〕*prep.* 在…之間 triumph〔'traɪəmf〕*n.* 大勝利

anxiety〔æŋ'zaɪətɪ〕*n.* 焦慮 shift〔ʃɪft〕*n.* 轉換

transfer〔'trænsfɚ〕*n.* 轉讓 accelerate〔æk'sɛlə,ret〕*v.* 加速

drift〔drɪft〕*n.* 趨勢 assault〔ə'sɔlt〕*n.* 攻擊<*against*>

seizure〔'siʒɚ〕*n.* 扣押 *enter into* 開始參加

negotiation〔nɪ,goʃɪ'eʃən〕*n.* 協商

architecture〔'ɑrkə,tɛktʃɚ〕*n.* 結構

28. (**B**)　(A) unveil〔ʌn'vel〕*v.* 揭露秘密
　　　　(B) *alleviate*〔ə'livɪ,et〕*v.* 緩和
　　　　(C) adopt〔ə'dɑpt〕*v.* 採取
　　　　(D) revise〔rɪ'vaɪz〕*v.* 修正

29. (**C**)　(A) embrace〔ɪm'bres〕*v.* 擁抱；欣然接受
　　　　(B) secure〔sɪ'kjʊr〕*v.* 使安全；獲得
　　　　(C) *merit*〔'mɛrɪt〕*v.* 應該得到；值得
　　　　(D) declaim〔dɪ'klem〕*v.* 巧辯；演講

30. (**C**)　(B) commit〔kə'mɪt〕*v.* 犯（罪）
　　　　(C) *trigger*〔'trɪgɚ〕*v.* 引起；觸發
　　　　(D) pledge〔plɛdʒ〕*v.* 保證給予

31. (**A**)　(A) *spark*〔spɑrk〕*v.* 點燃；發動
　　　　(B) clarify〔'klærə,faɪ〕*v.* 澄清
　　　　(C) prolong〔prə'lɔŋ〕*v.* 延長
　　　　(D) deploy〔dɪ'plɔɪ〕*v.* 部署

32. (**D**)　(A) discourage〔dɪsˈkɝɪdʒ〕*v.* 使氣餒
　　　　　(B) irritate〔ˈɪrəˌtet〕*v.* 使惱怒
　　　　　(C) interrupt〔ˌɪntəˈrʌpt〕*v.* 打斷
　　　　　(D) ***indulge***〔ɪnˈdʌldʒ〕*v.* 縱容；遷就

33. (**C**)　(A) intercept〔ˌɪntəˈsɛpt〕*v.* 攔截；妨礙
　　　　　(B) erode〔ɪˈrod〕*v.* 侵蝕
　　　　　(C) ***jeopardize***〔ˈdʒɛpəˌdaɪz〕*v.* 危害

VIII. 閱讀測驗：

【譯文】

　　根據國貿局的統計，從中國大陸進口與出口的金額，在一九九九年都雙雙創下歷史新高，分別為兩百一十二億三千六百萬美元與四十五億兩千兩百萬美元。對中國大陸出口的明顯升高肇因於幾項國內與國外因素的結和。

　　中華人民共和國宣布了一連串刺激當地出口的措施，因此對台灣的工業原料與產品的進口需求大增。

　　國際市場在一九九九年中期也開始反彈，導致從中國大陸出口產品的需求增加，因而增加了大陸從台灣進口工業原料的需求。

　　台灣對大陸的出口包括機械設備、電子組件與設備、塑膠、鋼鐵，與人工纖維。這些產品的出口，佔台灣對大陸出口總值的百分之七十五點八。

　　從中國大陸進口產品的增加，源自於對當地生產的原料需求大增，這些佔台灣一九九九年進口總額的百分之四點一。

　　根據中華人民共和國海關的說法，儘管從台灣的進口量有所成長，但台灣的市場佔有率卻小跌了百分之零點一。萎縮的原因主要是因為其他國家的市場佔有率的增加。馬來西亞、澳洲與日本，增加了在中國大陸市場的佔有率。

判斷下列的推論或敘述何者是錯的？

【答案】

34.（**D**）

【註】

export〔ˈɛksport〕*n.* 出口品
import〔ˈɪmport〕*n.* 進口品　〔ɪmˈport〕*v.* 進口
respectively〔rɪˈspɛktɪvlɪ〕*adv.* 分別地
statistics〔stəˈtɪstɪks〕*n., pl.* 統計數字
board〔bord〕*n.*（政府的）部；局；會
significantly〔sɪgˈnɪfəkəntlɪ〕*adv.* 顯著地
internal〔ɪnˈtɜnḷ〕*adj.* 內在的；國內的
external〔ɪkˈstɜnḷ〕*adj.* 外在的；國外的
boost〔bust〕*v.* 增加；提高　　***pick up*** 改進；恢復
steel〔stil〕*n.* 鋼鐵　　synthetic〔sɪnˈθɛtɪk〕*adj.* 合成的；人工的
fiber〔ˈfaɪbɚ〕*n.* 纖維　　***take up*** 佔據
raw material 原料　　customs〔ˈkʌstəmz〕*n., pl.* 海關
shrinkage〔ˈʃrɪŋkɪdʒ〕*n.* 收縮；減少
expansion〔ɪkˈspænʃən〕*n.* 膨脹
bilateral〔baɪˈlætərəl〕*adj.* 雙邊的
shrink〔ʃrɪŋk〕*v.* 收縮；減少　　***cut down*** 削減

IX. 閱讀表格：18％

【答案】

35.（**C**）

【註】

volume〔ˈvɑljəm〕*n.*（生產、交易等的）量；額
substantially〔səbˈstænʃəlɪ〕*adv.* 相當大量地；可觀地
project〔prəˈdʒɛkt〕*v.* 預計；推斷

心得筆記欄

國立台灣大學八十七學年度
碩士班研究生入學考試英文試題

Choose the BEST answer. Blacken the appropriate space on your computer card for each question to indicate your choice.

Example : It was Joan's first visit to the country, and everything was fresh and ＿＿＿＿＿ to her.
    (A) dull   (B) quickly
    (C) new   (D) excite

Answer : A   B   C   D   E

I. Vocabulary/Grammar/Usage (Choose the best answer to fill in the blank)

1. The child was unable to offer an ＿＿＿＿＿ description of what she had witnessed.
    (A) articulate   (B) enormous
    (C) clear   (D) artificial

2. The truck was equipped with a fuel tank which had a ＿＿＿＿＿ of 140 liters.
    (A) ability   (B) capacity
    (C) burden   (D) accommodate

3. While I was away at school, I ＿＿＿＿＿ regularly with my brothers and sisters.
    (A) called   (B) wrote
    (C) e-mailed   (D) corresponded

4. The acquired immune deficiency ＿＿＿＿＿ (AIDS) is likely to strike those whose immune system is already below par.
    (A) scene   (B) scenario
    (C) synopsis   (D) syndrome

5. According to the latest _____ information, the air
   crash did take place around midnight.
   (A) adjacent   (B) available
   (C) artful   (D) apprehend

6. Parents should _____ in their children a desire
   to learn and the habit of reading.
   (A) covet   (B) cover
   (C) cultivate   (D) crook

7. He is considered one of the best scientists in
   physics and plays a _____ role in the field.
   (A) dominant   (B) previous
   (C) prevalent   (D) notorious

8. The claim that there was life on Mars seemed to us
   _____.
   (A) civilized   (B) considerate
   (C) dubious   (D) undoubtedly

9. People without confidence tend to _____ their
   success to external causes such as luck.
   (A) distribute   (B) contribute
   (C) tribute   (D) attribute

10. A covering letter should never exceed one page;
    often a far shorter letter will _____.
    (A) survive   (B) surmise
    (C) suffice   (D) suspend

11. Mary was promoted to the position of executive
    manager, because her boss considered her _____
    in dealing with problems of the company.
    (A) complete   (B) competent
    (C) concrete   (D) complicated

12. The manager's boss felt _____ to give him a raise
    in salary, because he had done such a good job.
    (A) object   (B) obliged
    (C) obeyed   (D) obedient

13. The general sent all the soldiers out on maneuvers,
    leaving the fort ——————— to attack.
    (A) vivid   (B) vital
    (C) vulgar   (D) vulnerable

14. Modern men want to live a comfortable life at the
    ——————— of turning the Earth into a waste land.
    (A) expense   (B) dispense
    (C) expend   (D) inexpensive

15. The only ——————— for membership in this club is an
    IQ of over 150.
    (A) pretense   (B) prescription
    (C) presumption   (D) prerequisite

16. The senator declined to give a speech ——————— a sore
    throat.
    (A) with respect to   (B) in terms of
    (C) on behalf of   (D) on account of

17. Sometimes things don't ——————— the way we think
    they are going to.
    (A) turn out   (B) turn into
    (C) turn over   (D) turn down

18. I ——————— him for his valuable comments on my article.
    (A) indebted to   (B) indebt to
    (C) am indebted to   (D) am in debt to

19. The suspect claimed that he was not allowed ———————
    to a lawyer after he had been arrested.
    (A) award   (B) access
    (C) avail   (D) agreement

20. ——————— your summer house, would you rent it to
    us next year?
    (A) By means of   (B) On account of
    (C) With regard to   (D) Regardless of

II. Paraphrase(Choose the answer that best keeps the
    meaning of each of the underlined words or phrases)

Education, to have any meaning beyond the purpose
of creating well-informed dunces, must (21)elicit from
the pupil what is (22)latent in every human being—the
rule of reasoning, the inner knowledge of what is proper
for men to be and do, the ability to sift evidence and
come to conclusions that can generally (23)be assented
to by all open minds and warm hearts.

Pupils are more like oysters than sausages. The job
of teaching is not to (24)stuff them and then seal them
up, but to help them open up and reveal the riches
within. There are pearls in each of us, if only we know
how to cultivate them with (25)ardor and persistence.

21. (A) elevate   (B) draw out
    (C) eliminate   (D) rule out
22. (A) hidden   (B) impart
    (C) obvious   (D) oblivious
23. (A) be made   (B) be stipulated
    (C) be stimulated   (D) be agreed to
24. (A) press   (B) cram
    (C) give   (D) push
25. (A) fever   (B) knowledge
    (C) skill   (D) earnestness

III. Cloze Test(Choose the best answer to fill in the
     blank)

If UCLA researchers are accurate, dogs were domesticated about the time mankind first learned to grow
crops. This knowledge may prompt today's typical dog
lovers to wonder why their prehistoric ancestors took
so long to do something so important.

____(26)____ this decade, dogs have climbed to a new status in the lap of society. Thanks to a ____(27)____ in the relationships that animals enjoy within families, dogs have become surrogate children for some adults.

As a result, we want our pets to live as long and as well as possible, and veterinary medicine ____(28)____. Through improved preventive care, better nutrition and overall life-style management, dogs live longer. However, because dogs are living longer, they are more susceptible to diseases associated with age, including arthritis. More than one in five adult dogs experience restricted movement and ____(29)____ quality of life ____(30)____ arthritis.

26. (A) Inside   (B) Among
    (C) Along   (D) Within
27. (A) transaction   (B) transformation
    (C) transmission   (D) transport
28. (A) has responded   (B) has replied
    (C) has approved   (D) has referred
29. (A) enhanced   (B) warm
    (C) diminished   (D) disappearing
30. (A) by means of   (B) despite of
    (C) as a result of   (D) based upon

IV. Reading Comprehension
    Part One: Read each of the following paragraphs and choose the statement that BEST represents its main idea.

Child psychologists recognize the value of the toy a child holds in his hand at bedtime. It is different from his thumb, with which he can close himself in from the rest of the world, and it is different from the real world, to which he is learning to relate himself. Psychologists call these toys "transitional objects"; that is, objects that help the child move back and forth between the exactions of everyday life and the world of wish and dream.

31. (A) The toy a child holds functions like his or her thumb.
    (B) A child can close himself in the toy he holds.
    (C) Toys represent the real world to a child.
    (D) Toys help a child to live between the real world and the world of dreams.

  I can't help wondering what prompted murderers to speak out against killing as they entered the death house door. Did their newfound reverence for life stem from the realization that they were about to lose their own? Life is indeed precious, and I believe the death penalty helps to affirm this fact. Had the death penalty been a real possibility in the minds of these murderers, they might well have stayed their hand. They might have shown their moral awareness before their victims died, and not after.

32. (A) The author is against the death penalty.
    (B) The death penalty may help to prevent murders.
    (C) Murderers oftentimes showed reverence for life before their victims died.
    (D) Abolishing the death penalty helps to make life precious.

  Our deepest folly is the notion that we are in charge of the place, that we own it and can somehow run it. We are beginning to treat the earth as a sort of domesticated household pet, living in an environment invented by us, part kitchen garden, part park, part zoo. It is an idea we must rid ourselves of soon, for it is not so. It is the other way around. We are not separate beings. We are a living part of the earth owned and operated by the earth, probably specialized for functions on its behalf that we have not yet glimpsed.

33. (A) We are in charge of the earth.
    (B) We are part of the earth.
    (C) We have been doing something good to the earth.
    (D) We should change the earth into part kitchen
        garden, part park, and part zoo.

The remarkable thing about dinosaurs is not that
they became extinct, but that they dominated the earth
for so long. Dinosaurs held sway for 100 million years
while mammals, all the while, lived as small animals in
the interstices of their world. After 70 million years
on top, we mammals have an excellent track record and
good prospects for the future, but we have yet to display
the staying power of dinosaurs.

34. (A) Dinosaurs are noted for their staying power on
        earth.
    (B) It is certain that human beings will last longer
        than dinosaurs did.
    (C) Mammals did not exist when dinosaurs were
        around.
    (D) It's a good thing that dinosaurs became extinct.

It's often said that the United States has a skill
shortage in high technology—and the fact that Silicon
Valley recruits heavily around the world is said to be
evidence of that. But without more inquiry, we can't
know whether this is because American college graduates
are dumb, or because the high-technology sector has
grown so fast that it cannot possibly satisfy all its
demands for high-level skills from the United States.

35. (A) Silicon Valley recruits heavily around the world
    because U.S. college graduates are dumb.
    (B) The high technology sector has grown so fast that
    it cannot get enough skilled workers to satisfy
    its demands.
    (C) The real reason for a skill shortage in high
    technology in the U.S. is still unknown.
    (D) Demands for high-level skills from the United
    States have grown fast.

   People are often shocked by the blunt honesty of
Niccolo Machiavelli's *The Prince*, a sixteenth-century
book of practical advice for rulers. One of the basic
messages of *The Prince* is that a good image is more
important than virtues. Machiavelli lists five virtues
people claim to want in their rulers: mercy, faith-
fulness, piety, integrity, and kindness. Machiavelli
says that having all these virtues is not necessary for
rulers but that appearing to have them is essential.

36. According to Machiavelli,
    (A) it's important for rulers to have the virtues he
    has listed.
    (B) love of justice is more important than any of the
    virtues mentioned.
    (C) it's important for rulers to appear to have
    virtues.
    (D) rulers often possess the virtues he has listed.

   Once met by the public with wild enthusiasm for
their potential benefits to humanity, X-rays, radium,
nuclear energy, and nuclear arms now generate fear and
foreboding as their unforeseen side effects become
known. While it is true that radiation occurs naturally
from the sun and cosmic rays, these levels are minuscule

when compared to the levels that humans are exposed to from fallout, nuclear accidents, medical treatments, consumer products and nuclear waste.

37. (A) Nuclear fallout is less dangerous than radiation from the sun.
    (B) Side effects of X-rays, radium, and unclear energy are frightful.
    (C) Human beings benefit greatly from X-rays.
    (D) Radiation from consumer products poses little harm to human beings.

Advertisements — no matter how carefully "engineered" and packed with information — cannot succeed unless they capture our attention in the first place. Of the hundreds of advertising messages in store for us each day, very few will actually obtain our conscious attention. The rest are screened out. The people who design and write ads know about this screening process; they anticipate and accept it as a basic premise of their business. They expend a great deal of energy to guarantee that their ads will make it past our defenses and the distractions that surround us.

38. (A) An ad writer's primary job is to capture viewers' attention.
    (B) The basic premise of the advertising business is to screen out advertisements.
    (C) About 90% of the ads which viewers see each day catch their attention.
    (D) Almost all the ads that we see can pass the distractions that surround us.

Part Two: Read the passages carefully, then choose the best answer to each question.

Mary Wollstonecraft, an eighteen-century feminist, believed that most people care too much for money. In her view, people's excessive concern for money can explain most of the world's problems.

Calling talent and virtue natural distinctions, Wollstonecraft said that society had set up unnatural distinctions like money and property. She argued that people should be judged by their natural talent and their virtue, not by anything else. Her definition of virtue included both moral behavior and hard work. She felt that giving respect to money and property instead of to talent and virtue makes people dishonest.

Wollstonecraft disliked inherited wealth. Inheriting wealth and titles gives people no reason to work. And for her, hard work and virtue went hand in hand. In her view, because of inherited wealth many people never learn the joy of honest work.

Finally, Wollstonecraft also believed that wealthy people often thought they were virtuous when they really weren't. She said that false flatterers, who surround wealthy people, praise wealthy people for being virtuous whether they are or not—and that the wealthy people believe them.

39. Which of the statements is not true?
    (A) Most of the world's problems result from people's excessive concern for money.
    (B) Inheriting wealth gives people no reason to work.
    (C) Money and property are natural distinctions.
    (D) Wealthy people often think they are virtuous.

40. According to Mary Wollstonecraft, virtue includes
    (A) moral behavior and hard work.
    (B) inherited wealth and hard work.
    (C) moral behavior and inherited wealth.
    (D) talent and hard work.

Scientists and government officials have known for
several years that radiation causes the mutations I have
described, which lead to illness, genetic damage, and
death; yet, they continue to allow the unsuspecting
public to be exposed to dangerous levels of radiation,
and to have their food, water, and air contaminated by
it. Ernest Sternglass made the comment that because of
man's fascination with nuclear power, "it appears that
we have unwittingly carried out an experiment with
ourselves as guinea pigs on a worldwide scale." Millions
of innocent people have paid the price of nuclear power
through their suffering and untimely deaths. By inheriting genetic damage caused by radiation, the future
generations of mankind may bear the burden as well. A
multimillion dollar settlement was awarded to Utah
residents who proved that their cancers were caused by
radioactive fallout. Whether or not radiation is indeed
responsible for my own illness may never be proven.
Nevertheless, I must bear the knowledge that, because
of atmospheric bomb tests performed before I was born,
I am a prime candidate for developing some form of
cancer in my lifetime, and if that happens, it won't be
because of fate or the will of God, but because of man's
unleashing a power he cannot control.

41. Which of the following statements is true?
    (A) The public have been informed of the potential harm caused by radiation.
    (B) The public have suspected the potential harm of being exposed to radiation.
    (C) The public have not suspected the potential harm of being exposed to radiation.
    (D) The public have ordered their food, water, and air to be contaminated by radiation.

42. Because "we have unwittingly carried out an experiment with ourselves as guinea pigs on a worldwide scale,"
    (A) our future generations will benefit from the experiment.
    (B) scientists are fascinated with nuclear power.
    (C) worldwide use of nuclear power is possible.
    (D) millions of innocent people have suffered and probably have died.

43. The author declares that
    (A) her illness is caused by radiation.
    (B) she might have cancer someday.
    (C) she already suffers from cancer.
    (D) it's her fate to have cancer someday.

44. Readers of this passage may infer that there had been high nuclear fallout in
    (A) the world.   (B) all the states in America.
    (C) Utah.   (D) New York.

    Long before the United States was founded as a nation, Europeans were involved in Asia. As a continent with many colonies, Asia was the backyard of Europe where the adventuresome played. All that came to an abrupt stop when colonization was no longer fashionable or accepted. For about 40 years thereafter, Asia was wiped off the map as far as Europe was concerned. Unlike the United States, which has an ideology to promulgate and hence was continuously involved—notably in Japan, Korea, Taiwan and Vietnam—Europe simply disappeared from the region.

Things began to change in the past decade. Economic stagnation at home has driven European companies to look outward, and globalization brought on by technological advancements has added urgency. As a result, Europe has once again "discovered" Asia. Just as was the case 200 years ago, interest is still economically driven. The only difference this time is that it is more civil; there is no more gunboat diplomacy. In fact, as Europe remains consumed by internal affairs—namely European integration—there has been little diplomacy of any sort supporting European businessmen.

Governments in Europe do have other things to worry about. Decades of overemphasis on social welfare have produced many problems, including unemployment and a lack of competitiveness. Structural difficulties such as an inflexible labor force and chronic government budget deficits, coupled with long-standing cultural rigidity, have robbed European corporations of vitality.

Yet there are reasons Asia now welcomes Europe. Even before the recent economic turmoil, Asia wanted investment from Europe. European capital and technology are sought after to help with economic development; Asian producers covet European markets. Moreover, Europe is seen in Asia as a counterbalance to the United States. It is obviously more desirable to have two sources of funds and technology, as well as two export markets.

Does Europe need Asia? Asia is still one of the biggest markets in the world. After all, European companies have been losing market share to their American counterparts in some critical sectors and in certain regions such as South America. To be sure, the integrated European market is huge, but in these days of factory overcapacity, an Asian market of almost 3 billion people must be critically desirable.

All this means that Europe and Asia will move closer to each other. While America was the linchpin of the world in the decades following World War II, reaching out to both Europe and Asia, the coming century will see a tripolar arrangement. The hitherto weak link —between Europe and Asia—will be strengthened.

45. After World War II,
   (A) European countries had a close relationship with their Asian colonies.
   (B) The U.S. had close ties with Asian countries.
   (C) Asia was the backyard of Europe.
   (D) European involvement in Asia was supported by gunboat diplomacy.

46. The "rediscovery" of Asia by the Europeans in the past decade was due to
   (A) European businessmen supported by their governments.
   (B) an effort for European integration.
   (C) an economic interest and the trend of globalization.
   (D) a desire to treat Asia more civilly than before.

47. Which of the following statements is not true?
    (A) The labor force in Europe is inflexible.
    (B) Unemployment in Europe is caused by overemphasis on social welfare.
    (C) There are chronic government budget deficits in Europe.
    (D) Europe is free from the bondage of cultural rigidity.

48. What Asia and Europe see in each other is
    (A) an export market.
    (B) a source of technology.
    (C) investment from the other party.
    (D) the market share each of them is about to lose.

49. An Asian market of 3 billion people is desirable to Europe because
    (A) the integrated European market is huge, too.
    (B) after Asia, South America is the other market Europe is after.
    (C) Europe is seen as a counterbalance to the U.S.
    (D) the Europeans produce more products than they can consume nowadays.

50. The article predicts that in the coming century
    (A) the link between Europe and Asia will be stronger than that between America and Asia.
    (B) the link between Europe and Asia will be strengthened.
    (C) America will be the linchpin of the world.
    (D) colonization will no longer be fashionable or acceptable.

國立台灣大學八十七學年度
碩士班研究生入學考試英文試題詳解

I. 字彙、文法、用法：40%

1. (**A**) (A) *articulate* 〔 ɑr'tɪkjəlɪt 〕 *adj.* （言語）清楚的
   - (B) enormous 〔 ɪ'nɔrməs 〕 *adj.* 巨大的
   - (C) clear 〔 klɪr 〕 *adj.* 清楚的（由於空格前冠詞是 an，須選一母音開頭的字，故不合）
   - (D) artificial 〔 ˌɑrtə'fɪʃəl 〕 *adj.* 人造的
     witness 〔 'wɪtnɪs 〕 *v.* 目擊

2. (**B**) (A) ability 〔 ə'bɪlətɪ 〕 *n.* 能力
   - (B) *capacity* 〔 kə'pæsətɪ 〕 *n.* 容量
   - (C) burden 〔 'bɝdn̩ 〕 *n.* 負擔
   - (D) accommodate 〔 ə'kɑməˌdet 〕 *v.* 容納
     be equipped with 裝配有　*fuel tank* 油箱
     liter 〔 'litɚ 〕 *n.* 公升

3. (**D**) (B) write to *sb*. 寫信給某人
   - (C) e-mail *sb*. 寫電子郵件給某人
   - (D) *correspond with sb*. 與某人通信
     regularly 〔 'rɛgjələlɪ 〕 *adv.* 定期地

4. (**D**) (B) scenario 〔 sɪ'nɛrɪˌo 〕 *n.* 電影劇本
   - (C) synopsis 〔 sɪ'nɑpsɪs 〕 *n.* （論文、小說等的）大意；摘要
   - (D) *syndrome* 〔 'sɪndrəˌmi 〕 *n.* 症候群
     strike 〔 straɪk 〕 *v.* 襲擊
     par 〔 pɑr 〕 *n.* 標準；（健康等的）常態
     acquired 〔 ə'kwaɪrd 〕 *adj.* 後天的
     immune 〔 ɪ'mjun 〕 *adj.* 免疫的
     deficiency 〔 dɪ'fɪʃənsɪ 〕 *n.* 不足

5. (**B**)　(A)　adjacent〔ə'dʒesn̩t〕*adj.* 鄰近的
　　　　　(B)　***available***〔ə'veləbl̩〕*adj.* 可獲得的
　　　　　(C)　artful〔'ɑrtfəl〕*adj.* 狡猾的；巧妙的
　　　　　(D)　apprehend〔ˌæprɪ'hɛnd〕*v.* 逮捕；恐懼
　　　　　　　air crash 空難；墜機

6. (**C**)　(A)　covet〔'kʌvɪt〕*v.* 垂涎
　　　　　(C)　***cultivate***〔'kʌltəˌvet〕*v.* 培養
　　　　　(D)　crook〔krʊk〕*v.* 使彎曲

7. (**A**)　(A)　***dominant***〔'dɑmənənt〕*adj.* 支配的；主要的
　　　　　(B)　previous〔'privɪəs〕*adj.* 先前的
　　　　　(C)　prevalent〔'prɛvələnt〕*adj.* 普遍的
　　　　　(D)　notorious〔no'torɪəs〕*adj.* 惡名昭彰的
　　　　　　　field〔fild〕*n.* 領域

8. (**C**)　(A)　civilized〔'sɪvl̩ˌaɪzd〕*adj.* 文明的
　　　　　(B)　considerate〔kən'sɪdərɪt〕*adj.* 體貼的
　　　　　(C)　***dubious***〔'djubɪəs〕*adj.* 可疑的
　　　　　(D)　undoubtedly〔ʌn'daʊtɪdlɪ〕*adv.* 無疑地
　　　　　　　Mars〔mɑrz〕*n.* 火星

9. (**D**)　(A)　distribute〔dɪ'strɪbjut〕*v.* 分布
　　　　　(B)　contribute〔kən'trɪbjut〕*v.* 貢獻
　　　　　(C)　tribute〔'trɪbjut〕*n.* 貢物
　　　　　(D)　***attribute***〔ə'trɪbjut〕*v.* 歸因於
　　　　　　　external〔ɪk'stɜnl̩〕*adj.* 外在的

10. (**C**)　(A)　survive〔sɚ'vaɪv〕*v.* 生還
　　　　　(B)　surmise〔sɚ'maɪz〕*v.* 推測
　　　　　(C)　***suffice***〔sə'faɪs〕*v.* 足夠
　　　　　(D)　suspend〔sə'spɛnd〕*v.* 暫停
　　　　　　　covering letter 附函；說明書
　　　　　　　exceed〔ɪk'sid〕*v.* 超過

11. (**B**) (A)　complete〔kəm'plit〕*adj.* 完整的
　　　　　(B)　***competent***〔'kɑmpətənt〕*adj.* 能勝任的；能幹的
　　　　　(C)　concrete〔'kɑnkrit〕*adj.* 具體的
　　　　　(D)　complicated〔'kɑmplə͵ketɪd〕*adj.* 複雜的
　　　　　　　executive〔ɪg'zɛkjutɪv〕*adj.* 執行的；行政的
　　　　　　　promote〔prə'mot〕*v.* 升遷　　***deal with*** 處理

12. (**B**) (A)　object〔əb'dʒɛkt〕*v.* 反對
　　　　　(B)　***obliged***〔ə'blaɪdʒd〕*adj.* 有義務的
　　　　　(C)　obey〔o'be〕*v.* 遵守
　　　　　(D)　obedient〔ə'bidɪənt〕*adj.* 服從的
　　　　　　　raise〔rez〕*n.* 加薪

13. (**D**) (A)　vivid〔'vɪvɪd〕*adj.* 生動的；栩栩如生的
　　　　　(B)　vital〔'vaɪtl̩〕*adj.* 非常重要的
　　　　　(C)　vulgar〔'vʌlgɚ〕*adj.* 粗俗的
　　　　　(D)　***vulnerable***〔'vʌlnərəbl̩〕*adj.* 易受攻擊的
　　　　　　　general〔'dʒɛnərəl〕*n.* 將軍
　　　　　　　maneuvers〔mə'nuvɚz〕*n.pl.* 機動演習
　　　　　　　fort〔fɔrt〕*n.* 堡壘

14. (**A**) (A)　***expense***〔ɪk'spɛns〕*n.* 費用；代價
　　　　　(B)　dispense〔dɪ'spɛns〕*v.* 分配
　　　　　(C)　expend〔ɪk'spɛnd〕*v.* 花費（時間、精力）
　　　　　(D)　inexpensive〔͵ɪnɪk'spɛnsɪv〕*adj.* 便宜的
　　　　　　　at the expense of~ 以~代價　　***waste land*** 荒原

15. (**D**) (A)　pretense〔prɪ'tɛns〕*n.* 偽裝
　　　　　(B)　prescription〔prɪ'skrɪpʃən〕*n.* 藥方
　　　　　(C)　presumption〔prɪ'zʌmpʃən〕*n.* 假定；推測
　　　　　(D)　***prerequisite***〔͵pri'rɛkwəzɪt〕*n.* 先決條件
　　　　　　　membership〔'mɛmbɚ͵ʃɪp〕*n.* 會員資格

16.（ **D** ）(A)　with　respect　to　關於
　　　　　　(B)　in　terms　of　以～觀點
　　　　　　(C)　on　behalf　of　代表
　　　　　　(D)　***on　account　of***　由於
　　　　　　　　senator〔ˈsɛnətɚ〕*n.* 參議員　　decline〔dɪˈklaɪn〕*v.* 拒絕

17.（ **A** ）(A)　***turn　out***　結果（成為）
　　　　　　(B)　turn　into　轉變成
　　　　　　(C)　turn　over　把～翻過來；產生
　　　　　　(D)　turn　down　轉小聲；拒絕

18.（ **C** ）***be　indebted　to***～　感激～
　　　　　　comment〔ˈkɑmɛnt〕*n.* 評論

19.（ **B** ）(A)　award〔əˈwɔrd〕*n.* 獎
　　　　　　(B)　***access***〔ˈæksɛs〕*n.* 有接近～的權利
　　　　　　(C)　avail〔əˈvel〕*n.* 利益；效用
　　　　　　(D)　agreement〔əˈgrimənt〕*n.* 同意
　　　　　　　　suspect〔ˈsʌspɛkt〕*n.* 嫌疑犯　　arrest〔əˈrɛst〕*v.* 逮捕

20.（ **C** ）(A)　by　means　of　藉由
　　　　　　(B)　on　account　of　由於
　　　　　　(C)　***with　regard　to***　至於；關於
　　　　　　(D)　regardless　of　不管；不論
　　　　　　　　summer　house　避暑別墅

Ⅱ. 意譯：10%

【譯文】

　　若要使教育有意義，除了創造博學的蠢材這個目的之外，還必須從學生身上誘發出隱藏在每個人身上的潛力 —— 推論的原則、擁有熟知人所該有的合宜舉止的內在知識、篩選證據，達成為心胸開闊、充滿熱忱的人所能接受的結論的能力。

　　　學生比較像是牡蠣而非香腸。教學工作不是要將知識硬塞給學生，然後把它們密封起來，而是要幫助學生打開並顯露出隱藏其中的寶藏。只要我們都能知道如何用熱心與毅力來培養，我們每個人身上都有珍珠。

【註】

well-informed〔'wɛlɪn,fɔrmd〕*adj.* 見聞廣博的
dunce〔dʌns〕*n.* 蠢材；笨蛋
reasoning〔'riznɪŋ〕*n.* 推論；推理　　sift〔sɪft〕*v.* 過濾；仔細調查
pupil〔'pjupl〕*n.* 學生　　oyster〔'ɔɪstɚ〕*n.* 牡蠣；蠔
sausage〔'sɔsɪdʒ〕*n.* 香腸　　seal〔sil〕*v.* 封住
pearl〔pɝl〕*n.* 珍珠　　persistence〔pɚ'sɪstəns〕*n.* 毅力；堅持

21. (**B**) elicit〔ɪ'lɪsɪt〕*v.* 引出；誘出
    (A) elevate〔'ɛlə,vet〕*v.* 提高
    (B) ***draw out*** 引出
    (C) eliminate〔ɪ'lɪmə,net〕*v.* 除去
    (D) rule out 排除；駁回

22. (**A**) latent〔'letn̩t〕*adj.* 隱藏的
    (A) ***hidden***〔'hɪdn̩〕*adj.* 隱藏的
    (B) impart〔ɪm'pɑrt〕*v.* 告知（情報、知識等）
    (C) obvious〔'ɑbvɪəs〕*adj.* 明顯的
    (D) oblivious〔ə'blɪvɪəs〕*adj.* 健忘的；不注意的

23. (**D**) ***be assented to*** 被同意
    (B) stipulate〔'stɪpjə,let〕*v.* 規定
    (C) stimulate〔'stɪmjə,let〕*v.* 刺激
    (D) ***be agreed to*** 被同意

24. (**B**) stuff〔stʌf〕*v.* 填塞
    (A) press〔prɛs〕*v.* 壓
    (B) ***cram***〔kræm〕*v.* 填塞
    (D) push〔puʃ〕*v.* 推

25. (**D**)　ardor〔'ɑrdə〕*n.* 熱心；熱情
　　　　(A) fever〔'fivə〕*n.* 發燒；興奮；狂熱
　　　　(D) *earnestness*〔'ɝnɪstnɪs〕*n.* 熱心；認眞

III. 克漏字：10%

【譯文】

　　如果加州大學洛杉磯分校的研究人員，所說的是正確的，那麼狗在人類一開始學會種植農作物時，就被人類所飼養。這種說法可能會使現在典型的愛狗人士覺得奇怪，爲什麼史前時代的祖先，要花這麼久的時間，才會做如此重要的事？

　　近十年來，狗已爬升到一個新的社會地位。由於動物喜歡居家生活，因而狗與人的關係已有所轉變，對於某些成人而言，狗似乎已成爲小孩的代替品。

　　因此，我們都希望寵物能儘可能活得健康又長壽，而獸醫學方面也有了回應。由於對於狗的預防性保健已有改善，其營養以及整體生活方式的安排也比以往更好，使得狗可以活得更久。不過，因爲狗可以活得更久，所以更容易罹患與年老有關的疾病，包括關節炎。有五分之一以上的狗，曾經歷過因爲關節炎所造成的行動不便，以及生活品質的下降。

【註】

UCLA 加州大學洛杉磯分校（*=University of California, Los Angeles*）
researcher〔ri'sɝtʃə〕*n.* 研究人員
domesticate〔də'mɛstə,ket〕*v.* 馴養　　prompt〔prɑmpt〕*v.* 促使
prehistoric〔,prɪs'tɔrɪk〕*adj.* 史前的
ancestor〔'ænsɛstə〕*n.* 祖先　　decade〔'dɛked〕*n.* 十年
lap〔læp〕*n.* 環境；境遇
thanks to 由於　　surrogate〔'sɝəgɪt〕*n.* 替代者
veterinary〔'vɛtrə,nɛrɪ〕*adj.* 獸醫的　　nutrition〔nju'trɪʃən〕*n.* 營養
overall〔'ovə,ɔl〕*adj.* 全部的　　*be susceptible to* 容易罹患～
be associated with 與～有關　　arthritis〔ɑr'θraɪtɪs〕*n.* 關節炎

26. (**D**) 依句意,表「在～(時間)之內」,介系詞可用 in,*within*,
或 during,故選 (D)。而 (A) inside「在～(物體)內」,
(B) among「在～(三個以上)之中」,(C) along「沿著」,
用法均不合。

27. (**B**) (A) transaction〔træns'ækʃən〕*n.* 交易
(B) *transformation*〔ˌtrænsfɚ'meʃən〕*n.* 轉變
(C) transmission〔træns'mɪʃən〕*n.* 傳送
(D) transport〔træns'port〕*v.* 運送

28. (**A**) (A) *respond*〔rɪ'spɑnd〕*v.* 回應;反應
(B) reply〔rɪ'plaɪ〕*v.* 回答
(C) approve〔ə'pruv〕*v.* 贊成
(D) refer〔rɪ'fɝ〕*v.* 提到

29. (**C**) 依句意,狗因罹患關節炎,生活品質「降低」,選 (C)
diminished〔də'mɪnɪʃt〕*adj.* 減少的。而 (A) enhanced
〔ɪn'hænst〕*adj.* 增大的;提高的,(B) 溫暖的,(D) 逐漸消
失的,均不合句意。

30. (**C**) 依句意,選 (C) *as a result of*「由於」。而 (A) 藉由,
(B) despite「儘管」,其後不可加 of,(D) be based
upon「根據」,均不合句意。

IV. 閱讀測驗:40%

第一部份:選出最能代表段落大意的敘述

【譯文】

兒童心理學家認為,兒童在睡覺時手中握有玩具,是有其價值的。
這和大拇指不同,玩具能使孩子與外界隔絕,提供不同於現實生活的世
界,而孩子正好可以學習適應那樣的世界。心理學家稱這些玩具為「過
渡時期的物體」;也就是說,這樣的物體,可以幫助孩子來回穿梭於充
滿各種嚴格要求的日常生活,以及希望與夢想中的世界。

【註】

thumb〔θʌm〕*n.* 大拇指　　*close in* 包圍
relate oneself to 使自己適應～
transitional〔træn'zɪʃənl〕*adj.* 過渡時期的
back and forth 來回地　　exaction〔ɪg'zækʃən〕*n.* 嚴格要求

31.（**D**）(A) 孩子所拿的玩具，其功能就和孩子的大拇指一樣。
　　　　(B) 孩子可以藏身在自己所拿的玩具中。
　　　　(C) 玩具對孩子而言，代表的是現實世界。
　　　　(D) <u>玩具幫助孩子生活在真實世界與夢幻世界之間。</u>

【譯文】

　　我忍不住會想，到底是什麼，使殺人犯在進入死囚牢房時，會說自己反對殺人？是他們良心發現、重新尊重生命，難道是因為知道自己即將失去生命嗎？生命真的很寶貴，而且我也相信，死刑能證實這一點。如果自己真的有可能被判死刑的想法，曾出現在這些殺人犯的腦海中，他們很可能就會住手。他們可能在受害者死亡之前，就表現其道德意識，而不是在殺了人之後。

【註】

murderer〔'mɝdərə〕*n.* 殺人犯　　*death house* 死囚牢房
newfound〔'nju͵faʊnd〕*adj.* 新發現的
reverence〔'rɛvərəns〕*n.* 尊敬　　*stem from* 源自於
death penalty 死刑　　affirm〔ə'fɝm〕*v.* 證實
stay one's hand 住手不採取行動　　*moral awareness* 道德意識

32.（**B**）(A) 作者反對死刑。
　　　　(B) <u>死刑可能對防止謀殺案有幫助。</u>
　　　　(C) 殺人犯通常在受害者死亡之前，就表現出對生命的尊重。
　　　　(D) 廢除死刑有助於使生命變得珍貴。
　　　　　　abolish〔ə'bɑlɪʃ〕*v.* 廢除

【譯文】

我們最愚不可及的觀念就是，地球是由我們所主宰、擁有，而且我們能夠以某種方式來支配它。我們開始將地球當作家裏所飼養的寵物，生活在我們自己所發明的環境中，有部分是家庭菜園，有部份是公園，有些部份則是動物園。這個想法我們必須儘早去除，因為事實並非如此。情況正好相反。我們不是分開的個體，我們是地球生命中一個活生生的部份，被地球所擁有和操縱，可能是為了地球本身的利益，而發展出來的，只是我們自己並沒有看出來而已。

【註】

folly〔'falɪ〕*n.* 愚蠢　　notion〔'noʃən〕*n.* 觀念
be in change of 負責管理
somehow〔'sʌm,hau〕*adv.* 以某種方式
domesticated〔də'mɛstə,ketɪd〕*adj.* 被馴養的
household〔'haus,hold〕*adj.* 家庭的　　***rid…of~*** 除去…的~
the other way around 相反的情況
specialize〔'spɛʃəl,aɪz〕*v.* 為適應新環境或新功能而發展
behalf〔bɪ'hæf〕*n.* 利益　　glimpse〔glɪmps〕*v.* 瞥見

33.（ **B** ）(A) 我們負責管理地球。
　　　　　(B) 我們是地球生命的一部份。
　　　　　(C) 我們一直在做些對地球有益的事。
　　　　　(D) 我們應該將地球改成部份是家庭菜園、部份是公園，還有一部份是動物園。
　　　　　　　do good to~ 對~有益

【譯文】

關於恐龍，最引人注意的事不是絕種，而是牠們統治地球的時間相當久。恐龍支配全世界有十億年之久，而哺乳類動物，一直以來，就像小型動物般，在恐龍世界裏的縫隙中生存。經歷了七千萬年風光的日子後，我們哺乳類動物創造了優秀的成績，也對未來充滿了美好的憧憬，但我們仍須展現出恐龍所擁有的持久力。

【註】

remarkable〔rɪ'mɑrkəbḷ〕*adj.* 值得注意的
dinosaur〔'daɪnə,sɔr〕*n.* 恐龍　　extinct〔ɪk'stɪŋkt〕*adj.* 絕種的
dominate〔'dɑmə,net〕*v.* 統治；支配
hold sway 居統治地位；有支配力量
mammal〔'mæmḷ〕*n.* 哺乳類動物
all the while 一直；始終　　interstice〔ɪn'tɝstɪs〕*n.* 裂縫
on top 成功地；勝利地　　*track record* 成績記錄
prospect〔'prɑspɛkt〕*n.* 展望　　*staying power* 持久力；耐力

34.（**A**）(A) 恐龍以在地球上的持久力而聞名。
　　　　(B) 人類一定會比恐龍存在的時間久。
　　　　(C) 恐龍存在時，並沒有哺乳類動物。
　　　　(D) 恐龍絕種眞是太好了。
　　　　be noted for 因～而聞名

【譯文】

　　常有人說美國在高科技方面的技術不足 —— 據說矽谷在世界各地大量地招募新人，就是最好的證明。但是，沒有更進一步的研究，我們就無法得知，是否是因爲美國大學畢業生太笨，或是因爲高科技產業成長的速度太快，以致於美國境內可能無法滿足，所有高科技產業對於高水準技術的需求。

【註】

shortage〔'ʃɔrtɪdʒ〕*n.* 短缺
Silicon Valley 矽谷（美國加州舊金山灣南方廣大盆地，爲精密電子業之集中地。）
recruit〔rɪ'krut〕*v.* 招募（新人）
inquiry〔ɪn'kwaɪrɪ〕*n.* 詢問；調查
dumb〔dʌm〕*adj.* 笨的　　sector〔'sɛktə〕*n.* （產業）部門；領域

35. **(C)** (A) 矽谷在世界各地大量招募新人,是因為美國大學畢業生很笨。

(B) 高科技產業成長十分快速,以致於無法找到足夠的技術熟練的員工,來滿足它們的需求。

(C) 美國高科技產業技術人員很缺乏的真正原因,仍然無人知曉。

(D) 對於美國高科技人員的需求成長得很快。

【譯文】

　　馬基維利的「君王論」,是部十六世紀的作品,書中提供統治者一些實用的建議,其直言不諱的風格,常使人們十分震驚。「君王論」所要表達的基本訊息之一,就是良好的形象比美德更重要。馬基維利列出了人民聲稱,最希望統治者能具備的五項美德:慈悲、忠實、虔誠、正直,以及仁慈。馬基維利指出,統治者不必具備所有的這些美德,但是看起來像是具備了,是十分必要的。

【註】

blunt 〔blʌnt〕*adj.* 直率的;坦白的

Niccolo Machiavelli 馬基維利(1469-1527,義大利政治家及政治哲學家)

image 〔ˈɪmɪdʒ〕*n.* 形象　　virtue 〔ˈvɝtʃʊ〕*n.* 美德

claim 〔klem〕*v.* 宣稱　　mercy 〔ˈmɝsɪ〕*n.* 慈悲

piety 〔ˈpaɪətɪ〕*n.* 虔誠　　integrity 〔ɪnˈtɛgrətɪ〕*n.* 正直

appear 〔əˈpɪr〕*v.* 看起來像是　　essential 〔əˈsɛnʃəl〕*adj.* 必要的

36. **(C)** 根據馬基維利的說法,

(A) 統治者擁有他所列出的美德,是十分重要的。

(B) 熱愛正義比所提到的任何美德都要來得重要。

(C) 看起來像是具備了種種美德,對統治者而言,是十分重要的。

(D) 統治者通常具備了他所列出的美德。

　　　 justice 〔ˈdʒʌstɪs〕*n.* 正義

【譯文】

　　X 光、鐳、核能以及核子武器，其對人類可能產生的利益，曾經引起大家瘋狂的關切，現在卻使大家覺得恐懼，並且有不祥的預感，因為大家已經知道它們令人料想不到的副作用。雖然太陽以及宇宙光的確都會自然產生輻射，但與人類所接觸的輻射塵、核子意外、醫學治療、消費品，以及核廢料相比，實在是微不足道。

【註】

wild〔waɪld〕*adj.* 瘋狂的　　enthusiasm〔ɪn'θjuzɪˌæzəm〕*n.* 熱忱
radium〔'redɪəm〕*n.* 鐳　　***nuclear arms*** 核子武器
foreboding〔for'bodɪŋ〕*n.*（不祥的）預感
unforeseen〔ˌʌnfor'sin〕*adj.* 預料不到的
side effect 副作用　　radiation〔ˌredɪ'eʃən〕*n.* 輻射能；輻射線
cosmic〔'kɑzmɪk〕*adj.* 宇宙的　　level〔'lɛvḷ〕*n.* 程度
minuscule〔mɪ'nʌskjul〕*adj.* 微小的
fallout〔'fɔl'aut〕*n.*（來自核子爆炸的）輻射塵；原子塵

37.（**B**）(A) 核子輻射塵和太陽的輻射相比，較不具危險性。
　　　　(B) <u>X 光、鐳，以及核能的副作用是很可怕的。</u>
　　　　(C) 人類因 X 光而獲益良多。
　　　　(D) 消費品所產生的輻射對人類較不具傷害性。
　　　　　　pose〔poz〕*v.* 造成

【譯文】

　　廣告——不論是如何精心地「設計」，用資訊來包裝——除非能先吸引我們的注意，否則就無法成功。每天都有數以百計的廣告訊息提供給我們，但只有少數能吸引我們的注意。其餘的則被篩選後剔除。廣告的設計者與文案撰寫者，很清楚這種篩選的過程；他們期待並且接受這種篩選的過程為廣告業的基本前提。他們花費許多心力，保證他們所製作的廣告，能突破我們的防線，並且超越那些在我們周遭，容易使我們分心的事物。

【註】

engineer〔‚ɛndʒə'nɪr〕v. 設計；策畫　　pack〔pæk〕v. 包裝
capture〔'kæptʃə〕v. 捕捉；引起（注意）
in store for 替～準備著；即將發生在～的身上
screen out （經篩選）剔除　　premise〔'prɛmɪs〕n. 前提
expend〔ɪk'spɛnd〕v. 消耗；花費
guarantee〔‚gærən'ti〕v. 保證　　defense〔dɪ'fɛns〕n. 防禦
distraction〔dɪ'strækʃən〕n. 使人分散注意力的事物；消遣；娛樂

38. (**A**) (A) 廣告文案撰寫者的主要工作，就是要吸引觀眾的注意。
　　　　(B) 廣告業的基本前提就是要篩選剔除廣告。
　　　　(C) 觀眾每天所看到的廣告中，大約有百分之九十會吸引他們的注意。
　　　　(D) 我們所看見的廣告，幾乎都能超越那些會使我們分心的事物。

第二部份：仔細閱讀下列的文章，選出最適當的答案。24%

【譯文】

　　瑪麗·沃斯通克拉夫特是位十八世紀的女權運動者，認為大多數的人都太重視金錢。而人們過度重視金錢，是造成全世界大多數問題的原因。

　　沃斯通克拉夫特指出，才能和美德才是自然的特點，而社會卻訂定了不自然的區分特點，像是金錢與財產。她主張判斷一個人，要依據其天生的才能與美德，而不是其他任何事物。她對美德的定義包括道德行為與努力工作。她覺得重視金錢與財產，而不重視才能與美德，會使人變得不誠實。

　　沃斯通克拉夫特不喜歡繼承的財富。繼承了財富與頭銜，會使人覺得沒有理由要工作。對她而言，辛勤的工作和美德是密切相關的。她認為，由於有繼承的財富，使得許多人不知道誠實工作的樂趣。

　　最後，沃斯通克拉夫特也認為，有錢人常常會認為自己是很有品德的，即使事實上並非如此。她指出，有些圍繞在有錢人身邊的虛偽的奉承者，不管這些有錢人品德如何，都會稱讚其品德很高尚 — 偏偏有錢人就是會相信他們所說的話。

【答案】

　　39.（ **C** ）　　　　　40.（ **A** ）

【註】

feminist〔ˈfɛmənɪst〕*n.* 女權運動者

excessive〔ɪkˈsɛsɪv〕*adj.* 過度的

distinction〔dɪˈstɪŋkʃən〕*n.* 區別；特點

moral〔ˈmɔrəl〕*adj.* 道德的　　　***give respect to*** 尊重

inherited〔ɪnˈhɛrɪtɪd〕*adj.* 繼承的　　　title〔ˈtaɪtl̩〕*n.* 頭銜；封號

go hand in hand 密切關聯的

virtuous〔ˈvɝtʃʊəs〕*adj.* 有品德的

false〔fɔls〕*adj.* 虛偽的　　　flatterer〔ˈflætərə〕*n.* 奉承者

【譯文】

　　多年來，科學家以及政府官員都知道，輻射會造成我所描述的突變，會引起疾病、基因方面的損害、甚至死亡；然而他們卻繼續讓不知情的大眾，接觸具危險性的輻射，讓他們的食物、水、以及空氣，受到輻射的污染。鄂尼斯特‧斯騰格拉斯評論說，因為人類對核子力量太著迷，「我們似乎不知不覺地把全世界的人類當作實驗品。」數以百萬計的無辜人民，有人痛苦，有人早死，為了核動力付出了代價。遺傳了受輻射損害的基因，未來世世代代人類的子孫也有同樣的負擔。好幾百萬的和解金已發給了猶他州的居民，當地居民的癌症，經過證實，的確是由輻射落塵所造成的。我的病是不是由於輻射所造成的，也許永遠無法證實。不過，我必須具備這樣的知識，那就是，由於在我出生前在大氣中所進行的炸彈測試，使我成為在有生之年，可能罹患某種癌症的人，而且如果真的發生這種事，那將不是因為命中注定，或是上帝的旨意，而是因為我們人類，使用了一種自己無法控制的力量。

【答案】

41. (**C**)　　42. (**D**)　　43. (**B**)　　44. (**C**)

【註】

radiation〔ˏredɪ'eʃən〕*n.* 輻射　　mutation〔mju'teʃən〕*n.* 突變
genetic〔dʒə'nɛtɪk〕*adj.* 遺傳的；基因的
unsuspecting〔ˏʌnsə'spɛktɪŋ〕*adj.* 無懷疑的
be exposed to 接觸到　　contaminate〔kən'tæməˏnet〕*v.* 污染
comment〔'kɑmɛnt〕*n.* 評論
fascination〔ˏfæsn̩'eʃən〕*n.* 著迷
unwittingly〔ʌn'wɪtɪŋlɪ〕*adv.* 不知情地
guinea pig 天竺鼠；供作實驗之人或物
untimely〔ʌn'taɪmlɪ〕*adj.* 過早的
settlement〔'sɛtl̩mənt〕*n.* 解決；和解　　award〔ə'wɔrd〕*v.* 頒給
radioactive〔ˏredɪo'æktɪv〕*adj.* 有輻射能的；有放射性的
fallout〔'fɔlˏaut〕*n.* 輻射塵
atmospheric〔ˏætməs'fɛrɪk〕*adj.* 大氣的
prime〔praɪm〕*adj.* 第一的；最重要的
candidate〔'kændəˏdet〕*n.* 候選人　　*develop cancer* 得癌症
unleash〔ʌn'liʃ〕*v.* 發動；使用

【譯文】

　　早在美國建國前，歐洲和亞洲就有了密不可分的關係。亞洲是個有許多殖民地的國家，就像是歐洲的後花園，供歐洲愛冒險的人遊玩。當開拓殖民地的活動不再流行，而且不再為人們所接受時，這些現象就突然中止了。此後有四十年的時間，對歐洲而言，亞洲就像是被人從地圖上擦掉一樣。像是美國，喜歡散播其意識型態，因而持續和亞洲國家有往來，尤其是日本、韓國、台灣與越南 — 歐洲已從這個地區徹底地消失。

　　過去十年間，情況已開始有所改變。國內經濟不景氣，使得歐洲的公司放眼國外，而科技的進步所帶來的全球化，也增加了其迫切性。因此，歐洲又再次「發現」了亞洲。正如同二百年前的情況一樣，歐洲人對亞洲的興趣仍是以經濟爲主要考量。這次和過去最主要的不同點，那就是比較文明，不再採取船堅砲利的外交政策。事實上，當歐洲因其內部事務 — 也就是整合全歐洲 — 而耗損國力之際，幾乎沒有什麼外交政策來支持歐洲的商人。

　　歐洲各國的政府，的確有其他值得擔心的事情。幾十年來，過份重視社會福利，產生了許多的問題，包括失業及缺乏競爭力。由經濟結構所引起的困難，像是強硬的勞工，以及長期的政府預算赤字，再加上由來已久的文化的僵化，都使得歐洲公司缺乏活力。

　　然而現在亞洲很歡迎歐洲，其原因有很多。即使是在最近的經濟風暴之前，亞洲就很希望有歐洲的投資。亞洲渴望歐洲的資金與科技，能協助其經濟發展；亞洲的製造業者十分垂涎歐洲的市場。此外，亞洲也認爲，歐洲這股力量，能與美國相抗衡。很明顯的，同時擁有兩個資金與技術的來源，以及兩個外銷市場，的確是十分吸引人。

　　歐洲需要亞洲嗎？亞洲仍然是全世界最大的市場。畢竟，歐洲公司已經失去了一些重要產業的市場，以及某些特定的區域，如南美洲，這些都落入了它的對手美國的手中。的確，歐洲共同市場的確很大，但是在現今工廠產量過剩的情況下，亞洲這個大約三億人口的市場，一定是大家都想爭取的。

　　上述這些就意謂著，歐洲和亞洲將會變得更密切。由於二戰後的幾十年內，美國一直居於關鍵地位，其勢力往外延伸至歐洲與亞洲，下個世紀將會有三強鼎立的局面。此後也會加強歐洲與亞洲之間原本不太穩固的關係。

【答案】

45.（**B**）　46.（**C**）　47.（**D**）　48.（**A**）　49.（**D**）　50.（**B**）

【註】

colony〔ˈkɑlənɪ〕n. 殖民地

adventuresome〔ədˈvɛntʃəsəm〕adj. 大膽的；喜歡冒險的

abrupt〔əˈbrʌpt〕adj. 突然的

colonization〔ˌkɑlənaɪˈzeʃən〕n. 開拓殖民地

thereafter〔ðɛrˈæftə〕adv. 其後　　　*wipe off*　擦掉

ideology〔ˌɪdɪˈɑlədʒɪ〕n. 意識形態

promulgate〔prəˈmʌlget〕v. 散播（思想）

notably〔ˈnotəblɪ〕adv. 特別地；顯著地

stagnation〔stægˈneʃən〕n. 不景氣

globalization〔ˌglobəˌlaɪˈzeʃən〕n. 全球化

urgency〔ˈɝdʒənsɪ〕n. 迫切的事

drive〔draɪv〕v. 驅使　　　gunboat〔ˈgʌnˌbot〕n. 砲艇

structural〔ˈstrʌktʃərəl〕adj. 由經濟結構所引起的

inflexible〔ɪnˈflɛksəbḷ〕adj. 強硬的　　　*labor force*　勞工

chronic〔ˈkrɑnɪk〕adj. 慢性的；長期的

deficit〔ˈdɛfəsɪt〕n. 不足；赤字　　　*be coupled with*　結合

long-standing〔ˈlɔŋˈstændɪŋ〕adj. 由來已久的

rigidity〔rɪˈdʒɪdətɪ〕n. 僵化　　　*rob…of~*　剝奪…的~

corporation〔ˌkɔrpəˈreʃən〕n. 公司

vitality〔vaɪˈtælətɪ〕n. 活力

turmoil〔ˈtɝmɔɪl〕n. 動亂　　　capital〔ˈkæpətḷ〕n. 資金

covet〔ˈkʌvɪt〕v. 垂涎

counterbalance〔ˈkauntəˌbæləns〕n. 平衡力；對抗力

share〔ʃɛr〕n. 部份　　　counterpart〔ˈkauntəˌpɑrt〕n. 對手

critical〔ˈkrɪtɪkḷ〕adj. 決定性的；重要的

overcapacity〔ˌovəkəˈpæsɪtɪ〕n. 生產力過剩

linchpin〔ˈlɪntʃˌpɪn〕n. 樞紐；關鍵

reach out　伸展　　　tripolar〔traɪˈpolə〕adj. 三極的

hitherto〔ˌhɪðəˈtu〕adv. 至今　　　link〔lɪŋk〕n. 連結

國立政治大學八十七學年度
碩士班研究生入學考試英文試題

I. Vocabulary. 20%

Choose the word or phrase closest in meaning to the underlined word or phrase in each of the following sentences, and then write (A),(B),(C), or (D) on your answer sheet.

1. Experiments based on this hypothesis are designed and conducted to test each <u>contingency</u>.
   (A) stigma　　　　　　　(B) theory
   (C) possibility　　　　(D) belief

2. The loan officer suggested that we get someone to sign for us, since we didn't have any <u>collateral</u>.
   (A) guarantee　　　　　(B) payment
   (C) promise　　　　　　(D) currency

3. Nature is some sort of foe, some sort of <u>adversary</u> in the dominant culture's mentality.
   (A) villain　　　　　　(B) wilderness
   (C) gamble　　　　　　　(D) opponent

4. Similarly fascinating coincidences have <u>intrigued</u> scientists and nonscientists alike for many years.
   (A) tortured　　　　　(B) provoked
   (C) interested　　　　(D) involved

5. Registrars at most well-known colleges say they deal with <u>fraudulent</u> claims at the rate of about one per week.
   (A) phony　　　　　　　(B) reluctant
   (C) conceiving　　　　(D) apathetic

6. Attuned to history as much as to action, Archer is
   more fascinated by the past patterns of relationships
   that erupt into the present than by the immediacies
   of violence and personal <u>confrontation</u>.
   (A) detection   (B) fight
   (C) molestation   (D) reproach

7. The oldenlandia root is used to <u>accelerate</u> labor
   contractions in pregnant women.
   (A) speed up   (B) carry out
   (C) grind down   (D) put off

8. Together let us explore the stars, conquer the
   deserts, <u>eliminate</u> diseases, tap the ocean depths,
   and encourage the arts and commerce.
   (A) discharge   (B) condemn
   (C) eradicate   (D) challenge

9. It is extraordinary enough for a first novel, but is
   <u>prodigious</u> for an author of twenty-two.
   (A) enormous   (B) satisfactory
   (C) sterile   (D) ample

10. The pizza deliveryman's hearing and eyesight were
    <u>permanently</u> damaged.
    (A) deliberately   (B) incredibly
    (C) wholly   (D) forever

II. Structure. 20%

A. Questions 1-5 are incomplete sentences. Four phrases
   or clauses, marked (A),(B),(C), and (D), are given
   beneath each sentence. Choose the best answer and then
   write its corresponding letter on your answer sheet.

1. _____ influencing our idea of the perfect mate is our "lovemap" — a group of messages encoded in our brains — that describes our likes and dislikes.
   (A) The one most telling factors
   (B) The most telling one factor
   (C) The one of most telling factor
   (D) One of the most telling factors

2. _____ is as impossible as for an inexperienced man to build a bridge across a chasm obstructing his way.
   (A) For a spider to change the pattern of its web
   (B) A spider's changing the pattern of its web
   (C) A spider changing the pattern of its web
   (D) That a spider changes the pattern of its web

3. Only if they are extremely subordinate to the new arrival, and perhaps in serious trouble with him, _____ a likelihood of them taking the body-cross role.
   (A) then there will be   (B) so will there be
   (C) and there will be   (D) will there be

4. To some extent, the unrelenting sensationalism of the news and of life _____, added to the resistance to emotional responses.
   (A) when it has been portrayed on the daytime talk shows
   (B) as it has been portrayed on the daytime talk shows
   (C) having been portrayed on the daytime talk shows
   (D) to be portrayed on the daytime talk shows

5. The reason I didn't play well at the recital was

   _____
   (A) because I had sprained my little finger.
   (B) that I had sprained my little finger.
   (C) why I had sprained my little finger.
   (D) how badly I had sprained my little finger.

B. In questions 6-10, each sentence has four underlined
words or phrases marked A, B, C, and D. You are to
identify the one that should be corrected and then
write its corresponding letter on your answer sheet.

6. IDEA <u>officially</u> defines transition services as "a
         A
   <u>coordinated</u> set of activities for a student, designed
         B
   within an <u>outcome-oriented</u> process, <u>that promote</u>
                      C   D
   movement from school to post-school activities."

7. <u>Given</u> the choice between swapping work, play, and
   A
   freedom <u>for</u> housework and <u>wait</u> up late for a
            B   C
   husband, many women find little advantage in <u>tying</u>
                                                      D
   the knot.

8. It's the <u>balancing</u> out of sociological <u>likenesses</u> and
              A   B
   psychological differences <u>which</u> seems to point the
                                C
   way <u>for</u> the most solid lifelong romance.
        D

9. People should keep themselves <u>politically inform</u>;
                                    A
   <u>otherwise</u>, they will not <u>be living</u> <u>up to</u> their
     B   C   D
   democratic responsibilities.

10. <u>Knowing</u> her and other children <u>like</u> her has been a
     A   B
    humbling lesson in a world <u>where</u> places so <u>much</u>
                                   C   D
    emphasis on power, intellect, and glamour.

III. Cloze. 20%

In the following two passages, there are ten blanks where words or phrases are left out. For each blank, there are four choices marked (A), (B), (C), and (D). One of the choices best fits the blank. Choose the best answer and write its corresponding letter on the answer sheet.

Psychologists agree that most of us have creative ability that is greater than what we use in daily life. ___1___, we can be more creative than we realize! The problem is that we use mainly ___2___ hemisphere of our brain — the left. From childhood, in school, we're taught reading, writing, and mathematics; we are exposed to very ___3___ music or art. Therefore, many of us might not "exercise" our right hemisphere much, ___4___ through dreams, symbols, and those wonderful insights in which we suddenly find the answer to a problem that has been bothering us — and ___5___ without the need for logic. Can we be taught to use our right hemisphere more? Many experts believe so.

1. (A) Owing to this   (B) In other words
    (C) At the same time   (D) on the contrary

2. (A) one   (B) half   (C) another   (D) part

3. (A) fair   (B) little   (C) rare   (D) valuable

4. (A) not   (B) hardly   (C) besides   (D) except

5. (A) do so   (B) be it   (C) turn out   (D) be so

Some people considered careers that were not obvious progressions from their formal qualifications. Such a decision did not seem to make the searching process any easier. Fish farming was one very popular example, and ___6___ computing. Interestingly, none of the respondents had taken a degree in computer science,

___7___ well over one quarter had this down as a first or second career choice. People who ___8___ jobs in computing, say after a life sciences degree, met with little success: competing with graduates in computer science for vacancies, they felt a ___9___ disadvantage. In short, respondents said that finding a job in a ___10___ area was just as difficult as finding one where they would use what they had studied.

6. (A) as for   (B) the same
   (C) which was   (D) so was

7. (A) that   (B) once
   (C) yet   (D) thus

8. (A) stuck on (B) tried for
   (C) suffered from   (D) account for

9. (A) distinct (B) dull
   (C) tentative   (D) rival

10. (A) competitive   (B) non-relevant
    (C) productive   (D) resourceful

IV. Reading Comprehension. 20%
In this section you will find two reading passages followed by questions about the meaning of the material. You are to choose the best answer to each question, and then write its corresponding letter (A),(B),(C), or (D) on your answer sheet.

Passage One

The popularity of organic foods can be traced to many people's nostalgia for a simpler, more pioneerlike life-style. And many people believe that organic foods are safer than foods produced on a large scale by traditional methods. Many people also believe that these organic foods contain more and better nutrients than conventional food.

In fact, plants absorb all their food directly from the soil in inorganic form, no matter where the nutrients may originally have come from. Experiments in Michigan and in England that went on for twenty-five years were unable to find any difference in plants raised organically and plants raised with chemical fertilizers. Things that do affect nutrient content are climate, time of harvest, and genetics — but no difference results when plants are grown organically.

Neither are organically grown plants free from chemicals such as pesticides. Some pesticides leave traces in the soil for years; these traces may be absorbed by the plant that is "organically" grown. Rainfall may wash pesticides from neighboring farms onto "organic" fields, and sprays or other applications of chemicals may drift and cause the same problem.

Furthermore, all foods — whether grown conventionally or organically — may contain toxic substances to some degree; the Food and Drug Administration (FDA) maintains constant checks to ensure that these substances are kept at a harmless level, but aflatoxin, a mold that causes cancer, may grow on corn or peanuts or be present in milk. Lead and arsenic are sometimes present in bone meal or seafood. And many vegetables contain poisonous compounds such as oxalic acid and nitrite compounds. The point is that these may be present in a given food, no matter how the food was grown and cultivated. Toxic substances in food do not necessarily have to come from fertilizers or chemical sprays.

1. This passage is mainly about
   (A) the rise in demand for organic food in the last decade.
   (B) how organic plants are grown.
   (C) the toxic substances that are contained in both organically and inorganically grown food.
   (D) the numerous fallacies that exist about organically grown foods.

2. The popularity of organic foods can be traced to all of the following <u>except</u>
   (A) people's longing for a simpler life-style.
   (B) people's fear of vascular disease.
   (C) people's belief that organic foods are safer.
   (D) people's belief that plants grown conventionally are not as nutritious.

3. Which of the following can be concluded from the passage?
   (A) There is some risk of toxic substances in all types of food grown in the earth.
   (B) Organic foods are more expensive because of the expense of growing them.
   (C) Organic foods are more nutritious, though more expensive.
   (D) The FDA strongly recommends organically grown foods.

4. The passage suggests that
   (A) in the long run, inorganic foods are more dangerous than organic ones.
   (B) the organic food industry is preying on the public's misconceptions about its product.
   (C) organic foods are safe because they are controlled by the FDA.
   (D) higher food prices are a result of organic foods.

5. Organic food is used interchangeably with which term?
   (A) traditional food   (B) popular food
   (C) ethnic food   (D) natural food

6. The author's tone is
   (A) ironical.   (B) neutral.
   (C) negative.   (D) positive.

Passage Two

The cicada exemplifies an insect species which uses a combinatorial communication system. In their life cycle, communication is very important, for only through the exchange of sounds do cicadas know where to meet and when to mate. Three different calls are employed for this purpose. Because of their limited sound producing mechanisms, cicadas can make only ticks and buzzes. The only way they can distinguish between congregation and courtship calls is by varying the rate with which they make ticks and buzzes. The congregation call consists of 12 to 40 ticks, delivered rapidly, followed by a two-second buzz. It is given by males but attracts cicadas of both sexes. Once they are all together, the males use courtship calls. The preliminary call, a prolonged, slow ticking, is given when the male notices a female near him. The advanced call, a prolonged series of short buzzes at the same slow rate, is given when a female is almost within grasp. The preliminary call almost invariably occurs before the advanced call, although the latter is given without the preliminary call occurring first if a female is suddenly discovered very nearby. During typical courtship, though, the two calls together result in ticking followed by a buzzing

—the same pattern which comprises the congregation call but delivered at a slower rate. In this way, cicadas show efficient use of their minimal sound producing ability, organizing two sounds delivered at a high rate as one call and the same sounds delivered at a slow rate as two more calls.

7. The cicada congregation call _____
   (A) attracts only males.
   (B) is given by both sexes.
   (C) is given only by males.
   (D) attracts only females.

8. During typical courtship, when a male cicada first notices a female near him, he gives _____
   (A) the two courtship calls together.
   (B) a series of slow ticks.
   (C) 12 to 40 rapid ticks.
   (D) a two-second buzz.

9. According to this passage, why is communication so important for cicadas?
   (A) It helps them defend themselves against other insect species.
   (B) It warns them of approaching danger.
   (C) It separates the males from the females.
   (D) It is necessary for the continuation of the species.

10. How does the congregation call differ from the two courtship calls together?
    (A) It is delivered at a slower rate.
    (B) It is delivered at a faster rate.
    (C) The ticks precede the buzzes.
    (D) The buzzes precede the ticks.

V.　Translate the following into English. 20%

1. 對早期的印第安戰士而言，馬是身分的象徵。

2. 從馬匹身上的飾物，可以看出牠的主人的出身、地位、及經歷等。

3. 例如，從馬鼻子上的線條，可以知道馬的主人和別人交戰過多少次。

4. 但是，令人費解的是，他們從不給自己的馬命名。

5. 理由很簡單：即使他沒有給牠取名字，牠還是他的馬。

國立政治大學八十七學年度
碩士班研究生入學考試英文試題詳解

I. 選同義字：20%

1.（ **C** ） contingency〔kən'tɪndʒənsɪ〕*n.* 可能性
   - (A) stigma〔'stɪgmə〕*n.* 恥辱
   - (B) theory〔'θiərɪ〕*n.* 理論
   - (C) **possibility**〔͵pɑsə'bɪlətɪ〕*n.* 可能性
   - (D) belief〔bɪ'lif〕*n.* 信仰
     experiment〔ɪk'spɛrəmənt〕*n.* 實驗
     hypothesis〔haɪ'pɑθəsɪs〕*n.* 假說
     conduct〔kən'dʌkt〕*v.* 進行；做（實驗）

2.（ **A** ） collateral〔kə'lætərəl〕*n.* 抵押品
   - (A) **guarantee**〔͵gærən'ti〕*n.* 抵押品；擔保
   - (B) payment〔'pemənt〕*n.* 支付（金額）
   - (C) promise〔'prɑmɪs〕*n.* 承諾
   - (D) currency〔'kɝənsɪ〕*n.* 貨幣
     loan〔lon〕*n.* 貸款　　sign〔saɪn〕*v.* 簽名

3.（ **D** ） adversary〔'ædvɚ͵sɛrɪ〕*n.* 對手；仇敵
   - (A) villain〔'vɪlən〕*n.* 歹徒
   - (B) wilderness〔'wɪldɚnɪs〕*n.* 荒野
   - (C) gamble〔'gæmbḷ〕*n.* 賭博
   - (D) **opponent**〔ə'ponənt〕*n.* 對手
     foe〔fo〕*n.* 對手；敵人
     dominant〔'dɑmənənt〕*adj.* 支配的；主要的
     mentality〔mɛn'tælətɪ〕*n.* 心理；想法

4. (**C**) intrigue〔ɪn'trig〕*v.* 使感興趣
  (A) torture〔'tɔrtʃɚ〕*v.* 折磨
  (B) provoke〔prə'vok〕*v.* 激怒
  (C) ***interest***〔'ɪntrɪst〕*v.* 使感興趣
  (D) involve〔ɪn'vɑlv〕*v.* 牽涉
    fascinating〔'fæsn̩,etɪŋ〕*adj.* 令人著迷的
    coincidence〔ko'ɪnsədəns〕*n.* 巧合

5. (**A**) fraudulent〔'frɔdʒələnt〕*adj.* 騙人的
  (A) ***phony***〔'fonɪ〕*adj.* 假的
  (B) reluctant〔rɪ'lʌktənt〕*adj.* 勉強的
  (C) conceiving〔kən'sivɪŋ〕*adj.* 想像的
  (D) apathetic〔,æpə'θɛtɪk〕*adj.* 冷淡的
    registrar〔'rɛdʒɪ,strɑr〕*n.* 註冊主任
    claim〔klem〕*n.* 要求；聲明

6. (**B**) confrontation〔,kɑnfrən'teʃən〕*n.* 對抗
  (A) detection〔dɪ'tɛkʃən〕*n.* 察覺
  (B) ***fight***〔faɪt〕*n.* 爭鬥；戰鬥
  (C) molestation〔,moləs'teʃən〕*n.* 妨害
  (D) reproach〔rɪ'protʃ〕*n.* 責備
    attune〔ə'tjun〕*v.* 使一致
    immediacy〔ɪ'midɪəsɪ〕*n.* 直接

7. (**A**) accelerate〔æk'sɛlə,ret〕*v.* 加速
  (A) ***speed up*** 加速
  (B) carry out 實行
  (C) grind down 折磨
  (D) put off 延期
    labor〔'lebɚ〕*n.* 分娩
    contraction〔kən'trækʃən〕*n.* 收縮

8. (**C**) eliminate〔ɪˋlɪməˌnet〕v. 消除
    (A) discharge〔dɪsˋtʃɑrdʒ〕v. 解僱
    (B) condemn〔kənˋdɛm〕v. 譴責
    (C) *eradicate*〔ɪˋrædɪˌket〕v. 根除
    (D) challenge〔ˋtʃælɪndʒ〕v. 向～挑戰
       tap〔tæp〕v. 開發   commerce〔ˋkɑmɝs〕n. 商業

9. (**A**) prodigious〔prəˋdɪdʒəs〕adj. 龐大的
    (A) *enormous*〔ɪˋnɔrməs〕adj. 巨大的
    (B) satisfactory〔ˌsætɪsˋfæktərɪ〕adj. 令人滿意的
    (C) sterile〔ˋstɛrəl〕adj. 貧瘠的
    (D) ample〔ˋæmpl̩〕adj. 充足的

10. (**D**) permanently〔ˋpɝmənəntlɪ〕adv. 永久地
    (A) deliberately〔dɪˋlɪbərɪtlɪ〕adv. 故意地
    (B) incredibly〔ɪnˋkrɛdəblɪ〕adv. 難以置信地
    (C) wholly〔ˋholɪ〕adv. 完全地
    (D) *forever*〔fəˋɛvɚ〕adv. 永遠地

II. 結構：10%

A. 完成句子

1. (**D**) 能左右我們對於最佳伴侶的看法，最有力的關鍵之一，就是
我們的「愛情版圖」——那是一組訊息，像密碼一樣地被編
制在腦中——記錄著我們的好惡。
    * one of the most～ 最～之一
    telling〔ˋtɛlɪŋ〕adj. 有力的；顯著的
    encode〔ɛnˋkod〕v. 編成密碼

2.（**A**）讓一隻蜘蛛改變蜘蛛網的紋路，就像讓一個經驗不足的人去
建造一座橋，好讓他能跨越阻攔在他面前的峽谷一樣，都是
不可能的事。

* as…as「和～一樣」，為表比較的對等連接詞，須連接文
法結構的單字或片語。

spider〔'spaɪdɚ〕*n.* 蜘蛛　　web〔wɛb〕*n.*（蜘蛛）網
chasm〔'kæzəm〕*n.* 峽谷　　obstruct〔əb'strʌkt〕*v.* 阻礙

3.（**D**）只有當他們完全聽命於新來的長官，並且和他一起面對極大
的麻煩時，他們之間才有可能角色互換。

* only if 置於句首，句子須倒裝。

subordinate〔sə'bɔrdn̩ɪt〕*adj.* 順從的

4.（**B**）正如同充斥在白天脫口秀節目中的煽情內容一樣，這種不留
情面的聳動言論，不論是出現在新聞中，或日常生活中，在
某種程度上，都會加深情緒上的反感。

unrelenting〔ˌʌnrɪ'lɛntɪŋ〕*adj.* 無情的
sensationalism〔sɛn'seʃən̩ˌɪzəm〕*n.* 聳動的作品、語言
resistance〔rɪ'zɪstəns〕*n.* 反抗；反感

5.（**B**）我在獨奏會上表現不佳，原因就是我的小指扭傷了。

* the reason…was that～ …的理由，就是～

recital〔rɪ'saɪtl̩〕*n.* 獨奏會　　sprain〔spren〕*v.* 扭傷

B. 挑錯

6.（**D**）*that promotes*→***which promotes***　關代 that 前面不可有
介系詞或逗點。

transition〔træn'zɪʃən〕*n.* 轉變；變遷
coordinated〔ko'ɔrdn̩ɪtɪd〕*adj.* 協調的
outcome-oriented 以結果為取向的
promote〔prə'mot〕*v.* 促進；提倡

7. (**C**) *wait* → **waiting** and 為對等連接詞，須連接文法作用相同的
單字、片語，或子句。work，play，freedom 皆為名詞，故
wait 亦須改為動名詞 waiting。

swap〔swɑp〕*v.* 交換   *tie the knot* 結婚

8. (**D**) *for* → *to* *the way to~* ~的方法
sociological〔ˌsoʃɪəˈlɑdʒɪkḷ〕*adj.* 社會（學）的
solid〔ˈsɑlɪd〕*adj.* 穩固的
lifelong〔ˈlaɪfˈlɔŋ〕*adj.* 終身的

9. (**A**) *politically inform* → **politically informed**
informed〔ɪnˈfɔrmd〕*adj.* 消息靈通的
live up to 履行

10. (**C**) *where* → **which** 關代 which 代替先行詞 a world，作
places 的主詞。
humbling〔ˈhʌmblɪŋ〕*adj.* 令人羞辱的
glamour〔ˈglæmɚ〕*n.* 美貌；魅力

Ⅲ. 克漏字：20%

【譯文】

　　心理學家都認為，我們大多數人都有創造力，並且還遠遠大於我們每
天日常生活所使用的。換句話說，我們可以比我們所知道的，還要有想
像力！問題就在於我們大多只是使用半邊的頭腦，也就是左腦。從小，
學校老師都教我們閱讀、寫作和數學；很少接觸音樂和美術。因此，我
們大多數的人，很少「運動」右腦，除了當某個困擾我們已久的問題，
經由做夢、象徵、或超凡的洞察力，而得到答案時──是不需要邏輯思
考能力時。我們能被教會多使用右腦嗎？很多專家認為是可以的。

【答案】

1. (**B**)　　2. (**A**)　　3. (**B**)　　4. (**D**)　　5. (**A**)

【註】

hemisphere〔'hɛməs,fɪr〕*n.* 大腦半球　　***be exposed to*** 接觸
insight〔'ɪn,saɪt〕*n.* 洞察力　　logic〔'lɑdʒɪk〕*n.* 邏輯

【譯文】

　　有些人會考慮一些並非很明顯是其本科系的工作。這樣的決定並不會使找工作的過程更容易。養魚業就是一個非常普遍的例子,而電腦業也是如此。有趣的是,在受訪者當中,沒有一位是拿到電腦科學的學位,但是卻有遠超過四分之一的受訪者,都寫電腦業是他們選擇職業時的第一或第二順位。那些嘗試在電腦業工作的人,就擁有生命科學學位的人來說好了,通常不太可能成功:當他們和電腦科學領域的畢業生,一起爭取職務上的空缺時,馬上會處於明顯的劣勢。簡單地說,受訪者都認為,在一個毫不相關的領域裡找工作,和去找一個能夠學以致用的工作,是一樣困難的。

【答案】

6. (**D**)　　7. (**C**)　　8. (**B**)　　9. (**A**)　　10. (**B**)

【註】

progression〔prə'grɛʃən〕*n.* 進行;前進
qualifications〔,kwɑləfə'keʃənz〕*n.pl.* 資格
fish farming 養魚　　compute〔kəm'pjut〕*v.* 使用計算機
respondent〔rɪ'spɑndənt〕*n.* 受訪者
have this down 寫下 (= *put this down*)
try for 爭取;謀求　　vacancy〔'vekənsɪ〕*n.* (職務的) 空缺
distinct〔dɪ'stɪŋkt〕*adj.* 清楚的
tentative〔'tɛntətɪv〕*adj.* 試驗性的;暫時的
resourceful〔rɪ'sorsfəl〕*adj.* 足智多謀的

IV. 閱讀測驗：20%

【譯文】

有機食物的大爲流行，可以追溯到人們的懷古之情，那種追求較爲簡樸、以及像拓荒者般的生活型態。許多人認爲，有機食物和傳統大規模生產方式的食物相比，更爲安全。許多人還認爲，這些有機食物，比傳統的食物含有更多、更好的營養。

事實上，植物是以無機的形態，直接從土壤裏吸收它們所需的養分，無論這些養分到底是源自何方。在密西根以及英國所進行的實驗，已長達二十五年，這些實驗都無法找出，有機栽培的植物，和以化學肥料培養的植物之間有何不同。真正影響營養成分的關鍵是氣候、收成時間，和遺傳方面的因素——但是當植物以有機方式來種植時，卻沒有產生任何差異。

有機栽培的植物，並不是就沒有像殺蟲劑般的化學農藥。有些殺蟲劑可以殘留在土壤裏好幾年；後來栽培的「有機」植物便會吸收這些農藥殘留。此外，鄰近農田的殺蟲劑可能會被水沖到有機農田上，而噴灑、或用其他方式使用農藥，都還是會到處漂流，並造成同樣的問題。

此外，所有的食物——不論用傳統方式生產的，或是有機栽培出來的——都含有一定程度的有毒物質；食品藥物管理局（FDA）長久以來都有定期檢查，以確保這些有毒物質，是在不會傷害人體的標準之下，可是，有一種會導致癌症的黴菌，黃麴毒素，會在玉米、花生或牛奶裡滋生。有時在用作肥料的骨粉裡，或海鮮裡，會發現鉛和砷的成份。許多蔬菜更包含有毒的化合物，像是草酸和亞硝酸鹽的化合物。不過，重點在於：不論栽培過程是如何，這些都可能存在於特定的食物。而這些有毒物質不盡然是來自肥料或化學噴劑。

【答案】

1.（**D**）　2.（**B**）　3.（**A**）　4.（**B**）　5.（**D**）　6.（**C**）

【註】

trace〔 tres 〕*v.* 追溯　*n.* 微量

nostalgia〔 nɑ'stældʒɪə 〕*n.* 懷念

nutrient〔 'njutrɪənt 〕*n.* 營養素

conventional〔 kən'vɛnʃənḷ 〕*adj.* 傳統的

fertilizer〔 'fɜtḷ,aɪzɚ 〕*n.* 肥料

pesticide〔 'pɛstɪsaɪd 〕*n.* 殺蟲劑

spray〔 spre 〕*n.* 噴灑　　drift〔 drɪft 〕*v.* 漂流

toxic〔 'taksɪk 〕*adj.* 有毒的

aflatoxin〔 ,æflə'taksɪn 〕*n.* 黃麴黴毒素　　mold〔 mold 〕*n.* 黴

lead〔 lɛd 〕*n.* 鉛　　arsenic〔 'ɑrsnɪk 〕*n.* 砷

bone meal 磨碎的骨粉　　compound〔 'kampaʊnd 〕*n.* 化合物

oxalic〔 aks'ælɪk 〕*adj.* 酢漿草的　　**oxalic acid** 草酸

nitrite〔 'naɪtraɪt 〕*n.* 亞硝酸鹽

in the long run 到最後　　prey〔 pre 〕*v.* 壓榨

misconception〔 mɪskən'sɛpʃən 〕*n.* 錯誤的觀念

interchangeably〔 ,ɪntɚ'tʃendʒəbḷɪ 〕*adv.* 可替換地

ethnic〔 'ɛθnɪk 〕*adj.* 民族的　　ironical〔 aɪ'ranɪkḷ 〕*adj.* 諷刺的

neutral〔 'njutrəl 〕*adj.* 中立的

【譯文】

　　蟬是使用混合聯絡系統的昆蟲的最佳例證。在牠們的生命週期裡，相互聯絡是很重要的，因為只有經由聲音的交流，蟬才能知道去哪裡找同伴，去哪裡交配。於是，就有三種叫聲因應而生。因為受限於發聲結構，牠們只能嗶嗶叫，或是嗡嗡叫。因此，為了使找尋同伴和求偶的叫聲有所區別，唯一的方法就是改變其鳴叫時的速度。呼朋引伴的叫聲，包括了十二至四十次的急促嗶嗶聲，還有接下來長達兩秒的嗡嗡聲。發出這種聲音的蟬都是公的，不過卻能同時吸引公蟬和母蟬的到來。一旦牠們都聚集在一起了，公蟬便會開始發出求偶的叫聲。當公蟬發現母蟬在身旁，就會開始初步的鳴叫，那是一聲長而緩慢的嗶嗶聲。當母蟬幾

乎是垂手可得時，公蟬便會發出進一步的鳴叫，那就是以同樣緩慢的速度，發出一連串短暫的嗡嗡聲。這種初步的鳴叫，幾乎一定是在進一步的叫聲之前，雖然有時候，公蟬突然發現母蟬就在牠身旁時，牠便會略過初步的鳴叫，而直接發出進一步的叫聲。不過，在一般的求偶過程中，蟬會把兩種鳴叫聲混合在一起，先唧唧聲，然後才是嗡嗡聲——這種組合方式，基本上包含了呼朋引伴的叫聲，只不過求偶的叫聲速度比較慢。如此一來，蟬就充分利用了有限的發聲能力，將僅有的兩種聲音排列組合，速度快的，就是一種鳴叫方式；而同樣的聲音，速度慢的，就多形成兩種鳴叫方法。

【答案】

7.(**C**)   8.(**B**)   9.(**D**)   10.(**B**)

【註】

cicada〔sɪ'kɑdə〕*n.* 蟬
exemplify〔ɪg'zɛmplə,faɪ〕*v.* 做爲～之例
combinatorial〔,kɑmbənə'tɔrɪəl〕*adj.* 混合的
mate〔met〕*v.* 交配
mechanism〔'mɛkə,nɪzəm〕*n.* 結構
tick〔tɪk〕*n.* 滴答聲　　　buzz〔bʌz〕*n.* 嗡嗡聲
congregation〔,kɑŋgrɪ'geʃən〕*n.* 集合
courtship〔'kortʃɪp〕*n.* 求愛
preliminary〔prɪ'lɪmə,nɛrɪ〕*adj.* 初步的
prolonged〔prə'lɔŋd〕*adj.* 延長的
advanced〔əd'vænst〕*adj.* 更進一步的　　　grasp〔græsp〕*n.* 抓住
invariably〔ɪn'vɛrɪəblɪ〕*adv.* 一定
comprise〔kəm'praɪz〕*v.* 包含
minimal〔'mɪnɪml̩〕*adj.* 最低限度的
continuation〔kən,tɪnju'eʃən〕*n.* 繼續
precede〔prɪ'sid〕*v.* 在～之前

1. For the early Indian warriors, horses were a symbol of rank.

2. From the horse's ornaments, one could see its master's origin, status, and experiences, etc.

3. For example, from the lines on the horse's nose, one could tell how many times its master had engaged in battle.

4. However, what confuses people is that they never named their horses.

5. The reason is quite simple: even though the master didn't name his horse, it still belonged to him.

國立交通大學八十七學年度
碩士班研究生入學考試英文試題

A. Select the word that best fits the sentence. 20%

1. The temperature of the liquid _____ after oxygen was introduced.
   (A) inclined   (B) declined   (C) reclined

2. High energy costs seem certain to have a(n) _____ effect on the economy.
   (A) adverse   (B) diverse   (C) reverse

3. No amount of freedom at school can completely _____ the influence of a bad home.
   (A) react   (B) interact   (C) counteract

4. A solid link has been established between alcohol and _____ behavior.
   (A) aggressive   (B) progressive   (C) regressive

5. The government officials believed that drug _____ should be enforced at all costs.
   (A) exhibition   (B) inhibition   (C) prohibition

6. The _____ of the approach reflects the manager's multi-directional thinking mode.
   (A) relativity   (B) flexibility   (C) individuality

7. The files of correspondence are arranged _____.
   (A) sequentially   (B) consequentially
   (C) subsequently

8. The government has no _____ but to raise bus fares to solve the transportation problem.
   (A) adjustment   (B) variability   (C) alternative

9. The lawyers seriously considered the legal —————
of the charges.
(A) possibility　(B) probability　(C) plausibility

10. The victimized customer ————— her decision to sue
the company.
(A) summon　　　(B) rationalized (C) generalized

B. Select the word that is a synonym for the underlined word of each sentence. 20%

11. The barometer is used by weather forecasters to
detect changes in air pressure.
(A) announce　　　　(B) discover
(C) reduce　　　　　(D) justify

12. The argument is invalid because it is based on a
mistake.
(A) unsound　　　　(B) unfinished
(C) impracticable　(D) incomprehensible

13. Television experts play a dominant role in moulding
public opinion.
(A) interesting　　(B) relevant
(C) irreplaceable　(D) major

14. The job applicants are required to take a preliminary
test before an interview.
(A) conductive　　　(B) introductory
(C) preferential　　(D) precarious

15. The United States is a multicultural society, with
virtually every corner of the nation drawing people
from different national backgrounds.
(A) almost　　　　(B) absolutely
(C) definitely　　(D) undoubtedly

16. A hypothetical question is a question about something
that has not happened and might not happen.
(A) imaginative　　(B) practical
(C) tentative　　　(D) fundamental

17. The President's view about the matter was <u>explicitly</u>
    stated in the press conference.
    (A) plainly   (B) briefly
    (C) eloquently   (D) emphatically

18. The cabinet meeting was held for <u>assessment</u> of the
    country's political situation.
    (A) achievement   (B) involvement
    (C) evaluation   (D) development

19. The recent murder case on the Tsin-Hua campus was
    an <u>unprecedented</u> event.
    (A) unpredictable   (B) uncontrollable
    (C) unintelligible   (D) unexampled

20. There are a <u>considerably</u> greater number of nale than
    female students in NCTU.
    (A) numerically   (B) measurably
    (C) approximately   (D) substantially

C. Choose the best answer to complete a grammatically
   correct sentence. 12%

21. Everyone at the meeting should be allowed to express
    _____ opinion.
    (A) its   (B) his   (C) their

22. A number of business firms _____ moved from Taipei.
    (A) has   (B) have   (C) had

23. Pacing is a useful way to hold the _____ interest
    when you are speaking.
    (A) audience   (B) audiences'   (C) audience's

24. The oil reserves of Kuwait are richer than _____
    of many other countries.
    (A) that   (B) those   (C) the ones

25. As the police approached the house, they _____ hear the couple shouting.
(A) will　　　　(B) can　　　　(C) could

26. Five types of plants _____ eat insects are found in the United States.
(A) who　　　　(B) those　　　　(C) that

27. Hot-air balloons were first flown in France, _____ the two-hundredth anniversary of ballooning was celebrated in 1983.
(A) there　　　(B) where　　　　(C) whither

28. Comic strips in the newspaper entertain practically every reader because they appeal _____ us.
(A) to　　　　　(B) on　　　　　(C) at

29. _____ by the evidence provided by the witness, the suspect was not a stranger to the victim.
(A) Judged　　　(B) Judging　　　(C) To judge

30. Primarily _____ its scientific and ecological importance, many scientists feel that Antarctica should be reserved for research only.
(A) because　　　(B) because of　　(C) because that

31. Shopping malls have become major cultural centers that many Americans _____ to visit.
(A) often decide
(B) decide often
(C) have often decided

32. When _____ a résumé, the applicant should give precise information about his educational background, work experience, and interests.
(A) write　　　　(B) writes　　　　(C) writing

D. For each of the following paragraphs, cross out the extra sentence that is irrelevant to the main idea of the given paragraph and then identify the best topic for each. 12%

The Los Angeles Lakers is a championship basketball team. Their home court is the Forum, a modern stadium near Hollywood, California. Among their fans are many big names in the entertainment industry, including Jack Nicholson and Johnny Carson. Most basketball teams are based in large cities. Whenever the Lakers play home games, they can be sure of a few movie stars to cheer for them. Laker fans have a lot to cheer about: their team has won four championships in recent years.

33. Which sentence in the above paragraph should be crossed out?
   (A) The Los Angeles Lakers is a championship basketball team.
   (B) Their home court is the Forum, a modern stadium near Hollywood, California.
   (C) Among their fans are many big names in the entertainment industry, including Jack Nicholson and Johnny Carson.
   (D) Most basketball teams are based in large cities.

34. The best title for the above paragraph is
   (A) The Los Angeles Lakers Basketball Team.
   (B) Los Angeles Lakers Fans.
   (C) Movie Stars.
   (D) The Los Angeles Lakers' Basketball Court.

   Everybody knows that cigarette smoking is harmful to one's health. However, many parents who are smokers may not be aware that it is also bad for their children.

Cigarette smoke can have harmful effects not just on the
smoker, but also on people who live with the smoker.
Children, naturally, are more easily affected than
adults. In fact, studies have shown that children of
smokers get sick more often than children of non-smokers.
Many people smoke in order to feel more relaxed in
social situations. One experiment, for example, studied
a very common problem among small children: earaches.
The statistics clearly proved that children of smokers
got earaches more often than children of non-smokers.
Their earaches were also more difficult to cure and
tended to last longer.

35. Which sentence in the above paragraph should be
    crossed out?
    (A) Children, naturally, are more easily affected
        than adults.
    (B) In fact, studies have shown that children of
        smokers get sick more often than children of
        non-smokers.
    (C) Many people smoke in order to feel more relaxed
        in social situations.
    (D) One experiment, for example, studied a very
        common problem among small children: earaches.

36. The best title for the above paragraph is
    (A) How Cigarette Smoke Does Harm to One's Health
    (B) How Cigarette Smoke Affects the Children of
        Smokers
    (C) How the Children of Smokers Suffer from Disease
    (D) Why People Smoke

    If you ever get a blow-out while you are driving,
you should know what to do. A blow-out is a sudden flat
tire. It can be a very frightening experience, especially
if you are traveling at high speed. If your car gets a

blow-out, the first thing to do is to hold very tightly to the steering wheel. You can easily lose control of the car if you do not have a good hold on the steering wheel. The next step is to get off the road. You must not try to stop or turn too quickly, however. After you check the traffic, you should move over to the side of the road and slow down gradually. Then you should turn on your flashing lights so other cars will see you. This way you may learn it is a good idea to check the amount of air in your tires every week.

37. Which sentence in the above paragraph should be crossed out?
    (A) It can be a very frightening experience, espe-cially if you are traveling at high speed.
    (B) You can easily lose control of the car if you do not have a good hold on the steering wheel.
    (C) After you check the traffic, you should move over to the side of the road and slow down gradually.
    (D) This way you may learn it is a good idea to check the amount of air in your tires every week.

38. The best title for the above paragraph is
    (A) How You Feel If You Get a Blow-out.
    (B) What to Do If You Are Traveling at High Speed.
    (C) What to Do If You Get a Blow-out.
    (D) What to Do When You Check Your Tires.

E. Find the missing part from the given phrases/clauses to complete the following abstract of a journal article. 12%

    Companies with international linkages often ___39___, and the success of these expatriates is frequently critical to the success of the project on which they are

working. Many of these companies could potentially
benefit from including the spouse in the expatriation
process. For example, ___40___ because of their spouse's
career, and ___41___, especially in North America and
Western Europe. This may also ___42___, because of an
increasing number of working women, and women with
careers, in all parts of the world. Substantial research
has indicated that spouses are particularly important
to the success of the expatriate process, but, surprisingly, ___43___. This is especially true for spouses
with a career and for male spouses; little is known
of their situation and concerns. This paper draws on a
series of research projects that do address the spouse's
viewpoint to suggest practical means by which companies
can ___44___.

39. (A) this is expected to be a growing reason for
       rejection
    (B) improve the expatriation process by including
       the spouse
    (C) find it necessary to use expatriates for a variety
       of reasons
    (D) there is little research that looks at the
       expatriate process from the spouse's viewpoint

40. (A) about 15% of expatriate candidates were reported
       to have rejected a foreign assignment
    (B) there is little research that looks at the
       expatriate process from the spouse's viewpoint
    (C) this is expected to be a growing reason for
       rejection
    (D) find it necessary to use expatriates for a
       variety of reasons

41. (A) find it necessary to use expatriates for a variety of reasons
    (B) this is expected to be a growing reason for rejection
    (C) there is little research that looks at the expatriate process from the spouse's viewpoint
    (D) improve the expatriation process by including the spouse

42. (A) find it necessary to use expatriates for a variety of reasons
    (B) improve the expatriation process by including the spouse
    (C) about 15% of expatriate candidates were reported to have rejected a foreign assignment
    (D) be true in other parts of the world

43. (A) find it necessary to use expatriates for a variety of reasons
    (B) this is expected to be a growing reason for rejection
    (C) about 15% of expatriate candidates were reported to have rejected a foreign assignment
    (D) there is little research that looks at the expatriate process from the spouse's viewpoint

44. (A) find it necessary to use expatriates for a variety of reasons
    (B) there is little research that looks at the expatriate process from the spouse's viewpoint
    (C) improve the expatriation process by including the spouse
    (D) this is expected to be a growing reason for rejection

F. Reading Comprehension: 24%

A hoax, unlike an honest error, is a deliberately concocted plan to present an untruth as the truth. It can take the form of a fraud, a fake, a swindle, or a forgery, and can be accomplished in almost any field: successful hoaxes have been foisted on the public in fields as varied as politics, religion, science, art and literature.

A famous scientific hoax occurred in 1912 when Charles Dawson claimed to have uncovered a human skull and jawbone on the Piltdown Common in southern England. These human remains were said to be more than 500,000 years old and were unlike any other remains from that period; as such they represented an important discovery in the study of human evolution. These remains, popularly known as the Piltdown Man and scientifically named *Eoanthropus dawsoni* after their discoverer, confounded scientists for more than forty years. Finally in 1953 a chemical analysis was used to date the bones, and it was found that the bones were modern bones that had been skillfully aged. A further twist to the hoax was that the skull belonged to a human and the jaws to an orangutan.

45. The topic of this passage could best be described as
 (A) the Piltdown Man.
 (B) Charles Dawson's discovery.
 (C) *Eoanthropus dawsoni*.
 (D) a definition and example of a hoax.

46. The author's main point is that
    (A) various types of hoaxes have been perpetrated.
    (B) Charles Dawson discovered a human skull and jawbone.
    (C) Charles Dawson was not an honest man.
    (D) the human skull and jawbone were extremely old.

Lincoln's now famous Gettysburg Address was not, on the occasion of its delivery, recognized as the masterpiece it is today. Lincoln was not even the primary speaker at the ceremonies, held at the height of the Civil War in 1863, to dedicate the battlefield at Gettysburg. The main speaker was orator Edward Everett, whose two-hour speech was followed by Lincoln's shorter remarks. Lincoln began his small portion of the program with words that today are immediately recognized by most Americans: "Four score and seven years ago our fathers brought forth on this continent a new nation, conceived in liberty and dedicated to the proposition that all men are created equal." At the time of the speech, little notice was given to what Lincoln had said, and Lincoln considered his appearance at the ceremonies rather unsuccessful. It was after his speech appeared in print that it began receiving the growing recognition that today places it among the greatest speeches of all time.

47. The main idea of this passage is that
    (A) the Gettysburg Address has always been regarded as a masterpiece.
    (B) at the time of its delivery the Gettysburg Address was truly appreciated as a masterpiece.
    (C) it was not until sometime after 1863 that Lincoln's speech at Gettysburg took its place in history.
    (D) Lincoln is better recognized today than he was at the time of his presidency.

48. According to the passage, when Lincoln spoke at the Gettysburg ceremonies,
    (A) his words were immediately recognized by most Americans.
    (B) he spoke for only a short period of time.
    (C) he was enthusiastically cheered.
    (D) he was extremely proud of his performance.

49. When did Lincoln's Gettysburg Address begin to receive public acclaim?
    (A) After it had been published.
    (B) Immediately after the speech.
    (C) Not until the present day.
    (D) After Lincoln received growing recognition.

Rock-climbing is a challenging, sometimes dangerous sport. Harsh weather is the one challenge rock climbers might prefer to avoid. The rock climbers living in or near Seattle, Washington, no longer have to alter their plans because of rain or snow. Instead, they can visit the country's first indoor rock-climbing gym — the Vertical Club.

Inside a former warehouse, the Vertical Club offers a varied terrain to climbers of all levels of skill. The walls, made of four-foot-square panels, can be turned to create different degrees of steepness, from gentle slopes with easy handholds to sheer faces with sharply angled overhangs.

Working out at the club is not only more comfortable than climbing outdoors; it is also safer. Ropes stop climbers if they fall, and the areas below the climbing surfaces are cushioned. Better still, when climbers are finished, they don't have to face the long drive home from the mountains!

50. The story says that what rock climbers enjoy the least is
   (A) the danger involved.
   (B) the physical effort.
   (C) the thrill.
   (D) the harsh weather.

51. The Vertical Club has created rock-climbing surfaces
   (A) on a mountain.　　　　(B) in a field.
   (C) in a warehouse.　　　 (D) underground.

52. The story suggests that in addition to being comfortable and safe, indoor climbing is also
   (A) easy.　　　　　　　　(B) convenient.
   (C) dangerous.　　　　　 (D) bone-chilling.

國立交通大學八十七學年度
碩士班研究生入學考試英文試題詳解

A. 字彙：20%

1. (**B**)　(A)　incline〔ɪnˋklaɪn〕*v.* 傾向於
　　　　　　(B)　***decline***〔dɪˋklaɪn〕*v.* 下降
　　　　　　(C)　recline〔rɪˋklaɪn〕*v.* 斜倚
　　　　　　　　 liquid〔ˋlɪkwɪd〕*n.* 液體
　　　　　　　　 introduce〔͵ɪntrəˋdjus〕*v.* 引入

2. (**A**)　(A)　***adverse***〔ˋædvɝs〕*adj.* 不利的
　　　　　　(B)　diverse〔daɪˋvɝs〕*adj.* 不同的
　　　　　　(C)　reverse〔rɪˋvɝs〕*adj.* 相反的

3. (**C**)　(A)　react〔rɪˋækt〕*v.* 反應
　　　　　　(B)　interact〔͵ɪntəˋækt〕*v.* 相互作用
　　　　　　(C)　***counteract***〔͵kaʊntəˋækt〕*v.* 抵消

4. (**A**)　(A)　***aggressive***〔əˋgrɛsɪv〕*adj.* 具有攻擊性的
　　　　　　(B)　progressive〔prəˋgrɛsɪv〕*adj.* 進步的
　　　　　　(C)　regressive〔rɪˋgrɛsɪv〕*adj.* 退步的
　　　　　　　　 solid〔ˋsɑlɪd〕*adj.* 穩固的　　　link〔lɪŋk〕*n.* 關連

5. (**C**)　(A)　exhibition〔͵ɛksəˋbɪʃən〕*n.* 展覽
　　　　　　(B)　inhibition〔͵ɪnhɪˋbɪʃən〕*n.* 壓抑
　　　　　　(C)　***prohibition***〔͵proəˋbɪʃən〕*n.* 禁止
　　　　　　　　 enforce〔ɪnˋfors〕*v.* 實施

6. (**B**)　(A)　relativity〔͵rɛləˋtɪvətɪ〕*n.* 關聯性
　　　　　　(B)　***flexibility***〔͵flɛksəˋbɪlətɪ〕*n.* 變通性；彈性
　　　　　　(C)　individuality〔͵ɪndə͵vɪdʒʊˋælətɪ〕*n.* 個人性
　　　　　　　　 approach〔əˋprotʃ〕*n.* 方法
　　　　　　　　 thinking mode 思考方式

7. (**A**) (A) ***sequentially*** 〔 sɪ'kwɛnʃəlɪ 〕 *adv.* 按順序地
   (B) consequentially 〔 ˌkɑnsə'kwɛnʃəlɪ 〕 *adv.* 必然的
   (C) subsequently 〔 'sʌbsəkwəntlɪ 〕 *adv.* 隨後
   correspondence 〔 ˌkɔrə'spɑndəns 〕 *n.* 通信

8. (**C**) (A) adjustment 〔 ə'dʒʌstmənt 〕 *n.* 調整
   (B) variability 〔 ˌvɛrɪə'bɪlətɪ 〕 *n.* 可變性
   (C) ***alternative*** 〔 ɔl'tɜnətɪv 〕 *n.* 選擇
   fare 〔 fɛr 〕 *n.* 車費

9. (**C**) (A) possibility 〔 ˌpɑsə'bɪlətɪ 〕 *n.* 可能性
   (B) probability 〔 ˌprɑbə'bɪlətɪ 〕 *n.* 機率；可能性
   (C) ***plausibility*** 〔 ˌplɔzə'bɪlətɪ 〕 *n.* 似合法性
   the legal plausibility of a charge 指控的貌似合法性

10. (**B**) (A) summon 〔 'sʌmən 〕 *v.* 召喚
    (B) ***rationalize*** 〔 'ræʃənlˌaɪz 〕 *v.* 使合理化；爲~找藉口
    (C) generalize 〔 'dʒɛnərəlˌaɪz 〕 *v.* 概括出；歸納出
    victimize 〔 'vɪktɪmˌaɪz 〕 *v.* 使受害
    sue 〔 su 〕 *v.* 控告

B. 選同義字：20%

11. (**B**) detect 〔 dɪ'tɛkt 〕 *v.* 發現；察覺
    (A) announce 〔 ə'naʊns 〕 *v.* 宣布
    (B) ***discover*** 〔 dɪ'skʌɚ 〕 *v.* 發現
    (C) reduce 〔 rɪ'djus 〕 *v.* 減少
    (D) justify 〔 'dʒʌstəˌfaɪ 〕 *v.* 使成爲正當
    barometer 〔 bə'rɑmətɚ 〕 *n.* 氣壓計

12. (**A**) invalid 〔 ɪn'vælɪd 〕 *adj.* 無效的
    (A) ***unsound*** 〔 ʌn'saʊnd 〕 *adj.* 錯誤的
    (B) unfinished 〔 ʌn'fɪnɪʃt 〕 *adj.* 未完成的
    (C) impracticable 〔 ɪm'præktɪkəbḷ 〕 *adj.* 不切實際的
    (D) incomprehensible 〔 ˌɪnkɑmprɪ'hɛnsəbḷ 〕 *adj.* 不可思議的

13. (**D**)　dominant〔'dɑmənənt〕*adj.* 主要的
　　　(A)　interesting〔'ɪntrɪstɪŋ〕*adj.* 有趣的
　　　(B)　relevant〔'rɛləvənt〕*adj.* 相關的
　　　(C)　irreplaceable〔ˌɪrɪ'plesəbḷ〕*adj.* 不能代替的
　　　(D)　**major**〔'medʒɚ〕*adj.* 主要的
　　　　　mould〔mold〕*v.* 塑造

14. (**B**)　preliminary〔prɪ'lɪməˌnɛrɪ〕*adj.* 初步的
　　　(A)　conductive〔kən'dʌktɪv〕*adj.* 傳導的
　　　(B)　**introductory**〔ˌɪntrə'dʌktərɪ〕*adj.* 初步的
　　　(C)　preferential〔ˌprɛfə'rɛnʃəl〕*adj.* 優先的
　　　(D)　precarious〔prɪ'kɛrɪəs〕*adj.* 不安定的
　　　　　applicant〔'æpləkənt〕*n.* 申請人；應徵者

15. (**A**)　virtually〔'vɝtʃʊəlɪ〕*adv.* 幾乎
　　　(A)　**almost**〔'ɔlˌmost〕*adv.* 幾乎
　　　(B)　absolutely〔'æbsəˌlutlɪ〕*adv.* 絕對地
　　　(C)　definitely〔'dɛfənɪtlɪ〕*adv.* 必定
　　　(D)　undoubtedly〔ʌn'daʊtɪdlɪ〕*adv.* 無疑的
　　　　　draw〔drɔ〕*v.* 吸引

16. (**A**)　hypothetical〔ˌhaɪpə'θɛtɪkḷ〕*adj.* 假設的
　　　(A)　**imaginative**〔ɪ'mædʒəˌnetɪv〕*adj.* 想像的
　　　(B)　practical〔'præktɪkḷ〕*adj.* 實際的
　　　(C)　tentative〔'tɛntətɪv〕*adj.* 試驗性的
　　　(D)　fundamental〔ˌfʌndə'mɛntḷ〕*adj.* 基本的

17. (**A**)　explicitly〔ɪk'splɪsɪtlɪ〕*adv.* 明白地
　　　(A)　**plainly**〔'plenlɪ〕*adv.* 明白地
　　　(B)　briefly〔'briflɪ〕*adv.* 簡短地
　　　(C)　eloquently〔'ɛləkwəntlɪ〕*adv.* 雄辯地
　　　(D)　emphatically〔ɪm'fætɪkəlɪ〕*adv.* 強調地
　　　　　press conference 記者會

18. (**C**) assessment〔ə'sɛsmənt〕*n.* 評估
　　　　(A) achievement〔ə'tʃivmənt〕*n.* 成就
　　　　(B) involvement〔ɪn'vɑlvmənt〕*n.* 牽連
　　　　(C) *evaluation*〔ɪ,vælju'eʃən〕*n.* 評估
　　　　(D) development〔dɪ'vɛləpmənt〕*n.* 發展
　　　　　　cabinet〔'kæbənɪt〕*adj.* 內閣的

19. (**D**) unprecedented〔ʌn'prɛsə,dɛntɪd〕*adj.* 空前的
　　　　(A) unpredictable〔,ʌnprɪ'dɪktəbḷ〕*adj.* 不可預測的
　　　　(B) uncontrollable〔,ʌnkən'troləbḷ〕*adj.* 不能控制的
　　　　(C) unintelligible〔,ʌnɪn'tɛlədʒəbḷ〕*adj.* 難以理解的
　　　　(D) *unexampled*〔,ʌnɪg'zæmpḷd〕*adj.* 空前的

20. (**D**) considerably〔kən'sɪdərəblɪ〕*adv.* 相當多地
　　　　(A) numerically〔nju'mɛrɪkəlɪ〕*adv.* 數字地
　　　　(B) measurably〔'mɛʒərəblɪ〕*adv.* 可測量地
　　　　(C) approximately〔ə'prɑksəmɪtlɪ〕*adv.* 大約
　　　　(D) *substantially*〔səb'stænʃəlɪ〕*adv.* 大量地

C. 文法：12%

21. (**B**) everyone 的代名詞為 he，故所有格用 his。

22. (**B**) 主詞 firms 為複數形，故助動詞亦須用複數，依句意為現在完成式，選 (B)。

23. (**C**) audience「觀眾」為集合名詞，其所有格為 audience's。
　　　　pace〔pes〕*v.* 踱步

24. (**B**) 為了避免重複前面出現過的名詞，單數名詞可用 that 代替，複數名詞則用 those 代替，依句意為 the oil reserves，故代名詞用 those，選 (B)。
　　　　reserves〔rɪ'zɝvz〕*n.pl.*（礦）藏量

25.（ **C** ）　依句意為過去式，助動詞須用 could。

26.（ **C** ）　空格應填一關係代名詞，引導形容詞子句，修飾先行詞
　　　　　　　plants。

27.（ **B** ）　空格應填一表地點的關係副詞，故選 (B) *where*。
　　　　　　　(C) whither〔 'hwɪðə 〕*conj.* 向哪裏（ = *to which place* ）
　　　　　　　hot-air balloon 熱汽球
　　　　　　　anniversary〔 ˌænə'vɜsərɪ 〕*n.* 週年紀念
　　　　　　　ballooning〔 bə'lunɪŋ 〕*n.* 乘汽球

28.（ **A** ）　*appeal to* 吸引|　　*comic strip* 連環漫畫

29.（ **B** ）　*Judging by～* 由～判斷　　suspect〔 'sʌspɛkt 〕*n.* 嫌疑犯

30.（ **B** ）　空格後為名詞片語，故空格應填介系詞，選 (B) *because of*。
　　　　　　　primarily〔 'praɪˌmɛrəlɪ 〕*adv.* 主要地
　　　　　　　ecological〔 ˌɛkə'ladʒɪkəl 〕*adj.* 生態學的
　　　　　　　Antarctica〔 ænt'arktɪkə 〕*n.* 南極大陸

31.（ **A** ）　頻率副詞 often 須置於一般動詞之前。

32.（ **C** ）　原句為 When he writes a resume, the applicant
　　　　　　　should give⋯，因句意很明顯，主詞 he 可省略，但動詞
　　　　　　　writes 須改為現在分詞 writing。

D. 删除與本文不相關的句子，並且找出最適合的標題：12%

【譯文】

　　　洛杉磯湖人隊是一支冠軍籃球隊。他們的主場佛蘭，位於加州好萊
塢附近，是一個現代化的體育館。他們的球迷中有很多是娛樂界的名
人，包括傑克‧尼克遜和強尼‧卡森。許多籃球隊都以大城市為根據地。
每當湖人隊在主場比賽時，總會有一些電影明星到場加油。讓湖人隊球
迷高興的事可多了；最近幾年來，他們的球隊已經贏了四場冠軍。

┌─【答案】────────────────────────────┐
　　33. (**D**)　　　　　34. (**A**)
└──────────────────────────────────┘

【註】

home court　主場 (運動員在本國或本地比賽時的球場)
stadium〔'stedɪəm〕*n.* 體育館　　fan〔fæn〕*n.* 迷
big name　有名的人
home game　主場比賽；在本地球場舉行的比賽
cheer〔tʃɪr〕*v.* 加油　　*cross out*　刪除

【譯文】

　　每個人都知道抽煙有害健康。不過,很多抽煙的父母可能不知道,抽煙對他們的小孩也有害處。抽煙不但對吸煙者有害,也會影響跟吸煙者住在一起的人。而小孩自然比大人更容易受影響。事實上,研究顯示,吸煙者的小孩比非吸煙者的小孩更常生病。很多人抽煙,是為了在社交場合中放鬆自己。舉例來說,有一個實驗,研究在小孩當中很普遍的問題:耳痛。統計數字清楚地證明,吸煙者的小孩比非吸煙者的小孩更常有耳痛的情況,而且他們的耳痛也比較難治癒,持續的時間也較久。

┌─【答案】────────────────────────────┐
　　35. (**C**)　　　　　36. (**B**)
└──────────────────────────────────┘

【註】

social〔'soʃəl〕*adj.* 社交的
experiment〔ɪk'spɛrəmənt〕*n.* 實驗
earache〔'ɪr,ek〕*n.* 耳痛
statistics〔stə'tɪstɪks〕*n.pl.* 統計數字
tend to　易於～　　last〔læst〕*v.* 持續

【譯文】

　　如果你開車的時候爆胎，你應該要知道該如何處理。爆胎就是輪胎突然漏氣。這是很可怕的經驗，尤其是當你車速很快的時候。當你的車子爆胎時，第一件要做的事，就是緊握方向盤。如果方向盤沒握緊，車子很容易就失去控制。下一步就是將車子駛離馬路。不過，你不能突然停止或轉彎。在確定通狀況後，你應該將車子開到路邊，然後慢慢停下來。接著你要打開車子的閃光燈，這樣別的車子才能看到你。這麼一來，你才能學會，每個禮拜都要檢查車胎裡的空氣量。

【答案】

　37. (**D**)　　　　38. (**C**)

【註】

blow-out〔ˈbloˌaut〕*n.* 爆胎　　　　flat〔flæt〕*adj.* 洩了氣的

steering wheel 方向盤

E. 填充並完成整篇文章：12%

【譯文】

　　有些跨國企業會因為不同的原因，認為派遣駐外人員是必要的。而這些駐外人員的成功，通常對跨國企業所進行的計劃的關鍵。許多這一類公司，如果把駐外人員的配偶也包括在外派計劃中，可能會比較有利。舉例來說，約有百分之十五的駐外人員候選人，因為配偶職業的因素，而拒絕了國外的職務，尤其是在北美和西歐，這個因素越來越重要。在其他地方也是一樣，因為到處都有越來越多的職業婦女。充分的研究顯示，配偶對外派計劃的成功，是相當重要的，然而，令人訝異的是，我們沒有太多的研究，是從配偶的觀點來探討外派制度。特別是有工作的配偶，或是男性配偶，我們不太知道他們的情況，或是關切的重點。這篇論文利用一系列針對配偶的觀點，所做的研究計劃，建議一些實用的方法，這些公司可以採納這個方法，將配偶包含在外派計劃中，使外派計劃更成功。

【答案】

39. (**C**)　40. (**A**)　41. (**B**)　42. (**D**)　43. (**D**)　44. (**C**)

【註】

linkage〔 ˊlɪŋkɪdʒ〕*n.* 連結　　***work on*** 進行
potentially〔 pəˊtɛnʃəlɪ〕*adv.* 可能地
benefit〔 ˊbɛnəfɪt〕*v.* 獲益
expatriate〔 ɛksˊpetrɪˌet〕*n.* 駐外人員
critical〔 ˊkrɪtɪkḷ〕*adj.* 關鍵的　　spouse〔 spaʊz〕*n.* 配偶
candidate〔 ˊkændədɪt〕*n.* 候選人
assignment〔 əˊsaɪnmənt〕*n.* 指派；任務
substantial〔 səbˊstænʃəl〕*adj.* 充足的　　***draw on*** 利用
address〔 əˊdrɛs〕*v.* 提出

F. 閱讀測驗：24%

【譯文】

　　騙局是刻意設計，想要弄假成真的計劃，和真正的過失不同。它可能是詐欺、詭計、欺瞞或偽造，而且幾乎在各種領域都可能出現：欺騙大眾的成功的騙局，曾出現在許多不同的領域中，如政治、宗敎、科學、藝術及文學領域。

　　在一九一二年有一場著名的科學騙局，當時，查爾斯‧道森宣稱，他在英國南部的皮爾當，發現一個人類的頭蓋骨和下顎骨。據說這些人類的遺骸有五十萬年的歷史，而且和同時期的其他遺骸不同；因此，這些遺骸代表人類進化的研究上，一個重大的發現。便以這些遺骨的發現者姓名，爲它們命名爲道森曙人，一般則稱之爲皮爾當人，它們欺騙了科學家長達四十年之久。一直到一九五三年，人們採用一種化學分析法，來偵測這些骨頭的年代，這時才發現，那是一些被巧妙地加以老化的現代骨頭。這個騙局中更曲折的是：那個頭蓋骨是人類的，而下顎骨卻是屬於一頭猩猩。

【答案】

　45.（ **D** ）　　　　　46.（ **A** ）

【註】

hoax〔hoks〕*n.* 騙局　　deliberately〔dɪˈlɪbərɪtlɪ〕*adv.* 故意地

concoct〔kɑnˈkɑkt〕*v.* 捏造；虛構　　fraud〔frɔd〕*n.* 詐欺

fake〔fek〕*n.* 贗品　　swindle〔ˈswɪndl〕*n.* 欺騙；冒牌貨

forgery〔ˈfɔrdʒərɪ〕*n.* 偽造　　foist〔fɔɪst〕*v.* 矇騙

skull〔skʌl〕*n.* 頭蓋骨　　jawbone〔ˈdʒɔˈbon〕*n.* 下顎骨

evolution〔ˌɛvəˈluʃən〕*n.* 進化　　*as such* 像那樣

Piltdown Man n. 皮爾當人（1912 年在英國皮爾當發現的頭蓋骨，當時認
　爲是史前人類的化石，1953 年經鑑定爲偽造。）

Eoanthropus〔ˌioænˈθropəs〕*n.* 曙人（1911-1915 年在英國皮爾當地方發
　掘出，據稱是曙人的原始人頭骨化石，後發現係爲偽造。）

confound〔kɑnˈfaʊnd〕*v.* 使困惑　　age〔edʒ〕*v.* 使老化

orangutan〔oˈræŋʊˌtæn〕*n.* 猩猩

perpetrate〔ˈpɝpəˌtret〕*v.* 做（壞事）；犯（罪）

【譯文】

　　林肯著名的蓋茨堡演說詞，在發表的當時，並不像今天一樣，被認
爲是偉大的傑作。爲了要紀念在蓋茨堡的戰場，在一八六三年南北戰爭
最激烈時舉行了紀念典禮，而林肯甚至不是典禮中的主要演講者，主要
的演講者是演說家愛德華‧艾威雷特。他講了兩個小時之後，才是林肯
簡短的演說。他的演說只是典禮中的一小部份，但是今天大部份的美國
人，都可以立刻認出他的演講詞的開場白：「八十七年前，我們的祖先
在這塊土地上，創立了一個以自由爲立國之本的新國家，並主張人人生
而平等。」在演說的當時，林肯並沒有得到很多注意，他自己認爲那次
出席典禮是很不成功的。一直到他的演講詞被刊登出來之後，才漸漸得
到越來越多的認同。現在，蓋茨堡演說詞，已被認爲是有史以來最偉大
的演講之一。

【答案】

　　47. (**C**)　　　48. (**B**)　　49. (**A**)

【註】

Gettysburg Address 林肯的蓋茨堡演說
masterpiece〔ˈmæstəˌpis〕*n.* 傑作
ceremony〔ˈsɛrəˌmonɪ〕*n.* 典禮
dedicate〔ˈdɛdəˌket〕*v.* 奉獻　　orator〔ˈɔrətə〕*n.* 演說家
score〔skor〕*n.* 二十　　conceive〔kənˈsiv〕*v.* 產生；創立
proposition〔ˌprɑpəˈzɪʃən〕*n.* 主張
take *one's **place*** 獲得應有的地位　　acclaim〔əˈklem〕*n.* 稱讚

【譯文】

　　攀岩是一種具有挑戰性，有時又有危險性的運動。攀岩家都想避開惡劣天氣的挑戰。住在華盛頓州的西雅圖，或是附近的攀岩家，再也不需要因為下雨或下雪，而改變他們的計劃。相反地，他們可以到全國第一家室內攀岩健身房——垂直俱樂部。

　　垂直俱樂部的以前是一間倉庫，它提供了不同程度的攀岩家，各式各樣的場地。以四平方公尺的嵌板打造的牆，可以變化出不同的傾斜度，有的是微微的傾斜，並附帶方便的扶手，也有大角度突出的陡峭岩壁。

　　在俱樂部裡運動不但比在戶外攀岩舒適，而且也比較安全。如果攀岩家跌倒，有繩索可以防止他們往下掉，而且在岩壁下面的區域，也都鋪有軟墊。更好的是，當攀岩者運動完之後，他們不用再從山上，大老遠開車回家。

【答案】

　　50. (**D**)　　51. (**C**)　　52. (**B**)

【註】

rock-climbing〔'rɑk͵klaɪmɪŋ〕*n.* 攀岩

harsh〔hɑrʃ〕*adj.* 惡劣的　　alter〔'ɔltɚ〕*v.* 改變

gym〔dʒɪm〕*n.* 健身房　　warehouse〔'wɛr͵haʊs〕*n.* 倉庫

terrain〔'tɛren〕*n.* 地形　　panel〔'pænḷ〕*n.* 嵌板

handhold〔'hænd͵hold〕*n.*（攀岩時）可以抓手的地方

steepness〔'stipnɪs〕*n.* 陡峭　　gentle〔'dʒɛntḷ〕*adj.* 和緩的

slope〔slop〕*n.* 坡度　　sheer〔ʃɪr〕*adj.* 陡峭的

face〔fes〕*n.* 表面　　angle〔'æŋgḷ〕*v.* 使轉向成一角度

overhang〔'ovɚ͵hæŋ〕*n.* 突出　　***work out*** 運動

cushion〔'kʊʃən〕*v.* 裝置褥墊　　thrill〔θrɪl〕*n.* 刺激

bone-chilling〔'bon͵tʃɪlɪŋ〕*adj.* 令人毛骨悚然的

國立中正大學八十七學年度
碩士班研究生入學考試英文試題

A. Vocabulary: (40%)

You are to choose the one word or phrase that best keeps the meaning of the original sentence if it is substituted for the underlined word or phrase.

1. English is a <u>compulsory</u> subject in undergraduate programs.
   (A) difficult   (B) popular
   (C) required   (D) main

2. The government will <u>initiate</u> the building's construction soon.
   (A) begin   (B) supervise
   (C) approve   (D) resume

3. Don't miss the meeting because it is <u>mandatory</u>.
   (A) enjoyable   (B) necessary
   (C) worthwhile   (D) important

4. Jack was <u>frustrated</u> in his attempt to become an actor.
   (A) discouraged   (B) punished
   (C) discharged   (D) concerned

5. Books with <u>illustrations</u> often give the readers better ideas than those without them.
   (A) explanations   (B) definitions
   (C) pictures   (D) exercises

6. The only <u>remedy</u> for your poor pronunciation is to practice over and over again.
   (A) cure   (B) action
   (C) choice   (D) advance

7. Thoughtful modifications of the environment can make it more inviting and <u>accessible</u> to people with physical disabilities.
   (A) acceptable　　　　　(B) approachable
   (C) appreciable　　　　(D) favorable

8. When we catch a cold, the mucous membrane in the nose becomes <u>irritated</u> by the virus.
   (A) upset　　　　　　　(B) injured
   (C) sensitive　　　　　(D) congested

9. In some regions of the world, where volcanoes are more <u>prevalent</u>, lakes are created as water collects in volcanic craters.
   (A) gigantic　　　　　(B) common
   (C) unstable　　　　　(D) famous

10. Thousands of commuters in major cities depend upon <u>an intricate</u> network of trains to get to work every day and back to their homes every evening.
    (A) a convenient　　　(B) an advanced
    (C) a fast　　　　　　(D) a complex

11. His support of the measure has <u>jeopardized</u> his chances for re-election.
    (A) assured　　　　　(B) destroyed
    (C) increased　　　　(D) endangered

12. The scientist needed more <u>proof</u> before his theory could be accepted.
    (A) financing　　　　(B) publications
    (C) recognition　　　(D) evidence

13. We issue <u>an annual</u> report every September.
    (A) a comprehensive　(B) a yearly
    (C) a financial　　　(D) a product

14. Modern computer technology makes it possible for people to carry several on-line conversations <u>simultaneously</u>.
    (A) at the same time   (B) with safety
    (C) without distortion   (D) in little space

15. Nothing is more <u>deceitful</u> than the appearance of humility. It is often only carelessness of opinion, and sometimes an indirect boast.
    (A) dishonest   (B) essential
    (C) important   (D) offensive

16. To <u>grasp</u> the full significance of life is the actor's duty, to interpret it is his problem, and to express it his dedication.
    (A) understand   (B) clarify
    (C) simplify   (D) produce

17. There is no such thing as <u>perpetual</u> tranquillity of mind while we live here; because life itself is but motion, and can never be without desire, nor without fear, no more than without sense.
    (A) momentary   (B) powerful
    (C) senseless   (D) continuous

18. What a man calls his conscience is merely the mental action that follows a <u>sentimental</u> reaction after too much love or wine.
    (A) unwilling   (B) emotional
    (C) strong   (D) bitter

19. A man who exposes himself when he is <u>intoxicated</u>, has not the art of getting drunk.
    (A) poisoned   (B) hurt
    (C) saddened   (D) drunk

20. A doctrine serves no purpose in itself, but it is
    <u>indispensable</u> to have one if only to avoid being
    deceived by false doctrines.
    (A) harmful   (B) necessary
    (C) useless   (D) interesting

B. Reading Comprehension (30%)

In this section, you will read several passages. Each
one is followed by several questions about it. You
are to choose the one best answer.

Questions 21-23

Contrary to the old warning that time waits for no
one, time slows down when you are on the move. It also
slows down more as you move faster, which means ast-
ronauts someday may survive so long in space that they
would return to an Earth of the distant future. If you
could move at the speed of light, 186,282 miles a
second, your time would stand still. If you could move
faster than light, your time would move backward.

Although no form of matter yet discovered moves as
fast or faster than light, scientific experiments have
confirmed that accelerated motion causes a voyager's,
or traveler's time to be stretched. Albert Einstein
predicted this in 1905, when he introduced the concept
of relative time as part of his Special Theory of
Relativity. A search is now under way to confirm the
suspected existence of particles of matter that move
faster than light and, therefore, possibly might serve
as our passports to the past.

21. According to this passage, if you could move faster
    than light, your time would
    (A) speed up.   (B) reverse.
    (C) stop.   (D) remain the same.

22. What did Einstein predict in 1905?
    (A) No form of matter that moves as fast or faster than light can exist.
    (B) Time slows down when you are on the move.
    (C) Stretched time will cause accelerated motion.
    (D) If you know how to stretch your time, you can be a voyager.

23. According to the passage, particles of matter that move faster than light
    (A) have been found.
    (B) are believed to be in existence.
    (C) have been verified by scientists.
    (D) will soon be used in space traveling.

Questions 24-26

All students should discuss their academic program with their faculty advisors. Each student, however, is responsible for knowing and meeting the requirements for graduation. Except for required courses (such as freshman Chinese the first semester), students may select their own classes each semester. The usual schedule is four courses each semester, three courses being the minimum unless a student receives special permission. A student may not register for five or more courses in any semester.

24. According to the passage, the faculty advisor will assist the student in
    (A) taking as many courses as possible.
    (B) becoming independent.
    (C) completing the graduation requirements.
    (D) planning a course of study.

25. A student is required to get special permission when taking
    (A) two courses.　　　　　(B) three courses.
    (C) four courses.　　　　　(D) five courses.

26. The normal number of courses for a student in one semester is
    (A) one.　　　　　　　　　(B) two.
    (C) three.　　　　　　　　(D) four.

Questions 27-29

It's plain common sense — the more happiness you feel, the less unhappiness you experience. It's plain common sense, but it's not true. Recent research reveals that happiness and unhappiness are not really flip sides of the same emotion. They are two distinct feelings that, coexisting, rise and fall independently.

"You'd think that the higher a person's level of unhappiness, the lower their level of happiness and vice versa," says Edward Diener, a University of Illinois professor of psychology who has done much of the new work on positive and negative emotions. But when Diener and other researchers measure people's average levels of happiness and unhappiness, they often find little relationship between the two.

The recognition that feelings of happiness and unhappiness can coexist much like love and hate in a close relationship may offer valuable clues on how to lead a happier life. It suggests, for example, that changing or avoiding things that make you miserable may well make you less miserable but probably won't make you any happier. That advice is backed up by an extraordinary series of studies which indicate that

a genetic predisposition for unhappiness may run in
certain families. On the other hand, researchers have
found, happiness doesn't appear to be anyone's heritage.
The capacity for joy is a talent you develop largely for
yourself.

27. According to the passage, which of the following
    statements is true?
    (A) The higher a person's level of unhappiness, the
        higher their level of happiness.
    (B) The lower a person's level of unhappiness, the
        higher their level of happiness.
    (C) A person's level of happiness has little to do
        with their level of unhappiness.
    (D) A person's happiness depends on successful
        avoidance of things that make them miserable.

28. According to the passage, which of the following
    statements is true?
    (A) The tendency to be unhappy is inherited, and
        happiness is, too.
    (B) The tendency to be unhappy is inherited, but
        happiness is not.
    (C) The tendency to be happy is inherited, but
        unhappiness is not.
    (D) Neither happiness nor unhappiness can be
        inherited.

29. Edward Diener believes that
    (A) you can feel happiness and unhappiness at the
        same time.
    (B) your average levels of happiness and unhappiness
        are about the same.
    (C) unhappiness is the opposite side of happiness.
    (D) your unhappiness can be reduced if you are with
        your family.

Questions 30-32

His people said good-bye and watched him walk off
toward the mountains. They had little reason to fear
for his safety: the man was well dressed in insulated
clothing and equipped with tools needed to survive the
Alpine climate. However, as weeks passed without his
return, they must have grown worried, then anxious, and
finally resigned. After many years everyone who knew
him had died, and not even a memory of the man remained.

Then, on an improbably distant day, he came down
from the mountain. Things had changed a bit: it wasn't
the Bronze Age anymore, and he was a celebrity.

When a melting glacier released its hold on a
4,000-year-old corpse in September, it was quite rightly
called one of the most important archeological finds of
the century. Discovered by a German couple hiking at
10,500 feet in the Italian Tyrol near the Austrian
border, the partially freeze-dried body still wore
remains of leather garments and boots that had been
stuffed with straw for insulation.

30. According to the author, one of the most important
    archeological finds of the century is
    (A) that ancient people could survive the severe
        Alpine climate.
    (B) a 4000-year-old well-preserved human body.
    (C) the way ancient people living in Europe used
        to keep themselves warm.
    (D) the discovery of the Alpine climate 4000 years
        ago.

31. According to the passage, the man discovered by a German couple
    (A) walked down from the mountain.
    (B) woke up in the mountain.
    (C) was brought down from the mountain.
    (D) was released soon after he was found.

32. What would be an appropriate title for this passage?
    (A) The Ice Man
    (B) The Bronze Age
    (C) Hunter from the Past
    (D) A Celebrity in the Mountain

Questions 33-35

Fungi are seen as a diverse group of either single-celled or multicellular organisms that obtain food by direct absorption of nutrients. The food is dissolved by enzymes that the fungi excrete, is then absorbed through thin cell walls, and is distributed by simple circulation, or streaming, of the protoplasm. Together with bacteria, fungi are responsible for the decay and decomposition of all organic matter and are found wherever other forms of life exist. Some are parasitic on living matter and cause serious plant and animal diseases. The study of fungi is called mycology.

Fungi were traditionally classified as a division in the plant kingdom. They were thought of as plants that have no stems or leaves and that in the course of becoming food absorbers lost the pigment chlorophyll, which is needed for conducting photosynthesis. Most scientists today, however, view them as an entirely separate group that evolved from unpigmented flagellates and place them either in the protist kingdom or in their own kingdom, according to the complexity of organization. Approximately 100,000 species of fungi are known. The more complex groups are believed to have derived from the primitive types, which have flagellated cells at some stage in their life cycle.

33. Which of the following would be the best title for the passage?
    (A) The Plant Kingdom
    (B) The Bacteria Kingdom
    (C) Nature's Deccmposer
    (D) The Process of Photosynthesis

34. According to the passage, which of the following is correct?
    (A) Fungi are plants that use enzymes that produce themselves to dissolve food.
    (B) Fungi are plants that have no stems or leaves.
    (C) Fungi can't absorb food.
    (D) Fungi are not plants.

35. Which of the following can be inferred from the passage?
    (A) Fungi should be exterminated because they cause serious plant and animal diseases.
    (B) Fungi belong to a unique division in the plant kingdom.
    (C) The only difference between fungi and plants lies in the pigment chlorophyll, which is needed for conducting photosynthesis.
    (D) No plants or animals can live without fungi.

C. English Writing (30%)

Write a short composition in which you discuss love in 100-150 words. You may write about romantic love or some other kind of love, such as brotherly love or parental love. Remember to give a title to your writing. (30%: title 2%, grammar/spelling 8%, word choice 10%, contents and style 10%)

國立中正大學八十七學年度
碩士班研究生入學考試英文試題詳解

A. 字彙：40%

1. (**C**) compulsory〔kəm'pʌlsərɪ〕*adj.* 強制的；必修的
   (C) *required*〔rɪ'kwaɪrd〕*adj.* 必修的
   (D) main〔men〕*adj.* 主要的
   　　 undergraduate〔͵ʌndɚ'grædʒuɪt〕*adj.* 大學生的

2. (**A**) initiate〔ɪ'nɪʃɪ͵et〕*v.* 開始；創始
   (B) supervise〔͵supɚ'vaɪz〕*v.* 監督
   (C) approve〔ə'pruv〕*v.* 贊成
   (D) resume〔rɪ'zum〕*v.* 繼續
   　　 construction〔kən'strʌkʃən〕*n.* 建造

3. (**B**) mandatory〔'mændə͵torɪ〕*adj.* 強制性的
   (A) enjoyable〔ɪn'dʒɔɪəbḷ〕*adj.* 令人愉快的
   (C) worthwhile〔'wɝθ'hwaɪl〕*adj.* 值得的

4. (**A**) frustrated〔'frʌstretɪd〕*adj.* 失敗的；失意的
   (A) *discouraged*〔dɪs'kɝɪdʒd〕*adj.* 氣餒的
   (C) discharged〔dɪs'tʃɑrdʒd〕*adj.* 開除的
   (D) concerned〔kən'sɝnd〕*adj.* 擔心的
   　　 attempt〔ə'tɛmpt〕*n.* 嘗試

5. (**C**) illustration〔ɪ͵ləs'treʃən〕*n.* 插圖；圖解說明
   (A) explanation〔͵ɛksplə'neʃən〕*n.* 解釋
   (B) definition〔͵dɛfə'nɪʃən〕*n.* 定義
   (D) exercise〔'ɛksɚ͵saɪz〕*n.* 習題

6. (**A**) remedy〔 'rɛmədɪ 〕*n.* 補救方法
　　(A) *cure*〔 kjʊr 〕*n.* 補救方法
　　(D) advance〔 əd'væns 〕*n.* 進步
　　　pronunciation〔 prəˌnʌnsɪ'eʃən 〕*n.* 發音

7. (**B**) accessible〔 æk'sɛsəbḷ 〕*adj.* 易近的；可達到的
　　(B) *approachable*〔 ə'protʃəbḷ 〕*adj.* 可接近的
　　(C) appreciable〔 ə'priʃɪəbḷ 〕*adj.* 可察覺的
　　(D) favorable〔 'fevərəbḷ 〕*adj.* 贊成的
　　　thoughtful〔 'θɔtfəl 〕*adj.* 體貼的
　　　modification〔 ˌmɑdəfə'keʃən 〕*n.* 修改
　　　inviting〔 ɪn'vaɪtɪŋ 〕*adj.* 吸引人的
　　　disability〔 ˌdɪsə'bɪlətɪ 〕*n.* 身體殘障

8. (**A**) irritated〔 'ɪrəˌtetɪd 〕*adj.* 受刺激而不適的
　　(A) *upset*〔 ʌp'sɛt 〕*adj.* 不安的；不舒服的
　　(B) injured〔 'ɪndʒəd 〕*adj.* 受傷的
　　(C) sensitive〔 'sɛnsətɪv 〕*adj.* 敏感的
　　(D) congested〔 kən'dʒɛstɪd 〕*adj.* 擁塞的
　　　mucous membrane〔 'mjukəs 'mɛmbren 〕*n.* 黏膜
　　　virus〔 'vaɪrəs 〕*n.* 病毒

9. (**B**) prevalent〔 'prɛvələnt 〕*adj.* 普遍的
　　(A) gigantic〔 dʒaɪ'gæntɪk 〕*adj.* 巨大的
　　(C) unstable〔 ʌn'stebḷ 〕*adj.* 不穩定的
　　　region〔 'ridʒən 〕*n.* 地區
　　　volcanic crater〔 vɑl'kænɪk 'kretə 〕*n.* 火山口

10. (**D**) intricate〔 'ɪntrəkɪt 〕*adj.* 錯綜複雜的
　　(B) advanced〔 əd'vænst 〕*adj.* 進步的
　　(D) *complex*〔 'kɑmplɛks 〕*adj.* 複雜的
　　　commuter〔 kə'mjutə 〕*n.* 通勤者

11. (**D**) jeopardize〔ˈdʒɛpəˌdaɪz〕v. 使瀕於險境
    (A) assure〔əˈʃʊr〕v. 保證
    (B) destroy〔dɪˈstrɔɪ〕v. 毀滅
    (D) *endanger*〔ɪnˈdendʒɚ〕v. 危害
    measure〔ˈmɛʒɚ〕n. 措施
    re-election〔ˌriəˈlɛkʃən〕n. 再度當選

12. (**D**) proof〔pruf〕n. 證據
    (A) financing〔faɪˈnænsɪŋ〕n. 理財
    (B) publication〔ˌpʌblɪˈkeʃən〕n. 出版物
    (C) recognition〔ˌrɛkəgˈnɪʃən〕n. 認可；承認
    (D) *evidence*〔ˈɛvədəns〕n. 證據

13. (**B**) annual〔ˈænjʊəl〕adj. 一年一次的
    (A) comprehensive〔ˌkɑmprɪˈhɛnsɪv〕adj. 理解；全面的
    (B) *yearly*〔ˈjɪrlɪ〕adj. 一年一度的；每年的
    (C) financial〔faɪˈnænʃəl〕adj. 財務的
    (D) product〔ˈprɑdəkt〕n. 產品

14. (**A**) simultaneously〔ˌsaɪmḷˈtenɪəslɪ〕adv. 同時地
    (C) distortion〔dɪsˈtɔrʃən〕n. 扭曲
    on-line〔ˈɑnˌlaɪn〕adj. 連線的

15. (**A**) deceitful〔dɪˈsitfəl〕adj. 虛偽的
    (B) essential〔əˈsɛnʃəl〕adj. 必要的
    (D) offensive〔əˈfɛnsɪv〕adj. 冒犯的
    humility〔hjuˈmɪlətɪ〕n. 謙遜
    indirect〔ˌɪndəˈrɛkt〕adj. 間接的　　boast〔bost〕n. 直誇

16. (**A**) grasp〔græsp〕v. 了解
    (B) clarify〔ˈklærəˌfaɪ〕v. 使明確
    (C) simplify〔ˈsɪmpləˌfaɪ〕v. 簡單化
    interpret〔ɪnˈtɝprɪt〕v. 演出；詮釋
    dedication〔ˌdɛdəˈkeʃən〕n. 獻身；致力

17. (**D**) perpetual〔pəˋpɛtʃuəl〕*adj.* 永久的
    (A) momentary〔ˋmomənˏtɛrɪ〕*adj.* 短暫的
    (C) senseless〔ˋsɛnslɪs〕*adj.* 無感覺的
    (D) *continuous*〔kənˋtɪnjuəs〕*adj.* 持續的
        tranquility〔trænˋkwɪlətɪ〕*n.* 寧靜

18. (**B**) sentimental〔ˏsɛntəˋmɛntl̩〕*adj.* 感情的；情緒的
    (A) unwilling〔ʌnˋwɪlɪŋ〕*adj.* 不願意的
    (B) *emotional*〔ɪˋmoʃən̩l〕*adj.* 情感的
    (D) bitter〔ˋbɪtɚ〕*adj.* 苦的；痛苦的
        conscience〔ˋkɑnʃəns〕*n.* 良心

19. (**D**) intoxicated〔ɪnˋtɑksəˏketɪd〕*adj.* 喝醉酒的
    (A) poisoned〔ˋpɔɪzn̩d〕*adj.* 中毒的
        sadden〔ˋsædn̩〕*v.* 使悲傷
    (D) *drunk*〔drʌŋk〕*adj.* 喝醉的
        expose〔ɪkˋspoz〕*v.* 暴露

20. (**B**) indispensable〔ˏɪndɪsˋpɛnsəbl̩〕*adj.* 不可或缺的；必要的
    doctrine〔ˋdɑktrɪn〕*n.* 教條
    serve～purpose 符合～需要
    deceive〔dɪˋsiv〕*v.* 欺騙　　*if only* 如果～就好了

B. 閱讀測驗：30%

【譯文】

　　古老的警語說：「歲月不待人」，跟這句話相反的是，當你移動的時候，時間便會慢下來。而當你移動得越快時，時間的流逝就越慢，這意謂著將來有一天，若太空人在太空生存了相當久，當他們回到地球時，地球上的時間已經是在遙遠的未來。如果你可以像光速每秒 186,282 英哩的速度行進，你的時間將會是靜止的。如果你可以移動得比光快，你的時間會倒退。

　　雖然我們還沒有發現任何物質形式能移動得跟光速一樣快,或是比光還快,但科學實驗證實,加速運動會延長旅行者的時間。亞伯特·愛因斯坦在一九〇五年就預測了這一點,當時他提出時間相對的概念,作為他狹義相對論的一部份。現在我們正在調查,希望能確認是否有專種物質粒子,其移動的速度比光快,如果有的話,就有可能成為我們回到過去的通行證。

┌─【答案】──────────────────────────
│　　21.(**B**)　　　22.(**B**)　　　23.(**B**)
└──────────────────────────────────

【註】

contrary〔'kɑntrɛrɪ〕adj. 相反的　　　***on the move*** 在移動中
astronaut〔'æstrə‚nɔt〕n. 太空人　　　***stand still*** 靜止不動
backward〔'bækwəd〕adv. 向後地　　　matter〔'mætə〕n. 物質
accelerated motion 加速運動
voyager〔'vɔɪɪdʒə〕n. 旅行者
predict〔prɪ'dɪkt〕v. 預測
Special Theory of Relativity 狹義相對論
under way 正在進行中
suspected〔sə'spɛktɪd〕adj. 被懷疑可能存在的
particle〔'pɑrtɪkl̩〕n. 粒子　　　***serve as*** 充當
passport〔'pæs‚pɔrt〕n. 通行證;手段

【譯文】

　　所有的學生都必須跟指導教授討論自己的學術計畫。不過,每位學生都要知道,畢業所需的必要條件,並符合這些要求。除了必修課(如第一學期的大一國文)之外,每學期學生都可以自己選課。一般的課程表都是一學期四門課,除非有特別許可,否則至少要修三門課。每一學期學生都不得修五門以上的課。

【答案】

24.（ **D** ）　　25.（ **A** ）　　26.（ **D** ）

【註】

academic〔͵ækə'dɛmɪk〕*adj.* 學術的
faculty advisor 指導教授　　required〔rɪ'kwaɪrd〕*adj.* 必修的
schedule〔'skɛdʒul〕*n.* 課程表
minimum〔'mɪnəmən〕*n.* 最低限度　　*register for* 註冊選讀

【譯文】

　　「你越覺得快樂，就越不會不快樂」，這是一個普通常識，卻不是事實。最近的研究顯示，快樂和不快樂並不是同一種情緒的兩面。它們是兩種不同的感覺，雖然共同存在，但卻各自起伏。

　　伊利諾大學的心理學教授愛德華•第耶納，他做了很多新的，有關正面和負面情緒的研究，他指出：「一般人可能會認為，當一個人不快樂的程度越大，他快樂的程度就越小，而反之亦然。」但是當第耶納和其他研究者衡量一般人快樂和不快樂的平均程度時，他們經常發現，快樂和不快樂兩者之間，並沒有太大的關聯。

　　如果知道快樂和不快樂，就像夢與恨一樣，是密切地共存，就可以提供寶貴的線索，幫助你過得更快樂。比方說，改變或逃避讓人苦惱的事物，可能會讓你比較不痛苦，但是卻可能不會讓你更快樂。有一系列非常特別的研究，也支持這樣的意見，這些研究指出，某些家庭可能有不快樂的遺傳傾向。在另一方面，研究者發現，快樂似乎不是遺傳的。快樂是一種才能，而這種才能大部份是要靠自己培養的。

【答案】

27.（ **C** ）　　28.（ **B** ）　　29.（ **A** ）

【註】

flip side 相對應的人或物　　distinct〔dɪ'stɪŋkt〕*adj.* 不同的

coexist〔ˌkoɪg'zɪst〕*v.* 共存　*vice versa* 反之亦然

clue〔klu〕*n.* 線索　　miserable〔'mɪzərəbḷ〕*adj.* 悲慘的

back up 支持　　extraordinary〔ˌɛkstrə'ɔrdṇˌɛrɪ〕*adj.* 特殊的

genetic〔dʒə'nɛtɪk〕*adj.* 遺傳的

predisposition〔ˌpridɪspə'zɪʃən〕*n.* 傾向

run〔rʌn〕*v.* 世代相傳

heritage〔'hɛrətɪdʒ〕*n.* 繼承物　　capacity〔kə'pæsətɪ〕*n.* 能力

tendency〔'tɛndənsɪ〕*n.* 傾向

【譯文】

　　他的族人跟他道別，並目送他走向山裡。他們沒什麼理由擔心他的安危：穿著相當保暖的衣服，並且配帶可以幫他在高山氣候下存活的工具。但是，好幾個禮拜過去了，他卻還沒回來，他的族人們一定會感到擔憂，然後感到焦慮，最後只好放棄。許多年後，認識他的人都去世了，沒有留下任何關於他的記憶。

　　然後，在很久之後的某天，他從山上回來了。事情有一點改變：當時已經不是銅器時代，而他也變成一個名人。

　　九月時，冰河融化之後，出現了一個四千年前的屍體，這堪稱本世紀考古學上最重大的發現之一。這個屍體是被一對德國夫婦發現的，當時他們正在靠近奧地利邊境，海拔一千五百公尺高的義大利提洛爾區健行。這個部分被凍乾的屍體被發現時，還身穿殘餘的皮衣，以及塞滿稻草用以保暖的靴子。

【答案】

30. (**B**)　　　31. (**C**)　　　32. (**A**)

【註】

insulate〔ˈɪnsəˌlet〕v. 絕緣　　Alpine〔ˈælpaɪn〕adj. 高山的

improbably〔ɪmˈprɑbəblɪ〕adv. 不太可能地

Bronze Age 銅器時代　　celebrity〔səˈlɛbrətɪ〕n. 名人

melting〔ˈmɛltɪŋ〕adj. 融化的

resign〔rɪˈzaɪn〕v. 放棄（希望）

glacier〔ˈgleʃɚ〕n. 冰河

release one's **hold on~** 鬆手放開~

corpse〔kɔrps〕n. 屍體　　rightly〔ˈraɪtlɪ〕adv. 適當地

archeological〔ˌɑrkɪəˈlɑdʒɪkḷ〕adj. 考古學的

find〔faɪnd〕n. 發現　　hike〔haɪk〕v. 徒步旅行

remains〔rɪˈmenz〕n.pl. 剩餘物　　garment〔ˈgɑrmənt〕n. 衣服

stuff〔stʌf〕v. 填塞　　straw〔strɔ〕n. 稻草

insulation〔ˌɪnsəˈleʃən〕n. 絕緣　　severe〔səˈvɪr〕adj. 酷烈的

【譯文】

　　黴菌和單細胞或多細胞有機體不同，它們攝取食物的方式是直接吸收養分。食物在黴菌分泌的酵素中分解，通過薄薄的細胞壁吸收之後，經由原生物質的簡單循環或流動，分散到各處。黴菌和細菌在一起時，黴菌負責使有機物質腐爛並分解，而且它們存在於任何有生命的地方。有些黴菌寄生於生物體上，會導致嚴重的動、植物疾病。有關黴菌的研究被稱為黴菌學。

　　傳統上，黴菌被劃分為植物界的一個分支。它們被認為是沒有莖和葉的植物，在成為可獨立吸收養分的植物的過程中，失去了行光合作用所需的葉綠素。然而，現今大部份的科學家，認為黴菌是從無葉綠素的鞭毛蟲所進化而來的，並且根據其結構的複雜程度，將它們歸類於原生生物，或是自成一類。現在，我們知道的黴菌大約有十萬種。一般認為，比較複雜的黴菌是源自於原始的黴菌，這些原始黴菌，在其生命周期的某個階段中，擁有鞭毛形的細胞。

【答案】

33. (**C**)　　34. (**D**)　　35. (**D**)

【註】

fungi〔ˈfʌndʒaɪ〕*n.pl.* 黴菌　　diverse〔daɪˈvɝs〕*adj.* 不同的
multicellular〔ˈmʌltɪˈsɛljələ〕*adj.* 多細胞的
organism〔ˈɔrgən͵ɪzəm〕*n.* 生物
absorption〔əbˈsɔrpʃən〕*n.* 吸收
nutrient〔ˈnjutrɪənt〕*n.* 養分　　enzyme〔ˈɛnzaɪm〕*n.* 酵素
excrete〔ɛkˈskrit〕*v.* 分泌　　*cell wall* 細胞壁
circulation〔͵sɝkjəˈleʃən〕*n.* 循環
stream〔strim〕*v.* 流動
protoplasm〔ˈprotə͵plæzəm〕*n.* 原生質
bacteria〔bækˈtɪrɪə〕*n.pl.* 細菌　　decay〔dɪˈke〕*n.* 腐爛
decomposition〔͵dikɑmpəˈzɪʃən〕*n.* 分解
organic matter 有機物
parasitic〔͵pærəˈsɪtɪk〕*adj.* 寄生的
mycology〔maɪˈkɑlədʒɪ〕*n.* 黴菌學
plant kingdom 植物界
pigment〔ˈpɪgmənt〕*n.* 色素
chlorophyll〔ˈklorə͵fɪl〕*n.* 葉綠素
conduct〔kənˈdʌkt〕*v.* 進行；做
photosynthesis〔͵fotəˈsɪnθəsɪs〕*n.* 光合作用
evolve〔ɪˈvɑlv〕*v.* 進化
unpigmented〔͵ʌnpɪgˈmɛntɪd〕*adj.* 無色素的
flagellate〔ˈflædʒə͵let〕*n.* 鞭毛蟲
protist〔ˈprotɪst〕*n.pl.* 原生生物
species〔ˈspiʃɪz〕*n.* 種　　*derive from* 源自
primitive〔ˈprɪmətɪv〕*adj.* 原始的
terminate〔ˈtɝmə͵net〕*v.* 終結

C. 英文作文：30%

Romantic Love — The Ultimate Love

There are many cynics who sneer at the notion of romantic love. But for me it's the greatest thing life has to offer. The passion, idealism and sense of adventure that are its quintessential components lift our lives into the heavens. There is nothing else like it on earth!

I consider myself an incurable romantic because as many times as I have been in love and it has foundered, I keep coming back for more. The energy it produces is intoxicating.

In my heart of hearts I am convinced that one day I will find the girl of my dreams. In the meantime the search for her, though sometimes involving heartache, is always worthwhile for the chance at the biggest jackpot of all.

How can I be so sure? It is not only because of from my own experience but also because of the prodigious art on the subject created by some of the all time romantic greats, like the poets Byron and Pushkin, the novelists Faulbert and Tolstoy and the painters Renoir and Picasso. Such a group would not lead me astray.

國立中興大學八十七學年度
碩士班研究生入學考試英文試題

I. Vocabulary: 20%
To each question, choose one answer, (A),(B),(C), or
(D) that <u>best</u> completes the sentence.

Example : The witness said that he had _____ information
that could have a major effect on the case.
(A) bland   (B) pertinent
(C) contagious   (D) prestigious
Answer : B

1. Public administration consists of the _____ of
public policy by public authorities.
(A) excursion   (B) extermination
(C) execution   (D) acknowledgment

2. We shall pay any price, support any friend, _____
any foe to assure the survival and success of liberty.
(A) oppose   (B) rivalry
(C) level   (D) invent

3. The United States Constitution mandates two Houses
of Congress so that the large states will not be
_____ represented.
(A) illegally   (B) mistakenly
(C) discontentedly   (D) disproportionately

4. The scientific conquest of fusion energy is proving
to be _____ task.
(A) an arduous   (B) an intangible
(C) a superfluous   (D) an embellish

5. Although most birds have only a _____ sense of
smell, they have acute vision.
(A) faulty   (B) negligible
(C) condensed   (D) negative

6. Many pure metals have little use because they are
   too soft, rust too easily, or have some other _____.
   (A) properties   (B) additives
   (C) drawbacks   (D) disparities

7. Some of technology's negative aspects are extremely
   hard to _____.
   (A) obey   (B) inspire
   (C) invest   (D) remedy

8. The _____ temperature range for growing mushrooms
   is from 55°F to 72°F.
   (A) flexible   (B) obvious
   (C) optimal   (D) magnetic

9. Slang and substandard language are not generally
   _____ in published scientific papers.
   (A) abundant   (B) permitted
   (C) pragmatic   (D) withheld

10. The new operating system includes features that
    significantly _____ a computer's boot-up, shut-down,
    and applications-loading time.
    (A) rush   (B) accelerate
    (C) accentuate   (D) accredit

II. Grammar: 20%

   Each of the sentences below has four underlined
   expressions. The four underlined parts of the
   sentence are marked (A),(B),(C), and (D). Choose
   the one underlined expression that must be changed
   in order to make the sentence correct.
   選錯：請自下列各句劃線部份（ A, B, C 或 D ）挑出一個文法有錯
        誤的答案。

   Example : Maria knows English fairly well but she
                                  A
             cannot speak it quite well as she
             B   C
             is able to read it.
                       D
   Answer : C

11. <u>Even though</u> body language is <u>repeatedly</u> ignored or
      A   B
   misread, nonverbal communication is <u>still</u> less
                                    C
   <u>complication</u> than verbal communication.
    D

12. When Marshall completed his errands, <u>it was no time</u>
                                           A
   <u>left</u> to do <u>the very things</u> he <u>most wanted</u> to do.
   B   C   D

13. With the <u>exception</u> of aluminum, shiny metals such
          A
   as tin or copper <u>turns into</u> black <u>powders</u> when
                  B   C
   <u>ground fine</u>.
    D

14. Developmental psychologists <u>view</u> human development
                           A
   and behavior <u>as functions</u> of the interaction between
                B
   <u>biological</u> characteristics <u>also</u> environmental
    C   D
   influences.

15. <u>The first time</u> that Mr. Smith <u>went skiing</u>, he
      A   B
   <u>bruised</u> one of his legs and broke <u>another</u>.
    C   D

16. The policeman <u>wondered whether</u> he should <u>rely simply</u>
                 A   B
   on the drivers' accounts of the accident or <u>to search</u>
                                      C
   the neighborhood <u>for some witnesses</u>.
                D

17. When inflation is rampant, many families find
   <u>it difficult</u> to <u>maintain</u> the life-style <u>with which</u>
    A   B   C
   they <u>are accustomed</u>.
       D

18. The <u>central</u> idea of resource management is to make
       A
each action or judgment help <u>achievement</u> a <u>carefully</u>
                         B   C
<u>chosen</u> goal.
  D

19. Human beings are <u>social</u> animals <u>who</u> usually prefer
               A   B
not to live <u>in a</u> physical or psychological <u>isolation</u>.
          C   D

20. If television had been invented a thousand years ago,
<u>will</u> <u>nations</u> be significantly <u>more homogeneous</u>
 A   B   C
than <u>they are</u> now?
    D

III. Reading Comprehension: 20%
    Read the following passages carefully, and choose
    the best answer to each question.

A.
    Public goods are those commodities from whose
enjoyment nobody can be effectively excluded. Everybody
is free to enjoy the benefits of these commodities, and
one person's utilization does not reduce the possibility of anybody else enjoying the same good.

    Examples of public goods are not as rare as one
might expect. A flood control dam is a public good. Once
the dam is built, all persons living in the area will
benefit—irrespective of their own contribution to the
construction cost of the dam. The same holds true for
highway signs or aids to navigation. Once a lighthouse
is built, no ship of any nationality can be effectively
excluded from the utilization of the lighthouse for
navigational purposes. National defense is another

example. Even a person who voted against military expenditures or did not pay any taxes will benefit from the protection afforded.

It is no easy task to determine the social costs and social benefits associated with a public good. There is no practicable way of charging drivers for looking at highway signs, sailors for watching a lighthouse, and citizens for the security provided to them through national defense. Because the market does not provide the necessary signals, economic analysis has to be substituted for the impersonal judgment of the marketplace.

21. With what topic is the passage mainly concerned?
    (A) Mechanisms for safer navigation.
    (B) The economic structure of the marketplace.
    (C) A specific group of commodities.
    (D) The advantages of lowering taxes.

22. Which of the following would NOT be an example of a public good as described in the passage?
    (A) A taxicab.   (B) A bridge.
    (C) A fire truck.   (D) A stoplight.

23. In line 11, the word "holds" could best be replaced by which of the following?
    (A) has   (B) is
    (C) grasps   (D) carries

24. According to the passage, finding out the social costs of a public good is a
    (A) difficult procedure.
    (B) daily administrative duty.
    (C) matter of personal judgment.
    (D) citizen's responsibility.

25. Which of the following statements best describes the organization of the first two paragraphs?
    (A) Suggestions for the application of an economic concept are offered.
    (B) Several generalizations are presented from which various conclusions are drawn.
    (C) Persuasive language is used to argue against a popular idea.
    (D) A general concept is defined and then examples are given.

B.

　　The success of science, both its intellectual excitement and its practical application, depends upon the self-correcting character of science. There must be a way of testing any valid idea. It must be possible to reproduce any valid experiment. The character or beliefs of scientists are irrelevant; all that matters is whether the evidence supports their contentions. Arguments from authority simply do not count; too many authorities have been mistaken too often. I would like to see these very effective scientific modes of thought communicated by the schools and the media; and it would certainly be an astonishment and delight to see them introduced into politics. Scientists have been known to change their minds completely and publicly when presented with new evidence or new arguments. I cannot recall the last time a politician displayed a similar openness and willingness to change.

26. What does the passage mainly discuss?
    (A) The rewards of intellectual excitement.
    (B) Practical applications of an abstract theory.
    (C) An important characteristic of science.
    (D) Some similarities between politics and science.

27. According to the passage, if a scientist repeats an
    experiment several times and does not produce
    similar results each time, the experiment must be
    (A) invalid.   (B) incorrectly recorded.
    (C) extremely complex.   (D) scientific.

28. According to the passage, which of the following is
    most essential to scientists' work?
    (A) Character.   (B) Beliefs.
    (C) Authority.   (D) Evidence.

29. The author implies that, in science, arguments from
    authority are
    (A) irrelevant.   (B) effective.
    (C) uncomplicated.   (D) accountable.

30. The author suggests that the scientific way of
    thinking should be propagated by
    (A) justice departments. (B) newspapers.
    (C) businesses.   (D) research laboratories.

IV. Translation: 20%
    Translate the following passages into Chinese.
    請將下面兩段文字翻成中文。

A.

    Policy problems are often interpreted in different
ways by different policy stakeholders, i.e. the problems
are partly in the eye of the beholder. Successful
problem solving requires finding the right solution to
the right problem. We fail more often because we solve
the wrong problem than because we get the wrong solution
to the right problem.

B.

　　Beijing's political mood always colors its relations with the United States. So it's telling that ties
are now firmly on the mend. China ceased railing about
U.S. meddling before Jiang's visit to Washington last
year. A scheduled visit by Bill Clinton in June could
effectively close the books on 1989. Any crackdown
before then would put the trip in peril. Chinese
intellectuals understand this equation.

V. Composition: 20%
　　Write in two paragraphs your responses to the
　　following quotation in the context of the cross-
　　Taiwan Strait relations.

　　"Let us never negotiate out of fear.
　　But let us never fear to negotiate."
　　　　　　John F. Kennedy, Inaugural Address, 1961

國立中興大學八十七學年度
碩士班研究生入學考試英文試題詳解

I. 字彙：20%

1. (**C**) (A) excursion〔ɪk'skɜʒən〕*n.* 遠足
   (B) extermination〔ɪk,stɜmə'neʃən〕*n.* 消滅
   (C) ***execution***〔,ɛksɪ'kjuʃən〕*n.* 執行
   (D) acknowledgement〔ək'nɑlɪdʒmənt〕*n.* 承認
      administration〔əd,mɪnə'streʃən〕*n.* 行政；統治

2. (**A**) (A) ***oppose***〔ə'poz〕*v.* 反抗；反對
   (B) rivalry〔'raɪvl̩rɪ〕*n.* 敵對
   (C) level〔'lɛvl̩〕*v.* 使平等
      foe〔fo〕*n.* 敵人   assure〔ə'ʃur〕*v.* 確保

3. (**D**) (A) illegally〔ɪ'ligl̩ɪ〕*adv.* 不合法地
   (B) mistakenly〔mə'stekənlɪ〕*adv.* 錯誤地
   (C) discontentedly〔,dɪskən'tɛntɪdlɪ〕*adv.* 不滿地
   (D) ***disproportionately***〔,dɪsprə'porʃənɪtlɪ〕*adv.* 不成比例地
      mandate〔'mændet〕*v.* 授權；委任
      two Houses of Congress 議會兩院

4. (**A**) (A) ***arduous***〔'ɑrdʒuəs〕*adj.* 困難的
   (B) intangible〔ɪn'tændʒəbl̩〕*adj.* 無形的
   (C) superfluous〔su'pɜfluəs〕*adj.* 多餘的
   (D) embellish〔ɪm'bɛlɪʃ〕*v.* 裝飾
      conquest〔'kɑŋkwɛst〕*n.* 征服
      fusion〔'fjuʒən〕*n.* 熔合

5. (**B**) (A) faulty〔ˈfɔltɪ〕*adj.* 有缺點的

   (B) ***negligible***〔ˈnɛglədʒəbḷ〕*adj.* 極小的；微不足道的

   (C) condensed〔kənˈdɛnst〕*adj.* 濃縮的

   (D) negative〔ˈnɛgətɪv〕*adj.* 否定的；消極的

   acute〔əˈkjut〕*adj.* 敏銳的

6. (**C**) (A) property〔ˈprɑpɚtɪ〕*n.* 特性

   (B) additive〔ˈædətɪv〕*n.* 添加物

   (C) ***drawback***〔ˈdrɔˌbæk〕*n.* 缺點

   (D) disparity〔dɪsˈpærətɪ〕*n.* 不同

   pure〔pjʊr〕*adj.* 純的 rust〔rʌst〕*v.* 生銹

7. (**D**) (A) obey〔əˈbe〕*v.* 遵守

   (B) inspire〔ɪnˈspaɪr〕*v.* 激勵；給予靈感

   (C) invest〔ɪnˈvɛst〕*v.* 投資

   (D) ***remedy***〔ˈrɛmədɪ〕*v.* 補救；消除

   aspect〔ˈæspɛkt〕*n.* 方面

8. (**C**) (A) flexible〔ˈflɛksəbḷ〕*adj.* 有彈性的

   (B) obvious〔ˈɑbvɪəs〕*adj.* 明顯的

   (C) ***optimal***〔ˈɑptəməl〕*adj.* 最佳的

   (D) magnetic〔mægˈnɛtɪk〕*adj.* 有磁性的

   range〔rendʒ〕*n.* 範圍

   mushroom〔ˈmʌʃrum〕*n.* 洋菇

9. (**B**) (A) abundant〔əˈbʌndənt〕*adj.* 豐富的

   (B) ***permitted***〔pɚˈmɪtɪd〕*adj.* 被許可的

   (C) pragmatic〔prægˈmætɪk〕*adj.* 忙碌的

   (D) withheld〔wɪθˈhɛld〕*adj.* 被限制的

   slang〔slæŋ〕*n.* 俚語

   substandard〔sʌbˈstændɚd〕*adj.* 不合標準的

10. (**B**) (A) rush 〔 rʌʃ 〕 v. 衝

(B) ***accelerate*** 〔 æk'sɛlə‚ret 〕 v. 加速

(C) accentuate 〔 æk'sɛntʃu‚et 〕 v. 強調

(D) accredit 〔 ə'krɛdɪt 〕 v. 信賴

boot-up 〔 'but‚ʌp 〕 n. (電腦) 開機

load 〔 lod 〕 v. 裝載

II. 文法：20%（挑錯）

11. (**D**) *complication* → ***complicated***

nonverbal 〔 nɑn'vɝbḷ 〕 adj. 不靠語言表達的

verbal 〔 'vɝbḷ 〕 adj. 以語言表示的

12. (**A**) *it was no time* → ***there was no time***

errand 〔 'ɛrənd 〕 n. 任務；使命

13. (**B**) *turns into* → ***turn into***

aluminum 〔 ə'lumɪnəm 〕 n. 鋁   tin 〔 tɪn 〕 n. 錫

copper 〔 'kɑpɚ 〕 n. 銅   grind 〔 graɪnd 〕 v. 磨

fine 〔 faɪn 〕 adj. 極細的

14. (**D**) *also* → ***and***

15. (**D**) *another* → ***the other***

* 表「兩者之另一個」，用 the other。三者或三者以上的
另一個，才用 another。

bruise 〔 bruz 〕 v. 瘀傷   break 〔 brek 〕 v. 折斷

16. (**C**) *to search* → ***search***

account 〔 ə'kaunt 〕 n. 說明   witness 〔 'wɪtnɪs 〕 n. 目擊者

17. (**C**) *with which* → ***to which***

inflation 〔 ɪn'fleʃən 〕 n. 通貨膨脹

rampant 〔 'ræmpənt 〕 adj. 瘋狂的；猖獗的

be accustomed to 習慣於

18. (**B**)　*achievement → **achieve***

19. (**C**)　*in　a → **in***
social〔ˈsoʃəl〕*adj.* 群居的
isolation〔ˌaisḷˈeʃən〕*n.* 孤立（爲不可數名詞）

20. (**A**)　*will → **would***　　與現在事實相反的假設，須用過去式助動詞。
significantly〔sɪgˈnɪfəkəntlɪ〕*adv.* 相當多地；顯著地
homogeneous〔həˈmɑdʒənəs〕*adj.* 同性質的

Ⅲ. 閱讀測驗：20％

【譯文】

　　公共財就是一般的公共設施，沒有人可以完全不使用到這些設備。每個人都可以自由享用公共設施所帶來的好處；多一個人的使用，並不會減少其他人使用相同設施的可能性。

　　公共財的實例，並不如一般人想像中的那麼少。水門就是公共財的一種。一旦水門建好了，所有住在附近地區的人都能受惠，不論他們是否有捐錢來建造這座水門。此外，高速公路號誌，導航器材也是同樣的道理。一旦設立了一座燈塔，任何國籍的船隻，都不可能不利用這座燈塔來導航。國防也是公共財之一。即使是反對國防預算的人，或是不繳稅的人，也都能蒙受其利。

　　判定一個公共財所帶來的社會成本及社會福利，並不容易。要駕駛人因爲看了高速公路的號誌而付錢，要水手爲了利用燈塔而付錢，或是要人民爲了國防所提供的安全而付錢，都是行不通的。因爲這種需求並沒有必要的指標，必須用經濟分析來取代客觀的市場判斷。

┌─【答案】────────────────────────
│　　21.（ **C** ）　　22.（ **A** ）　　23.（ **B** ）　　24.（ **A** ）　　25.（ **D** ）
└──────────────────────────────

【註】

public good 公益；公共財產
commodity〔kə'mɑdətɪ〕*n.* 日常必需品
utilization〔,jutḷə'zeʃən〕*n.* 利用　　rare〔rɛr〕*adj.* 罕見的
irrespective of 不管；不論　　aid〔ed〕*n.* 輔助器具
navigation〔,nævə'geʃən〕*n.* 航行
lighthouse〔'laɪt,haʊs〕*n.* 燈塔
purpose〔'pɝpəs〕*n.* 用途　　***vote against*** 投票反對
expenditure〔ɪk'spɛndɪtʃɚ〕*n.* 經費
impersonal〔ɪm'pɝsṇḷ〕*adj.* 客觀的
mechanism〔'mɛkə,nɪzəm〕*n.* 方法
fire truck 救火車　　procedure〔prə'sidʒɚ〕*n.* 程序
administrative〔əd'mɪnə,stretɪv〕*adj.* 行政的
generalization〔,dʒɛnərələ'zeʃən〕*n.* 概論

【譯文】

　　科學的成功，無論是智慧上的激發，或是實際上的應用，都是取決於科學的自我修正的特性。任何一種合理的想法，一定有其證明的方式。而重新做一次已經被認爲是有確實根據的實驗，也是有可能的。這和科學家的性格、信念無關，眞正有關係的，在於這個證據是否能支持他們的論點。重要的不是權威的論點，已有太多的權威是錯的。我很希望看到這些具有影響力的科學思考模式，能藉由學校和媒體宣揚開來，若能看到它們被引薦到政治領域上，那肯定是件令人又驚又喜的事。大家都知道，每當科學家一有新的證據或論點，他們就會完全並且公開地改變他們的想法。不過我卻不記得，上一次有哪位政治人物，表現出類似的直率和改變的意願。

【答案】

26. (**C**)　　27. (**A**)　　28. (**D**)　　29. (**A**)　　30. (**B**)

【註】

character〔'kærɪktɚ〕*n.* 特性
valid〔'vælɪd〕*adj.* 有效的；有事實根據的
reproduce〔,riprə'djus〕*v.* 複製；仿造
irrelevant〔ɪ'rɛləvənt〕*adj.* 不相關的
contention〔kən'tɛnʃən〕*n.* 爭論
count〔kaʊnt〕*v.* 重要　　mode〔mod〕*n.* 模式
communicate〔kə'mjunə,ket〕*v.* 傳達
recall〔rɪ'kɔl〕*v.* 回想起
openness〔'opənnɪs〕*n.* 率直；寬大
willingness〔'wɪlɪŋnɪs〕*n.* 願意
abstract〔'æbstrækt〕*adj.* 抽象的
invalid〔ɪn'vælɪd〕*adj.* 無效的；無價值的
accountable〔ə'kaʊntəbl̩〕*adj.* 可說明的
propagate〔'prɑpə,get〕*v.* 傳達

IV. 翻譯：20％

【譯文】

　　握有政治籌碼的人不同，政策問題的解讀方式也就經常不一樣，也就是在旁觀者的眼裡，只能看到問題的一部分。想要成功地解決問題，必須對症下藥。我們之所以無法解決問題，大多是因為我們解錯問題，而不是給錯答案。

【註】

interpret〔ɪn'tɝprɪt〕*v.* 詮釋
stakeholder〔'stek,holdɚ〕*adj.* 有效的；有事實根據的
beholder〔bɪ'holdɚ〕*n.* 觀看者；旁觀者

【譯文】

　　北京的政治氣氛，總是能影響它和美國的關係。所以，很明顯地，它們之間的關係正在穩定改變中。去年，在江澤明訪問華府之前，中國停止一切有關於美國干預中國內政的謾罵。而柯林頓六月訪華的既定行程，可能可以有效地結束自一九八九年來，中美的冷凍關係。因此，北京當局任何鎮壓的行動，都可能危及這次的訪華行程。中國的知識分子非常了解這種平衡關係。

【註】

mood〔mud〕*n.* 氣氛　　color〔'kʌlɚ〕*v.* 影響

telling〔'tɛlɪŋ〕*adj.* 顯著的　　ties〔taɪz〕*n.pl.* 關係

on the mend 在改善中　　rail〔rel〕*v.* 罵

meddle〔'mɛdḷ〕*v.* 干涉　　scheduled〔'skɛdʒuld〕*adj.* 排定的

close the books on 停止；中止

crackdown〔'kræk͵daʊn〕*n.* 制裁；鎮壓

peril〔'pɛrəl〕*n.* 危險　　intellectual〔͵ɪntḷ'ɛktʃʊəl〕*n.* 知識分子

equation〔ɪ'kweʒən〕*n.* (涉及平衡的) 關係狀態

V. 英文作文：20%

Negotiations and Fear

　　Due to China's sheer size and military strength in contrast to Taiwan's, it is easy for Beijing to instill fear into the hearts and minds of its small neighboring country's citizens. China has used this tactic whenever it has felt that Taiwan was getting out of line or becoming too independent. The effect has been that Taiwan often concedes, meekly restating public policy towards China. But the new point of view as enunciated by President Lee in 1999 of state to state relations more truly reflects the views of many Taiwanese.

Taiwan is open to negotiations with China and sees itself returning to China in the future, but only under democratic negotiations, not coercive ones based on fear. Mr. Soong, a Taiwanese presidential candidate, stated he will view sees negotiations with China seriously, only after the Chinese government becomes democratic. Until then, it looks like both sides will smile at each other and choose their words carefully, continuing cross-strait talks at the methodical, stop and go pace seen over the last few years.

私立淡江大學八十七學年度
碩士班研究生入學考試英文試題

Part A

I. Vocabulary in context: Each of the following questions has four answers, of which only one is correct. 20%

1. Many citizens objected vigorously to the _____ of the county offices, which could not be reached without traveling considerable distances.
   (A) inaccessibility   (B) lack
   (C) inefficiency   (D) insufficiency

2. A fortunate but small number of people work at jobs which are in themselves _____ and are not performed chiefly for the return which they bring.
   (A) painful   (B) wearisome
   (C) necessary   (D) pleasurable

3. The sailors made a _____ attempt to save the ship.
   (A) futile   (B) tardy
   (C) fulfill   (D) mimicking

4. He sometimes looks on the sly. The phrase "on the sly" means _____.
   (A) roughly   (B) wildly
   (C) abruptly   (D) secretly

5. If a person feels "enervated," he is _____.
   (A) full of ambition   (B) full of strength
   (C) exhausted   (D) troubled

6. A callous person is one who is _____.
   (A) benevolent   (B) unsympathetic
   (C) incorrigible   (D) proud

7. Some people think that too much reliance on mechanical
   devices is —————— to health.
   (A) conducive   (B) contagious
   (C) advantageous   (D) inimical

8. The surest way of keeping the citizenry ——————
   is to limit the means by which the intellectuals
   can agitate.
   (A) docile   (B) healthy
   (C) rebellious   (D) indomitable

9. "Use of our beauty cream will —————— your skin,"
   the advertisement claimed.
   (A) regulate   (B) reinstate
   (C) relegate   (D) rejuvenate

10. He refused to see anyone and remained a —————— to
    the end of his life.
    (A) heretic   (B) fugitive
    (C) recluse   (D) veteran

11. She looked closely at the bug for a long time,
    —————— every detail in it.
    (A) visualizing   (B) jeopardizing
    (C) dissecting   (D) scrutinizing

12. Something which can be seen or recognized is ——————.
    (A) discernible   (B) despicable
    (C) detestable   (D) delectable

13. I am sure her decision will be fair and just, for
    she has a reputation for being ——————.
    (A) imperative   (B) impervious
    (C) impertinent   (D) impartial

14. Despite the many bribes they offered the player, the
    "fixers" did not succeed in —————— his integrity.
    (A) discovering   (B) discouraging
    (C) reducing   (D) undermining

15. His success in converting the people to his way
    of thinking was largely a result of his _____
    criticisms of the existing order.
    (A) compromising   (B) indiscreet
    (C) persuasive   (D) emotional

16. Since Peter did not expect to speak and had not
    prepared any remarks, his talk was _____.
    (A) inadvertent   (B) impromptu
    (C) contingent   (D) propaganda

17. Those who live in cities think country folk have
    _____ manners.
    (A) manifest   (B) sheer
    (C) exclusive   (D) rustic

18. We had to start at exactly the same time, so we had
    our watches _____.
    (A) transfixed   (B) stabilized
    (C) temporized   (D) synchronized

19. If a parachute can be easily seen, we say that it
    is _____ .
    (A) desolate   (B) vigorous
    (C) picturesque   (D) conspicuous

20. There is a _____ of flies on the table.
    (A) flock   (B) herd
    (C) swarm   (D) drove

II. Vocabulary without context: Choose the one word or
    phrase whose meaning is most nearly the same as the
    one given. 10%

21. *ostensible*
    (A) gaudy   (B) stubborn
    (C) apparent   (D) elastic

22. *imminent*
   (A) hazardous
   (C) astounding
   (B) impending
   (D) disastrous

23. *a wanderer*
   (A) immigrant
   (C) pilgrim
   (B) pedestrian
   (D) vagabond

24. *trifling or silly*
   (A) pertinent
   (C) tentative
   (B) sardonic
   (D) frivolous

25. *required*
   (A) perfunctory
   (C) methodical
   (B) paramount
   (D) mandatory

26. *to depart from or to differ*
   (A) convert
   (C) alternate
   (B) deviate
   (D) fluctuate

27. *genuine or reliable*
   (A) substantial
   (C) feasible
   (B) authentic
   (D) tangible

28. *pensive*
   (A) obstinate
   (C) thoughtful
   (B) lustful
   (D) fanciful

29. *to deny an opportunity*
   (A) the most unusual feature
   (B) the plan in operation
   (C) hold back a privilege
   (D) to prove very helpful

30. *the general run of things*
   (A) to withdraw from life
   (B) a method of study
   (C) to be determined about
   (D) usual course of events

III. Completing sentences: Each of the following
     questions consists of a sentence, part of which
     is missing. From the four phrases or clauses,
     choose the one that best completes the sentence. 5%

31. Charles Ives gave away the Pulitzer Prize money
    because he _____.
    (A) felt that he deserved the award
    (B) he needed a vast amount of financial assistance
    (C) had little regard for people with money
    (D) thought the honor was sufficient

32. There's many a crown for those _____.
    (A) who match their desire with action
    (B) who could sometimes arrive their goals
    (C) who ambitiously reach for it easily
    (D) who thought it worth doing it

33. The veterans spent a year _____.
    (A) in the hospital yet they emerged well entirely
    (B) in the hospital and they entirely emerged well
    (C) in the hospital but they entirely emerged
    (D) in the hospital; consequently, they emerged
        entirely well

34. For all _____, he is not happy.
    (A) so much money
    (B) the riches he possesses
    (C) he is rich
    (D) his merry life

35. Modern cars _____.
    (A) of today, unlike the old cars of yesterday, can
        be driven faster without danger than the old ones
    (B) unlike the old cars of yesterday can be driven
        faster without danger than the old ones
    (C) , unlike the old ones, can be driven faster
        without danger
    (D) unlike the old ones, can be driven faster without
        danger than the old ones.

IV. Choice: From the five sentences lettered (a) through (e), choose the one that has most nearly the same meaning as the sentence preceeding (a). 5%

36. There are no special tricks for concentrating and none are necessary.
(A) Concentration, although difficult, does not require the use of particular tricks.
(B) Concentration is an art which college students will find very necessary in their studying.
(C) It is necessary to learn to concentrate quickly.
(D) There are tricks to all trades.
(E) Concentration is a result of a series of special studies by a student.

37. Geographical factors have something to do with the method of living.
(A) There is no connection between geography and living habits.
(B) Influence of climate is quite apparent in weather maps.
(C) Religious faith is a result of geographical location.
(D) Developments in civilization that affect one's way of living are often determined by physical conditions in any given locality.
(E) Human behavior varies according to the weather.

38. Surveying the site for the new highway was very difficult because of the rugged terrain.
(A) Surveying for the new highway took almost three months due to the moisture in the soil.
(B) Final location of the new highway is always of important interest to the people through whose land it might go.
(C) Engineers had difficulty in surveying the land for the new highway because of the very rough terrain over which they worked.

(D) The new highway would have been moved to another section of the country if the terrain had been smoother.

(E) Surveying is not a difficult thing to do if the land is smooth and the land owner are cooperative.

39. One of the students' problem is to recognize what should be known and then to fix it in memory so that it will be there when wanted.

(A) Success of an individual depends on how well he adjusts to the new school environment.

(B) Repeated learning is highly desirable for students so that they may have the facts needed always in mind.

(C) Many students find that one difficulty in studying is to be able to recognize what is important and to apply procedures for remembering ideas.

(D) A good way to study is to read the lesson at least twice, and then listen closely to the instructor.

(E) Explaining the problems is the best way to learn important facts.

40. The process of change is one in which an invention comes before we anticipate its social effects.

(A) Social effects of the inventions that occur are relatively unimportant.

(B) A delay should be declared on invention and scientific discovery until the social institutions of man catch up.

(C) Before this process of change can be controlled, it must first be anticipated.

(D) Inventions come before the social effects which they are bound to cause.

(E) The problem of the control of social change resolves itself largely into the problem of the control of the effects of the environment.

V. Reading comprehension: Read the following passages and answer the questions. Choose the one best answer from the four. 28%

A house without books is like a room without windows. No man has a right to bring up his children without surrounding them with books if he has the means to buy them. It is wronging his family. Children learn to read by being in the presence of books. The love of knowledge comes with reading and grows upon it. And the love of knowledge, in a young mind, is almost a warrant against the inferior excitement of passions and vices.

41. The author reveals a fear of _____.
    (A) improper exercise of passions
    (B) knowledge learned from books
    (C) lack of school education
    (D) people's ability to obey laws and regulations

42. The author attempts to convince the reader through _____.
    (A) citing examples
    (B) appealing to the reader's sentiment
    (C) logical development of an idea
    (D) generalizations

43. The author stresses the importance of _____ in the learning process.
    (A) ability of the instructor
    (B) the type of textbooks being used
    (C) environment
    (D) the educational level of one's friends and relatives

44. According to the author the best that a parent can give his child must include _____.
    (A) sensibility to the rights of others
    (B) understanding of self
    (C) love of knowledge for its own sake
    (D) fear of propaganda

    I feel that you are justified in looking to the future with true assurance, because you have a model in which we find the joy of life and the joy of work harmoniously combined. Added to this is the spirit of ambition which pervades your very being, and seems to make the day's work like that of a happy child at play.

45. The author's use of "I," "you," "we" serve to _____.
    (A) show his disapproval of mixing play with work
    (B) confuse the reader
    (C) show his disapproval of the actions of the other
    (D) show how both he and others have evaluated the deeds of the person

46. The tone of the passage is best termed _____.
    (A) cynical   (B) approving
    (C) dogmatic   (D) pessimistic

47. In this selection the author aims to _____.
    (A) be neutral
    (B) persuade his reader to evaluate his own life aims
    (C) show the advantages of his idea
    (D) present a model to be followed

    Even the fairest and most impartial newspaper is a medium of propaganda. Every daily newspaper has an editorial page. Its opinions on events and personalities in the news are expressed. But editorial judgment is so persuasively presented that many people accept these opinions as facts. Good journalists uphold a code of ethics which distinguishes between news and editorial opinion. This code holds that in an editorial column the publisher is entitled to advocate any cause he chooses. It is understood that there he is speaking as a partisan and may express any view he desires. Because modern newspapers have increasingly become big business organizations, these large newspapers tend to reflect the views of their owners in their editorials on economic and political matters. In the news columns, however, the complete and unbiased facts should be reported. The better metropolitan newspapers and the great press associations usually can be relied on to keep their news impartial. But the less ethical publications often deliberately "color" the news to favor or oppose certain groups or movements.

48. The author states that no modern newspaper _____.
   (A) is free of propaganda
   (B) separates fact and opinion
   (C) is controlled by big business interests
   (D) operates according to a code of ethics

49. According to the passage, all daily newspapers _____.
   (A) have an editorial page
   (B) tend to ignore their code of ethics
   (C) are operated by an unbiased publisher
   (D) are supported by a big industrial organization

50. According to the journalistic code of ethics, a newspaper must _____.
    (A) accept only responsible advertisers
    (B) separate editorials from news
    (C) refrain from interpreting news according to its editorial viewpoint
    (D) determine what the reader should know about the news

51. According to the passage, a newspaper publisher may use the editorial page to support _____.
    (A) only the cause which is most popular
    (B) any cause supported by the advertisers
    (C) any cause he believes in
    (D) only the cause of the owners

52. When news is often mixed with editorial opinion, the reader may assume that the _____.
    (A) paper is a member of a large press association
    (B) paper's ethical standards are suspect
    (C) paper is in financial trouble
    (D) paper upholds the journalistic code of ethics

53. Newspapers have entered the category of large business organizations because of _____.
    (A) their influence on the reading public
    (B) their reports of stock market activity
    (C) the millions of copies sold daily
    (D) the tremendous costs of its establishment and operation

54. The word "color" in the last sentence most nearly means _____.
    (A) dye   (B) bias
    (C) describe   (D) reverse

Part B

VI. Combine the following items or sentences into a
statement using the suggested phrases in the
parentheses. Add or delete words if necessary. 12%

1. (a) zeppelin and mackintosh
   (b) An invention sometimes becomes known by the name
       of its inventor.
       (such ... as) (good examples of the fact that)

2. (a) A literary character occasionally adds a new
       word to the English language.
   (b) The Spanish character Don Quixote gave us the
       word quixotic.
       (can be illustrated)

3. (a) Some people, through their bad deeds, live on in
       the language long after they have died.
   (b) Vidkun Quisling was a Norwegian politician who
       betrayed his country.
       (such a person as) (exemplifies)

私立淡江大學八十七學年度
碩士班研究生入學考試英文試題詳解

I. 字彙：20%

1. (**A**) (A) ***inaccessibility*** 〔,ɪnæk,sɛsə'bɪlətɪ 〕 *n.* 很難到達
    (B) lack 〔 læk 〕 *n.* 缺乏
    (C) inefficiency 〔 ,ɪnə'fɪʃənsɪ 〕 *n.* 無效率
    (D) insufficiency 〔 ,ɪnsə'fɪʃənsɪ 〕 *n.* 不足
    object 〔 əb'dʒɛkt 〕 *v.* 反對
    vigorously 〔 'vɪgərəslɪ 〕 *adv.* 強烈地
    county 〔 'kaʊntɪ 〕 *n.* 縣；郡
    considerable 〔 kən'sɪdərəbḷ 〕 *adj.* 相當大的

2. (**D**) (A) painful 〔 'penfəl 〕 *adj.* 痛苦的
    (B) wearisome 〔 'wɪrɪsəm 〕 *adj.* 令人疲倦的
    (D) ***pleasurable*** 〔 'plɛʒərəbḷ 〕 *adj.* 令人愉快的
    perform 〔 pɚ'fɔrm 〕 *v.* 做（工作）
    return 〔 rɪ'tɝn 〕 *n.* 收入；利益

3. (**A**) (A) ***futile*** 〔 'fjutḷ 〕 *adj.* 徒勞的
    (B) tardy 〔 'tɑrdɪ 〕 *adj.* 遲緩的
    (C) fulfill 〔 fʊl'fɪl 〕 *v.* 實現；滿足
    (D) mimicking 〔 'mɪmɪkɪŋ 〕 *adj.* 模仿的
    attempt 〔 ə'tɛmpt 〕 *n.* 嘗試

4. (**D**) (A) roughly 〔 'rʌflɪ 〕 *adv.* 粗魯地；大約
    (B) wildly 〔 'waɪldlɪ 〕 *adv.* 瘋狂地
    (C) abruptly 〔 ə'brʌptlɪ 〕 *adv.* 突然地
    (D) ***secretly*** 〔 'sikrɪtlɪ 〕 *adv.* 秘密地
    on the sly 秘密地
    sly 〔 slaɪ 〕 *n.* 秘密；狡猾

5. (**C**) (A) ambition〔æm'bɪʃən〕*n.* 抱負
　　　(B) strength〔strɛŋθ〕*n.* 力量
　　　(C) ***exhausted***〔ɪg'zɔstɪd〕*adj.* 筋疲力盡的
　　　(D) troubled〔'trʌbḷd〕*adj.* 煩惱的
　　　　enervated〔ɪ'nɝvɪtɪd〕*adj.* 無力的

6. (**B**) (A) benevolent〔bə'nɛvələnt〕*adj.* 慈善的
　　　(B) ***unsympathetic***〔ˌʌnsɪmpə'θɛtɪk〕*adj.* 無情的
　　　(C) incorrigible〔ɪn'kɔrɪdʒəbḷ〕*adj.* 固執的；根深蒂固的
　　　　callous〔'kæləs〕*adj.* 無情的

7. (**D**) (A) conducive〔kən'djusɪv〕*adj.* 有益的
　　　(B) contagious〔kən'tedʒəs〕*adj.* 傳染性的
　　　(C) advantageous〔ˌædvən'tedʒəs〕*adj.* 有利的
　　　(D) ***inimical***〔ɪn'ɪmɪkḷ〕*adj.* 有害的
　　　　reliance〔rɪ'laɪəns〕*n.* 依賴
　　　　mechanical devices 機械裝置

8. (**A**) (A) ***docile***〔'dɑsɪl〕*adj.* 溫順的
　　　(C) rebellious〔rɪ'bɛljəs〕*adj.* 反叛的
　　　(D) indomitable〔ɪn'dɑmətəbḷ〕*adj.* 不屈不撓的
　　　　citizenry〔'sɪtəzṇrɪ〕*n.* 公民
　　　　intellectual〔ˌɪntḷ'ɛktʃʊəl〕*n.* 知識分子
　　　　agitate〔'ædʒəˌtet〕*v.* 煽動；鼓動

9. (**D**) (A) regulate〔'rɛgjəˌlet〕*v.* 管制；調整
　　　(B) reinstate〔ˌriɪn'stet〕*v.* 復職
　　　(C) relegate〔'rɛləˌget〕*v.* 降級調職
　　　(D) ***rejuvenate***〔rɪ'dʒuvəˌnet〕*v.* 使恢復青春活力

10. (**C**) (A) heretic〔'hɛrətɪk〕*n.* 異教徒
　　　　　(B) fugitive〔'fjudʒətɪv〕*n.* 逃亡者
　　　　　(C) *recluse*〔rɪ'klus〕*n.* 隱士
　　　　　(D) veteran〔'vɛtərən〕*n.* 退伍軍人

11. (**D**) (A) visualize〔'vɪʒʊəl,aɪz〕*v.* 想像
　　　　　(B) jeopardize〔'dʒɛpəd,aɪz〕*v.* 使陷入危險
　　　　　(C) dissect〔dɪ'sɛkt〕*v.* 分析；解剖
　　　　　(D) *scrutinize*〔'skrutn̩,aɪz〕*v.* 仔細觀察
　　　　　　bug〔bʌg〕*n.* 小蟲

12. (**A**) (A) *discernible*〔dɪ'sɝnəbl̩〕*adj.* 可辨別的
　　　　　(B) despicable〔'dɛspɪkəbl̩〕*adj.* 卑鄙的
　　　　　(C) detestable〔dɪ'tɛstəbl̩〕*adj.* 非常令人討厭的
　　　　　(D) delectable〔dɪ'lɛktəbl̩〕*adj.* 令人愉快的

13. (**D**) (A) imperative〔ɪm'pɛrətɪv〕*adj.* 緊急的；必須的
　　　　　(B) impervious〔ɪm'pɝvɪəs〕*adj.* 不透（水、空氣等）的
　　　　　(C) impertinent〔ɪm'pɝtn̩ənt〕*adj.* 魯莽的；無禮的
　　　　　(D) *impartial*〔ɪm'parʃəl〕*adj.* 公平的；無偏見的
　　　　　　reputation〔,rɛpjə'teʃən〕*n.* 名聲

14. (**D**) (B) discourage〔dɪs'kɝɪdʒ〕*v.* 使氣餒
　　　　　(C) reduce〔rɪ'djus〕*v.* 減少
　　　　　(D) *undermine*〔,ʌndɚ'maɪn〕*v.* 暗中破壞
　　　　　　bribe〔braɪb〕*n.* 賄賂　　　fixer〔'fɪksɚ〕*n.* 仲介人
　　　　　　integrity〔ɪn'tɛgrətɪ〕*n.* 正直

15. (**C**) (A) compromising〔'kɑmprə,maɪzɪŋ〕*adj.* 妥協的
　　　　　(B) indiscreet〔,ɪndɪ'skrit〕*adj.* 輕率的
　　　　　(C) *persuasive*〔pɚ'swesɪv〕*adj.* 有說服力的
　　　　　(D) emotional〔ɪ'moʃənl̩〕*adj.* 感情的
　　　　　　convert〔kən'vɝt〕*v.* 改變

16. (**B**) (A) inadvertent〔͵ɪnəd'vɝtn̩t〕*adj.* 不注意的；偶然的

    (B) *impromptu*〔ɪm'prɑmptu〕*adj.* 即席的

    (C) contigent〔kən'tɪndʒənt〕*adj.* 附帶的；偶然的

    (D) propaganda〔͵prɑpə'gændə〕*n.* 宣傳

17. (**D**) (A) manifest〔'mænə͵fɛst〕*adj.* 顯然的

    (B) sheer〔ʃɪr〕*adj.* 全然的；陡峭的

    (C) exclusive〔ɪk'sklusɪv〕*adj.* 除外的；獨享的

    (D) *rustic*〔'rʌstɪk〕*adj.* 鄉村的；粗野的

       folk〔fok〕*n.* 人（= *people*）

18. (**D**) (A) transfix〔træns'fɪks〕*v.* 刺穿

    (B) stabilize〔'stebl̩͵aɪz〕*v.* 使穩定

    (C) temporize〔'tɛmpə͵raɪz〕*v.* 拖延；順應時勢

    (D) *synchronize*〔'sɪnkrə͵naɪz〕*v.* 對（鐘錶的）時間

19. (**D**) (A) desolate〔'dɛsl̩ɪt〕*adj.* 荒涼的

    (B) vigorous〔'vɪgərəs〕*adj.* 精力充沛的

    (C) picturesque〔͵pɪktʃə'rɛsk〕*adj.* 風景如畫的；生動的

    (D) *conspicuous*〔kən'spɪkjuəs〕*adj.* 顯然的；引人注目的

       parachute〔'pærə͵ʃut〕*n.* 降落傘

20. (**C**) (A) flock〔flɑk〕*n.*（鳥）群；（羊）群

    (B) herd〔hɝd〕*n.*（牛）群

    (C) *swarm*〔swɔrm〕*n.*（昆蟲）群

    (D) drove〔drov〕*n.*（驅趕中的）成群的家畜

       fly〔flaɪ〕*n.* 蒼蠅

II. 同義字：10%

21. (**C**) ostensible〔as'tɛnsəbl̩〕*adj.* 明顯的
    (A) gaudy〔'gɔdɪ〕*adj.* 俗麗的
    (B) stubborn〔'stʌbən〕*adj.* 頑固的
    (C) *apparent*〔ə'pɛrənt〕*adj.* 明顯的
    (D) elastic〔ɪ'læstɪk〕*adj.* 有彈性的

22. (**B**) imminent〔'ɪmənənt〕*adj.* 即將來臨的
    (A) hazardous〔'hæzədəs〕*adj.* 危險的
    (B) *impending*〔ɪm'pɛndɪŋ〕*adj.* 即將發生的
    (C) astounding〔ə'staundɪŋ〕*adj.* 令人震驚的
    (D) disastrous〔dɪz'æstrəs〕*adj.* 災難性的；極不幸的

23. (**D**) wanderer〔'wandərə〕*n.* 流浪者
    (A) immigrant〔'ɪmə,grænt〕*n.*（自外國移入的）移民
    (B) pedestrian〔pə'dɛstrɪən〕*n.* 行人
    (C) pilgrim〔'pɪlgrɪm〕*n.* 朝聖者
    (D) *vagabond*〔'vægə,band〕*n.* 流浪者

24. (**D**) trifling〔'traɪflɪŋ〕*adj.* 微不足道的；無關緊要的
    silly〔'sɪlɪ〕*adj.* 愚蠢的
    (A) pertinent〔'pɝtnənt〕*adj.* 有關係的；中肯的
    (B) sardonic〔sar'danɪk〕*adj.* 諷刺的
    (C) tentative〔'tɛntətɪv〕*adj.* 暫時的
    (D) *frivolous*〔'frɪvələs〕*adj.* 微不足道的；無價值的

25. (**D**) required〔rɪ'kwaɪrd〕*adj.* 必須的
    (A) perfunctory〔pə'fʌŋktərɪ〕*adj.* 敷衍的；表面的
    (B) paramount〔'pærə,maunt〕*adj.* 至高的；卓越的
    (C) methodical〔mə'θadɪkl̩〕*adj.* 有方法的
    (D) *mandatory*〔'mændə,tɔrɪ〕*adj.* 強制性的

26. (**B**) depart from 背離

   differ〔ˈdɪfɚ〕v. 不同

   (A) convert〔kənˈvɝt〕v. 使轉變

   (B) *deviate*〔ˈdivɪˌet〕v. 背離

   (C) alternate〔ˈɔltɚˌnet〕v. 輪流；互相交替

   (D) fluctuate〔ˈflʌktʃʊˌet〕v. 起伏；波動

27. (**B**) genuine〔ˈdʒɛnjʊɪn〕adj. 真正的

   reliable〔rɪˈlaɪəbl〕adj. 可靠的

   (A) substantial〔səbˈstænʃəl〕adj. 實質的

   (B) *authentic*〔ɔˈθɛntɪk〕adj. 真正的

   (C) feasible〔ˈfizəbl〕adj. 可實行的

   (D) tangible〔ˈtændʒəbl〕adj. 實體的；有形的

28. (**C**) pensive〔ˈpɛnsɪv〕adj. 沉思的

   (A) obstinate〔ˈɑbstənɪt〕adj. 頑固的

   (B) lustful〔ˈlʌstfəl〕adj. 渴望的；好色的

   (C) *thoughtful*〔ˈθɔtfəl〕adj. 沈思的

   (D) fanciful〔ˈfænsɪfəl〕adj. 奇特的；想像的

29. (**C**) to deny an opportunity 別人不給機會

   deny〔dɪˈnaɪ〕v. 拒絕給予

   (A) feature〔ˈfitʃɚ〕n. 容貌；特徵

   (B) in operation 實行中

   (C) *hold back a privilege* 保留特權

      hold back 扣留；保留

      privilege〔ˈprɪvlɪdʒ〕n. 特權；優待

30. (**D**) the general run of things 事情的普遍運作過程
　　　　run〔rʌn〕n. 運作；路程
　　　　(A) to withdraw from life 與世隔絕
　　　　　　withdraw〔wɪθ'drɔ〕v. 撤退
　　　　(B) a method of study 學習的方法
　　　　(C) to be determined about 決定
　　　　(D) *usual course of event* 事件的普遍發展過程

Ⅲ. 完成句子：5%

31. (**D**) 查爾斯·艾微斯放棄普利茲獎的獎金，因為他認為只要有這項
　　　　榮譽就足夠了。
　　　　give away 放棄　　*Pulitzer Prize* 普利茲獎
　　　　award〔ə'wɔrd〕n. 獎　　vast〔væst〕adj. 巨大的
　　　　regard〔rɪ'gɑrd〕n. 尊敬

32. (**A**) 能將想法付諸行動者，未來必有許多榮耀。
　　　　crown〔krɑʊn〕n. 王冠；榮耀
　　　　match〔mætʃ〕v. 使一致
　　　　ambitiously〔æm'bɪʃəslɪ〕adv. 有抱負地

33. (**D**) 那些退伍軍人住院一年，後來他們出院時，就完全康復了。
　　　　veteran〔'vɛtərən〕n. 退伍軍人
　　　　emerge〔ɪ'mɝdʒ〕v. 出來

34. (**B**) 儘管他擁有財富，他卻不快樂。
　　　　* for all「儘管」，其後須接名詞或名詞片語，不可接句子。
　　　　riches〔'rɪtʃɪz〕n.pl. 財富
　　　　merry〔'mɛrɪ〕adj. 快樂的

35. (**C**) 現代的車不同於以往，可以開得較快，而且不會有危險。

IV. 選出同義的句子：5%

36.（**A**）專心沒有什麼特殊訣竅，也不需要任何訣竅。

　　　　trick〔trɪk〕*n.* 訣竅

　　　　concentrate〔'kɑnsn̩‚tret〕*v.* 專心

37.（**D**）地理方面的因素與生活方式有關。

　　　　have something to do with 與～有關

　　　　physical〔'fɪzɪkl̩〕*adj.* 自然的

　　　　given〔'gɪvən〕*adj.* 特定的

　　　　locality〔lo'kælətɪ〕*n.* 地區；位置

38.（**C**）勘察新的公路地點非常困難，因為地形崎嶇不平。

　　　　survey〔sə've〕*v.* 勘察

　　　　rugged〔'rʌgɪd〕*adj.* 崎嶇不平的

　　　　terrain〔tɛ'ren〕*n.* 地形

　　　　moisture〔'mɔɪstʃ ＞〕*n.* 濕度

　　　　rough〔rʌf〕*adj.* 崎嶇不平的

39.（**C**）學生所面臨的問題之一，就是要認清什麼是該知道的，將之存入記憶中，以備不時之需。

　　　　adjust〔ə'dʒʌst〕*v.* 適應

　　　　apply〔ə'plaɪ〕*v.* 應用

　　　　procedure〔prə'sidʒ ＞〕*n.* 程序

　　　　instructor〔ɪn'strʌktə˞〕*n.* 教師

40.（**D**）改變的過程就是，在我們還沒預料到會對社會造成什麼影響時，發明就先推出了。

　　　　be bound to 一定

　　　　resolve *oneself* ***into*** 使變成

V. 閱讀測驗：28%

【譯文】

　　房子裏沒有書，就如同房間內沒有窗戶一樣。有財力買書，而不讓書圍繞著子女的人，沒有權利養育他的子女。有錢而不肯買書給子女讀是不對的。孩子們要有書在他們面前，才能學會讀書。對知識的愛來自於讀書，並因讀書而逐漸熱愛讀書。在年輕人的心中，對知識的愛，幾乎就是免於熱情與罪惡的次等刺激之保證。

【答案】

　　41.（ **A** ）　　　42.（ **C** ）　　43.（ **C** ）　　44.（ **C** ）

【註】

surround〔səˋraʊnd〕v. 使圍繞
in the presence of 在～面前
grow upon ～ 對～有愈來愈大的影響
warrant〔ˋwɔrənt〕n. 保證
inferior〔ɪnˋfɪrɪɚ〕adj. 次等的　　　vice〔vaɪs〕n. 罪惡
cite〔saɪt〕v. 引用　　　***appeal to*** 訴諸
sentiment〔ˋsɛntəmənt〕n. 感情
generalization〔͵dʒɛnərəlaɪˋzeʃən〕n. 概論
propaganda〔͵prɑpəˋgændə〕n. 宣傳活動

【譯文】

　　我認為你理所當然，可以真的非常有信心地看待未來。因為我們發現，你的生活方式，是將生活中的樂趣與工作的快樂，很和諧地結合在一起。除此之外，你的人生中充滿抱負的精神，似乎能使你一天的工作，變成像是在玩耍中的快樂小孩。

【答案】

45.（ **D** ）　　46.（ **B** ）　　47.（ **D** ）

【註】

be justified in 做～是理所當然的

assurance〔əˈʃʊrəns〕*n.* 信心

harmoniously〔hɑrˈmonɪəslɪ〕*adv.* 和諧地

pervade〔pɚˈved〕*v.* 瀰漫；充滿

being〔ˈbiɪŋ〕*n.* 存在；生存　　***at play*** 玩耍

evaluate〔ɪˈvæljʊˌet〕*v.* 評估　　term〔tɝm〕*v.* 稱為

cynical〔ˈsɪnɪkḷ〕*adj.* 諷刺的憤世嫉俗的

dogmatic〔dɔgˈmætɪk〕*adj.* 武斷的

neutral〔ˈnjutrəl〕*adj.* 中立的；公平的

【譯文】

　　就算是最公平、最不偏私的報紙，也會淪為宣傳的工具。每份日報都有社論。在社論中，報社表達對新聞中的事件及人物的看法。但是因為社論中的評斷，非常具有說服力，所以有很多人，就把報社的意見，看作是事實。好的新聞從業人員會遵守道德規範，將新聞及社論區別開來。這種道德規範中規定，報紙的出版業者，有權利在社論專欄中，提倡其所支持的理想。一般人都可理解，出版者可在社論中，以某黨派的支持者身份發表看法，表達出他所想表達的意見。因為現代的報紙已逐漸成為大型的商業組織。儘管有少數例外，但許多大型的報社，常會在社論中，反映其擁有者，對於政治與經濟事務的看法。但是，在新聞專欄中，應該完整報導出不偏不倚的事實。比較好的大都會中的報紙，以及大型的新聞協會，通常較值得信賴，能公正地報導新聞。但是比較沒有道德的出版業者，則常會刻意「渲染」新聞，以支持或反對某些團體或活動。

【答案】

48. (**A**)　49. (**A**)　50. (**C**)　51. (**C**)　52. (**B**)
53. (**C**)　54. (**B**)

【註】

impartial〔ɪm'parʃəl〕*adj.* 公正的；不偏坦的
medium〔'midɪəm〕*n.* 工具；媒體
editorial〔͵ɛdə'tɔrɪəl〕*adj.* 社論的　*n.* 社論
personality〔͵pɜsn̩'ælətɪ〕*n.* 人物
journalist〔'dʒɜnl̩ɪst〕*n.* 新聞工作者
uphold〔ʌp'hold〕*v.* 支持　　*code of ethics* 道德規範
column〔'kaləm〕*n.* 專欄　　*be entitled to* 有權利~
advocate〔'ædvə͵ket〕*v.* 提倡　cause〔kɔz〕*n.* 理想
partisan〔'partəzn̩〕*n.* (黨派的) 支持者
unbiased〔ʌn'baɪəst〕*adj.* 無偏見的；公平的
metropolitan〔͵mɛtrə'palətn̩〕*adj.* 大都會的
color〔'kʌlɚ〕*v.* 渲染；扭曲報導　　favor〔'fevɚ〕*v.* 支持；贊同
suspect〔'sʌspɛkt〕*adj.* 值得懷疑的
stock market 股巾　bias〔'baɪəs〕*v.* 使有偏見

VI. 完成句子：12%

1. Words such as zeppelin and mackintosh are good
   examples of the fact that an invention sometimes
   becomes known by the name of its inventor.

   有些發明會以發明者的名字為大家所熟知，像是齊柏林式飛船以及
   麥金塔這些字都是很好的例子。

   zeppelin〔'zɛpəlɪn〕*n.* 齊柏林式飛船 (因德籍發明者 Zeppelin 得名)
   mackintosh〔'mækɪn͵taʃ〕*n.* 橡膠布雨衣 (因發明者英國人 Charles
   　 Mackintosh 的姓而得名)

2. That a literary character occasionally adds a new word to the English language can be illustrated by the Spanish character Don Quixote, who gave us the word quixotic.

文學作品中的物有時會增加英文字的字彙，例如西班牙人物 Don Quixote（唐吉軻德），就給了我們 quixotic 這個字。

character〔'kærɪktɚ〕n. 人物
illustrate〔'ɪləstret〕v. 舉例證明
Don Quixote〔,dɑnkɪ'hotɪ〕n. 唐吉軻德〔西班牙作家塞凡提斯（Cervantes）諷刺小說中的人物〕
quixotic〔kwɪks'ɑtɪk〕adj. 唐吉軻德式的；幻想的；不實際的

3. Such person as Vidkun Quisling, a Norwegian politician who betrayed his country, exemplifies that some people, through their bad deeds, live on in the language long after they have died.

有些人因其惡劣的行為，在死後很久，仍存活在語言中，像是挪威的政客 VidKun Quisling，就是很好的例子。

quisling〔'kwɪzlɪŋ〕n. 賣國賊；內奸（源自挪威政客 Vidkun Quisling，1887-1945，因賣國投向納粹德國，被立為挪威傀儡政府之首領。）
Norwegian〔nɔr'widʒən〕adj. 挪威的
politician〔,pɑlə'tɪʃən〕n. 政客
betray〔bɪ'tre〕v. 出賣；背叛
exemplify〔ɪg'zɛmplə,faɪ〕v. 例證
deed〔did〕n. 行為

心得筆記欄

國立台灣大學八十五學年度
碩士班研究生入學考試英文試題

Choose the BEST answer. Blacken the appropriate space on your computer card for each question to indicate your choice.

Example: It was Joan's first visit to the country, and everything was fresh and_____to her.
(A) dull　　　　　　　　(B) quickly
(C) new　　　　　　　　 (D) excite
(E) familiar

Answer :　　A　　B　　C　　D　　E

I. Vocabalary/Grammar/Usage: 40%

Choose the best answer to fill in the blank.

1. The environmental_____of these chemicals went unrecognized for many years.
(A) force　　　　　　　　(B) impression
(C) power　　　　　　　　(D) impact
(E) control

2. I couldn't attend the meeting because the date_____with my holidays.
(A) opposed　　　　　　　(B) clashed
(C) occurred　　　　　　　(D) struck
(E) jumped

3. The tennis player couldn't_____the possibility of withdrawing from the championship because of injury.
(A) do without　　　　　　(B) pass over
(C) come off　　　　　　　(D) put on
(E) rule out

4. This new advertising campaign is not_____with our company policy.
(A) consistent　　　　　　(B) congenial
(C) matched　　　　　　　(D) helping
(E) allied

5. Recent surveys have focused_____on the nation's health.
(A) responsibility　　　　　(B) tension
(C) direction　　　　　　　(D) ideas
(E) attention

6. Children may be difficult to teach because of their short attention_____.
   (A) time　　　　　　　(B) distance
   (C) span　　　　　　　(D) duration
   (E) limit

7. Passengers are_____not to leave their cases and packages here unattended.
   (A) forbidden　　　　(B) forfeited
   (C) advocated　　　　(D) advised
   (E) allowed

8. All the applicants for the job are thoroughly_____ for their suitability.
   (A) instructed　　　(B) searched
   (C) voted　　　　　　(D) dismissed
   (E) scrutinized

9. Because of road construction, traffic is restricted to one_____in each direction.
   (A) alley　　　　　　(B) street
   (C) lane　　　　　　　(D) row
   (E) line

10. The famous director expressed his_____for certain kinds of cheaply produced movies.
    (A) distaste　　　　(B) dispute
    (C) disagreement　　(D) display
    (E) disloyalty

11. He was deaf to everything_____than what he wanted to hear.
    (A) except　　　　　(B) besides
    (C) other　　　　　 (D) else
    (E) apart

12. In his absence, I would like to thank all concerned on my brother's_____.
    (A) business　　　　(B) part
    (C) interest　　　　(D) behalf
    (E) side

13. When I finally got my suitcase back from the airport, it had been damaged_____repair.
    (A) above　　　　　　(B) beyond
    (C) over　　　　　　 (D) further
    (E) under

14. I am afraid that you will be_____responsible if
    anything goes wrong.
    (A) brought   (B) carried
    (C) forgiven   (D) taken
    (E) held

15. The young man was_____of shoplifting by the
    court.
    (A) convicted   (B) condemned
    (C) accused   (D) concluded
    (E) disobeyed

16. If you_____too long, you may miss a wonderful
    opportunity.
    (A) hesitate   (B) insist
    (C) suspect   (D) loiter
    (E) hurry

17. It is regretted that there can be no_____to this rule.
    (A) exclusion   (B) alternative
    (C) exception   (D) example
    (E) deviation

18. The government clearly had not the slightest_____of
    changing the legislation, in spite of the continued
    protest from the public.
    (A) mood   (B) emotion
    (C) intention   (D) ambition
    (E) mind

19. He has an excellent_____as a criminal lawyer.
    (A) circulation   (B) notion
    (C) regard   (D) reputation
    (E) honor

20. The dealer wanted to sell the camera for $4000, I wanted
    to pay $3000, and we finally agreed to_____the differ-
    ence.
    (A) drop   (B) give up
    (C) decrease   (D) increase
    (E) split

II. Paraphrase: 10%

Choose the answer that best keeps the meaning of the underlined words.

Tom Dolan's accomplishments in swimming are remarkable, despite his physical limitations. At 20, he is already world champion and world-record holder in the demanding 400-meter individual (21)<u>medley</u>, which requires 100 meters each of butterfly, backstroke, breast stroke and freestyle. He has been twice voted U.S. Swimmer of the Year. But Tom is the perfect swimmer in an imperfect swimming machine. He has this most improbable trouble: he has difficulty breathing. He was born with a narrow windpipe, which at times reduces his oxygen (22)<u>intake</u> to 20 percent of normal, and his breathing problems are compounded by (23)<u>exercise-induced</u> asthma and allergies.

With the Olympic trials looming, Dolan dropped out of college for the fall semester, enabling him to ignore distractions like classes. Left to his own designs, he (24) <u>practically lived in the pool</u>, swimming 18,000 meters--almost 12 miles--a day. Dolan's blasé attitude may simply reflect how much he has already overcome. Almost all medications that might help his breathing contain substances that are illegal under swimming's stringent (25)<u>doping rules</u>. So Dolan is left to rely on his inhaler, which he always keeps poolside. The question in future will be whether he has preserved enough of his spirit so that he can pursue his Olympic dream in Atlanta.

21. (A) performance   (B) race
    (C) combination of items   (D) competition
    (E) long-distance swim

22. (A) acceptance   (B) intention
    (C) instant   (D) mistake
    (E) increase

23. (A) prevented from doing exercise
    (B) cured by doing exercise
    (C) injured by doing exercise
    (D) generated by doing exercise
    (E) reduced from doing exercise

24. (A) actually lived in the pool
    (B) spent almost all his time swimming
    (C) lived in a tent beside the pool
    (D) ate and slept by the pool
    (E) lived next door to the pool

25. (A) IQ tests   (B) rules of competition
    (C) dress codes   (D) pool manners
    (E) regulations of drug usage

III. Cloze Test: 30%

Choose the best answer to fill in the blank.

___26___to ourselves, we should look for the most reasonable ways to work them out. For some of us, just___27___
our problem with a sympathetic friend or adviser helps to
clear the air. It can often help to relieve any feelings of
guilt we have about our own disagreeable thoughts and
feelings___28___others experience similar feelings. ___29___
of group discussions which give people a chance to exchange
ideas and viewpoints that lead to insights and better understanding. ___30___may be eased by an open exchange in a relaxed atmosphere.

26. (A) In spite of keeping all worries and tensions
    (B) In order to keep all worries and tensions
    (C) Besides keeping all worries and tensions
    (D) Instead of keeping all worries and tensions
    (E) All worries and tensions should be kept

27. (A) talking with   (B) talking over
    (C) talking in   (D) talking out
    (E) talking for

28. (A) whoever we discover that
    (B) than we discover that
    (C) where we discover that
    (D) that we discover
    (E) when we discover that

29. (A) This is one of the values
    (B) One of the values is
    (C) In which one of the values
    (D) So that one of the values
    (E) Even if one of the values

30. (A) Young people's conflicts and their parents
    (B) Conflicting young people and their parents
    (C) Conflicts between young people and their parents
    (D) Parents' conflicts and their young people
    (E) Between young people and their parents' conflicts

Today items of clothing, hundreds at a time, all the same size, style, and color, 31 the assembly line in rapid succession. Soon new technology will change all that. New laser machines will produce any item of clothing 32 cheaply and quickly than the old mass-production methods. 33 you will be able to contact a clothing manufacturer by phone and give your personal measurements and preferences to a computer. A laser machine will produce exactly the kind of clothing you want for little or no extra cost. The days of standardized sizes of clothing will 34 . In fact, factories may be able to produce many products, such as cars and furniture, with the style, size, and color you prefer, just 35 the factory computer.

31. (A) come with   (B) come without
    (C) come off   (D) come up
    (E) come in

32. (A) one at a time more
    (B) more than one at a time
    (C) once in a while more
    (D) more at times
    (E) from time to time more

33. (A) Since the day will come
    (B) When the day will come
    (C) Come a day when
    (D) Will the day come when
    (E) The day will come when

34. (A) someday belong to the past
    (B) belong to the past a day
    (C) that day belong to the past
    (D) be past someday
    (E) belong to the past tense

35. (A) by you call up   (B) by you calling up
    (C) by your call up   (D) by your calling up
    (E) by calling you up

    Insomnia is usually caused by a ____36____ of the natural sleep rhythm. The reasons are many and they ____37____ from drugs that are being taken to treat a separate medical condition to anxiety. A sudden change in life-style or climate could do it, or just that you've fallen into the habit of ____38____ for forty winks in front of the television.

    Certainly the body must have enough sleep. Tests that ____39____ people of sleep have proved lack of it can cause fairly rapid physical and mental deterioration. But on the other hand, it doesn't need too much. So if you're sleeping in front of the TV, you won't sleep soundly at night. Similarly, if you're holidaying in Hawaii, and spending your days sleeping on the beach, ____40____ that you'll be wide awake at bedtime.

36. (A) degeneration   (B) disruption
    (C) apprehension   (D) contention
    (E) alteration

37. (A) measure   (B) reinforce
    (C) range   (D) proportion
    (E) ration

38. (A) dozing off   (B) slouching off
    (C) lagging off   (D) dreaming off
    (E) idling off

39. (A) deviated   (B) depreciated
    (C) depressed   (D) devastated
    (E) deprived

40. (A) then most likely   (B) notwithstanding
    (C) despite the fact   (D) chances are
    (E) it is unlikely

IV. Reading Comprehension: 20%

Read the passage carefully, then choose the best answer to each question.

The prevention of child abuse is a difficult and multifaceted task. The importance of preventing it, however, cannot be overemphasized, because the physical and psychological consequences of abuse can be very serious. Child abuse can result not only in physical handicaps but also in severe neurological problems. A blow to the head can cause bleeding inside a child's skull, ultimately leading to brain damage. What is particularly surprising and disturbing is that infants, whose skulls are much larger than their brains (which are still growing) can suffer hemorrhages throughout the brain simply by being shaken. Known as the *shaken baby syndrome,* this form of abuse can cause brain damage as well as visual problems and deficits in language and motor skills.

Besides the neurological consequences of abuse, abused children also suffer from disturbances in emotional and social development. They have learned from their home life that their involvement with other people carries with it a great deal of pain, and they tend to be inhibited and socially unresponsive, often backing away when a friendly caregiver or another child approaches them. Such children have also been found to be overly compliant or to exhibit violent and aggressive behavior toward adults and peers. Some abused children are "hypervigilant," meaning that they are constantly on the lookout for danger, scanning the environment and ever-ready to attack. A variety of underlying processes may account for such behavior among abused children. It may well be the case that because of the ill treatment they have received, these children failed to develop the social skills required to engage in harmonious social interactions. Or, they may be imitating the hostile interpersonal exchanges that they have experienced.

41. The prevention of child abuse is a difficult and multifaceted task,
    (A) therefore we should not do anything at all.
    (B) and all we need to do is to simplify it and make it manageable.
    (C) yet our efforts turn out to be in vain no matter how hard we have tried.
    (D) however, it is a necessary evil in the character development of children.
    (E) but we still have to do our best to prevent children from getting harmed.

42. "Hypervigilant" children
    (A) are ever-ready to welcome people.
    (B) have a greater chance of achievement.
    (C) are usually hyperactive.
    (D) have better awareness of danger.
    (E) have more concern for the living environment.

43. According to this passage, abused children generally
    (A) have difficulty interacting with people.
    (B) are more adjusted to difficult situations.
    (C) are better trained to take challenges.
    (D) are encouraged to fight for their own future.
    (E) are prone to engage in harmonious social interactions.

44. The author's purpose in this passage is
    (A) to tell another story of child abuse.
    (B) to evaluate the importance of child development.
    (C) to give new information about a social problem.
    (D) to analyze the social issue of child abuse.
    (E) to arouse human sympathy in readers.

45. The main idea in this passage is that
    (A) the problem of child abuse is easy to prevent so long as we understand the consequences.
    (B) abused children are constantly on the lookout for danger.
    (C) abused children suffer from disturbances in social and emotional development.

 (D) *shaken baby syndrome* is abuse characterized by brain damage and other problems.
 (E) the physical and psychological consequences of child abuse are very serious.

 Once I found myself in the house of a famous living poet without at first realizing it. It was in wartime England, in the summer of 1944. I was travelling from my home in Edinburgh to my job in the Foreign Office, my department of which was in a county outside London. In the train I sat next to a girl who was also going back to her job. She was a mother's helper, she told me, in a professor's family. The train arrived with five hours' delay, too late for me to cross London and make my connection to the county. My new friend asked me to come and spend the night with her at the house where she worked; her employers were away, she said.

 It was a warm summer evening, still light enough to see the small, tangled garden in front of the house. We entered a large room almost entirely filled by a long worktable of plain wood, just such a table as I myself always write on now. The place was generally unconventional. I thought, at first, unnecessarily so. It looked like eccentricity for its own sake. One room had nothing but a mattress-bed on the floor. There was a handsome writing desk and a marvellous library of books. It was a decidedly literary collection. I began looking through the titles.

 I found two of the books, and then more, inscribed by famous novelists. Another was dedicated to a famous poet, and so was yet another. I called upstairs to my friend, who was now having a bath. "Is this the house of a famous poet?" "Yes," she called out, "he writes poetry."

 The famous poet was Matthew Arlington, whose work I loved and admired tremendously. I was rather embarrassed when

I found myself in Matthew Arlington's house. I made my new friend assure me there was no likelihood of his return that night. I saw the house with new eyes, the functional rightness and nobility of all it held.

I ran outside to look at the house from the point of view of my new knowledge. I had never met a real poet. I have always known that this occasion vitally strengthened my resolve to become a writer.

46. How did the author come to spend the night at the poet's house?
 (A) It was too late to go back to Edinburgh.
 (B) She thought it sounded an interesting place to visit.
 (C) She had arranged to stay there with a friend.
 (D) She didn't have anywhere to stay in London.
 (E) She couldn't complete her journey to her workplace.

47. When she found out that the house belonged to a famous poet,
 (A) she began reading his poems.
 (B) she wanted to leave.
 (C) she was eager to meet him.
 (D) she was taken by surprise.
 (E) she understood certain aspects of the house.

48. How did the visit affect her later life?
 (A) It established her as a writer.
 (B) It determined her career.
 (C) It changed her views on poetry.
 (D) She decided to become a poet.
 (E) She wanted to become famous.

49. What, for the author, was exciting about the house she visited?
 (A) The unconventional house made her feel embarrassed.
 (B) The poet's presence could be sensed from his possessions.
 (C) The house had been visited by so many famous people.
 (D) The poet's possessions were on display for the public.
 (E) The exterior of the house was unusual.

50. Which of the following statements is probably not
    correct?
    (A) The famous poet planned to be home that very night.
    (B) The author had read the works of the poet before.
    (C) The house was a two-story home.
    (D) The employer of the author's new friend was a
        professor.
    (E) At present the author uses a writing table similar
        to one found in the house she visited.

國立台灣大學八十五學年度
碩士班研究生入學考試英文試題詳解

I. 字彙、文法與用字：40％

1. (**D**) (A) force〔fɔrs〕*n.* 力量
　　　　(B) impression〔ɪm'prɛʃən〕*n.* 印象
　　　　(C) power〔'pauɚ〕*n.* 動力；力量
　　　　(D) ***impact***〔'ɪm͵pækt〕*n.* 影響
　　　　(E) control〔kən'trol〕*n.* 控制
　　　　　　unrecognized〔ʌn'rɛkəg͵naɪzd〕*adj.* 未經承認的

2. (**B**) (A) oppose〔ə'poz〕*v.* 反對
　　　　(B) ***clash***〔klæʃ〕*v.* 衝突
　　　　(C) occur〔ə'kɝ〕*v.* 發生
　　　　(D) strike〔straɪk〕*v.* 打擊；使想起
　　　　(E) jump〔dʒʌmp〕*v.* 跳躍

3. (**E**) (A) cannot do without 不能沒有
　　　　(B) pass over 經過　　　(C) come off （鈕扣）脫落
　　　　(D) put on 穿上；增加　　(E) ***rule out*** 排除
　　　　　　withdraw〔wɪð'drɔ〕*v.* 退出
　　　　　　championship〔'tʃæmpɪən͵ʃɪp〕*n.* 錦標賽
　　　　　　injury〔'ɪndʒərɪ〕*n.* 傷

4. (**A**) (A) ***consistent***〔kən'sɪstənt〕*adj.* 符合的；前後一致的
　　　　　　be consistent with ～ 與～符合
　　　　(B) congenial〔kən'dʒinjəl〕*adj.* 性格相同的
　　　　　　be congenial to ～ 與～意氣相投
　　　　(C) match〔mætʃ〕*v.* 相配（不加 with ）
　　　　(D) help〔hɛlp〕*v.* 幫助（不加 with ）
　　　　(E) ally〔ə'laɪ〕*v.* 聯合；結合　be allied with 與～聯盟
　　　　　　campaign〔kæm'pen〕*n.* 活動

5. (**E**) (A) responsibility〔rɪˌspɑnsəˈbɪlətɪ〕 *n.* 責任
   (B) tension〔ˈtɛnʃən〕 *n.* 緊張
   (C) direction〔dəˈrɛkʃən〕 *n.* 方向
   (D) idea〔aɪˈdiə〕 *n.* 主意；想法
   (E) *attention*〔əˈtɛnʃən〕 *n.* 注意
   survey〔səˈve〕 *n.* 調查　　focus〔ˈfokəs〕 *v.* 集中
   focus attention on ～　集中注意力於～

6. (**C**) (A) time *n.* 時間（無 attention time 的用法）
   (B) distance〔ˈdɪstəns〕 *n.* 距離
   (C) *span*〔spæn〕 *n.* 精神活動之持續時間
   attention span 集中注意力的時間
   (D) duration〔djʊˈreʃən〕 *n.* （時間的）持續；持久
   (E) limit〔ˈlɪmɪt〕 *n.* 限制

7. (**D**) (A) forbid〔fəˈbɪd〕 *v.* 禁止
   (B) forfeit〔ˈfɔrfɪt〕 *v.* 喪失
   (C) advocate〔ˈædvəˌket〕 *v.* 提倡
   (D) *advise*〔ədˈvaɪz〕 *v.* 勸告
   (E) allow〔əˈlaʊ〕 *v.* 允許
   unattended〔ˌʌnəˈtɛndɪd〕 *adj.* 無人照顧的

8. (**E**) (A) instruct〔ɪnˈstrʌkt〕 *v.* 教導
   (B) search〔sɝtʃ〕 *v.* 尋找
   (C) vote〔vot〕 *v.* 投票
   (D) dismiss〔dɪsˈmɪs〕 *v.* 解散
   (E) *scrutinize*〔ˈskrutəˌnaɪz〕 *v.* 詳細審查
   suitability〔ˌsutəˈbɪlətɪ〕 *n.* 適合

9. (**C**) (A) alley〔ˈælɪ〕 *n.* 小巷　　(C) *lane*〔len〕 *n.* 車道
   (D) row〔ro〕 *n.* 排　　(E) line〔laɪn〕 *n.* 線

10. (**A**) 　(A) *distaste* 〔 dɪsˋtest 〕 *n.* 嫌惡
　　　　　(B) dispute 〔 dɪˋspjut 〕 *n.* 爭論
　　　　　(C) disagreement 〔 ͵dɪsəˋgrimənt 〕 *n.* 意見不合
　　　　　(D) display 〔 dɪˋsple 〕 *n.* 展示
　　　　　(E) disloyalty 〔 dɪsˋlɔɪəltɪ 〕 *n.* 不忠

11. (**C**) 　*other than* 除了～　　be deaf to ～ 不聽～

12. (**D**) 　(A) business 〔 ˋbɪznɪs 〕 *n.* 事務
　　　　　(B) part 〔 pɑrt 〕 *n.* 部分
　　　　　(C) interest 〔 ˋɪnt(ə)rɪst 〕 *n.* 興趣
　　　　　(D) *behalf* 〔 bɪˋhæf 〕 *n.* 代替　　*on one's behalf* 代替～
　　　　　(E) side 〔 saɪd 〕 *n.* 方面

13. (**B**) 　*beyond repair* 無法修理的

14. (**E**) 　*hold sb. responsible for* ～ 要某人為～負責

15. (**A**) 　(A) *convict* 〔 kənˋvɪkt 〕 *v.* 判定
　　　　　　　convict sb. of ～ 判定某人犯～罪
　　　　　(B) condemn 〔 kənˋdɛm 〕 *v.* 譴責
　　　　　　　condemn *sb.* for *sth.* 為～而譴責某人
　　　　　(C) accuse 〔 əˋkjuz 〕 *v.* 指控
　　　　　　　accuse *sb.* of ～ 控告某人～罪
　　　　　(D) conclude 〔 kənˋklud 〕 *v.* 下結論
　　　　　(E) disobey 〔 ͵dɪsəˋbe 〕 *v.* 不服從
　　　　　　　shoplifting 〔 ˋʃɑp͵lɪftɪŋ 〕 *n.* 順手牽羊
　　　　　　　court 〔 kɔrt 〕 *n.* 法院

16. (**A**) 　(A) *hesitate* 〔 ˋhɛzə͵tet 〕 *v.* 猶豫
　　　　　(B) insist 〔 ɪnˋsɪst 〕 *v.* 堅持
　　　　　(C) suspect 〔 səˋspɛkt 〕 *v.* 懷疑
　　　　　(D) loiter 〔 ˋlɔɪtɚ 〕 *v.* 閒蕩
　　　　　(E) hurry 〔 ˋhɝɪ 〕 *v.* 匆忙

17. (**C**) (A) exclusion〔ɪk'skluʒən〕*n.* 排除；除外
   (B) alternative〔ɔl'tɝnətɪv〕*n.* 選擇
   (C) ***exception***〔ɪk'sɛpʃən〕*n.* 例外
   (D) example〔ɪg'zæmpḷ〕*n.* 例子
   (E) deviation〔͵divɪ'eʃən〕*n.* 脫軌

18. (**C**) (A) mood〔mud〕*n.* 心情
   (B) emotion〔ɪ'moʃən〕*n.* 情緒
   (C) ***intention***〔ɪn'tɛnʃən〕*n.* 意圖；打算
   (D) ambition〔æm'bɪʃən〕*n.* 抱負
   (E) mind〔maɪnd〕*n.* 心智
   　legislation〔͵lɛdʒɪs'leʃən〕*n.* 立法；法令

19. (**D**) (A) circulation〔͵sɝkju'leʃən〕*n.* 循環；發行量
   (B) notion〔'noʃən〕*n.* 概念
   (C) regard〔rɪ'gɑrd〕*n.* 關心；注意
   (D) ***reputation***〔͵rɛpjə'teʃən〕*n.* 聲譽
   (E) honor〔'ɑnɚ〕*n.* 榮譽
   　criminal lawyer 刑事律師

20. (**E**) (A) drop〔drɑp〕*v.* 落下
   (B) give up 放棄
   (C) decrease〔dɪ'kris〕*v.* 減少
   (D) increase〔ɪn'kris〕*v.* 增加
   (E) ***split***〔splɪt〕*v.* 分攤　　***split the difference*** 互相讓步

II. 意譯：10 ％

【譯文】

　　儘管湯姆・多倫在生理方面受到某些限制，但他在游泳方面卻有著令人矚目的成就。二十歲時，他已是高難度的個人四百公尺混合式的世界冠軍與世界紀錄保持人。混合式要求必須以蝶式、仰式、蛙式和自由式各游一百公尺。他曾經兩度被選為美國年度最佳游泳選手。

而湯姆是不完美游泳機器中的完美選手。他有令人難以置信的毛病：呼吸困難。湯姆天生氣管就特別狹窄，有時候會使他吸入的氧氣量減少，少到只有正常人的百分之三十，而且他的呼吸問題還包含了由運動引發的氣喘和過敏。

　　由於奧運預賽即將來臨，多倫在大學上學期時辦理休學，以使他能不去在意像課業那些會使他分心的事物。湯姆不受任何的約束，他幾乎是住在游泳池裏，一天游一萬八千英尺──差不多十二英里。多倫這種刻苦耐勞的態度，反映出他所克服的種種困難。幾乎所有能幫他於改善呼吸問題的藥物，都含有在嚴格的游泳禁藥規定下，不合法的物質。所以多倫只能依靠一直放在游泳池畔的呼吸器。未來的問題在於他是否能秉持一貫的精神，以追求他的亞特蘭大奧運之夢。

【註】

remarkable〔rɪˋmɑrkəbḷ〕*adj.* 引人注目的
demanding〔dɪˋmændɪŋ〕*adj.* 過分要求的
butterfly〔ˋbʌtɚˏflaɪ〕*n.* 蝶式
backstroke〔ˋbækˏstrok〕*n.* 仰式　　***breast stroke*** 蛙式
freestyle〔ˋfriˏstaɪl〕*n.* 自由式　　windpipe〔ˋwɪndˏpaɪp〕*n.* 氣管
compound〔kɑmˋpaʊnd〕*v.* 混合
asthma〔ˋæsmə〕*n.* 氣喘　　allergy〔ˋælədʒɪ〕*n.* 過敏
trial〔ˋtraɪəl〕*n.* 預賽　　loom〔lum〕*v.* 逼近　　***drop out*** 輟學
distraction〔dɪˋstrækʃən〕*n.* 使分心的事物
be left to *one's* ***own designs*** 不受任何約束
designs〔dɪˋzaɪnz〕*n.pl.* 目的　　blase〔blɑˋze〕*adj.* 厭倦於享樂的
stringent〔ˋstrɪndʒənt〕*adj.* 嚴格的　　inhaler〔ɪnˋhelɚ〕*n.* 吸入器

21.（ **C** ）medley〔ˋmɛdlɪ〕*n.* 混合式
　　　　（C）item〔ˋaɪtəm〕*n.* 項目

22.（ **A** ）intake〔ˋɪnˏtek〕*n.* 吸入
　　　　（A）***acceptance***〔əkˋsɛptəns〕*n.* 接受；收納
　　　　（B）intention〔ɪnˋtɛnʃən〕*n.* 意圖；打算
　　　　（C）instant〔ˋɪnstənt〕*adj.* 立即的

23. (**D**) exercise-induced〔`ˈɛksɚˌsaɪz ɪnˈdjust`〕*adj.* 運動引起的
　　　　(C) injure〔`ˈɪndʒɚ`〕*v.* 傷害
　　　　(D) generate〔`ˈdʒɛnəˌret`〕*v.* 引起

24. (**B**) practically lived in the pool 幾乎是住在泳池裏

25. (**E**) doping rules 用藥規定
　　　　(C) dress codes 服裝規定　　　code〔`kod`〕*n.* 規定
　　　　(E) 用藥規定　　　regulation〔`ˌrɛgjəˈleʃən`〕*n.* 規定

Ⅲ. 克漏字：30%

【譯文】

　　我們應該找尋最合理的方式來解決問題，而不要只把憂慮和緊張留給自己。對某些人來說，只要與富有同情心的朋友或顧問談論問題，就可以助其消除疑慮。當我們發現別人也有過和我們類似的感受時，常有助於減輕自己很討厭的想法和感覺所產生的罪惡感。這就是團體討論的價值之一。團體討論能提供人們一個交換意見和觀點的機會，使我們擁有洞察力並對問題有更深入的了解。父母與子女之間的衝突，在輕鬆的氣氛下，可藉由坦然交換意見而較為緩和。

【註】

reasonable〔`ˈriznəbl`〕*adj.* 合理的　　　***work out*** 解決（問題）
clear the air 消除誤解；澄清疑慮
disagreeable〔`ˌdɪsəˈgriəbl`〕*adj.* 討厭的
insight〔`ˈɪnˌsaɪt`〕*n.* 洞察力

26. (**D**) (A) in spite of 儘管　　(B) in order to 為了～
　　　　(C) besides 除了～之外，還有…
　　　　(D) ***instead of*** 而不要　　　tension〔`ˈtɛnʃən`〕*n.* 緊張

27. (**B**) 依句意，選 (B) ***talk over*** 討論。而 (A) talk with 與～交談，
　　　　(D) talk out 談個明白，皆不合句意。(C)、(E) 無此用法。

28. (**E**)　依句意，選 (E) *when we discover that ~* 　當我們發現~。

29. (**A**)　依句意，「這就是集體討論的價值之一」，選 (A)。

30. (**C**)　「父母與子女之間的衝突」可較為緩和，選 (C)。

今日的服裝，一次好幾百件，同樣的大小、款式和顏色，都是由連續不斷快速運作的裝配線製造出來。再過不久，新的科技會改變這一切。新的雷射機器能一次製造一件衣服，比古老的大量生產的方法更快更便宜。到時候就可以用電話和服飾製造商聯絡，把個人的尺寸和喜好輸入電腦。雷射機器會製造出你所想要的服裝，而只要一點點或者根本不需要付額外的費用。服裝尺寸規格化的時代將成為過去。事實上，工廠可能可以製造出許多你比較喜歡的款式、大小和顏色的產品，像是汽車和傢俱，只要打通電話給工廠的電腦就可以了。

【註】

assembly line 裝配線　　　*in succession* 連續地

laser 〔 ′lezɚ 〕 *n.* 雷射

mass-production 〔 ′mæsprə′dʌkʃən 〕 *n.* 大量生產

standardized 〔 ′stændɚˌdaɪzd 〕 *adj.* 規格化的

31. (**C**)　依句意，選 (C) *come off* 自~離開。而 (A) come with 和~一起來，(D) come up 上升，(E) come in 進來，皆不合句意。(B) 則無此用法。

32. (**A**)　依句意，「一次製造一件，而且更快更便宜」，選 (A) *one at a time more* cheaply and quickly …。而 (C) once in a while 偶爾，(D) at times 有時候，(E) from time to time 有時候，皆不合句意。

33. (**E**)　when 引導表「時間」的副詞子句，其中動詞須用現在式代替未來式，故 (B)，(D) 不合。依句意，選 (E) *The day will come when*。

34. (**A**) 依句意,「將來有一天規格化的時代將成爲過去」,選 (A)
The days of standardized sizes of clothing will *someday belong to the past*。

35. (**D**) by 爲介系詞,其後須接受詞,而 calling up 爲動名詞片語,
可用所有格修飾,故依句意,選 (D) *by your calling up*。

失眠通常是由於自然的睡眠規律被擾亂所引起。失眠的原因很多,
從爲治療特定疾病所服用的藥物,到焦慮都有。生活方式或氣候突然
改變,或是你有在電視機前打瞌睡的習慣,也都會造成失眠。

身體當然需要充足的睡眠。有些剝奪人們睡眠的實驗,其結果證
實,缺乏睡眠會使人身心狀況急速惡化。但是另一方面,人們並不需
要太多睡眠。所以如果你在電視前睡著,那你晚上就無法睡得很熟。
同樣地,如果你在夏威夷度假,白天在沙灘上睡覺,很可能你在就寢
時間就會非常清醒。

【註】

insomnia〔ɪn'samnɪə〕*n.* 失眠　　rhythm〔'rɪðəm〕*n.* 節奏;規律
separate〔'sɛpərɪt〕*adj.* 個別的　　anxiety〔æŋ'zaɪətɪ〕*n.* 焦慮
forty winks 小睡　　deterioration〔dɪˌtɪrɪə'reʃən〕*n.* 惡化

36. (**B**) *disruption*〔dɪs'rʌpʃən〕*n.* 混亂
　　(A) degeneration〔dɪˌdʒɛnə'reʃən〕*n.* 墮落
　　(C) apprehension〔ˌæprɪ'hɛnʃən〕*n.* 了解;憂慮
　　(D) contention〔kən'tɛnʃən〕*n.* 爭論
　　(E) altercation〔ˌɔltə'keʃən〕*n.* 口角

37. (**C**) *range from ~ to …* 範圍從~到…都有
　　而 (A) 測量,(B) reinforce〔'riɪnˌfors〕*v.* 加強,(D) 比例,
　　(E) ration〔'reʃən〕*v.* 分配,皆不合句意。

38. (**A**) 依句意,選 (A) *doze off* 打瞌睡。而 (B) slouch〔slaʊtʃ〕*v.* 垂
頭彎腰地坐,(C) lag〔læg〕*v.* 延遲;落後,(E) idle〔'aɪdl̩〕*v.* 鬼
混,皆不合句意。

39. (**E**)　***deprive sb. of ~***　剝奪某人的~
　　(A) deviate〔ˈdivɪˌet〕*v.* 偏離
　　(B) depreciate〔diˈpriʃɪˌet〕*v.* 貶值
　　(C) depress〔dɪˈprɛs〕*v.* 使沮喪；使蕭條
　　(D) devastate〔ˈdɛvəsˌtet〕*v.* 毀壞

40. (**D**)　***chances are that ~***　很有可能~
　　(B) notwithstanding〔ˌnɑwɪθˈstændɪŋ〕*prep. , adv.* 儘管

Ⅳ. 閱讀測驗：20 %

【譯文】

　　防止兒童受虐是項艱鉅且多方面的工作，然而其重要性再怎麼強調也不爲過，因爲虐待會對兒童的身心造成重大的影響。虐待兒童不只會造成身體上的殘障，也會產生嚴重的神經方面的問題。重擊頭部可能會造成孩子的頭內出血，因而導致大腦受損。特別令人驚訝且憂心的是，嬰兒的頭顱比腦大了許多（腦還在生長），只要受到搖晃，整個腦就可能會出血。這種虐待就是大家所熟知的「嬰兒搖晃徵候群」，會造成腦部受損、產生視覺問題，以及語言能力和運動技能的不足。

　　虐待除了會造成神經上的影響，也會妨礙受虐兒在情感和社交方面的發展。他們從家庭生活中學習到與人相處時，常會伴隨許多痛苦。因此受虐兒常會壓抑自己，在與人交往時沒什麼反應。通常當別人友善地照顧他們或有其他小孩接近時，他們都會退縮。受虐兒通常會非常順從別人，或是會對成人或同儕表現出暴力和侵略性的行爲。有些受虐兒會「過度警戒」，也就是他們會一直提高警覺，注意危險，審視周遭環境，而且隨時準備好要攻擊別人。各種潛在的過程都可以解釋受虐兒的這種行爲。我們很有理由相信，受虐兒是因爲受到虐待，才會使他們無法培養和諧的人際關係所需要的社交技巧。或者，受虐兒可能模仿了其所經歷的那種充滿敵意的與人交往的模式。

【答案】
　　41. (**E**)　　42. (**D**)　　43. (**A**)　　44. (**D**)　　45. (**E**)

【註】

multifaceted〔͵mʌltɪˈfæsətɪd〕*adj.* 多方面的

handicap〔ˈhændɪ͵kæp〕*n.* 殘障　　severe〔səˈvɪr〕*adj.* 嚴重的

neurological〔͵njʊrəˈlɑdʒɪkḷ〕*adj.* 神經的

skull〔skʌl〕*n.* 頭顱　　　hemorrhage〔ˈhɛmərɪdʒ〕*n.* 出血

syndrome〔ˈsɪn͵drom〕*n.* 徵候群　　deficit〔ˈdɛfəsɪt〕*n.* 不足

motor〔ˈmotɚ〕*adj.* 運動的　　inhibited〔ɪnˈhɪbɪtɪd〕*adj.* 受抑制的

caregiver〔ˈkɛrˈgɪvɚ〕*n.* 給予關心的人

overly〔ˈovəlɪ〕*adv.* 非常；過度地

compliant〔kəmˈplaɪənt〕*adj.* 順從的

aggressive〔əˈgrɛsɪv〕*adj.* 侵略性的　　peer〔pɪr〕*n.* 同儕

hypervigilant〔͵haɪpɚˈvɪdʒələnt〕*adj.* 過度警戒的

on the lookout 注意；警戒　　scan〔skæn〕*v.* 審視

underlying〔͵ʌndɚˈlaɪɪŋ〕*adj.* 根本的；潛在的

hostile〔ˈhɑstɪl〕*adj.* 有敵意的

manageable〔ˈmænɪdʒəbḷ〕*adj.* 易於管理的

hyperactive〔͵haɪpɚˈæktɪv〕*adj.* 極為活躍的

【譯文】

　　有一次我發現自己置身在一位當代著名的詩人家裏，但起初我並不知道。那是在一九四四年的夏天，戰時的英格蘭。我正要從位於愛丁堡的家前往外交部上班。我所屬的部門是位於倫敦郊外的一郡。搭火車時，我坐在一位女孩隔壁，她也是要回去上班。她告訴我，她是一位教授家裏的女傭。火車延誤五個小時才到達，所以我已經來不及經過倫敦，趕上開往那個郡的車子。我的新朋友要我到她雇主家裏過夜；她說她老闆不在。

　　那是個暖和的夏夜，光線還夠亮，可以看到屋前那個小小的、枝葉纏繞的花園。我們進入一間大房間，房間幾乎完全被一張很長的原木工作桌所佔滿，就像我自己現在用來寫字用的這張桌子。整個看來，這間房子十分與眾不同。起初我認為沒必要這樣。似乎這房間本身就讓人覺得有點古怪。有間房間裏面只有一張放在地上的床墊、一張漂亮的書桌和許多藏書。這些書顯然都是一些文學作品。我開始瀏覽書名。

　　我發現有兩本書，接著又發現更多本，全都是著名小說家所簽名贈送的書。有一本是獻給一位十分著名的詩人，另一本也是。我對正在樓上洗澡的朋友喊道：「這間是不是一位著名詩人的房子？」她大聲答道：「是啊，他寫詩。」

　　這位名詩人就是馬休‧阿靈頓，我熱愛他的作品而且十分欽佩他。當我發現自己身在馬休‧阿靈頓的房子裏時，我感到相當尷尬。我要我的新朋友保證當晚他絕不會回來。我用新的眼光來看待這個房子，這房子的一切是那麼實用、合適，並且高貴。

　　我跑到屋外，以我最新了解到的觀點看著它。我從未遇到過真正的詩人。我一直深信，就是這次的經歷，使我想成為作家的決心更加堅定。

【答案】

　　46.（ **E** ）　　47.（ **E** ）　　48.（ **B** ）　　49.（ **B** ）　　50.（ **A** ）

【註】

Edinburgh（'ɛdən,bɝo）*n.* 愛丁堡（蘇格蘭首府）
tangled（'tæŋgḷd）*adj.* 纏繞的；糾結的
unconventional（,ʌnkən'vɛnʃənḷ）*adj.* 不落俗套的
eccentricity（,ɛksən'trɪsɪtɪ）*n.* 古怪
for one's own sake 為了~　　mattress（'mætrɪs）*n.* 床墊
decidedly（dɪ'saɪdɪdlɪ）*adv.* 明確地；無疑地
inscribe（ɪn'skraɪb）*v.* 把…（書寫上姓名）贈送給~
be dedicated to 題獻給~
tremendously（trɪ'mɛndəslɪ）*adv.* 非常地
likelihood（'laɪklɪ,hʊd）*n.* 可能性
functional（'fʌŋkʃənḷ）*adj.* 實用的　　rightness（'raɪtnɪs）*n.* 合適
vitally（'vaɪtəlɪ）*adv.* 極重要地　　resolve（rɪ'zɑlv）*n.* 決心
be taken by surprise 大吃一驚
establish（ə'stæblɪʃ）*v.* 就任；開業　　presence（'prɛzəns）*n.* 存在
possessions（pə'zɛʃənz）*n.pl.* 所有物

國立清華大學八十五學年度
碩士班研究生入學考試英文試題

I. Vocabulary: 20%

Part One: Select the word that <u>best</u> completes the meaning of the sentence as a whole.

1. Leftist rebels killed 31 soldiers in an_____on an army patrol early Tuesday in Colombia's southwestern province of Narino.
   (A) anguish   (B) avalanche
   (C) ambush   (D) alteration

2. A Los Angeles jury Wednesday recommended life in prison without the possibility of_____for the Menendez brothers for the 1989 shotgun slayings of their wealthy parents.
   (A) probation   (B) parole
   (C) promotion   (D) permission

3. The Senate_____approved an anti-terrorism bill Wednesday, two days before the anniversary of the Oklahoma City bombing. Congress is trying to fulfill President Clinton's request to give him the bill before the bombing's one-year anniversary.
   (A) accidentally   (B) overwhelmingly
   (C) incidentally   (D) scarcely

4. A 62-year-old gunman, whose name wasn't immediately _____, critically injured a security guard and slightly injured two employees.
   (A) dissolved   (B) dispelled
   (C) disclosed   (D) disposed

5. The Justice Department has defended the widespread practice of_____the property of convicted drug dealers as an important weapon in the narcotics war.
   (A) confiscating   (B) complimenting
   (C) contradicting   (D) comprehending

6. Two Marines who refused to give blood samples for a DNA registry were found guilty Tuesday of disobeying a lawful order. They were_____and placed on seven days restriction to base.
   (A) suspected   (B) apprehended
   (C) recommended   (D) reprimanded

7. The Duke and Duchess of York are to divorce and necessary
   legal_____are under way.
   (A) propositions　　　　　　(B) precedings
   (C) proceedings　　　　　　 (D) provisions

8. A Kansas man identified by the FBI as a member of the
   anti-government Freemen group was being held Wednesday
   on explosives charges as the_____in Montana entered
   its 24th day.
   (A) compromise　　　　　　 (B) standoff
   (C) embargo　　　　　　　　(D) campaign

9. The leader of Liberian rebels holding hostages at a
   military camp packed with refugees is considering an
   offer of_____from Nigeria.
   (A) asylum　　　　　　　　 (B) negotiation
   (C) sanction　　　　　　　 (D) extradition

10. The Chinese dishes served at those restaurants in the
    U.S. are not_____; that is, they don't taste like real
    Chinese food.
    (A) acquisitive　　　　　　(B) authoritative
    (C) authentic　　　　　　　(D) autocratic

Part Two: For each numbered blank, choose the one word which
         is most appropriate. Each of the words should be
         used exactly once.

It was an evening to___11___but not the one expected.
Dressed in dinner jackets and formal gowns, 450 elite,
mostly foreign business people and diplomats___12___on
Beijing's Holiday Inn Lido for a sold-out banquet that
promised a five-course dining extravaganza and exciting
raffles. The___13___was to raise money for Chinese orphans.
But an hour before dinner, 40 Chinese security___14___
descended on the five-star hotel's grand ballroom and pro-
nounced the event___15___because it did not have a permit.
Authorities, who were still___16___from last January's
Human Rights Watch/Asia report, which alleged rampant abuse
of children in Shanghai's state-run orphanage, did not want
the subject___17___up again. The police, though,___18___
allowed the fete to continue as long as there was no raffle

and no speeches--not even the scheduled keynote by Chinese-
American author Amy Tan. Said one ___19___ : "These thugs must
have suspected that a political trick was planned when they
heard the buzzword___20___."

AB. event	AC. illegal	AD. remember
AE. converged	BC. police	BD. smarting
BE. orphanage	CD. grudgingly	CE. brought
DE. attendee		

II. Grammar. Identify the one word or phrase that <u>should be
corrected or rewritten.</u> 20%

21. If I <u>tell</u> him <u>the truth</u>, he may never <u>speak</u> to me again.
　　　A　　　　　B　　　　　　　　　C

<u>On the contrary</u>, he may thank me later.
　　　D

22. The university in the small town has <u>clearer</u> <u>focusing</u>
　　　　　　　　　　　　　　　　　　　　　A　　　B

and orientation <u>in</u> <u>its</u> academic programs.
　　　　　　　　　C　　D

23. Classes are small, <u>and it allowing</u> a lot of contact
　　　　　　　　　　　　　　A

<u>among</u> all the members of <u>the community</u>, often in the
　B　　　　　　　　　　　　　　C

professor's home <u>after class</u>.
　　　　　　　　　　D

24. I don't get angry easily, enjoy <u>being</u> around people <u>like</u>
　　　　　　　　　　　　　　　　　　　A　　　　　　　　　B

my own age, find young children <u>a little irritating</u>, and
　　　　　　　　　　　　　　　　　C

<u>would rather</u> spend time at a party than in a library.
　D

25. <u>In these respects</u> my twin feels <u>the same like me</u>. But
　　　A　　　　　　　　　　　　　　B

my twin likes loud music and <u>modern dances</u>, <u>while</u> I find
　　　　　　　　　　　　　　C　　　　　D

that nightclubs give me a headache.

26. I have discovered three rules <u>with</u> <u>making friends</u> in a
　　　　　　　　　　　　　　　　　A　　　　B
foreign country. My first rule is that you should say
<u>the opposite</u> of <u>what</u> you really feel.
　　　C　　　　　　D

27. For example, when I first arrived, I was tired and
uncomfortable, but I <u>realized</u> that when people asked me
　　　　　　　　　　　　　A
<u>how I was getting along</u>, they <u>only really</u> wanted to hear
　　　　　　B　　　　　　　　　　　　C
how <u>excited</u> I was and how pleasant everything was.
　　　D

28. My second rule is never <u>to show</u> enthusiasm <u>for anything</u>
　　　　　　　　　　　　　A　　　　　　　　B
<u>unless</u> after I find out <u>if it is fashionable.</u>
　　C　　　　　　　　　　D

29. My third rule is to <u>suppose</u> that people know nothing
　　　　　　　　　　A
about me or my home city. I <u>have grown tired of</u> telling
　　　　　　　　　　　　　　　　B
people that I do not ride a horse to work, that I keep
my food in the refrigerator, that I have electricity
<u>in my house</u>, and that there are <u>streets and traffic</u>
　　C　　　　　　　　　　　　　　D
lights in my town.

30. I eventually got to <u>high school</u>, and <u>surprising</u> enough,
　　　　　　　　　　A　　　　　　B
the most positive influence <u>on</u> my life was a group of
　　　　　　　　　　　　　　C
wild friends <u>I met there.</u>
　　　　　　D

31. In my country, <u>most of people</u> were very conservative and
　　　　　　　　A
believed that getting along with others, <u>even if</u> it meant
　　　　　　　　　　　　　　　　　　B
<u>ignoring</u> one's own feelings, was <u>of primary importance.</u>
　C　　　　　　　　　　　　　D

32. They studied, but <u>instead of</u> accepting the <u>moderate</u> and
    　　　　　　　　　　　　　A　　　　　　　　　　　　　　B
    uninteresting interpretations of the teachers, they
    asked questions that often <u>irritating</u> those <u>in charge of</u>
    　　　　　　　　　　　　　　　C　　　　　　　　　　　D
    <u>the school</u>.

33. Rather than <u>following</u> all the socially accepted <u>norms</u>,
    　　　　　　　　　A　　　　　　　　　　　　　　　　　　B
    like dressing prettily and saying all the polite things,
    we developed more honest friendships and were quite
    frank, sometimes <u>almost insulting</u>, when we <u>disagreed to</u>
    　　　　　　　　　　　C　　　　　　　　　　　　　　D
    <u>people</u>.

34. Fossil fuel <u>resources</u> in the United States are running
    　　　　　　　　A
    out faster than nuclear fuels can <u>substitute</u> them, and
    　　　　　　　　　　　　　　　　　　　B
    the <u>growing</u> reliance on nuclear fuels <u>could be</u> dangerous
    　　　　C　　　　　　　　　　　　　　　　　　D
    and environmentally damaging.

35. <u>For the present</u>, the U.S. energy industry is <u>firmly</u>
    　　A
    <u>structured around</u> petroleum, and it <u>is likely to</u>
    　　B　　　　　　　　　　　　　　　　　C
    <u>remaining</u> that way for some time.
    　　D

36. Not only is natural gas the cheapest and <u>most</u> versatile
    　　　　　　　　　　　　　　　　　　　　　A
    fossil fuel <u>available</u> but, perhaps <u>most important</u>, it is
    　　　　　　　B　　　　　　　　　　C
    also the <u>less</u> polluting.
    　　　　　D

37. <u>Opposition to</u> nuclear power plants <u>on environmental</u>
    　A　　　　　　　　　　　　　　　　B
    <u>ground</u> has <u>led to</u> bitter dispute <u>over</u> their siting and
    　　　　　　C　　　　　　　　D
    delays in their construction.

38. The remaining problems <u>require</u> concerted effort <u>as well</u>
    　　　　　　　　　　　　　A　　　　　　　　　　　　　　B
    <u>as</u> a substantial <u>amount</u> of money for exploration and
    　　　　　　　　　　　C
    <u>technology</u> development.
    　　D

39. <u>In response to</u> <u>persistently</u> questioning of plant safety,
    　　　A　　　　　　　　B
    Schlesinger <u>argued</u> that the <u>chance</u> of a catastrophic
    　　　　　　　　　C　　　　　　　　D
    accident was "virtually zero."

40. After I <u>got out of</u> the plane and walked to <u>customs</u>, I
    　　　　　A　　　　　　　　　　　　　　　　　　　　B
    got in the line that said "Citizens Only" because I
    <u>didn't understand</u> what they said, and then had to go
    　　　　C
    <u>all the way</u> back through the other line.
    　　D

III. Reading Comprehension. Read each of the following
     passages and choose the one best answer for each
     question. 20%

A.
　　For two millennia, an intellectual divide separated
scholars' views of the natural world, one essentially
Platonic, the other Aristotelian. On the Aristotelian side,
mechanists said that living organisms are "nothing but
machines," and are completely explicable by the laws of
mechanics, physics, and chemistry. Platonics agreed that
living organisms obeyed these physical laws, but insisted
that the essence of life itself was something extra, a vital
force breathed into mere material. To vitalists, therefore,
many of the more interesting properties of organisms were,
by their nature, beyond scientific analysis.

　　By the early decades of this century, the mechanists
had prevailed, for two reasons. First, because scientific
discovery had shown repeatedly that properties of organisms

that previously were considered inexplicable indeed had
mechanistic explanations. And second, mechanists had moved
away from the strict "nothing but machines" position to
accepting that living and nonliving objects were indeed
different. The differences resided in the organization of
physical material, so that organisms possessed properties
not shared by nonliving objects. Mainstream biology therefore
became essentially mechanistic.

41. What is this reading mainly about?
    (A) explanation in science
    (B) Plato and Aristotle
    (C) the problems with mechanism
    (D) the struggle between two views of living things

42. If science could not explain many important character-
    istics of living things, this would
    (A) be evidence for the Platonic view.
    (B) be evidence for the Aristotelian view.
    (C) not provide any evidence.
    (D) indicate that the debate is confused.

43. The phrase "nothing but machines" describes whose view
    of living organisms?
    (A) mechanists
    (B) early mechanists
    (C) Platonists
    (D) mainstream biologists

B.
    One difficulty with the idea of a static universe is
that each star in the universe ought to be attracted towards
every other star. If so, how could they stay motionless, at
a constant distance from each other? Wouldn't they all fall
together? Newton was aware of this problem. In a letter to
Richard Bentley, a leading philosopher of the time, he
agreed that a *finite* collection of stars could not remain
motionless; they would all fall together to some central
point. However, he argued, an infinite collection of stars
would not fall together, for there would not be any central
point for them to fall to. This argument is an example of

the pitfalls that one can encounter when one talks about
infinite systems. By using different ways to add up the
forces on each star from the infinite number of other stars
in the universe, one can get different answers to the question of whether the stars can remain at constant distances
from each other. We now know that the correct procedure is
to consider the case of a *finite* region of stars, and then
to add more stars, distributed roughly uniformly outside the
region. A finite collection of stars will fall together, and
adding more stars outside the region will not stop the collapse. Thus, an infinite collection of stars cannot remain
in a motionless state. If they are not moving relative to
each other at one time, the attraction between them will
cause them to start falling towards each other. Alternatively, they can be moving away from each other, with gravity
slowing down the velocity of the recession.

44. What is this reading mainly about?
    (A) a problem with the idea that the universe doesn't
        change
    (B) proper calculation of gravitational forces
    (C) the expanding universe
    (D) the static universe

45. The author says the idea that an infinite collection of
    stars could stay in fixed positions
    (A) is right.
    (B) is wrong.
    (C) was rejected by Newton.
    (D) is still controversial.

46. What does the word recession in the last line mean?
    (A) moving away   (B) slowing down
    (C) speeding up   (D) attraction

C.
    In a tradition-filled country like Japan, where scores
of ancient festivals dot the calendar, the Sapporo Snow
festival, begun in 1950, is something of a Johnny-come-
lately to the cultural scene. Its popularity, however, is

none the worse for it. During its relatively short existence,
in fact, this seven-day event has grown steadily in both
size and scope to become the country's largest wintertime
celebration. Today, about two million people attend the
annual show to marvel at the luminous displays of more than
300 creations painstakingly hewn by hand from snow and ice.
A festival in honor of the snow seems only too fitting in
this sub-frigid zone where winter holds an icy grip for up
to six months each year.

47. Which of the following would be the most appropriate
    title for the article?
    (A) Japan's Largest Festival
    (B) The Sapporo Snow Festival
    (C) The Origins of the Sapporo Snow Festival
    (D) Winter in Japan

48. The author suggests that the Sapporo Snow festival
    (A) is a Japanese tradition.
    (B) should be held in Tokyo.
    (C) is relatively new in Japan.
    (D) is not very popular.

49. How long does the festival last?
    (A) one week
    (B) six months
    (C) a full year
    (D) The article does not say.

50. According to the article, the festival includes
    (A) various traditional cultural activities.
    (B) performances of Japanese drama.
    (C) ice and snow sculpting.
    (D) skiing.

IV. Translation: 20%

Part One: Translate the following passage into Chinese. 10%

    While the hazards of pesticide exposure have been un-
derstood for decades, the warnings have been ignored by
skeptics unable to grasp the urgency of the problem. It has
now escalated to the point of presenting a threat to the

future of mankind. Exposure-related issues such as decreasing
sperm counts and fetal abnormalities are affecting humans
and other species. Nowhere are the genetic consequences more
readily seen than in the post-Vietnam War era. Only the naive
may find comfort in thoughts of a golden future; the decline
of man has begun.

Part Two: Translate the following passage into English. 10%

解嚴後，觀念上威權解體是師生關係之間第一波的衝擊。許多教師發現，
今日的學生與「我們那一代」不同了。他們有話要說，勇於表達，而且
方式強烈、直接，「不知道如何對待學生」，是不少教師心頭或多或少
的結。

V. English Composition. Write an English composition
(approximately 100-150 words) on the following subject.
20%

The effect of electronic communications (the Internet)
on modern life.

國立清華大學八十五學年度
碩士班研究生入學考試英文試題詳解

I. 字彙：20 %

Part 1：

1. (**C**) (A) anguish〔'æŋgwɪʃ〕*n.* 苦惱
   (B) avalanche〔'ævə,læntʃ〕*n.* 山崩；雪崩
   (C) ***ambush***〔'æmbuʃ〕*n.* 埋伏
   (D) alteration〔,ɔltə'reʃən〕*n.* 變更
   leftist〔'lɛftɪst〕*n.* 左派分子　　patrol〔pə'trol〕*n.* 巡邏

2. (**B**) (A) probation〔pro'beʃən〕*n.* 緩刑
   (B) ***parole***〔pə'rol〕*n.* 假釋
   (C) promotion〔prə'moʃən〕*n.* 升遷；提倡
   (D) permission〔pɚ'mɪʃən〕*n.* 許可
   jury〔'dʒurɪ〕*n.* 陪審團　　shotgun〔'ʃat,gʌn〕*n.* 獵槍
   slay〔sle〕*v.* 殺害

3. (**B**) (A) accidentally〔,æksə'dɛntḷɪ〕*adv.* 偶然地；意外地
   (B) ***overwhelmingly***〔,ovɚ'hwɛlmɪŋlɪ〕*adv.* 壓倒性地
   (C) incidentally〔,ɪnsə'dɛntḷɪ〕*adv.* 偶然地；附帶地
   (D) scarcely〔'skɛrslɪ〕*adv.* 幾乎不
   senate〔'sɛnɪt〕*n.* 參議院
   anti-terrorism〔,æntɪ'tɛrə,rɪzm̩〕*n.* 反恐怖主義
   anniversary〔,ænə'vɝsərɪ〕*n.* 週年紀念（日）

4. (**C**) (A) dissolve〔dɪ'zalv〕*v.* 溶解
   (B) dispel〔dɪ'spɛl〕*v.* 驅散
   (C) ***disclose***〔dɪs'kloz〕*v.* 透露
   (D) dispose〔dɪ'spoz〕*v.* 處置
   gunman〔'gʌn,mæn〕*n.* 持槍搶劫及殺人者
   critically〔'krɪtɪkəlɪ〕*adv.* 危急地

5. (**A**)　(A) ***confiscate*** 〔 'kɑnfɪs,ket 〕 *v.* 沒收；充公
　　　　　(B) compliment 〔 'kɑmpləmənt 〕 *v.* 稱讚
　　　　　(C) contradict 〔 ,kɑntrə'dɪkt 〕 *v.* 矛盾；牴觸
　　　　　(D) comprehend 〔 ,kɑmprɪ'hɛnd 〕 *v.* 理解
　　　　　the Justice Department 司法部
　　　　　defend 〔 dɪ'fɛnd 〕 *v.* 支持　　***drug dealer*** 毒販
　　　　　narcotic 〔 nɑr'kɑtɪk 〕 *n.* 麻醉劑；吸毒者
　　　　　convicted 〔 kən'vɪktɪd 〕 *adj.* 定罪的

6. (**D**)　(A) suspect 〔 sə'spɛkt 〕 *v.* 懷疑
　　　　　(B) apprehend 〔 ,æprɪ'hɛnd 〕 *v.* 憂慮；領悟
　　　　　(C) recommend 〔 ,rɛkə'mɛnd 〕 *v.* 推薦
　　　　　(D) ***reprimand*** 〔 ,rɛprə'mænd 〕 *v.* 懲戒
　　　　　marine 〔 mə'rin 〕 *n.* 海軍陸戰隊士兵

7. (**C**)　(A) proposition 〔 ,prɑpə'zɪʃən 〕 *n.* 提議
　　　　　(B) preceding 〔 prɪ'sidɪŋ 〕 *adj.* 前面的
　　　　　(C) ***proceedings*** 〔 prə'sidɪŋz 〕 *n.pl.* 訴訟程序
　　　　　(D) provisions 〔 prə'vɪʒənz 〕 *n.pl.* 食物；糧食
　　　　　duchess 〔 'dʌtʃɛs 〕 *n.* 公爵夫人　　***under way*** 進行中

8. (**B**)　(A) compromise 〔 'kɑmprə,maɪz 〕 *n.* 妥協
　　　　　(B) ***standoff*** 〔 'stænd,ɔf 〕 *n.* 旁觀；平手
　　　　　(C) embargo 〔 ɪm'bɑrgo 〕 *n.* 禁運
　　　　　(D) campaign 〔 kæm'pen 〕 *n.* 運動；活動
　　　　　explosive 〔 ɪk'splosɪv 〕 *n.* 爆炸物

9. (**A**)　(A) ***asylum*** 〔 ə'saɪləm 〕 *n.* 庇護
　　　　　(B) negotiation 〔 nɪ,goʃɪ'eʃən 〕 *n.* 談判
　　　　　(C) sanction 〔 'sæŋkʃən 〕 *n.* 批准；制裁
　　　　　(D) extradition 〔 ,ɛkstrə'dɪʃən 〕 *n.* 引渡
　　　　　Liberian 〔 laɪ'bɪrɪə 〕 *adj.* 賴比瑞亞的
　　　　　hostage 〔 'hɑstɪdʒ 〕 *n.* 人質　　refugee 〔 ,rɛfju'dʒi 〕 *n.* 難民
　　　　　Nigeria 〔 naɪ'dʒɪrɪə 〕 *n.* 奈及利亞

10. (**C**)　(A) acquisitive〔ə'kwɪzətɪv〕*adj.* 渴望得到的
　　　　　 (B) authoritative〔ə'θɔrə,tetɪv〕*adj.* 權威式的
　　　　　 (C) ***authentic***〔ɔ'θɛntɪk〕*adj.* 眞正的；道地的
　　　　　 (D) autocratic〔,ɔtə'krætɪk〕*adj.* 專制的

Part 2 :

【譯文】

　　那是個令人難忘,但卻出人意料的夜晚。有四百五十位社會菁英,身著晚禮服與正式的長禮服,其中大部分都是外籍商人和外交官,爲了參加這場座無虛席的盛宴,而群集於北京假日飯店。這場盛宴有五道菜以及令人興奮的摸彩銷售。這次的活動是要爲中國孤兒募款。但在晚宴前一小時,有四十位中國公安,進入這家五星級飯店的大舞廳,並宣稱此次活動不合法,因爲未經核准。政府仍爲一則亞洲人權瞭望的報導耿耿於懷,因其中揭露了上海國營孤兒院嚴重虐待兒童的情形,他們不希望再引起同樣的話題。不過警方仍勉強同意晚宴繼續進行,只要不舉行摸彩銷售和演講就可以 —— 即使是原本排定由華裔美國作家唐艾咪報告這次晚宴舉行的主旨也不被允許。一位與會人士說:「當這些惡棍聽到孤兒院這個流行的行話時,一定懷疑我們籌畫了什麼政治把戲。」

【答案】

11. (**AD**)	12. (**AE**)	13. (**AB**)	14. (**BC**)	15. (**AC**)
16. (**BD**)	17. (**CE**)	18. (**CD**)	19. (**DE**)	20. (**BE**)

【註】

dinner jacket 男用無尾晚禮服　　gown〔gaʊn〕*n.* 長禮服
elite〔ɪ'lit〕*n.* 菁英　　converge〔kən'vɝdʒ〕*v.* 聚集
Lido〔'lido〕*n.* 戶外豪華舒適的海濱遊地
sold-out〔'sold,aʊt〕*adj.* 售完的　　banquet〔'bæŋkwɪt〕*n.* 宴會
extravaganza〔ɛk,strævə'gænzə〕*n.* 盛典;盛事
raffle〔'ræfl〕*n.* 摸彩出售　　smart〔smɑrt〕*v.* 憤慨
ballroom〔'bɔl,rum〕*n.* 舞廳　　allege〔ə'lɛdʒ〕*v.* 聲言
rampant〔'ræmpənt〕*adj.* 激烈的;猖獗的

state-run〔ˈstetˌrʌn〕*adj.* 國營的
orphanage〔ˈɔrfənɪdʒ〕*n.* 孤兒院　　***bring up*** 提出
grudgingly〔ˈgrʌdʒɪŋlɪ〕*adv.* 勉強地　　　fete〔fet〕*n.* 慶典；慶宴
keynote〔ˈkiˌnot〕*n.* 主旨　　　attendee〔əˌtɛnˈdi〕*n.* 出席者
thug〔θʌg〕*n.* 惡棍　　　buzzword〔ˈbʌzˌwɝd〕*n.* 流行的行話

Ⅱ. 文法：20 %

21.（ **D** ）*On the contrary* → ***However***

22.（ **B** ）*focusing* → ***focus***　　and 為對等連接詞，須連接文法作用相
　　　　同的單字、片語，或子句。orientation 為名詞，故 focusing
　　　　亦須改為名詞 focus。

23.（ **A** ）*and it allowing* → ***which allows***　　which 為補述用法的關
　　　　係代名詞，代替前面一整句。

24.（ **B** ）*like* → ***of***　　*of one's age* 像～的年紀

25.（ **B** ）*the same like* → ***the same as***

26.（ **A** ）*with* → ***for***

27.（ **C** ）*only really* → ***really only***

28.（ **C** ）*unless* → ***until***

29.（ **A** ）*suppose* → ***assume***

30.（ **B** ）*surprising* → ***surprisingly***
　　　　surprisingly enough 令人驚訝的是

31.（ **A** ）*most of people* → ***most people***　　most 作「大部分的」解，
　　　　為形容詞，其後應直接加名詞。

32.（ **C** ）*irritating* → ***irritated***　　that 引導的子句缺少動詞，故 (C) irri-
　　　　tating 應改為動詞，依句意為過去式。

33.（ **D** ）*disagreed to people* → ***disagreed with people***

34.（ **B** ） *substitute* → ***substitute for***

35.（ **D** ） *remaining* → ***remain***　be likely to + V　可能~

36.（ **D** ） *less* → ***least***　依句意，爲最高級，故比較級 less 須改爲 least。

37.（ **B** ） *on environmental ground* → ***on environmental grounds***
　　　　　nuclear power plant　核電廠
　　　　　grounds〔graʊndz〕*n. pl.* 理由

38.（ **D** ） *technology* → ***technological***　　修飾名詞 development 須用
　　　　　形容詞。

39.（ **B** ） *persistently* → ***persistent***　修飾名詞 questioning「質疑」，
　　　　　須用形容詞 persistent。
　　　　　catastrophic〔͵kætə'strɑfɪk〕*adj.* 毀滅性的；悲慘的
　　　　　virtually〔'vɝtʃʊəlɪ〕*adv.* 幾乎

40.（ **A** ） *got out of* → ***got off***　***get off*** 下（車、飛機）

Ⅲ. 閱讀測驗：20％

A.

【譯文】

　　　　兩千年來，學者對自然界的觀點可區分成兩派。依其本質可分爲柏拉圖學派與亞里斯多德學派。亞里斯多德學派的機械論者指出，生物「只不過是機械而已」，且可完全以機械論、物理學，和化學法則來解釋。柏拉圖學派同意生物是遵循著這些自然法則，不過仍堅持生命本身的本質不止於此，在單純的物質中存在著生命力。因此，對生機論者而言，生物有許多更耐人尋味的特性，本來就是無法用科學來分析的。

　　　　在本世紀初，機械論者就已較佔優勢，其原因有二。首先，因爲科學的發現不斷顯示，以前認爲無法解釋的生物特性，的確可由機械論來解釋。其次，機械論者從嚴格的「所有事物皆爲機械」之立場，轉變爲接受生物與非生物之間確有其不同之處的觀點。兩者的差異存在於物質的結構，所以生物擁有非生物所沒有的特性。因此生物學的主流，其本質仍是機械論。

【答案】

　41.（ **D** ）　　　42.（ **A** ）　　　43.（ **B** ）

【註】

millennia〔məˈlɛnɪə〕*n. pl.* 爲 millennium「一千年」的複數形
intellectual〔ˌɪntəˈlɛktʃuəl〕*adj.* 知性的
divide〔dəˈvaɪd〕*n.* 劃分；分界
Platonic〔pleˈtɑnɪk〕*adj.* 柏拉圖學派的
Aristotelian〔ˌærɪstəˈtilɪən〕*adj.* 亞里斯多德學派的
mechanist〔ˈmɛkəˌnɪst〕*n.* 機械論者
organism〔ˈɔrgəˌnɪzəm〕*n.* 生物
explicable〔ˈɛksplɪkəbḷ〕*adj.* 可解釋的
mechanics〔məˈkænɪks〕*n.* 機械學　　essence〔ˈɛsn̩s〕*n.* 本質
vital force　生命力；活力
vitalist〔ˈvaɪtḷɪst〕*n.* 生機論者　　property〔ˈprɑpətɪ〕*n.* 特性
by nature　本來　　prevail〔prɪˈvel〕*v.* 佔優勢
previously〔ˈprivɪəslɪ〕*adv.* 以前
inexplicable〔ɪnˈɛksplɪkəbḷ〕*adj.* 無法解釋的
mechanistic〔ˌmɛkəˈnɪstɪk〕*adj.* 機械論的；機械作用的
reside in　在於　　mainstream〔ˈmenˌstrim〕*n.* 主流

B.

【譯文】

　　關於靜態宇宙的觀點有項難題，那就是宇宙中每顆星球應該會彼此互相吸引。如果是這樣的話，它們如何能維持不動，相互之間保持固定的距離呢？它們不會聚集在一起嗎？牛頓察覺到這個問題。在寫給當代一流的哲學家，理查‧班特利的信中，牛頓同意一群「有限的」星球無法靜止不動，它們會集中至某個中心點。然而，他認爲無限的星球不會聚集在一起，因爲根本沒有中心點可供聚集。這個論點是在討論無限系統時，常犯的錯誤。藉由不同的方式，把宇宙中無限量的星球加諸其他星球之力量加在一起,關於星球間是否能保持固定距離的問題,就可以得到不同的答案。我們現在知道正確的程序,應是先考慮在有限區域內的星球,然後再加上更多的星球,大致上平均地散佈在區域的外圍。有限區域內的星球會聚集在一起,而在區域外增加更多星球並不會停止這項毀滅。因此,無限的星球無法保持在靜止的狀態。如果它們不能同時彼此相應地移動,其間的吸引力就會使它們聚集在一起。或者,會因為重力會減緩其後退的速度,所以它們可以彼此遠離。

【答案】

44. (**A**)　　　　45. (**B**)　　　　46. (**A**)

【註】

static〔ˈstætɪk〕*adj.* 靜止的　　finite〔ˈfaɪnaɪt〕*adj.* 有限的
collection〔kəˈlɛkʃən〕*n.* 集合;聚集
infinite〔ˈɪnfənɪt〕*adj.* 無限的　　pitfall〔ˈpɪtˌfɔl〕*n.* 易犯的錯誤
procedure〔prəˈsidʒɚ〕*n.* 程序　　roughly〔ˈrʌflɪ〕*adv.* 大約地
uniformly〔ˈjunəˌfɔrmlɪ〕*adv.* 一樣地;均等地
collapse〔kəˈlæps〕*n.* 崩潰
alternatively〔ɔlˈtɝnətɪvlɪ〕*adv.* 兩者取一地
gravity〔ˈgrævətɪ〕*n.* 重力
velocity〔vəˈlɑsətɪ〕*n.* 速度　　recession〔rɪˈsɛʃən〕*n.* 後退
gravitational〔ˌgrævəˈteʃən̩〕*adj.* 重力的

C.

【譯文】

　　像日本這種充滿傳統的國家,很多古老的節日都會標示於日曆上。像札幌雪祭,開始於一九五○年,就文化發展上來說是較晚些,但是它受歡迎的程度卻不受影響。事實上,雖然札幌雪祭存在的時間不長,但這為期七天的活動,在其大小及規模上,已是全日本冬季最大的慶祝活動。現在大約有兩百萬人會去觀賞這一年一度的表演，欣賞這包含了三百多件費盡心力之雪雕作品光輝燦爛的展覽。這種紀念雪的節慶似乎非常適合這個副嚴寒地區，在這裏每年冬季都長達六個月之久。

【答案】

47.（ B)	48.（ C)	49.（ A)	50.（ C)

【註】

scores of 很多　　dot〔dɑt〕*v.* 打小點
Sapporo Snow Festival 札幌雪祭
Johnny-come-lately 新來者；遲來的人
annual〔'ænjuəl〕*adj.* 一年一度的
marvel〔'mɑrvḷ〕*v.* 驚歎
luminous〔'lumənəs〕*adj.* 光輝的
painstakingly〔'penz,tekɪŋlɪ〕*adv.* 費力地
hew〔hju〕*v.* 砍；劈　　grip〔grɪp〕*n.* 緊握
frigid〔'frɪdʒɪd〕*adj.* 嚴寒的
sculpting〔'skʌlptɪŋ〕*n.* 雕刻

IV. 翻譯：20 ％

Part One ：英譯中

【譯文】

　　雖然幾十年來人們都了解接觸殺蟲劑的危險，但是這些警告卻一直為懷疑論者所忽視，他們無法了解這個問題的迫切性。現在這問題已提升至足以威脅人類未來生活的程度。像是精蟲數量減少及畸型兒這類與接觸殺蟲劑有關的問題，都影響著人類及其他生物。越戰後的時期所產生的遺傳結果是最明顯的。只有天真的人才會因想到未來美好的歲月而覺得舒坦；人類已經開始衰退了。

【註】

hazard〔'hæzəd〕*n.* 危險　　pesticide〔'pɛstɪˌsaɪd〕*n.* 殺蟲劑

exposure〔ɪk'spoʒɚ〕*n.* 暴露；接觸

skeptic〔'skɛptɪk〕*n.* 懷疑論者　　escalate〔'ɛskəˌlet〕*v.* 升高

sperm〔spɝm〕*n.* 精蟲　　count〔kaʊnt〕*n.* 總數

fetal〔'fitl〕*adj.* 胎兒的

abnormality〔ˌæbnɔr'mælətɪ〕*n.* 畸型

genetic〔dʒə'nɛtɪk〕*adj.* 遺傳的　　naive〔nɑ'iv〕*adj.* 天眞的

Part Two：中譯英

【譯文】

After lifting the martial law, the first impact between teachers and students was the disintegration of authority Many teachers have found that students today are different from those of "our generation." They have something to say, dare to express their ideas and do it in a fierce, direct way. "Having no idea how to treat students" is more or less the worry in many a teacher's mind.

V. 作文：20%

The Effect of Electronic Communication on Modern Life

The effect of electronic communication on modern life has been dramatic. The Internet has been growing so fast that every day the world gets closer to total dependency on it. Every day, more and more people connect to the Internet in an attempt to improve their daily lives. People from house-wives to company presidents are beginning to spend any spare time they have searching the Internet. What once had been a hobby for the academics in life, is now becoming a way of life for everybody.

The Internet makes it possible for people to do anything they need to in the privacy of their own homes. People can work, bank, shop, send mail, do library research, play games, attend school and do many other things previously unheard of, without ever leaving home. Electronic communication is changing the way people live their lives today.

國立交通大學八十五學年度
碩士班研究生入學考試英文試題

I. Choose the one word that does not have the same meaning as the other three words. 13%

1. The software engineer's _____ was limited to one area.
   (A) expertise   (B) intelligence
   (C) proficiency   (D) mastery

2. They undertook their _____ after making careful calculations.
   (A) venture   (B) risky undertaking
   (C) challenge   (D) decision

3. Silent film actors had to _____ their emotions clearly when they performed in a dramatic scene.
   (A) adopt   (B) express
   (C) project   (D) convey

4. As a state-of-the-art entertainment medium, television revolutionized the entertainment industry and caused a _____ drop in movie attendance.
   (A) marked   (B) striking
   (C) temporary   (D) dramatic

5. When humans _____ animals, meat became a basic part of their diet.
   (A) expanded   (B) raised
   (C) tamed   (D) domesticated

6. People _____ an excessive amount of food at Roman banquets.
   (A) consumed   (B) ate
   (C) cultivated   (D) devoured

7. The birth of twins was considered an unnatural _____ in some cultures.
   (A) relationship   (B) event
   (C) phenomenon   (D) occurrence

8. Scientists _____ that the earth is billions of years old.
   (A) speculate   (B) think
   (C) decide   (D) guess

9. A deaf person who is _____ at lip reading can often
   adapt himself to college life.
   (A) capable   (B) coherent
   (C) competent   (D) proficient

10. The computer programmer discovered a (an)_____ of
    details that had to be changed before the program would
    be effective.
    (A) myriad   (B) multitude
    (C) abundance   (D) obstacle

11. The fickle behavior of nature both_____life and
    destroys it.
    (A) supports   (B) maintains
    (C) sustains   (D) produces

12. The_____winds of hurricanes and tornadoes move in a
    clockwise direction in the Southern Hemisphere and in
    a counterclockwise direction in the Northern Hemisphere.
    (A) disabling   (B) revolving
    (C) rotating   (D) turning

13. Weather satellites provide information about weather
    conditions over_____areas.
    (A) widespread   (B) isolated
    (C) broad   (D) extensive

II. Read the following passage and choose the appropriate
    logical connectors (transitional words). 12%

　　　Most people like to talk, but few people like to listen,
____14____ listening well is a rare talent that everyone should
treasure. Because they hear more, good listeners tend to
know more and to be more sensitive to what is going on
around them than most people. ____15____ , good listeners are
inclined to accept or tolerate rather than to judge and
criticize. ____16____ , they have fewer enemies than most people.
____17____ , they are probably the most loved of people. However, there are exceptions to that generality. ____18____ , John
Steinbeck, a famous American writer, is said to have been an
excellent listener, yet he was hated by some of the people
he wrote about. No doubt his ability to listen contributed

to his capacity to write. ___19___ , the results of his listening did not make him popular. Thus, depending on what a
good listener does with what he hears, he may pay a price
for his talent or go unappreciated in his lifetime.

14. (A) or   (B) yet
    (C) for   (D) because

15. (A) In addition   (B) Consequently
    (C) However   (D) But

16. (A) However   (B) Still
    (C) For example   (D) Therefore

17. (A) Moreover   (B) On the contrary
    (C) Notwithstanding   (D) In fact

18. (A) Therefore   (B) Of course
    (C) For example   (D) Indeed

19. (A) Nevertheless   (B) Similarly
    (C) Besides   (D) In addition

III. Complete the following passage by selecting the appropriate statements from the list below. 15%

    ___20___ . We know a great deal about the mechanics of
sleep and we are beginning to know about the biochemical
changes involved. ___21___ as how much sleep a person needs.
While the physiological bases of sleep remain very much a
matter for conjecture, we do nevertheless have considerable
evidence on ___22___ . We still need to know more about the
kinds of effects that sleep deprivation causes. In spite of
the considerable effort devoted to investigating why we
sleep, ___23___ . The fact that sleep deprivation causes numerous harmful effects suggests that the body requires sleep
to restore itself. However, more research is needed to determine whether this is so or ___24___ . There is also the possibility that these two alternatives may not be incompatible.

(A) how much sleep people do in fact obtain
(B) However, we are still a long way from finding out
    answers to such questions
(C) whether sleep is the result of adaptation to the
    environment
(D) there is still disagreement in this area
(E) Much research has been carried out in recent years
    into sleep

IV. Read the following passages and choose the best statement of the author's main idea. 15%

25. The average age of the population of many countries is getting older. That means that businesses in those countries must adjust to older customers. In fact, many companies are working to respond to the special needs of the elderly. One example of this is the medical industry. New medicines and technologies are being developed especially for the health problems of older people. Another business that offers services for the elderly is the tourist industry. Many travel agents offer special trips for groups of older people. And, finally, there are many different kinds of products made for the elderly. These include everything from shoes and shampoos to magazines and furniture.
   (A) The medical industry is developing new medicines for the elderly.
   (B) New products and services are being developed by many companies.
   (C) Many companies are developing products and services for the increasing elderly population.
   (D) Elderly people have lots of money to spend on medicine and traveling.

26. In industrialized countries today, many elderly people suffer from depression. The main cause of this is loneliness. In the past, older people usually lived with other members of the family. They usually had some responsibilities around the home. For example, older women could help take care of the children or prepare meals. Older men could help their sons at work or around the house. These days, married children often prefer to live on their own, sometimes far away from their parents. Thus, older people may be cut off from family ties. They may feel cut off from the world around them. Life has changed so much so quickly that older people sometimes feel that they do not belong any more.
   (A) The elderly people in industrialized countries are often depressed because of loneliness.
   (B) Older people used to live with other family members and helped take care of the children.
   (C) Some elderly people may feel the world has changed too quickly for them.
   (D) Young people in industrialized countries prefer to live on their own.

27. The idea of a small electric car is not new. A number of different car manufacturers already sell such cars. But now a French company, Renault, has designed a very special kind of electric car. By pushing a button, you can make it fold up! The back of the car folds into the car body. These cars were designed mainly for use in cities. They have several advantages over regular cars. Their small size makes them much easier to drive around busy, narrow streets. They are also much easier to park in city parking spaces. Like other electric cars, these autos do not pollute the air. This is an important consideration these days when many cities have serious pollution problems.
    (A) Electric cars do not pollute the air.
    (B) The new folding electric car has many advantages over regular cars.
    (C) French car manufactures are the only ones interested in developing an electric car.
    (D) These electric cars are used mainly in cities.

28. Many studies have shown that it is better to wear your seat belt when you are traveling in a car. Seat belts greatly reduce the risk of death or injury in an accident. This fact is widely recognized and many governments have passed laws requiring seat belt use. However, many people still do not wear seat belts. Researchers have found several reasons for this. Some people feel uncomfortable with the seat belt. They are afraid of being trapped in the car in an accident. Others do not think that the seat belt can protect them. They believe that people have no power over their fate. Fate will decide whether they will have an accident and whether they will be injured or die. They think that wearing a seat belt or not will make no difference.
    (A) In spite of the risks, some people do not wear seat belts.
    (B) All new cars must now be equipped with seat belts.
    (C) Some people feel uncomfortable wearing seat belts.
    (D) Seat belts greatly reduce the risk of death or injury in an accident.

29. The country with the most crowded roads is Italy. In 1992, there were an average of 101.1 vehicles (cars, trucks, and buses) per kilometer of road in Italy. This can be compared with the vehicles-per-kilometer ratios of other European countries. The ratio varies from 35.8 in France to 74.2 in Great Britain. In the United States, the ratio is 30.6. Part of the reason for Italy's higher ratio lies in its geography. Because much of the country is mountainous, there are fewer roads. Thus the traffic is more concentrated on those

few roads. This fact has caused some serious problems.
Many cities and highways are often blocked by terrible
traffic jams. The heavy traffic has also meant a high
accident rate for Italy. And finally, all those cars add
to Italy's air pollution.
(A) Because of the mountains, there are fewer roads in
    Italy.
(B) Crowded roads create traffic jams, accidents, and
    air pollution.
(C) There were an average of 101.1 vehicles per kilometer
    of road in Italy in 1992.
(D) Italy's roads are the most crowded in the world.

V. Choose the best ending for each of the following
   paragraphs. 15%

30. The Japanese love to eat raw fish. Dishes of uncooked
    fish, called sushi or sashimi, are prepared at most
    Japanese restaurants. Japanese cooks use many kinds of
    fish or shellfish for these dishes. Whatever kind of
    fish they use, however, it must always be very fresh.
    To prove that the fish is fresh, some restaurants will
    even serve
    (A) fish cooked on a grill.
    (B) fish that is still alive.
    (C) whole fish.
    (D) many unusual kinds of fish.

31. What would you do if you got lost in a desert? The most
    important thing is to find water. But where can you find
    drinking water in the middle of all that sand? The an-
    swer is simple: in the desert plants. In fact, the most
    common desert plant, the cactus, contains lots of good
    water. With the right method and some simple tools, you
    (A) can get only a few drops of water a day.
    (B) will get water that is undrinkable.
    (C) will be able to find a drinking fountain.
    (D) can get about a liter of water a day.

32. Do you know what to do if someone falls off a small
    boat? The first thing to do is to throw out a life ring.
    Don't lose sight of the person. You should try to get
    close with the boat. At the same time, you must be very
    careful not to hurt the person in the water. Then you
    should try to help him or her climb back into the boat.
    This is not always easy, especially if
    (A) the weather is warm.
    (B) there are several people to help.
    (C) the person is hurt or cold.
    (D) the person is a good swimmer.

33. Cars are the most important cause of air pollution in
    many cities. This is especially true in cities, such as
    Los Angeles, where most people go to work by car. In
    order to reduce pollution, the city must reduce the
    number of cars on the road. This is only possible,
    however, if people have another way to get to work. For this
    reason, many city governments are working to improve the
    (A) highway system.
    (B) quality of life.
    (C) connections between cities.
    (D) public transportation system.

34. In different parts of the world, people build their
    houses of different materials. In areas where there is a
    lot of wood, houses are made of wood. In hot, dry areas
    with little wood, houses are often made of clay bricks.
    In the far northern areas, people even build their
    houses of ice. Generally,
    (A) people build their houses with whatever they can
        find.
    (B) people prefer houses made of stone.
    (C) wooden houses are dangerous because they can burn.
    (D) people in some areas build their houses of leaves.

VI. Reading Comprehension: 30%
Passage 1

There is reason to believe that when teachers feel that
a certain child will do well in school, that child will in
fact do well. The self-fulfilling prophecy –a phenomenon by
which people act as they are expected to--has been documented
in many different situations (Rosenthal & Jacobson, 1968).

In the Oak School experiment, some teachers in a California elementary school were told at the beginning of the term
that some of their pupils had shown unusual potential for
intellectual growth. Actually, the children identified as
potential "bloomers" had been chosen at random. There was
absolutely no basis for thinking that their IQs would rise
anymore than would those of any other children. But on sub-
sequent tests several months or more later, many of the
selected children--especially the first and second graders--
showed unusual gains in IQ scores. Furthermore, the teachers
seemed to like the "bloomers" better.

35. The self-fulfilling prophecy has been documented by
    (A) Rosenthal and Jacobson.　(B) Smith and Rutland.
    (C) Vincent and Gardenia.　(D) Olson and Wertheimer.

36. The children named as having potential for intellectual
    growth were chosen
    (A) on the basis of their IQ scores.
    (B) on the basis of teachers' reports.
    (C) at random.
    (D) on the basis of their work in school.

37. These "gifted" children were called
    (A) "spurters."
    (B) "gifted students."
    (C) "high-potential students."
    (D) "bloomers."

38. According to the passage, these children experienced
    (A) periodic depressions.
    (B) actual increase in IQ scores.
    (C) abuse from the other children.
    (D) no change in their IQ scores.

39. The gains of the "bloomers" were greatest if they were
    in
    (A) third or fourth grade.　(B) sixth or seventh grade.
    (C) eighth or ninth grade.　(D) first or second grade.

Passage 2

　　One of the most serious respiratory diseases is influenza, for it is able to attack people of all ages throughout
the world. Incidence frequently is highest in young adults.
It is an example of a disease that has inreased in virulence
throughout the years, although since 1942 it seems to have
become milder again. Influenza periodically has been epidemic
in the United States from 1918 to the present time. Several
tragic world-wide pandemics have occurred. One of the most
dreadful was the 1918-1919 outbreak, in which there were some
20 million cases of influenza and pneumonia and approximately
850,000 deaths occurred.

Influenza is an acute disease of the respiratory tract that affects the whole body. It is characterized by a sudden onset, with chills, a fever of around 102 degrees that may rise to 104 degrees, headache, muscular pains, prostration, sore throat, and cough. Like the common cold, it paves the way for secondary infections such as hemolytic streptococci and pneumonia. Most deaths are due to complications from pneumonia. Recovery is usual in four or five days.

40. Influenza deserves attention as an important respiratory disease because it
    (A) usually results in pneumonia or death.
    (B) has a long recovery period.
    (C) attacks all age groups in all countries.
    (D) occurs most frequently among young adults.

41. Influenza is a disease which
    (A) has generally increased in virulence.
    (B) was unknown in the United States.
    (C) has remained constant in its toxicity.
    (D) is not difficult to control.

42. In the 1918-1919 world influenza outbreak,
    (A) there were 5,000 deaths.
    (B) a count of deaths was impossible to take.
    (C) there were 2 million deaths.
    (D) there were 850,000 deaths.

43. Influenza is a serious disease because
    (A) it frequently leads to heart disease.
    (B) high fevers usually accompany it.
    (C) it confers no immunity.
    (D) quarantine is the only really effective control.

44. Most deaths from influenza are due to
    (A) parainfluenza.
    (B) faulty diagnosis.
    (C) complications due to pneumonia.
    (D) complications leading to hepatitis.

國立交通大學八十五學年度
碩士班研究生入學考試英文試題詳解

I. 選出不同義的字：13%

1. (**B**)　*intelligence*〔 ɪn'tɛlədʒəns 〕*n.* 才智
　　　(A) expertise〔 ˌɛkspɚ'tis 〕*n.* 專門技術
　　　(C) proficiency〔 prə'fɪʃənsɪ 〕*n.* 精通
　　　(D) mastery〔 'mæstərɪ 〕*n.* 精通
　　　　software〔 'sɔftˌwɛr 〕*n.* 軟體

2. (**D**)　*decision*〔 dɪ'sɪʒən 〕*n.* 決定
　　　(A) venture〔 'vɛntʃɚ 〕*n.* 冒險事業
　　　(B) risky undertaking　冒險事業
　　　(C) challenge〔 'tʃælɪndʒ 〕*n.* 挑戰
　　　　undertake〔 ˌʌndɚ'tek 〕*v.* 開始

3. (**A**)　*adopt*〔 ə'dɑpt 〕*v.* 採用
　　　(B) express〔 ɪk'sprɛs 〕*v.* 表達
　　　(C) project〔 prə'dʒɛkt 〕*v.* 投射；傳達
　　　(D) convey〔 kən've 〕*v.* 傳達
　　　　silent film　默片

4. (**C**)　*temporary*〔 'tɛmpəˌrɛrɪ 〕*adj.* 暫時的
　　　(A) marked〔 mɑrkt 〕*adj.* 明顯的
　　　(B) striking〔 'straɪkɪŋ 〕*adj.* 顯著的
　　　(D) dramatic〔 drə'mætɪk 〕*adj.* 戲劇性的；重大的
　　　　state-of-the-art　應用已有的最高技術的
　　　　revolutionize〔 ˌrɛvə'luʃəˌnaɪz 〕*v.* 大事改革

5 (**A**)　*expand*〔 ɪk'spænd 〕*v.* 擴張
　　　(B) raise〔 rez 〕*v.* 飼養
　　　(C) tame〔 tem 〕*v.* 馴服
　　　(D) domesticate〔 də'mɛstəˌket 〕*v.* 馴養

6. (**C**)　***cultivate*** 〔 'kʌltə,vet 〕 v. 培養
　　　　　(A) consume 〔 kən'sum 〕 v. 消耗；吃（喝）掉
　　　　　(D) devour 〔 dɪ'vaur 〕 v. 吞食；狼吞虎嚥
　　　　　　excessive 〔 ɪk'sɛsɪv 〕 adj. 過度的
　　　　　　banquet 〔 'bæŋkwɪt 〕 n. 盛宴

7. (**A**)　***relationship*** 〔 rɪ'leʃən,ʃɪp 〕 n. 關係
　　　　　(B) event 〔 ɪ'vɛnt 〕 n. 事件
　　　　　(C) phenomenon 〔 fə'namə,nan 〕 n. 現象
　　　　　(D) occurrence 〔 ə'kɝəns 〕 n. 事件
　　　　　　twins 〔 'twɪnz 〕 n.pl. 雙胞胎

8. (**C**)　***decide*** 〔 dɪ'saɪd 〕 v. 決定
　　　　　(A) speculate 〔 'spɛkjə,let 〕 v. 推測
　　　　　(D) guess 〔 gɛs 〕 v. 猜測

9. (**B**)　***coherent*** 〔 ko'hɪrənt 〕 adj. 前後一致的
　　　　　(A) capable 〔 'kæpəbl̩ 〕 adj. 有能力的
　　　　　(C) competent 〔 'kampətənt 〕 adj. 能勝任的
　　　　　(D) proficient 〔 prə'fɪʃənt 〕 adj. 精通的
　　　　　　adapt 〔 ə'dæpt 〕 v. 使適應

10. (**D**)　***obstacle*** 〔 'abstəkl̩ 〕 n. 障礙
　　　　　(A) myriad 〔 'mɪrɪəd 〕 n. 無數
　　　　　(B) multitude 〔 'mʌltə,tjud 〕 n. 眾多
　　　　　(C) abundance 〔 ə'bʌndəns 〕 n. 豐富

11. (**D**)　***produce*** 〔 prə'djus 〕 v. 生產；製造
　　　　　(A) support 〔 sə'port 〕 v. 支持
　　　　　(B) maintain 〔 men'ten 〕 v. 維持
　　　　　(C) sustain 〔 sə'sten 〕 v. 支持
　　　　　　fickle 〔 'fɪkl̩ 〕 adj. 多變的

12. (**A**) *disabling* 〔 dɪsˈeblɪŋ 〕 *adj.* 使人殘廢的
　　　　(B) revolving 〔 rɪˈvɑlvɪŋ 〕 *adj.* 旋轉的
　　　　(C) rotating 〔 ˈrotetɪŋ 〕 *adj.* 旋轉的
　　　　hurricane 〔 ˈhɝɪˌken 〕 *n.* 颶風
　　　　tornado 〔 tɔrˈnedo 〕 *n.* 龍捲風
　　　　hemisphere 〔 ˈhɛməsˌfɪr 〕 *n.* 半球

13. (**B**) *isolated* 〔 ˈaɪsəˌletɪd 〕 *adj.* 孤立的
　　　　(A) widespread 〔 ˈwaɪdˌsprɛd 〕 *adj.* 廣泛的
　　　　(C) broad 〔 brɔd 〕 *adj.* 廣闊的
　　　　(D) extensive 〔 ɪkˈstɛnsɪv 〕 *adj.* 廣泛的

II. 克漏字 —— 連接詞與轉承語： 12 ％

【譯文】

　　大部分的人都喜歡說話，但是很少人喜歡聆聽。不過，能夠好好聆聽別人說話是項每個人都須珍惜的稀有天分。專心聽別人說話的人，因為聽得多，所以知道的會比別人多，而且對於周遭所發生的事，會比別人更敏感。此外，善於傾聽的人，較容易接受或容忍，而不會妄下評斷或任意批評。因此，他們的敵人比大多數的人少。事實上，他們可能是人們的最愛。但是這項概論也有例外。例如，著名的美國作家約翰・史坦貝克，據說是一位絕佳的聽眾，但是有些成為他筆下角色的人卻很恨他。無疑地，史坦貝克傾聽的能力對於他的寫作十分有幫助，然而他聆聽的結果卻並沒有使他受到人們的歡迎。因此，端看好的聽眾如何處理他所聽到的事，他可能要為他的才能付出代價，或是終其一生都未獲賞識。

【答案】
　　14. (**B**)　15. (**A**)　16. (**D**)　17. (**D**)　18. (**C**)　19. (**A**)

【註】
generality 〔 ˌdʒɛnəˈrælətɪ 〕 *n.* 通論；概論
unappreciated 〔 ˌʌnəˈpriʃɪˌetɪd 〕 *adj.* 未獲賞識的

Ⅲ. 選擇適當的句子，完成下列的文章：15%

【譯文】

近年來有許多關於睡眠的研究。我們對於睡眠的結構十分了解，也開始注意到睡眠所牽涉的生化方面的變化。然而，我們仍需多加努力，才能找到像是人需要多少睡眠這類問題的答案。儘管睡眠的生理方面的根據大半仍在臆測階段，不過關於人們睡眠時數的多寡，則已有相當多的證據。我們仍需要知道更多有關缺乏睡眠所造成的各種影響。儘管大家十分努力要研究人為什麼需要睡眠，但在這方面每個人仍持有不同的看法。缺乏睡眠會造成許多不良的影響，因為人體需要藉由睡眠來恢復。但是，仍須做更進一步的研究才能確定，究竟情況就是如此，還是睡眠只是適應環境的結果，也有可能這兩項並不互相衝突。

【答案】

20. (**E**)　21. (**B**)　22. (**A**)　23. (**D**)　24. (**C**)

【註】

mechanics〔 mə'kænɪks 〕*n.* 結構；方法
biochemical〔 ˌbaɪo'kɛmɪkḷ 〕*adj.* 生物化學的
physiological〔 ˌfɪzɪə'lɑdʒɪkḷ 〕*adj.* 生理的
conjecture〔 kən'dʒɛktʃɚ 〕*n.* 臆測
considerable〔 kən'sɪdərəbḷ 〕*adj.* 相當多的
deprivation〔 ˌdɪprə'veʃən 〕*n.* 喪失；剝奪
be devoted to 致力於　investigate〔 ɪn'vɛstəˌget 〕*v.* 調查
restore〔 rɪ'stor 〕*v.* 恢復
alternative〔 ɔl'tɝnətɪv 〕*n.* 選擇
incompatible〔 ˌɪnkəm'pætəbḷ 〕*adj.* 不相容的
carry out 執行；實現
adaptation〔 ˌædəp'teʃən 〕*n.* 適應

IV. 釋義：15 %

25. (**C**) 許多國家人口的平均年齡正逐漸老化。這意謂著這些國家的
企業必須配合年老的顧客。事實上，已有許多公司正努力要
因應老年人的特殊需求。醫療業就是一例。他們爲解決老人
的健康問題，特別研發出新的醫藥與技術。另一個爲老人提
供服務的行業則是旅遊業。許多旅行業者爲老人團體提供特
別的行程。也有許多不同種類的產品，是專爲老人所製造的。
這些產品像是鞋子、洗髮精、雜誌，和傢俱等東西都包括在內。
adjust to 適合　　　***travel agent*** 旅遊業者

26. (**A**) 在現代的工業化國家中，有很多老人都感到沮喪。主要的原
因是由於寂寞。在過去，老人多半和家人住在一起，通常會
爲家庭擔負一些責任。例如，年老的婦女可以幫忙照顧小孩
或準備三餐。年老的男人可以幫忙兒子處理工作上或家裏的
事。最近，已婚的子女多半喜歡自己住，有時候會遠離父母。
因此，老人可能會被切斷與家人的關係，也可能會覺得周遭
的世界都與他們隔離。生活上重大而迅速的改變使得老人有
時會覺得自己不再有任何的歸屬感。
depression〔dɪ'prɛʃən〕*n.* 沮喪　　***cut off*** 切斷
family ties 家族關係

27. (**B**) 小型電動車的點子並不算新。許多不同的汽車製造商已經出
售過這種車子。但是現在有家法國公司——雷諾，設計出一
種非常特別的電動車。按個鈕，就可把車子摺疊起來！車尾
摺進車身裏。這種車的設計，主要適用於城市，並且有幾項
超越一般車種的優點。體積小使它們更容易穿梭於繁忙窄小
的街道，在都市裏停車也更加容易。這些車子和其他的電動
車一樣，並不會污染空氣。當許多城市都有嚴重的污染問題
之際，這是一項相當重要的考量。
electric〔ɪ'lɛktrɪk〕*adj.* 電動的
fold〔fold〕*v.* 摺疊
consideration〔kən‚sɪdə'reʃən〕*n.* 考慮

28. (**A**) 許多研究顯示，乘車時最好繫上安全帶。安全帶能大幅地減
少在車禍致死或受傷的危險。這個事實廣爲大衆所接受，而
且許多政府已經通過法律，規定要使用安全帶。然而許多人
仍然不繫安全帶。研究人員發現有幾項原因。有些人覺得安
全帶不舒服，他們害怕發生意外時被困在車上，人認爲安全
帶無法保護他們。他們認爲人類沒有力量來掌控命運。命運
會決定他們是否會發生意外，以及他們是否會受傷或是死亡，
並且覺得繫不繫安全帶並沒有差別。

seat belt 安全帶　　　trap〔træp〕*v.* 困住

29. (**D**) 義大利是道路最爲擁擠的國家。在 1992 年，義大利的馬路平
均每公里有 101.1 輛車（包括汽車、卡車和公車）。這可以
拿來和其他歐洲國家每公里車輛數的比例來作比較。每公里
車輛數的比例從法國的 35.8 到英國的 74.2 都有。在美國，比
例是 30.6。義大利的比例較高，其部分原因在於地理因素。
因爲義大利多山，且道路較少，所以交通會較集中於少數的
道路上。這個現象已造成一些嚴重的問題。許多城市和高速
公路都被嚴重的塞車所阻礙。繁忙的交通也意謂著義大利的
高車禍率。因此，過多的車輛也使得義大利的空氣污染更加
嚴重。

ratio〔'reʃo〕*n.* 比例；比率
mountainous〔'mautənəs〕*adj.* 多山的
block〔blɑk〕*v.* 阻礙

V. 選出每段最適合的結尾： 15 ％

30. (**B**) 日本人非常愛吃生魚片。沒有烹調過的魚，被稱爲壽司或生
魚片，在大部分的日本餐館都有。日本廚師使用各種魚類或
貝類來做這類菜餚。不過，不論他們使用何種魚類，一定要
非常新鮮。爲了證明魚很新鮮，有些餐廳甚至供應活魚。

raw〔rɔ〕*adj.* 生的　　shellfish〔'ʃɛl.fɪʃ〕*n.* 貝類
grill〔grɪl〕*n.* 烤架

31.（ **D** ） 如果在沙漠裏迷路了，該怎麼辦？最重要的就是要找到水。
但是在沙漠中哪裏可以找到可飲用的水呢？答案很簡單：就
在沙漠的植物裏。事實上，最普通的沙漠植物 —— 仙人掌，
就含有大量水分。只要方法正確，並準備一些簡單的工具，
一天就能獲得大約一公升的水。
cactus〔ˈkæktəs〕*n.* 仙人掌
fountain〔ˈfauntn̩〕*n.* 泉水；水源　　liter〔ˈlitə〕*n.* 公升

32.（ **C** ） 如果有人從小船跌入水中，你知道該怎麼辦嗎？首先就是要
把救生圈丟下去。別讓那個人離開視線。應該要儘量使船靠
近。同時必須很小心，不要傷害到水中的人。接著必須協助
落水的人爬回船上。這有時並不簡單，尤其是如果這個人受
傷或很冷的話。　　　　 *life ring* 救生圈

33.（ **D** ） 在許多城市中，汽車是主要的空氣污染源，在像洛杉磯這類
的城市尤其如此。在這些城市中，大部分的人都開車上班。
為了減少污染，必須減少城市中路上汽車的數量。但是這只
有在人們有另一種到達辦公室的方式才有可能。基於這個理
由，許多市政府都在努力改善大衆運輸系統。

34.（ **A** ） 在世界各地，人們建造房子所採用的材料都不相同。在樹木
茂密的地區，房子多用木頭建造。在乾燥炎熱、樹木稀少的
地區，房子常用泥磚來建造。在偏遠的北方，人們甚至用冰
來蓋房子。一般而言，人們會用他們找到的材料來建造房子。

Ⅵ. 閱讀測驗：30 %

Passage 1

【譯文】

　　我們有理由相信，當老師認為某個小孩在學校會表現得很好時，
那個小孩的確會表現得不錯。自我實現預言，就是人們會表現得如別
人所預期的這種現象，已經在許多不同的情況下得到驗證。（ Rosenthal ＆ Jacobson, 1968 ）

在橡樹學校的實驗中，有些加州小學的老師，在學期開始，就被告知，有些學生在智力成長方面表現出不尋常的潛力。事實上，這些被認為是有潛力的「資優生」，是隨機挑選出來的。我們完全沒有任何根據，可以認定他們的智商的成長，會比其他小孩來得高。但是在稍後幾個月或更晚的後續測驗中，許多被選出來的小孩 —— 特別是一、二年級學生 —— 在智商成績上，都有不尋常的成長。此外，似乎老師也比較喜歡這些「資優生」。

【答案】

　　35. (**A**)　　36. (**C**)　　37. (**D**)　　38. (**B**)　　39. (**D**)

【註】

prophecy〔'prɑfəsɪ〕*n.* 預言
document〔'dɑkjumənt〕*v.* 提供文件證明
pupil〔'pjupḷ〕*n.* 小學生　　identify〔aɪ'dɛntə,faɪ〕*v.* 鑑定；認出
potential〔pə'tɛnʃəl〕*adj.* 有潛力的；可能的
bloomer〔'blumə〕*n.* 資優生　　*at random* 隨機地
subsequent〔'sʌbsɪ,kwɛnt〕*adj.* 隨後的
grader〔'gredə〕*n.* ～年級生　　spurter〔'spɜtə〕*n.* 發芽者
periodic〔,pɪrɪ'ɑdɪk〕*adj.* 周期的

Passage 2

【譯文】

　　流行性感冒是種十分嚴重的呼吸方面的疾病，因為它會侵襲全世界各年齡層的人。罹患率最高的往往是年輕人。流行性感冒是近幾年來，疾病罹患率劇增的典型例子，雖然從 1942 年開始，似乎有較為緩和的跡象。從 1918 年到現在，流行性感冒定期地會在美國蔓延開來，已經有過好幾次可怕的世界大流行。最嚴重的一次是在 1918 年到 1919 年爆發，當時大約有二千萬人感染流行性感冒和肺炎，造成將近八十五萬人死亡。

　　流行性感冒是呼吸道的急性病症，會影響到全身。其症狀是突然發病、發冷、發燒高達 102 度左右，甚至升至 104 度、頭痛、肌肉痠痛、身體虛弱、喉嚨痛，以及咳嗽。流行性感冒和一般的感冒一樣，可能會併發由溶血性鏈球菌和肺炎所造成的二度感染。大部分的死亡都是由於肺炎引起的併發症。復元通常需要四到五天的時間。

【答案】

40. (**C**)　　41. (**A**)　　42. (**D**)　　43. (**B**)　　44. (**C**)

【註】

respiratory〔ˈrɛspərəˌtorɪ〕*adj.* 呼吸的

influenza〔ˌɪnfluˈɛnzə〕*n.* 流行性感冒

incidence〔ˈɪnsədəns〕*n.* (疾病) 發生率

virulence〔ˈvɪrʊləns〕*n.* 毒性兇惡　　mild〔maɪld〕*adj.* 緩和的

periodically〔ˌpɪrɪˈɑdɪkəlɪ〕*adv.* 定期地

epidemic〔ˌɛpəˈdɛmɪk〕*adj.* 流行性的

pandemic〔pænˈdɛmɪk〕*n.* 全國 (世界) 性的流行病

outbreak〔ˈaʊtˌbrek〕*n.* 爆發　　pneumonia〔njuˈmonjə〕*n.* 肺炎

acute〔əˈkjut〕*adj.* 急性的　　tract〔trækt〕*n.* 道

onset〔ˈɑnˌsɛt〕*n.* 襲擊；(疾病的) 開始　　chill〔tʃɪl〕*n.* 寒冷

prostration〔prɑˈstreʃən〕*n.* (極度的) 疲勞；虛弱

pave the way for 為～舖路；使～容易進行

hemolytic〔hɪˈmɑlɪtɪk〕*adj.* 溶血性的

streptococcic〔ˌstrɛptəˈkɑksɪk〕*adj.* 鏈球菌的

complication〔ˌkɑmpləˈkeʃən〕*n.* 併發症

toxicity〔takˈsɪsətɪ〕*n.* 毒性　　confer〔kənˈfɝ〕*v.* 賦與

immunity〔ɪˈmjunətɪ〕*n.* 免疫力

quarantine〔ˈkwɔrənˌtin〕*n.* 隔離

parainfluenza〔ˌpærəˌɪnfluˈɛnzə〕*n.* 副流行性感冒

hepatitis〔ˌhɛpəˈtaɪtɪs〕*n.* 肝炎

國立彰化師範大學八十五學年度
碩士班研究生入學考試英文試題

I. Choose the Best Answer for Each Blank: 20%

1. The mature person understands that a positive attitude is crucial in making the transition successful. Being negative will never_____the feelings of frustration.
   (A) alleviate   (B) aviate
   (C) indiscreet   (D) increase

2. Registering for school the first time is a very complicated process. In order to_____this long, confusing process, you had better consult an experienced person first.
   (A) eliminate   (B) disturb
   (C) squander   (D) facilitate

3. The Congressman was forced to resign his position when his bribe-taking practices were_____to the public.
   (A) disposed   (B) exposed
   (C) supposed   (D) composed

4. Martha did not make enough money on her job, so she took a part-time job on weekends in order to_____her income.
   (A) profit   (B) supplement
   (C) defray   (D) install

5. Dennis does not want to gain any weight. He also does not want to lose weight. Therefore, he is trying to_____his present weight by eating carefully.
   (A) maintain   (B) contain
   (C) attain   (D) detain

6. Do you agree_____what Tom said about this issue?
   (A) to   (B) with
   (C) in   (D) on

7. Carol loved baseball. She listened enthusiastically to the baseball games_____the radio.
   (A) to   (B) in
   (C) on   (D) with

8. Susan is very quiet and shy. She finds it very difficult
   to cope_____meeting new people.
   (A) in   (B) with
   (C) to   (D) for

9. It is very convenient for John to go to school by bus
   because he can get_____the bus right in front of the
   school gate.
   (A) out of
   (B) out from
   (C) off
   (D) down

10. Many people are opposed_____the use of nuclear power.
    (A) with   (B) to
    (C) in   (D) on

II. Grammar: 30%

11. Having been served lunch, _____.
    (A) the problem was discussed by the members of the
        committee
    (B) the committee members discussed the problem
    (C) it was discussed by the committee members the
        problem
    (D) a discussion of the problem was held by the members
        of the committee

12. The first commercial film_____in California was
    completed in 1907.
    (A) made   (B) to make
    (C) was made   (D) making

13. _____with his girlfriend, he bought her a dozen roses.
    (A) He wanted to make up
    (B) He was trying to make up
    (C) To make up
    (D) Wanted to make up

14. When a bacterium becomes too large, it splits in half
    and forms two new bacteria,_____its own cell wall and
    protoplasm.
    (A) each has
    (B) with each
    (C) has each
    (D) each with

15. The New Frontier,_____, got off to a slow start.
    (A) the name of the program which John F. Kennedy gave
    (B) the name John F. Kennedy gave to his program
    (C) John F. Kennedy named his program
    (D) while the program named by John F. Kennedy

16. Not only_____, but he also owned a movie studio.
    (A) Hughes owned Las Vegas hotels
    (B) did Hughes own Las Vegas Hotels
    (C) owned Hughes Las Vegas hotels
    (D) Las Vegas hotels owned by Hughes

17. Spanish claim to California began in 1542_____its
    discovery by Cabrillo.
    (A) since   (B) when
    (C) for   (D) with

18. _____, he would have been able to pass the exam.
    (A) If he studied more
    (B) If he were studying to a greater degree
    (C) Studying more
    (D) Had he studied

19. Was it_____the professor regarded with such contempt?
    (A) them   (B) them whom
    (C) he   (D) he who

20. The committee members were of the same opinion_____
    the new tax measure.
    (A) in regard to
    (B) regarding to
    (C) with regards to
    (D) for regarding

21. Here_____notebook and report that I promised you last
    week.
    (A) is the   (B) are the
    (B) was the   (D) were the

22. _____, Georgia O'Keeffe is famous for the subtle color
    of her landscapes of the New Mexican desert.
    (A) She is an outstanding American painter
    (B) An outstanding American painter
    (C) An outstanding American painter who is
    (D) Despite an outstanding American painter

23. I asked Helen about Bill's disappearance, but she didn't know_____
    (A) why he had gone away
    (B) why he hadn't returned back
    (C) where he had gone to
    (D) where he was at

24. I was proud that_____was able to attend the reunion.
    (A) my whole entire family
    (B) all of my entire family
    (C) every member of my family
    (D) the sum total of my family

25. "Whose fault was it?" "The accident clearly resulted
    _____ your carelessness."
    (A) in   (B) on
    (C) from   (D) for

III. Read the following passages and give the most appropri-
     ate answer to each of the following questions by giving
     the letter (A, B, C, or D) which indicates the answer.
     30%

It is not often realized that women held a high place
in southern European societies in the 10th and 11th centuries.
As a wife, the woman was protected by the setting up of a
dowry or *decimum*. Admittedly, the purpose of this was to
protect her against the risk of desertion, but in reality
its function in the social and family life of the time was
much more important. The *decimum* was the wife's right to
receive a tenth of all her husband's property. The wife had
the right to withhold consent, in all transactions the
husband would make. And more than just a right: the documents show that she enjoyed a real power of decision, equal
to that of her husband. In no case do the documents indicate
any degree of difference in the legal status of husband and
wife.

The wife shared in the management of her husband's personal property, but the opposite was not always true. Women
seemed perfectly prepared to defend their own inheritance
against husbands who tried to exceed their rights, and on

occasion they showed a fine fighting spirit. A case in point
is that of Maria Vivas, a Catalan woman of Barcelona. Having
agreed with her husband Miro to sell a field she had inherited, for the needs of the household, she insisted on compensation. None being offered, she succeeded in dragging her
husband to the scribe to have a contract duly drawn up assigning her a piece of land from Miro's personal inheritance.
The unfortunate husband was obliged to agree, as the contract
says, "for the sake of peace." Either through the dowry or
through being hot-tempered, the Catalan wife knew how to win
herself, within the context of the family, a powerful economic position.

1. A *decimum* was_____
   (A) the wife's inheritance from her father.
   (B) a gift of money to the new husband.
   (C) a written contract.
   (D) the wife's right to receive one-tenth of her
       husband's property.

2. In the society described in the passage, the legal
   standing of the wife in marriage was_____
   (A) higher than that of her husband.
   (B) lower than that of her husband.
   (C) the same as that of her husband.
   (D) higher than that of a single woman.

3. What compensation did Maria Vivas get for the field?
   (A) some of the land Miro had inherited
   (B) a tenth of Miro's land
   (C) money for household expenses
   (D) money from Miro's inheritance

4. Could a husband sell his wife's inheritance?
   (A) no, under no circumstances
   (B) yes, whenever he wished to
   (C) yes, if she agreed
   (D) yes, if his father-in-law agreed

5. Which of the following is not mentioned as an effect of
the dowry system?
(A) The husband had to share the power of decision in
marriage.
(B) The wife was protected from desertion.
(C) The wife gained a powerful economic position.
(D) The husband was given control over his wife's property.

Misconceptions about alcoholism are common. Many people,
for example, think that alcoholics are careless, pleasure-
seeking people who have moral problems that make them easier
prey for liquor. Actually, alcoholics often feel guilty about
their drinking and are very self-conscious around other people. Alcoholics quite often have a low self-esteem and are
too sensitive about what people may think of them. Another
common myth is that the alcoholic is always drunk, but experts say this is not so. In truth, there are three types of
alcoholics. Episodic drinkers, for example, drink only now
and then, but each of the their drinking episodes ends in
overindulgence. Habitual excess drinkers are also only occasionally drunk, but their episodes are much more frequent
than those of the episodic drinker. The addict is a person
who must drink continually simply in order to function. It
is the addict who needs medical assistance to withdraw from
the support of alcohol.

6. This passage is mainly about
(A) therapy for alcoholics.
(B) alcoholism.
(C) common misconceptions about alcoholism.
(D) three types of alcoholics.

7. The best title for this passage is
(A) What About the Habitual Drinker?
(B) Alcoholism: Fact and Fiction.
(C) Curing the Alcoholic.
(D) Alcoholism in America.

8. According to the passage, which of the following
statements is not true?
(A) Many alcoholics feel guilty about their drinking.
(B) The habitual drinker is only occasionally drunk.
(C) The addict needs medical help with his problem.
(D) Episodic drinkers never overindulge.

9. We can conclude from the passage that_____
   (A) few alcoholics are episodic drinkers.
   (B) episodic drinkers' "bouts" are worse than those
       of habitual drinkers.
   (C) most alcoholics are emotionally disturbed people.
   (D) the addict-type alcoholic is always drunk.

10. The author's tone is_____
    (A) ironical.   (B) sarcastic.
    (C) subjective.   (D) objective.

    One major problem facing the further development of
non-chemical methods of pest control is their specificity.
Because these methods usually are effective against only
one kind of pest, crops still require chemical or other
treatments to handle threats from other species of pests.
The second important issue for non-chemical, and chemical
control methods is the possibility that health or environmental hazards may be introduced which have effects at least
as severe as those methods they are intended to replace.
This is particularly true in the cases of hormonal control
and chemical sterilization techniques.

    A third major drawback in the use of non-chemical meas-
ures is the cost of developing and marketing them. Because
of the specificity of these measures, a feature that many
environmentalists consider desirable, any single product
will have a limited market. So, even if a product could
capture the entire market for the control of a particular
species of pest, its limited demand might not justify the
cost of development.

11. What is one of the biggest difficulties in controlling
    pests by non-chemical means?
    (A) A particular non-chemical product may only work
        against one type of pest.
    (B) All crops require non-specific chemical measures to
        remain healthy.
    (C) Many species of pests can only be controlled by
        chemical sterilization.
    (D) Chemical or other treatments are always more
        effective than non-chemical methods.

12. According to the passage, a possible effect of non-
    chemical and chemical methods of control could be
    (A) the replacement of hormones in animals.
    (B) infertility in man and animals.
    (C) the introduction of health controls.
    (D) severe weather changes.

13. Many non-chemical products are not fully developed
    because_____
    (A) they are dangerous to sell.
    (B) environmentalists object to them.
    (C) they are very expensive to produce.
    (D) they have a narrow market.

14. Why is there a limited demand for non-chemical products?
    (A) Chemical products have much larger markets.
    (B) Most species of pests don't respond to non-chemical
        products.
    (C) They can never capture the entire specificity.
    (D) It is impossible to control their development
        effectively.

15. The passage would most likely be assigned reading for
    courses in which one of the following subjects?
    (A) Business management
    (B) Medicine
    (C) Botany
    (D) Biochemistry

IV. Cloze Test: Choose an appropriate word from the given
    list by giving the corresponding letter to fill in each
    of the blanks in the passages. 20%

A. around	B. react	C. during
D. up	E. making	F. while
G. distraction	H. fading	I. deal
J. comprising	K. bust	L. officials
M. sector	N. delay	O. but

Hang up and drive.

   If you don't, Brazil will___1___you. It's now a crime
in that country to use a cellular phone while driving, even
when stopped at a stop light.

   Exception: Voice-activated phones that let drivers keep
hands on the wheel.

Violators can be fined___2___to \$25.20. Repeaters can lose their drivers' licenses.

A U.S. study says only lighting a cigarette is more distracting. Experts say that___3___causes wrecks.

A 1990 phone study, by the American Automobile Association Foundation, says drivers aged 26 to 50 take an average 0.9 seconds longer to___4___in an emergency___5___making a phone call.

At 30 mph, their cars travel 37 feet during that___6___. Drivers over 50 average 1.4 seconds, or nearly 62 feet.

A complex conversation, such as a business___7___, slows reaction time about 0.8 seconds for most drivers.

___8___experts say no data directly link phones to crashes,___9___it difficult to justify a ban in the U.S.A.

But the real reason anti-phone laws aren't likely, says Jim Baxter, head of the National Motorists Association, is because, "A lot of elected___10___like to use cellular phones."

國立彰化師範大學八十五學年度
碩士班研究生入學考試英文試題詳解

I. 字彙：20%

1. (**A**)　(A) *alleviate* 〔ə'lɪvɪ,et〕 v. 減輕
　　　　　(B) aviate 〔'ævɪ,et〕 v. 飛行
　　　　　(C) indiscreet 〔,ɪndɪ'skrit〕 adj. 輕率的
　　　　　(D) increase 〔ɪn'kris〕 v. 增加
　　　　　　transition 〔træn'zɪʃən〕 n. 轉變；轉移

2. (**D**)　(A) eliminate 〔ɪ'lɪmə,net〕 v. 消除
　　　　　(B) disturb 〔dɪ'stɝb〕 v. 打擾
　　　　　(C) squander 〔'skwɑndɚ〕 v. 揮霍
　　　　　(D) *facilitate* 〔fə'sɪlə,tet〕 v. 使便利；使容易
　　　　　　register 〔'rɛdʒɪstɚ〕 n. 註冊

3. (**B**)　(A) dispose 〔dɪ'spoz〕 v. 處置
　　　　　(B) *expose* 〔ɪk'spoz〕 v. 使暴露
　　　　　(C) suppose 〔sə'poz〕 v. 假定；認爲
　　　　　(D) compose 〔kəm'poz〕 v. 組成；作曲
　　　　　　Congressman 〔'kɑŋgrəsmən〕 n. 國會議員
　　　　　　bribe 〔braɪb〕 n. 賄賂　　practices 〔'præktɪsɪz〕 n.pl. 惡習

4. (**B**)　(A) profit 〔'prɑfɪt〕 v. 獲益；有利
　　　　　(B) *supplement* 〔'sʌplə,mənt〕 v. 補充
　　　　　(C) defray 〔dɪ'fre〕 v. 給付
　　　　　(D) install 〔ɪn'stɔl〕 v. 安裝
　　　　　　income 〔'ɪn,kʌm〕 n. 收入

5. (**A**)　(A) *maintain* 〔men'ten〕 v. 維持
　　　　　(B) contain 〔kən'ten〕 v. 包含
　　　　　(C) attain 〔ə'ten〕 v. 達到
　　　　　(D) detain 〔dɪ'ten〕 v. 拘留；監禁

6.（ **B** ）*agree with* 同意

7.（ **C** ）*on the radio* 在無線廣播中
　　　　　enthusiastically〔 ɪn,θjuzɪˈæstɪkəlɪ 〕*adv.* 熱心地

8.（ **B** ）*cope with* 應付

9.（ **C** ）*get off* 下（車）

10.（ **B** ）*be opposed to* 反對

II. 文法：30％

11.（ **B** ）分詞 Having 之前的主詞被省略，故分詞構句意義上的主詞
　　　　　與主要子句的主詞相同，依句意，主詞應為人，故選 (B)。

12.（ **A** ）空格原本應填 which was made，而 which was 可省略，
　　　　　故選 (A) made 。　　commercial〔 kəˈmɝʃəl 〕*adj.* 商業的

13.（ **C** ）(A)，(B) 缺少連接詞，而 (D) 應改為 Wanting to make up ，
　　　　　故選 (C) To make up「為了要和好」。
　　　　　make up 和好

14.（ **D** ）with 引導的介詞片語修飾 each 。
　　　　　bacterium〔 bækˈtɪrɪəm 〕*n.* 細菌（複數形為 bacteria ）
　　　　　split〔 splɪt 〕*v.* 分裂
　　　　　protoplasm〔ˈprotə,plæzəm 〕*n.* 原生質

15.（ **B** ）原句是由 the name which John F. Kennedy gave to
　　　　　his program ，省略當受詞的關代 which 而來。
　　　　　get off 出發

16.（ **B** ）否定詞 not only 放在句首，句子要倒裝。

17.（ **D** ）依句意，選 (D) *with* 由於。

18.（ **D** ）依句意為「與過去事實相反的假設」，主要子句應用過去完
　　　　　成式：If he had studied, … 而 If 可省略，再將句子倒裝：
　　　　　Had he studied, … ，故選 (D)。

19. (**D**) 此句爲「It is (was)＋強調部分＋that (who)＋其餘部分」
的「強調語氣」句型。直述句爲：The professor regarded
him with such contempt. 強調句型爲：It was he who
the professor regarded with such contempt.

20. (**A**) ***in regard to＝with regard to＝regarding*** 關於（＝*about*）

21. (**B**) 主詞爲 notebook and report 爲複數，故動詞也應用複數
動詞，依句意爲現在式，選 (B)。

22. (**B**) 原句是由 Being an outstanding American painter 省略
Being 而來。
subtle〔ˊsʌtl̩〕*adj.* 巧妙的
landscape〔ˊlænskep〕*n.* 風景

23. (**A**) (B)應改爲 why he didn't return，(C)應改爲 where he
had gone，(D)則應改爲 where he was，故選(A)。

24. (**C**) that 引導的名詞子句，其動詞爲單數動詞 was，故主詞亦爲
單數，選 (C)。

25. (**C**) ***result from*** 起因於　　(A)result in 導致

Ⅲ. 閱讀測驗：30 ％

【譯文】

　　一般人通常不知道，在西元十、十一世紀時，女人在南歐社會裏
地位很高。爲人妻時，女人可藉由嫁妝或十分之一財產制度的確立，
而受到保護。不可否認地，這樣做的目的是要保護她免受被遺棄的危
險，但事實上這在當時的社會和家庭中的功能更爲重要。十分之一財
產制是指妻子擁有獲得丈夫十分之一財產的權利。丈夫生意上的全部
交易，妻子都保有同意權。而且不僅僅只是權利而已，文件上也寫明
妻子擁有眞正的、與丈夫同等的決定權。文件上指出丈夫和妻子在法
定地位上並無任何不同。

　　妻子得以分享丈夫個人財產的管理權,但反之則不然。女人似乎隨時準備好要保衛她們自己的遺產,不容丈夫越界侵犯,甚至有時還會表現出高度的戰鬥力。瑪莉亞‧菲佛就是一例,她是一位巴塞隆納加泰隆的婦女,為了家計所需,同意丈夫米羅出售她所繼承的一塊土地,但卻堅持要獲得賠償。丈夫沒有提出任何補償,於是瑪麗亞便成功地拉她先生到代書那裏,簽下草擬好的合約,要米羅從他的遺產中撥出一塊土地登記在她的名下。這位不幸的丈夫被迫同意,正如合約中所記載:「為了和平的緣故。」不論因其嫁妝或其暴躁的脾氣,這位加泰隆妻子知道如何在家庭裏,為自己贏得強而有力的經濟地位。

【答案】

1.(**D**)　　2.(**C**)　　3.(**A**)　　4.(**C**)　　5.(**D**)

【註】

dowry〔'daʊrɪ〕*n.* 嫁妝　　deci-〔'dɛsɪ〕*n.* 十分之一的…
admittedly〔əd'mɪtɪdlɪ〕*adv.* 不可否認地
withhold〔wɪð'hold〕*v.* 保留　　transaction〔træn'sækʃən〕*n.* 交易
document〔'dɑkjəmənt〕*n.* 文件　　Catalan〔'kætələn〕*adj.* 加泰隆的
inheritance〔ɪn'hɛrətəns〕*n.* 遺產　　exceed〔ɪk'sid〕*v.* 超越
on occasion 有時　　***in point*** 適當的
inherit〔ɪn'hɛrɪt〕*v.* 繼承　　household〔'haʊs,hold〕*n.* 家庭
drag〔dræg〕*v.* 拖;拉　　scribe〔skraɪb〕*n.* 代書
duly〔'dulɪ〕*adv.* 適當地;及時地
draw up 草擬(文件)　　***be obliged to*** 被迫
hot-tempered〔'hɑt'tɛmpɚd〕*n.* 暴躁的;易怒的

【譯文】

　　一般人對於酒精中毒常有誤解。舉例來說,很多人認為酗酒者是不負責的尋歡之人,他們有道德上的問題,使他們容易猛灌黃湯。事實上,酗酒者對於他們的豪飲常會有罪惡感,而且和別人在一起,會十分不自在。酗酒者很自卑,而且對於別人的看法很敏感。另一個普

遍的想法是，酗酒的人總是爛醉如泥，但專家說並非如此。事實上，酗酒者有三種。舉例來說，間歇性酗酒者只是偶爾喝酒，但他們每一次喝酒，到後來都會過於沈迷。習慣於飲酒過量的酗酒者也是偶爾才會喝醉，但他們的酗酒次數，比間歇性酗酒者來得頻繁。有酒癮的人必須一直喝酒，才能讓體內器官正常運作。有酒癮的人，需要借助醫藥的幫助，才能消除對酒的依賴。

【答案】

6. (**C**)　　7. (**B**)　　8. (**D**)　　9. (**C**)　　10. (**D**)

【註】

misconception〔͵mɪskən'sɛpʃən〕*n.* 誤解；錯誤的觀念
alcoholism〔'ælkəhɔl͵ɪzəm〕*n.* 酒精中毒
alcoholic〔͵ælkə'hɔlɪk〕*n.* 酗酒者
prey〔pre〕*n.* 犧牲者；被害者　　liquor〔'lɪkɚ〕*n.* 酒
self-conscious〔'sɛlf'kɑnʃəs〕*adj.* 羞怯的
sensitive〔'sɛnsətɪv〕*adj.* 敏感的
episodic〔͵ɛpɪ'sɑdɪk〕*adj.* 間歇的
now and then 偶爾　　episode〔'ɛpə͵sod〕*n.* 插曲
overindulgence〔'ovəɪn'dʌldʒəns〕*n.* 過度耽溺
habitual〔hə'bɪtʃuəl〕*adj.* 習慣性的
excess〔ɪk'sɛs〕*adj.* 過量的　　addict〔'ædɪkt〕*n.* 上癮的人
function〔'fʌŋkʃən〕*v.* 起作用　　bout〔baut〕*n.* 一回

【譯文】

　　關於以非化學的方法防治害蟲已有進一步的發展，不過主要的問題在於其個別性。因為這些方法通常只對一種害蟲有效，農作物仍得藉助化學藥物或其他方法，以對抗他種害蟲的威脅。使用非化學藥品及化學控制方法的第二個嚴重問題，是仍有可能危害健康和環境，而這所帶來的影響至少和我們原本想取代的一樣嚴重，這在荷爾蒙控制和化學絕育科技方面最為明顯。

　　第三個使用非化學方法的主要缺點，是花費於研發及行銷此方法的成本。這些方法的個別性是許多環境學家都滿意的特性，但由於其個別性，任何一種產品的市場都有限。所以，即使產品能獨占整個市場、控制某種特別的害蟲，其有限的需求可能也無法證明其研發成本的合理性。

【答案】

11. (**A**)　　12. (**B**)　　13. (**C**)　　14. (**C**)　　15. (**D**)

【註】

pest〔pɛst〕n. 害蟲　　specificity〔ˌspɛsəˈfɪsətɪ〕n. 特效；獨特

species〔ˈspiʃɪz〕n. 種　　hazard〔ˈhæzɚd〕n. 危險

hormonal〔ˈhɔrmon̩〕adj. 荷爾蒙的

sterilization〔ˌstɛrələˈzeʃən〕n. 使貧瘠；絕育

drawback〔ˈdrɔˌbæk〕n. 缺點　　market〔ˈmɑrkɪt〕v. 行銷

environmentalist〔ɪnˌvaɪrənˈmɛntl̩ɪst〕n. 環境學家

desirable〔dɪˈzaɪrəbl̩〕adj. 合意的

justify〔ˈdʒʌstəˌfaɪ〕v. 證明～爲正當

infertility〔ˌɪnfɝˈtɪlətɪ〕n. 貧瘠　　botany〔ˈbɑtənɪ〕n. 植物學

biochemistry〔ˌbaɪoˈkɛmɪstrɪ〕n. 生物化學

IV. 克漏字：20％

【譯文】

　　掛上電話開車吧。

　　如果你不這樣做，巴西政府會逮捕你。現在在巴西，開車時使用行動電話是違法的行爲，即使在停紅燈時也不行。

　　例外：駕駛員仍能手握方向盤的聲控電話。

　　違規者得處高達＄25.20 的罰金。再犯者會被吊銷駕照。

　　美國一項研究指出，打行動電話是僅次於點燃香煙最易使駕駛人分心的事。專家指出開車不專心易釀成車禍。

　　1990 年由美國汽車協會基金會所作的電話研究顯示，26 至 50 歲的駕駛人，若在使用電話時發生緊急事故，平均要多花 0.9 秒的時間來應變。

　　在每小時 30 英里的速度中，那個延遲的反應會使車子多開 37 英尺。50 歲以上的駕駛人平均要多花 1.4 秒，車子會多開將近 62 英尺。

　　複雜的對話，例如生意交易，使大部分駕駛人的應變時間，平均慢了 0.8 秒。

　　專家指出，並沒有資料顯示電話與車禍有直接的關連，這使得美國要讓禁令合理化很困難。

　　國家汽車協會主席吉姆‧白斯特說，反對使用行動電話的法律不大可能會通過的真正理由是因為「有許多被選出的官員喜歡使用行動電話。」

【註】

hang up 掛電話　　***cellular phone*** 行動電話
activate〔'æktə‚vet〕v. 使起反應
violator〔'vaɪə‚letə˞〕n. 違反者
distract〔dɪ'strækt〕v. 使分心　　ban〔bæn〕n. 禁止

1. (**K**) bust〔bʌst〕v. 逮捕；突擊
2. (**D**) ***up to*** 高達
3. (**G**) distraction〔dɪ'strækʃən〕n. 分心
4. (**B**) react〔rɪ'ækt〕v. 反應
5. (**F**) while〔hwaɪl〕conj. 當～時候
6. (**N**) delay〔dɪ'le〕n. 延遲
7. (**I**) deal〔dil〕n. 交易
8. (**O**) but　但是
9. (**E**) make〔mek〕v. 使得
10. (**L**) official〔ə'fɪʃəl〕n. 官員

國立中興大學八十五學年度
碩士班研究生入學考試英文試題

I. Vocabulary(20%): Following the context, choose the one word or phrase which is closest in meaning to the underlined word.

Example: No one can be sure if the war is <u>imminent</u> or not.
    (A) dangerous   (B) severe
    (C) about to take place (D) coming to an end
The best answer is (C).

1. The Court may <u>presume</u> incorrectly that the choices made by plaintiffs are free and uncoerced.
    (A) manage   (B) assume
    (C) imply   (D) quote

2. They argued that law enforcement against prostitution would be <u>facilitated</u> if the law dispensed with proof of actual hire.
    (A) made complicated
    (B) made less difficult
    (C) legalized
    (D) canceled

3. Under the Prison Rules a prisoner might be granted <u>temporary</u> release for any special purpose.
    (A) effective   (B) temporal
    (C) not permanent   (D) conditional

4. Attempts to <u>extradite</u> him from Taiwan were not pursued.
    (A) send back   (B) transfer by air
    (C) smuggle   (D) assassinate

5. A psychiatrist had earlier underlined certified that there were serious grounds for supposing that the applicant suffered from a mental disorder.
(A) argued　　　　　　　　(B) supposed
(C) affirmed　　　　　　　(D) interpreted

6. Variations among companies in the application of generally accepted accounting principles may hamper comparability.
(A) accelerate　　　　　　(B) improve
(C) enact　　　　　　　　(D) impede

7. Depreciation is the process of allocating the cost of an asset to expense over its useful life in a rational manner.
(A) assigning　　　　　　(B) cutting
(C) alienating　　　　　　(D) increasing

8. The museum has been heavily criticized over its acquisition of the four-million-dollar sculpture.
(A) exchange　　　　　　(B) appreciation
(C) gaining　　　　　　　(D) inflation

9. As soon as the board of elections promulgates the list of candidates, a secret vote is prepared.
(A) critically reviews　　(B) quickly contacts
(C) informally discusses　(D) officially declares

10. The Taichung Port Authorities have seized over a million dollars
(A) measured　　　　　　(B) delivered
(C) confiscated　　　　　(D) stolen

11. Though the evidence is overwhelming, if one juror is still skeptical, the case must be retried.
(A) not convinced　　　　(B) not pleased
(C) not present　　　　　(D) not worried

12. Diplomatic misunderstandings can often be traced back
    to blunders in translation.
    (A) arguments   (B) insults
    (C) mistakes   (D) attempts

13. A cut in the budget put 20 percent of the state
    employees' jobs in jeopardy.
    (A) review   (B) danger
    (C) perspective   (D) reservation

14. Primary education in Taiwan is compulsory.
    (A) easy   (B) excellent
    (C) free of charge   (D) required

15. Historical records reveal that Confucius reiterated
    his ideas about a meritocracy.
    (A) repeated   (B) furthered
    (C) changed   (D) published

16. Everyone rejoiced at the news of his safe return.
    (A) confirmed
    (B) was surprised
    (C) desired to make sure
    (D) showed great happiness

17. He has been an ardent patriot of Zionism.
    (A) enthusiastic   (B) reluctant
    (C) ignorant   (D) financial

18. The noise from the street diverted his mind from
    studying.
    (A) overwhelmed   (B) disturbed
    (C) distracted   (D) isolated

19. He sat at his desk, brooding over why she had left him.
    (A) talking loudly   (B) thinking silently
    (C) arguing   (D) wondering

20. In every western country the State <u>subsidizes</u> education, housing and health provision.
    (A) encourages   (B) promotes
    (C) ignores   (D) finances

II. Grammar (20%)

Part A

　　Each sentence below has four words or phrases un-derlined. The four underlined parts of the sentence are marked (A),(B),(C), and (D). You are to identify the one underlined word or phrase that should be corrected or rewritten.

Example: <u>Many</u> water <u>is</u> needed <u>for people</u> <u>living</u> in the
　　　　　　A　　　　　B　　　　　C　　　　　D
　　　　　dry area.
　　　　　You should choose answer (A).

21. <u>As</u> you study his face, you are <u>struck</u> <u>by</u> the look
    A   B   C
    of a man <u>in peace with</u> himself.
               D

22. The river <u>murmured</u> to the shores in musically, <u>told</u>
                   A   B
    of its <u>release</u> from icy <u>fetters</u>.
              C   D

23. She saw a <u>Venetian</u> cross of gold <u>setting with</u> precious
                  A   B
    ous <u>stones</u> of wonderful <u>workmanship</u>.
          C   D

24. The people <u>whom</u> <u>live</u> across the street always <u>share</u>
                   A   B   C
    their surplus <u>vegetables</u>.
                     D

25. The old man, <u>broke</u> and <u>had</u> no friends to <u>turn to</u>,
             A   B   C
    simply <u>disappeared</u> from the neighborhood.
             D

26. Eagles have <u>such the</u> long, <u>broad wings</u> and tails that
                 A   B
    they <u>look</u> clumsy <u>while</u> they are on the ground.
         C   D

27. The winner of the first auto race <u>held</u> in the United
                            A
    States, in 1895, <u>drived</u> his car at a <u>speed</u> of 7.5
                B   C
    <u>miles per hour</u>.
        D

28. Penny <u>has</u> <u>always</u> enjoyed <u>walking through</u> the park
        A   B   C
    and <u>looking the flowers</u>.
        D

Part B

The following sentences are incomplete ones Four words or phrases, marked (A),(B),(C), and (D), are given beneath each sentence. Choose the one word or phrase that best completes the sentence.

Example: I came to _____ your birthday.
         (A) take (B) stay (C) celebrate (D) saving
         The best answer is (C).

29. _____ brings about happiness has utility, according to the doctrine of utilitarianism.
    (A) Why   (B) Each
    (C) Whatever   (D) It

30. Mary just called the office and said she _____ within the hour.
    (A) will arrive   (B) would arrive
    (C) arrives   (D) is arriving

31. Paul's comments were not relevant _____ the
    topic under discussion.
    (A) with   (B) to
    (C) at   (D) on

32. Doctor, for the last two days I haven't been able to
    keep any food down. Every time I try to eat something,
    I throw _____ soon afterward.
    (A) out   (B) off
    (C) up   (D) down

33. _____ the necessary qualifications, he was not
    considered for the job.
    (A) He lacked   (B) Lacked
    (C) Lacking   (D) Lacked of

34. Peter, _____, suggested stopping at the next
    station.
    (A) whom had been driving all day
    (B) who had been driving all day
    (C) that had been driving all day
    (D) which had been driving all day

35. No one knows what I _____ while I was waiting
    for the verdict.
    (A) went on   (B) went round
    (C) went down   (D) went through

III. Reading Comprehension(30%). Read the following three
     passages carefully, and then choose the best answer
     to each question.

(1)
     YOU'RE THE BOSS! announce campaign posters plas-
tered the length and breadth of Taiwan, and it's a good,
beefy, democratic message. When Taiwan's 12 million voters
choose a President in balloting on March 23, the man they

anoint will be the first popularly elected chief executive in more than 40 centuries of Chinese history. The candidate grinning toothily on those posters, incumbent President Lee Teng-hui, helped engineer his island state's swift conversion to democracy, giving the slogan a subtext: if the people now have the power, he was the guy who delivered it to them.

But as events last week showed all too alarmingly, Taiwan's citizens are not the sole bosses of their destiny as long as mainland China, 175km across the Taiwan Strait, considers the island a renegade province. Beijing sees the election as a conscious move by Taiwan, and Lee, toward a political status independent of the mainland, and the People's Republic has literally gone ballistic.

On March 5 (Tuesday) China announced it would test-fire missiles into the waters off the Taiwanese ports of Kaohsiung and Keelung during the penultimate week of the campaign. Three M-9 medium-range ballistic missiles (Chinese versions of the Scud) splashed down Friday, and they were reportedly unarmed. But at week's end Beijing announced that missile tests starting this week in the South China Sea would use live ammunition.

36. When was this passage most likely written?
    (A) Between March 5 and March 9
    (B) Between March 10 and March 16
    (C) Between March 17 and March 23
    (D) Between March 24 and March 29

37. The author said that the presidential election in Taiwan was
    (A) to make Taiwan's citizens the sole bosses of their destiny.
    (B) the first one in more than 4000 years of Chinese history.
    (C) to make the people's Republic of China go ballistic.
    (D) to affirm Taiwan's resolution not to be terrorized by the giant nation across the strait.

38. According to the author, Lee Teng-hui's campaign posters implied that
    (A) he was the one who delivered power to people.
    (B) an incumbent president could make people his bosses.
    (C) he should have helped engineer his island state's swift conversion to democracy.
    (D) when Taiwan voters chose a President, he was the most popular one.

39. Why did Beijing test-fire missiles into the waters off Taiwan? Which of the following descriptions is correct?
    (A) Taiwan's citizens are not the sole bosses of their destiny.
    (B) Beijing considers the island a renegade province.
    (C) Beijing sees the presidential election a move toward an independent political status.
    (D) All the above.

40. The first three missiles test-fired
    (A) were loaded with live ammunition.
    (B) were unarmed M-9 Medium-range missiles.
    (C) fell short and missed the target.
    (D) were launched without warning.

(2)

On July 4, 1997, a collection of computers, lasers and cameras is expected to land on the surface of Mars, roll around at the rate of one centimeter per second and start taking pictures. This roving scientific envoy, the future of the American space program, weighs about 23 pounds and takes up as much shelf space as a microwave oven. Its creators call it Rocky.

This is the face of NASA in the '90s--and beyond. The mission is small, has limited goals and uses off-the-shelf technology, the kind of stuff found in personal computers and cellular phones. Rocky is cheap, too. Back in 1976, a Viking visit to the red planet cost $1 billion; next year NASA will spend less than $260 million to send its new rover to Mars. The budget cap is strict: ''If you go over that, they just cancel your thing,'' says Tom Rivellini, an engineer at the Jet Propulsion Laboratory in Pasadena, Calif., where the spacecraft is being designed and as-sembled.

The Mars Global Surveyor Program--five missions are planned over the next decade--is one of the boldest steps NASA has taken in years. In the months that followed the 1986 Challenger disaster, the space agency floated in a state of shock. It grounded shuttle flights for nearly three years. Confusion reigned. ''There were some people on the outside who said that we ought to cancel the whole space program,'' says Bryan O'Connor, head of NASA's shuttle program.

41. Which of the following descriptions is incorrect?
   (A) Rocky is the creator of a roving scientific envoy.
   (B) The roving scientific envoy weighs about 23 pounds.
   (C) The scientific envoy is expected to land on Mars in 1997.
   (D) The envoy is a collection of computers, lasers and cameras.

42. Rocky's mission
   (A) is to make a Viking visit to Mars for the first time.
   (B) costs $1 billion.
   (C) uses the same technology as that of personal computers.
   (D) is going to be canceled because of the strict budget cap.

43. This roving scientific envoy
   (A) is being designed and assembled at NASA.
   (B) caused the 1986 Challenger disaster.
   (C) grounded shuttle flights for nearly three years.
   (D) is part of the Mars Global Surveyor Program.

44. NASA is the abbreviation for
   (A) Naval Air Station and Association.
   (B) National Association of Spaceship Agency.
   (C) National Aeronautics and Space Administration.
   (D) Naval Airplanes and Ships Administration.

45. The US space agency once floated in a state of shock because
   (A) the shuttle program cost $1 billion.
   (B) of the 1986 Challenger disaster.
   (C) some people said that the whole space program ought to be canceled.
   (D) NASA took bold steps.

(3)

　　When I first met Nina, I disliked her at once. She was wearing skintight pedal pushers, a flashy, floppy top, and sneakers with no socks--bizarrely inappropriate even at our very informal company. Soon, Nina was doggedly pumping me for information about the new department I was running, where she hoped to get a permanent job. Not a chance, I thought. Not if I have anything to say about it.

　　However, I didn't. Within a few days she was "trying out" for me. I gave her a moderately difficult, uninteresting, and unimportant project that I didn't need for months. It took that long for her successor to untangle the mess she had made out of it. Although I couldn't have predicted exactly what Nina would do, in three minutes flat I had assessed her as someone who could not be relied upon to get a job done.

46. On what occasion did the author first meet Nina?
　(A) A date.
　(C) An interview.
　(B) A formal meeting.
　(D) A party.

47. Since the author disliked Nina at first sight, why did she hire her?
　(A) She did not have a say in this case.
　(B) She wanted to try out for Nina.
　(C) She wanted to challenge Nina.
　(D) She knew that first impressions could be deceptive.

48. What happened to Nina after she got the job?
　(A) She did the job well, but couldn't get along well with the author.
　(B) With the help of her successor, she got her job done.
　(C) She did not do her job well, but she stayed.
　(D) She could not get her job done and she left.

49. Which of the following descriptions of Nina is incorrect?
    (A) Pushy.
    (B) Conscientious.
    (C) Insensitive.
    (D) Aggressive.

50. What does this passage imply?
    (A) First impressions can be misleading.
    (B) Snap judgments about strangers do make sense.
    (C) Females may not be relied on to get a job done.
    (D) One who doggedly pumps for information may not be a good employee.

IV. Composition(20%): Write a well-organized and fully-developed composition on the topic--"The Importance of Independent Thinking.''

國立中興大學八十五學年度
碩士班研究生入學考試英文試題詳解

I. 字彙：20%

1. (**B**) presume〔prɪ'zum〕*v.* 假定；推測
   (B) ***assume***〔ə'sjum〕*v.* 假定
   (D) quote〔kwot〕*v.* 引用
   plaintiff〔'plentɪf〕*n.* 原告
   uncoerced〔ˌʌnko'ɝst〕*adj.* 未經逼迫的

2. (**B**) facilitate〔fə'sɪləˌtet〕*v.* 使便利
   (C) legalize〔'ligḷˌaɪz〕*v.* 使合法化
   prostitution〔ˌprɑstə'tjuʃən〕*n.* 賣淫
   dispense with 免除

3. (**C**) temporary〔'tɛmpəˌrɛrɪ〕*adj.* 暫時的
   (A) effective〔ə'fɛktɪv〕*adj.* 有效的
   (B) temporal〔'tɛmpərəl〕*adj.* 世俗的
   (C) ***not permanent*** 不是永久的
   (D) conditional〔kən'dɪʃənḷ〕*adj.* 有條件的

4. (**A**) extradite〔'ɛkstrəˌdaɪt〕*v.* 引渡
   (C) smuggle〔'smʌgḷ〕*v.* 走私
   (D) assassinate〔ə'sæsṇˌet〕*v.* 暗殺

5. (**C**) certify〔'sɝtəˌfaɪ〕*v.* 證明
   (C) ***affirm***〔ə'fɝm〕*v.* 證明
   (D) interpret〔ɪn'tɝprɪt〕*v.* 解釋
   psychiatrist〔saɪ'kaɪətrɪst〕*n.* 精神科醫師
   ground〔graʊnd〕*n.* 理由

6. (**D**) hamper〔'hæmpɚ〕*v.* 妨礙
　　　　(A) accelerate〔æk'sɛlə,ret〕*v.* 加速
　　　　(C) enact〔ɪn'ækt〕*v.* 制定
　　　　(D) ***impede***〔ɪm'pid〕*v.* 阻礙
　　　　　variation〔,vɛrɪ'eʃən〕*n.* 不同
　　　　　accounting〔ə'kaʊntɪŋ〕*n.* 會計
　　　　　comparability〔,kɑmpərə'bɪlətɪ〕*n.* 相似

7. (**A**) allocate〔'ælə,ket〕*v.* 分配
　　　　(A) ***assign***〔ə'saɪn〕*v.* 分配
　　　　(B) cut〔kʌt〕*v.* 減少
　　　　(C) alienate〔'eljən,et〕*v.* 使疏遠
　　　　　depreciation〔dɪ,priʃɪ'eʃən〕*n.* 跌價；貶值
　　　　　asset〔'æsɛt〕*n.* 資產

8. (**C**) acquisition〔,ækwə'zɪʃən〕*n.* 獲得
　　　　(B) appreciation〔ə,priʃɪ'eʃən〕*n.* 欣賞
　　　　(C) ***gain***〔gen〕*n.* 獲得
　　　　(D) inflation〔ɪn'fleʃən〕*n.* 通貨膨脹
　　　　　sculpture〔'skʌlptʃɚ〕*n.* 雕刻品

9. (**D**) promulgate〔prə'mʌlget〕*v.* 宣布
　　　　(A) critically review 批判性的評論
　　　　(D) ***officially declare*** 正式公布
　　　　　board〔bɔrd〕*n.* 委員會
　　　　　candidate〔'kændə,det〕*n.* 候選人
　　　　　secret vote 不記名投票

10. (**C**) seize〔'siz〕*v.* 沒收
　　　　(A) measure〔'mɛʒɚ〕*v.* 測量
　　　　(C) ***confiscate***〔'kɑnfɪs,ket〕*v.* 沒收

11. (**A**) skeptical〔'skɛptɪkəl〕*adj.* 懷疑的
　　　(A) ***not convinced*** 不相信的
　　　(B) not pleased 不滿意的
　　　(C) not present 不在場的
　　　overwhelming〔,ovɚ'hwɛlmɪŋ〕*adj.* 壓倒性的
　　　juror〔'dʒʊrɚ〕*n.* 陪審員
　　　retry〔ri'traɪ〕*v.* 重審

12. (**C**) blunder〔'blʌndɚ〕*n.* 錯誤
　　　(B) insult〔'ɪnsʌlt〕*n.* 侮辱
　　　diplomatic〔,dɪplə'mætɪk〕*adj.* 外交的

13. (**B**) jeopardy〔'dʒɛpɚdɪ〕*n.* 危險
　　　(A) review〔rɪ'vju〕*n.* 複習；評論
　　　(C) perspective〔pɚ'spɛktɪv〕*n.* 正確的眼光
　　　(D) reservation〔,rɛzɚ'veʃən〕*n.* 預訂
　　　budget〔'bʌdʒɪt〕*n.* 預算

14. (**D**) compulsory〔kəm'pʌlsərɪ〕*adj.* 強迫的；義務的
　　　(C) free of charge 免費的
　　　(D) ***required***〔rɪ'kwaɪrd〕*adj.* 必須的

15. (**A**) reiterate〔ri'ɪtə,ret〕*v.* 重述
　　　(A) ***repeat***〔rɪ'pit〕*v.* 重述
　　　(B) further〔'fɝðɚ〕*v.* 促進
　　　(D) publish〔'pʌblɪʃ〕*v.* 出版
　　　meritocracy〔,mɛrə'tɑkrəsɪ〕*n.* 賢能統治主義

16. (**D**) rejoice〔rɪ'dʒɔɪs〕*v.* 高興
　　　(A) confirm〔kən'fɝm〕*v.* 確認

17. (**A**) ardent〔'ɑrdn̩t〕*adj.* 熱心的
　　(A) ***enthusiastic***〔ɪn͵θjuzɪ'æstɪk〕*adj.* 熱心的
　　(B) reluctant〔rɪ'lʌktənt〕*adj.* 不情願的
　　(C) ignorant〔'ɪgnərənt〕*adj.* 無知的
　　(D) financial〔faɪ'nænʃəl〕*adj.* 財務的
　　　patriot〔'petrɪət〕*n.* 愛國者
　　　Zionism〔'zaɪən͵ɪzəm〕*n.* 猶太復國運動

18. (**C**) divert〔daɪ'vɝt〕*v.* 使轉向
　　(A) overwhelm〔͵ovɚ'hwɛlm〕*v.* 使感動
　　(B) disturb〔dɪ'stɝb〕*v.* 擾亂
　　(C) ***distract***〔dɪ'strækt〕*v.* 使分心
　　(D) isolate〔'aɪsl̩͵et〕*v.* 使孤立

19. (**B**) brood〔brud〕*v.* 沈思
　　(B) ***thinking silently*** 靜靜地思考

20. (**D**) subsidize〔'sʌbsə͵daɪz〕*v.* 資助
　　(B) promote〔prə'mot〕*v.* 升遷；提倡
　　(D) ***finance***〔'faɪnæns〕*v.* 資助
　　　provision〔prə'vɪʒən〕*n.* 供應；（政府提供的）錢和設備

II. 文法：20 %

A.

21. (**D**) *in peace with* → ***at peace with***
　　at peace with oneself 心平氣和

22. (**B**) *told* → ***telling***　　兩動詞間無連接詞，第二個動詞須改為現
　　在分詞。
　　murmur〔'mɝmɚ〕*v.*（小河、風等）潺潺聲
　　fetter〔'fɛtɚ〕*n.* 束縛

23. (**B**) *setting* → *set*　　set 爲過去分詞，原句是由形容子句 which
was　set　with …簡化而來。
set〔sɛt〕*v.* 鑲嵌　　*set A with B* 將 B 鑲嵌於 A 中
Venetian〔və'niʃən〕*adj.* 威尼斯的
workmanship〔'wɜkmən,ʃɪp〕*n.* 手藝

24. (**A**) *whom* → *who*　　surplus〔'sɜpləs〕*adj.* 剩餘的

25. (**B**) *had* → *having*　　原句是由補述用法的形容詞子句… who
was　broke　and　had　no　friends　to　turn　to 簡化而來。
broke〔brok〕*adj.* 沒錢的

26. (**A**) *such the* → *such*　　clumsy〔'klʌmzɪ〕*adj.* 笨拙的

27. (**B**) *drived* → *drove*

28. (**C**) *looking the flowers* → *looking at the flowers*

B.

29. (**C**) whatever 爲複合關係代名詞，相當於 anything that，引導
名詞子句做爲整句的主詞。
utility〔ju'tɪlətɪ〕*n.* 用處　　doctrine〔'dɑktrɪn〕*n.* 教條
utilitarianism〔,jutɪlə'tɛrɪənɪzm〕*n.* 實用主義

30. (**B**) 依句意，爲過去式，選 (B)。

31. (**B**) *be relevant to* 與～相關

32. (**C**) 依句意，選 (C) *throw up*「嘔吐」。而 (A) throw out「否
決；發表」，(B) throw off「擺脫；發出」，(C) throw down
「扔下；推翻」，皆不合句意。

33. (**C**) Lacking the necessary qualifications 爲分詞構句，是由
副詞子句：As he lacks the necessary qualifications
簡化而來。

34.（ **B** ）代替人且為主格時，關代用 who ，此為補述用法，不可用
　　　that 。

35.（ **D** ）依句意，選 (D) ***go through*** 「忍受；經歷」。而 (A) go on
　　　「繼續」，(B) go round 「足夠分配」，(C) go down 「沈
　　　沒；下降」，皆不合。　　verdict〔ˈvɝdɪkt〕*n.* 判決

Ⅲ. 閱讀測驗：30 ％

(1)【譯文】

　　人民是頭家！整個台灣地區都貼滿了競選的海報，這傳達了良好
的而穩固的民主訊息。全台灣一千二百萬的選民，於三月廿三日當天
投票選舉總統，當選的人將是四千多年來，中國有史以來第一位民選
總統。現任總統李登輝亦是候選人之一，海報中的他露齒而笑，透過
他的監督、指揮，使得台灣迅速地轉向民主政治，這使得那句口號隱
含著另一層意義：如果現在人民擁有權力，是他所賦予的。

　　但是上星期發生的事件，令人膽顫心驚。只要海峽對岸，與我們
相隔 175 公里的中國大陸認為台灣是背叛的一省，台灣的人民就不是
自己命運的唯一主宰。北京當局將這次的選舉，視為台灣民眾和李登
輝有意的行動，目的是要台灣脫離中國大陸而獨立。中共已經開始採
取口頭上的攻擊。

　　3 月 5 日（星期二）大陸宣布，在選舉前的二個星期，舉行飛彈試
射，目標為高雄和基隆二港的水域。到了星期五，三顆 M-9 中程飛彈
（中國版的飛毛腿飛彈）射入海中，根據報導，這些是未裝彈藥的飛
彈。但在周末時，北京當局又宣布，這星期開始，在中國南海域的演
習會使用真正的飛彈。

【答案】
　36.（ **A** ）　　37.（ **B** ）　　38.（ **A** ）　　39.（ **D** ）　　40.（ **B** ）

【註】

campaign〔kæmˈpen〕*n.* 競選活動

poster〔ˈpostɚ〕*n.* 海報　　plaster〔ˈplæstɚ〕*v.* 張貼

the length and breadth 到處

beefy〔ˈbifɪ〕*adj.* 強壯的　　ballot〔ˈbælət〕*v.* 投票

anoint〔əˈnɔɪnt〕*v.* 照天意選定　　grin〔grɪn〕*v.* 露齒而笑

toothily〔ˈtuθəlɪ〕*adv.* 露出牙齒地

incumbent〔ɪnˈkʌmbənt〕*adj.* 現任的

engineer〔ˌɛndʒəˈnɪr〕*v.* 監督

conversion〔kənˈvɜʒən〕*n.* 轉變

slogan〔ˈslogən〕*n.* 口號；標語

subtext〔ˈsʌbˌtɛkst〕*n.* 字面下的文本；潛台詞

deliver〔dɪˈlɪvɚ〕*v.* 交給

alarmingly〔əˈlɑrmɪŋlɪ〕*adv.* 驚人地

renegade〔ˈrɛnɪˌged〕*adj.* 反叛的

ballistic〔bæˈlɪstɪk〕*adj.* 彈道的；發射的

test-fire〔ˈtɛstˈfaɪr〕*v.* 試射　　missile〔ˈmɪsḷ〕*n.* 飛彈

penultimate〔pɪˈnʌltəmɪt〕*adj.* 倒數第二的

unarmed〔ʌnˈɑrmd〕*adj.* 未武裝的

live〔laɪv〕*adj.* 未爆炸的；可用的

ammunition〔ˌæmjəˈnɪʃən〕*n.* 彈藥

load〔lod〕*v.* 裝　　launch〔lɑntʃ〕*v.* 發射

(2)【譯文】

　　一九九七年七月四日，一套包括有電腦、雷射和照相機的裝備登陸火星表面，以每秒一公分的速度運轉，並開始攝影。這個可自由移動的科學特使，是美國太空計劃未來的希望所在，它的重量只有廿三磅，擱板面積大約是微波爐的大小，其創造者稱之為「洛基」。

　　這是關乎美國航空暨太空總署九○年代，甚至是以後的面子問題。這項任務規模不大，有特定的目標，而且採用的是現有的科技，這種裝備可在個人電腦和行動電話中找到。「洛基」的花費也不高。一九七六年到火星的維京探測就花費十億美元；明年太空總署要把新的移動器送至火星，這項花費不到二億六千萬美元。預算的上限規定很嚴格，湯姆・瑞凡里尼說：「如果你超過預算，他們就取消你的計畫。」他是噴進推進實驗室的工程師，實驗室位於加州的帕薩迪納市，這裡是設計和裝配太空船的地方。

火星全貌探測計畫，包括五項任務，將在未來十年中規劃完成，這也是太空總署這幾年來，最大膽的行動之一。一九八六年「挑戰者號」失事後的幾個月內，太空總署受到很大的衝擊。將近三年的時間，停止所有的太空梭飛行，也逐漸引起大家的疑惑。BASA 太空梭計劃的指揮者布萊恩・奧康納說：「有些局外人認為，我們應該取消整個太空計劃。」

【答案】

41. (**A**)　　42. (**C**)　　43. (**D**)　　44. (**C**)　　45. (**B**)

【註】

roving〔ˈrovɪŋ〕adj. 移動的　　envoy〔ˈɛnvɔɪ〕n. 使者
take up 占有　　shelf〔ʃɛlf〕n. 擱板；架子
NASA 美國航空暨太空總署　　off-the-shelf〔ˈɔfðəˈʃɛlf〕adj. 現有的
stuff〔stʌf〕n. 裝備　　**cellular phone** 行動電話
rover〔ˈrovɚ〕n. 流浪者　　cap〔kæp〕n. 最高限額
jet propulsion 噴氣推進　　laboratory〔ˈlæbrəˌtorɪ〕n. 實驗室
disaster〔dɪzˈæstɚ〕n. 災禍；不幸
ground〔graund〕v. 停止（飛行）　　shuttle〔ˈʃʌtl̩〕n. 太空梭
reign〔ren〕v. 佔優勢；盛行
abbreviation〔əˌbrivɪˈeʃən〕n. 縮寫

(3)【譯文】

　　當我第一次見到妮娜，我就不喜歡她。她穿著緊身的女用運動短褲，頭髮的裝扮很俗氣又邋遢，腳上穿的是膠底運動鞋，但沒有穿襪子。這樣的裝扮，即使在非常不正式的公司，也是非常地奇特、不適當的。不久，妮娜不斷地追問我所管理的新的部門的情形，她想在我的部門找一份固定的工作。我心想這是不可能的事，即使我有發言權也不可能給她機會。

　　但是，我並沒有這麼做。幾天之內，她接受了我給她的考驗。後來我交給她一項不太難、不怎麼有趣又不太重要的計劃，幾個月內還不會執行。但是後來接手的人，卻必須花費很長的時間，才收拾好她所留下的爛攤子。雖然當時我無法準確地預測妮娜會做什麼，但是在三分鐘之內，我就把她歸類為無法信賴，而且是一事無成的人。

【答案】

46. (**C**)　47. (**A**)　48. (**D**)　49. (**B**)　50. (**B**)

【註】

skintight〔'skɪn'taɪt〕*adj.* 緊身的　***pedal pushers*** 女用運動短褲
flashy〔'flæʃɪ〕*adj.* 俗氣的　　floppy〔'flɑpɪ〕*adj.* 邋遢的
sneaker〔'snikɚ〕*n.* 膠底運動鞋
bizarrely〔bɪ'zɑrlɪ〕*adv.* 古怪地
doggedly〔'dɔgɪdlɪ〕*adv.* 頑強地　　pump〔pʌmp〕*v.* 追問
permanent〔'pɝmənənt〕*adj.* 固定的；永久的
try out for （為爭取資格而）接受考驗
successor〔sək'sɛsɚ〕*n.* 繼任者
untangle〔ʌn'tæŋgl〕*v.* 解決　　flat〔flæt〕*adv.* 正好
assess〔ə'sɛs〕*v.* 評估　　pushy〔'puʃɪ〕*adj.* 進取的；強求的
conscientious〔͵kɑnʃɪ'ɛnʃəs〕*adj.* 正直的
snap〔snæp〕*adj.* 倉促的

IV. 作文：20%

The Importance of Independent Thinking

The importance of independent thinking can not be emphasized enough. In today's fast-paced and growing world, independent thinking is especially essential. Without in-dependent thinkers, everyone would be doing the same thing, and nothing would ever change. It's important for people to go their own way, do their own thing, and not to worry so much about being part of the crowd. Independent thinking is the key to progress. Without independent thinkers, there would be no scientific or technological advancements within society.

I believe that it is high time the government took hold of the education system and pushed for a reform. As it is, the school system in Taiwan tends to discourage independent thinking. Instead, it stresses the importance of memorization, which it believes to be the best method to study for the infamous JCEE. That is one reason why Taiwan lags behind in original scientific and technological discoveries. THINK, and become free.

國立中正大學八十五學年度
碩士班研究生入學考試英文試題

A. Grammar in Context: Choose the best answer to each statement.(20%)

1. Peter's jacket cost _____ Jack's.
   (A) twice more than   (B) two times more as
   (C) twice as much as   (D) twice more as

2. In the War of 1812, the British living in Canada _____.
   (A) helped the Indians for fight the Americans
   (B) helped the Indians fight the Americans
   (C) helped the Indians for fighting Americans
   (D) helped the Indians to fighting the Americans

3. _____ both the largest and northernmost state in the United States, Alaska has the smallest population.
   (A) Despite it is   (B) In spite being
   (C) In spite of to be   (D) Despite being

4. Astigmatism _____ caused by a flat spot on the eyeball.
   (A) a type of visual impairment
   (B) which is a type of visual impairment
   (C) it's a type of visual impairment
   (D) is a type of visual impairment

5. The speed of communications today, as opposed to _____, has greatly altered the manner in which business today is conducted.
   (A) the one of yesterday
   (B) communications yesterday
   (C) that of yesterday
   (D) communication's speed a long time ago

6. When the court was in session, the judge would not permit entrance by _____.
   (A) no one　　　　　　　　(B) anyone
   (C) someone　　　　　　　(D) none

7. If silver _____ scarcer than gold, it will no doubt have a greater value.
   (A) became　　　　　　　　(B) will become
   (C) becomes　　　　　　　(D) had become

8. The salmon spends its adult life in rivers and seas but _____.
   (A) its eggs are laid in streams
   (B) it lays its eggs in streams
   (C) in streams are laid its eggs
   (D) laid in streams are its eggs

9. A reward of five hundred dollars will be given _____ can identify the bank robber.
   (A) to whoever　　　　　　(B) to whomever
   (C) whomever　　　　　　　(D) whoever person

10. _____, follow the directions on the bottle carefully.
    (A) When taken drugs　　(B) When one takes drugs
    (C) When, in taking drugs　(D) When taking drugs

B. Dialogue: Choose the appropriate response to each statement.(20%)

Bob : Hello, Sam. ___11___?
Sam : Oh, hello, Bob. I've lost my spectacles, and I can't see without them.

Bob : ___12___ I can help you look for them. How can you be sure you dropped them here in the dormitory? Could you have left them somewhere else, ___13___?
Sam : I can't be sure of anything; ___14___. I just can't think where I last had them.

Bob : ___15___ you can't even remember when you had them last? Can't you remember putting them down some-where?

Sam : I know I had them in class this morning, because I can remember ___16___.

Bob : But if you had them then, they could be on your desk, ___17___? I mean, you could have left them there.

Sam : Perhaps I might have...but no, wait, I remember. They ___18___ be on my desk, for I think I had them after class, at lunch time. But after lunch I can't remember taking them ___19___.

Bob : Oops! ___20___.

Sam : Oh, no! My spectacles!

11. (A) What's the matter   (B) I beg your pardon
    (C) What's on   (D) So what

12. (A) Take care.   (B) Swell!
    (C) My hands are tied.   (D) Don't worry.

13. (A) O.K.   (B) perhaps
    (C) could you   (D) really

14. (A) that's no problem   (B) that's the trouble
    (C) it's a deal   (D) it's on me

15. (A) Do you mean that   (B) Do you think
    (C) Why   (D) How

16. (A) putting on them   (B) to put them on
    (C) putting them on   (D) to put on them

17. (A) couldn't they   (B) had you
    (C) do you   (D) could they

18. (A) may not   (B) need not
    (C) must not   (D) cannot

19. (A) over   (B) off   (C) on   (D) out

20. (A) I must have stepped on something.
    (B) Behave yourself!
    (C) I'm not out of cash.
    (D) Take it easy.

C. Reading comprehension: Choose the best answer of each statement.(20%)

Naturalists have long been fascinated with the social behavior of elephants. Traveling in herds usually numbering around 25, the elephant is a remarkably loyal and gregarious animal. These herds exhibit familial characteristics, caring for the young of the disabled, and even killing an incurable member to put an end to its suffering. Indeed, the herds are generally composed of several generations of relatives, including several sets of monogamous couples.

Because elephants are such large animals, reaching up to 12 feet and 6 tons, they are constantly moving in order to search for food, sometimes in migratory routes that take 10 years to complete. Because elephants are not fully grown until they are about 5 years old, babies often have trouble keeping up with the herd. When this happens, or when an elephant is injured, several members of the herd will stay behind to help and protect it. It is extremely common to see older elephants using their trunks to help support less mature relatives. Occasionally, a single elephant will become belligerent. These elephants, called ''rogues,'' are then actually excluded from the herd and sent to live alone.

21. What does this passage mainly discuss?
    (A) the migration of elephants
    (B) the social habits of elephants
    (C) the life cycle of the elephant
    (D) man's fascination with elephants

22. According to the passage, when does an elephant reach maturity?
    (A) twelve years   (B) six years
    (C) five years   (D) ten years

23. Which of the following is NOT mentioned as one of the social characteristics of elephants?
    (A) life long mating
    (B) banishment of unruly herd members
    (C) helping injured herd members
    (D) excluding immature elephants

24. A "rogue" elephant is one who
    (A) has not reached maturity.
    (B) has exhibited overly aggressive behavior.
    (C) has been injured.
    (D) has been recognized as the leader of the herd.

25. If a group of four to five elephants is sighted, it is probably
    (A) a group of rogue elephants.
    (B) an average sized herd.
    (C) a portion of a herd helping an injured member.
    (D) a group of elephants performing mating rituals.

For many years, sociologists and historians have referred to the United States as a cultural "melting pot," in order to suggest the successful integration into American society of the massive waves of immigration which have marked American history. This term has been primarily a complimentary one, implying that immigrants invariably embrace not only American ideals, but a pervasive "American" culture. Also, the term suggests that American immigrants successfully leave behind the turmoil of their home countries which has caused them to come to the United States, thus "melting" into American society.

However, in recent years, this term has lost much of its popularity, primarily because of an increasing em-phasis on diversity among ethnic groups. Ironically, this emphasis springs from another American ideal, strong individuality. Instead, many prefer to refer to the U.S. as a ''salad bowl,'' viewing each of the many ethnic groups in America as a component of a salad. Thus, each group preserves its own identity in the salad, but, at the same time, inter-acting with the other vegetables to create a delightful mix and variety. Certainly the term makes a great deal of sense with regard to geography, as ethnic distribution in the United States is hardly uniform. Now York, with its Chinatown and Little Italy, is an excellent example of this separation. However, the term is primarily used with reference to the various cultures and sensibilities of ethnic groups in the U.S.

26. The author suggests that all of the following are implied by the phrase ''melting pot'' EXCEPT
   (A) a pervasive American culture.
   (B) a successful integration of immigrants into American society.
   (C) the preservation of ethnic distinctiveness.
   (D) the leaving behind of trouble in an immigrants home land.

27. According to the passage, why does the term " salad bowl'' make sense geographically?
   (A) Ethnic groups in the U.S. often live in distinctive areas.
   (B) There is great diversity in the cultures of ethnic groups in the U.S.
   (C) The term appeals to the American ideal of individuality.
   (D) Immigrants to the U.S. come from many different parts of the world.

28. According to the author, why has there been a change
    in the terminology with reference to the ethnic di-
    versity of the U.S.?
    (A) a change in the ethnic distribution of the U.S.
    (B) a change in American ideals
    (C) a natural evolution of language
    (D) an emphasis on diversity

29. For whom is the author probably writing this passage?
    (A) ethnic groups
    (B) general audiences
    (C) cooks
    (D) sociologists and historians

30. The organization of this passage is best described as
    (A) a hypothesis followed by arguments against the
        hypothesis
    (B) two different analogies about the same subject
    (C) a statement followed by an analogy which
        supports it
    (D) a comparison of two hypotheses

D. Write a story about the picture and give a title to
   your story(40%). Title(5%) Story(35%)

國立中正大學八十五學年度
碩士班研究生入學考試英文試題詳解

A. 文法：20％

1. (**C**) 倍數的用法爲：「～ times ＋as ＋形容詞或副詞＋as ～」，
故選 (D)。
Peter's jacket cost *twice as much as* Jack's.
＝Peter's jacket cost *two times as much as* Jack's.

2. (**B**) help ＋*sb.* ＋ $\begin{cases} \text{to ＋V.} \\ \text{V} \end{cases}$ 幫助某人～

3. (**D**) despite ＝in spite of 「儘管～」，用法與介系詞相同，其後
須接名詞或動名詞，故選 (D)。
northernmost〔ˈnɔrðən͵most〕*adj.* 最北的；極北的

4. (**D**) 本句缺少動詞，故選 (D)。而 caused by a flat spot on the
eyeball 是由形容詞子句簡化而來的分詞片語，省略了 which
is。
astigmatism〔əˈstɪgmə͵tɪzəm〕*n.* 散光
impairment〔ɪmˈpɛrmənt〕*n.* 損傷

5. (**C**) 爲避免重覆，可用 that 代替前面出現過的名詞。
alter〔ˈɔltɚ〕*v.* 改變
conduct〔kənˈdʌkt〕*v.* 做（生意）

6. (**B**) 依句意，「任何人」都不准進入，選 (B)。
session〔ˈsɛʃən〕*n.* 開庭

7. (**C**) If 所引導的條件句爲直說法，而非假設語氣。若表示未來的情
況，If 子句須用現在簡單式，而主要子句則用未來式，故選 (C)。

8. (**B**) 依句意,選 (B) 鮭魚卻是在溪流裏產卵。

salmon〔'sæmən〕*n.* 鮭魚　　lay〔le〕*v.* 產卵

9. (**A**) whoever 爲複合關係代名詞,相當於 anyone who,引導名詞子句。　　reward〔rɪ'wɔrd〕*n.* 獎賞

10. (**D**) 原句是由:When you are taking drugs, follow …簡化而來。副詞子句中,若句意很明確,可將主詞與 be 動詞省略。

B. 對話:20%

鮑伯:哈囉,山姆。<u>你怎麼啦?</u>
　　　　　　　　　　　　　　11

山姆:噢,哈囉,鮑伯。我把我的眼鏡弄丟了。沒有眼鏡,我什麼也看不見。

鮑伯:<u>別擔心</u>,我幫你找找看。你確定一定是掉在宿舍裡嗎?有沒有
　　　　12
　　　<u>可能</u>放在其他地方?
　　　13

山姆:<u>問題是</u>我完全無法確定。我根本想不起來最後戴著眼鏡時,是
　　　14
　　　在哪裡。

鮑伯:<u>你是說你</u>不記得最後一次戴眼鏡,是什麼時候?你難道想不起
　　　15
　　　來把它們放在哪裡嗎?

山姆:我知道今天早上上課時有戴眼鏡,因爲我記得<u>有戴上</u>。
　　　　　　　　　　　　　　　　　　　　　　　　　　　16

鮑伯:如果你有戴,那可能會在書桌上,<u>不是嗎</u>?我是說你有可能把
　　　　　　　　　　　　　　　　　17
　　　它們放在桌上。

山姆:有可能…不對,等一下,我想起來了。<u>不可能</u>在桌上,因爲下
　　　　　　　　　　　　　　　　　　　　18
　　　課後,吃中飯時我還戴著眼鏡。但是我不記得吃完中飯後有把
　　　眼鏡拿<u>下來</u>。
　　　　　　19

鮑伯:哎呀!<u>我一定踩到什麼東西了。</u>
　　　　　　　20

山姆:噢,糟糕!我的眼鏡!

11.（**A**)　(A) 怎麼了　　　　　　(B) 對不起
　　　　　　(C) 電視在演什麼　　(D) 那又怎樣

12.（**D**)　(A) 保重。　(B) 太棒了！　(C) 很忙。　　　(D) 別擔心。

13.（**B**)　(A) 好吧　(B) 也許　　(C) 可以嗎　　　(D) 真地

14.（**B**)　(A) 沒問題　　　　　(B) 問題就在這裏
　　　　　　(C) 一言為定　　　　(D) 我請客

15.（**A**)　(A) 你是說　(B) 你認為　(C) 為什麼　　(D) 如何

16.（**C**)　*put sth. on* 戴上～

17.（**A**)　由於前面助動詞為 could，故附加問句須用 couldn't they。

18.（**D**)　(A) 也許不　(B) 不需要　(C) 不可以；禁止　(D) 不可能

19.（**B**)　*take sth. off* 拿下～

20.（**A**)　(A) 我一定是踩到某樣東西了。
　　　　　　(B) 守規矩點！
　　　　　　(C) 我不缺錢。
　　　　　　(D) 放輕鬆。

C. 閱讀測驗：20%

【譯文】

　　長久以來，動物學家對大象的社會行為，非常感興趣。大象會集體行動，數量大約廿五隻左右，是非常忠心並且合群的動物。大象會表現出其家族特性，即照顧幼象或行動不便的大象，有時甚至將無法治癒的大象殺死，以結束其痛苦。事實上，整群大象是由好幾代的親屬所組成，其中有些是成雙成對的。

　　大象的體型非常龐大，身長達十二英尺，重達六公噸，所以必須不斷地遷徙，以找尋食物，有時遷移的路線，得花上十年的時間才能完成。因爲大象在五歲時，才完全發育成熟，所以小象常常跟不上象群的速度。如果有這種情況發生，或是有大象受傷，就會有幾隻大象留在後頭幫忙和保護牠們。我們經常可以看到年長的大象用象鼻來扶持未成熟的小象。有時候，若有大象變得好鬥，這樣的大象就被稱爲「無賴」，會受到象群的排斥，只能獨自地生活。

```
┌─【答案】─────────────────────────────────────────┐
│   21.（ B ）   22.（ C ）   23.（ D ）   24.（ B ）   25.（ C ）   │
└─────────────────────────────────────────────────┘
```

【註】

naturalist〔ˈnætʃərəlɪst〕n. 動（植）物學家

fascinate〔ˈfæsn̩ˌet〕v. 使著迷　　herd〔hɝd〕n. 獸群

gregarious〔grɪˈgɛrɪəs〕adj. 群居的

familial〔fəˈmɪljəl〕adj. 家族的

disabled〔dɪsˈeb!d〕adj. 殘廢的

monogamous〔məˈnɑgəməs〕adj. 一夫一妻制的

trunk〔trʌŋk〕n. 象鼻　　belligerent〔bəˈlɪdʒərənt〕adj. 好鬥的

rogue〔rog〕n. 無賴；惡棍

banishment〔ˈbænɪʃmənt〕n. 驅逐

unruly〔ʌnˈrulɪ〕adj. 不聽話的

ritual〔ˈrɪtʃuəl〕n. 儀式；慣例

　　多年來，社會學家和歷史學家把美國稱爲文化的「大熔爐」，這顯示了在美國歷史上著名的移民潮時期中，移民者成功地融入美國的社會。這種說法基本上是一種讚美，表示移民者一定會接受美國的理想和普遍的美國文化。此外，這種說法也暗示，因爲本國的動亂而移居美國的人能成功地忘記那些動亂，真正地「融入」美國社會中。

　　但是，最近這幾年，這種說法已不受到歡迎，主要是因為大家愈來愈重視族群之間的多元性。諷刺的是，這正是因為美國人的另一種意識型態強烈的個人主義所造成。相反地，現在有許多人比較喜歡把美國比喻成一個「沙拉盆」，將每個種族視為沙拉中的某一項成份，在沙拉中，不僅能保留原有的特性，同時又能和其他蔬菜相互作用，產生令人喜愛的融合與多樣性。若以地理的角度來解釋，這個名詞亦具有重大意義，因為美國境內的種族分布是非常不平均的。紐約的中國城和小義大利，就是這種區隔的最佳寫照。然而，這個名詞最主要是用來說明美國境內族群的多樣文化和感受。

【答案】

　　26.（ **C** ）　　27.（ **A** ）　　28.（ **D** ）　　29.（ **B** ）　　30.（ **B** ）

【註】

melting pot 大熔爐
integration〔͵ɪntə'greʃən〕*n.* 整合
mark〔mɑrk〕*v.* 顯示
complimentary〔͵kɑmplə'mɛntərɪ〕*adj.* 讚美的
invariably〔ɪn'vɛrɪəblɪ〕*adv.* 必定；不變地
pervasive〔pɚ'vesɪv〕*adj.* 流行的；普遍的
turmoil〔'tɝmɔɪl〕*n.* 混亂；動亂
diversity〔daɪ'vɝsətɪ〕*n.* 多樣性；多元化
ethnic〔'ɛθnɪk〕*adj.* 種族的
ironically〔aɪ'rɑnɪk!ɪ〕*adv.* 諷刺地
spring〔sprɪŋ〕*v.* 出現
component〔kəm'ponənt〕*n.* 成份
uniform〔'junə͵fɔrm〕*adj.* 相同的
sensibilities〔͵sɛnsə'bɪlətɪz〕*n.pl.* 感受

D. 作文：40%

【譯文】根據下圖，用英文寫一篇故事，並須附標題。

The Obese Lord Bennington

When Randal, the manager, went to check on the obese Lord Bennington, he was very happy. Lord Bennington was pleased again, and was sure to return. It always made Randal nervous when Lord Bennington came to the restaurants, because Lord Bennington was a very demanding patron. Once, he stopped coming to dine for a whole month, because his rolls were not warm enough.

Since Lord Bennington was very wealthy and influential, it was important to keep him happy. He often entertained groups of business associates, and that meant high revenues for the restaurant. At those times, there was not much to worry about, because Lord Bennington drank more than he ate, and his pickiness was outdone by his drunkenness, which distorted his memory. It was at times when he dined alone, however, that Lord Bennington drank moderately, and paid careful attention to the preparation of

國立中央大學八十五學年度
碩士班研究生入學考試英文試題

Read the following story:

``You! You! You bitch!'' He slaps her face. It's five o'clock in the morning...again. Oh, Jesus, look at her. She is all blue and black. He continues hitting her. She is weeping with some strange sound which makes me think that it may be a dog, not a woman, that gets beaten. Nobody comes to her rescue or shows up to intercede with the man on her behalf...as usual. But I believe there must be many pairs of eyes looking curiously at this scene across the street every day. ``What do you want? I work so hard every day to buy you everything. Do I treat you badly? Why do you still go for other men? Tell me! Tell me! Why? Is he much stronger than I? Can't I satisfy you? Hum? Bitch!'' As usual she, wearing her pink dressing gown and bare-footed, sits on the ground, says nothing, and keeps on weeping. She shakes her head, but it is almost imperceptible.

I go to make a cup of coffee for myself. I go back to my bed to enjoy it and to wait for what shall go on.... Am I a bitch too? Why can't I enjoy any other man's love when you treat me like this? I feel lonely when you're not by my side. You come to see me once a week and disappear for the rest of the week. The difference between a woman and a plant is that she needs not only food but much love and caring. He kicks her, but she doesn't run away. She sits there motionlessly, looking at the ground with empty eyes.

She is a bitch! Me too! If every bitch deserves that treatment, then what about me? Why don't you beat me up? Don't look sadly at me and say ``Suit yourself!'' Don't. Please.... Come and beat me hard with anger so that I can make sure you do care about me.... Who likes to act like this!? Who likes to fool around with so many men!? Who wouldn't like to be faithful to her lover!?.... I love you! ...and--I need to be loved!

The man shouts at her with many four-letter words. The morning is still quiet and dark. Nobody comes out to end this war.... The man seems to wait for someone to do this job. Still, nobody.... He yells at her with the most dirty words possible and kicks her again. Then he goes into the house. The woman (or shall I call her the bitch?) still sits on the ground, in the same position, with the same empty eyes.

Although the woman called "bitch" remains silent throughout the story, she is not incapable of speech. If she is to tell her side of the story, what would it be? Be the woman, write a first person narrative, and verbalize her feelings. Create a situation in which she retells the story. It can be an interior monologue (when and where does she speak?), a letter (addressed to whom?), or a phone conversation in which only her voice is heard (again, whom is she speaking to?). Alternatively, you may retell the story as a neighbor or a friend of hers or a spectator of the scene. There are other possibilities still. Be imaginative. (100%)

國立中央大學八十五學年度
碩士班研究生入學考試英文試題詳解

英文作文： 100 ％——閱讀下面的文章

【譯文】

　　「妳！妳！妳這個淫婦！」他打了她一巴掌。現在又是早上五點。噢！天啊，看看她，全身青一塊、紫一塊的。他不停地打她。她的哭聲很奇怪，讓我誤以為是一隻狗，而不是個女人遭到毆打。和以前一樣，沒有人去救她，或是替她向男人求情，但我相信，每天一定有許多雙眼睛越過街道，好奇地觀看這一幕。「妳到底要什麼？我每天辛苦地工作，買給妳所有的東西，我對妳還不夠好嗎？妳為什麼還要去找別的男人？告訴我！妳告訴我！這是為什麼？他比我強嗎？我不能滿足妳嗎？哼，賤貨！」她還是和往常一樣，身穿粉紅色的長袍，赤腳坐在地上，什麼話也不說，只是不停地哭。她搖頭，但幾乎察覺不出來。

　　我幫自己泡了一杯咖啡，然後回到床上品嚐，等等看還會發生什麼事。我也是淫婦嗎？你如此地對待我，為什麼我不可以擁有別的男人的愛？當你不在身邊時，我覺得很孤單，你一星期才來看我一次，其餘的時間就不見人影，女人和植物的差別在於，女人不僅需要食物，還需要更多的愛和關心。那男人踢她，但是她沒有逃走，只是一動也不動地坐在那兒，眼神空洞地望著地上。

　　她是淫婦！我也是！如果每位淫婦都應該受到那樣的對待，那我呢？你為什麼不打我？不要哀傷地看著我，然後說「隨你高興！」千萬不要，求求你……請憤怒而用力地打我，這樣我才能確定你是真的在乎我……誰願意這樣做!?有誰喜歡和這麼多的男人廝混!誰不希望能忠於自己的愛人!? 我愛你！而我也需要被愛！

男人對著女人罵髒話。清晨時分，周遭仍是十分寧靜與黑暗，沒有人出來結束這場戰爭……男人似乎在等待有人能這樣做。但是一個人也沒有……他用最不堪入耳的字眼對她嘶吼，又踢了她一腳。然後就走進屋裏。那女人（或是我該叫她淫婦？）仍坐在地上，有著同樣的姿勢和同樣空洞的眼神。

【註】

bitch〔bɪtʃ〕*n.* 娼婦；淫婦
slap〔slæp〕*v.* 打耳光　　weep〔wip〕*v.* 哭泣
intercede〔͵ɪntɚˋsid〕*v.* 代爲求情
on one's behalf 爲了某人
go for 喜歡　　***dressing gown*** 晨袍
bare-footed〔ˋbɛr͵fʊtɪd〕*adj.* 赤腳的
imperceptible〔͵ɪmpɚˋsɛptəb!〕*adj.* 無法察覺的
beat up 毒打　　***four-letter word*** 髒話

【說明】

雖然那被叫做「淫婦」的女人，在整篇故事中，一直保持沈默，但是她不是無法說話。如果以她的角度來敘述故事，會是什麼內容呢？把你自己當作是那位女人，用第一人稱來敘述，具體描述她的感覺。你要創造一個她在重述故事的情境，可以是內心獨白（她在何時、何地說的？），也可以是一封信（寫給誰的？）或是電話中的對話，但只能聽到她的聲音（同樣地，她在對誰說？）或者，你也可以以一位鄰居、朋友，或是目擊者的身分，來重述這個故事。還有其他的可能性。請發揮你的想像力。（100％）

【英文作文】

Dear Ungrateful,

Is that what I am to you, a bitch, an animal, a lowly dog? Maybe that is what I have become.

You once treated me so well. You treated me like a princess, and you indeed were my prince. You were so regal and fine that people thought we were the perfect couple. Then, then you changed. When you began to belittle me day after day, I began to lose my humanity. You started paying attention to everything else except me. You started treating me like dirt, and to you, that is what I became. I became your property, and no longer your love. To you, I became something to be kicked around and abused.

When someone else offered me love and comfort, I went to him quickly, just as an animal would, because that is what I became. If you never stopped treating me with humanity, I would still be your princess, and you would still be my prince.

Sincerely,

Your Bitch

私立逢甲大學八十五學年度
碩士班研究生入學考試英文試題

I. Vocabulary:(Choose the most appropriate word in accordance with the context.) 20%

1. Investors buy large amounts of _____ and hope that the price increases.
   (A) conveniences   (B) commodities
   (C) communities   (D) commercials

2. We are much impressed with Thomas's new job as a computer programmer; I hear that the company plans on _____ him soon.
   (A) promoting   (B) upgrading
   (C) evaluating   (D) quitting

3. With the increasingly wide-spread computer network, preventing the intrusion of _____ becomes an important task.
   (A) minors   (B) pilots
   (C) hackers   (D) informers

4. The accident that delayed our bus gave us a _____ reason for being late.
   (A) expertise   (B) extravagant
   (C) legitimate   (D) dispassionate

5. The badly wounded take _____ for medical attention over those only slightly hurt.
   (A) authority   (B) minority
   (C) celebrity   (D) priority

6. The increase in the output of Factory B is due to the
　　_____ of the production methods in effect there.
　(A) influence 　　　　　　　(B) efficiency
　(C) discrimination 　　　　(D) inflation

7. Give a(n) _____ example of the abstract statement,
　``Honesty is the best policy.''
　(A) remote 　　　　　　　　(B) enormous
　(C) complicated 　　　　　(D) concrete

8. We will replace this _____ lens with a perfect one.
　(A) defective 　　　　　　　(B) creative
　(C) convicted 　　　　　　　(D) abundant

9. I should like to consult a _____ financier before
　we proceed with such a far-reaching enterprise.
　(A) reliable 　　　　　　　　(B) reluctant
　(C) persistent 　　　　　　　(D) diligent

10. Misleading advertising may _____ the public.
　(A) investigate 　　　　　　(B) shield
　(C) relieve 　　　　　　　　(D) deceive

II. Grammar & Structure: (Choose from the following
　underlined parts the incorrect one.) 20%

11. The differences <u>in</u> American English <u>and</u> British
　　　　　　　　　 A 　　　　　　　　　　　B
　English are not as <u>great</u> as the differences <u>among</u>
　　　　　　　　　　　 C 　　　　　　　　　　　　　　 D
　Chinese dialects.

12. <u>If</u> you major <u>in</u> teacher education, Carlos, <u>one</u> will
　　 A 　　　　　 B 　　　　　　　　　　　　　　　 C
　spend some time <u>as</u> an apprentice in a classroom.
　　　　　　　　　　 D

13. Although I was famished, I did not have time to go to
    $\qquad$ A $\qquad\qquad\qquad$ B
    the cafeteria, where is on the fifth floor of the
    $\qquad$ C $\qquad\qquad$ D
    building across the street.

14. Despite the heavy rain, there have more than one
    $\quad$ A $\qquad\qquad\qquad$ B $\qquad\qquad$ C
    thousand fans at the baseball game.
    $\qquad\qquad$ D

15. He still remembers to be kidnapped one day when he
    $\qquad$ A $\qquad\qquad$ B $\qquad\qquad$ C
    was a small child studying at an elementary school.
    $\qquad\qquad\qquad$ D

16. When the accused person was found innocence, the
    $\qquad$ A $\qquad\qquad\qquad$ B
    robbery case was closed.
    $\quad$ C $\qquad\qquad$ D

17. Mr. Turner's physician does not think it advise for
    $\qquad\qquad\qquad$ A $\qquad\qquad$ B
    him to make the trip at this time.
    $\quad$ C $\qquad\qquad$ D

18. Although your sales plan is not impossible, but it is
    $\qquad$ A $\qquad\qquad\qquad\qquad$ B
    impracticable owing to our great distance from the
    $\qquad\qquad$ C $\qquad\qquad\qquad$ D
    market.

19. The world is full of brilliant poets who can't balance
    $\qquad$ A
    a checkbook, and genius physicists who incapable of
    $\qquad\qquad$ B $\qquad\qquad$ C $\qquad\qquad$ D
    driving a manual-shift car.

20. It's worth remembering that IQ isn't quite the same
    A $\qquad$ B $\qquad\qquad\qquad\qquad$ C
    thing like intelligence.
    $\qquad$ D

III. Reading Comprehension:(Read the following passages carefully and then answer the questions below them.) 20%

A.

　　The number of animal species that have died out since 1600 has increased sharply. As far as experts can tell, fewer than twenty animal species became extinct between the beginning of the modern historical period and the beginning of the seventeenth century. Between 1600 and 1699, in just one century, however, seventeen animal species are known to have disappeared. The next ninety -nine years saw the extinctions of thirty-six animals. The number of pre-1600 extinction nearly quintupled, increased by five times, in the 1800s (eighty-one). In the first seventy-five years of the twentieth century, eighty-three more species have already disappeared. Obviously, the rate of extinction has not been slowed.

21. According to experts, how many animal species died out in the eighteenth century?
 (A) 17　　　(B) 36　　　(C) 83　　　(D) 20

22. Which sentence best states the main idea?
 (A) More animal species had already become extinct by 1975 than had in the previous century.
 (B) The number of animal species that become extinct has increased each century.
 (C) If people do not make an animal-saving plan soon, the world will lose all its wild animals.
 (D) There is not enough food for all the wild animals.

B.

　　This isn't just idle conjecture. New York's Citibank plans to have more than half its 2.5 million account-holders on-line by 1995. Major retail chains like

Penney's are experimenting with at-home shopping systems, and computer-based news, sports, and entertainment
services such as QUBE and Teletext are already available.
A shopping mall near Washington, D.C., offers shoppers a
"window shopping" service accessible through a modem. The
service lists sales and specials in a store-by-store index.
Users can call up price comparisons of particular items,
place orders, and request gift suggestions for women,
men, children, pets, older relatives, secretaries, or a
variety of other recipient categories. The wide availa-
bility of inexpensive computers could have a dramatic
impact on our society.

23. Which is the main idea of the passage?
    (A) Computers could have a great influence on our
        lives.
    (B) New York's Citibank and J.C. Penney's are idle
        conjectures.
    (C) Now window shopping is accessible.
    (D) QUBE and Teletext are computer-based entertain-
        ment services.

24. Which statement is NOT true?
    Users of the "window shopping" service
    (A) can check a store-by-store index.
    (B) can compare prices of particular items.
    (C) can order merchandise.
    (D) can receive gifts from women.

C.
    Some people get headaches when they eat very cold ice
cream. A neurologist (a doctor who is a nerve expert) told
me why these headaches happen. The extreme cold of the ice
cream acts on a certain nerve in the face. The nerve is

located in the cheek and fans out to reach the chin, jaw, and temples. The extreme cold causes pain, which the nerve sends to the temples. The result: a headache.

If that happens to you, relax. Try drinking something warmer than the ice cream. The warmer liquid may help calm the nerve. Whatever you do, remember that the pain won't last long. Let your remaining ice cream warm up just a bit...and eat slowly.

Choose the best answer for each question.

25. What is the source of the information about the cause of ice cream headaches?
(A) the author of the article
(B) a neurologist
(C) a survey about ice cream headaches
(D) The source is not given.

26. In the author's opinion, ice cream headaches are _____.

(A) temporary   (B) dangerous
(C) rare   (D) relaxing

27. The main purpose of the article is to _____.
(A) explain the cause of headaches
(B) describe the function of the nerves
(C) suggest a remedy for a certain kind of headache
(D) define the word neurologist

D.

Robert Spring, a 19th century forger, was so good at his profession that he was able to make his living for 15 years by selling false signatures of famous Americans. Spring was born in England in 1813 and arrived in Philadelphia in 1858 to open a bookstore. At first he prospered by selling his small but genuine collection of early U.S. autographs. Discovering his ability at copying handwriting, he began imitating signatures of George Washington and Ben Franklin and writing them on the title pages of old books. To lessen the chance of detection, he sent his forgeries to England and Canada for sale and circulation.

Forgers have a hard time selling their products. A forger can't approach a respectable buyer but must deal with people who don't have much knowledge in the field. Forgers have many ways to make their work look real. For example, they buy old books to use the aged paper of the title page, and they can treat paper and ink with chemicals.

In Spring's time, right after the Civil War, Britain was still fond of the Southern states, so Spring invented a respectable maiden known as Miss Fanny Jackson, the only daughter of General "Stonewall" Jackson. For several years Miss Fanny's financial problems forced her to sell a great number of letters and manuscripts belonging to her famous father. Spring had to work very hard to satisfy the demand. All this activity did not prevent Spring from dying in poverty, leaving sharp-eyed experts the difficult task of separating his forgeries from the originals.

28. Robert Spring spent 15 years _____
    (A) running a bookstore in Philadelphia.
    (B) corresponding with Miss Fanny Jackson.
    (C) as a forger.
    (D) as a respectable dealer.

29. According to the passage, forgeries are usually sold
    to _____
    (A) sharp-eyed experts.
    (B) persons who aren't experts.
    (C) book dealers.
    (D) owners of old books.

30. Who was Miss Fanny Jackson?
    (A) the only daughter of General "Stonewall" Jackson
    (B) a little-known girl who sold her father's papers
        to Robert Spring
    (C) Robert Spring's daughter
    (D) an imaginary person created by Spring

IV. Cloze Test: (Fill in each of the following blanks with
    an appropriate word from the four possible choices
    provided.) 20%

    One must find the source of contentment within
oneself. That is one of the great ___31___ of old-age
activities like ___32___ and ___33___. The golden rule for
old age is ___34___. When you can't ___35___ to read, you
can listen. When the weather is good, go out and ___36___;
if you can't garden you should still go out and make the
most of the sunshine. Above all, keep ___37___, vary your
interests, turn from one thing to ___38___ as the mood
takes you--always ___39___ an objective ahead and Never
Give ___40___.

    So one way or another, in old age I manage to have
quite a good time!

31. (A) advantages   (B) disadvantages
    (C) advantage   (D) disadvantage
32. (A) read   (B) reading
    (C) study   (D) studying

33. (A) garden   (B) gardening
    (C) clean   (D) cleaning
34. (A) Adapt   (B) Move   (C) Complain   (D) Watch
35. (A) see   (B) take   (C) make   (D) study
36. (A) study   (B) listen   (C) smile   (D) garden
37. (A) alive   (B) awake   (C) asleep   (D) active
38. (A) other   (B) others   (C) another   (D) either
39. (A) come   (B) do   (C) have   (D) bring
40. (A) Out   (B) Away   (C) Off   (D) In

V. Composition: 20%

Write a composition of about 120 words on the following topic: Why I LIKE (DISLIKE) CITY LIFE IN TAIWAN. Give at least THREE reasons to support your position.

私立逢甲大學八十五學年度
碩士班研究生入學考試英文試題詳解

I. 字彙：20 %

1. (**B**) (A) convenience 〔 kən'vinjəns 〕 *n.* 方便
　　　　(B) ***commodity*** 〔 kə'mɑdətɪ 〕 *n.* 貨物；商品
　　　　(C) community 〔 kə'mjunətɪ 〕 *n.* 社區
　　　　(D) commercial 〔 kə'mɝʃəl 〕 *n.* 商業廣告　*adj.* 商業的
　　　　　investor 〔 ɪn'vɛstɚ 〕 *n.* 投資者

2. (**A**) (A) ***promote*** 〔 prə'mot 〕 *v.* 升遷；促進
　　　　(B) upgrade 〔 'ʌp'gred 〕 *v.* 改良
　　　　(C) evaluate 〔 ɪ'vælju,et 〕 *v.* 評估
　　　　(D) quit 〔 kwɪt 〕 *v.* 辭職
　　　　　programmer 〔 'progræmɚ 〕 *n.* 程式設計者

3. (**C**) (A) minor 〔 'maɪnɚ 〕 *n.* 未成年者
　　　　(B) pilot 〔 'paɪlət 〕 *n.* 飛行員；領航員
　　　　(C) ***hacker*** 〔 'hækɚ 〕 *n.* 非法進入電腦通訊網的人
　　　　(D) informer 〔 ɪn'fɔrmɚ 〕 *n.* 告密者
　　　　　intrusion 〔 ɪn'truʒən 〕 *n.* 入侵

4. (**C**) (A) expertise 〔 ,ɛkspɚ'tiz 〕 *n.* 專門知識
　　　　(B) extravagant 〔 ɪk'strævəgənt 〕 *adj.* 奢侈的
　　　　(C) ***legitimate*** 〔 lɪ'dʒɪtəmɪt 〕 *adj.* 正當的；合法的
　　　　(D) dispassionate 〔 dɪs'pæʃənɪt 〕 *adj.* 冷靜的

5. (**D**) (A) authority 〔 ə'θɔrətɪ 〕 *n.* 權威
　　　　(B) minority 〔 maɪ'nɔrətɪ 〕 *n.* 少數
　　　　(C) celebrity 〔 sə'lɛbrətɪ 〕 *n.* 名人
　　　　(D) ***priority*** 〔 praɪ'ɔrətɪ 〕 *n.* 優先權

6. (**B**)　(B) *efficiency* 〔 ə'fɪʃənsɪ 〕 *n.* 效率
　　　　　(C) discrimination 〔 dɪ͵skrɪmə'neʃən 〕 *n.* 區別；歧視
　　　　　(D) inflation 〔 ɪn'fleʃən 〕 *n.* 通貨膨脹
　　　　　output 〔 'aut͵put 〕 *n.* 產量

7. (**D**)　(A) remote 〔 rɪ'mot 〕 *adj.* 遙遠的
　　　　　(B) enormous 〔 ɪ'nɔrməs 〕 *adj.* 巨大的
　　　　　(C) complicated 〔 'kamplə͵ketɪd 〕 *adj.* 複雜的
　　　　　(D) *concrete* 〔 'kankrit 〕 *adj.* 具體的
　　　　　abstract 〔 æb'strækt 〕 *adj.* 抽象的

8. (**A**)　(A) *defective* 〔 dɪ'fɛktɪv 〕 *adj.* 有瑕疵的
　　　　　(B) creative 〔 krɪ'etɪv 〕 *adj.* 有創造力的
　　　　　(C) convicted 〔 kən'vɪktɪd 〕 *adj.* 定罪的；犯罪的
　　　　　(D) abundant 〔 ə'bʌndənt 〕 *adj.* 豐富的
　　　　　lens 〔 lɛnz 〕 *n.* 鏡頭

9. (**A**)　(A) *reliable* 〔 rɪ'laɪəbḷ 〕 *adj.* 可靠的
　　　　　(B) reluctant 〔 rɪ'lʌktənt 〕 *adj.* 不情願的
　　　　　(C) persistent 〔 pə'sɪstənt 〕 *adj.* 頑固的；持續不斷的
　　　　　(D) diligent 〔 'dɪlədʒənt 〕 *adj.* 勤勉的
　　　　　financier 〔 ͵faɪnən'sɪr 〕 *n.* 財政家；金融業者
　　　　　proceed 〔 prə'sid 〕 *v.* 繼續進行
　　　　　far-reaching 〔 'far'ritʃɪŋ 〕 *adj.* (計畫等) 遠大的

10. (**D**)　(A) investigate 〔 ɪn'vɛstə͵get 〕 *v.* 調查
　　　　　(B) shield 〔 ʃild 〕 *v.* 保護
　　　　　(C) relieve 〔 rɪ'liv 〕 *v.* 減輕；緩和
　　　　　(D) *deceive* 〔 dɪ'siv 〕 *v.* 欺騙
　　　　　misleading 〔 mɪs'lidɪŋ 〕 *adj.* 引起誤解的

II. 文法與結構： 20 %

11. (**A**)　*in → between*
　　difference between A and B A 與 B 之間的不同
　　dialect〔ˈdaɪəlɛkt〕*n.* 方言

12. (**C**)　*one → you*
　　apprentice〔əˈprɛntɪs〕*n.* 學徒；初學者

13. (**C**)　*where → which*
　　which 為關係代名詞，引導形容詞子句修飾 cafeteria，
　　而 where 為關係副詞，在此用法不合。
　　famished〔ˈfæmɪʃt〕*adj.* 非常饑餓的

14. (**B**)　*there have → **there were*** 「 there ＋ be 動詞」，表「有～」。
　　there 不可和 have 連用。

15. (**B**)　*to be kidnapped → **being kidnapped***
　　remember $\begin{cases} \text{to V.} & \text{記得要～} \\ \text{V-ing} & \text{記得曾經～} \end{cases}$
　　kidnap〔ˈkɪdnæp〕*v.* 綁架

16. (**B**)　*innocence → **innocent***　　innocent 為受詞補語，用來修飾
　　find 的受詞 the accused person。
　　accused〔əˈkjuzd〕*adj.* 被控告的
　　robbery〔ˈrɑbərɪ〕*n.* 搶劫

17. (**B**)　*advise → **advisable***　　advisable 為受詞補語。
　　physician〔fəˈzɪʃən〕*n.* 內科醫生

18. (**B**)　*but* 去掉　　although 為連接詞，不可和 but 連用。
　　impracticable〔ɪmˈpræktɪkəbl̩〕*adj.* 無法實行的
　　owing to 由於

19. (**C**) *who → who are* 或直接將 *who* 去掉　　原句是由 physicists who are incapable of driving a manual-shift car 省略關代 who 與 be 動詞 are 而來的分詞構句。
physicist〔ˈfɪzəsɪst〕*n.* 物理學家
manual-shift〔ˈmænjuəlˈʃɪft〕*adj.* 手排的

20. (**D**) *like → as*　　*the same thing as* ~　與~相同的事

III. 閱讀測驗：20%

A. 【譯文】

　　自一六○○年以來，絕種的動物急速增加。根據專家的了解，自有歷史記載以來至十七世紀初期之間，絕種的動物不到二十種。一六○○年至一六九九年，只有一世紀的時間，就有十七種動物消失了。之後的九十九年間，共有三十六種動物絕跡。在一八○○年代，絕種的動物增為一六○○年之前的五倍（共八十一種）。二十世紀初的七十五年間，又有八十三種動物絕跡。很顯然，動物絕種的速度並未減緩。

┌─【答案】─────────────────
│　　　21. (**B**)　　　　22. (**B**)
└────────────────────

【註】

species〔ˈspiʃɪz〕*n.* 種；類　　*die out* 絕種
sharply〔ˈʃɑrplɪ〕*adv.* 急速地；明顯地
extinct〔ɪkˈstɪŋkt〕*adj.* 絕種的
quintuple〔ˈkwɪntjupl̩〕*v.* 成為五倍

B.【譯文】

　　這將不再只是毫無意義的空想。擁有二百五十萬名帳戶持有人的紐約花旗銀行，計劃在一九九五年以前，讓一半以上的客戶連線。大型零售連鎖機構，如 J.C. Penney's，正在試行家庭購物系統，其他以電腦為基礎的新聞、體育和娛樂服務，如雙向有線電視系統和泰萊克思，都已正式使用，華盛頓特區附近的購物中心，利用數據機連線，為顧客提供「櫥窗瀏覽」服務，他們會在每家商店的索引中，列出所有銷售商品和特價品。使用者還可叫出某項商品的比價下訂單，並要求提供送給女性、男性、兒童、寵物、年長親屬和祕書的禮品建議，或是其他各式各樣的贈禮種類。這種垂手可得又價格低廉的電腦，對我們的社會必定會產生重大的影響。

【答案】

　　23.（**A**）　　　　24.（**D**）

【註】

idle〔ˈaɪdḷ〕*adj.* 無意義的；無聊的

conjecture〔kənˈdʒɛktʃɚ〕*n.* 推測；猜想

retail〔ˈritel〕*n.* 零售　　chain〔tʃen〕*n.* 連鎖機構

UBE〔kjub〕*n.* 雙向有線電視系統（商標名）

Teletext〔ˈtɛlətɛkst〕*n.* 泰萊泰思（商標名，一種使用互相連結的計算機終端的數據處理和通信系統）

mall〔mɔl〕*n.* 購物中心

accessible〔ækˈsɛsəbḷ〕*adj.* 可獲得的

modem〔ˈmoˌdɛm〕*n.* 數據機　　special〔ˈspɛʃəl〕*n.* 特價品

index〔ˈɪndɛks〕*n.* 索引　　order〔ˈɔrdɚ〕*n.* 訂購

pet〔pɛt〕*n.* 寵物　　recipient〔rɪˈsɪpənt〕*n.* 接受者

category〔ˈkætəˌgorɪ〕*n.* 種類

dramatic〔drəˈmætɪk〕*adj.* 重大的

C.【譯文】

有些人如果吃了很冰的冰淇淋，就會頭痛。有位神經科醫師（神經科專家）告訴我為什麼這樣會產生頭痛。極度低溫的冰淇淋會對臉部的某條神經產生作用。這條神經位於臉頰部位，然後在下巴、顎和太陽穴部位呈扇形散開。極度低溫會產生疼痛，這條神經會將疼痛的感覺傳至太陽穴，因而造成頭痛。

如果有這種情形發生，要放鬆。試著喝點比冰淇淋溫熱的東西。較溫熱的液體有助於鎮定神經。不論你怎麼做，記住，這種疼痛不會持續很久，等冰淇淋較不冰的時候，再慢慢地吃。

【答案】

25. (**B**)　　　26. (**A**)　　　27. (**C**)

【註】

neurologist〔nju'rɑlədʒɪst〕*n.* 神經科醫師
cheek〔tʃik〕*n.* 臉頰　　fan〔fæn〕*v.* 作扇形散開
chin〔tʃɪn〕*n.* 下巴　　jaw〔dʒɔ〕*n.* 顎
temple〔'tɛmpl̩〕*n.* 太陽穴

D.【譯文】

羅伯特・史賓是十九世紀的仿冒專家，非常善於偽造，十五年來，一直以販賣偽造的美國名人簽名來謀生。史賓於一八一三年出生於英國，在一八五八年來到費城，開了一家書店。起初，他因為出售自己所收集一些美國早期名人的親筆簽名而生意興隆。在發現自己有模仿別人筆跡的能力之後，就開始模仿華盛頓和富蘭克林的簽名，並寫在舊書的書名頁上。為了避免被識破，他把自己的偽造品送往英國和加拿大銷售和發行。

　　僞造者在出售產品時，會遇到許多困難，他們不能和有名望的買主接洽，只能推銷給對這方面不太熟悉的民衆。僞造者有許多方法，能讓作品看起來和眞的一樣。例如，他們會購買舊書，使用其陳舊的書名頁，再利用化學藥品處理紙張和墨水。

　　在史賓生長的年代，正是南北戰爭結束後不久，英國仍非常喜愛南方各州，所以史賓就創造一位有身分地位的女士，名爲范妮傑克生小姐，是「史東威爾」傑克生將軍的獨生女。多年來，范妮小姐因爲財務問題，不得不大量出售這位著名父親的信件和手稿。史賓必須努力趕工，才能滿足需求。儘管如此，他最後仍窮困潦倒而死，留給那些目光敏銳的專家們十分吃力的工作，要去分辨哪些是僞造品，哪些才是眞品。

【答案】

28. (**C**)　　　　29. (**B**)　　　　30. (**D**)

【註】

forger〔ˈfɔrdʒɚ〕*n.* 僞造者　　signature〔ˈsɪɡnətʃɚ〕*n.* 簽名
prosper〔ˈprɑspɚ〕*v.* 成功；發達
genuine〔ˈdʒɛnjʊɪn〕*adj.* 眞正的
autograph〔ˈɔtəˌɡræf〕*n.* 親筆簽名
handwriting〔ˈhændˌraɪtɪŋ〕*n.* 筆跡
forgery〔ˈfɔrdʒərɪ〕*n.* 僞造品
detection〔dɪˈtɛkʃən〕*n.* 看穿；發現
circulation〔ˌsɝkjəˈleʃən〕*n.* 發行
manuscript〔ˈmænjəˌskrɪpt〕*n.* 手稿
sharp-eyed〔ˈʃɑrpˈaɪd〕*adj.* 目光敏銳的
original〔əˈrɪdʒənḷ〕*n.* 原作；原物

IV. 克漏字：20％

【譯文】

　　每個人都必須發掘自己內心滿足的來源，這就是老年人活動，如閱讀和園藝的眾多好處之一。老年人的守則就是要活動筋骨，如果無法閱讀，就可以用聽的，如果天氣很好，就出門去種種花草，如果不能種花草，還是要走出戶外，曬曬太陽。最重要的是，要保持活力，多培養興趣，隨興之所至，做不同的事——永遠要把目標擺在前方，絕不輕言放棄。

　　所以，我會用盡各種辦法，讓我的老年生活過得愉快！

【註】

source〔sɔrs〕n. 來源
contentment〔kən'tɛntmənt〕n. 滿足
golden rule 金科玉律　　*make the most of* 善加利用
above all 最重要的是　　vary〔'vɛrɪ〕v. 變換
objective〔əb'dʒɛktɪv〕n. 目標
one way and another 用種種方法

31. (**A**) 依句意，許多「好處」之一，選 (A)。one of + 複數名詞，表「～之一」。

32. (**B**) 依句意，選 (B) *reading*〔'ridɪŋ〕n. 閱讀。

33. (**B**) 依句意，選 (B) *gardening*〔'gɑrdṇɪŋ〕n. 園藝。

34. (**A**) adapt〔ə'dæpt〕v. 適應

35. (**A**) see〔si〕v. 看見

36. (**D**) garden〔'gɑrdṇ〕v. 種植花草

37. (**D**) 依句意，選 (D) *active* 〔'æktɪv 〕 *adj.* 活躍的；積極的。而 (A) alive 〔 ə'laɪv 〕 *adj.* 活著的，(B) awake 〔 ə'wek 〕 *v.* 叫醒，(D) asleep 〔 ə'slip 〕 *adj.* 睡著的，均不合句意。

38. (**C**) from one thing to *another* 從某件事到另一件事

39. (**C**) *have* an objective 有一個目標

40. (**D**) 依句意，選 (D) *give in* 「屈服」。而 (A) give out 「用完；疲倦」，(B) give away 「洩露；贈送」，(C) give off 「發出（光熱、味道）」，均不合句意。

IV. 作文： 20 %

Why I Like City Life in Taiwan

I have only lived in the city since entering high school, but I've really come to like it. I can find and do things very easily in the city. Although the country has fewer people and cars, and cleaner air, it leaves a lot to be desired in terms of convenience and facilities.

Taipei, the capital city of Taiwan, is now my home. I like it, because it is a city that never sleeps. There is always something to do here twenty-four hours a day. Another thing I like is that the best food from around the world can be found here. I can find food from almost any country in the numerous hotel and department store restaurants. The convenience of the city is also to my liking. Except during rush hour, I can get to most places I need to go very quickly. That is why I like the city life in Taiwan.

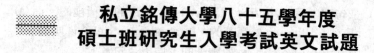

私立銘傳大學八十五學年度
碩士班研究生入學考試英文試題

I. Vocabulary: choose the most suitable definition of the following words. 30%

1. When IBM announced that the Company would be down-sizing in 1995, it meant that IBM would _____.
   (A) lay off employees
   (B) give a raise to its employees
   (C) decrease the pay to its employers
   (D) merge with other companies

2. The principal of a loan which I take from the National Taiwan Bank is _____.
   (A) the bonds I bought
   (B) the additional amount that I have to pay
   (C) the service charge from the Bank
   (D) the sum of money I borrowed

3. Portfolio diversity means that one should invest one's money in _____.
   (A) one specific product
   (B) various products
   (C) personal products
   (D) hair products

4. There are many who practice voodoo economics nowadays. This means that the economist who proclaims it, _____
   (A) will not clearly identify the objective of the theory.
   (B) uses the ups and downs in currency for profit.
   (C) uses a vague or questionable formula for computation.
   (D) uses a witch spell for computation.

5. The <u>interest</u> that I earn from the stocks is the money
   that I _____.
   (A) make in addition to my capital
   (B) lose on the stock market
   (C) invest in the stock market
   (D) save in a bank

6. AIDS is a <u>contagious</u> disease which means that the
   disease will _____
   (A) be transmitted through talking.
   (B) not be transmitted through bodily contact.
   (C) be transmitted through education or earning
       potential.
   (D) be transmitted through bodily contact.

7. If one needs to ask for a loan, one must show his/
   her <u>assets</u> as an indication of potential ability of
   paying it back. Assets are _____.
   (A) valuable property and possession
   (B) children
   (C) clothes   (D) education

8. The <u>means of production</u> is referring to _____.
   (A) stock holders
   (B) the owners
   (C) the instrument, tools
   (D) the workers

9. <u>Pollution</u> has been a major focus in the green movement
   of improving the quality of our living environment.
       Pollution means _____ a certain object.
   (A) to clean   (B) to wash
   (C) to work on   (D) to make foul

10. I will <u>collaborate</u> with someone I hate if she has a
    compassion for the less fortunate people. Collaborate
    means _____.
    (A) to substitute   (B) to work with
    (C) to replace   (D) to join

II. Reading Comprehension: 20%

　　According to J. Wallach & G. Metcalf in ''Working with Americans'', Americans believe that self-promotion is not a bad thing, after all, no one would know more than oneself about the merits of oneself. Asians, on the other hand, operate differently. Any merit or special abilities will be valued more highly if it is brought out by others and not by oneself. The American bosses consider Asians are over-humble and tend to send their Asian workers to assertiveness training classes. They believe the reasons for these Asian people being so humble is because these Asians have a lack of ability or self-assurance. The Asians regard the Americans as persons who do not understand the meaning of humbleness and who love to exaggerate and bluff. Asians practice humbleness in order to avoid the chance of ''losing face,'' which is the major issue in interpersonal relations. Americans who do not have the concept of ''face'' do not considered it a disgrace if they do not achieve what they have boasted of or set up to reach.

1. Americans believe that ＿＿＿＿＿＿ is the right thing to do because they know their merit the best.
   (A) self-assurance　　　　　(B) assertiveness
   (C) humbleness　　　　　　(D) self-promotion

2. American bosses tend to misunderstand their Asian employees' humbleness as a sign of ＿＿＿＿＿＿.
   (A) self-assurance
   (B) pride
   (C) a lack of ability
   (D) confidence

3. The likely reason for Asians to practice humbleness
   is ─────.
   (A) fear of losing face
   (B) self-confidence
   (C) that it is a fun game
   (D) that interpersonal interaction is a complicated
       matter

4. In the eyes of Asians, Americans are ─────.
   (A) humble   (B) braggarts
   (C) noisy   (D) irresponsible

5. Based on the above statements predicate what an Asian
   (AS) and an American(AM) would say if they both take
   lessons on learning Russian language for a year: ─────.
   (A) AS: I can only speak a little
   (B) AM: I can only speak a little
   (C) AS: I speak Russian
   (D) AM: I don't speak Russian

III. Translation: 20%

1. Modern women are trapped in two kinds of war zones.
   They face constant struggles: they want to search
   and develop their potential ability and at the same
   time to be a mother.

2. 目前的經濟不景氣連在菜市場買菜的主婦都可以感受到。

IV. Identify any grammatical errors (underline the errors)
    and make corrections at the end of the sentence. There
    might be more than one error in a sentence and it/
    they are not necessary in the same places. Using C for
    correct sentences and IC for incorrect sentences: 30%

E.g. _C_ 1. I have been to the Library twice since I came
            back from my vacation in March.
     _IC_ 2. The Michael Bolton concert will be taken
            place in Taipei soon. Will take place.

1. The lunch that I had with Mr. Robinson went very well. We enjoyed chatting with each other.

2. Managing people is a quite challenging task because people are the biggest, most unpredictable variable.

3. Life is usually filled with surprises. At any moment, there might had something different happen.

4. Jack Chan is one of the world famous action actors. He was one of the hosts of this year's Oscar Award Ceremony.

5. Marketing have became a popular instrument in identifying the potentiality of a product in modern days.

6. Everybody is using credit cards, yet not everyone knows the potential of using plastic appropriately.

7. Going to the train station is not a difficulty thing. It is fun and health.

8. The creditability of a company will help a consumer making decisions in purchasing.

9. Living in the present world is a challenging task. The present and the past is so different that it confused our value judgment.

10. Taking examination is extreme exhausting.

私立銘傳大學八十五學年度
碩士班研究生入學考試英文試題詳解

I. 字彙：30 ％

1. (**A**) down-size〔ˈdaʊnˌsaɪz〕*v.* 縮小
   (A) *lay off employees* 解僱員工
   (B) raise〔rez〕*n.* 加薪
   (D) merge〔mɝdʒ〕*v.* 合併

2. (**D**) principal〔ˈprɪnsəpl̩〕*n.* 本金
   (A) bond〔bɑnd〕*n.* 債券
   (C) service charge　服務費
   (D) *the sum of money I borrowed* 借貸總額
   　　loan〔lon〕*n.* 貸款

3. (**B**) portfolio diversity　多種有價證券
   (A) specific〔spəˈsɪfɪk〕*adj.* 特定的
   (B) *various products* 不同的產品

4. (**C**) voodoo economics　巫術經濟學
   (B) currency〔ˈkɝənsɪ〕*n.* 貨幣
   (C) vague〔veg〕*adj.* 模糊的
   　　formula〔ˈfɔrmjələ〕*n.* 公式
   　　computation〔ˌkɑmpjəˈteʃən〕*n.* 計算
   (D) witch spell　巫咒

5. (**A**)　interest〔ˈɪntrɪst〕*n.* 利息
   (A) capital〔ˈkæpətl̩〕*n.* 資本
   (B) stock market　股票市場

6. (**D**)　contagious〔kənˈtedʒəs〕*adj.* 接觸傳染的
   (A) transmit〔trænsˈmɪt〕*v.* 傳染

7. (**A**)   assets〔ˈæsɛts〕*n.pl.* 資產
      (A) property〔ˈprɑpətɪ〕*n.* 財產
        possession〔pəˈzɛʃən〕*n.* 擁有物
      indication〔ˌɪndəˈkeʃən〕*n.* 指標

8. (**C**)   means of production 生產工具
      (A) stock holders 股東
      (C) *the instrument, tools* 儀器和工具

9. (**D**)   pollution〔pəˈluʃən〕*n.* 污染
      (C) work on 影響
      (D) *make foul* 弄髒

10. (**B**)   collaborate〔kəˈlæbəˌret〕*v.* 合作
      (A) substitute〔ˈsʌbstəˌtjut〕*v.* 代替
      (B) *work with* ～ 與～合作
      compassion〔kəmˈpæʃən〕*n.* 同情

II. 閱讀測驗：20%

【譯文】

　　根據瓦勒其和麥特卡夫在「與美國人共事」一書中的說法，美國人認爲毛遂自薦不是一件壞事。畢竟，只有自己最了解自己的優點。然而，另一方面，亞洲人的態度卻不一樣。由別人發現的優點和特殊才能比毛遂自薦的要有價值。美國主管認爲亞洲人過於謙虛，因此常常派亞裔的員工去接受自我表現的訓練課程。他們認爲，亞洲人之所以如此謙虛，是因爲缺乏能力或自信。而亞洲人則認爲美國人不懂得謙虛，喜歡誇耀和吹噓自己。亞洲人習慣性的謙虛，是爲了避免「丟臉」，因爲這是人際關係中，最重要的問題。但是美國人沒有「面子」的觀念，所以如果他們沒有完成先前所誇耀的事情，或沒能達到預期的目標，也不會覺得羞恥。

【答案】

1. (**D**)　　2. (**C**)　　3. (**A**)　　4. (**B**)　　5. (**A**)

【註】

merit〔'mɛrɪt〕 *n.* 優點　　***bring out*** 提出；顯示
assertiveness〔ə'sɝtɪv͵nɪs〕 *n.* 強烈主張己見
self-assurance〔͵sɛlfə'ʃurəns〕 *n.* 自信
bluff〔blʌf〕 *v.* 虛張聲勢
interpersonal〔͵ɪntɚ'pɝsənl̩〕 *adj.* 人與人之間的
disgrace〔dɪs'gres〕 *n.* 恥辱　　boast〔bost〕 *v.* 誇耀
braggart〔'brægɚt〕 *n.* 自誇的人
predicate〔'prɛdɪ͵ket〕 *v.* 宣稱；斷言

III. 翻譯：20%

1. 現代婦女正陷入兩難的情況，她們必須面臨不斷的掙扎：她們想要去追尋、發展自己的潛力，但同時又要做一位母親。

2. The present economic depression can be felt even by the housewives who buy vegetables and meat in the marketplace.

IV. 文法：30%（挑錯並改正）

1. (**C**)　chat〔tʃæt〕 *v.* 閒談

2. (**IC**)　*a quite challenging task→**quite a challenging task***
　　quite 須置於定冠詞 a / an 之前。
　　unpredictable〔͵ʌnprɪ'dɪktəbl̩〕 *adj.* 不可預測的
　　variable〔'vɛrɪəbl̩〕 *n.* 變數

3. (**IC**) *there might had something different happen*
   → **something different might happen**

4. (**IC**) *one of the world famous* → **one of the world's most famous**

5. (**IC**) *have became* → **has become**　　主詞 marketing 為單數名詞，助動詞須和主詞一致。
   marketing〔ˈmɑrkɪtɪŋ〕*n.* 行銷

6. (**C**)

7. (**IC**) *difficulty* → **difficult**　　*health* → **healthy**

8. (**IC**) *making decisions in purchasing* → **(to) make decisions in purchasing**
   creditability〔͵krɛdəˈbɪlətɪ〕*n.* 可靠性

9. (**IC**) *is so different that it confused* → **are so different that they confuse**

10. (**IC**) *examination* → **examinations**
    extreme → **extremely**　　修飾形容詞 exhaustive，須用副詞。

國立台灣大學八十三學年度
碩士班研究生入學考試英文試題

Choose the BEST answer. Put a cross--"X"--in the appropriate space for each question to indicate your choice.

Example: It was Joan's first visit to the country, and everything was fresh and_____to her.
(A) dull　　(B) quickly　　(C) new　　(D) excite

Answer :　A　　B　　C　　D
　　　　　□　　□　　☒　　□

I. Cloze Test (Choose the best answer to fill in the blank)

　　There is a bargain sale in the department store downtown; of all merchandise is being sold at a ___1___ of 50% off. But before you go shopping there, you need to plan in advance your ___2___ and the things you want to buy, otherwise you will b bankrupt and waste much money getting things you don't really need. Besides, make sure the things you buy are not defective or damaged items; you know, during sale time most department stores in Taiwan are notorious for treating customers rudely and disregarding ___3___ rights. By the way, I know you are a fashion clothes faddist, so how about ___4___ those outdated clothes in your closet to a charity institution?

1. (A) discharge　　　　　　(B) discredit
　　(C) discount　　　　　　(D) disorder

2. (A) budget　　　　　　　(B) income
　　(C) charge　　　　　　　(D) balance

3. (A) service　　　　　　　(B) consumer
　　(C) clerk　　　　　　　(D) claim

4. (A) donor　　　　　　　(B) donate
　　(C) donation　　　　　　(D) donating

Many large cities today are increasing in size because of a___5___in population from the country to the city. This rapid increase has caused a___6___in housing and transportation. There has also been a___7___in living standards. As a result, living in the big cities has become a problem. Overcrowding, traffic, crime and pollution are serious problems. The___8___of improvement in big city life does not seem encouraging at all. One___9___would be to limit city growth, but that decision would require the___10___of a strong, brave government.

5. (A) exchange   (B) shift
   (C) transaction   (D) turn

6. (A) deterioration   (B) distance
   (C) pollution   (D) recession

7. (A) disdain   (B) disgust
   (C) decline   (D) depression

8. (A) design   (B) approach
   (C) perspective   (D) prospect

9. (A) tradition   (B) alternative
   (C) altercation   (D) treatment

10. (A) initiative   (B) introduction
    (C) issue   (D) initial

There are apparently very few areas of agreement___11___ doctors and nutritional experts these days, upon what constitutes a safe and healthy diet and what is to be avoided. ___12___ is a product declared by one group of scientists to be the key to vigor and longevity,___13___ it is dismissed by another group as being acutely dangerous to health.

11. (A) between   (B) among
    (C) against   (D) over

12. (A) Immediately   (B) Whenever
    (C) As soon as   (D) No sooner

13. (A) then　　　　　　　　(B) than
　　(C) that　　　　　　　　(D) so that

　　My grandma's moods are very changeable. Sometimes she
can be very domineering and difficult; ___14___ she'll be
pleasant and quite happy. But whichever it is, the good is
___15___ quite as good as it might be and the bad is always
worse—whenever my mother and I are involved. ___16___, she
seems happier to hear about our problems than our successes.
I haven't seen ___17___ of her since I married, although my
mother still sees her about every three or four weeks.
Occasionally she has outbursts about me and tells mother I'm
no good. Other relatives ___18___ this treatment and have
moved away or lost contact. My mother tells me about her
visits and I feel weighed ___19___ just by listening. She is
my grandmother, and is not getting any younger and I'm
taking the easy way ___20___ by not going to visit her.

14. (A) whereas　　　　　　(B) when
　　(C) at other times　　　(D) at a time

15. (A) always　　　　　　(B) never
　　(C) neither　　　　　　(D) nevertheless

16. (A) While　　　　　　(B) Frankly
　　(C) As soon as　　　　(D) Since

17. (A) very much　　　　　(B) always
　　(C) occasionally　　　　(D) too many

18. (A) have never　　　　(B) have had
　　(C) have done　　　　　(D) have been

19. (A) against　　　　　　(B) up
　　(C) down　　　　　　　(D) out

20. (A) up　　　　　　　　(B) on
　　(C) over　　　　　　　(D) out

II. Paraphrase (Choose the answer that best keeps the meaning of the underlined words)

21. The human body is sometimes seen as a <u>microcosm</u> of the universe.
    (A) study of microbes
    (B) well-ordered system
    (C) miniature representation
    (D) power of microscopes

22. Even if the police <u>postulate</u> that the suspect had a motive for the murder, that still doesn't mean that he did it.
    (A) advocate   (B) claim
    (C) question   (D) admit

23. Feeling <u>omniscient</u>, brilliant people can destroy themselves by ignoring possible risks.
    (A) especially greedy   (B) knowing everything
    (C) present everywhere   (D) able to do anything

24. It w~ the defense lawyer's <u>contention</u> that his client could not have committed the crime.
    (A) defiance   (B) proof
    (C) announcement   (D) assertion

25. She used <u>devious</u> means to gain power.
    (A) cautious   (B) thoughtless
    (C) clever   (D) deceitful

26. One can scarcely expect to escape <u>reproof</u> for such irresponsible behavior.
    (A) additional confirmation
    (B) expression of disapproval
    (C) silence
    (D) violent agitation

27. Nowadays, the word "individualism" seems to <u>connote</u> selfishness.
    (A) imply   (B) confuse
    (C) draw closer   (D) point out

28. The government should no longer ignore the political <u>aspirations</u> of the local people.
    (A) resentment   (B) freedom
    (C) challenge   (D) ambition

29. The man did not grasp the <u>enormity</u> of betraying his comrades in arms.
    (A) foolishness   (B) stupidity
    (C) grandeur   (D) great wickedness

30. People nowadays are more able to tolerate <u>ambiguous</u> attitudes toward controversial issues.
    (A) encircling   (B) not clear
    (C) unusually skillful   (D) forgetful

    Outside protected areas, Asian tigers are a vanishing breed, disappearing faster than any other large mammal with the possible exception of the rhinoceros. No more than 5,000 to 7,500 of the majestic tigers remain on the planet--a population decline of roughly 95% in this century. Unless something (31)<u>dramatic</u> is done to reverse the trend, tigers will be seen only in (32)<u>captivity</u>, prowling in zoos or performing in circuses. The wild tigers of old will be gone forever, their glory surviving merely in storybooks, on film--and in dreams.

    Preventing such a tragedy is supposed to be the main goal of the governing body of CITES, the Convention on International Trade in (33)<u>Endangered</u> Species. Last September, CITES warned China and Taiwan, two countries where the illicit trade in tiger and rhino parts is prevalent, to (34)<u>take steps</u> to shut down their black markets or face possible (35)<u>trade sanctions</u>. Both nations claim to have curbed the illegal commerce, but environmentalists have gathered evidence to the contrary.

31. (A) difficult   (B) terrible
    (C) drastic   (D) playful

32. (A) capitalization   (B) captivation
    (C) immobilization   (D) imprisonment

33. (A) dangerous   (B) almost extinct
    (C) extraordinary   (D) distinguished

34. (A) take measures   (B) take walks
    (C) take advantage of   (D) take apart

35. (A) trade penalties   (B) trade exchanges
    (C) trade profits   (D) trade approvals

III. Reading Comprehension (Read the passage carefully, then answer the questions)

One of the complications of modern life is that when you're waiting for an up elevator, the first one to arrive is usually going down. Apparently, this observation turns out to be true for reasons built into the laws of nature.

Why is the first elevator usually going in the wrong direction? The answer is relatively simple: In most buildings, when you're on a low floor, the chances are that you probably want to go up because there are more possible destinations above you than below you. However, there are also probably more elevators above you than below you, which means that when they reach you, they will be going down. Similarly, when you're on a high floor, you probably want to go down, but because there are more elevators below you, when they get to you they are going up.

This analysis does not apply to the first floor or to the top floor of a building. All elevators at the first floor go up, and all elevators at the top floor go down. Of course, as any elevator rider will attest, you will still probably have to wait a long time for one. During the morning rush hour, most people want to go up, and during the evening rush hours, most people want to go down.

There are psychological factors at work in our perceptions of elevators as well. Since negative emotions are felt more acutely than positive ones, we tend to remember our disappointments with elevators more keenly than we remember our satisfactions. We forget the times that the right elevator came and focus on the times that it didn't.

36. Elevators always seem to be going in the wrong direction
because
(A) there is no exception.
(B) we are going in the opposite drection.
(C) waiting is invariably frustrating.
(D) we focus our thoughts too keenly on waiting for
elevators.

37. While waiting for elevators, if you are on the first
floor of a building and you want to go up, the chances
are high that
(A) you probably don't have to wait at all.
(B) you probably don't have to wait during the rush
hour.
(C) you probably still have to wait for a long time.
(D) you probably still have to wait for a down elevator.

38. In most buildings when you are on the second or third
floor, you probably want to go up because
(A) there are more elevators below you than above you.
(B) there are more destinations below you than above
you.
(C) there are more elevators above you than below you.
(D) there are more destinations above you than below
you.

39. According to this article, which of the following situation is most likely to occur?
(A) Your chances of getting an elevator in your direction are better when you are going up than when you
are going down.
(B) Your chances of getting an elevator that is going
up are better in the morning than in the evening.
(C) Your chances of getting an elevator that is going
up are better in the evening than in the morning.
(D) Your chances of getting the right elevator the
first time are usually good.

40. This article gives the general impression that
(A) waiting for elevators may involve psychological
factors as well as personal emotions.
(B) positive emotions are more strongly felt than
negative emotions.
(C) the higher floor you are on, the more positive
emotions you will have.
(D) we are usually more satisfied than disappointed
when waiting for elevators.

Tropical rain forests are located near the equator between 30 degrees north and 20 degrees south, spanning 4 continents and nearly 50 countries. Tropical rain forests cover 7% of the world's land, and they flourish in the relatively constant hot temperatures and abundant rainfall of the equatorial regions.

We need rain forests for several reasons. First, we need them because the trees act as a watershed, holding the water and then gradually releasing it into the surrounding land, preventing erosion. Deforestation sometimes results in a loss of rainfall. The average rainfall in Panama is 17 inches less per year than historical averages, as a result of the stripping of forest land. The forests also help deter sedimentation of streams, rivers, and hydro-electric dams. In Thailand, many rivers are no longer navigable due to sedimentation because many rain forests have been destroyed.

Second, we need rain forests to inhibit the greenhouse effect. Tropical rain forests absorb an enormous amount of sunlight, preventing the sun's rays from being reflected back into the atmosphere. However, as deforestation occurs through the burning of tropical forests, the CO_2 released, along with emissions from industry and automobiles, traps the sun's rays. This phenomenon, now known as the "greenhouse effect," can lead to a shift of the world's weather pattern, raising of global temperatures and causing the melting of the polar ice caps.

Finally, we need rain forests because they contribute to medicine and science. For instance, curare, used in muscle relaxants, comes from tropical plants. Genetic engineers and other medical researchers are realizing that tropical forests are a valuable resource for other chemicals. A promising new cure for cancer may come from the chemical phyllanthostatin, which is found in the jungles of Costa

Rica. Scientists have also used tropical rain forests to
upgrade the genes of rice, peanuts, and sugar cane.

We need the tropical rain forests because they help to
maintain the soil and the balance in the climate. In addition, they provide a resource for scientific research and
advancement.

41. The theme of this article is concerned with
    (A) saving endangered species.
    (B) promoting environmental protection.
    (C) facing energy crisis.
    (D) exploiting natural resources.

42. Rain forests are so named and characterized by the
    fact that
    (A) these forests can reduce rainfall to the minimum.
    (B) too much rainfall in these forests often causes
        flood damage.
    (C) the average rainfall is less than 17 inches per year.
    (D) the rainfall in these forests is heavy and plentiful.

43. Deforestation means
    (A) increasing the acres of forests.
    (B) planting more trees in forests.
    (C) preventing the greenhouse effect.
    (D) cutting down the trees in forests.

44. Which of the following situations will definitely not be
    a consequence of deforestation?
    (A) Rainfall will be greatly reduced and land erosion
        will not be preventable.
    (B) Rivers will not be able to maintain regular flow so
        boats will not be able to sail.
    (C) The weather pattern will be changed because of the
        greenhouse effect.
    (D) We will lose all hope of curing cancer and for
        biochemical research.

45. The problem of the shrinking rain forests is
    (A) serious because it influences the global ecosystem.
    (B) something trivial because they cover only 7% of the
        world's land.
    (C) exaggerated by scientists and environmentalists.
    (D) merely a natural consequence of evolution.

To understand the nature of the liberal arts college and its function in our society, it is important to understand the difference between education and training. Training is intended primarily for the service of society; education is primarily for the individual. Society needs doctors, lawyers, engineers, and teachers to perform specific tasks necessary to its operation, just as it needs carpenters and plumbers. Training supplies the immediate and specific needs of society so that the work of the world may continue. Our training centers--the professional and trade schools--fill these needs.

But although education is for the improvement of the individual, it also serves society by providing a leavening of men and women of understanding, of perception and wisdom. They are our intellectual leaders, the critics of our culture, the defenders of our free traditions, the instigators of our progress. They serve society by examining its function, appraising its needs, and criticizing its direction. They may be earning their livings by practicing one of the professions, or in pursuing a trade, or by engaging in business enterprise. They may be rich or poor. They may occupy positions of power and prestige, or they may be engaged in some humble employment. Without them, however, society either disintegrates or else becomes an anthill.

46. In professional and trade schools, students should be taught
    (A) the ways of living in a modern world.
    (B) to follow closely the progress of new technology.
    (C) the specific skills of certain occupations.
    (D) the ways of handling social problems.

47. Liberal arts education is intended
    (A) to give further training to talented artists.
    (B) to cultivate the individual who is to play the leading role in our society.
    (C) to generate the opinion that everyone has a promising future in every trade.
    (D) to claim genuine equality between men and women, and between the rich and the poor.

48. The argument of this passage is based on the writing mode of
    (A) comparison and contrast.
    (B) narration.
    (C) cause and effect.
    (D) description.

49. This passage seems to imply that
    (A) professional training is the only thing that improves our society.
    (B) liberal arts education educates people who can inspect and re-evaluate our social system.
    (C) professional training is more important because it improves the whole society rather than the individual.
    (D) liberal arts education is like a castle in the air with goals too idealistic to fulfill.

50. The suggested title of this passage would be
    (A) The Function of Liberal Arts Education in Our Society.
    (B) The Importance of Society and the Individual.
    (C) Professional Training Meets Our Social Needs.
    (D) Liberal Arts Education Meets Our Social Needs.

國立台灣大學八十三學年度
碩士班研究生入學考試英文試題詳解

Ⅰ. 克漏字：40％

【譯文】

　　市中心的百貨公司正舉行大拍賣，所有的商品都打五折。但是在去那裏購物之前，必須事先計畫好你的預算，以及想要購買的物品，否則，你可能會破產，浪費錢去買你並不需要的東西。此外，必須確定你所買的物品沒有瑕疵或故障；你知道的，台灣的百貨公司，在拍賣期間惡名昭彰，待客十分無禮，而且不重視消費者的權利。對了，我知道你是個熱愛新潮服飾的人，何不將你衣櫥裏那些過時的衣服捐給慈善機構呢？

【註】

bargain sale 大拍賣　　merchandise〔ˈmɝtʃən͵daɪz〕*n.* 商品
bankrupt〔ˈbæŋkrʌpt〕*adj.* 破產的
defective〔dɪˈfɛktɪv〕*adj.* 瑕疵的
notorious〔noˈtorɪəs〕*adj.* 惡名昭彰的
disregard〔͵dɪsrɪˈgɑrd〕*v.* 忽視　　faddist〔ˈfædɪst〕*n.* 趕時髦的人
charity institution 慈善機構

1.（ C ）　(A) discharge〔dɪsˈtʃɑrdʒ〕*n.* 開除
　　　　　(B) discredit〔dɪsˈkrɛdɪt〕*n.* 懷疑；不信任
　　　　　(C) *discount*〔ˈdɪskaʊnt〕*n.* 折扣
　　　　　(D) disorder〔dɪsˈɔrdɚ〕*n.* 無秩序；混亂

2.（ A ）　(A) *budget*〔ˈbʌdʒɪt〕*n.* 預算　　(B) income〔ˈɪn͵kʌm〕*n.* 收入
　　　　　(C) charge〔tʃɑrdʒ〕*n.* 收費　　(D) balance〔ˈbæləns〕*n.* 平衡

3.（ B ）　依句意，百貨公司在拍賣期間，會忽視「消費者」的權利，故選(B) *consumer*〔kənˈsumɚ〕*n.* 消費者。而(A)服務，(C)職員，(D)宣稱，皆不合句意。

4.（ D ）　about 為介系詞，其後須接名詞或動名詞為受詞，故選 (D)
donating。donate〔ˈdonet〕*v.* 捐贈

【譯文】

現在有許多大城市正逐漸擴大，因為人口多由鄉村流入都市。這種快
速增加的現象，導致居住品質及交通運輸的惡化，生活品質也隨之下降。
因此，住在都市裏，變成一種進退兩難的困境。過度擁擠、交通、犯罪，
以及污染，都是十分嚴重的問題。大都市裏的生活將來是否能有所改善，
情況似乎並不樂觀。抑制都市的成長是種可行的辦法，但需要有強勢而且
勇敢的政府來發起，才能做此決定。

【註】

living standard 生活水準

5.（ B ）　(A) exchange〔ɪksˈtʃændʒ〕*n.* 交換
(B) *shift*〔ʃɪft〕*n.* 移動
(C) transaction〔trænsˈækʃən〕*n.* 交易
(D) turn〔tɜn〕*n.* 轉變

6.（ A ）　依句意，選 (A) *deterioration*〔dɪˌtɪrɪəˈreʃən〕*n.* 惡化。而 (B)
距離，(C) 污染，(D) recession〔rɪˈsɛʃən〕*n.* 不景氣，皆不合
句意。

7.（ C ）　依句意，選 (C) *decline*〔dɪˈklaɪn〕*n.* 衰退。而 (A) disdain
〔dɪsˈden〕*v.* 輕視，(B) disgust〔dɪsˈgʌst〕*v.* 厭惡，(D)
depression〔dɪˈprɛʃən〕*n.* 沮喪，皆不合句意。

8.（ D ）　(A) design〔dɪˈzaɪn〕*n.* 設計
(B) approach〔əˈprotʃ〕*n.* 方法
(C) perspective〔pɚˈspɛktɪv〕*n.* 正確的看法
(D) *prospect*〔ˈprɑspɛkt〕*n.* 預期；展望

9.（ B ）　*alternative*〔ɔlˈtɜnətɪv〕*n.* 選擇
而 (A) 傳統，(C) altercation〔ˌɔltɚˈkeʃən〕*n.* 爭辯，與 (D) 治療；
處理，皆不合句意。

10. **(A)** (A) ***initiative*** 〔 ɪˋnɪʃɪ͵etɪv 〕 *n.* 發起；首倡

(B) introduction 〔 ͵ɪntrəˋdʌkʃən 〕 *n.* 引進；介紹

(C) issue 〔 ˋɪʃʊ 〕 *n.* 發行

(D) initial 〔 ɪˋnɪʃəl 〕 *adj.* 最初的

【譯文】

　　最近很顯然地，醫師和營養專家們，對於哪一種飲食才是既安全又健康，以及哪些飲食應該避免，大多抱持不同的看法。當一群科學家們宣稱某種產品是補充活力與使人長壽的秘訣時，就會有另一群科學家認為，這種產品會對健康造成極大的危害。

【註】

nutritional 〔 njuˋtrɪʃən̩ 〕 *adj.* 營養方面的

constitute 〔 ˋkɑnstə͵tjut 〕 *v.* 組成

vigor 〔 ˋvɪgɚ 〕 *n.* 活力　　longevity 〔 lɑnˋdʒɛvətɪ 〕 *n.* 長壽

dismiss 〔 dɪsˋmɪs 〕 *v.* 摒棄；忘却

acutely 〔 ˋækjutlɪ 〕 *adv.* 急劇地

11. **(A)** 依句意，表二個群體之間，介系詞用 between。

12. **(D)** No sooner … than ～ ……就～

13. **(B)** 同上。

【譯文】

　　我的祖母是個性情多變的人。有時候她非常蠻橫，十分難以相處；有時候她又心情很好，十分愉快。但不管情況如何，當我和媽媽牽涉在內時，她的心情好時，絕不會太好；心情不好時，情況一定很糟。坦白說，似乎聽說我們有困難比知道我們成功，還要令她高興。結婚之後，我不常見到她，然而我母親大約每隔三、四週就會去探望她。有時她提到我時，心情十分激動，告訴媽媽說我很不好。其他的親戚都曾遭受這樣的待遇，所以都搬了家，失去了連絡。媽媽會告訴我去探望祖母的情形，而聽她提起這些，就足以讓我心情十分沈重。她是我祖母，而且已不再年輕了，所以我採取比較容易的辦法，那就是不去探望她。

【註】

domineering〔͵dɑmə'nɪrɪŋ〕*adj.* 蠻橫的
difficult〔'dɪfəkəlt〕*adj.* 難以相處的
outburst〔'aʊt͵bɝst〕*n.*（感情的）爆發
weighted〔'wetɪd〕*adj.* 痛苦的

14.（**C**）　*at other times* 在其他時候
　　　　　　(A) 然而；由於　(D) 曾經；一度

15.（**B**）　依句意，選(B)絕不。而(A)總是，(C)也不，(D)儘管如此，皆不合句意。

16.（**B**）　*frankly*〔'fræŋklɪ〕*adv.* 坦白說（＝*frankly speaking*）
　　　　　　(A) 然而，(C) 一…就～，(D) 既然，皆不合。

17.（**A**）　依句意，「我不常見到她」，選(A)。而(B)總是，(C)偶爾，(D)太多，句意不合。

18.（**B**）　*have had* ～ 已經有過～

19.（**C**）　*be weighted down* 心情沈重

20.（**D**）　*take* ～ *way out* 以～方法解決

Ⅱ. 同義字：30 %

21.（**C**）　microcosm〔'maɪkrə͵kɑzm̩〕*n.* 微觀世界；縮圖
　　　　　　(A) microbe〔'maɪkrob〕*n.* 微生物
　　　　　　(C) *miniature representation* 縮版的呈現

22.（**B**）　postulate〔'pɑstʃə͵let〕*v.* 假定
　　　　　　(A) advocate〔'ædvə͵ket〕*v.* 提倡
　　　　　　(B) *claim*〔klem〕*v.* 聲稱

23.（**B**）　omniscient〔ɑm'nɪʃənt〕*adj.* 無所不知的；全知的

24.(**D**)　contention〔kən'tɛnʃən〕*n.* 爭論
　　　　(A) defiance〔dɪ'faɪəns〕*n.* 挑戰；違抗
　　　　(C) announcement〔ə'naʊnsmənt〕*n.* 宣布
　　　　(D) **assertion**〔ə'sɝʃən〕*n.* 斷言

25.(**D**)　devious〔'dɪvɪəs〕*adj.* 不正直的
　　　　(A) cautious〔'kɔʃəs〕*adj.* 小心謹慎的
　　　　(D) **deceitful**〔dɪ'sitfəl〕*adj.* 欺騙的

26.(**B**)　reproof〔rɪ'pruf〕*n.* 譴責
　　　　(D) agitation〔,ædʒə'teʃən〕*n.* 辯論

27.(**A**)　connote〔kə'not〕*v.* 含意；包涵

28.(**D**)　aspiration〔,æspə'reʃən〕*n.* 渴望；希望
　　　　(A) resentment〔rɪ'zɛntmənt〕*n.* 憤恨
　　　　(D) **ambition**〔æm'bɪʃən〕*n.* 雄心；企圖

29.(**D**)　enormity〔ɪ'nɔrmətɪ〕*n.* 殘暴
　　　　(C) grandeur〔'grændʒɚ〕*n.* 富麗堂皇
　　　　(D) **wickedness**〔'wɪkɪdnɪs〕*n.* 邪惡；罪惡
　　　　* betray〔bɪ'tre〕*v.* 背叛
　　　　　comrade in arms 武裝同志；戰友

30.(**B**)　ambiguous〔æm'bɪgjʊəs〕*adj.* 含糊的
　　　　(A) encircle〔ɪn'sɝkḷ〕*v.* 環繞；包圍
　　　　* controversial〔,kɑntrə'vɝʃəl〕*adj.* 引起爭論的
　　　　　issue〔'ɪʃʊ〕*n.* 問題

【譯文】

　　在保護區之外，亞洲虎是一種快要絕種的動物。亞洲虎消失的速度，比除了河馬之外的其他大型哺乳類動物都要快得多。這種威猛的老虎，現今地球上只剩五千至七千五百隻──在本世紀，亞洲虎總數大約已減少了百分之九十五。除非採取強硬的措施，否則就只有當亞洲虎被監禁、在動物園裏徘徊，或在馬戲團表演時，我們才能看得到牠們。從前的野生老虎，將永遠消失，其光輝將只存留在故事書、電影──以及我們的夢裏。

　　「瀕臨絕種動物國際貿易會議」（CITES）管理機構的首要目標就是要防止這樣的悲劇產生。去年九月，該組織已警告買賣老虎與犀牛各部位十分盛行的台灣與中國大陸，必須採取行動禁止這種黑市交易，否則將受到貿易制裁。這兩個國家都宣稱已抑止這種非法的買賣，但環保人士卻已蒐集到相反的證據。

【註】

vanishing〔'vænɪʃɪŋ〕*adj.* 逐漸消滅的　　breed〔brid〕*n.* 種；族
mammal〔'mæml̩〕*n.* 哺乳類動物
rhinoceros〔raɪ'nɑsərəs〕*n.* 犀牛
majestic〔mə'dʒɛstɪk〕*adj.* 有威嚴的　　roughly〔'rʌflɪ〕*adv.* 大約
reverse〔rɪ'vɝs〕*v.* 使倒轉；使顛倒　　prowl〔praʊl〕*v.* 徘徊
circus〔'sɝkəs〕*n.* 馬戲團　　tragedy〔'trædʒədɪ〕*n.* 悲劇
governing body 管理機構　　convention〔kən'vɛnʃən〕*n.* 會議；大會
species〔'spiʃɪz〕*n.pl.* 種；類　　illicit〔ɪ'lɪsɪt〕*adj.* 不法的；非法的
prevalent〔'prɛvələnt〕*adj.* 普遍的　　***shut down*** 停止營運
curb〔kɝb〕*v.* 控制　　commerce〔'kɑmɝs〕*n.* 商業；交易
to the contrary 相反地；相反的

31.（ **C** ）　dramatic〔drə'mætɪk〕*adj.* 戲劇的；重大的
　　　(C) ***drastic***〔'dræstɪk〕*adj.* 強烈的
　　　(D) playful〔'plefəl〕*adj.* 開玩笑的

32.（ **D** ）　captivity〔kæp'tɪvətɪ〕*n.* 囚禁
　　　(A) capitalization〔ˌkæpətl̩ə'zeʃən〕*n.* 資本化
　　　(B) captivation〔ˌkæptə'veʃən〕*n.* 迷惑
　　　(C) immobilization〔ɪmˌmoblaɪ'zeʃən〕*n.* 固定
　　　(D) ***imprisonment***〔ɪm'prɪzn̩mənt〕*n.* 監禁

33.（ **B** ）　endangered〔ɪn'dendʒɚd〕*adj.* 瀕臨絕種的
　　　(B) ***extinct***〔ɪk'stɪŋkt〕*adj.* 絕種的
　　　(C) extraordinary〔ˌɛkstrə'ɔrdn̩ˌɛrɪ〕*adj.* 特別的
　　　(D) distinguished〔dɪs'tɪŋgwɪʃt〕*adj.* 卓越的

34.(**A**)　take steps 採取行動

　　　　(A) ***take measures*** 採取措施

　　　　(C) take advantage of 利用

35.(**A**)　trade sanctions 貿易制裁

　　　　(A) ***trade penalties*** 貿易制裁

　　　　(C) profit〔'prɑfɪt〕*n.* 利潤

　　　　(D) approval〔əˈpruvḷ〕*n.* 批准；認可

Ⅲ. 閱讀測驗：30％

【譯文】

　　現代生活中常會面臨一種麻煩的情況，那就是等電梯上樓時，先到的電梯一定是往下，而要等電梯下樓時，先到的通常是往上。顯然地，這樣的觀察結果是對的，這是自然法則的一部份。

　　爲什麼先到的通常是反方向的電梯呢？這個問題相當簡單：在大部份的建築物裏，當位於較低的樓層時，要上樓的機率較大，因爲往上的目的地要比往下的多。然而在你樓上的電梯可能要比樓下的多，也就是當電梯來的時候，可能就是往下。同樣地，當你在較高的樓層時，你可能是要下樓，但因爲在你樓下的電梯較多，所以當你等到電梯時，它通常是往上。

　　這樣的分析並不適用於建築物的一樓或頂樓。所有的電梯在一樓時，都會上升，在頂樓時，則會往下降。當然，所有搭乘電梯的人都能證實，要搭電梯可能還是得等上一段時間。在早上尖峯時間，大部份的人都會上樓，而在晚上尖峯時間，大部份的人都會下樓。

　　此外，我們對電梯也會產生一種心理作用。由於負面的感受要比正面感受來得強烈，我們對電梯失望的感覺會比滿意的感覺來得更強烈，因而常會忘記來得正是時候的電梯，但卻會把注意力集中在等到反方向電梯的情形。

【答案】

| 36.(**C**) | 37.(**C**) | 38.(**D**) | 39.(**B**) | 40.(**A**) |

【註】

complication〔͵kɑmplə'keʃən〕*n.* 麻煩的情況

elevator〔'ɛlə͵vetɚ〕*n.* 電梯；升降機

be built into ～　成爲～的一部份

relatively〔'rɛlətɪvlɪ〕*adv.* 相當地

attest〔ə'tɛst〕*v.* 證明　　*rush hours* 尖峯時間

at work 起作用　　perception〔pɚ'sɛpʃən〕*n.* 感覺

negative〔'nɛɡətɪv〕*adj.* 負面的；否定的

acutely〔ə'kjutlɪ〕*adv.* 深刻地

keenly〔'kinlɪ〕*adv.* 劇烈地　　*focus on* 集中於

【譯文】

　　熱帶雨林位於北緯三十度與南緯二十度之間，橫越四大洲，涵蓋近五十個國家。熱帶雨林覆蓋全球百分之七的陸地面積，因赤道地區持續性的相對高溫以及充沛的雨水而十分繁盛。

　　我們需要雨林的原因有許多。首先，雨林可作爲河川的集水區，先涵養水源，再逐漸將水釋放至鄰近的土地，預防雨水沖蝕。森林砍伐有時會導致降雨量的損失。由於林地被砍伐，使得巴拿馬的降雨量，和以往的平均雨量相比，每年減少十七英寸。在泰國，由於雨林被破壞，使得許多河川因泥沙淤積而無法航行。

　　其次，我們需要雨林來抑制溫室效應。熱帶雨林吸收大量的陽光，防止陽光被反射回大氣層。然而，由於熱帶森林被焚毀、遭受砍伐，以及工業與汽車排放的二氧化碳，使得太陽的光線無法散射出去，這種現象，就是大家所熟知的「溫室效應」，它會改變全世界的氣候型態，而使全球氣溫上升，也使得極地的冰帽逐漸融化。

　　最後，雨林在醫藥與科學方面也極有貢獻。例如，可供作肌肉緩和劑的箭毒，就來自於熱帶植物。遺傳工程師和其他的醫學研究者已逐漸了解，對於其他化學藥品而言，熱帶雨林是種十分有價值的資源。在哥斯大黎加的叢林裏發現的化學藥物 phyllanthostatin，就是種極有希望的癌症新療法。科學家們也利用熱帶雨林，來提升稻米、花生以及甘蔗的基因品質。

　　我們需要熱帶雨林來幫助我們穩固土壤，並且使氣候均衡。此外，熱帶雨林也是提供科學研究與發展的一項資源。

【答案】

41.（B） 42.（D） 43.（D） 44.（D） 45.（A）

【註】

equator〔ɪˈkwetɚ〕*n.* 赤道　　span〔spæn〕*v.* 延伸

flourish〔ˈflɝɪʃ〕*v.* 茂盛；繁茂

watershed〔ˈwɑtɚˌʃɛd〕*n.*（河川的）集水區；流域

erosion〔ɪˈroʒən〕*n.* 侵蝕

deforestation〔dɪˌfɔrɪsˈteʃən〕*n.* 森林砍伐

stripping〔ˈstrɪpɪŋ〕*n.* 除去；脫去　　deter〔dɪˈtɝ〕*v.* 阻礙

sedimentation〔ˌsɛdəmənˈteʃən〕*n.* 沈澱作用

hydro-electric〔ˌhaɪdro·ɪˈlɛktrɪk〕*adj.* 水力發電的

dam〔dæm〕*n.* 水壩　　navigable〔ˈnævəgəbḷ〕*adj.* 可航行的

inhibit〔ɪnˈhɪbɪt〕*v.* 抑制　　*greenhouse effect* 溫室效應

emission〔ɪˈmɪʃən〕*n.* 放射物　　global〔ˈglobḷ〕*adj.* 全球的

polar〔ˈpolɚ〕*adj.* 極地的　　*ice cap* 冰帽

curare〔kjʊˈrɑrɪ〕*n.* 箭毒　　relaxant〔rɪˈlæksənt〕*n.* 緩和劑

upgrade〔ˈʌpˌgred〕*v.* 使提高品質　　gene〔dʒin〕*n.* 基因

【譯文】

　　想要了解文理學院的本質與在我們社會上的功能，必須了解教育與訓練之間的差別，這是很重要的。訓練主要是爲了服務社會；而教育則主要是針對個人。社會的運作需要醫生、律師與老師，來從事專門的工作，正如同社會需要木匠與水管工人一樣。訓練能立即提供社會特殊的需要，使世界的工作有可能持續下去。

　　但是儘管教育是爲了個人的成長，它也提供了社會一群具有理解力、知覺智慧、以及有影響力的男男女女。他們是聰明的領導者、文化的批判者、自由傳統的保衞者，也是引導我們進步的鼓動者。他們會藉著檢視社會的功能、評估其需要，並且批評其方向來服務社會。他們也許是靠從事其專門的職業、做生意、或從事某種事業來謀生。他們可能富有也可能貧窮；可能位居權貴；也可能只是做著十分卑微的工作。然而，沒有他們，社會可能會瓦解，或是變成人群聚集的地方而已。

【答案】

46. (C)	47. (B)	48. (D)	49. (B)	50. (A)

【註】

liberal arts 文理科　　　primarily〔'praɪm,ɛrəlɪ〕*adv.* 主要地
plumber〔'plʌmɚ〕*n.* 水管工人
leavening〔'lɛvənɪŋ〕*n.* 影響;感化
perception〔pɚ'sɛpʃən〕*n.* 知覺;理解
instigator〔'ɪstə,getɚ〕*n.* 煽動者
appraise〔ə'prez〕*v.* 評估;鑑定
enterprise〔'ɪntɚ,praɪz〕*n.* 事業;企業
prestige〔'prɛstɪdʒ〕*n.* 聲望　　　humble〔'hʌmbḷ〕*adj.* 卑微的
disintegrate〔dɪs'ɪntəgret〕*v.* 瓦解;崩潰
anthill〔'ænt,hɪl〕*n.* 蟻丘;人群聚集的地方

國立政治大學八十三學年度
碩士班研究生入學考試英文試題

I. Vocabulary: 30%

In each of the following 15 sentences, there is a word underlined. Below each sentence are four other words, marked A, B, C, and D. You are to choose the one that best keeps the meaning of the original sentence if it is substituted for the underlined word. Choose the best answer and write its corresponding letter on the answer sheet.

1. These students are greedy for knowledge.
   (A) fervent   (B) inexhaustible
   (C) harsh   (D) affable

2. The bargain hunters swarmed into the store.
   (A) pounced   (B) surged
   (C) fluctuated   (D) thronged

3. Laws have been passed against sex discrimination.
   (A) hindrance   (B) bias
   (C) harassment   (D) scandal

4. The government should do something to defuse the crisis.
   (A) clarify   (B) reduce
   (C) challenge   (D) sustain

5. As a pilot, he is still a fledgling.
   (A) an apple polisher   (B) a greenhorn
   (C) a lame duck   (D) a bootlicker

6. The steak was quite palatable.
   (A) tasty   (B) tender
   (C) tough   (D) tardy

7. The lunch is virtually ready, I only have to finish the vegetables.
   (A) obviously   (B) vividly
   (C) practically   (D) ghastly

8. Something must be done to <u>alleviate</u> the traffic congestion.
   (A) diminish　　　　　　(B) enhance
   (C) solve　　　　　　　 (D) justify

9. It is illegal to <u>dodge</u> taxes.
   (A) scramble　　　　　　(B) camouflage
   (C) evade　　　　　　　 (D) peddle

10. By doing so, they <u>escalated</u> the problems.
    (A) encountered　　　　 (B) resolved
    (C) unraveled　　　　　 (D) intensified

11. Many people are beginning to call for <u>sterner</u> measures.
    (A) stricter　　　　　　(B) gentler
    (C) more adequate　　　 (D) more advanced

12. The teacher <u>reprimanded</u> the class for being noisy.
    (A) suppressed　　　　　(B) admonished
    (C) confronted　　　　　(D) extolled

13. Price increases <u>trigger</u> demands for wage increases.
    (A) necessitate　　　　 (B) require
    (C) facilitate　　　　　(D) spark

14. Malaria is still <u>rampant</u> in some swampy regions.
    (A) unchecked　　　　　 (B) unsteady
    (C) shabby　　　　　　　(D) prudent

15. The dark clouds suggest an <u>impending</u> storm.
    (A) a potential　　　　 (B) a strong
    (C) an oncoming　　　　 (D) a compelling

II. Grammar: 30%

Each of the following 15 questions is followed by 4 possible answers, of which only one is correct. Choose the correct answer and write its corresponding letter on the answer sheet.

1. He will never forget_____the party in Taichung last week.
   (A) to go to　　　　　　(B) gone to
   (C) having gone to　　　(D) that he has gone to

2. Please sing it_____.
   (A) the way it was written
   (B) by the way which it was written
   (C) in the way of which it was written
   (D) as the way how it was written

3. We walked_____.
   (A) since where he had left us
   (B) from where he left us
   (C) where he left us from
   (D) where he had left us since

4. _____, he was in Hualien.
   (A) When was seen last   (B) When last seen
   (C) When he last seen   (D) When had been last seen

5. I tried_____some aspirin, but I couldn't get the cap
   off the bottle.
   (A) and took   (B) taking
   (C) to take   (D) to have taken

6. The three elements required in all photographic typeset-
   ting_____: a master character image, a light source,
   and a photo- or light-sensitive material.
   (A) is following   (B) is the following
   (C) are as follow   (D) are as follows

7. The government of the Republic of China_____5 Yuans:
   the Executive, the Legislative, the Judicial, the
   Control, and the Examination.
   (A) is composed by   (B) constitutes
   (C) comprises   (D) is consisted of

8. People who want_____don't drive drunkenly.
   (A) to arrive safe
   (B) to arrive at safely
   (C) to have arrived safe
   (D) to have arrived at safely

9. They decided to wait for dawn,_____his two-hour turn
   at watch.
   (A) each hiker took
   (B) every hiker took
   (C) every hiker to take
   (D) each hiker taking

10. Mount Everest is_____in the world.
    (A) taller than any mountains
    (B) taller than any another mountains
    (C) taller than any other mountain
    (D) taller than any mountain

11. Which of the following sentences is correct?
    (A) Whenever you don't know the meaning of a new word,
        consult with a dictionary.
    (B) Please contact with him immediately.
    (C) He has graduated from high school for 3 years.
    (D) The meeting is scheduled for 10 p.m. tomorrow.

12. Which of the following sentences is NOT correct?
    (A) Be sure to brush among your teeth.
    (B) The Red Cross distributes food among the needy.
    (C) Careful writers distinguish between ludicrous,
        preposterous, and ridiculous.
    (D) We have to choose between arriving early and
        perhaps having to wait and arriving late and
        perhaps missing the beginning.

13. Which of the following sentences is NOT correct?
    (A) He acts as if he is the only person in the world.
    (B) Would that Mary were able to come with me.
    (C) Do you recommend that he take the GRE again?
    (D) Not for nothing does Paris claim to be the world's
        most beautiful city.

14. Which of the following sentences is NOT correct?
    (A) We should have an answer to our letter soon.
    (B) I would much appreciate if you would remove my
        name from your mailing list.
    (C) They would have remodeled the house, but they ran
        out of money.
    (D) Children should be read to as often as possible.

15. Which of the following sentences is NOT correct?
    (A) The mere fact that he went surprised me.
    (B) The age 7 is an awkward age.
    (C) There is a rumor that the foreign minister is going
        to resign.
    (D) I don't like the color red.

III. Reading Comprehension: 30%

Read the following 3 selections closely and then choose the correct answer for each of the 15 questions that follow.

Part A

Almost overcome with fear, Digit turned unarmed to face the spears and dogs of Munyarukiko and his five companions. He would have to gain time for his family to escape up the mountain slopes. It was his role, his "duty"--and although he may well have known it would mean his death, Digit stood his ground. To Munyarukiko and the other poachers, the silverback male gorilla, erect with his canines bared, was doubtless a terrifying sight, one made more terrifying by the quick demise of one of their dogs, whose frenzy at the smell of the gorilla's fear brought it too close to Digit's powerful arms. But gorillas, strong as they are, are sadly vulnerable to the weapons of their physically weaker human relatives. Digit bought the time for his family group to flee, but he took five mortal spear thrusts in the proccess.

1. According to the selection, Digit is
   (A) an Indian.   (B) a dog.
   (C) a poacher.   (D) an ape.

2. What did Digit do when confronted by Munyarukiko and his companions?
   (A) ran away in fear
   (B) fought and managed to save his family
   (C) died immediately from a well-aimed bullet
   (D) escorted his family members to a safe place

3. Which of the following is closest to the meaning of the word "demise"?
   (A) death   (B) injury
   (C) extinction   (D) casualties

4. This selection is most likely extracted from an article on
   (A) environmental protection
   (B) the preservation of endangered species
   (C) human rights issues
   (D) deforestation

5. What can be inferred about Digit's fate?
   (A) He defeated the poachers.
   (B) He died.
   (C) He was set free.
   (D) His family came to save him.

Part B

    The ancient Hebrews regarded the body of a dead person as something unclean and not to be touched. The early American Indians talked about the evil spirits and shot arrows in the air to drive the spirits away. Many other cultures have rituals to take care of the "bad" dead person, and they all originate in this feeling of anger which still exists in all of us, though we dislike admitting it. The tradition of the tombstone may originate in this wish to keep the bad spirits deep down in the ground, and the pebbles that many mourners put on the grave are left-over symbols of the same wish. Though we call the firing of guns at military funerals a last salute, it is the same symbolic ritual as the Indian used when he shot his spears and arrows into the skies.

    I give these examples to emphasize that man has not basically changed. Death is still a fearful, frightening happening, and fear of death is a universal fear even if we think we have mastered it on many levels. What has changed is our way of coping and dealing with death and dying and our dying patients.

    We would think that our great emancipation, our knowledge of science and of man, has given us better ways and means to prepare ourselves and our families for this inevitable happening. Instead the days are gone when a man was allowed to die in peace and dignity in his own home. The more advancements we make in science, the more we seem to fear and deny the reality of death. How is this possible?

We use euphemisms; we make the dead look as if they were asleep; we ship the children off to protect them from the anxiety and turmoil around the house if the patient is fortunate enough to die at home; we have long and controversial discussions about whether patients should be told the truth--a question that rarely arises when the dying person is tended by the family physician who has known him from delivery to death.

I think there are many reasons for this flight away from facing death calmly. One of the most important facts is that dying nowadays is more gruesome in many ways, namely, more lonely, mechanical, and dehumanized, at times it is even difficult to determine technically when the time of death has occurred.

6. Pebbles are put on the grave to
(A) keep the bad spirits deep down in the ground.
(B) make special marks on the tomb.
(C) drive the spirits away.
(D) commemorate the dead.

7. According to the writer, which of the following is correct?
(A) The firing of guns at military funerals is a sign of last salute to the dead.
(B) The firing of guns at military funerals is to drive the spirits away.
(C) The early American Indians regarded the body of a dead person as something unclean and not to be touched.
(D) The ancient Hebrews shot arrows in the air to drive the spirits away.

8. According to the writer, which of the following is NOT correct?
(A) The advancement we made in medical science has given us better means to treat the dying person.
(B) Funeral rituals originated from man's fear of death.
(C) Family physicians used to have open discussion with the dying patients about their illness.
(D) Our advancement in science has not decreased the degree of fear we have towards death.

9. We can infer that modern people face death in one of the
   following ways.
   (A) Children are allowed to visit their dying relatives
       in the hospitals.
   (B) We talk about death in front of the dying person.
   (C) Most dying people are put in the hospitals.
   (D) A critically ill patient is informed of the truth
       of his condition.

10. The writer's main purpose is to
    (A) describe different funeral rituals.
    (B) criticize the modern way of treating the dying
        person.
    (C) praise the ancient funeral rituals.
    (D) proclaim that man's fear of death originated from
        early cultures.

Part C

　　Psychodynamic theorists emphasize that when threat
becomes especially serious it may lead to intense and widespread inhibitions. In the psychodynamic view, such defensive inhibition is desperate and primitive. It is a massive,
generalized inhibitory reaction rather than a discriminative
response to the specific danger. This denial defense is
called forth when the person can neither escape nor attack
the threat. If the panic is sufficient, the only possible
alternative may be to deny it. Outright denial may be possible for the young child because he is not yet upset by
violating the demands of reality testing. When the child
becomes cognitively too mature to deny objective facts in
the interests of defense, denial becomes a less plausible
alternative and he may resort to repression.

　　Repression was one of the initial concepts in Freud's
theory and became one of its cornerstones. Material in the
unconscious that is relatively inaccessible to conscious
awareness is said to be in a state of repression. The ego
may become aware that the expression of a particular in-
stinctual demand would be dangerous, and the demand must
therefore be suppressed, removed, made powerless.

Freud believed that the mechanisms of denial and repression were the most fundamental or primitive defenses and
played a part in other defenses. Indeed he thought that
other defenses started with a massive inhibition of an impulse, which was followed by various elaborations. In pro-
jection the person's own unacceptable impulses are inhibited
and the source of the anxiety is attributed to another person. Replacement in consciousness of an anxiety-producing
impulse by its opposite is another defense; it is termed
reaction formation. Intellectualization is the third kind of
defense mechanism. It is the tendency to transform emotional
conflicts into abstract, quasi-intellectual terms.

11. What does *inhibitions* mean in this selection?
    (A) aggressions
    (B) restraints
    (C) pretensions
    (D) tensions

12. Which of the following statements about repression is
    not supported by the selection?
    (A) Repression is a defense mechanism of the ego.
    (B) It is a type of denial: the rejection from con-
        sciousness.
    (C) It is a discriminative reaction to the specific
        danger.
    (D) It is the suppression of a dangerous instinctual
        demand.

13. What is the source of repression?
    (A) outright denial of threat
    (B) cognitive maturity
    (C) serious threat
    (D) emotional impulse

14. Which of the following is not a defense mechanism
    discussed in the selection?
    (A) sublimation
    (B) intellectualization
    (C) reaction formation
    (D) projection

15. Based on the selection, which defense mechanism does the
    following situation illustrate?
    A man who has unconscious, deeply hostile impulses
    toward his wife invents elaborate excuses, such as
    "Pressures at the office", "a hectic schedule" to
    disrupt their relationship without admitting his true
    feelings.
    (A) sublimation
    (B) intellectualization
    (C) reaction formation
    (D) projection

IV. Paragraph Writing: 10%

    What is the one most important quality that you think a
    student must have in order to have a meaningful life in
    college? Write ONE paragraph of no more than 150 words
    arguing why you think this quality is important. You
    will be graded according to the following criteria:
    Content 3%; Organization 2%; Grammar 3%; Diction and
    Spelling 2%.

國立政治大學八十三學年度
碩士班研究生入學考試英文試題詳解

I. 字彙：30％

1. (**A**)　greedy〔′gridɪ〕*adj*. 渴望的
　　　　(A) ***fervent***〔′fɜvənt〕*adj*. 熱切的
　　　　(B) inexhaustible〔,ɪnɪg′zɔstəbl̩〕*adj*. 無窮盡的
　　　　(C) harsh〔hɑrʃ〕*adj*. 嚴厲的　　(D) affable〔′æfəbl̩〕*adj*. 和藹的

2. (**D**)　swarm〔swɔrm〕*v*. 群集
　　　　(A) pounce〔paʊns〕*v*. 猛撲　(B) surge〔sɜdʒ〕*v*. 起伏
　　　　(C) fluctuate〔′flʌktʃʊ,et〕*v*. 波動
　　　　(D) ***throng***〔θrɔg〕*v*. 群集；擠滿
　　　　　　bargain hunter 到處找便宜貨的人

3. (**B**)　discrimination〔dɪ′skrɪmə′neʃən〕*n*. 歧視
　　　　(A) hindrance〔′hɪndrəns〕*n*. 阻礙　(B) ***bias***〔′baɪəs〕*n*. 偏見
　　　　(C) harassment〔hə′ræsmənt〕*n*. 騷擾
　　　　(D) scandal〔′skændl̩〕*n*. 醜聞

4. (**B**)　defuse〔dɪ′fjuz〕*v*. 緩和
　　　　(A) clarify〔′klærəfaɪ〕*v*. 澄清
　　　　(B) ***reduce***〔rɪ′djus〕*v*. 降低
　　　　(C) challenge〔′tʃælɪndʒ〕*v*. 挑戰
　　　　(D) sustain〔səs′ten〕*v*. 支持
　　　　　　crisis〔′kraɪsɪs〕*n*. 危機

5. (**B**)　fledgling〔′flɛdʒlɪŋ〕*n*. 生手
　　　　(A) apple polisher 馬屁精
　　　　(B) ***greenhorn***〔′grin,hɔrn〕*n*. 新手
　　　　(C) lame duck 起不了作用的人
　　　　(D) bootlicker〔′but,lɪkə〕*n*. 拍馬屁的人

6. (A)　palatable〔'pælətəbḷ〕 *adj.* 美味的
　　　　(A) *tasty*〔'testɪ〕 *adj.* 美味的　(B) tender〔'tɛndɚ〕 *adj.* 溫柔的
　　　　(C) tough〔tʌf〕 *adj.* 困難的　　(D) tardy〔'tɑrdɪ〕 *adj.* 遲鈍的

7. (C)　virtually〔'vɝtʃəlɪ〕 *adv.* 實際上
　　　　(A) obviously〔'ɑbvɪəslɪ〕 *adv.* 明顯地
　　　　(B) vividly〔'vɪvɪdlɪ〕 *adv.* 生動地
　　　　(C) *practically*〔'præktɪkḷɪ〕 *adv.* 實際上
　　　　(D) ghastly〔'gæstlɪ〕 *adj.* 可怕的

8. (A)　alleviate〔ə'livɪ,et〕 *v.* 減輕
　　　　(A) *diminish*〔də'mɪnɪʃ〕 *v.* 減少　(B) enhance〔ɪn'hæns〕 *v.* 加強
　　　　(D) justify〔'dʒʌstə,faɪ〕 *v.* 證明～為正當
　　　　　　traffic congestion 交通阻塞

9. (C)　dodge〔dɑdʒ〕 *v.* 逃避
　　　　(A) scramble〔'skræmbḷ〕 *v.* 攀登
　　　　(B) camouflage〔'kæmə,flɑʒ〕 *v.* 掩飾；偽裝
　　　　(C) *evade*〔ɪ'ved〕 *v.* 躲避　(D) peddle〔'pɛdḷ〕 *v.* 販賣

10. (D)　escalate〔'ɛskə,let〕 *v.* 擴大；增強
　　　　(A) encounter〔ɪn'kaʊntɚ〕 *v.* 遭遇
　　　　(B) resolve〔rɪ'zɑlv〕 *v.* 下決心
　　　　(C) unravel〔ʌn'rævḷ〕 *v.* 解開
　　　　(D) *intensify*〔ɪn'tɛnsə,faɪ〕 *v.* 使強烈

11. (A)　sterner〔'stɝnɚ〕 *adj.* 更嚴格的
　　　　(A) *stricter*〔'strɪktɚ〕 *adj.* 更嚴格的
　　　　(B) gentler〔'dʒɛntlɚ〕 *adj.* 較溫柔的
　　　　(C) adequate〔'ædəkwɪt〕 *adj.* 適當的
　　　　(D) advanced〔əd'vænst〕 *adj.* 進步的
　　　　　call for 要求　　measure〔'mɛʒɚ〕 *n.* 措施

12.(**B**)　reprimand〔,rɛprə'mænd〕*v.* 斥責
　　　　(A) suppress〔sə'prɛs〕*v.* 鎮壓
　　　　(B) ***admonish*** 〔əd'mɑnɪʃ〕*v.* 訓誡
　　　　(C) confront〔kən'frʌnt〕*v.* 遭遇
　　　　(D) extol〔ɪk'stɑl〕*v.* 稱讚

13.(**D**)　trigger〔'trɪgɚ〕*v.* 引起
　　　　(A) necessitate〔nə'sɛsə,tet〕*v.* 使成為必要
　　　　(C) facilitate〔fə'sɪlə,tet〕*v.* 促進　(D) ***spark***〔spɑrk〕*v.* 引起
　　　　wage〔wedʒ〕*n.* 工資

14.(**A**)　rampant〔'ræmpənt〕*adj.* 猖獗的；蔓延的
　　　　(A) ***unchecked*** 〔ʌn'tʃɛkt〕*adj.* 不受抑制的
　　　　(B) unsteady〔ʌn'stɛdɪ〕*adj.* 不穩定的
　　　　(C) shabby〔'ʃæbɪ〕*adj.* 破爛的
　　　　(D) prudent〔'prudn̩t〕*adj.* 謹慎的
　　　　malaria〔mə'lɛrɪə〕*n.* 瘧疾　swampy〔'swɑmpɪ〕*adj.* 沼澤的

15.(**C**)　impending〔ɪm'pɛndɪŋ〕*adj.* 即將發生的
　　　　(A) potential〔pə'tɛnʃəl〕*adj.* 可能的
　　　　(C) ***oncoming*** 〔,ɑn'kʌmɪŋ〕*adj.* 即將到來的
　　　　(D) compelling〔kəm'pɛlɪŋ〕*adj.* 強制性的

II. 文法：30%

1.(**C**)　$\begin{cases} \text{forget +Ving　忘記曾～} \\ \text{forget + to V　忘記去～} \end{cases}$　依句意，表「曾經做過」，故選(C)。

2.(**A**)　the way 前省略了介系詞 in，在命令句中，in 通常都省略。

3.(**B**)　依句意「從他離開我們的地方」，故選(B)。而(A) since 之後必須
　　　　接時間（片語）。

4.(**B**)　原句是由When he was last seen, …簡化而來。

5.（ **C** ）　$\begin{cases} \text{try to V　試圖要～} \\ \text{try Ving　試試看～} \end{cases}$ 依句意，選(C) try to take 。

　　　　　cap〔kæp〕*n.* 蓋子

6.（ **D** ）　主詞 elements 為複數名詞，故動詞亦用複數動詞，依句意選(D)
　　　　　are as follows。
　　　　　as follows 如下

7.（ **C** ）　依句意，選(C) comprise〔kəm'praɪz〕*v.* 包括。而(A)應改為 is
　　　　　composed of「由～所組成」，(B)應改為 is constituted by
　　　　　「由～所組成」，(D) consists of「由～組成」，無被動語態。

8.（ **A** ）　依句意，「想要安全抵達」，故選(A) want to arrive safe
　　　　　（ = *safely* ）。

9.（ **D** ）　兩句間無連接詞，故將第二個動詞改為現在分詞，選(D)。
　　　　　dawn〔dɔn〕*n.* 黎明　hiker〔'haɪkə〕*n.* 徒步旅行者

10.（ **C** ）　使用比較級時，必須把本身除外，故須與 other 連用。

11.（ **D** ）　*be scheduled for* 排定在～
　　　　　(A) *consult with → consult* 查閱
　　　　　(B) *contact with → contact* 　與～聯絡
　　　　　(C) 須改為 He graduated from high school three years ago.

12.（ **A** ）　brush「刷」為及物動詞，後面直接接受詞，故(A)須改為 Be sure
　　　　　to brush your teeth 。

13.（ **A** ）　表與現在事實相反的假設，be 動詞一律用 were，故(A)須改為：
　　　　　He acts as if he *were* the only person in thc world.

14.（ **B** ）　(B) 應改為：I would much appreciate it if you would have
　　　　　remove my name from the mailing list.

15.（ **B** ）　(B) 應改為 Age 7 is the awkward age. 不須加定冠詞 the 。
　　　　　awkward〔'ɔkwəd〕*adj.* 笨拙的

Ⅲ. 閱讀測驗：30％

Part A

【譯文】

　　弟吉特害怕得不得了，他轉身手無寸鐵地面對Munyarukiko以及他五個同伴的長矛和狗。他必須爭取時間，好讓他的家人逃到山坡上。這是他的任務，他的「責任」——雖然弟吉特很可能知道這將意味著他的死期，他仍死守崗位。對Munyarukiko和其他的侵入者來說，這隻露齒站著的銀背雄猩猩，無疑是個令人畏懼的景象。尤其是當其中一隻狗嗅到大猩猩的恐懼後，狂吠不已，因而太靠近弟吉特有力的雙臂，而很快地死亡，這使得景象更可怕。但，這隻大猩猩雖然強壯，卻可悲地受到那些體格比他弱小的人類，拿著武器攻擊著。弟吉特爭取時間讓家人逃跑，但在這過程中，他卻受到了五次致命的長矛攻擊。

【答案】

　　1.（D）　　2.（B）　　3.（A）　　4.（B）　　5.（B）

【註】

spear〔spɪr〕*n.* 矛　　companion〔kəmˈpænjən〕*n.* 同伴

slope〔slop〕*n.* 斜坡　　***stand one's ground*** 堅守崗位

gorilla〔gəˈrɪlə〕*n.* 大猩猩　　canine〔ˈkenaɪn〕*n.* 犬齒

demise〔dɪˈmaɪz〕*n.* 死亡　　frenzy〔ˈfrɛnzɪ〕*n.* 狂亂

vulnerable〔ˈvʌlnərəbḷ〕*adj.* 易受攻擊的

buy〔baɪ〕*v.* (以犧牲)換得

flee〔fli〕*v.* 逃跑　　mortal〔ˈmɔrtḷ〕*adj.* 致命的

thrust〔θrʌst〕*n.* 刺

Part B

【譯文】

　　古希伯來人認為人的屍體是種不潔的東西，不可以碰觸。早期美國印地安人談論著邪惡的靈魂，並對空射箭以驅逐惡靈。在很多其他的文化中，有儀式祭典來安撫「惡劣的」死人，這些都起源於一種憤怒的感覺，雖然我們不願承認，但它仍然存在我們的心中。墓碑的傳統可能是起源於希望惡靈永遠深深埋在地下，許多送葬者把小圓石放在墳墓上，也是象徵著同樣的希望。雖然我們把軍中葬禮的鳴槍稱為最後的致敬，但這和印地安人把長矛和箭射入天空的儀式具有相同的象徵性意義。

　　我舉出這些例子，是為了強調人類基本上並沒有改變。死亡仍是可怕而且令人恐懼的事。即使我們認為自己能以不同的層次，來克制對死亡的恐懼，但死亡的恐懼仍是世人皆有。有所改變的只是我們處理死亡、垂死及我們垂死的病人的方法。

　　我們會認為我們極大的解放、以及對科學和對人類的知識，會讓我們有更好的方法，來針對這不可避免的事，為自己和家人做好準備。然而，一個人能安詳、有尊嚴地死在自己家中的日子已經過去了。我們在科學方面愈進步，似乎就愈恐懼並否定死亡的事實。這怎麼可能呢？

　　我們使用較委婉的說法；我們讓死者看起來像是在睡覺；假如病人很幸運地死在家裏，我們會把小孩趕走，以遠離家中的焦慮和混亂。長久以來，我們有著具爭議性的討論，探討病人是否應被告知真相——而當垂死的病人由自出生就認識他的家庭醫師照顧時，這個問題卻很少被提起。

　　我認為無法平靜地面對死亡的原因有很多。其中一項重要的事實是，垂死的情況在許多方面都變得更恐怖，那就是說，更孤獨、更機械化，而且毫無人性；有時就技術上而言，要斷定死亡的時間變得更困難了。

【答案】

6. (A)　　7. (B)　　8. (C)　　9. (C)　　10. (B)

【註】

Hebrew〔'hibru〕 *n*. 希伯來人　　ritual〔'rɪtʃʊəl〕 *n*. 儀式；祭典

originate〔ə'rɪdʒə,net〕 *v*. 起源於　　tombstone〔'tum,ston〕 *n*. 墓碑

pebble〔'pɛbḷ〕 *n*. 小圓石　　mourner〔'mɔrnɚ〕 *n*. 送葬者

funeral〔'fjunərəl〕 *n*. 葬禮　　salute〔sə'lut〕 *v*. 致敬

master〔'mæstɚ〕 *v*. 克制　　emancipation〔ɪ,mænsə'peʃən〕 *n*. 解放

inevitable〔ɪn'ɛvətəbḷ〕 *adj*. 不可避免的　　dignity〔'dɪgnətɪ〕 *n*. 尊嚴

euphemism〔'jufə,mɪzəm〕 *n*. 委婉的說法　　***ship off*** 送走

controversial〔,kɑntrə'vɝʃəl〕 *adj*. 引起爭論的

gruesome〔'grusəm〕 *adj*. 恐怖的　mechanical〔mə'kænɪkḷ〕 *adj*. 機械化的

dehumanized〔di'hjumə,naɪzd〕 *adj*. 無人性的

Part C
【譯文】

　　精神動力理論家強調，當威脅變得特別嚴重時，會導致強烈且廣泛的壓抑。以精神動力的觀點來說，這種防禦性的抑制是不顧一切且十分原始的。這是種強大而廣泛的抑制反應，而不是對特定的危險做出不同的反應。當一個人無法逃離或反擊威脅時，這種否認的防衛方式就會出現。假如處於極度的恐慌，唯一的選擇便是否認它。對於兒童而言，因為他們不會因違反現實考驗的要求而心煩，所以可能可以完全否認。當兒童在認知方面變得很成熟，而不能否定客觀事實來防衛自己時，否認就成了比較行不通的辦法，便可能會訴諸於壓抑。

　　壓抑是佛洛依德理論中最初的概念，並成為他理論的基礎之一。存在於潛意識中而比較無法變成有意識的資訊，就是種處於壓抑的狀態。自我可能會察覺，若將特殊的本能需求抒發出來會很危險，因此這種需要必須壓抑、轉移，並使它威力減弱。

　　佛洛依德認為，否認和壓抑的機制是最基本且原始的防衛，並且在其他的防衛中，扮演某種角色。事實上，他認為其他的防衛開始是種一時衝動的強大壓抑，接著便需要花費各種心思。在爆發時，個人會壓抑住本身不被人接受的衝動，而認為焦慮來自於另一人。對於會產生焦慮的衝動，以相反的方式的有意識替代，是另一種防衛；這被稱為反應形態。理性思考是第三種防衛機制。它是種把情感上的衝突，轉換成抽象的、似理性說法的傾向。

【答案】

11. (B)　　12. (C)　　13. (C)　　14. (A)　　15. (B)

【註】

psychodynamic〔,saɪkodaɪ'næmɪk〕*adj.* 精神動力的

theorist〔'θɪə,rɪst〕*n.* 理論家　　inhibition〔,ɪnhɪ'bɪʃən〕*n.* 壓抑

defensive〔dɪ'fɛnsɪv〕*adj.* 防禦的

desperate〔'dɛspərɪt〕*adj.* 不顧一切的

primitive〔'prɪmətɪv〕*adj.* 最早的；原始的

massive〔'mæsɪv〕*adj.* 強大的

discriminative〔dɪ'skrɪmə,netɪv, -,nətɪv〕*adj.* 有差別的

denial〔dɪ'naɪəl〕*n.* 否認　　panic〔'pænɪk〕*n.* 恐慌

outright〔'aʊt'raɪt〕*adj.* 完全的；徹底的

cognitively〔'kɑgnətɪvlɪ〕*adv.* 在理解力方面

plausible〔'plɔzəbl̩〕*adj.* 好像有道理的

resort to 訴諸於　　repression〔rɪ'prɛʃən〕*n.* 壓抑

cornerstone〔'kɔrnə,ston〕*n.* 基礎

inaccessible〔,ɪnək'sɛsəbl̩〕*adj.* 難懂的

instinctual〔ɪn'stɪŋktʃʊəl〕*adj.* 本能的；直覺的

mechanism〔'mɛkə,nɪzəm〕*n.* 機制

impulse〔'ɪmpʌls〕*n.* 衝動

elaboration〔ɪ,læbə'reʃən〕*n.* 苦心經營

projection〔prə'dʒɛkʃən〕*n.* 投射；發射

formation〔fɔr'meʃən〕*n.* 構造；形態

intellectualization〔,ɪntl̩,ɛktʃʊəl,aɪ'zæʃən〕*n.* 理智

quasi-〔字首〕表「類似；準」

Ⅳ. 作文：10%

　　The most important quality a student must have in order to have a meaningful life in college is the ability to recognize his priorities in life. Compared to school life, college life offers more independence and therefore more opportunities for various extracurricular activities. As a result, many college students take up hobbies and interests. Some of these interests, if left unchecked, may turn into bad habits; for instance, love for video games may turn into an addiction to gambling. A student's priority in life is to study. He may indulge in other activities, but he should not pay more attention to them than to his studies; otherwise, it may prove disastrous. On the other hand, a student who knows his priorities well would never let anything distract him from his goals. He will eventually succeed in life.

國立清華大學八十三學年度
碩士班研究生入學考試英文試題

I. Vocabulary: 20%

Part One: Select the word that best completes the meaning of the sentence as a whole. 10%

1. The police informed underaged smokers about the law and _____their cigarettes.
   (A) confiscated　　　　　(B) castigated
   (C) conjugated　　　　　(D) conjured

2. I'm_____of the team's chances of winning.
   (A) susceptible　　　　　(B) skeptical
   (C) surpass　　　　　　(D) suspect

3. Those who act on _____ tend to make mistakes and feel regretful afterwards.
   (A) institution　　　　　(B) intelligence
   (C) impatience　　　　　(D) impulse

4. Machines have changed society_____. It's doubtful that we will voluntarily return to the days when we used human muscles to do most of our work.
   (A) irrevocably　　　　　(B) flexibly
   (C) tentatively　　　　　(D) influentially

5. One look at today's best-selling books and popular magazines will demonstrate America's_____with physical appearance.
   (A) precept　　　　　　(B) preconception
   (C) precedence　　　　　(D) preoccupation

6. Tight-fitting jeans that_____a thin, youthful appearance are the fashion of the day.
   (A) appreciate　　　　　(B) accentuate
   (C) alleviate　　　　　　(D) associate

7. In order to predict whether an idea will become part of our daily lives, it's important to know if the idea is technologically and economically_____.
   (A) formidable　　　　　(B) forcible
   (C) feasible　　　　　　(D) flammable

8. Science fiction movies surve an important function. They help people to think and_____about life in the future.
   (A) speculate   (B) stimulate
   (C) circulate   (D) concentrate

9. Oil and natural gas exist on this planet in a limited supply. Therefore it's essential for us to develop _____to these nonrenewable energy sources.
   (A) architectures   (B) artifacts
   (C) alternatives   (D) additives

10. Hospitals usually do not_____a patient until the doctors feel the person is ready to go home.
    (A) dissociate   (B) disapprove
    (C) dissolve   (D) discharge

Part Two: Select the word or phrase <u>nearest in meaning</u> to the key word. 10%

11. benevolent
    (A) industrious   (B) malicious
    (C) ridiculous   (D) virtuous

12. provoke
    (A) arouse   (B) deprive
    (C) resolve   (D) appeal

13. complacent
    (A) futile   (B) angry
    (C) satisfied   (D) peculiar

14. friction
    (A) intrusion   (B) disagreement
    (C) transition   (D) operation

15. catastrophe
    (A) accident   (B) disaster
    (C) fragment   (D) comedy

16. illustrious
    (A) momentous   (B) implausible
    (C) famous   (D) diligent

17. dismiss
    (A) despise   (B) reject
    (C) confront   (D) perplex

18. bizarre
    (A) mischieveous   (B) strenuous
    (C) carnival   (D) weird

19. antagonistic
    (A) hostile   (B) friendly
    (C) hilarious   (D) egocentric

20. convert
    (A) interact with   (B) change into
    (C) focus on   (D) impose upon

II. Grammar and written expression: 20%

Part One: Choose the one expression that <u>best</u> completes
          the sentence. 10%

21. _____we can devise an IQ test that can be administered
    to an embryo in utero, there is no way of deciding what
    are the limits of a person's intelligence potential.
    (A) Besides   (B) Owing to
    (C) Unless   (D) On the contrary

22. For digital operation,_____simply switched on and off
    to generate pulses, linearity is not essential.
    (A) where the light is   (B) the light is
    (C) the light where is   (D) where is the light

23. The result is a forecast of_____warming of the globe
    than has previously been thought likely, setting in by
    the end of the present decade.
    (A) so rapid and pronounced
    (B) much more rapid and pronounced
    (C) very rapid and pronounced
    (D) much rapid and pronounced

24. John is worrying that his great social popularity_____
    a discouraging effect on the girl he wants to marry.
    (A) should be
    (B) had been
    (C) could has
    (D) might have

25. _____Harry Boot made his greatest contribution and by which he will be long remembered.
    (A) This is to the cavity magnetron
    (B) To the cavity magnetron it is
    (C) It is to the cavity magnetron that
    (D) It is the cavity magnetron that

26. The natural resources of Kentucky include rich soils and mineral deposits,_____, and plentiful plant and animal life.
    (A) forests thick   (B) thick forests
    (C) thickly forested   (D) forested thickly

27. Documentary evidence of the economic damage_____has only recently become available.
    (A) caused by these animals
    (B) these animals cause it
    (C) was caused by these animals
    (D) causing these animals

28. Tungsten, a gray metal with the_____, is used to form the wires in electric light bulbs.
    (A) point melts is the highest of any metal
    (B) melting point is the highest of any metal
    (C) highest melting point of any metal
    (D) melting highest point of any metals

29. At root, however, they are very similar, their different behaviors_____their differences in wavelength.
    (A) are traceable to   (B) being traceable to
    (C) which trace to   (D) have traced to

30. _____an obstacle to the flow, forcing the fluid to change direction and accelerate around the object.
    (A) As an immersed object necessarily acts
    (B) An immersed necessary object acts
    (C) As an object immersed necessarily
    (D) An immersed object necessarily acts as

Part Two: Identify the one word or phrase that should be corrected or rewritten. 10%

31. The earth behaves pretty much like a particle if we are
                         ‾‾‾‾‾‾‾‾‾‾‾   ‾‾
                              A   B

    interested in it's orbital motion around the sun.
                    ‾‾‾‾   ‾‾‾‾‾‾
                      C   D

32. We are <u>then</u> presented with three of <u>the</u> remaining
　　　　　A　　　　　　　　　　　　　　　　B

　　<u>quantities</u> and asked to find <u>fourth</u>.
　　　　C　　　　　　　　　　　　　D

33. The <u>boldface</u> symbol always <u>refers to</u> both <u>properties</u> of
　　　　　A　　　　　　　　　B　　　　　　　C

　　the vector, magnitude <u>and</u> direction.
　　　　　　　　　　　　　D

34. The <u>useful</u> of unit <u>vectors</u> is that we can express <u>other</u>
　　　　A　　　　　　B　　　　　　　　　　　　　　　　C

　　vectors in <u>terms</u> of them.
　　　　　　　D

35. These two <u>algebraic</u> equations, <u>taking together</u>, are
　　　　　　　A　　　　　　　　　　B

　　<u>equivalent</u> to <u>the</u> single equation 9.
　　　C　　　　D

36. Actually, <u>we all</u> experience <u>uniform</u> circular motion
　　　　　　　A　　　　　　　　B

　　<u>because</u> the <u>rotation</u> of the earth.
　　　C　　　　　D

37. The <u>minus</u> sign tells us that this acceleration <u>component</u>
　　　　A　　　　　　　　　　　　　　　　　　　B

　　points <u>vertical</u> downward <u>in</u> Fig. 18.
　　　　　C　　　　　　　D

38. <u>Everyday</u> experience tells us that <u>a given</u> force <u>will</u>
　　　A　　　　　　　　　　　　　　B

　　<u>produce</u> different accelerations in different <u>body</u>.
　　　C　　　　　　　　　　　　　　　　　　D

39. <u>Suppose</u> that gravity <u>were</u> suddenly turned off, <u>so that</u>
　　　A　　　　　　　B　　　　　　　　　　　C

　　the earth becomes a free object rather than <u>is</u> confined
　　　　　　　　　　　　　　　　　　　　　　D

　　to orbit the sun.

40. <u>As</u> could be predicted, <u>addict</u> tended to be more permis-
      A   B

    sive <u>on</u> the question of legalization of drugs such as
          C

    marijuana, cocaine, and heroin <u>than</u> the Gallup sample.
                               D

III. Reading comprehension: 20%

Each passage in this section is followed by questions
based on its content. Choose the <u>best</u> answer to each
question on the basis of what is stated or implied in
that passage.

Passage One

When I say that Machiavelli is not scientific, I do not
mean merely that many of his conclusions are questionable or
even superficial. A writer who is not a scientist may sometimes be right where a scientist is mistaken. For example,
I should say that Montesquieu comes much closer than Machiavelli to being a political scientist, though he too reaches
many questionable and superficial conclusions. Montesquieu
expresses opinions about a much wider variety of subjects,
and is therefore probably much more often wrong than is
Machiavelli. But he does at least attempt to make a systematic study of different types of government; he takes many
examples; he aims at an exhaustive classification; he is
concerned about the methods he uses. We may say that his
study is not as systematic as he thought it was, that his
examples are not well chosen, that his classification is
not exhaustive, and that his ideas about his methods are
confused; we may say all this, and yet concede that he aims
at making a scientific study of society, and that he has some
notion of what distinguishes a scientific from an unscien-
tific study. But we cannot say this of Machiavelli. He is
not, as Montesquieu is, a very imperfect social and political
scientist; he is not a political scientist at all, but a man
of genius with considerable practical experience who writes
about politics.

41. The author implies that a scientist may be characterized
    as
    (A) being full of imagination.
    (B) being open-minded in all matters.
    (C) having wide-ranging interests.
    (D) having a conscious concern for method.

42. We have learned that valuable opinions about politics
    and society are
    (A) never acquired without much genius.
    (B) only obtained by rigorous empirical methods.
    (C) attainable by scientists as well as nonscientists.
    (D) seldom appreciated by politicians in office.

43. According to the passage, Montesquieu's political
    opinions are wrong much more often than those of
    Machiavelli because Machiavelli
    (A) restricts his remarks to a narrower range of topics.
    (B) is lucky enough to be a genius.
    (C) uses scientific and systematic methods in his
        studies.
    (D) has been a politician for many years.

44. According to the passage, scientific methodology refers
    to a quality that we may
    (A) gain from considerable practical experience.
    (B) learn only through formal instruction.
    (C) interpret in a more or less rigorous sense.
    (D) attribute only to certain sensible people.

45. We can infer from the last sentence of the passage that
    (A) scientific efforts cannot affect the work of genius.
    (B) some excellent political writing is unscientific.
    (C) Machiavelli is a less brilliant political scientist.
    (D) diligence may substitute for scientific methodology.

Passage Two

　　There is something romantic and mysterious about the
great deserts. So many writers have glorified them--Burton,
T.E. Lawrence and Saint-Exupery. Rudolph Valentino's
throbbing movie, *The Sheik*, wafted countless millions of
smitten women into dreams of frenzied thrashings in the
dunes. Exploits of fictitious foreign legionaries and the
galloping armies of Araby gave men visions that steamed
hotter than the sands themselves.

Those visions, alas, are for the books. What experts have learned and what they are now telling the world at large is that desert-like conditions, which reign over roughly one-third of the globe's land masses, have become one of civilization's major environmental menaces. In Nairobi last week, 1,500 delegates from 110 nations gathered under the auspices of the United Nations to compare notes. Their findings: deserts everywhere are spreading relentlessly and with alarming speed--often emerging in places separate from existing wasteland. The phenomenon is awkwardly but accurately known as desertification. And thanks largely to Man's own folly, desertification now threatens the fragile existence of about 630 million people who dwell in these regions.

The U.S. Agency for International Development reported that in the past half-century, an estimated 650,000 sq.km (250,000 sq. miles) of farming and grazing lands have been swallowed up by the Sahara along the great desert's southern fringe. Egyptian-born geologist Farouk El-Baz has found that a great sea of sand is moving towards the fertile Nile delta at about 13 km (8 miles) a year.

46. Which of the following four statements is the most accurate in defining "desertification"?
(A) Deserts are romantic and mysterious.
(B) One-third of the globe's land masses are deserts.
(C) Deserts everywhere are spreading relentlessly and with alarming speed.
(D) Regions receiving no more than 100 mm (4 inches) of rain are deserts.

47. According to this article, what should be mainly responsible for the global desertification phenomenon?
(A) the weather
(B) man's own folly
(C) the United Nations
(D) armies of Araby

Passage Three

To claim that malaria is on the rampage in Sri Lanka is
something of an understatement. The official figure stands
at a staggering 304,000, about 2% of the national population.
The carrier, the female Anopheles mosquito has resurged in
freshwater swamps and river areas. But another major factor
in the return of malaria has been human greed and the desire
for fast money. On the western coast of Sri Lanka, there are
rich pickings for gem hunters prepared to dig shallow holes
in the river mud of the surrounding area. Since Sri Lankan
rubies and other gems fetch such high prices among foreign
tourists, many dealers collect at the height of the mining
season. They dig, work and then desert thousands of holes.
It is these water-filled pits which have provided the most
ideal breeding grounds for the mosquito carriers of malaria.
The government's Anti-Malarial Campaign is directing its
full force against these avaricious miners who have no
regard for the ruined land they leave in their wake.

48. What is the most suitable title for the above passage?
    (A) Malaria Plagues Sri Lanka
    (B) Where Greed Breeds Death
    (C) Malaria in Sri Lanka
    (D) Sri Lanka's Anti-Malarial Campaign

49. In Sri Lanka, mosquito carriers of malaria tend to be
    found
    (A) on the western coast of the country
    (B) wherever foreign tourists stay
    (C) in deserted water-filled holes
    (D) in inland areas

50. This article blames the rampage of malaria in Sri
    Lanka on
    (A) mosquitoes.
    (B) miners.
    (C) the government.
    (D) foreign tourists.

IV. Translation: 20%

Translate the following two passages into Chinese.

51. China challenges foreign critics because it does not easily fit into a mold. In recent decades, the other communist countries simultaneously repressed and impoverished their citizens. But China is presiding over rapidly rising living standards for the society as a whole, even as it suppresses the minority of intellectuals and workers who take a stand for democracy.

52. There is nothing to prepare you for the experience of growing old. Living is a process, an irreversible progression toward old age and eventual death....The cellular clock differs for each one of us, and is profoundly affected by our own life experiences, our heredity, and perhaps most important, by the concepts of aging encountered in society and in oneself.

V. Composition: 20%

Suppose that you divide all your friends into three basic categories. Write an essay which explains your classification. A humorous approach is entirely acceptable but not required. The length of your essay will be about 250 words.

國立清華大學八十三學年度
碩士班研究生入學考試英文試題詳解

I. 字彙：20%

Part One :

1. (A) (A) ***confiscate*** 〔'kɑnfɪs,ket〕 *v.* 沒收
   (B) castigate 〔'kæstə,get〕 *v.* 嚴懲
   (C) conjugate 〔'kɑndʒə,get〕 *v.* (動詞) 變化
   (D) conjure 〔'kʌndʒɚ〕 *v.* 施魔法

2. (B) (A) susceptible 〔sə'sɛptəbḷ〕 *adj.* 易感動的
   (B) ***skeptical*** 〔'skɛptɪkḷ〕 *adj.* 多疑的
   (C) surpass 〔sɚ'pæs , -'pɑs〕 *v.* 超越
   (D) suspect 〔sə'spɛkt〕 *v.* 懷疑

3. (D) (A) institution 〔,ɪnstə'tjuʃən〕 *n.* 學會
   (B) intelligence 〔ɪn'tɛlədʒəns〕 *n.* 智能
   (C) impatience 〔ɪm'peʃəns〕 *n.* 沒耐心
   (D) ***impulse*** 〔'ɪmpʌls〕 *n.* 衝動

4. (A) (A) ***irrevocably*** 〔ɪ'rɛvəkəblɪ〕 *adv.* 不能挽回地
   (B) flexibly 〔'flɛksəblɪ 〕 *adv.* 有彈性地
   (C) tentatively 〔'tɛntətɪvlɪ〕 *adv.* 暫時地
   (D) influentially 〔 ɪnflʊ'ɛnʃəlɪ 〕 *adv.* 有影響力地

5. (D) (A) precept 〔'prisɛpt〕 *n.* 教訓
   (B) preconception 〔,prikən'sɛpʃən〕 *n.* 偏見
   (C) precedence (prɪ'sidn̩s) *n.* 優勢
   (D) ***preoccupation*** (pri,ɑkjə'peʃən) *n.* 全神貫注
   demonstrate 〔'dɛməns,tret〕 *v.* 證明

6. (**B**) (A) appreciate 〔ə'priʃɪ,et〕 v. 欣賞
　　　　　(B) ***accentuate*** 〔æk'sɛntʃʊ,et, ək-〕 v. 加重；強調
　　　　　(C) alleviate 〔ə'livɪ,et〕 v. 減輕（痛苦）
　　　　　(D) associate 〔ə'soʃɪ,et〕 v. 聯想

7. (**C**) (A) formidable 〔'fɔrmɪdəbl̩〕 *adj.* 艱鉅的
　　　　　(B) forcible 〔'forsəbl̩, 'fɔrs-〕 *adj.* 有力的
　　　　　(C) ***feasible*** 〔'fizəbl̩〕 *adj.* 可實行的
　　　　　(D) flammable 〔'flæməbl̩〕 *adj.* 易燃的

8. (**A**) (A) ***speculate*** 〔'spɛkjə,let〕 v. 沈思
　　　　　(B) stimulate 〔'stɪmjə,let〕 v. 刺激
　　　　　(C) circulate 〔'sɝkjə,let〕 v. 循環
　　　　　(D) concentrate 〔'kɑnsn̩,tret〕 v. 專心

9. (**C**) (A) architecture 〔,ɑrkɪ'tɛktʃɚ〕 n. 建築
　　　　　(B) artifact 〔'ɑrtɪfækt〕 n. 人工製品
　　　　　(C) ***alternative*** 〔ɔl'tɝnətɪv〕 n. 選擇
　　　　　(D) additive 〔'ædətɪv〕 n. 添加物

10. (**D**) (A) dissociate 〔dɪ'soʃɪ,et〕 v. 分離
　　　　　(B) disapprove 〔,dɪsə'pruv〕 v. 不贊成
　　　　　(C) dissolve 〔dɪ'zɑlv〕 v. 溶解
　　　　　(D) ***discharge*** 〔dɪs'tʃɑrdʒ〕 v. 送走

Part two : 10％

11. (**D**) benevolent 〔bə'nɛvələnt〕 *adj.* 仁慈的
　　　　　(A) industrious 〔ɪn'dʌstrɪəs〕 *adj.* 勤勉的
　　　　　(B) malicious 〔mə'lɪʃəs〕 *adj.* 惡意的
　　　　　(C) ridiculous 〔rɪ'dɪkjələs〕 *adj.* 荒謬的
　　　　　(D) ***virtuous*** 〔'vɝtʃʊəs〕 *adj.* 善良的

12.(**A**) provoke〔prə'vok〕*v.* 引起
    (A) ***arouse***〔ə'rauz〕*v.* 引起 (B) deprive〔dɪ'praɪv〕*v.* 剝奪
    (C) resolve〔rɪ'zɑlv〕*v.* 決定 (D) appeal〔ə'pil〕*v.* 吸引

13.(**C**) complacent〔kəm'plesṇt〕*adj.* 自滿的
    (A) futile〔'fjutḷ〕*adj.* 徒勞的
    (B) angry〔'æŋgrɪ〕*adj.* 生氣的
    (C) ***satisfied***〔'sætɪs,faɪd〕*adj.* 滿意的
    (D) peculiar〔pɪ'kjuljɚ〕*adj.* 奇特的

14.(**B**) friction〔'frɪkʃən〕*n.* 衝突；摩擦
    (A) intrusion〔ɪn'truʒən〕*n.* 闖入
    (B) ***disagreement***〔,dɪsə'grimənt〕*n.* 不一致；不同意
    (C) transition〔,træn'zɪʃən〕*n.* 轉變
    (D) operation〔,ɑpə'reʃən〕*n.* 運作

15.(**B**) catastrophe〔kə'tæstrəfɪ〕*n.* 大災難
    (A) accident〔'æksədənt〕*n.* 意外
    (B) ***disaster***〔dɪ'zæstɚ〕*n.* 大災難
    (C) fragment〔'frægmənt〕*n.* 碎片
    (D) comedy〔'kɑmədɪ〕*n.* 喜劇

16.(**C**) illustrious〔ɪ'lʌstrɪəs〕*adj.* 著名的
    (A) momentous〔mo'mɛntəs〕*adj.* 重大的
    (B) implausible〔,ɪm'plɔzəbḷ〕*adj.* 難以置信的
    (C) ***famous***〔'feməs〕*adj.* 著名的
    (D) diligent〔'dɪlədʒənt〕*adj.* 勤勉的

17.(**B**) dismiss〔dɪs'mɪs〕*v.* 拒絕
    (A) despise〔dɪs'paɪz〕*v.* 輕視
    (B) ***reject***〔rɪ'dʒɛkt〕*v.* 拒絕
    (C) confront〔kən'frʌnt〕*v.* 面對
    (D) perplex〔pɚ'plɛks〕*v.* 使困惑

18. (**D**) bizarre 〔bɪ'zɑr〕 *adj*. 奇怪的
    (A) mischievous 〔'mɪstʃɪvəs〕 *adj*. 淘氣的
    (B) strenuous 〔'strɛnjuəs〕 *adj*. 費力的
    (C) carnival 〔'kɑrnəvḷ〕 *n*. 嘉年華會
    (D) *weird* 〔wɪrd〕 *adj*. 奇怪的

19. (**A**) antagonistic 〔æn,tægə'nɪstɪk〕 *adj*. 敵對的
    (A) *hostile* 〔'hɑstɪl〕 *adj*. 敵對的
    (B) friendly 〔'frɛndlɪ〕 *adj*. 友善的
    (C) hilarious 〔hə'lɛrɪəs〕 *adj*. 高興的
    (D) egocentric 〔,igo'sɛntrɪk〕 *adj*. 自我中心的

20. (**B**) convert 〔kən'vɝt〕 *v*. 轉變
    (A) interact with 與～相互作用　　(B) *change into* 變成
    (C) focus on 專注於　　　　　　　(D) impose upon 施加於

Ⅱ. 文法：20％

Part One

21. (**C**) 依句意選(C) Unless　除非。
    administer 〔əd'mɪnɪstɚ〕 *v*. 給予；執行
    embryo 〔'ɛmbrɪ,o〕 *n*. 胎兒　　utero 〔'jutəro〕 *n*. 子宮

22. (**A**) 兩逗點間為由關係副詞 where 引導，補述用法的形容詞子句。
    digital 〔'dɪdʒətḷ〕 *adj*. 手指的；數字的
    pulse 〔pʌls〕 *n*. 脈搏
    linearity 〔,lɪnɪ'ærətɪ〕 *n*. 直線性

23. (**B**) 由連接詞 than 可知，本句為比較級，而修飾形容詞比較級的副詞，須用 much，故選(B)。
    the globe 地球

24. (**D**) 依句意選(D) 可能。

25.(**C**) 本句爲強調句型，其公式爲：It is＋強調部分＋that＋其餘
部分，又依句意，「對～有貢獻」須用 make a contribution
to ～，故選(C)。
cavity〔'kævətɪ〕*n.* 洞穴
magnetron〔'mægnə,trɑn〕*n.* 磁控管

26.(**B**) 本句中逗點及對等連接詞 and 連接的皆爲名詞，故選(B)。
mineral〔'mɪnərəl〕*n.* 礦物質　deposit〔dɪ'pɑzɪt〕*n.* 沈澱

27.(**A**) 本句中，主詞和動詞已出現，故空格中應爲修飾先行詞 damage
的形容詞子句，而子句中關係代名詞和 be 動詞可省略，選(A)。
documentary〔,dɑkjə'mɛntərɪ〕*adj.* 文書的
documentary evidence 書面證據

28.(**C**) 兩逗點間爲 Tungsten 的同位語，爲一名詞片語，而(A)、(B)中有
動詞，故不合。又依句意，「最高熔點」爲 highest melting
point，故選(C)。

29.(**B**) 兩動詞間無連接詞，第二個動詞須改爲現在分詞，而前後主詞不
一致，第二個主詞須保留，選(B)。

30.(**D**) 逗點之後並非一獨立完整的句子，故前句不可能爲從屬子句，
(A)、(C)不選。又依句意，「一個沈沒的物體必須扮演～」，故
選(D)。
accelerate〔æk'sɛlə,ret〕*v.* 加速

Part Two：10 %

31.(**C**) *it's* → ***its***
orbital〔'ɔrbɪtl̩〕*adj.* 軌道的

32.(**D**) *fourth* → ***the fourth***　序數前要加定冠詞 the 。

33.(**A**) *boldface* → ***boldfaced***
boldfaced〔'bold'fest〕*adj.* 黑體字的
vector〔'vɛktɚ〕*n.* 向量；方位
magnitude〔'mægnə,tjud〕*n.* 重要

34.(A) *useful → usage*

usage 〔'jusɪdʒ〕 *n.* 用法

in terms of 以…觀點

35.(B) *taking together → taken together* 依句意「被放在一起」，

應為被動語態。

algebraic 〔,ældʒə'bre·ɪk〕 *adj.* 代數的

algebraic equation 代數方程式

equivalent 〔ɪ'kwɪvələnt〕 *adj.* 相等的

36.(C) *because → because of* because 接子句，而 because of 則

接名詞片語。

uniform 〔'junə,fɔrm〕 *adj.* 相同的

rotation 〔ro'teʃən〕 *n.* 旋轉

37.(C) *vertical → vertically* 修飾動詞須用副詞。

minus 〔'maɪnəs〕 *adj.* 負的

vertically 〔'vɜtɪkəlɪ〕 *adv.* 垂直地

38.(D) *body → bodies*

39.(D) 將 is 去掉。… rather than 所連接的前後部份，其文法結構須

一致，前面是 becomes ＋補語，而後面也應是 becomes ＋補語

的形式，而 becomes 可省略。

40.(B) *addict → addicts* 或 *an addict*

addict 〔'ædɪkt〕 *n.* 上癮者

permissive 〔pə'mɪsɪv〕 *adj.* 表示准許的

marijuana 〔,mærə'wɑnə〕 *n.* 大麻

cocaine 〔ko'ken〕 *n.* 古柯鹼

heroin 〔'hɛro·ɪn〕 *n.* 海洛因

Ⅲ. 閱讀測驗：20%

Passage One ：

【譯文】

　　我說馬基維利不合乎科學，並不是僅僅指他的結論令人懷疑，或甚至很膚淺。一個非科學家的作家，有時也會在科學家犯錯的地方，表現得正確無誤。舉例來說，雖然孟德斯鳩也有太多令人懷疑又很膚淺的結論，但我覺得他比馬基維利更像個政治科學家。孟德斯鳩在發表意見時，其主題更廣泛、更富多樣性。因此，他可能比馬基維利更常犯錯。但他至少會嘗試對各種政府形態做有系統的研究；他舉了很多例子，並希望能做徹底的分類，而且他很關心自己所使用的方法。我們可以說他的研究並不像他所想的那樣有系統，他選的例子也不是很妥當，做的分類也不詳盡，對於方法的觀念也很混淆；我們都可以這麼說，但是我們得承認他有志於對社會做科學的研究，而且他對於區分科學和非科學的研究有一些概念。但是，我們就不能這樣說馬基維利了。他並不像孟德斯鳩是個很不完美的社會與政治科學家；馬基維利根本就不是個政治科學家，但他是個很有天賦，而且擁有很多實際經驗的政治作家。

【答案】

41.（ D ）　　42.（ C ）　　43.（ A ）　　44.（ C ）　　45.（ B ）

【註】

superficial〔ˌsupɚˈfɪʃəl〕*adj*. 表面的；膚淺的

systematic〔ˌsɪstəˈmætɪk〕*adj*. 有系統的

exhaustive〔ɪgˈzɔstɪv〕*adj*. 徹底的

classification〔ˌklæsəfəˈkeʃən〕*n*. 分類　concede〔kənˈsid〕*v*. 承認

Passage Two ：

【譯文】

　　大沙漠有種浪漫又神秘的氣息。很多作家都曾歌頌過沙漠——柏頓，T.E. 勞倫斯，和 Saint-Exupery・魯道夫。范倫鐵諾令人悸動的電影「酋長」，將數以百萬墜入情網的女人，送入了狂亂潰敗的沙丘之夢中。片中虛構的外籍兵的功績，和阿拉伯疾如風的軍隊，使男人展現出一種比沙漠中的沙還要灼熱的景象。

啊！這些景象只在書上才會出現。而就專家所知，並召告全世界的事實是，這些沙漠般的情況，約占全球陸地的三分之一，已成為一種文明中，主要的環境威脅。上週在奈洛比，來自一百一十個國家的一千五百位代表，在聯合國的贊助下，比較各項紀錄。他們發現，各地的沙漠正以驚人的速度大肆擴張，而且通常出現在現存的沙漠荒地之外。這種現象很可怕，但我們已能確切知道這就叫「沙漠化」。而由於人類的愚蠢，沙漠化已威脅到此地的六十三億居民微弱的生命力。

根據美國國際發展機構報告指出，在上半個世紀裏，撒哈拉沙漠南方邊緣地帶的農耕和放牧地，據估計約有六十五萬平方公里（二十五萬平方英里）已被撒哈拉沙漠吞噬。埃及地質學家Farouk El-Baz已發現，有大量的沙漠正以每年十三公里（八英里）的速度，向肥沃的尼羅河三角洲逼進。

【答案】

46.(C)　　　47.(B)

【註】

glorify〔'glorə,faɪ〕*v.* 讚美；歌頌　throbbing〔'θrɑbɪŋ〕*adj.* 悸動的
waft〔wæft〕*v.* 飄送　smitten〔'smɪtn̩〕*adj.* 墜入情網的
frenzied〔'frɛzɪd〕*adj.* 瘋狂的　thrashing〔'θræʃɪŋ〕*n.* 潰敗
dune〔djun〕*n.* 沙丘　exploit〔ɪk'splɔɪt〕*n.* 功績
legionary〔'lidʒən,ɛrɪ〕*n.*（古羅馬的）軍團兵
galloping〔'gæləpɪŋ〕*adj.* 疾馳的　steam〔stim〕*v.* 冒蒸氣
menace〔'mɛnɪs〕*n.* 威脅　delegate〔'dɛlə,get〕*n.* 代表
auspice〔'ɔspɪs〕*n.* 主辦；贊助　relentlessly〔rɪ'lɛntlɪslɪ〕*adv.* 無情地
emerge〔ɪ'mɝdʒ〕*v.* 出現　awkwardly〔'ɔkwədlɪ〕*adv.* 侷促不安地
folly〔'fɑlɪ〕*n.* 愚蠢　fragile〔'frædʒəl〕*adv.* 脆弱地
grazing〔'grezɪŋ〕*n.* 放牧　swallow〔'swɑlo〕*v.* 吞噬
fringe〔frɪndʒ〕*n.* 邊緣　*a great sea of* 大量的
fertile〔'fɝtl̩〕*adj.* 肥沃的

Passage Three

【譯文】

　　瘧疾在斯里蘭卡大肆蔓延，只是種輕描淡寫的說法。官方的數字驚人地顯示出，該國有百分之二的人口，也就是三十萬四千人受害。瘧疾傳染者——阿諾非拉斯雌蚊，又再次從淡水沼澤和河流區域竄起。然而，瘧疾再度興起的另一原因是人類的貪婪和對快速賺錢的渴望。斯里蘭卡西岸盛產寶石，那些採集寶石者，便在周圍地區的河流汙泥中挖洞來採集。因為斯里蘭卡的紅寶石以及其他的寶石可對外來遊客以高價出售，許多交易商便在採礦季紛紛湧入採集。他們挖掘、工作，然後再將成千的洞廢棄。就是這些充滿水的坑洞，為瘧疾病蚊提供了最佳繁殖場所。政府的反瘧疾活動，正嚴厲譴責這些貪婪的礦工，四處留下已遭破壞的土地並棄之不顧。

【答案】

48.(B)　　49.(C)　　50.(B)

【註】

malaria〔mə'lɛrɪə〕*n*. 瘧疾
rampage〔'ræmpedʒ〕*n*. 猖獗
understatement〔,ʌndə'stetmənt〕*n*. 輕描淡寫
staggering〔'stægərɪŋ〕*adj*. 驚人的　carrier〔'kærɪə〕*n*. 帶菌者
resurge〔rɪ'sɝdʒ〕*v*. 再興起　freshwater〔'frɛʃ,wɔtə〕*adj*. 淡水的
gem〔dʒɛm〕*n*. 寶石　　fetch〔fɛtʃ〕*v*. 賣得
pit〔pɪt〕*n*. 坑　　avaricious〔,ævə'rɪʃəs〕*n*.貪婪的
miner〔'maɪnə〕*n*. 礦工　　***in** one's **wake*** 在～之後

Ⅳ. 翻譯：20%

51. 中國考驗了外國評論家的能力，因為要把它歸類於某種模式並不容易。
在最近幾十年來，其他共產國家，同時壓迫人民又使人民貧困。但是即
便是當中共鎮壓少數主張民主的知識份子和工人時，整體看來，中共的
統治仍快速地提高了社會生活水準。
* simultaneously〔,sɪml̩'tenɪəslɪ〕*adv*. 同時地
impoverish〔ɪm'pɑvərɪʃ〕*v*.使貧困　preside〔prɪ'zaɪd〕*v*. 管理

52. 你無法為衰老的過程做任何準備。生命是一種過程，只有前進，無法
　　倒退，一直到達年老，最後到死亡…。每個人細胞的生理時鐘不同，
　　它完全取決於我們的生活經歷、遺傳，也許最重要的是取決於社會上，
　　或自身對變老的看法。

* irreversible〔,ɪrɪ'vɝsəbl̩〕*adj.* 不能倒退的
　cellular〔'sɛljələ〕*adj.* 細胞的　heredity〔hə'rɛdətɪ〕*n.* 遺傳

V. 作文：20%

　　Since I have many friends and I enjoy socializing, if I had to divide my friends into three categories, these categories would necessarily be rather broad. In any case, I'll divide them as follows: One, "spiritual friends", two, "practical friends" and three, "friends who are drifters".

　　The first group, "spiritual friends", all strongly believe that life has real meaning and that there is a reason for man's existence on earth. Some of these people believe that love is the key to our existence; others believe that man's progress through civilization has achieved a lot; and I have many other kinds of spiritual friends as well. These spiritual friends are my best friends.

　　The second category, "practical friends," meanwhile, is typified by students studying something such as engineering which will enable them to get a good job, and of course some of them have already graduated and are working at such a job. These friends are concerned mainly with living life here and now, and I feel that I can learn a lot about living from them.

　　The third and final category, "drifters", includes those of my friends who have no real goals in life. These people drift around, change occupations a lot, and generally waste all their leisure time in bars, etc., since they have no set goals. Usually these people are somewhat unhappy and cynical about life. When I speak with these people, I often become depressed as they remind me of mankind's relative insignificance. I feel it's often quite a challenge to talk with these people.

國立交通大學八十三學年度
碩士班研究生入學考試英文試題

I. Mark the synonym for the underlined word. 10%

1. The host and hostess <u>cordially</u> welcomed their foreign guests.
   (A) excitedly   (B) warmly
   (C) calmly   (D) with hostility

2. One man arose from the crowd and <u>staunchly</u> accepted the challenge.
   (A) politely   (B) quietly
   (C) firmly   (D) secretly

3. The dog's bite slowly <u>penetrated</u> my skin.
   (A) pierced   (B) poisoned
   (C) destroyed   (D) excited

4. Cockroaches seem to <u>flourish</u> everywhere around that old house.
   (A) run   (B) spread disease
   (C) leave garbage   (D) thrive

5. Nancy's ability to skate is <u>phenomenal</u>.
   (A) admirable   (B) remarkable
   (C) surprising   (D) impossible

6. Pollution is becoming more <u>prevalent</u> year by year in our country.
   (A) harmful   (B) disgusting
   (C) tolerated   (D) widespread

7. That story Professor Lee told us two days ago was <u>hilarious</u>!
   (A) exciting   (B) incredible
   (C) disgusting   (D) funny

8. <u>Famine</u> is not a big problem in many European countries.
   (A) shortage of housing
   (B) shortage of food
   (C) shortage of drinking water
   (D) poverty

9. They will meet us in front of the planetarium.
   (A) cafeteria   (B) fish museum
   (C) plant museum   (D) star museum

10. Hitler's holocaust of the Jews will never be forgotten.
    (A) destruction   (B) fear
    (C) hatred   (D) treatment

II. Use the following words or phrases to complete the passage below. 26%

a. consumption	b. has revealed	c. balance
d. cycle	e. cellular	f. adverse
g. interference	h. identify	i. region
j. forms	k. far-reaching	l. survive
m. incorporation		

The Effect of Oil on Marine Organisms

In recent years the number of oil spills has been increasing. These spills, some of which have occurred directly at the site of extraction and others during transportation, have had an __11__ effect on marine organisms. Because of the importance of these organisms in the life __12__, research has been carried out in order to __13__ more accurately the reactions of these organisms to oil. A recent study __14__ that it is essential to understand that there is not one, but rather at least four possible ways in which oil can affect an organism.

First, as a result of an organism's ingestion of oil, direct lethal toxicity, that is, death by poisoning, can occur. However, in cases where the effect is less extreme, sub-lethal toxicity occurs. While __15__ and physiological processes are involved in both cases, in the latter the organism continues to __16__. Second, in some cases, oil __17__ a covering on the organism. This covering, referred to as coating, can result in smothering, that is, death of the organism due to lack of air. In instances where the effects of coating are less severe __18__ with movement and loss of insulative properties of feathers or fur may occur. The third effect of oil on marine organisms is the tainting or contamination of edible organisms. This results from the __19__ of hydrocarbons into the organism, thus making it unfit for human__20__. The final effect which this study has revealed is that of habitat changes. The alterations in the physical and chemical environment brought about by oil spills result in a change in the species composition of a __21__.

The implications of this most recent study are__22__. An oil spill in a particular region could critically upset the __23__ of nature, the total effect only becoming apparent after many years.

III. Choose the correct form from the words in parentheses. 5%

24. Professor Smith said that Halley's Comet, a large bright comet with a tail millions of kilometers long,_____ every seventy-six years.
    (A) appear   (B) appears
    (C) appeared   (D) has appeared

25. Carl Lewis is admired by the public for his dedication to his sport and for the excitement he brings to the track_____he enters a race.
    (A) whenever   (B) whatever
    (C) whoever   (D) however

26. Despite_____up all night, Ross seems alert.
    (A) stay   (B) staying
    (C) stayed   (D) having stayed

27. A cardiologist spoke to our physical education class on jogging and_____effects on the cardiovascular system.
    (A) his   (B) her
    (C) its   (D) their

28. The Vietnam War Memorial in Washington,_____to the American soldiers killed in Vietnam, attracts thousands of visitors every week.
    (A) dedicate   (B) dedicates
    (C) dedicated   (D) dedicating

IV. Choose the incorrect sentence (Only one of the three sentences is incorrect.) 10%

29. (A) Encouraged by Dan's attention, Shirley improved her appearance.
    (B) Working at maximum efficiency, the job should be completed on time.
    (C) To be precise, while they are not the most beautiful creatures, women are the most necessary.

30. (A) When you consider how much money the government collects in taxes, it makes a person wonder where it all goes.
    (B) If the committee of bigwigs has control, it might just refuse your request.
    (C) What I had really wanted to say is ..—but then I guess I'd better not say it.

31. (A) A piece was played at the dance which was composed of dissonant chords.
    (B) Pablo Casals was a great cellist who claimed that he had practiced playing the cello every day for almost eighty years.
    (C) Kent was so impressed by the lecture given by the astronomer that he decided to major in astronomy.

32. (A) The negotiations committee presented their recommendations for wages and benefits to the union members and officers.
    (B) Many of his customers transferred their business to another company.
    (C) Some members of American Indian tribes do not want anthropologists digging up their ancient burial sites.

33. (A) Whereas only ten years ago there were vast deserts of uninhabited space here, there now stand equally vast housing projects.
    (B) He finds, much to his chagrin, that his main support is Bruno and Bela and that Nancy and Ann are not much help at all.
    (C) The significant points to be incorporated in the "Major Requirements" list was discussed at a meeting in my office.

V. Select, out of the list below, the most appropriate
   preposition for each blank. (The same preposition may
   be chosen twice.) 9%

   Preposition list:

   a. in   b. at   c. of   d. to   e. for
   f. with g. during h. upon

   Levi Strauss was born___34___Bad Ocheim, Germany, in
1829, and___35___the European political turmoil___36___1848
decided to take his chances in New York,___37___which his
two brothers already had emigrated.___38___arrival, Levi
soon found that his two brothers had exaggerated their tales
of an easy life in the land of the main chance. They were
landowners, they had told him; instead, he found them
pushing needles, thread, pots, pans, ribbons, yarn, scissors,
and buttons to housewives.___39___two years he was a lowly
peddler, hauling some 180 pounds of sundries door-to-door to
eke out a marginal living. When a married sister in San
Francisco offered to pay his way West in 1850, he jumped
___40___the opportunity, taking___41___him bolts of canvas
he hoped to sell___42___a living.

VI. Thinking skills. (Choose the best answer) 10%

43. The whale swims like a fish and lives in the ocean. But
    it is not a fish. Fish stay under water all the time.
    But whales must have air. They can go down deep in the
    ocean for many minutes. But they always need to
    (A) find a fish to eat.   (B) swim a long way.
    (C) act like a fish.   (D) come up again for air.

44. In New England, the weather changes often. It may be
    sunny in the morning. Then it can be very cold and rainy
    in the afternoon. That is why a famous writer said: "If
    you don't like the weather in New England,
    (A) go home."
    (B) wait a few hours."
    (C) bring an umbrella."
    (D) listen to the radio."

45. In the United States, many children do not read books.
    They watch TV many hours every day. These children are
    not good readers because they
    (A) have no books.
    (B) go to school.
    (C) read books all day.
    (D) watch too much TV.

46. Fishermen today have large boats and special nets. They
    can catch thousands of fish in a short time. But this
    may be a problem. Some scientists are afraid
    (A) there will be too many fish soon.
    (B) the boats will not be large enough.
    (C) the fish will swim away.
    (D) there soon will not be any fish.

47. Doctors say they can tell that some people will get
    heart trouble. These people are too heavy. They work too
    hard. They smoke cigarettes. Some doctors get heart
    attacks. Maybe they do not
    (A) smoke cigarettes.   (B) work to hard.
    (C) do what they say.   (D) eat too much.

VII. Find the topic sentence (the main idea sentence) of
     each paragraph. 15%

48. (A) Man is a singular creature.
    (B) He has a set of gifts which make him unique among
        the animals: so that, unlike them, he is not a
        figure in the landscape--he is a shaper of the land-
        scape.
    (C) In body and in mind he is the explorer of nature,
        the ubiquitous animal, who did not find but has
        made his home in every continent.

49. (A) Albert Einstein, one of the world's geniuses, failed
        his university entrance examinations on his first
        attempt.
    (B) William Faulkner, one of America's noted writers,
        never finished college because he could not pass his
        English courses.
    (C) Sir Winston Churchill, who is considered one of the
        masters of the English language, had to have special
        tutoring in English during elementary school.
    (D) These few examples show that failure in school does
        not always predict failure in life.

50. (A) Synonyms, words that have the same basic meaning, do
       not always have the same emotional meaning.
    (B) For example, the words "stingy" and "frugal" both
       mean "careful with money".
    (C) However, to call a person stingy is an insult, while
       the word frugal has a much more positive connotation.
    (D) Similarly, a person wants to be slender but not
       skinny, and aggressive but not pushy.
    (E) Therefore, you should be careful in choosing words
       because many so-called synonyms are not really
       synonymous at all.

51. (A) The earth is always changing.
    (B) One way it changes is by erosion.
    (C) Some erosion is caused by the weather.
    (D) For example, the wind causes erosion.
    (E) In a desert, the wind blows the sand around.
    (F) Rain also causes erosion.
    (G) It washes away earth and even changes the shape of
       some rocks.
    (H) Another kind of erosion is caused by rivers.
    (I) When a river goes through a mountain, it cuts into
       the mountain.
    (J) After a long time, the mountain is lower and the
       land is flatter.

52. (A) There are two major differences between the European
       and American university systems.
    (B) In European universities, students are not required
       to attend classes.
    (C) In fact, professors in Germany generally do not know
       the names of the students enrolled in their courses.
    (D) In the United States, however, students are required
       to attend all classes and may be penalized if they
       don't.
    (E) Furthermore, in the European system, there is
       usually just one comprehensive examination at the
       end of the students' entire four or five years of
       study.
    (F) In the American system, on the other hand, there are
       usually numerous quizzes, tests, and homework as-
       signments, and there is almost always a final ex-
       amination in each course at the end of the semester.
    (G) The requirement for class attendance and the evalua-
       tion of student performance, therefore, are the two
       major differences between the European and American
       university systems.

VIII. Making inferences. 15%

53. Surveys reveal that most adults consider themselves
    "well informed about the affairs of the nation and the
    world." Yet a regularly taken Roper poll that asks,
    "From where do you obtain most of your information about
    the world?" has found the percentage of people who reply,
    "Television" has been increasing steadily over the past
    decade. The latest questionnaire found that well over 60
    percent of the respondents chose television over other
    media as their major source of information. These two
    facts are difficult to reconcile since even a casual
    study of television news reveals it is only a headline
    service and not a source of information enabling one to
    shape a world view.

    Choose the correct inference:
    (A) Most adults obtain most of their information about
        world affairs from the newspaper.
    (B) The author does not believe that television provides
        enough information to make people well informed.
    (C) The number of people answering the questionnaire has
        increased.
    (D) Sixty percent of the people questioned get all their
        news from television.
    (E) Most adults are well informed about the affairs of
        the nation and the world.

54. By voting against mass transportation, voters have
    chosen to continue on a road to ruin. Our interstate
    highways, those much praised golden avenues built to
    whisk suburban travelers in and out of downtown, have
    turned into the world's most expensive parking lots.
    That expense is not only economic--it is social. These
    highways have created great walls separating neighbor-
    hood from neighborhood, disrupting the complex social
    connections that help make a city livable.

    Choose the correct inference:
    (A) Interstate highways have done more good than harm.
    (B) Highways create complex social connections.
    (C) By separating neighborhoods, highways have made
        cities more livable.
    (D) The author supports the idea of mass transportation.
    (E) The author agrees with a recent vote by the
        citizens.

55. There was a time when scholars held that early humans lived in a kind of beneficent anarchy, in which people were granted their rights by their fellows and there was no governing or being governed. Various early writers looked back to this Golden Age, but the point of view that humans were originally children of nature is best known to us in the writings of Rousseau, Locke, and Hobbes. These men described the concept of social contract, which they said had put an end to the state of nature in which the earliest humans were supposed to have lived.

Choose the correct inference:
(A) According to the author, scholars today do not hold that early humans lived in a state of anarchy.
(B) Only Rousseau, Locke, and Hobbes wrote about early humans as children of nature.
(C) The early writers referred to in this passage lived through the Golden Age of early humans.
(D) The author believes the earliest humans were governed by social contract.
(E) Anarchy is a kind of social contract.

國立交通大學八十三學年度
碩士班研究生入學考試英文試題詳解

I. 字彙：10 ％

1. (B)　cordially〔'kɔrdʒəlɪ〕*adv*.熱忱地
   (B) ***warmly***〔'wɔrmlɪ〕*adv*.熱忱地
   (D) hostility〔hɑs'tɪlətɪ〕*n*.敵意

2. (C)　staunchly〔'stɔntʃlɪ〕*adv*.堅定地
   (C) ***firmly***〔'fɜmlɪ〕*adj*.堅定地

3. (A)　penetrate〔'pɛnə,tret〕*v*.穿透
   (A) ***pierce***〔pɪrs〕*v*.穿透

4. (D)　flourish〔'flɜɪʃ〕*v*.茂盛；繁盛
   (D) ***thrive***〔θraɪv〕*v*.繁衍；旺盛
   　　cockroach〔'kɑk,rotʃ〕*n*.蟑螂

5. (B)　phenomenal〔fə'nɑmənḷ〕*adj*.非凡的
   (B) ***remarkable***〔rɪ'mɑrkəbḷ〕*adj*.非凡的

6. (D)　prevalent〔'prɛvələnt〕*adj*.普遍的
   (D) ***widespread***〔'waɪd'sprɛd〕*adj*.普及的

7. (D)　hilarious〔haɪ'lɛrɪəs〕*adj*.有趣的
   (B) incredible〔ɪn'krɛdəbḷ〕*adj*.令人難以置信的
   (D) ***funny***〔'fʌnɪ〕*adj*.有趣的

8. (B)　famine〔'fæmɪn〕*n*.饑荒
   (B) ***shortage of food*** 缺乏食物

9. (D)　planetarium〔,plænə'tɛrɪəm〕*n*.天文館
   (D) ***star museum*** 天文館

10. (A)　holocaust〔'hɑlə,kɔst〕*n*.大破壞；大屠殺
   (A) ***destruction***〔dɪ'strʌkʃən〕*n*.破壞

Ⅱ. 填入適當的字詞：26 %

【譯文】

石油對海洋生物的影響

　　近年來，石油外漏次數持續增加。有些外漏直接發生在石油提煉地，有些則發生在運送途中，這些外漏對於海洋生態有不良的影響。因為這些海洋生物在生物圈十分重要，人們便進行許多研究，以便精確地辨識出這些生物對石油的反應。最近一項調查顯示，我們必須了解石油對生物的影響，有四種可能的途徑，而不是只有一種而已。

　　首先，由於生物吃了石油這種能直接致命的有毒物質，便發生中毒死亡事件。然而，在影響較不嚴重的地區，也會有潛在的致命有毒物質。當生物在此二種情況下進行細胞及生理作用時，後者仍能繼續生存。第二，在某些情況下，石油在生物體表形成一個覆蓋物。這層像表皮一樣的覆蓋物，會造成窒息，也就是會使生物缺少空氣而死亡。在覆蓋物的影響較不嚴重的事件中，便導致了生物活動受到妨礙，身上具有保護作用的羽毛或毛皮也可能會脫落。石油對海洋生物所造成的第三種影響，是會造成可食用的海洋生物的腐敗及污染，這是因為碳氫化合物在生物體內結合，使它不適合人類食用。研究報告中最後一項影響是生物棲息地的改變。石油外漏帶來的物理和化學環境的改變，會造成各地區組成生物種類的改變。

　　這項最新研究結果影響深遠。某一特定地區的石油外漏可能會嚴重破壞自然平衡，但要在許多年之後，所有的影響才會比較顯著。

【註】

marine〔məˈrin〕*adj.* 海洋的　　organism〔ˈɔrgən,ɪzəm〕*n.* 生物

spill〔spɪl〕*n.* 洩漏；外漏　　extraction〔ɪkˈstrækʃən〕*n.* 提煉

ingestion〔ɪnˈdʒɛstʃən〕*n.* 攝取

lethal〔ˈliθəl〕*adj.* 致命的　　toxicity〔tɑksˈɪsətɪ〕*n.* 毒性

physiological〔,fɪzɪəˈlɑdʒɪkl̩〕*adj.* 生理的

smother〔ˈsmʌðɚ〕*v.* 使窒息　　severe〔səˈvɪr〕*adj.* 嚴重的

insulative〔ɪnˈsʌlə,tɪv〕*adj.* 保護的

hydrocarbon〔,haɪdrəˈkɑrbən〕*n.* 碳氫化合物

habitat〔ˈhæbə,tæt〕*n.* 棲息地

11. (f) adverse〔'ædvɜs〕*adj.* 不利的

12. (d) cycle〔'saɪkḷ〕*n.* 循環

13. (h) identify〔aɪ'dɛntə,faɪ〕*v.* 辨認

14. (b) reveal〔rɪ'vil〕*v.* 顯示

15. (e) cellular〔'sɛljələ〕*adj.* 細胞的

16. (l) survive〔sə'vaɪv〕*v.* 存活

17. (j) form〔fɔrm〕*v.* 形成

18. (m) interference〔,ɪntə'fɪrəns〕*n.* 妨礙

19. (g) incorporation〔ɪn,kɔrpə'reʃən〕*n.* 合併;結合

20. (a) consumption〔kən'sʌmpʃən〕*n.* 消耗;消費

21. (i) region〔'ridʒən〕*n.* 地區

22. (k) far-reaching〔'fɑr'ritʃɪŋ〕*adj.* 深遠的

23. (c) balance〔'bæləns〕*n.* 平衡

Ⅲ. 選擇:5%

24. (B) 表不變的眞理,用現在簡單式。
　　　　* *Halley's Comet* 哈雷彗星

25. (A) 依句意,表時間的關係副詞,須用 whenever(=no matter when)。

26. (D) despite 爲介系詞,後須接名詞或動名詞,又句意指「動作持續整晚」,故用完成式。

27. (C) 依句意指慢跑的效果,故代名詞用 its。
　　　　* cardiologist〔,kɑrdɪ'alədʒɪst〕*n.* 心臟學家
　　　　cardiovascular〔,kɑrdɪo'væskjulə〕*adj.* 循環系統的

28. (C) 兩逗點間爲補述用法的形容詞子句,原句爲 which is dedicated to～,關係代名詞和 be 動詞可省略,故選(C)。

Ⅳ. 選出錯誤的句子：10 %

29. (**B**) *Working* → $\begin{cases} \textbf{\textit{If you are working}} \\ \textbf{\textit{With you working}} \end{cases}$

　　* 分詞構句中，前後主詞不一致，則須保留主詞。原句是由 If you work at … 簡化而來。

30. (**C**) *had* → **have** 或將 *had* 去掉

　　* 依句意爲現在簡單式，故須將 had 改爲 have。
　　bigwig〔'bɪg,wɪg〕*n.* 大人物；大亨

31. (**A**) *which* → **, which**

　　* which 引導補述用法的形容詞子句，其前面須有逗點。
　　dissonant〔'dɪsənənt〕*adj.* 不和諧的
　　chord〔kɔrd〕*n.* 和弦

32. (**A**) *their* → **its**

　　* committee〔kə'mɪtɪ〕*n.* 委員會（爲一集合名詞，視爲一整
　　體，所有格用 its）　　tribe〔traɪb〕*n.* 部落
　　anthropologist〔,ænθro'pɑlədʒɪst〕*n.* 人類學家

33. (**C**) *was* → **were**

　　* points 爲複數名詞，須配合複數動詞。
　　chagrin〔ʃə'grɪn〕*n.* 懊惱
　　incorporate〔ɪn'kɔrpə,ret〕*v.* 使合併

Ⅴ. 選出正確的介系詞：9 %

【譯文】

　　李維‧史特勞斯於西元一八二九年出生於德國的 Bad Ocheim，一八四八年歐洲發生政治動亂時，他決定冒險到紐約闖一闖，他的兩個哥哥都早已移民到紐約了。到達紐約時，李維很快地發現兩位哥哥誇大其辭，紐約並不像他們所說的是個容易生存、充滿機會的地方。哥哥曾告訴李維他們是地主。相反地，他卻發現他們向家庭主婦推銷針線、茱鍋、平底鍋、絲帶、紗線、剪刀、和鈕扣。兩年來，李維是個卑微的小販，拖著一百八十磅的雜貨，挨家挨戶地叫賣，以維持最低限度的生計。一八五〇年，在

舊金山已婚的姊姊願意給他錢到西部，他欣然接受了這個機會，並帶了一袋的螺栓，希望能以販賣螺栓維生。

【註】

turmoil〔'tɜmɔɪl〕*n.* 動亂　　emigrate〔'ɛmə,gret〕*v.* 移民
exaggerate〔ɪg'zædʒə,ret〕*v.* 誇張
peddler〔'pɛdlə〕*n.* 小販　　haul〔hɔl〕*v.* 拉；拖
sundries〔'sʌndrɪz〕*n. pl.* 雜貨
marginal〔'mɑrdʒɪnl〕*adj.* 最低限度的
bolt〔bolt〕*n.* 螺栓；帶帽的螺絲釘　　canvas〔'kænvəs〕*n.* 帆布袋

34. (a)　在～都市裏，介系詞用 in 。

35. (g)　during 「在～期間」

36. (a)　在～年，介系詞用 in 。

37. (d)　emigrate to～ 移居至～

38. (h)　(up)on arrival （人）一到就～

39. (e)　表「時間的長短」，介系詞用 for 。

40. (b)　*jump at* 欣然接受

41. (f)　表示「帶在～身上」，介系詞用with 。

42. (e)　*for a living* 維持生計

Ⅵ. 選出最適當的答案：10 ％

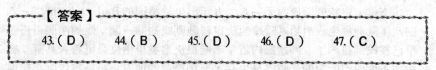

【答案】

43. (D)　　44. (B)　　45. (D)　　46. (D)　　47. (C)

【註】

whale〔hwel〕*n.* 鯨魚　　*heart attack* 心臟病發作

Ⅶ. 找出每段的主題句：15 ％

48. (**A**)　singular〔'sɪŋgjələ˞〕*adj.* 奇特的
　　　　　　ubiquitous〔ju'bɪkwətəs〕*adj.* 無所不在的

49. (**D**)　noted〔'notɪd〕*adj.* 著名的
　　　　　　tutor〔'tutə˞, 'tju-〕*v.* 家庭指導

50. (**A**)　synonym〔'sɪnə,nɪm〕*n.* 同義字
　　　　　　stingy〔'stɪndʒɪ〕*adj.* 小氣的
　　　　　　frugal〔'frugḷ〕*adj.* 節儉的
　　　　　　connotation〔,kɑnə'teʃən〕*n.* 含意
　　　　　　slender〔'slɛndə˞〕*adj.* 苗條的
　　　　　　skinny〔'skɪnɪ〕*adj.* 皮包骨的
　　　　　　aggressive〔ə'grɛsɪv〕*adj.* 積極的
　　　　　　pushy〔'puʃɪ〕*adj.* 強求的

51. (**B**)　erosion〔ɪ'roʒən〕*n.*（土地的）侵蝕

52. (**A**)　enroll〔ɪn'rol〕*v.* 登記；註冊　penalize〔'pɛnḷ,aɪz〕*v.* 處罰
　　　　　　comprehensive〔,kɑmprɪ'hɛnsɪv〕*adj.* 綜合性的
　　　　　　quiz〔kwɪz〕*n.* 小考

Ⅷ. 推論：15 ％

53. (**B**)　調查顯示，大部分的成年人認為他們自己對於國家及世界大事有
　　　　　　全盤的了解。然而根據洛帕民意調查做的正式訪問，問題是：「你
　　　　　　從哪裏獲得世界各地的消息？」，結果發現，在過去幾十年中，
　　　　　　回答「電視」的人在持續增加中。最新的問卷調查發現，在所有
　　　　　　的傳播媒體中，有百分之六十以上的人選擇電視作為資訊的主要
　　　　　　來源。這兩項調查結果很難同時成立，因為即使是對電視新聞非
　　　　　　正式的研究，也顯示電視新聞只提供新聞提要。它並不是一種能
　　　　　　使人們建立世界觀的資訊來源。

　　　　　　＊ poll〔pol〕*n.* 意見調查
　　　　　　　questionnaire〔,kwɛstʃən'ɛr〕*n.* 問卷調查表
　　　　　　　reconcile〔'rɛkən,saɪl〕*v.* 使調合；使並存

54.(**D**) 選民們否決了大衆運輸,選擇了毀滅之路。那些曾被稱爲黃金道路、使市郊的遊人快速出入城鎮的州際公路,已成爲世上最昂貴的停車場。這不僅是經濟上,也是社會上的損失。這些公路築起了高牆,使人們和鄰居疏離,分裂了使城市更值得居住的社會關係。

> * interstate〔ˈɪntɚ͵stet〕*adj.* 州際的
> whisk〔hwɪsk〕*v.* 迅速帶走
> avenue〔ˈævə͵nju〕*n.* 街道
> suburban〔səˈbɝbən〕*adj.* 市郊的

55.(**A**) 學者曾一度認爲,早期人類生活在友善的無政府狀態下,人們的權力由同伴們授與,並沒有統治或被統治的情況。有許多早期的作家都回溯這段黃金時代,但作品中,以人類原本是「自然之子」的觀念著稱的有羅素、洛克和霍布士。這些作家描述了「社會契約」的理念,並表示這種觀念,已爲一般認爲早期人類所居住的「自然之國」劃下句點。

> * beneficent〔bəˈnɛfəsn̩t〕親切的
> anarchy〔ˈænəkɪ〕*n.* 無政府(狀態)

國立中正大學八十三學年度
碩士班研究生入學考試英文試題

I. Reading comprehension : 60%

After reading the following passages, choose one best answer to each of the questions below them.

One of the deepest of minor pleasures is the common one of collecting. I say deep because it is rooted in the soil of the primitive. It is akin to the pleasure we take in being snug and warm when outside the elements are raging. It must respond to the caveman within. The philatelist will tell you that stamps are educational, that they are valuable, that they are beautiful. All that is quite true, but only part of the truth. Such reasoning can hardly account for the fact that collecting can be and often is a passion, saturated with the irrational. My notion is that collecting is a symbolic gesture. The collection is a hedge, a comfort, a shelter into which the sorely beset mind can withdraw. It is orderly, it grows toward completion, it is something, as we say, that can't be taken away from us. The miser is merely a collector gone mad; but all collectors are a little mad in that they draw from an assemblage of inanimate objects a pleasure that is profoundly emotional and tied to the core of their being.

1. In the passage, the pleasure of collecting is compared to
   (A) a civilized hobby.
   (B) something that is unique.
   (C) a symbolic gesture.
   (D) being safe and warm during a storm.

2. Collectors who carry their hobby too far can become
   (A) philatelists.
   (B) primitive people.
   (C) inanimate objects.
   (D) misers.

3. The speaker says that all collectors are a little mad because they
   (A) have one-track minds.
   (B) can never complete their collections.
   (C) are saturated with passion.
   (D) obtain excessive pleasure from objects.

4. From this passage we can assume that collecting fulfills
   (A) physical drives.
   (B) emotional needs.
   (C) intellectual desires.
   (D) spiritual yearnings.

5. The speaker views collectors with
   (A) amazement.   (B) scorn.
   (C) understanding.   (D) pity.

　　Misconceptions about alcoholism are common. Many people, for example, think that alcoholics are careless, pleasure-seeking people who have moral problems that make them easier prey for liquor. Actually, alcoholics often feel guilty about their drinking and are very self-conscious around other people. Alcoholics quite often have a low self-esteem and are sensitive about what people may think of them. Another common myth is that the alcoholic is always drunk, but experts say this is not so. In truth, there are three types of alcoholics. Episodic drinkers, for example, drink only now and then, but each of their drinking episodes ends in overindulgence. Habitual excess drinkers are also only occasionally drunk, but their episodes are much more frequent than those of the episodic drinker. The addict is a person who must drink continually simply in order to function. It is the addict who needs medical assistance to withdraw from the support of alcohol.

6. The best title for this passage is
   (A) What About the Habitual Drinker?
   (B) Alcoholism: Fact and Fiction.
   (C) Curing the Alcoholic.
   (D) Alcoholism in America.

7. According to the passage, which of the following
   statements is NOT TRUE?
   (A) Many alcoholics feel guilty about their drinking.
   (B) The habitual drinker is only occasionally drunk.
   (C) The addict needs medical help with his problem.
   (D) Episodic drinkers never overindulge.

8. We can conclude from the passage that
   (A) few alcoholics are episodic drinkers.
   (B) episodic drinkers' "bouts" are worse than those of
       habitual drinkers.
   (C) most alcoholics are emotionally disturbed people.
   (D) the addict-type alcoholic is always drunk.

9. The passage suggests that
   (A) the addict has an emotional and physical dependence
       on alcohol.
   (B) more habitual drinkers become addicts than do
       episodic drinkers.
   (C) addicts can be helped by chemical control of their
       drinking urges.
   (D) alcoholics are basically immoral.

10. As used in this passage, the word "episodic" means
    (A) constant.   (B) periodic.
    (C) suicidal.   (D) uncontrollable.

Vitamin research may be the fastest growing area of research in medicine. Despite the fact that the public apparently trusts vitamins to do exactly what their manufacturers
say they will do and rushes to buy vitamins, there are a
great many misunderstandings and myths about what vitamins
are and how consumers should use them. And research is consistently proving these myths wrong.

First of all, many vitamins simply will not do what is
often claimed. Vitamin C has never been proven to aid in the
prevention of colds. B vitamins do not get rid of "the
rundown feeling"; any effect a person feels when taking a
B-12 capsule, for example, is purely a psychological effect.
B-12 deficiencies are rare, and even in cases where B-12
treatment is necessary, the vitamin must be injected because
it is ineffective when taken orally.

Vitamin E is often said to prevent heart disease, improve virility, and slow the aging process, but there has been no experimental proof of any of these claims. The fact that male rats become sterile when deprived of vitamin E does not mean that the same thing happens to humans who are deprived of vitamin E. In fact, it is nearly impossible to study vitamin E deprivation in human beings because vitamin E is present in almost all sources of human food.

The same is true of almost every other vitamin. They are abundantly present in a balanced diet. The most common vitamins are A, B-1, B-2, C, and D; and if a person eats a balanced diet that provides these vitamins, all the other vitamins will be present in enough quantity. Though many people claim that vitamins are rare and that you should eat special foods or take vitamin pills daily to make sure you are getting the correct quantity, this is simply not true. In fact, you can overdo vitamin supplements. Some vitamins are toxic if you take in too much of them. Vitamin C over- dose can cause diarrhea and kidney stones. Large amounts of A can cause pressure to build up in the brain or cause dryness in the skin, headaches, general pains. Vitamin D overdoses can cause mental and physical retardation, nausea, and high blood pressure. In fact, vitamin overdose is often more severe than vitamin deficiency and is becoming more common.

Another myth about vitamins is that "natural" ones are superior to those produced in the lab. People will often pay high prices for vitamins made up of natural ingredients-- such as C from rose hips--when synthetic, lab-produced vitamins are available at much cheaper prices. In fact, a vitamin always has exactly the same molecular structure, whether its source is a plant, animal, or test tube; any change in its structure would make it a different substance altogether. There is not any difference between a synthetic

and a "natural" vitamin, so the body cannot possibly make a
distinction between the two.

11. The main idea of this passage is that
    (A) since vitamins are rare in our diets, we need to
        take vitamin supplements regularly.
    (B) vitamin supplements are dangerous.
    (C) natural vitamins are no better than synthetic ones.
    (D) vitamin overdose can cause serious problems.

12. According to this passage, which of the following
    statements is TRUE?
    (A) Most vitamins are not effective when taken orally.
    (B) Vitamin E can be toxic.
    (C) Synthetic vitamins are better than natural ones.
    (D) All the vitamins we need are present in a balanced
        diet.

13. Slowing the "aging process" has been associated with
    (A) vitamin C.   (B) vitamin E.
    (C) vitamin B-12.   (D) vitamin D.

14. Which of the following conclusions does the passage
    support?
    (A) Vitamin supplements need to be controlled by law.
    (B) If you take vitamin supplements, you should take
        natural ones.
    (C) "Junk" foods do not provide enough vitamins.
    (D) People should try to eat balanced diets instead of
        taking vitamin supplements.

15. The author probably
    (A) is a vegetarian.
    (B) avoids taking vitamins A and D.
    (C) uses only natural vitamins.
    (D) doesn't take vitamin supplements.

16. A good title for this passage might be
    (A) The Use of Common Vitamins.
    (B) Myths About Vitamin Supplements.
    (C) Vitamins.
    (D) Natural and Synthetic Vitamins.

17. As used in this passage, the word virility means
    (A) emotions.   (B) life.
    (C) good health.   (D) physical strength.

18. As used in this passage, the word <u>sterile</u> means
    (A) stronger.
    (B) lacking ability to produce offspring.
    (C) female.
    (D) clean.

19. As used in this passage, the word <u>toxic</u> means
    (A) poisonous.   (B) deadly.
    (C) useful.   (D) harmful.

20. As used in this passage, the word <u>synthetic</u> means
    (A) artifical.   (B) natural.
    (C) useless.   (D) expensive.

II. Translation: 20%

Translate the following passage from Lien-ho Pao (United Daily News, December 16, 1993) into English.

黃石城的養生方法之一是「褲袋哲學」，他說，即使再冷，他也不會把手放在褲袋內，因爲將手插進褲袋即意味著，不想做事了。

黃石城說，時下常有人沒事就把手放進褲袋，無意間也傳達了自詡頗有成就或了不起的意念，但是把手放進口袋裡，還能做甚麼呢？

手不收進褲袋，則可以和自然維持接觸，也象徵不服輸的想法，和隨時以旺盛活力去忙的肢體語言。

III. Composition: 20%

Write a short essay (100-120 words) to persuade your readers that they ought to contribute to making and keeping our environment clean and healthy. Your writing will be evaluated on the strength of your argument, grammar, structure, use of words, spelling, capitalization, and punctuation.

國立中正大學八十三學年度
碩士班研究生入學考試英文試題詳解

I. 閱讀測驗：50 %

【譯文】

　　在較次要的樂趣中，一般的收集是最深刻的樂趣之一。我說深刻是因為它深植於原始的土地中。這就像是當外頭狂風暴雨，而我們卻在家享受舒適和溫暖所得到的快樂一樣。這一定能與穴居者的內心相呼應。集郵者會告訴你郵票具有教育性，有價值又美麗。這些都相當正確，但只是事實的一部分。這樣的理由很難解釋收集通常是一種狂熱，是非理性的。我的觀念是，收集是一種象徵性的行為。收集是藩籬、是慰藉、是庇護所，被苦痛包圍的心可以回來安歇。它是井然有序的，它會逐漸圓滿，就如我們說的，它是別人無法從我們身邊帶走的東西。守財奴只是一個發了瘋的收集者；但所有的收集者都有點瘋，他們將無生命的東西收集在一起，並將之視為一種樂趣，這種樂趣完全是情感上的，並與他們生命的核心緊緊相繫。

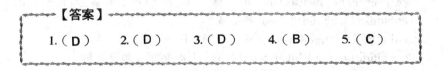

【答案】

1.（ D ）　　2.（ D ）　　3.（ D ）　　4.（ B ）　　5.（ C ）

【註】

primitive〔ˈprɪmətɪv〕*adj.* 原始的

akin〔əˈkɪn〕*adj.* 類似的　　snug〔snʌg〕*adj.* 舒適的

philatelist〔fəˈlætlɪst〕*n.* 集郵者

saturate〔ˈsætʃəˌret〕*v.* 浸透

hedge〔hɛdʒ〕*n.* 藩籬　　miser〔ˈmaɪzɚ〕*n.* 守財奴

【譯文】

　　一般人對於酒精中毒常有誤解。舉例來說，很多人認為酗酒者是不負責的尋歡之人，他們有道德上的問題，使他們容易猛灌黃湯。事實上，酗酒者對於他們的豪飲常會有罪惡感，而且和別人在一起，會十分不自在。酗酒者很自卑，而且對於別人的看法很敏感。另一個普遍的想法是，酗酒的人總是爛醉如泥，但專家說並非如此。事實上，酗酒者有三種。舉例來說，間歇性酗酒者只是偶爾喝酒，但他們每一次喝酒，到後來都會過於沈迷。習慣於飲酒過量的酗酒者也是偶爾才會喝醉，但他們的酗酒次數，比間歇性酗酒者來得頻繁。有酒癮的人必須一直喝酒，才能讓體內器官正常運作。有酒癮的人，需要借助醫藥的幫助，才能消除對酒的依賴。

【答案】

6.（B）　　7.（D）　　8.（C）　　9.（C）　　10.（B）

【註】

misconception〔ˌmɪskən'sɛpʃən〕*n.* 誤解
alcoholism〔'ælkəhɔlˌɪzəm〕*n.* 酒精中毒
alcoholic〔ˌælkə'hɔlɪk, -'hɑl-〕*n.* 酗酒者
self-esteem〔ˌsɛlfə'stim〕*n.* 自尊　　myth〔mɪθ〕*n.* 迷思；憑空想像
episodic〔ˌɛpə'sɑdɪk〕*adj.* 插曲式的
episode〔'ɛpəˌsod〕*n.* 插曲；一個事件
overindulgence〔'ovərɪn'dʌldʒəns〕*n.* 放縱；過度耽溺
addict〔'ædɪkt〕*n.* 耽溺於不良嗜好的人

【譯文】

　　維他命的研究可能是醫學研究中，成長最快速的領域。儘管一般民眾相信維他命真有其製造商所說的效用，並且急著去購買，然而，關於維他命究竟是什麼，以及顧客要如何使用，仍存有許多誤解和傳說。研究便一次又一次地證明傳聞是錯的。

　　首先，許多維他命實在不能達到其所宣稱的效果。維他命 E 從未被證明能有助於預防感冒。維他命 B 並不能消除疲憊的感覺。舉例來說，人們服用維他命 B_{12} 膠囊後所感到的效果，純粹是心理作用。人體很少發生維他命 B_{12} 不足，即使在必須用 B_{12} 治療的情況下，也必須用注射的，因為口服不會發生效用。

　　人們常說維他命 E 能預防心臟病，增強活力，及降低老化速度，但是這些說法尚未經過實驗證明。公鼠失去了維他命 E 會變得無法生育，但這項事實並不表示人類失去維他命 E 也會發生相同的事。事實上，要想研究人類在失去維他命 E 之後的情況幾乎不可能，因為幾乎在所有人類食物來源中，都存有維他命 E。

　　幾乎其他每種維他命都是如此。在均衡的飲食中皆含有足夠的維他命。最常見的是維他命 A，B_1，B_2，C 和 D，如果人吃了均衡的一餐，其中提供了這些維他命，那麼其他的維他命也會十分充足。雖然許多人聲稱維他命很罕見，應該每天吃特別的食物或服用維他命丸，以確保攝取充足的維他命，但這實在是錯誤的。事實上，你可能會攝取過量的維他命。有些維他命，如果你吃太多，是有毒的。過量的維他命 C 會造成腹瀉和腎結石。大量的維他命 A 會增加腦中壓力，或造成皮膚乾燥、頭痛、全身疼痛。過量的維他命 D 會導致身心遲鈍、噁心、以及高血壓。事實上，維他命攝取過量總是比維他命不足更嚴重，也更普遍。

　　另一項關於維他命的傳聞是天然的比實驗室中製造出來的好。當實驗室中製造的合成維他命可以更低價購得時，人們卻會以高價去購買天然原料製成的維他命——像是由玫瑰花莢製成的維他命 C。事實上，同一種維他命有同樣的分子構造，不管它是來自植物、動物、還是試管；任何構造上的改變都會使它變成另一種物質。合成維他命和天然維他命之間並沒有差別，所以，我們的身體不可能分辨得出二者有何不同。

【答案】

11.（D）	12.（D）	13.（B）	14.（D）	15.（D）
16.（B）	17.（D）	18.（B）	19.（A）	20.（A）

【註】

vitamin〔'vaɪtəmɪn〕 *n.* 維他命
manufacturer〔‚mænjə'fæktʃərə〕 *n.* 製造業者
rundown〔'rʌn'daʊn, 'rʌn‚daʊn〕 *adj.* 疲憊的
capsule〔'kæpsḷ〕 *n.* 膠囊
psychological〔‚saɪkə'lɑdʒɪkḷ〕 *adj.* 心理上的
virility〔və'rɪlətɪ, vaɪ-〕 *n.* 活力   sterile〔'stɛrəl〕 *adj.* 不孕的
deprivation〔‚dɛprɪ'veʃən〕 *n.* 剝奪
toxic〔'tɑksɪk〕 *adj.* 有毒的   overdose〔'ovə‚dos〕 *n.* 藥量過多
diarrhea〔‚daɪə'riə〕 *n.* 腹瀉   kidney〔'kɪdnɪ〕 *n.* 腎
retardation〔‚rɪtɑr'deʃən〕 *n.* 遲鈍   hip〔hɪp〕 *n.* 玫瑰花莢
synthetic〔sɪn'θɛtɪk〕 *adj.* 合成的
molecular〔mə'lɛkjələ〕 *adj.* 分子

Ⅱ. 翻譯：20％

Huang Shih Cheng's method of living well is a so-called "pocket philosophy". He says that if it's cold, he won't put his hands in his pockets because to put one's hands in one's pockets gives an impression that one lacks motivation.

Huang Shih Cheng says that at times when people have nothing to do and they put their hands in their pockets, they will merely boast about past achievements or think of things that can't be done. However, at this time, when someone puts his hands in his pockets, what can he do?

If the hands are outside the pockets, then it's possible to keep in touch with the situation, and it symbolizes a person who refuses to be defeated, and who at the same time has an air of vitality and of being prosperous. This is the sort of body language that it portrays.

Ⅲ. 作文：20%

It ought to be obvious that a clean environment is essential to man's continuing existence upon this earth. Unfortunately, many people don't give much thought to their environment; they just live as their culture tells them to. But in these modern times man's ability to pollute his environment has increased dramatically. We can no longer avoid thinking about the impact our actions have on our environment.

Today cancers and other lifestyle / environmental diseases are on the increase. Such diseases shorten people's lives and reduce the quality of life. These diseases in turn cost society billions of dollars in health care. Likewise, poisoned air, soil and water etc. also reduce the length and quality of life and again have great economic costs.

Too many people care more about their own personal convenience (i.e. money) than they do about their environment. They are oblivious to getting cancer etc. and they apparently don't care about the future of their children. In fact, they don't believe in anything, and this is the essence of the problem. Our culture today is empty, and must be changed. Our sick environment is just a symptom of our own cultural disease.

國立中興大學八十三學年度
碩士班研究生入學考試英文試題

I. Vocabulary: 20%

To each question, choose one answer, A, B, C, or D that best completes the sentence.

Example: I＿＿＿＿＿you are happy.
　　　　　(A) think　　(B) sink　　(C) thank　　(D) seek
Answer : A

1. I used to dislike cheese, but I＿＿＿＿＿a taste for it when I was in college.
   (A) inquired   (B) acquired
   (C) requested   (D) required

2. The immigrant＿＿＿＿＿to living in his new country.
   (A) adapted   (B) adopted
   (C) adjured   (D) addicted

3. An optical＿＿＿＿＿is a visual trick.
   (A) allusion   (B) delusion
   (C) illusion   (D) derision

4. The jury are＿＿＿＿＿the case.
   (A) deliberating   (B) elaborating
   (C) illustrating   (D) demonstrating

5. She hoped to get rich by＿＿＿＿＿in the stock market.
   (A) inspecting   (B) investing
   (C) calculating   (D) insinuating

6. You can choose your friends, but you can't choose your ＿＿＿＿＿.
   (A) religions   (B) relations
   (C) relatives   (D) regulars

7. The fire claimed fifty lives; people suspected＿＿＿＿＿.
   (A) murder   (B) arson
   (C) intrigue   (D) war

8. The_____to which our solar system belongs is also
   called the Milky Way.
   (A) star   (B) planet
   (C) supernova   (D) galaxy

9. Come to see me. I'll be_____every Monday afternoon.
   (A) available   (B) valuable
   (C) avoidable   (D) vulnerable

10. They_____how to solve the problem.
    (A) disputed   (B) dispelled
    (C) disrupted   (D) distributed

11. Are you paid in_____to the number of hours you work?
    (A) preparation   (B) preposition
    (C) disposition   (D) proportion

12. The good weather will_____ all the week.
    (A) resist   (B) persist
    (C) insist   (D) assist

13. In England, women were given the_____ in 1918.
    (A) framework   (B) fraternity
    (C) freedom   (D) franchise

14. These paper plates are_____after use.
    (A) disputable   (B) respectable
    (C) disposable   (D) responsible

15. Love_____age and religion.
    (A) defies   (B) delays
    (C) destroys   (D) differs

16. At this_____in our nation's affairs, we need firm
    leadership.
    (A) junction   (B) function
    (C) juncture   (D) structure

17. Finally, we_____the power of the law to prevent a
    crime.
    (A) provoke   (B) evoke
    (C) invoke   (D) involve

18. We have to know the difference between_____and
    poisonous berries.
    (A) edible   (B) portable
    (C) drinkable   (D) equable

19. He_____a secret wish to be a painter.
    (A) harasses   (B) harbours
    (C) harnesses   (D) harangues

20. That government governs best that governs most justly
    and most_____.
    (A) beneficially   (B) benevolently
    (C) belovedly   (D) belligerently

II. English Structure and Writing Ability: 30%

(1) On the answer sheet, put down under the number of each
    question the parenthesized capital letter that precedes
    the expression that best completes the sentence.

    Example:_____beautiful was Akina that everybody
             looked at her in admiration.
             (A) So   (B) Too   (C) Very   (D) Such
    Answer : (A)

21. The amount of specialized training_____a physicist or
    chemist today is enormous.
    (A) requires   (B) requires of
    (C) required of   (D) required

22._____, his grandfather died.
    (A) When three years old
    (B) When he was three years old
    (C) When he is three years old
    (D) Three years old

23. He ran to the station and_____.
    (A) took the train
    (B) the train was taken by him
    (C) he took the train
    (D) had taken the train

24. If I were a rich man and if my father_____still alive,
    my life would be different.
    (A) was   (B) would be
    (C) were   (D) will be

25. To open this door,_____a sudden push.
    (A) to give it   (B) it must be given
    (C) giving   (D) give it

26. Paul_____.
(A) looked neither hurt or discouraged
(B) neither looked hurt nor discouraged
(C) looked neither hurt nor discouraged
(D) neither looked hurt nor looked discouraged

27. We judge our friends both_____.
(A) by what they say and what they do
(B) both by what they say and do
(C) by what they say and by what they do
(D) by what they say and by their doings.

(2) To each question, choose the one underlined expressions that is grammatically mistaken, and put the capital letter beneath it under the number of each question on the answer sheet.

Example: "No evil can real hurt a good man," said
    A   B   C   D
   Socrates.

Answer : B

28. That we ought to seek everything that is really good for
  A   B   C

us is self-evident true.
   D

29. Having asserted the existence of natural, human and,
  A

therefore, inalienable rights, the Declaration goes on
  B   C

to say that among those rights are life, liberty, and

the pursue of happiness.
  D

30. All what I want are those things I need.
  A B   C   D

31. A criterion of the justice of governments is that they
             A   B

derive their powers from the consent of governed.
     C   D

32. Economic <u>rights</u>, <u>like</u> political rights, are rights to
           A   B
    <u>good</u> that every human being <u>needs</u> in order to lead a
     C   D
    decent human life.

33. If we look <u>forward</u> to the turn of the century, the
                A
    <u>prospects</u> are <u>bright</u> <u>still</u>.
     B   C   D

34. Should we abolish the death penalty <u>for all</u> capital
                                          A
    offenses, <u>replacing</u> it with life imprisonment, <u>permit</u>
               B   C
    no release from prison <u>on parole</u>?
                            D

35. Without freedom of choice we would not be political
    animals, but merely instinctively gregarious <u>ones</u>, and
                                                  A
    <u>our to be</u> political by nature is the basis <u>for</u> our
     B   C
    natural right <u>to</u> political liberty.
                   D

III. Reading Comprehension: 30%
    Read the following three passages carefully, and then
    choose the best answer to each question.

    LADY FRIENDS, which opened last night at the Roxy
Theater, suffers from such a threadbare screenplay and
tentative personality that one can't help marveling at its
sloppy appeal. A person built and clad this wretchedly would
appear to be sinking fast.

    Although the film aspires to contrast the characters
and career choices of two young women, Susan Weinblatt and
Anne Munroe, who are first observed as roommates in an
apartment on New York's Upper West Side, the script barely

establishes the girls as nodding acquaintances let alone
friends destined to diverge along exemplary, if conflicting,
paths.

Some screenwriters possess enough flair or experience
to suggest a great deal through an artful minimum of ex-
position and characterization. Vicki Pound doesn't have that
rare kind of finesse, and the director, Claudia Scott,
doesn't demonstrate enough dash or resourcefulness to con-
ceal Pound's patchy work.

36. What is LADY FRIENDS?
    (A) a play   (B) a movie
    (C) a novel   (D) a textbook

37. Who wrote LADY FRIENDS?
    (A) Susan Weinblatt   (B) Anne Munroe
    (C) Vicki Pound   (D) Claudia Scott

38. The review clearly states that_____.
    (A) LADY FRIENDS will be an unqualified success at the
        box office
    (B) it will attract no one
    (C) everything about LADY FRIENDS is weak and unappealing
    (D) the reviewer will reserve judgment until a later
        date

39. The two main characters in LADY FRIENDS are supposed to
    be_____.
    (A) passengers about to sink
    (B) poorly built and clothed relatives
    (C) writers and directors from the Upper West Side
    (D) friends and roommates

Most of the intelligent land animals have prehensile,
grasping organs for exploring their environment--hands in
man and his anthropoid relatives, the sensitive, inquiring
trunk in the elephant. One of the surprising things about
the porpoise is that his superior brain is unaccompanied by
any type of manipulative organ. He has, however, a remarkable range-finding ability involving some sort of echo-

sounding. Perhaps this acute sense--far more accurate than any man has been able to devise artificially--brings him greater knowledge of his watery surroundings than might at first seem possible. Human beings think of intelligence as geared to things. The hand and the tool are to us the unconscious symbols of our intellectual attainment. It is difficult for us to visualize another kind of lonely, almost disembodied intelligence floating in the wavering green fairyland of the sea--an intelligence possibly near or comparable to our own but without hands to build, to transmit knowledge by writing, or to alter by one hairsbreadth the planet's surface. Yet at the same time there are indications that this is a warm, friendly, and eager intelligence, quite capable of coming to the assistance of injured companions and striving to rescue them from drowning. Porpoises left the land when mammalian brains were still small and primitive. Without the stimulus provided by agile exploring fingers, these great sea mammals have yet taken a divergent road toward intelligence of a high order. Hidden in their sleek bodies is an impressively elaborated instrument, the reason for whose appearance is a complete enigma. It is as though both man and porpoise were each part of some great eye which yearned to look both outward on eternity and inward to the sea's heart--that fertile entity like the mind in its swarming and grotesque life.

40. According to the author, in which way are porpoises better equipped than man?
    (A) They can rescue people in the water.
    (B) They can transmit knowledge.
    (C) They can look into eternity.
    (D) They have a range-finding ability.

41. Which literary device appears in the last sentence?
    (A) simile   (B) allusion
    (C) paradox   (D) alliteration

42. Which statement about porposies does the author make?
    (A) They have always lived in the water.
    (B) They once had prehensile organs.
    (C) They lived on land a long time ago.
    (D) Their brains are no longer mammalian.

43. This passage is primarily about
    (A) prehensile organs.
    (B) intelligence and the porpoise.
    (C) sea life.
    (D) land animals.

44. The author suggests that our failure to understand the
    intelligence of the porpoise is due to
    (A) a lack of equipment.
    (B) our inferiority.
    (C) a lack of a common language.
    (D) our inclination to judge other life by our own
        standards.

　　Whereas George Gershwin worked in the glare of critical
and commercial success, Charles Ives worked in obscurity.
Though Ives created the bulk of his output before Gershwin
appeared on the scene, his music was almost completely
neglected until he was "rediscovered" in the 1940s and
1950s. He earned his livelihood, for most of his adult
life, in the insurance business and created some of the most
striking examples of American music in his spare time.
Ives's composing was restricted to weekends, holidays,
vacations, and long evenings. Ives, himself, was quite
philosophic about this and never considered his business
career a handicap to artistic production. On the contrary,
he regarded his music and the business in which he earned
his livelihood as complementary activities.

　　His raw material for all of his work was the ordinary
musical life of a small New England town. In evolving his
highly individualistic musical language, Ives used popular
dance hall tunes, fragments of hymns and patriotic anthems,
brass band marches, country dances, and songs--which he
integrated into works of enormous complexity.

But Ives's music was hardly popular with the broad public at the time it was written. The composer found it all but impossible to get his music performed. For example, Ives's Second Symphony, which he worked on between 1897 and 1902, received its first performance in 1951 when it was played by the Philharmonic-Symphony Orchestra of New York, under Leonard Bernstein. His Third Symphony, completed in 1911, was first performed in 1945. The Fourth Symphony, written between 1910 and 1916, received its premiere in 1965 under the direction of Leopold Stokowski. Not until he was awarded the Pulitzer Prize for his Third Symphony, in 1947, did Charles Ives receive any degree of recognition for his work.

45. Charles Ives's success in music could be called unusual because he
   (A) had a physical handicap.
   (B) was trained to be a philosopher.
   (C) did not devote his entire career to music.
   (D) did not have much financial backing.

46. According to the passage, how did Ives feel about the business and musical sides of his life?
   (A) They lent support to each other.
   (B) They each satisfied his need for recognition.
   (C) They represented a conflict in his nature.
   (D) They took too much of his time.

47. It can be inferred that all of the following were sources of inspiration for Ives in his early career except
   (A) church music.
   (B) folk tunes.
   (C) Gershwin's compositions.
   (D) patriotic songs.

48. Ives's Third Symphony was first performed in the
   (A) late nineteenth century.
   (B) first decade of the twentieth century.
   (C) mid-nineteen forties.
   (D) mid-nineteen sixties.

49. Who conducted the first performance of Ives's Fourth
    Symphony?
    (A) Pulitzer
    (B) Bernstein
    (C) Gershwin
    (D) Stokowski

50. It can be inferred from the passage that Ives's
    symphonies were NOT popular with the general public
    for many years because they were
    (A) heard by very few people.
    (B) based on nonclassical themes.
    (C) inferior to Gershwin's music.
    (D) composed in his spare time.

IV. Composition: 20%

    Write a well-organized and fully-developed composition
    on the topic "How to Become a Successful Communicator".

國立中興大學八十三學年度
碩士班研究生入學考試英文試題詳解

I. 字彙：10％

1. (B) (A) inquire〔ɪn'kwaɪr〕*v.*詢問 (B) ***acquire***〔ə'kwaɪr〕*v.*獲得
   (C) request〔rɪ'kwɛst〕*v.*請求 (D) require〔rɪ'kwaɪr〕*v.*需要

2. (A) (A) ***adapt***〔ə'dæpt〕*v.*使適應 (B) adopt〔ə'dɑpt〕*v.*收養
   (C) adjure〔ə'dʒʊr〕*v.*命令；懇請
   (D) addict〔ə'dɪkt〕*v.*使沈溺於
   immigrant〔'ɪməgrənt〕*n.*移民

3. (C) (A) allusion〔ə'luʒən〕*n.*暗示
   (B) delusion〔dɪ'luʒən〕*n.*欺騙
   (C) ***illusion***〔ɪ'luʒən〕*n.*幻影；幻想
   (D) derision〔dɪ'rɪʒən〕*n.*嘲笑
   optical〔'ɑptɪkḷ〕*adj.*視覺的

4. (A) (A) ***deliberate***〔dɪ'lɪbə‚ret〕*v.*慎重考慮
   (B) elaborate〔ɪ'læbə‚ret〕*v.*用心做
   (C) illustrate〔'ɪləstret〕*v.*舉例說明
   (D) demonstrate〔'dɛmən‚stret〕*v.*證明
   jury〔'dʒʊrɪ〕*n.*陪審團

5. (B) (A) inspect〔ɪn'spɛkt〕*v.*檢查
   (B) ***invest***〔ɪn'vɛst〕*v.*投資
   (C) calculate〔'kælkjə‚let〕*v.*計算
   (D) insinuate〔ɪn'sɪnjʊ‚et〕*v.*暗示
   stock〔stɑk〕*n.*股票

6. (C) (A) religion〔rɪ'lɪdʒən〕*n.*宗教 (B) relation〔rɪ'leʃən〕*n.*關係
   (C) ***relative***〔'rɛlətɪv〕*n.*親戚 (D) regular〔'rɛgjələ〕*n.*老主顧

7. (B) (A) murder〔'mɝdɚ〕*n.* 謀殺　(B) *arson*〔'ɑrsn̩〕*n.* 縱火
(C) intrigue〔ɪn'trig〕*n.* 陰謀　(D) war〔wɔr〕*n.* 戰爭
claim〔klem〕*v.* 要求；（意外）奪去（生命）
suspect〔sə'spɛkt〕*v.* 懷疑

8. (D) (A) star〔stɑr〕*n.* 星星
(B) planet〔'plænɪt〕*n.* 行星
(C) supernova〔,supɚ'novə〕*n.* 超級新星
(D) *galaxy*〔'gæləksɪ〕*n.* 銀河
solar system 太陽系　　*the Milky Way* 銀河

9. (A) (A) *available*〔ə'veləbl̩〕*adj.* 可找得到的
(B) valuable〔'væljuəbl̩〕*adj.* 有價值的
(C) avoidable〔ə'vɔɪdəbl̩〕*adj.* 可避免的
(D) vulnerable〔'vʌlnərəbl̩〕*adj.* 易受傷害的

10. (A) (A) *dispute*〔dɪ'spjut〕*v.* 爭論
(B) dispel〔dɪ'spɛl〕*v.* 驅散
(C) disrupt〔dɪs'rʌpt〕*v.* 使分裂
(D) distribute〔dɪ'strɪbjut〕*v.* 分配

11. (D) (A) preparation〔,prɛpə'reʃən〕*n.* 準備
(B) preposition〔,prɛpə'zɪʃən〕*n.* 介系詞
(C) disposition〔,dɪspə'zɪʃən〕*n.* 配置
(D) *proportion*〔prə'porʃən〕*n.* 比例
in proportion to～ 與～成比例

12. (B) (A) resist〔rɪ'zɪst〕*v.* 抵抗　(B) *persist*〔pɚ'sɪst〕*v.* 持續
(C) insist〔ɪn'sɪst〕*v.* 堅持　(D) assist〔ə'sɪst〕*v.* 幫助

13. (D) (A) framework〔'frem,wɝk〕*n.* 骨架
(B) fraternity〔frə'tɝnətɪ〕*n.* 博愛
(C) freedom〔'fridəm〕*n.* 自由
(D) *franchise*〔'fræntʃaɪz〕*n.* 參政權

14.（ **C** ）(A) disputable〔dɪ'spjutəbl̩〕 *adj.* 易引起爭論的
　　　　　(B) respectable〔rɪ'spɛktəbl̩〕 *adj.* 可敬的
　　　　　(C) ***disposable***〔dɪ'spozəbl̩〕 *adj.* 用後即可丟棄的
　　　　　(D) responsible〔rɪ'spɑsəbl̩〕 *adj.* 負責任的

15.（ **A** ）(A) ***defy***〔dɪ'faɪ〕 *v.* 不顧　　(B) delay〔dɪ'le〕 *v.* 延緩
　　　　　(C) destroy〔dɪ'strɔɪ〕 *v.* 破壞　(D) differ〔'dɪfɚ〕 *v.* 不同

16.（ **C** ）(A) junction〔'dʒʌŋkʃən〕 *n.* 連接 (B) function〔'fʌŋkʃən〕 *n.* 功能
　　　　　(C) ***juncture***〔'dʒʌŋktʃɚ〕 *n.* 時機 (D) structure〔'strʌktʃɚ〕 *n.* 構造

17.（ **C** ）(A) provoke〔prə'vok〕 *v.* 激怒　(B) evoke〔ɪ'vok〕 *v.* 喚起
　　　　　(C) ***invoke***〔ɪn'vok〕 *v.* 求助於 (D) involve〔ɪn'vɑlv〕 *v.* 牽涉在內

18.（ **A** ）(A) ***edible***〔'ɛdəbl̩〕 *adj.* 可食的
　　　　　(B) portable〔'portəbl̩〕 *adj.* 可攜帶的
　　　　　(C) drinkable〔'drɪŋkəbl̩〕 *adj.* 可飲用的
　　　　　(D) equable〔'ikwəbl̩〕 *adj.* 一致的；穩定的

19.（ **B** ）(A) harass〔hə'ræs〕 *v.* 騷擾
　　　　　(B) ***harbour***〔'hɑrbɚ〕 *v.* 心懷～
　　　　　(C) harness〔'hɑrnɪs〕 *v.* 束以馬具
　　　　　(D) harangue〔hə'ræŋ〕 *v.* 大聲疾呼

20.（ **B** ）(A) beneficially〔,bɛnə'fɪʃəlɪ〕 *adv.* 有益地
　　　　　(B) ***benevolently***〔bə'nɛvələntlɪ〕 *adv.* 仁慈地
　　　　　(C) belovedly〔bɪ'lʌvɪdlɪ〕 *adv.* 親愛地
　　　　　(D) belligerently〔bə'lɪdʒərəntlɪ〕 *adv.* 好戰地

Ⅱ. 文法與修辭：30％
(1) 文法

21.（ **C** ）… training required of a physicist … 是由… training which
　　　　is required of a physicist 簡化而來。

22.（ B ）前後主詞不同不能省略，故(A)(D)均不合。而依句意，爲過去式，
　　　　選(B)。

23.（ A ）依句意，表示連續動作，且主詞相同可省略，故選(A)。而(B)搭乘
　　　　交通工具要用主動，(D) and 爲對等連接詞，所連接之動詞時態要
　　　　一致，故皆不合。

24.（ C ）表「與現在事實相反的假設」，if 子句中 Be 動詞一律用 were。

25.（ D ）依句意，爲祈使命令句，選(D) give it，主詞 you 可省略。

26.（ C ）依句意，選(C)，neither … nor ～「既不…，也不～」，連接兩個
　　　　形容詞 hurt 與 discouraged。

27.（ C ）依句意，其重點是在於兩個不同的觀念，故第二個介詞不予省略，
　　　　選(C)。

(2) 挑錯

28.（ D ）*self-evident* → ***self-evidently***　修飾形容詞 true，應用副詞。

29.（ D ）*pursue* → ***pursuit***　定冠詞 the 應接名詞。

30.（ B ）*what* → ***that***　　all　that = what，what 爲複合關代，不需先行詞。

31.（ D ）*governed* → ***the governed***　依句意，of 須接名詞。而形容詞（過
　　　　去分詞）前面須加定冠詞 the，才可當名詞用，表「被統治者」。

32.（ C ）*good* → ***the good***　　*to the good* 有益；有好處

33.（ C ）*bright* → ***brighter***　形容詞比較級＋ still 表「更～」。

34.（ C ）*permit* → ***permitting***　依句意，兩動詞間無連接詞，第二個動
　　　　詞須改爲現在分詞。
　　　　abolish〔ə'bɑlɪʃ〕*v.* 廢止　　penalty〔'pɛnəltɪ〕*n.* 處罰
　　　　capital〔'kæpətl〕*adj.* 可處死刑的　　parole〔pə'rol〕*n.* 假釋

35.（ B ）*our to be* → ***our being***　所有格＋動名詞＝主詞＋動詞，所以
　　　　and our being political = and that we are political … 。
　　　　gregarious〔grɪ'gɛrɪəs〕*adj.* 群居的

Ⅲ. 閱讀測驗：30％

【譯文】

　　昨晚在羅西戲院上映的「淑女朋友」，由於其過時的劇本以及沒有把握的人物，令人忍不住為它草率的訴求而感到奇怪。一個在訴求的塑造及表現很糟糕的人，似乎很快就會跌落至谷底。

　　雖然影片一心想造成兩名年輕女子——蘇珊‧溫布拉特和安‧穆羅的個性及其對職業生涯的選擇之強烈對比，她們兩人一開始看起來好像是住在紐約西北邊公寓裏的室友，而劇本僅將兩個女孩塑造成點頭之交，根本不可能讓她們變得像朋友般，如果是個性上相互衝突的朋友，就注定很典型地，兩人到最後分道揚鑣。

　　有些劇作家有足夠的天賦或經驗，能夠經由巧妙的最少之說明及描述，而表現出極豐富的內涵。維基‧龐德並沒有那種罕見的技巧，而導演克勞迪亞‧史考特，並未表現出足夠的活力與智謀去遮掩龐德破綻百出的作品。

【答案】

| 36.（ B ） | 37.（ C ） | 38.（ C ） | 39.（ D ） |

【註】

threadbare〔'θrɛd,bɛr〕adj. 陳腐的
screenplay〔'skrin,ple〕n. 電影劇本
tentative〔'tɛntətɪv〕adj. 試驗性的　　sloppy〔'slɑpɪ〕adj. 草率的
wretchedly〔'rɛtʃɪdlɪ〕adv. 惡劣地　　aspire〔ə'spaɪr〕v. 渴望
barely〔'bɛrlɪ〕adv. 僅僅　　script〔skrɪpt〕n. 脚本
nodding acquaintance 點頭之交　　**let alone** 更不用說
diverge〔daɪ'vɝdʒ〕v. 分歧　　exemplary〔ɪg'zɛmpləɪ〕adj. 可為模範的
screenwriter〔'skrin,raɪtɚ〕n. 劇作家　　flair〔flɛr〕n. 天賦
exposition〔,ɛkspə'zɪʃən〕n. 說明　　finesse〔fə'nɛs〕n. 技巧
demonstrate〔'dɛmən,stret〕v. 表現出
dash〔dæʃ〕n. 活力
resourcefulness〔rɪ'sorsfəlnɪs〕n. 智謀
patchy〔'pætʃɪ〕adj. 破綻百出的；拼湊的

【譯文】

　　大多數有智力的陸上動物，都具有可用以盤捲或握持的器官，讓他們去探索周遭環境——像是人類及與其同屬的人猿的手，還有大象敏感又愛探索的鼻子。而海豚令人驚奇的事情之一是，在牠高等的腦部，並沒有任何形式的操控器官。然而，海豚有著極不尋常的測距能力，這包括某種利用回音來探測水深的能力。或許這種靈敏的感官——遠比任何人類人為所能發明出來的東西都要來得正確——讓海豚對他的水底環境能有更多的認識，這似乎是超乎我們原本所想像的。人類認為智力適用於所有的東西。手和工具對我們來說，是我們智力成就之無意識的象徵。我們很難想像還有另一種孤獨的、幾乎是不成形的智力，漂浮在大海盪漾的綠色仙境中——一種可能和人類智力很接近，或已足堪匹敵的智力，但是牠們並沒有手來寫字、來建立、傳遞知識，或是在間不容髮的一刻去改變行星的表面。然而，在同時，也有跡象顯示，這是一種溫暖、友善，而且又熱心的智力，能夠去協助受傷的同伴，並拯救快淹死的同伴。當海豚哺乳類的頭腦還很小而且不發達的時候，牠們便離開了陸地。雖然沒有靈敏的手指供牠們去探險，獲得刺激，然而這些了不起的海上哺乳動物選擇了一條不同的路邁向高等智力。隱藏在他們光滑身體下的，是一部令人注目的精巧儀器，其成因則是個全然的謎。就彷彿人和海豚是某個偉大眼睛的一部分，該眼睛渴望向外看到永恆，又渴望向內看到大海的心——那豐富的本質就如同具有創造力而且奇特生命的心靈。

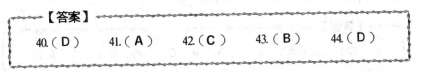

【答案】

40.（ D ）　　41.（ A ）　　42.（ C ）　　43.（ B ）　　44.（ D ）

【註】

prehensile〔prɪˈhɛnsɪl〕 *adj.* 能握住或盤住的
anthropoid〔ˈænθrəpɔɪd〕 *adj.* 似人類的　　porpoise〔ˈpɔrpəs〕 *n.* 海豚
visualize〔ˈvɪʒʊəlˌaɪz〕 *v.* 想像　　*a hairsbreadth* 間不容髮之際
mammalian〔mæˈmelɪən〕 *adj.* 哺乳類的
agile〔ˈædʒɪl〕 *adj.* 敏捷的　　sleek〔slik〕 *adj.* 光滑的
enigma〔ɪˈnɪgmə〕 *n.* 謎　　eternity〔ɪˈtɜnətɪ〕 *n.* 永恆
entity〔ˈɛntətɪ〕 *n.* 實體　　swarming〔ˈswɔrmɪŋ〕 *adj.* 成群的；擁擠的
grotesque〔groˈtɛsk〕 *adj.* 古怪的

【譯文】

當喬治‧葛希文在評論及商業方面都十分成功，而且引人注目地創作時，查爾斯‧艾伍茲卻正没没無聞地創作著。雖然艾伍茲在葛希文出現前曾創作了大量作品，但直到一九四〇及一九五〇年代被重新發掘前，艾伍茲的音樂幾乎完全被忽視。就其大部分成長以後的生活而言，艾伍茲都是在保險業中營生，並於閒暇時創作了美國音樂最引人注目的幾首作品。艾伍茲只在週末、節日、假期及漫長的夜晚才作曲。艾伍茲本人對此相當地達觀，從不認為他的商界事業會是藝術創作的障礙。相反地，艾伍茲認為他的音樂和他謀生的事業是相輔相成的。

新英格蘭小鎮的平凡音樂生活，是艾伍茲全部作品的原始資料。在開展艾伍茲高度個人主義的音樂語言中，使用了流行的舞廳曲調，片斷的聖歌及愛國歌曲、銅管樂隊進行曲、鄉村舞曲與歌曲——他將這些融入極為複雜的作品中。

但是艾伍茲的音樂在完成之時，並不太受廣大群眾的歡迎。這位作曲家發現，幾乎無法讓他的音樂得以被演奏。比如說，艾伍茲於一八九七至一九〇二年間所致力完成的第二號交響曲，一九五一年才首次被由連納德‧貝恩斯坦所指揮的紐約愛樂交響樂團演奏出來。艾伍茲的第三號交響曲，於一九一一年完成，一九四五年方被首度演奏。第四號交響曲，寫於一九一〇至一九一六年間，於一九六五年在利奧波德‧斯多考夫斯基的指揮之下，才獲得首度公演。直到於一九四七年因第三號交響曲獲頒普立茲獎之後，查爾斯‧艾伍茲的作品才受到肯定。

【答案】

45.（ C ）　46.（ A ）　47.（ C ）　48.（ C ）　49.（ D ）　50.（ A ）

【註】

glare〔glɛr〕*n.* 強光；引人注目　　obscurity〔əbˋskjʊrətɪ〕*n.* 没没無聞

bulk〔bʌlk〕*n.* 大量　　complementary〔͵kɑmpləˋmɛntərɪ〕*adj.* 互補的

evolve〔ɪˋvɑlv〕*v.* 開展　　fragment〔ˋfrægmənt〕*n.* 片斷

hymn〔hɪm〕*n.* 讚美詩　　patriotic〔͵petrɪˋɑtɪk〕*adj.* 愛國的

anthem〔ˋænθəm〕*n.* 頌歌　　***brass band*** 銅管樂隊

philharmonic〔͵fɪləˋmɑnɪk〕*adj.* 愛好音樂的

premiere〔prɪˋmɪr〕*n.* 首次公演

Ⅳ. 作文：20％

How to Become a Successful Communicator

Most people, even children, are good communicators in subjects that they are very familiar with and hence confident about. For example, children are almost always capable of ordering exactly what food they want in a restaurant. However, a young child would often be quite lost when it came to discussing a topic such as God or heart surgery. So if we lack knowledge or experience of a thing or haven't thought about it much, we will have problems talking about it. In such a situation, one would probably also lack confidence, which would create a further barrier to communication. Some subjects that our society regards as taboo, for example, sex, may also be difficult to talk about, simply because one doesn't have much experience in talking about it. Similarly, many people are nervous talking about something they know well in front of a large crowd. In most cases, experience will allow people to become more confident.

So, in most situations, we will be good communicators if we know what we are talking about, and we feel confident and comfortable about communicating.

However, there are other factors, too. For example, some people write essays that are very boring or use words and sentences which are not easy to comprehend. In such cases, the key is knowing and understanding other people. You must, through experience, learn how to keep people interested and speak in words they can understand.

私立淡江大學八十三學年度
碩士班研究生入學考試英文試題

I. Cloze Test: 20%
Choose the best answer to fill in the blank.

Samoan parents do not___1___anything from their children; they tell them no fairy tales about the birth of
babies___2___do they pack them off to a relative until after
a funeral. They believe quite literally that children should
be seen but not heard, should be present but make no comments, should learn the important facts of life from careful
___3___, not from random, groping experimentation. And the
children grow up,___4___with the rhythm of life and death,
accepting life as___5___and as unrebelliously as do their
parents.

1. (A) prevent   (B) hide
   (C) take   (D) ask

2. (A) and   (B) or
   (C) nor   (D) so

3. (A) observation   (B) organization
   (C) imagination   (D) education

4. (A) wiser   (B) friendly
   (C) pleased   (D) acquainted

5. (A) interesting   (B) uneasy
   (C) simply   (D) sad

There were, of course, critics who called Norman Rockwell
the Lawerence Welk of the art world,___6___that bubbles
floated off the ends of his brushes and___7___his work was
sticky with sweetness. There were others who___8___him,
saying that he was the artist___9___con artists. But now

they can both be heard calling him an artistic ___10___ to our
past, a visual historian.

6. (A) insisting　　　　　　(B) insist
   (C) insisted　　　　　　 (D) to insist

7. (A) also　　　　　　　　(B) about
   (C) that　　　　　　　　(D) as

8. (A) misunderstood　　　　(B) adored
   (C) irritated　　　　　　(D) despised

9. (A) in　　　　　　　　　(B) of
   (C) among　　　　　　　 (D) above

10. (A) success　　　　　　 (B) failure
    (C) genius　　　　　　　(D) link

　　　Individual reactions differ. We do not know yet whether
people who are by ___11___ early risers adjust at rates different from late-night, late-morning types. Experience and
some ___12___ evidence indicate that older people ___13___ more
from jet lag than the young. One interesting suggestion is
that people who ___14___ relatively isolated on arrival, with
few time cues and little physical activity, seem to take
longer to adjust than those who travel in groups, go outdoors more, and get more social stimulus. Research in this
area is still patchy, but social cues and influences are
generally thought to be important in ___15___ human circadian
rhythms.

11. (A) degree　　　　　　　(B) part
    (C) nature　　　　　　　(D) interest

12. (A) obvious　　　　　　 (B) experimental
    (C) important　　　　　 (D) surprising

13. (A) suffer　　　　　　　(B) enjoy
    (C) benefit　　　　　　 (D) learn

14. (A) like　　　　　　　　(B) hate
    (C) delay　　　　　　　 (D) stay

15. (A) putting   (B) having
    (C) setting   (D) getting

Math anxiety is more___16___among women. This should not be too startling. For years, "Don't bother your pretty head with numbers, "has been the all too common attitude toward women's___17___with mathematical problems. And we are all familiar with the___18___of the bungling housewife who has to get her husband to___19___the checkbook, even though that afternoon she has probably gone through elaborate mental calculations while shopping at the supermarket.

Yet studies show that girls generally do better at math than do boys up through elementary school, and it is___20___ when they reach junior high that their performance begins to slip. By high school, most girls are taking far fewer math courses than are boys.

16. (A) unexpected   (B) harmful
    (C) incredible   (D) prevalent

17. (A) struggle   (B) do
    (C) IQ   (D) dealing

18. (A) impression   (B) fact
    (C) studipity   (D) stereotype

19. (A) check   (B) balance
    (C) calculate   (D) write

20. (A) until   (B) just
    (C) only   (D) approximately

II. Vocabulary: 20%

Each of the following sentences has a word or phrase underlined. Below each sentence are four other words or phrases. Choose the letter of the word or phrase that keeps the meaning of the original sentence.

21. Despite name-calling from friends, Steve left a party
    when kids headed for the bedrooms.
    (A) calling somebody's name
    (B) attacking somebody by using abusive names
    (C) forgetting somebody's name
    (D) using a fake name

22. There is a lot of truth in the aphorism, "Morals are
    caught, not taught."
    (A) a wise saying
    (B) a traditional custom
    (C) a special message
    (D) a critical event

23. Disrespect to parents or siblings shouldn't be part of
    any loving home.
    (A) relatives   (B) grandparents
    (C) neighbors   (D) brothers and sisters

24. Chronic complainers bemoan their jobs, marriages or life
    in general.
    (A) habitual   (B) serious
    (C) unhappy   (D) depressed

25. Commitment and vision form a momentum of their own,
    which brings about a successful conclusion.
    (A) a critical moment
    (B) a sense of value
    (C) the force gained by the movement or development of
        events
    (D) an ability of analysis and synthesis

26. Because of their important place in the family and in
    the community, the aged retain a feeling of individual
    self worth and importance.
    (A) respect   (B) enjoy
    (C) possess   (D) emphasize

27. Suddenly on that mountain road, its time and my need
    had converged.
    (A) conflicted
    (B) come together towards the same point
    (C) departed
    (D) appeared

28. All human rights must be <u>observed</u>.
    (A) seen and noticed
    (B) acted in accordance with law or custom
    (C) respected
    (D) valued

29. Once in a lifetime, perhaps, one escapes the actual
    <u>confines</u> of the flesh.
    (A) limits   (B) death
    (C) corruption   (D) strength

30. He has <u>exquisite</u> taste in music.
    (A) old and unique   (B) terrible and poor
    (C) sensitive and delicate (D) long and lasting

31. Peking admitted that the Qiando Lake tragedy was
    "robbery, murder, and <u>arson</u>."
    (A) the crime of forcing people to kill
    (B) the crime of deceiving people to buy things
    (C) the crime of frightening people to obey orders
    (D) the crime of setting fire to property

32. An interministerial <u>ad hoc</u> committee passed a nine-point
    plan on April 20, 1994 to enhance wildlife conservation
    on Taiwan.
    (A) big
    (B) arranged for a special purpose
    (C) national
    (D) pre-arranged for common affairs

33. The well-born young Athenians who gathered around
    Socrates found it quite <u>paradoxical</u> that their hero was
    so intelligent, so brave, so honorable, so deductive and
    so ugly.
    (A) absolutely crazy
    (B) definitely impossible
    (C) seemingly impossible but truthful
    (D) obvious

34. What is <u>lamentable</u> is that beauty is the only form of
    power that most women are encouraged to seek.
    (A) very unsatisfactory
    (B) very surprising
    (C) relatively true
    (D) commonly accepted

35. There seems to be a <u>vogue</u> for Chinese food at present.
(A) big change
(B) popular fashion that does not last long time
(C) mixture of foreign flavours
(D) declination of popularity

36. The abolition of sex roles and the complete economic independence of women would <u>undermine</u> both a family's authority and its financial structure.
(A) remove support for
(B) strengthen
(C) increase difficulty for
(D) slow down

37. It's too early to <u>assess</u> the effects of the new legislation.
(A) predict   (B) give up
(C) oppose   (D) judge

38. Any increase in sexual freedom for women in the period 1930-60 is probably due less to social change than to better technology in the manufacture of contraceptive devices and thei‧ <u>proliferation</u>.
(A) side effect   (B) influence
(C) rapid increase   (D) variety

39. We still use this machine though it is <u>obsolete</u>.
(A) expensive   (B) old
(C) borrowed   (D) not productive

40. Economics and politics are best studied together as the two subjects <u>overlap</u>.
(A) become more and more important
(B) are totally different
(C) partly cover the same material
(D) make most money

III. Reading Comprehension: 30%

Each passage below is followed by questions based on its content. Answer all questions following a passage on the basis of what is stated or implied in that passage.

During the '50s, each TV season offered 39 weeks of new shows, and 13 weeks of repeats. Slowly, the ratio has

reversed. The ultimate goal may be a one-week season, 50
week of repeats, and one week off for good behaviour.

41. The central idea of this passage is that
    (A) television shows are being repeated more often than
        ever.
    (B) shows must be repeated to allow time to prepare new
        shows.
    (C) repeated shows are used to gain good ideas for new
        shows.
    (D) repeating shows cuts down costs.

42. When did the change in television that the passage
    describes take place?
    (A) during the past year
    (B) only very recently
    (C) over a period of time
    (D) several years ago

43. What does the writer most probably think of the situa-
    tion in television that he or she is telling us about?
    (A) It is better than it was before.
    (B) It cannot be helped.
    (C) It may soon improve.
    (D) It is becoming ridiculous.

    The very success of communications satellite systems
has raised widespread concern about their future. Some countries are already using satellites for domestic communications in place of conventional telephone lines on land.
Although this technique is extremely useful for linking
widely scattered villages in remote or mountainous regions,
in heavily built-up areas where extensive telephone and
telegraph systems already exist, domestic satellites (or
"domsats") are seen by the land-line networks as unfair
competition. Despite such opposition, domsats are gaining
support from many businesses and public interest groups in
the United States and seem likely to be more widely utilized
in the future.

44. The passage mentions which of the following as a major
    advantage of domsats?
    (A) They are inexpensive to operate.
    (B) They easily connect distant points.
    (C) They can be directed by remote control.
    (D) They can be built to be very light.

45. According to the passage, the use of domsats is
    especially valuable for which of the following?
    (A) mountainous areas
    (B) busy cities
    (C) small countries
    (D) private businesses

46. Who objects to the use of domsats?
    (A) managers of international business groups
    (B) people in small villages
    (C) operators of conventional communications systems
    (D) large public interest groups

47. According to the passage, future United States domsats
    will probably
    (A) be produced competitively.
    (B) carry telephone messages only.
    (C) become a government monopoly.
    (D) increase in use.

Decades before the American Revolution of 1776, Jesse
Fish, a native New Yorker, retreated to an island off St.
Augustine, Florida, to escape an unpleasant family situation.
In time he became Florida's first orange baron and oranges
were in great demand in London throughout the 1770s. The
English found them juicy and sweet and preferred them to
other varieties, even though they had thin skins and were
hard to peel.

There would probably have been some other successful
commercial growers before Fish if Florida had not been under
Spanish rule for some two hundred years. Columbus first
brought seeds for citrus trees to the New World and planted
them in the Antilles. But it was most likely Ponce de Leon
who introduced oranges to the North American continent when

he discovered Florida in 1513. For a time, each Spanish
sailor on a ship bound for America was required by law to
carry one hundred seeds with him. Later, because seeds
tended to dry out, all Spanish ships were required to carry
young orange trees. The Spaniards planted citrus trees only
for medical purposes, however. They saw no need to start
commercial groves because oranges were so abundant in Spain.

48. What is the main topic of the passage?
    (A) the role of Florida in the American Revolution
    (B) the discovery of Florida by Ponce de Leon in 1513
    (C) the history of the cultivation of oranges in Florida
    (D) the popularity of Florida oranges in London in
        1770s

49. Jesse Fish came from
    (A) London.   (B) St. Augustine.
    (C) the Antilles.   (D) New York.

50. Jesse Fish went to Forida to
    (A) grow oranges commercially.
    (B) buy an island off St. Augustine.
    (C) get away from his family.
    (D) work for the British government.

51. Londoners liked the oranges grown by Jesse Fish because
    they
    (A) had a lot of juice.
    (B) were not too sweet.
    (C) were not hard to peel.
    (D) had thin skins.

52. Oranges were most probably introduced to Florida by
    (A) Jesse Fish.   (B) Ponce de Leon.
    (C) Columbus.   (D) British sailors.

53. According to the passage, Spanish vessels began to
    bring orange tree seedlings to North American when
    (A) the United States agricultural laws were revised.
    (B) ambitious sailors began to smuggle seeds.
    (C) doctors reported a lack of medical supplies.
    (D) authorities realized that seeds did not travel
        well.

54. According to the passage, Florida oranges were valued by the Spanish primarily
(A) as a medium of exchange.
(B) for their unusual seeds.
(C) for their medical use.
(D) as a source of food for sailors.

55. The Spaniards did not grow oranges commercially in the New World because
(A) oranges tended to dry out during shipping.
(B) Florida oranges were very small.
(C) there was no great demand for oranges in Europe.
(D) oranges were plentiful in their home country.

IV. Composition: 30%

Choose only ONE of the two topics listed below and state in English your own ideas or arguments about it in several paragraphs.

Topic 1: Corporal (Physical) Punishment in Schools

Topic 2: Sexual Harassment on Campus

私立淡江大學八十三學年度
碩士班研究生入學考試英文試題詳解

Ⅰ. 克漏字：20％

【譯文】

　　薩摩亞人的父母不會對他們的子女隱瞞任何事情；他們不對子女說有關嬰兒出生的神話故事，也不會把子女打發到親戚那兒去直到葬禮結束。薩摩亞人的父母認為孩子們應該在身邊但要少說話，應該在場但不發表意見，應該經由仔細的觀察知道人生的重要事實，而非經由隨便的、摸索性的實驗。等到孩子們長大，已瞭解人生中生與死之間的規律，就會像他們父母般純然且不反抗地接受人生。

【註】

fairy tale 神話故事　　**pack off** 打發走

literally〔ˈlɪtərəlɪ〕*adv.* 完全　　random〔ˈrændəm〕*adj.* 隨便的

grope〔grop〕*v.* 摸索　　unrebelliously〔ˌʌnrɪˈbɛlɪəslɪ〕*adv.* 不反抗地

1. (B) 依句意，應選(B) **hide** *v.* 隱瞞。

2. (C) **nor** 也不～

3. (A) 依句意，應選(A) **observation**〔ˌɑbzəˈveʃən〕*n.* 觀察。而(B) organization〔ˌɔrgənaɪˈzeʃən〕*n.* 組織，(C) imagination〔ɪˌmædʒəˈneʃən〕*n.* 想像，(D) education〔ˌɛdʒəˈkeʃən〕*n.* 教育，均不合句意。

4. (D) **be acquainted with** ～ 熟知

5. (C) 空格應填入副詞修飾動詞 accept，故選(C) **simply** *adv.* 純然地。

【譯文】

　　當然有一些評論家會稱諾曼·羅克維爾為美術界的勞倫斯·維耳克，強調說泡沫從諾曼畫筆的末端漂浮出來，而且他的作品還黏著甜味。也有其它的評論家輕視諾曼，說他是欺世盜名的藝術家之一。但是現在可以聽見兩派評論家都稱諾曼是一位能銜接我們過去的藝術家，也就是一位視覺的歷史學家。

【註】

sticky〔'stɪkɪ〕*adj.* 黏的　　visual〔'vɪʒʊəl〕*adj.* 視覺的
con〔kɑn〕*adj.* 詐欺的

6.（**A**）兩個句子中沒有連接詞，第二個動詞須改為現在分詞，選(A)
　　　insisting。insist〔ɪn'sɪst〕*v.* 堅持

7.（**C**）對等連接詞 and 連接兩個由 that 所引導的名詞子句，作為
　　　insisting 的受詞，故選(C) that。

8.（**D**）依句意，應選(D) *despise*〔dɪ'spaɪz〕*v.* 輕視。而(A) misunder-
　　　stand〔'mɪsʌndə'stænd〕*v.* 誤解，(B) adore〔ə'dor〕*v.* 崇拜，
　　　(C) irritate〔'ɪrə,tet〕*v.* 激怒，均不合句意。

9.（**C**）依句意，應選(C) among　在…之中。

10.（**D**）依句意，應選(D) *link*〔lɪnk〕*n.* 連結。而(A) success 成功，(B)
　　　failure 失敗，(C) genius 天才，均不合句意。

【譯文】

　　每一個人的反應都不一樣。我們還不知道是否生來就早起的人，對時間的調適和晚睡晚起型的人不同。經驗及一些實驗的證據顯示，老年人比年輕人更會為時差所苦。一種有趣的說法是，那些如果在搭機飛行直到抵達之期間，幾乎都是孤單一人的，沒什麼時間概念，身體也不太運動的人，比起那些團體出遊，常到戶外，得到較多社會外界刺激的人，似乎得花更多的時間去調適。這一方面的研究似乎仍不夠完整，不過一般認為，社會的刺激和影響在人類調適生理節奏方面是很重要的。

【註】

rate〔ret〕*n.* 比例；速度　　*jet lag* 時差感；飛行時差反應
isolated〔'aɪsḷ,etd〕*adj.* 孤立的　　cue〔kju〕*n.* 線索；暗示
stimulus〔'stɪmjələs〕*n.* 刺激（物）　　patchy〔'pætʃɪ〕*adj.* 雜湊的
circadian〔sɜ'kedɪən〕*adj.* 以 24 小時為周期的
circadian rhythm 生理節奏

11.（ **C** ）　*by nature* 天生地

12.（ **B** ）　*experimental*〔ɪkˏspɛrəˈmɛntḷ〕*adj.* 實驗的

13.（ **A** ）　*suffer*〔ˈsʌfɚ〕*v.* 受苦　(C) benefit〔ˈbɛnəˏfɪt〕*v.* 獲益

14.（ **D** ）　*stay* *v.* 保持　(C) delay〔dɪˈle〕*v.* 延遲

15.（ **C** ）　依句意，應選(C) setting。set〔sɛt〕*v.* 調整

【譯文】

　　數學焦慮症在女性中較爲普遍。這應該是不會讓人太吃驚的。多年來，「不要讓數學困擾妳美麗的頭腦」是對於女人和數學問題奮戰之極爲普遍的態度。我們都非常熟悉一種刻板形象，一個笨手笨脚的家庭主婦，必須要她先生結算出支票簿的收支餘額，即使是當天下午她可能在逛超級市場的時候，已經先在心裡費力地算過了。

　　然而研究顯示，一般說來，直到唸完小學時，女生的數學成績要比男生好，只有當上了國中以後，女生在數學方面的表現才開始下滑。到了高中時，大部分的女生修的數學課都比男生少。

【註】

anxiety〔æŋˈzaɪətɪ〕*n.* 憂慮　　startling〔ˈstɑrtlɪŋ〕*adj.* 令人驚訝的
all too 太過於　　bungling〔ˈbʌŋglɪŋ〕*adj.* 笨拙的
checkbook〔ˈtʃɛkˏbʊk〕*n.* 支票簿
elaborate〔ɪˈlæbərɪt〕*adj.* 精心的　　slip〔slɪp〕*v.* 下滑

16.（ **D** ）　依句意，應選(D) prevalent〔ˈprɛvələnt〕*adj.* 普遍的。(A)料想不到的，(B)有害的，(C) incredible〔ɪnˈkrɛdəbḷ〕*adj.* 令人難以置信的，皆不合句意。

17.（ **A** ）　struggle〔ˈstrʌgḷ〕*n.* 奮鬥

18.（ **D** ）　stereotype〔ˈstɛrɪəˏtaɪp〕*n.* 刻板印象

19.（ **B** ）　balance〔ˈbæləns〕*v.* 結算；核算（帳戶）收支平衡
而(A)檢查，(C)計算（分數，費用），(D)寫，皆不合句意。

20.（ **C** ）　*only* 只有　(D) approximately〔əˈprɑksəmɪtlɪ〕*adv.* 大約

II. 字彙：20％

21. (**B**)　name-calling〔'nem,kɔlɪŋ〕*n.* 辱罵
　　　　　　abusive〔ə'bjusɪv〕*adj.* 辱罵的　　fake〔fek〕*adj.* 假的

22. (**A**)　aphorism〔'æfə,rɪzəm〕*n.* 格言　　moral〔'mɔrəl〕*n.* 道德
　　　　　　saying〔'seɪŋ〕*n.* 諺語　　critical〔'krɪtɪkl̩〕*adj.* 重要的

23. (**D**)　sibling〔'sɪblɪŋ〕*n.* 兄弟或姊妹
　　　　　　disrespect〔,dɪsrɪ'spɛkt〕*n.* 無禮

24. (**A**)　chronic〔'krɑnɪk〕*adj.* 習慣性的；慢性的
　　　　　　(D) depressed〔dɪ'prɛst〕*adj.* 沮喪的

25. (**C**)　momentum〔mo'mɛntəm〕*n.* 動力
　　　　　　synthesis〔'sɪnθəsɪs〕*n.* 綜合

26. (**C**)　retain〔rɪ'ten〕*v.* 保留

27. (**B**)　converge〔kən'vɝdʒ〕*v.* 集中於一點
　　　　　　(A) conflict〔kən'flɪk〕*v.* 衝突

28. (**C**)　observe〔əb'zɝv〕*v.* 注意
　　　　　　accordance〔ə'kɔrdəns〕*n.* 一致

29. (**A**)　confine〔'kɑnfaɪn〕*n.* 界限　　flesh〔flɛʃ〕*n.* 肉體

30. (**C**)　exquisite〔'ɛkskwɪzɪt〕*adj.* 細膩的
　　　　　　unique〔ju'nik〕*adj.* 獨特的
　　　　　　delicate〔'dɛlə,kɪt〕*adj.* 纖細的

31. (**D**)　arson〔'ɑrsn̩〕*n.* 縱火　　the Qiando Lake 千島湖
　　　　　　tragedy〔'trædʒədɪ〕*n.* 悲劇　　deceive〔dɪ'siv〕*v.* 欺騙
　　　　　　property〔'prɑpətɪ〕*n.* 財產

32. (**B**)　ad hoc〔'æd'hɑk〕*adj.* 特別的

33. (**C**)　paradoxical〔pærə'dɑksɪkl̩〕*adj.* 矛盾的

34. (**A**)　lamentable〔'læməntəbl̩〕*adj.* 令人惋惜的；可悲的

35.(**B**)　vogue〔vog〕*n.* 時尙　　flavor〔'flevɚ〕*n.* 口味
　　　　declination〔,dɪ,klə'neʃən〕*n.* 衰微；拒絕

36.(**A**)　undermine〔,ʌndɚ'maɪn〕*v.* 逐漸損壞
　　　　abolition〔,æbə'lɪʃən〕*n.* 廢止

37.(**D**)　assess〔ə'sɛs〕*v.* 評估
　　　　(A) predict〔prɪ'dɪkt〕*v.* 預測　　(B) give up 放棄
　　　　(C) oppose〔ə'poz〕*v.* 反對　　(D) **judge**〔dʒʌdʒ〕*v.* 評判
　　　　legislation〔,lɛdʒɪs'leʃən〕*n.* 立法

38.(**C**)　proliferation〔pro,lɪfə'reʃən〕*n.* 繁殖；增多
　　　　(A) side effect 副作用
　　　　(D) variety〔və'raɪətɪ〕*n.* 種類
　　　　due to 由於　　contraceptive〔,kɑntrə'sɛptɪv〕*adj.* 避孕的

39.(**B**)　obsolete〔'ɑbsə,lit〕*adj.* 過時的

40.(**C**)　overlap〔'ovɚ,læp〕*v.* 部份重疊

Ⅲ. 閱讀測驗：30％

【譯文】

在五〇年代，每一個電視季都播出卅九週的新節目，另外十三週重播。慢慢地，比例開始顛倒過來。最終目標可能是一週當季的節目，五十週重播，以及一週因爲表現良好而休播。

【答案】

　　　41.(**A**)　　　　42.(**C**)　　　　43.(**D**)

【註】

ratio〔'reʃo〕*n.* 比例　　reverse〔rɪ'vɝs〕*v.* 顛倒
ultimate〔'ʌltəmɪt〕*adj.* 最終的

【譯文】

通訊衛星系統的成功，已引起了大家對它未來的廣泛關切。有些國家已使用衛星做為國內通訊之用，以代替傳統的陸上電話線。雖然這項技術就連接遍佈在偏遠地區或山區的村莊而言非常地有用，但在那些已裝有範圍廣泛的電話和電報系統的建築物密布區，陸上通信網路認為國內衛星是種不公平的競爭。雖然有如此的抗議，國內衛星在美國仍受到許多來自商業和公益團體的支持，而且似乎在將來有可能被更廣泛地利用。

【答案】

44.（ B ）　　45.（ A ）　　46.（ C ）　　47.（ D ）

【註】

satellite〔'sætḷ,aɪt〕*n.* 人造衛星　　domestic〔də'mɛstɪk〕*adj.* 國內的
in place of 代替　　conventional〔kən'vɛnʃənḷ〕*adj.* 傳統的
scatter〔'skætɚ〕*v.* 散佈　　remote〔rɪ'mot〕*adj.* 遙遠的
built-up〔'bɪlt'ʌp〕*adj.* 建築物多的　　utilize〔'jutə,laɪz〕*v.* 利用

【譯文】

在一七七六年美國獨立革命的好幾十年前，一名紐約人傑西‧菲什來到了弗羅里達州的聖奧古斯丁帝旁的一座島上，以逃避一個不愉快的家庭處境。在那時他變成弗羅里達州第一個柑橘的大老闆，而在整個一七七〇年代，柑橘在倫敦的需求量都非常大。英國人發現柑橘多汁味甜，他們喜歡柑橘勝過其它種類的水果，即使是柑橘有又薄又難剝的皮。

如果不曾受西班牙統治差不多兩百年的話，弗羅里達州在菲什去之前，可能會有其它成功的商業栽培業者。哥倫布首先把柑橘樹的種子帶到新大陸，並將之種在安地列斯群島。但最有可能是旁沙‧里昂於一五 ‧三年發現弗羅里達州時，才將柑橘引進北美大陸。有一段期間，每一名在要駛往美國的船隻上之西班牙水手，依法都被要求攜帶一百顆種子。後來，因為種子容易乾掉，所有的西班牙船隻都被要求攜帶幼小的柑橘樹，這只是為了醫藥上的目的。他們覺得沒必要開闢能大量生產柑橘的樹林，因為柑橘在西班牙的產量很豐富。

【答案】

48.(C)	49.(D)	50.(C)	51.(A)
52.(B)	53.(D)	54.(C)	55.(D)

【註】

decade〔'dɛked〕n. 十年   retreat〔rɪ'trit〕v. 退隱

baron〔'bærən〕n. 大老闆   peel〔pil〕v. 剝皮

citrus〔'sɪtrəs〕n. 柑橘   bound〔baʊnd〕adj. 駛往～的

Spaniard〔'spænjəd〕n. 西班牙人   grove〔grov〕n. 小樹林

abundant〔ə'bʌndənt〕adj. 豐富的

Ⅳ. 作文：30％

Corporal Punishment in Schools

　　Traditionally, corporal punishment has been employed by those who believe that if you spare the rod, you will spoil the child. Recently, however, the use of corporal punishment has been declining. Now parents are much more inclined to sue a teacher who physically harms their child. In fact, many people now agree that violence only breeds more violence.

　　Although some youths are violent and difficult to manage, beating them up will hardly make them better people. Indeed the whole idea of corporal punishment is to break the student's spirit.

　　I think that corporal punishment is cruel and thoughtless. There is already too much violence in the world. Schools should be teaching children that violence is not the answer to our problems.

國立台灣大學八十一學年度
碩士班研究生入學考試英文試題

Choose the BEST answer. Put a cross--"X"--in the appropriate
space for each question to indicate your choice.

I. Vocabulary/Grammar/Usage

Example: It was Joan's first visit to the country, and
everything was fresh and_____to her.
(A) dull　(B) quickly　(C) new　(D) excite

Answer :　A　　B　　C　　D
　　　　　　□　　□　　□　　□

A.
1. I'm not going_____he tells me to.
(A) even　　　　　　　　(B) even if
(C) in spite　　　　　 (D) no matter

B.
2. Although most of the people in my class are traveling
abroad this summer vacation,_____plan on staying at
home to study.
(A) but I've　　　　　 (B) but
(C) I've　　　　　　　　(D) I

C.
3. Jack will graduate_____.
(A) recently　　　　　 (B) lately
(C) in a near future　(D) soon

D.
4. I live in_____, not a house.
(A) an apartment　　　 (B) a compartment
(C) a department　　　 (D) a ceiling

E.
　　　Geri was born twenty-five years ago in Buffalo, New
York.___5___ Geri was only eighteen months old, her parents
learned that Geri's brain had been damaged ___6___ birth.
The damage she suffered would affect the way she talked
and moved.

Her early teenage years were the most ___7___ of her life. "With one disappointment after another, I started behaving like a clown, and I was always joking. I was always trying to___8___attention. It was my way of___9___with dreams I could not even tell anybody, because I thought they would laugh at me."

5. (A) Until   (B) Since
   (C) When   (D) During

6. (A) to   (B) of
   (C) at   (D) on

7. (A) valuable   (B) satisfying
   (C) frustrating (D) ashamed

8. (A) get   (B) take
   (C) raise   (D) send

9. (A) associating (B) treating
   (C) meeting   (D) coping

F.

  Neckties are decorative but useless and uncomfortable articles of ___10___ clothing. They originated in military attire. The use of scarves soaked in water and wrapped around the neck to___11___the bodies of Roman soldiers in battle was recorded in the first century B.C. Much later, in the seventeenth century, French troops who fought in Croatia came back ___12___ France wearing scarves around their necks. French men and women___13___the idea, and called the fashion a "cravat", after the Croats who inspired it.

10. (A) man   (B) man's
    (C) men   (D) men's

11. (A) cool   (B) be cooled
    (C) have cooled (D) cooling

12. (A) in   (B) to
    (C) by   (D) of

13. (A) copy　　　　　　　　　　(B) to copy
　　(C) copied　　　　　　　　　 (D) copying

G.

　　　Thomas Jefferson, the third president of the United
States, was many___14___ besides a statesman. Ideas of all
kinds fascinated him. Jefferson was a good musician and the
best American architect ___15___ his day. He studied the
languages of the American Indians. He was ___16___ the
American money of dollars and cents. Following the work of
leading scientists, he became an inventor who wanted to see
the study of science ___17___ to some practical use.
___18___, he was also interested in ideas just as ideas.

14. (A) things　　　　　　　　　 (B) matters
　　(C) titles　　　　　　　　　 (D) positions

15. (A) within　　　　　　　　　 (B) to
　　(C) on　　　　　　　　　　　 (D) of

16. (A) blamed for　　　　　　　 (B) responsible for
　　(C) attributed to　　　　　　(D) contributed to

17. (A) turn　　　　　　　　　　 (B) to turn
　　(C) turning　　　　　　　　　(D) turned

18. (A) However　　　　　　　　　(B) Consequently
　　(C) Therefore　　　　　　　　(D) Incidentally

H.

　　　If the Earth was an icehouse 18,000 years___19___, it
was a hothouse 100 million years ago. In those days, there
was not a speck of permanent ice___20___ on the planet--at
least geologists have ___21___ no trace of it, even at the
poles.

19. (A) from now　　　　　　　　 (B) before
　　(C) ago　　　　　　　　　　　(D) once

20. (A) somewhere　　　　　　　　(B) anywhere
　　(C) everywhere　　　　　　　 (D) nowhere

21. (A) find   (B) found
    (C) been found   (D) to find

I.

      __22__ rather unpleasant persons are making a lot of money these days. They gain entry into people's homes by acting as salesmen, tradesmen, or local officials.__23__, having won the confidence of the elderly, the sick or the lonely, they either steal their life savings or persuade them to pay for goods which they never receive. Sometimes they claim they are from the gas or electricity company, __24__ the householder that they have come to read the meter.__25__they pretend to be salesmen, asking people to buy something which later turns__26__to be worthless.

22. (A) A number of   (B) A lot
    (C) Lots   (D) The number of

23. (A) For   (B) Because
    (C) Then   (D) Previously

24. (A) tell   (B) to tell
    (C) told   (D) telling

25. (A) On other occasions   (B) In any situations
    (C) In one situation   (D) On all occasions

26. (A) on   (B) out
    (C) over   (D) up

J.

    It is hard to imagine the conditions in our school when I was a boy. The food was not only bad, but it was__27__insufficient. Never before or since__28__I seen butter or jam scraped on bread so thinly. I__29__not think I can be imagining the fact that we were underfed, when I remember the __30__ we would go to in order to steal some stale bread from the pantry.

27. (A) also   (B) either
    (C) neither   (D) more

28. (A) have　　　　　　　(B) haven't
    (C) had　　　　　　　　(D) hadn't

29. (A) do　　　　　　　　(B) may
    (C) did　　　　　　　　(D) might

30. (A) lengths　　　　　　(B) difficulties
    (C) details　　　　　　(D) breadths

K.
　　There are some things we do in life that seem to have
small rewards, and___31___after a great deal of hard work--
___32___still those things are worth___33___. Acting in a
play is an example that comes to mind. It's at___34___95
percent hard, hard work, and the audience's appreciation
comes for only a few seconds at the end of a performance--
but the satisfaction is beyond___35___.

31. (A) seldom　　　　　　(B) only
    (C) barely　　　　　　 (D) rarely

32. (A) so　　　　　　　　(B) unless
    (C) or　　　　　　　　 (D) but

33. (A) this　　　　　　　(B) that
    (C) them　　　　　　　(D) it

34. (A) most　　　　　　　(B) least
    (C) best　　　　　　　(D) worst

35. (A) description　　　　(B) a description
    (C) the description　　(D) descriptions

L.
　　It's not___36___for passengers on a jumbo jet to burst
out in spontaneous applause when the wheels of the airliner
touch down. Flying can be___37___experience, and after a
bouncing, stomach-turning ride through a thunderstorm at
thirty thousand feet, few words can describe the joy of
feeling terra firma beneath your feet. It doesn't___38___
how many times you've flown, how many hours you've logged
in the air. There___39___when you feel frightened, when

you're positive the plane is not working just right, when
you wonder ___40___ is making those strange noises you've
seemingly never heard before. Thoughts turn to the inevitable "Will we make it?"

36. (A) unusual   (B) exotic
    (C) tropical   (D) additional

37. (A) a frightened   (B) a frightening
    (C) an afraid   (D) a scared

38. (A) care   (B) matter
    (C) differentiate   (D) additional

39. (A) come time   (B) come times
    (C) comes time   (D) comes times

40. (A) which   (B) where
    (C) how   (D) what

II. Error Recognition:

In questions 41 to 45, each sentence has four parts
underlined, marked A, B, C, and D. You are to identify
the one part that is incorrect.

41. Social disapproval <u>of</u> people's activities can serve both
                        A

<u>as</u> powerful punishment for <u>and</u> as a strong deterrent <u>in</u>
B   C   D

crime.

42. Difficulties <u>are arisen</u> when one or another party over-
                 A

steps the tacitly understood limits, <u>when he</u> attempts
                                      B

to connect up with <u>some module</u> not relevant to the
                    C

function <u>at hand</u>.
         D

43. The remark <u>got to</u> Bill. "I <u>suddenly dawned</u>," he says,
    　　　　　　　A　　　　　　　　　B

    that I was the one in charge of me, and that I had the

    power to change. <u>Then and there</u>, I resolved to stop
    　　　　　　　　　　　　　C

    drinking and to <u>make something of myself</u>.
    　　　　　　　　　　D

44. "Don't miss <u>this opportunity</u>," he said <u>excitingly</u>. "My
    　　　　　　　　A　　　　　　　　　　　　　　　B

    <u>cousin Michael</u> was in a traffic accident a few years
    　　　　C

    ago, and he <u>sued</u> the driver who caused the accident."
    　　　　　　　　D

45. The door <u>shut</u>, the firm, heavy steps recrossed the
    　　　　　　A

    bright carpet, the fat body <u>plumped</u> down in the spring
    　　　　　　　　　　　　　　　　　B

    chair, and <u>leaning</u> forward, the boss <u>covering</u> his face
    　　　　　　　C　　　　　　　　　　　　　D

    with his hands.

III. Reading Comprehension:

　　Read the following passages carefully, then choose the
　　<u>best</u> answer to each question.

A.

　　Mrs. Bennet rang the bell, and Miss Elizabeth was
summoned to the library.

　　"Come here, child," cried her father as she appeared.
"I understand that Mr. Collins has made you an offer of
marriage. Is it true?" Elizabeth replied that it was. "Very
well--and this offer of marriage you have refused?"

　　"I have, sir."

　　"Very well. We now come to the point. Your mother
insists upon your accepting it. Is it not so, Mrs. Bennet?"

"An unhappy choice is before you, Elizabeth. From this day you must be a stranger to one of your parents. Your mother will never see you again if you do not marry Mr. Collins, and I will never see you again if you do."

46. What had apparently been happening immediately before this passage?
(A) Mr. Bennet had been talking with Mrs. Bennet.
(B) Mrs. Bennet had been talking with Elizabeth.
(C) Elizabeth had been talking with Mr. Collins.
(D) Mr. Bennet had been talking with Elizabeth.

47. What do we learn about Mr. Bennet from this conversation?
(A) That he is afraid Elizabeth will leave home if she marries.
(B) That he agrees with his wife's choice of a husband for Elizabeth.
(C) That he consents to what Elizabeth has said to Mr. Collins.
(D) That he objects to Elizabeth's choice of a husband.

B.

Peter Ilyich Tchaikovsky was born in a Russian mining town in 1840. When he was eight, his family moved to St. Petersburg where he was sent first to boarding school, then later to law school. His mother, whom he loved dearly, died of cholera when Peter was just fourteen. He took a position as a clerk in the Ministry of Justice when he was nineteen, but at the same time he studied music at the newly-opened St. Petersburg Conservatory. By 1866 he was professor of harmony at the new Moscow Conservatory, and in the same year he wrote his first symphony.

In spite of being homosexual, Tchaikovsky married in 1877. He eventually attempted to commit suicide by jumping into the Volga River. Later a sympathetic admirer corresponded with him and provided him with a regular income, which allowed him to concentrate his energies on composing rather than teaching. The support was suddenly discontinued in 1890, but the composer was now able to support himself.

Nine days after conducting the premiere of his famous
Nutcracker ballet in St. Petersburg in 1893, Tchaikovsky is
said to have drunk a glass of unboiled water, and subsequently to have died of cholera.

48. Tchaikovsky had various occupations during his lifetime.
    Which of the following does the passage not mention as
    being one of Tchaikovsky's occupations?
    (A) miner   (B) clerk
    (C) composer   (D) professor

49. Right after leaving boarding school, Tchaikovsky studied
    (A) music.   (B) medicine.
    (C) carpentry.   (D) law.

50. Tchaikovsky's marriage was
    (A) illegal.
    (B) doomed from the start.
    (C) arranged by a rich admirer.
    (D) successful.

國立台灣大學八十一學年度
碩士班研究生入學考試英文試題詳解

I. 字彙與文法：

A. 1.（ B ） *even if* 即使

B. 2.（ D ）空格應填一主詞，且由動詞 plan 可知，應為現在簡單式，故選
(D) I 。由於前面是由連接詞 though 所引導的從屬子句，所以空
格不可出現另一連接詞 but，故(B)不選。

C. 3.（ D ）由於此句的時態是未來式，故應選(D) soon 。而(A) recently 多用
於過去式或現在完成式，(B) lately 通常與現在完成式連用，(D)
則須改為 in the near future 才能選。

D. 4.（ A ）依句意，選(A) apartment *n.* 公寓。而(B) compartment〔kəm'part-
mənt〕*n.* 隔間，(C) department *n.* 部門，(D) ceiling〔'silɪŋ〕
n. 天花板，均不合句意。

E.

【譯文】

　　傑芮在二十五年前出生於紐約的水牛城。當她才十八個月大時，她的
雙親就知道她在出生時，腦部受到損害，而且將會對傑芮說話或是走動的
方式有所影響。

　　她十多歲的時候，是她一生中最沮喪的時期。「由於一次又一次的失
望，我開始學習小丑的行為，總是和大家開玩笑，以獲得大家的注意。這
是我巧妙地處理我的夢想的方式，我無法把這些夢想告訴別人，因為我怕
遭人取笑。」

5.（ C ）依句意，選(C) when 　當…時候。

6.（ C ）*at birth* 出生時

7.（ C ）依句意，選(C) frustrating *adj.* 令人沮喪的。而(A) valuable *adj.*
珍貴的，(B) satisfying *adj.* 令人滿意的，(D) ashamed *adj.* 慚
愧的，均不合句意。

8.（ **A** ）她扮小丑是爲「獲得」別人的注意，故選(A) get *v.* 獲得。

9.（ **D** ）*cope with* 巧妙地處理；應付

F.

【譯文】

　　在男士的服裝裏，領帶除了具有裝飾作用外，並無其他用途，而且佩戴時又會使人不太舒服。領帶起源自軍裝。根據記載，在西元前第一世紀時，曾在戰場上使用浸濕的領巾，圍在羅馬士兵屍體的脖子上，使其冷卻。很久以後，西元十七世紀時，在克羅埃西亞打仗的法國軍隊回國時，就曾在他們脖子上圍著領巾。法國的男士與婦女就模仿他們，並且由於這種風尚是由克羅埃西亞人所賜與的靈感，所以法國人便將這些領巾稱爲「領帶」。

【註】

article〔ˊɑrtɪkl〕*n.* 物品　　　attire〔əˊtaɪr〕*n.* 服飾

scarf〔skɑrf〕*n.* 領巾；圍巾（複數爲 scarves）

battle〔ˊbætl〕*n.* 戰爭　　　troop〔trup〕*n.* 軍隊

cravat〔krəˊvæt〕*n.* 領帶；領結　　　inspire〔ɪnˊspaɪr〕*v.* 啓發

10.（ **D** ）men's clothing 男人的服裝

11.（ **A** ）不定詞：「to ＋原形動詞」，故選(A) cool。

12.（ **B** ）come back to France 回到法國

13.（ **C** ）依句意，應用過去式動詞，故選(C) copied。

G.

【譯文】

　　湯瑪士‧傑弗遜是美國的第三任總統，他除了是位政治家之外，還身兼數職。各式各樣的想法都能使他十分著迷。在他那個時代，傑弗遜是位很好的音樂家，也是當時最好的建築師。他曾學過美國印地安人的語言，也使美國擁有一元及一分的硬幣。傑弗遜承繼了一流科學家的工作，他成爲一位發明家，希望能看見科學研究的成果，能有實用的價值。然而對於純粹的概念，他一樣很感興趣。

【註】

fascinate〔'fæsn̩,et〕*v.* 使著迷 leading〔'lidɪŋ〕*adj.* 領導的；主要的

14.(**A**) …was many things besides a statesman.…除了是位政治家之外，他還身兼數職。在此 things 可泛指與 a statesman 同類的名詞，在此指其他職業。

15.(**D**) *of one's day* 在某人的那個時代

16.(**B**) *be responsible for* ～ 是～的起因
attribute〔ə'trɪbjʊt〕*v.* 歸因於
contribute〔kən'trɪbjʊt〕*v.* 對～有貢獻

17.(**D**) see 爲感官動詞，「感官動詞＋受詞＋過去分詞」表被動，依句意，科學成就的成果應是被轉變成實際的用途，故選(D) turned。

18.(**A**) 空格應塡一承轉詞，依句意，選(A) however 然而。(B)因此，(C)因此，(D)順便一提，皆不合句意。

H.

【譯文】

如果在一萬八千年前地球是間冰屋，那麼一億年前的地球，就可算是間熱屋了。在那時候，地球上沒有任何永不融化的冰。至少地質學家們並未發現，即使在兩極地區也沒有。

【註】

speck〔spɛk〕*n.* 微片
permanent〔'pɝmənənt〕*n.* 永久的 trace〔tres〕*n.* 踪跡
pole〔pol〕*n.* （南、北）極

19.(**C**) 時間長短＋ago，表「（多久）之前」。而(B) before 則無此用法。

20.(**B**) not … anywhere ＝ nowhere 到處都沒有

21.(**B**) 依句意，應用現在完成式：「have＋過去分詞」，且爲主動語態，故選(B) found。

I.

【譯文】

　　最近有許多惹人厭的人賺了很多錢。他們常假扮推銷員、送貨員或地方官員以進入民宅。然後在獲得老年人、病人或是孤獨的人的信任之後，就會偷取他們一生的積蓄，或是說服他們買一些永遠都得不到的東西。有時他們會自稱是電力公司或瓦斯公司派來的，告訴屋主說是要來抄錶的。有時候他們會假扮推銷員，要人們買一些沒什麼價值的東西。

【註】

entry〔'ɛntrɪ〕*n*. 進入　　　tradesman〔'trezmən〕*n*. 送貨員；零售商
claim〔klem〕*v*. 宣稱　　　meter〔'mitɚ〕*n*. 計量器

22.(**A**) *a number of* 許多

23.(**C**) 依句意，選(C)然後。

24.(**D**) 兩動詞間無連接詞，第二個動詞要改成現在分詞，故選(D) telling。

25.(**A**) *on other occasions* 在其他情況下

26.(**B**) *turn out* 結果（成爲）

J.

【譯文】

　　很難想像我小時候學校的情況。食物不但差，而且又不充足。麵包上所塗的奶油，是我所見過最薄的。當我想起當時從食品室要偷一些乾硬的麵包需要費多大的工夫時，我還是覺得很難想像我們營養不良的事實。

【註】

scrape〔skrep〕*v*. 擦　　　underfed〔͵ʌndɚ'fɛd〕*adj*. 營養不良的
stale〔stel〕*adj*. 不新鮮的；乾硬的　　pantry〔'pæntrɪ〕*n*. 食品室

27.(**A**) *not only … but also* ～ 不僅…而且～

28.(**A**) 否定副詞 never 放句首，句子須倒裝，且依句意，表過去到現在的經驗，應用現在完成式，故選(A) have 。

29.(**A**) 由後面助動詞 can 可知，應用現在簡單式，且依句意，應選(A) do 。

30.(**A**) *go lengths* 全力以赴；盡力而爲

K.

【譯文】

　　在人生當中，有些事情必須花費很大的心力去完成，而得到的報酬卻很微薄——但一切都是十分值得的。我想演戲就是個很好的例子。你至少必須花費百分之九十五的努力，而觀眾所給予的掌聲，卻只出現在表演快結束時短短的幾秒鐘而已——但那種滿足感卻是難以形容的。

31.（ B ）依句意，選(B) only 只有。

32.（ D ）依句意，選(D) but 但是。

33.（ D ）爲了避免重覆前面所提過的名詞 hard work，故用代名詞 it 代替。

34.（ B ）*at least* 至少

35.（ A ）*beyond description* 難以形容

L.

【譯文】

　　對搭乘巨無霸噴射客機的乘客而言，當飛機的輪子碰到地面時，他們通常都會忍不住鼓掌叫好。搭乘飛機可能是種可怕的經驗。如果在暴風雨期間，飛機在三萬英尺的高空，在經歷一陣跳動、反胃的飛行之後，那種踏上土地的喜悅，是很難用言語形容的。無論你搭乘過多少次飛機，無論你在空中飛行了多久，還是會有相同的感受。常常當你覺得恐懼，當你很肯定飛機出問題時，當你想知道到底是什麼發出那種你從來沒聽過的聲音時，你一定會想，「這次眞的會沒事嗎？」

【註】

jumbo jet 巨無霸型噴射機　　　*burst out* 突然…起來
airliner〔͵ɛr'laɪnɚ〕*n.* 班機　　*terra firma* 土地
log〔lɑg〕*v.* 累積（飛行時數）

36.（ A ）(A) *unusual adj.* 不尋常的
　　　　　(B) exotic〔ɪg'zɑtɪk〕*adj.* 外來的
　　　　　(C) tropical *adj.* 熱帶的
　　　　　(D) additional *adj.* 額外的

37.(B) *a frightening experience* 可怕的經驗。而 (A) 受到驚嚇的，
　　　　(B) 害怕的，(C) 受到驚嚇的，均不合句意。

38.(B) It doesn't matter … 不管…

39.(B) There come times … 有好幾次…

40.(D) 空格需填一複合關係代名詞，一方面作 wonder 的受詞，且須為
　　　　空格後句子的主詞，故填(D) what。

Ⅱ. 挑錯：

41.(D) *in → from*
　　　　deterrent〔dɪˈtɜrənt, -ˈtɛr-〕*n.* 阻礙之物；制止物

42.(A) *are arisen → arise*　　arise〔əˈraɪz〕*v.* 產生；出現，為一
　　　　不及物動詞，無被動語態。

43.(B) *I suddenly dawned …→ It suddenly dawned on me …*
　　　　dawn〔dɔn〕*v.* 使明白，此動詞不可用被動語態，故須以事物
　　　　當主詞。

44.(B) *excitingly → excitedly*　　excitingly *adv.* 令人興奮地，但依
　　　　句意，應改為 excitedly *adv.* 興奮地。

45.(D) *covering → covered*
　　　　shut〔ʃʌt〕*v.* 關；閉　　recross〔rɪˈkrɔs, -ˈkrɑs〕*v.* 再橫越
　　　　carpet〔ˈkɑrpɪt〕*n.* 地毯　　plump〔plʌmp〕*v.* 撲通一聲坐下

Ⅲ. 閱讀測驗：

A.

【譯文】

　　貝內特太太按了鈴，伊麗莎白就被叫到書房裏了。

　　「過來，孩子」，貝內特先生大聲道。「聽說柯林斯先生向妳求婚。
是真的嗎？」伊麗莎白回答說是真的。「很好，妳拒絕了，是嗎？」

　　「是的，爸爸。」

「很好。現在我們進入正題吧。妳的母親堅持要你答應他的求婚。是嗎？貝內特太太？」

「伊麗莎白，現在你得面臨一個令人不太愉快的抉擇。從今天開始，你必須和父母親之中的一個人形同陌路。如果你不嫁給柯林斯先生，妳的母親就不願和妳見面，但如果妳真的嫁給他，我就不再和你見面了。」

【答案】

46.(A)   47.(C)

【註】

summon〔'sʌmən〕 *v*. 召喚

B.

【譯文】

　　柴可夫斯基於一八四○年出生於俄國的一座礦城。在他八歲時，全家遷往聖彼得堡，就在當地，他首度被送往供膳宿的學校就讀。後來又進入法律學校就讀。當柴可夫斯基十四歲時，他摯愛的母親死於霍亂。十九歲時，他在司法部擔任職員，同時他也在新創辦的聖彼得堡音樂學校研習音樂。一八六六年，柴可夫斯基成為莫斯科音樂學校和聲學的教授，就在這一年他寫出了生平第一首交響曲。

　　儘管柴可夫斯基是位同性戀者，他卻於一八七七年結婚。到最後他曾想跳入莫加河自盡。後來有位同情他的仰慕者和他通信，並且提供他固定的收入，使他可以更專心致力於寫作而非教學上。這項資助於一八九○年突然中止，但這位作曲家已經能夠供養自己了。

　　一八九三年，柴可夫斯基著名的芭蕾舞曲「胡桃鉗」首度在聖彼德堡公演，在他指揮完首演之後九天，據說他因為飲用了一杯未煮沸的水，因而死於霍亂。

【答案】

48.(A)   49.(D)   50.(B)

【註】

boarding school 供膳宿的學校　　cholera〔'kɑlərə〕*n.* 霍亂
conservatory〔kən'sɝvə,torɪ〕*n.* 音樂學校
harmony〔'hɑrmənɪ〕*n.* 和聲學　　symphony〔'sɪmfənɪ〕*n.* 交響樂
homosexual〔,homə'sɛkʃəl〕*n.* 同性戀者
premiere〔prɪ'mɪr〕*n.* 首次公演
nutcracker〔'nʌt,krækɚ〕*n.* 胡桃鉗

國立台灣師範大學八十一學年度
碩士班研究生入學考試英文試題

I. Vocabulary in Context: 20%

For each of the blanks, find an appropriate word whose initial and final letters are given. Write the word on your answer sheet.

1. The nurse took the patient's temperature with a t____r.

2. Her parents e____ted from Taiwan to the United States when she was six years old.

3. He was such a m____s man that he forgave those people who had insulted him.

4. He was very unhappy; he led a w____ed life.

5. He gets paid for playing baseball. He is a p____l athlete.

6. Peaches are in s____n now and can be bought at any supermarket.

7. An a____t is a self-service restaurant where food and drink are obtained, by the customers themselves, from coin-operated closed compartments.

8. When a son does not act as he should act toward his parents, we say that he falls short in f____l consideration.

9. A person skilled in the management of money, especially public money, is a f____er.

10. Traffic signs should be co____s, or drivers will not be able to see them.

II. Grammar: 20%

Supply the correct form of the given verb in each of the following sentences. Put the form on your answer sheet.

1. The doctor suggested that he____(stop) smoking.

2. If I had money, I_____(buy) a large house.

3. He had great difficulty in _____(get) a ticket to the concert.

4. How do you want your beef, sir? I prefer it well_____ (do).

5. Although I am not active in politics, I've been an_____ (interest) observer of the political scene for many years.

6. All visitors_____(tour) the art museum were asked to sign the guest book.

7. Had I known that you didn't have a key, I_____(not lock) the door.

8. Unless he_____(try) his best, he will fail.

9. When_____(ask) to help, he always says "no." He will never help others.

10. She would have liked to swim, but they did not allow _____ (swim) there.

III. Word Forms: 20%

Supply the correct form of the word in parenthesis for each sentence. Put the word on your answer sheet.

1. He was_____(exceed) drunk.

2. The_____(melody) songs of the birds soothed our nerves.

3. Will you_____(companion) me to the concert tonight?

4. I enjoy reading_____(describe) writing.

5. Doctors work hard to relieve human_____(miserable).

6. Influenza is an_____(infect) disease.

7. They put the prisoner in solitary_____(confine).

8. Don't be so_____(greed)! There's enough for everyone.

9. His _____ (determine) to succeed helped him overcome all difficulties.

10. They have noted the_____(mystery) changes on the top
    of the mountain.

IV. Choose the most appropriate answer for each blank. Put
    the letter representing the answer on your answer sheet.
    20%

   One of the distinctions between man and the other
animals is that man in all his operations makes __1__ ;
animals make none. Did you ever hear of such a thing as a
bird sitting disconsolate on a twig, lamenting over her
half-finished nest, and puzzling her little poll to know how
to complete it? Or did you ever see the cells of a bee-hive
in clumsy irregular shapes, or observe anything __2__ a
discussion in the little community as if there __3__ a difference of opinion__4__ the architects? The lower animals
are even better __5__ than we are; for when they are ill,
they will, many of them, seek out some particular herb which
they do not use as food, and which possesses a medicinal
quality exactly suited to the__6__; whereas the whole
college of medical doctors will dispute for a century
__7__ the virtues of a single drug. Man undertakes nothing
in which he is not more or less__8__; he must try number-
less experiments before he can bring his undertakings to
anything like perfection; even the simplest operations of
domestic life are not well performed__9__some experience;
and the term of man's life is half wasted__10__ he has done
with his mistakes and begins to profit by his lessons.

1. (A) progress   (B) improvements
   (C) mistakes   (D) corrections

2. (A) similar   (B) like
   (C) familiar   (D) the same

3. (A) were   (B) have been
   (C) is   (D) be

4. (A) between   (B) on
   (C) in   (D) among

5. (A) physicians   (B) inventors
   (C) physicists   (D) chemicals

6. (A) sick   (B) complaint
   (C) fever   (D) ill

7. (A) as   (B) among
   (C) about   (D) between

8. (A) puzzling   (B) puzzles
   (C) puzzle   (D) puzzled

9. (A) with   (B) without
   (C) within   (D) withdraw

10. (A) after   (B) and
    (C) but   (D) before

V. Write a composition of about 120 words on the following topic. 20%

How to Achieve Success in Life

國立台灣師範大學八十一學年度
碩士班研究生入學考試英文試題詳解

I. 文意字彙：20％

1. *thermometer*〔θə'mɑmətɚ〕*n.* 溫度計

2. *emigrated*〔'ɛmə,gretɪd〕*v.* 移居（為動詞 emigrate 的過去式）

3. *magnanimous*〔mæg'nænəməs〕*adj.* 度量寬大的

4. *wretched*〔'rɛtʃɪd〕*adj.* 可憐的；悲慘的

5. *professional*〔prə'fɛʃənl〕*adj.* 職業的；專業的

6. *season*〔'sizn̩〕*n.* 季節　　*in season* 盛產期的；正當時令的
   peach〔pitʃ〕*n.* 桃子

7. *automat*〔'ɔtə,mæt〕*n.* 使用自動販賣機販賣食物之餐館；自動販賣機
   compartment〔kəm'pɑrtmənt〕*n.* 隔間

8. *filial*〔'fɪlɪəl, -ljəl〕*adj.* 子女的；孝順的

9. *financier*〔,fɪnən'sɪr, ,faɪnən-〕*n.* 財政家；金融業者

10. *conspicuous*〔kən'spɪkjʊəs〕*adj.* 顯著的；明顯的

II. 文法：20％

1. *stop v.* 停止
   * 由於 suggest 為一慾望動詞，故 that 子句中應出現 should ＋原形動詞，而 should 通常會省略，故填原形動詞 stop。

2. *buy → would buy*

   * 本題為與現在事實相反的假設，其公式為 If ＋過去式動詞…　　$\left\{\begin{array}{l}\text{should}\\\text{would}\\\text{could}\\\text{might}\end{array}\right.$
   ＋原形 V，故空格應填 would buy。

3. *get → getting*
   * 由於 in 為介系詞，其後須接名詞或動名詞，故填 getting。

4. *do → **done***　　well　done 全熟

5. *interest → **interested***
　　* 修飾名詞 observer 須用形容詞, 且依句意, 應填 interested *adj.*
　　感興趣的。

6. *tour → **who toured** 或 **touring***
　　* who tourred the art museum 爲形容詞子句, 修飾 visitors, 而此
　　子句亦可化簡爲 touring the art museum。

7. *not lock → **would not have locked***
　　* 本句爲與過去事實相反的假設, 其公式爲 If … had ＋過去分詞 …
　　$\left.\begin{array}{l} should \\ would \\ could \\ might \end{array}\right\}$ ＋ have ＋過去分詞, 故須改爲 would not have locked。

8. *try → **tries***
　　* unless 所引導的條件句中, 用現在簡單式代替未來式, 又 he 爲第三
　　人稱單數, 故 try 須改爲 tries。

9. *ask → **asked***
　　* 依句意, 應是當人家要求他幫忙, 故原句應是 When he was asked
　　to help, 化簡爲 When asked to help。

10. *swim → **swimming***　　allow ＋ Ving 允許〜

Ⅲ. 詞類變化：20％

1. *exceedingly* 〔 ɪk'sidɪŋlɪ 〕 *adv.* 太甚地
　　* 修飾形容詞 drunk, 應用副詞, 故填 exceedingly。

2. *melodious* 〔 mə'lodɪəs 〕 *adj.* 悅耳的
　　* 修飾名詞 songs 應用形容詞, 故填 melodious。

3. *accompany* 〔 ə'kʌmpənɪ 〕 *v.* 伴隨

4. **descriptive** 〔dɪˈskrɪptɪv〕 *adj.* 描寫的；敘述的
   * 形容詞 descriptive 修飾名詞 writing 。

5. **misery** 〔ˈmɪzərɪ〕 *n.* 痛苦

6. **infectious** 〔ɪnˈfɛkʃəs〕 *adj.* 有傳染性的
   influenza 〔ˌɪnfluˈɛnzə〕 *n.* 流行性感冒

7. **confinement** 〔kənˈfaɪnmənt〕 *n.* 拘留；監禁
   solitary confinement 單獨監禁

8. **greedy** 〔ˈgridɪ〕 *adj.* 貪心的

9. **determination** 〔dɪˌtɜməˈneʃən〕 *n.* 決心
   * 所有格 his 之後應接名詞，故改為 determination 。

10. **mysterious** 〔mɪsˈtɪrɪəs〕 *adj.* 神秘的
    * 修飾名詞 changes ，須用形容詞 mysterious 。

Ⅳ. 請選出最適當的答案：20％

【譯文】

　　人類和其他動物的差別之一就是人類在從事某些活動會犯錯，而動物卻不會。你有沒有聽說過鳥會悶悶不樂地坐在樹枝上，為了牠蓋了一半的巢傷心，苦思要如何才能蓋好牠的巢？或者你是否曾見過歪七扭八的蜂巢，或是觀察到蜜蜂之間會起爭執，就好像這些建築師之間意見不合一樣？低等動物在內科方面比人類還在行。當牠們生病時，牠們會找出不曾食用過的某種特殊的藥草，剛好具有醫治該病的療效。然而大學裏的醫學博士們，可能會為了一種藥的效力而爭論一世紀之久。人類會從事其或多或少覺得困惑的事情，在他達到完美之前，必須做過無數次的實驗。即使是最簡單的居家生活中的事情，也必須實驗過幾次才能做得好。而人的一生，大半都浪費在處理錯誤方面，然後才能從所得到的教訓裏獲益。

【註】

disconsolate〔dɪs'kɑnslɪt〕*adj.* 哀傷的；淒涼的
twig〔twɪg〕*n.* 小樹枝　　lament〔lə'mɛnt〕*v.* 悲傷
poll〔pol〕*n.* 頭　　virtue〔'vɝtʃʊ〕*n.* 效力
domestic life 家庭生活　　term〔tɝm〕*n.* 期限；期間

1. (C)　(A) 進步　(B) 改良　(C) 錯誤　(D) 修正

2. (B)　由於空格後爲名詞 a discussion，故填介系詞 like，選(B)。
而(A)須改爲 similar to，(C)應改爲 familiar with，(D)須改爲
the same as 才能選。

3. (A)　依句意，應是與現在事實相反的假設，故 be 動詞應用 were，選(A)。

4. (D)　表在三者或三者以上之間，用介系詞 among，選(D)。

5. (A)　依句意，選(A) physician〔fə'zɪʃən〕*n.* 醫生；內科醫生。而
(B) 發明家，(C) 物理學家，(D) 化學藥品，均不合句意。

6. (B)　(A) 生病的　(B) *complaint*〔kəm'plent〕*n.* 疾病
(C) fever〔'fivɚ〕*n.* 發燒　(D) 生病的

7. (C)　*argue about*～ 爭論關於～

8. (D)　空格應填一形容詞，且依句意選(D) puzzled〔'pʌzld〕*adj.* 困惑的。
而(A) puzzling〔'pʌzlɪŋ〕*adj.* 莫名其妙的，不合句意。

9. (B)　依句意，選(B) without *prep.* 沒有。

10. (D)　(A) 在…之後　(B) 而且　(C) 但是　(D) 在…之前

V. 作文：20%

How to Achieve Success in Life

Achieving success is not easy. However, I think everyone
can be successful if they set a reasonable goal for themselves
and pursue it patiently and diligently. It is important to really believe in this goal and be optimistic about its achievement.

We should also be friendly and sincere with people. It is good to have many friends since friends can help you and give you good advice. Another important thing is to know what is going on in the world in order to make the right decisions.

In order to stay informed it is essential to read newspapers and news magazines diligently. Reading books, and traveling whenever you can will also help keep you aware. Furthermore, since English has become the international language, you must learn it well, and practice as much as possible. Diligence is the key. We must be prepared to persevere and do what's necessary in order to succeed.

國立政治大學八十一學年度
碩士班研究生入學考試英文試題

I. Vocabulary & idioms: 30%

A. In each of the following sentences, there is a blank where a word is left out. Choose the best answer from the following four choices and write the corresponding letter on the answer sheet.

1. It is amazing to think that so many languages_____from a common ancestor.
   (A) ascend   (B) descend
   (C) derive   (D) degenerate

2. The general_____is that the original Indo-European civilization developed somewhere in eastern Europe about 3000 years ago.
   (A) consensus   (B) concession
   (C) council   (D) censure

3. It is not true that you need protein when you exercise _____.
   (A) energetically   (B) hardly
   (C) strenuously   (D) essentially

4. Body language is not easy to comprehend because it is full of_____.
   (A) nucleus   (B) nuisances
   (C) nonsense   (D) nuances

5. The best salespeople try to build_____with the customers before they try to sell them anything.
   (A) rapport   (B) confidence
   (C) fraternity   (D) potency

6. If there is an immovable object, there can be no_____ force.
   (A) impossible   (B) unidentifiable
   (C) irresistible   (D) undeniable

7. They send information every week,_____of whether it is useful or not.
   (A) tenacious   (B) irrespective
   (C) despite   (D) destitute

8. One of the problems_____ in having children is deciding how to educate them.
   (A) inherent   (B) inherited
   (C) heritage   (D) hereditary

9. A large glass of brandy at this time may_____his recovery.
   (A) deprive   (B) effect
   (C) arouse   (D) diminish

B. In each of the following sentences, there is a portion underlined. Choose its synonym from the four choices that follow and write the corresponding letter on the answer sheet.

10. A good counsellor knows how to create a common ground upon which to build trust between himself and his client.
    (A) an ordinary living place
    (B) a pleasant physical environment
    (C) a friendly atmosphere
    (D) an area of agreement

11. Children must be taught to take care of themselves or they will always expect their mothers to pick up the pieces for them.
    (A) solve their problems
    (B) repair items that get broken
    (C) pick up the children's clothing
    (D) help them to do homework

12. If a friendship deteriorates into enmity, friends become enemies.
    (A) continues to grow
    (B) get worse
    (C) maintains its present state
    (D) delineates against

13. When we feel guilty and down in the dumps, friends can reassure us.
    (A) dirty
    (B) ashamed
    (C) sad and spiritless
    (D) cheerful

14. I think the tolerance of the Chinese is in excess of anything that Europeans can imagine from their experience at home.
(A) in their house　　　　(B) in their country
(C) easy and comfortable　(D) in China

15. By bottling up their emotions, men deprive themselves of a natural outlet for their negative feelings.
(A) putting in a bottle
(B) turning to drinks
(C) controlling and restraining
(D) releasing

II. Grammar: 20%

In each of the following sentences, there is a blank where a word is missing. Choose the best answer to fill the blank from the four choices below so that the sentence can be complete.

1. A group of 30 experts on the Soviet Union concluded that Khrushchev's memoirs_____authentic and received the approval of the present Soviet leadership.
(A) had been　　　　(B) were
(C) was　　　　　　(D) were being

2. Her spectacles caught the light and prevented_____ seeing where she was looking.
(A) him　　　　(B) he
(C) he's　　　　(D) his

3. A sale of_____nylon stockings is advertised in today's paper.
(A) ladies'　　　　(B) ladie's
(C) lady's　　　　(D) lady

4. The man_____real estate men call Bill is in debt to numerous creditors.
(A) him　　　　(B) that
(C) who　　　　(D) whom

5. Handel's "Saul" is one of those works that_____ remained in limbo, not quite forgotten but probably never performed entirely.
(A) have　　　　(B) has
(C) having　　　(D) had

6. If the Gorgons looked at a person,_____was turned into stone..
   (A) he
   (B) it
   (C) who
   (D) one

7. What other steps can be taken in that direction_____ discussed by the steering group in Washington.
   (A) are being
   (B) are been
   (C) has
   (D) is being

8. After_____for more than 150 years, Beethoven is still loved by many people.
   (A) being died
   (B) being dead
   (C) dying
   (D) having dead

9. _____English, he can speak Russian and French.
   (A) In addition
   (B) Beside
   (C) Besides
   (D) Except

10. The enforcement of the First Amendment has a different meaning today _____ what it had at the end of the eighteenth century.
    (A) from
    (B) than
    (C) to
    (D) about

IJI. Reading comprehension: 30%

A. Cloze. In the following paragraph, some words are deleted. Please find them in the following choices and write the corresponding letters on the answer sheet.

In my own life, anxiety, trouble, and sorrow have been alloted to me at times in such abundant___1___that had my nerves not___2___so strong, I would have broken___3___under the weight. Heavy is the burden of fatigue and responsibility which has___4___upon me without a break for years. I have not much of my life for myself, not even the hours I should like to___5___to my wife and child.

1. (A) extent
   (B) degrees
   (C) measure
   (D) manner

2. (A) be
   (B) being
   (C) been
   (D) was

3. (A) away
   (B) down
   (C) apart
   (D) up

4. (A) lied   (B) lay
   (C) laid   (D) lain

5. (A) spend   (B) contribute
   (C) attribute   (D) devote

B. Read the following selection and answer the questions
   that follow.

　　Intimacy feeds on time. Specifically, there are two
time-bound factors that foster intimacy. First is the duration of the relationship; the longer you know a person, the
more likely you are to become intimate with him or her.
Second is the frequency of informal meetings. For intimacy
to grow, you need to see the other person often, and these
meetings should occur outside the context of formal roles
(employer-employee, teacher-student, clerk-customer). Such
roles, because they set rather strict rules for interactions,
prevent the sort of relaxed self-revelation, mutual explora-
tion, and general breeze-shooting that promote intimacy.

　　It is precisely the scarcity of these two factors--
long-standing relationships and frequent informal meetings--
that seem to work against intimacy in our time. As we have
seen, modern mobility tends to keep our friendships brief.
As for frequent and informal meetings with friends and acquaintances, these have almost gone out of style, at least
for the working adult with a family. Neighbors, in general,
are discouraged from simply appearing at the back door; good
fences make good neighbors, as they say. Friends, too, are
often discouraged from dropping in. We tend to see them,
instead, at dinners and parties, where our roles are more
strictly defined. Modern styles of architecture and city
planning contribute to this lack of opportunity for informal
meetings. Gone is the town square, where people used to
gather and gossip. Gone is the front porch, where people
used to sit and greet their neighbors. The modern American

couple is to be found behind closed (and often locked) doors.
If you want to see them, call before you come.

6. Which of the following statements is not a reason for
   the lack of intimacy in modern times?
   (A) We frequently move from one place to another.
   (B) Neighbors usually see each other on the front porch.
   (C) Friends meet mostly at dinners and parties.
   (D) Once a person has a family, he/she does not have
       much time to spend with friends and acquaintances.

7. Which of the following is true of the passage?
   (A) It takes people to cultivate intimacy.
   (B) It takes effort to cultivate intimacy.
   (C) It takes time to cultivate intimacy.
   (D) It takes gifts to cultivate intimacy.

8. Which of the following is most likely to result in
   intimacy?
   (A) an annual neighborhood party
   (B) a monthly get-together
   (C) a parent-teacher conference
   (D) asking neighbors in for a cup of coffee

9. Intimacy develops from
   (A) formal roles.
   (B) employer-employee relations.
   (C) long relationships and frequent informal meetings.
   (D) modern styles of architecture and city planning.

10. When the author says, "Good fences make good neighbors,
    as they say," he means
    (A) fences are a barrier to intimacy.
    (B) fences are necessary for neighbors.
    (C) fences promote intimacy among neighbors.
    (D) fences are a part of modern architecture.

11. The sentence "these have almost gone out of style" (in
    lines 5-6, paragraph 2) means
    (A) the working adult with a family does not have
        frequent and informal meetings with friends and
        acquaintances.
    (B) the working adult with a family has a very different
        style of informal meetings with friends and ac-
        quaintances.
    (C) the working adult with a family does not have
        friends and acquaintances.
    (D) the working adult with a family has a lot of friends
        and acquaintances.

12. Which of the following statements is true according to
    the passage?
    (A) The author is happy that the town square is gone.
    (B) The author is not happy that the town square is gone.
    (C) The author does not care whether the town square is
        gone or not.
    (D) The author likes to gossip at the town square.

13. The word "breeze-shooting" in paragraph 1 probably means
    (A) playing outdoors.　　　(B) catching cold.
    (C) chatting.　　　　　　　(D) killing.

14. Which of the following is probably the worst way for
    fostering intimacy among family members?
    (A) The whole family go for an outing.
    (B) The whole family watch TV in silence.
    (C) The whole family have dinner together.
    (D) The phone is taken off the hook.

15. The author feels that
    (A) the modern American couple should stay behind closed
        doors.
    (B) the modern American couple should stay behind locked
        doors.
    (C) the modern American couple should not stay behind
        closed and locked doors.
    (D) the modern American couple should not close and
        lock their doors.

IV. Translate the following sentences into English. 20%

1. 母愛不同於男女之愛；母親對子女的愛是沒有條件的。

2. 佛洛伊德（Freud）曾說過「沒有人是能保得住秘密的」。

3. 大多數人都以為年紀愈大，愈難學另一個語文。

4. 雖然有些參考書還有參考價值，但多數已經不合時宜了。

5. 在中國的傳統下，婚姻是家族的事情，而不是個人的事情。

國立政治大學八十一學年度
碩士班研究生入學考試英文試題詳解

I. 字彙與成語：30 %

PART A

1.(**C**)　(A) ascend 〔əˋsɛnd〕*v.* 上升　(B) descend 〔dɪˋsɛnd〕*v.* 下降
　　　(C) *derive* 〔dəˋraɪv〕*v.* 源自　(D) degenerate〔dɪˋdʒɛnə͵ret〕*v.* 墮落
　　　　derive from 源自

2.(**A**)　(A) *consensus* 〔kənˋsɛnsəs〕*n.* 共識
　　　(B) concession 〔kənˋsɛʃən〕*n.* 讓步
　　　(C) council 〔ˋkaʊnsl̩〕*n.* 會議　(D) censure 〔ˋsɛnʃɚ〕*n.* 譴責

3.(**C**)　(A) energetically 〔͵ɛnɚˋdʒɛtɪkl̩ɪ〕*adv.* 精力充沛地
　　　(B) hardly 〔ˋhɑrdlɪ〕*adv.* 幾乎不
　　　(C) *strenuously* 〔ˋstrɛnjʊəslɪ〕*adv.* 激烈地
　　　(D) essentially 〔ɪˋsɛnʃəlɪ〕*adv.* 必要地
　　　　protein 〔ˋprotiɪn〕*n.* 蛋白質

4.(**D**)　(A) nucleus 〔ˋnjuklɪəs〕*n.* 核心
　　　(B) nuisance 〔ˋnjusn̩s〕*n.* 討厭的人或物
　　　(C) nonsense 〔ˋnɑnsɛns〕*n.* 無意義的話或舉動
　　　(D) *nuances* 〔njuˋɑnsɪz, ˋnju-〕*n.pl.* (音調、措辭、感情等的)細微差異

5.(**A**)　(A) *rapport* 〔ræˋport, -ˋpɔrt〕*n.* 密切的關係
　　　(B) confidence 〔ˋkɑnfədəns〕*n.* 信心
　　　(C) fraternity 〔frəˋtɝnətɪ〕*n.* 手足之情
　　　(D) potency 〔ˋpotənsɪ〕*n.* 潛力；效力

6.(**C**)　(A) impossible 〔ɪmˋpɑsəbl̩〕*adj.* 不可能的
　　　(B) unidentifiable 〔͵ʌnaɪˋdɛntə͵faɪəbl̩〕*adj.* 無法確認的
　　　(C) *irresistible* 〔͵ɪrɪˋzɪstəbl̩〕*adj.* 不能抵抗的
　　　(D) undeniable 〔͵ʌndɪˋnaɪəbl̩〕*adj.* 無法否認的

7. **(B)** (A) tenacious 〔tə'neʃəs〕 *adj.*固執的

(B) ***irrespective*** 〔,ɪrɪ'spɛktɪv〕 *adj.* 不顧的

(C) despite 〔dɪ'spaɪt〕 *prep.* 不管

(D) destitute 〔'dɛstə,tjut,-tut〕 *adj.* 窮困的

　　irrespective of 不管；無論

8. **(A)** (A) ***inherent*** 〔ɪn'hɪrənt〕 *adj.* 固有的；與生俱來的

(B) inherited 〔ɪn'hɛrɪtɪd〕 *adj.* 遺傳的

(C) heritage 〔'hɛrətɪdʒ〕 *n.* 遺產

(D) hereditary 〔hə'rɛdə,tɛrɪ〕 *adj.* 世襲的

9. **(D)** (A) deprive 〔dɪ'praɪv〕 *v.* 剝奪

(B) effect 〔ə'fɛkt,ɪ-〕 *n.* 效果

(C) arouse 〔ə'rauz〕 *v.* 喚起

(D) ***diminish*** 〔də'mɪnɪʃ〕 *v.* 減少

PART B

10. **(D)** ***common ground*** 共同立場

　　counsellor 〔'kaunslə〕 *n.* 律師　　client 〔'klaɪənt〕 *n.* 客戶

11. **(A)** ***pick up the pieces*** 解決問題；收拾殘局

12. **(B)** deteriorate 〔dɪ'tɪrɪə,ret〕 *v.* 惡化

　　delineate 〔dɪ'lɪnɪ,et〕 *v.* 描繪

13. **(C)** ***down in the dumps*** 沮喪；憂鬱

　　dumps 〔dʌmps〕 *n.* 憂鬱　　reassure 〔,riə'ʃur〕 *v.* 使恢復信心

　　spiritless 〔'spɪrɪtlɪs〕 *adj.* 垂頭喪氣的

14. **(B)** ***at home*** 在國內

　　in excess of ～　比～多

15. **(C)** ***bottle up*** 抑制；隱藏

　　deprive sb. of sth. 剝奪某人的某物

　　outlet 〔'aut,lɛt〕 *n.* 發洩

　　negative 〔'nɛgətɪv〕 *adj.* 消極的；負面的

Ⅱ. 文法選擇：20 ％

1.(B) 依句意空格應填一過去式動詞，而 memoirs 為複數名詞，故選
   (B) were 。
   Khrushchev 〔xruʃ'tʃɔf〕*n.* 赫魯雪夫
   memoir 〔'mɛmwar,-wɔr〕*n.* 傳記；(*pl.*) 回憶錄
   authentic 〔ɔ'θɛntɪk〕*adj.* 可靠的；有根據的

2.(D) 使某人無法做某事，可用 prevent sb. from V-ing 或 prevent
   one's V-ing 表示，故選(D)。

3.(A) 指屬於女性的，或是女用的，應用 ladies'，選(A)。

4.(D) 空格應填一關係代名詞，做 call 的受詞，故選(D) whom 。
   in debt to ～ 對～負債　creditor 〔'krɛdɪtɚ〕*n.* 債主

5.(A) that 引導形容詞子句，修飾先行詞 works ，因 works 為複數名
   詞，且由現在式 be 動詞 is 可知，應選(A) have 。
   limbo 〔'lɪmbo〕*n.* 不確定的狀態

6.(A) 主要子句中缺乏主詞，由 if 子句中的 a person 可知，須填代名
   詞，選(A)。
   Gorgon 〔'gɔrgən〕*n.* (希臘神話中的)蛇髮女妖

7.(D) 本句的主詞是 what 所引導的名詞子句，視為單數，故須用單數
   動詞，且依句意應用被動語態，故選(D) is being 。

8.(B) 死亡是一種狀態，而非持續的動作，故選(B) being dead 。

9.(C) 依句意應該是除了英語之外，他還會說俄語和法語，故選(C)
   Besides「除了～之外，還有～」。(A)應改為 In addition to ，
   (B)「在～旁邊」，(D)用 except「除了～之外」則表示英語不包
   括在內，與句意不合。

10.(A) *different from* 和～不同
   enforcement 〔ɪn'fɔrsmənt, -'fɔrs-〕*n.* (法律等的)實行；執行
   amendment 〔ə'mɛndmənt〕*n.* 修正案

III. 閱讀測驗：30 %

PART A 克漏字

【譯文】

　　在我的生命中，有時憂慮、麻煩和悲哀加諸在我身上的份量實在太多，如果不是我的精神夠堅強的話，在如此沈重的負擔之下，我一定早就崩潰了。我所受的疲憊和責任的負擔是如此沈重，讓我好幾年都沒有喘息的機會。我沒有多少屬於自己的生活，更不用說應該留給我的妻子和孩子的時間了。

【註】

allot〔ə'lɑt〕*v.* 分配　　abundant〔ə'bʌndənt〕*adj.* 很多的；豐富的
weight〔wet〕*n.* 負荷；重擔　　burden〔'bɝdn〕*n.* 負擔
fatigue〔fə'tig〕*n.* 疲勞

1. (**C**)　由介系詞 in 可知，須選(C) measure *n.* 分量。而(A) extent 和(B) degree 也可表程度或範圍，但介系詞要用 to，如 to a certain extent 在某個程度內，to a degree 非常。(D) manner 則表方式；方法，與句意不合。

2. (**C**)　had my nerves not … 為與過去事實相反的假設語氣的倒裝，原句應為 if my nerves had not been so strong。

3. (**B**)　***break down*** 崩潰。(A) break away 脫離，(C) break apart 破碎，與(D) break up 停止，皆不合句意。

4. (**D**)　lie on～ 在～身上，而動詞 lie 的三態變化為 lie, lay, lain，故選(D)。

5. (**D**)　依句意選(D) devote。devote to～ 奉獻給～。而(A)應改為 spend 時間 with 人，(B) contribute to「有助於～」，(C) attribute to「歸因於～」，均與句意不合。

PART B 閱讀測驗

【譯文】

親密關係要靠時間培養。說得清楚一點，有兩個與時間有關的因素，有助於培養親密關係。第一是關係的持久。你認識一個人愈久，就愈可能和他或她變得親近。第二是經常有非正式的聚會。為了要培養親密關係，你必須常常去看對方，而這種聚會應該發生在正式角色（雇主—雇員、老師—學生、店員—顧客）之外。這些角色因為彼此互動關係的規則嚴謹，而阻礙了能促進親密關係的途徑：輕鬆的自我表白、相互的了解，以及一般的閒聊。

在現代，這二項要素的缺乏——長而持久的關係和頻繁的非正式聚會，似乎的確與親密關係的培養背道而馳。正如我們所見，現代的流動性使我們的友誼日趨簡短，至於與朋友及相識之人經常有非正式的聚會，更已經過時而幾乎不存在了，至少對於有家室的上班族而言是如此。鄰居通常連僅僅出現在後門都很難得，因為俗話說：有好籬笆才有好鄰居。朋友也常常無法順道來訪，相反地，我們卻常在晚宴或舞會上見到他們，不過在這些場合中，我們的角色都有更嚴格的限制。建築和都市計畫的現代風格，同樣使得我們缺乏非正式的聚會。人們從前聚集閒談的市區廣場消失了。人們從前常坐著和鄰居打招呼的前門門廊也消失了。現在的美國夫婦總躲在緊閉的（而且常是鎖住的）門後，如果你要來看他們，來之前先打個電話吧！

【答案】

6.（B）	7.（C）	8.（D）	9.（C）	10.（B）
11.（A）	12.（B）	13.（C）	14.（B）	15.（C）

【註】

feed on 以～爲食　　foster〔'fɑstɚ, 'fɔs-〕v. 養育
duration〔djʊ'reʃən〕n. 持續的時間　context〔'kɑntɛkst〕n. 情況
interaction〔,ɪntɚ'ækʃən〕n. 交互作用；互動關係
revelation〔,rɛvl̩'eʃən〕n. 揭露　　**shoot the breeze** 聊天
scarcity〔'skɛrsətɪ〕n. 缺乏　　mobility〔mo'bɪlətɪ〕n. 流動性
drop in 順道拜訪　　porch〔portʃ, pɔrtʃ〕n. 門廊

Ⅳ. 中翻英：20 %

1. Maternal love $\left\{\begin{array}{l}\text{differs from} \\ \text{is different from}\end{array}\right\}$ love affairs; a mother
   loves her children unconditionally.

2. Freud once said, "Nobody can keep a secret."

3. Most people think that it's harder to learn another language
   when one gets older.

4. Although some reference books are still of referential value,
   most of them are already out of date.

5. According to Chinese tradition, marriage is a family matter,
   not a personal affair.

國立清華大學八十一學年度
碩士班研究生入學考試英文試題

I. Vocabulary: 20%

For each of the following questions, choose the letter of the one answer which is closest in meaning to the under-lined word.

1. The story contains an interesting <u>dialogue</u> between the main characters.
   (A) quarrel   (B) conversation
   (C) decision   (D) relationship

2. Officer Smith <u>pursued</u> the criminal for many years.
   (A) chased   (B) hated
   (C) arrested   (D) studied

3. This petition <u>merits</u> more serious attention than it has so far received.
   (A) needs   (B) receives
   (C) lacks   (D) deserves

4. This student is very <u>inquisitive</u>.
   (A) strange   (B) curious
   (C) inconsiderate   (D) clever

5. So far the results of the experiment are encouraging, but the <u>ultimate</u> outcome is still in doubt.
   (A) final   (B) real
   (C) best   (D) other

6. The government feared there would be an <u>uprising</u> over its taxation policies.
   (A) approval   (B) boost
   (C) revolt   (D) protest

7. The workers were <u>irate</u> about the amount of work they were now expected to do.
   (A) angry   (B) sad
   (C) concerned   (D) pleased

8. A large amount of <u>counterfeit</u> money was discovered at the scene.
   (A) opposition　　　　　(B) hot
   (C) stolen　　　　　　　(D) fake

9. The author is best known for his <u>zany</u> science fiction stories.
   (A) crazy　　　　　　　(B) realistic
   (C) popular　　　　　　(D) funny

10. The official celebration was an extremely <u>tedious</u> affair.
    (A) boring　　　　　　(B) exciting
    (C) brief　　　　　　　(D) uplifting

II. Correcting Grammar: 20%

   Each of the following sentences contains one grammatical problem. For each sentence, choose the letter of the position in which the problem occurs.

11. <u>Before choosing</u> <u>which school to attend</u>, <u>you have to</u>
    　　　A　　　　　　　　B　　　　　　　　　　C
    <u>deciding what you really want to study</u>.
    　　　　　　　　D

12. <u>Four years ago</u>, <u>when I am a senior high school student</u>,
    　　　A　　　　　　　　　B
    I spent <u>a lot of time</u> <u>studying English</u>.
    　　　　　C　　　　　　　D

13. <u>I found the incident</u> <u>too disturbing that</u> <u>I was hardly</u>
    　　　A　　　　　　　　B　　　　　　　　　C
    able to <u>tell the police what had happened</u>.
    　　　　　　　　D

14. I can't <u>imagine</u> <u>what I am like</u> <u>if such a terrible thing</u>
    　　　　A　　　　　B　　　　　　　C
    <u>ever happened to me</u>.
    　　　　D

15. <u>When I returned</u> <u>to my office</u>, I found that <u>the money</u>
    　　　A　　　　　　B　　　　　　　　　C
    <u>was disappeared</u>.
    　　　D

16. <u>After this bad experience</u>, <u>I told to myself</u> <u>that I should</u>
　　　　　A　　　　　　　　　　　　　　B　　　　　　　　　　C

　　<u>never go there again</u>.
　　　　　D

17. <u>The child always</u> <u>had to endure</u> <u>the threaten by the old</u>
　　　　　A　　　　　　　　　B　　　　　　　　C

　　people that <u>they would eat her dog</u>.
　　　　　　　　　　D

18. <u>In the fall</u>, <u>the tree produces</u> a <u>yellow fruit smells</u>
　　　　A　　　　　　　　B　　　　　　　　　　　C

　　<u>incredibly foul</u>.
　　　　D

19. <u>Come home late</u> <u>last night</u>, <u>we found</u> <u>the house dark</u>.
　　　　A　　　　　　　B　　　　　C　　　　　　D

20. <u>The purpose</u> <u>of the rehearsal</u> is to <u>make everything</u> <u>to</u>
　　　　A　　　　　　B　　　　　　　　　　C

　　go smoothly <u>during the actual performance</u>.
　　　　　　　　　D

III. Fill in the Blank: 20%

　　For each of the following sentences, choose the letter
　　of the one answer which best fits in the blank space.

21. ＿＿＿＿is a good thing that Ms. Lopez is a lawyer and
　　not a journalist.
　　(A) There　　　　　　　　(B) It
　　(C) She　　　　　　　　　(D) What

22. The plans for a new highway are now being＿＿＿＿.
　　(A) consider　　　　　　　(B) considering
　　(C) consideration　　　　　(D) considered

23. Two weeks ago, Wills told us that he＿＿＿＿finish the
　　work last week.
　　(A) would　　　　　　　　(B) will
　　(C) is　　　　　　　　　　(D) can

24. There are four possible answers to this question; your
　　job is to pick＿＿＿＿the correct one.
　　(A) out　　　　　　　　　(B) for
　　(C) through　　　　　　　(D) up

25. I_____ you can come to the party tonight.
(A) want　　　　　　　　(B) hope
(C) desire　　　　　　　(D) wish

26. That was the first time that I_____.
(A) successed　　　　　(B) success
(C) succeeded　　　　　(D) succeed

27. Jones gave a long speech, but no one knew what he was
_____.
(A) talk　　　　　　　　(B) talked
(C) talking　　　　　　(D) talking about

28. They all like to take pictures_____beautiful scenery.
(A) of　　　　　　　　　(B) about
(C) for　　　　　　　　(D) under

29. _____the supervisor was not happy with the proposal,
he accepted it anyway.
(A) Since　　　　　　　(B) But
(C) Although　　　　　(D) Yet

30. The students were generally happy about the manner
_____the assignment was graded.
(A) how　　　　　　　　(B) that
(C) how that　　　　　(D) in which

IV. Reading Comprehension: 20%
For each of the following paragraphs, read the paragraph
and then answer each question which follows. For each
question, choose the letter of the one best answer.

A.
　　Because pressure varies from place to place, the air
tends to move from high to low-pressure areas in order to
create equilibrium. This air movement is the familiar wind,
but, because of the rotation of the Earth, the wind does not
move in a straight line from high to low. At the equator the
surface of the Earth is moving at about 1,000 miles an hour,
while at the poles the speed is zero, although anyone standing at a pole will rotate once every 24 hours. If an object
--be it a cricket ball, an artillery shell or a mass of

air--moves away from the equator, it will be travelling west to east at 1,000 miles an hour in addition to its speed away from the equator. When it lands it will be at a place where the Earth's west-east velocity is less than 1,000 miles an hour, so the object will land to the east of where it was aiming when it left the equator. This "kick" to the east can be represented mathematically as a force, analogous to centrifugal force, which is known as the Coriolis force. In general, the Coriolis force turns straight-line travel into a curved path, with the direction of the curve depending on whether the movement is toward the equator or away from it.

31. What is this paragraph mainly about?
    (A) air movements   (B) pressure differences
    (C) climate   (D) the Earth's speed of rotation

32. What reason is given in this paragraph for the fact that air does not move directly from high pressure areas to low pressure areas?
    (A) Pressure differences are constantly changing.
    (B) Air movements are affected by gravity.
    (C) The Earth's surface rotates at different speeds, varying with latitude.
    (D) The wind affects air movements.

33. Because of the Coriolis force, air moving south from the north pole will
    (A) be "kicked" eastward.
    (B) be "kicked" westward.
    (C) be "kicked" either eastward or westward, depending on the season.
    (D) move directly south.

34. Why does the writer mention a cricket ball and an artillery shell?
    (A) because their movements are similar to air movements
    (B) because their movements are different from air movements
    (C) because their movements are affected by air movements
    (D) because they move at high speeds

B.

Like the great religions, the communist doctrine offered several layers of analysis, ranging from the simplest explanation to rather more complex philosophical concepts. To the semi-literate, it sufficed to learn that all life is defined by the class struggle and that a state of social bliss will be achieved by the communist society. Especially gratifying from a psychological point of view to the disadvantaged was the justification of brutal violence against "enemies of the people," those previously endowed with greater material wealth, who could now be pleasurably humbled, oppressed, and destroyed. But communism was not only a passionate response to deeply felt concerns or just a self-righteous creed of social hate. It was also a readily understandable system of thought, seemingly providing a unique insight into the future as well as the past. Thus, to the intellectually more discriminating, Marxist theory seemed to provide the key to understanding human history, economic life, social motivation, and social and political change. At the same time, the emphasis placed on political action to promote a redemptive "revolution," and on all-embracing state control to achieve a rationally planned, just society, appealed especially to the intellectuals' craving for action seemingly based on reason. Communism thus appealed to the simpletons and to the sophisticates alike: It gave each a sense of direction, a satisfactory explanation, and a moral justification.

35. What is this paragraph mainly about?
    (A) why communism was attractive to many people
    (B) the intellectual status of communism
    (C) why communism appealed to intellectuals
    (D) why communism was wrong

36. In the last sentence, the word simpleton refers to
    (A) believers in communism.
    (B) intellectuals who accepted communism.
    (C) semi-literates who accepted communism.
    (D) communist leaders.

37. Which of the following is <u>not</u> given in the paragraph as
    a reason for intellectuals accepting communism?
    (A) It justified revenge against rich people.
    (B) It told them how they could create a better society.
    (C) It seemed to explain why societies change.
    (D) It offered an explanation of human history.

C.

The poets of the Norse mythology are the only spokesmen
for the beliefs of the whole Teutonic race--of which England
is a part, and ourselves through the first settlers in
America. Everywhere else in northwestern Europe the early
records, the traditions, the songs and stories, were oblit-
erated by the priests of Christianity, who felt a bitter
hatred for the paganism they had come to destroy. It is
extraordinary how clean a sweep they were able to make. A
few bits survived: Beowulf in England, the Nibelungenlied in
Germany, and some stray fragments here and there. But if it
were not for the two Icelandic Eddas we should know practically nothing of the religion which molded the race to which
we belong. In Iceland, naturally by its position the last
northern country to be Christianized, the missionaries seem
to have been gentler, or, perhaps, they had less influence.
Latin did not drive Norse out as the literary tongue. The
people still told the old stories in the common speech, and
some of them were written down, although by whom or when we
do not know. The oldest manuscript of the Elder Edda is
dated at about 1300, three hundred years after the Chris-
tians arrived, but the poems it is made up of are purely
pagan and adjudged by all scholars to be very old. The
Younger Edda, in prose, was written down by one Snorri
Sturluson in the last part of the twelfth century. The chief
part of it is a technical treatise on how to write poetry,
but it also contains some prehistoric mythological material
which is not in the Elder Edda.

38. Why does the author devote so much space to the discussion of Iceland?
    (A) because it was Christianized by missionaries
    (B) because it was never Christianized
    (C) because important Norse works have survived there
    (D) because it is so far north

39. Beowulf and the Nibelungenlied are examples of
    (A) Christian beliefs.
    (B) Norse mythology.
    (C) Icelandic myths.
    (D) anti-pagan works.

40. The author of this paragraph is
    (A) Latin.
    (B) Icelandic.
    (C) English.
    (D) American.

V. Composition: 20%

Write a one-paragraph composition about your experience with music.

國立清華大學八十一學年度
碩士班研究生入學考試英文試題詳解

I. 字彙：20％

1. (B) dialogue〔'daɪə,lɔg〕*n*. 對話
   (A) quarrel〔'kwɔrəl〕*n*. 爭吵

2. (A) pursue〔pə'su〕*v*. 追捕
   (A) *chase*〔tʃes〕*v*. 追　　(C) arrest〔ə'rɛst〕*v*. 逮捕

3. (D) merit〔'mɛrɪt〕*v*. 應得
   (C) lack〔læk〕*v*. 缺乏　　(D) *deserve*〔dɪ'zɜv〕*v*. 應得

4. (B) inquisitive〔ɪn'kwɪzətɪv〕*adj*. 好問的
   (B) *curious*〔'kjʊrɪəs〕*adj*. 好奇的
   (C) inconsiderate〔,ɪnkən'sɪdərɪt〕*adj*. 不體貼的

5. (A) ultimate〔'ʌltəmɪt〕*adj*. 最終的
   outcome〔'aʊt,kʌm〕*n*. 結果

6. (C) uprising〔'ʌp,raɪzɪŋ〕*n*. 叛變；暴動
   (B) boost〔bust〕*n*. 提高　　(C) *revolt*〔rɪ'volt〕*n*. 叛變
   (D) protest〔'protɛst〕*n*. 抗議

7. (A) irate〔aɪ'ret〕*adj*. 生氣的
   (D) concerned〔kən'sɜnd〕*adj*. 擔心的

8. (D) counterfeit〔'kaʊntəfɪt〕*adj*. 偽造的
   (A) opposition〔,ɑpə'zɪʃən〕*n*. 反對
   (D) *fake*〔fek〕*adj*. 假的

9. (A) zany〔'zenɪ〕*adj*. 瘋狂的

10. (A) tedious〔'tidɪəs〕*adj*. 沈悶的；乏味的
    (D) uplifting〔ʌp'lɪftɪŋ〕*adj*. 令人意氣昂揚的

Ⅱ. 文法：20%

11. (**C**)　*deciding → decide*　　have to = must「必須」，其後須接原形動詞。

12. (**B**)　*am → was*　　依句意，為過去式，故須用過去式 be 動詞。

13. (**B**)　*too → so*　　*so … that ~* 如此…以致於~

14. (**B**)　*what I am like → what I would be like*　　依句意，為與現在事實相反的假設，故用過去式。

15. (**D**)　*was disappeared → had disappeared*　　disappear 為一不及物動詞，無被動語態。

16. (**B**)　*to myself → myself*　　tell 為一及物動詞，須直接接受詞。

17. (**C**)　*the threaten by the old people → the threat of the old people*　　endure 為一及物動詞，其後須接受詞，故須將動詞 threaten 改為名詞 threat。

18. (**C**)　*smells → smelling* 或 *that smells*　　兩動詞間無連接詞，第二個動詞須改為現在分詞，或改為形容詞子句。
foul〔faʊl〕*adj.* 有惡臭的

19. (**A**)　*Come → Coming*　　原句為 When we came home late, we ~, 連接詞與相同主詞 we 可省略，came 須改為 coming，形成分詞構句。

20. (**D**)　*to go → go*　　make 為使役動詞，接受詞之後，須接原形動詞表主動。

Ⅲ. 填空：20%

21. (**B**)　用虛主詞 it，代替 that 子句。
journalist〔ˈdʒɝn!ɪst〕*n.* 新聞記者

22. (**D**)　依句意為被動語態，其公式為「be 動詞＋p.p.」，故選(D)。

23. (**A**)　依句意，為過去式，故選(A) would。

24. (**A**)　pick out　選出

25. (**B**)　依句意，選(B) hope 希望。而(A) want 不可接子句，(C) desire，
(D) wish 之後所接的子句，須用假設語氣，在此不合。

26. (**C**)　依句意，爲過去式，故選(C) succeeded 。

27. (**D**)　talk about　談論

28. (**A**)　take pictures of ～　拍攝～照片

29. (**C**)　依句意，選(C) although　儘管。而(A)旣然，(B)但是，(D)然而，
皆不合句意。
supervisor〔‚supɚˈvaɪzɚ〕*n.* 管理者

30. (**D**)　空格應塡一關係代名詞，代替先行詞manner，又依句意，表
「以～方式」須用 in ～manner，可將 in 加在關代which 之前，
故選(D) in which 。

Ⅳ. 閱讀測驗：20%

Part A.

【譯文】

　　因爲氣壓各地不同，而空氣會從高氣壓處移轉到低氣壓處，以取得平
衡。這種空氣的移動就是我們熟知的風，但是因爲地球自轉的緣故，風從
高壓處到低壓處並不是呈直線運動。在赤道地區，地球表面以每小時一千
英里的速度轉動，而在兩極地區，儘管任何站在極點上的人會每二十四小
時轉一圈，其速度卻是零。如果有一個物體——不管是板球、砲彈，或是
一團空氣——偏離赤道移動，它將會由西向東，以每小時一千英里，再加
上其原先偏離赤道的速度而移動。當它落地時，會降在地球由西向東轉動
的速度小於每小時一千英里的地方，所以該物體會落在當初它離開赤道時，
所瞄準的地方的東邊。這種向東的「後坐力」在數學上就代表一股力量，
也就是我們所知的科氏力，它很像離心力。大體而言，科氏力會把直線運
動變成曲線路徑，而彎曲的方向是決定於其移動是向著赤道，或是偏離赤
道。

【答案】

31.（ A ）　　32.（ C ）　　33.（ B ）　　34.（ A ）

【註】

equilibrium〔͵ikwə'lɪbrɪəm〕*n.* 平衡；平均

rotation〔ro'teʃən〕*n.* 迴轉；旋轉　　equator〔ɪ'kwetɚ〕*n.* 赤道

cricket ball 板球　　artillery〔ɑr'tɪlərɪ〕*n.* 大砲

artillery shell 砲彈　　velocity〔və'lɑsətɪ〕*n.* 速度

kick〔kɪk〕*n.* 反彈；後坐力　　analogous〔ə'næləgəs〕*adj.* 類似的

centrifugal〔sɛn'trɪfjʊgl̩〕*adj.* 離心（力）的

Coriolis force 科氏力

Part B

【譯文】

　　跟其它大宗教一樣，共產黨的教義也提供許多層的解釋，範圍從最簡單的解釋到較複雜的哲學理念。對教育程度不高的人來說，只要知道所有生活的定義，就是階級鬥爭，而只有共產社會才能達成社會大同就夠了。對處於劣勢的人，從心理學的角度來看，特別令他們感到高興的是，能將野蠻暴力合理化，來「對抗人民的公敵」。因此那些從前擁有較多財富的人，現在可以叫他們低聲下氣，可以壓迫他們，毀滅他們。但共產主義不只是對人們切身之事做出熱烈反應，也不只是社會仇恨，自以為是的教條而已。它也是一套立即可理解的思想體系，表面上看來是在對過去和未來提出一種獨到的見解。因此，對才智較出眾者，馬克思理論似乎提供了瞭解人類歷史、經濟生活、社會動機、社會及政治變動的答案。同時，共產主義強調以政治活動來促進救贖式的「革命」，強調無所不包的國家控制，以便達成一個經過理性規畫的社會，對渴望理性行動的知識分子特別有吸引力。因此，共產主義可同時吸引傻瓜和世故之人：它給每個人方向感、滿意的解釋、以及道德上的理由。

【答案】

35. (**A**)　　　36. (**C**)　　　37. (**A**)

【註】

communist〔'kɑmju,nɪst〕*n*. 共產黨員　　doctrine〔'dɑktrɪn〕*n*. 教條
semi-literate〔,sɛmə'lɪtərɪt〕*n*. 知識程度不高者
suffice〔sə'faɪs〕*v*. 使滿足　　gratifying〔'grætə,faɪɪŋ〕*adj*. 令人滿足的
the disadvantaged 處於劣勢者　　endow〔ɪn'daʊ〕*v*. 賦予
discriminating〔dɪ'skrɪmə,netɪŋ〕*adj*. 有識別力的
redemptive〔rɪ'dɛmptɪv〕*adj*. 救贖的　　all-embracing *adj*. 無所不包的
appeal to 吸引　　craving〔'krevɪŋ〕*n*. 渴望；熱望
simpleton〔'sɪmpl̩tən〕*n*. 笨蛋
sophisticate〔sə'fɪstɪ,ket〕*n*. 世故的人
justification〔,dʒʌstəfə'keʃən〕*n*. 正當化；理由

Part C

【譯文】

　　寫下北歐挪威神話的詩人，並不是整個條頓民族信仰的唯一代言人；英國是條頓民族的一部分，而我們則是美國第一批移民中的一群。西北歐其他所有的地方，早期的記錄、傳統、歌謠及故事，都被基督教的傳教士所消滅了，而這些教士對於他們所摧毀的異教信仰，感到深惡痛絕。極不尋常的是，他們能把當地文化清除得非常乾淨。只有一小部分殘存下來：那就是英國的「貝奧武夫」，德國的「尼白龍根」，以及一些四散佚失的斷簡殘篇。如果沒有兩部冰島的「埃達」詩文集，我們就根本無從了解塑成我們所屬民族的宗教了。因其地理位置的緣故，冰島成為最後一個皈依基督教的國家，因此，傳教士看起來比較溫和，或者該說，他們比較沒有影響力。拉丁文並沒有取代挪威語而成為文學所用的語言。人們仍然在日常的談話中，說著古老的故事，而其中有一些已被寫下來，成為文字，儘管我們並不知道是誰或是在何時所寫的。「大埃達」最古老的手稿被鑑定是在西元一三〇〇年所寫的，那是在基督教徒來了三百年之後的事。但其中的詩純粹都是非基督教的作品，因此，學者都認其為極古老的作品。散文寫成的「小埃達」是在十二世紀末葉由一位叫蘇諾里•史德魯森的人所寫成的。它主要的部分，是一篇關於教人如何寫詩的學術論文，但它也包括了一些在「大埃達」中沒有包含的史前神話題材。

【答案】

38.(C)　　39.(B)　　40.(D)

【註】

Norse〔nɔrs〕*adj.* 北歐的；挪威的　mythology〔mɪ'θɑlədʒɪ〕*n.* 神話集
spokesman〔'spoksmən〕*n.* 代言人；發言人
Teutonic〔tju'tɑnɪk〕*adj.* 條頓民族的
obliterate〔ə'blɪtə,ret〕*v.* 使消滅
Beowulf〔'beə,wulf〕*n.* 貝奧武夫(八世紀初古英語的一篇史詩中的主人翁)
Nibelungenlied〔'nibə,luŋən,lit〕*n.* 尼白龍根(十三世紀上半葉完成於
　　德國南部的長篇敍事)
fragment〔'frægmənt〕*n.* 片斷；斷簡殘篇
missionary〔'mɪʃən,ɛrɪ〕*n.* 傳教士　manuscript〔'mænjə,skrɪpt〕*n.* 手稿
pagan〔'pegən〕*adj.* 異教的　　adjudge〔ə'dʒʌdʒ〕*v.* 宣判；判決
technical treatise 學術論文

V. 作文：20%

My Experience with Music

　　With regard to listening, I can say that for the most part I
quite enjoy listening to all kinds of music, except pop music.　I
often enjoy listening to CDs（I have 122！）.　Unfortunately I
can't play any musical instrument; when I was a child I tried to
learn violin and piano, but I didn't have enough patience.　Then,
I tried to play the guitar but I found I didn't have enough time
to practice since I was always so busy studying.　Perhaps when
I'm older and have more time, I will try to play the guitar again.
In any case, I really enjoy music, and I don't feel that I could
live without it.

國立交通大學八十一學年度
碩士班研究生入學考試英文試題

I. Select the word that fits the sentence. (Write the letters that identify the words, not the words, for answers.) (40%)

Vocabulary list:

a. accommodate	b. addicted	c. adequate
d. alternative	e. chaos	f. compromise
g. counterpart	h. defiance	i. enforce
j. enhance	k. hemisphere	l. illiterate
m. perspective	n. promote	o. status
p. stereotypes	q. susceptible	r. therapist
s. versatility	t. vulnerable	

1. Clothing may indicate a person's social_____.

2. People can be_____to many things: drugs, alcohol, TV, etc.

3. Music may express a state of meaning for which there exists no_____word in any language.

4. A study of the English language reveals a dramatic history and astonishing _____.

5. Electrical efficiency can_____industrial competitiveness.

6. People working under stress are more_____to health problems such as heart attacks and stomach ulcers.

7. The left_____of our brain is responsible for language, vision, the senses, and movement on the right side of the body.

8. The theory is_____to proof.

9. The citywide blackout caused_____.

10. New hotels, and new restaurants are being built to _____the increasing number of visitors.

11. The students gathered at the campus park in_____of the curfew order.

12. The problem reflected the government's inability to
_____its laws and regulations.

13. In Mainland China,_____people comprise up to eighty
percent of its population.

14. The Foreign Minister, Mr. Chang, met his Nicaragua
_____in Managua.

15. A meeting was held to_____better understanding between
the two parties.

16. To offset the deficit, the president had no_____but
to raise taxes.

17. After a long talk, the factory and the employees agreed
to_____.

18. Pastor Chen always views things from a religious_____.

19. John went to a_____for help with his psychological
problems.

20. People world-wide believe in a lot of_____about
Americans; they think all Americans drive big cars,
drink beer, and eat hot dogs.

II. Choose the right word for each sentence. (Write the
accompanying letters.) (10%)

21. Life in its biological_____is an unfathomable secret.
(A) aspects　　　　　　　(B) respects

22. To know ourselves means to overcome the_____we have
about ourselves.
(A) illusions　　　　　　(B) allusions

23. The_____of science on the everyday life of modern
people is great.
(A) compact　　　　　　(B) impact

24. To prevent the epidemics from spreading, certain
policies must be_____.
(A) implemented　　　　(B) complemented

25._____approaches are needed to increase services for
the disabled people.
(A) Innovative　　　　　(B) Renovative

26. The first duty of the state is to_____that law-abiding people are protected from crime.
    (A) assure   (B) ensure

27. The ocean provides the island people rich_____ for living.
    (A) sources   (B) resources

28. In the U.S., Blacks, Hispanics and Chinese are some _____ minorities.
    (A) ethic   (B) ethnic

29. Martin Luther King was a great hero who led the black Americans in fighting against_____.
    (A) congregation   (B) segregation

30. Only graduate students had_____to the newly installed equipment.
    (A) access   (B) assess

III. Match the words on the left with those on the right to make sensible expressions. (Write the letters.) (10%)

31. (an) affluent   a. areas

32. (a) benign   b. diseases

33. (a) controversial   c. family

34. (an) eloquent   d. issue

35. (a) flexible   e. order

36. hereditary   f. power

37. hierarchical   g. schedule

38. hypnotic   h. speaker

39. superfluous   i. tumor

40. urban   j. words

IV. Select the clause or sentence connectors. (Write the letters.) (20%)

Connectors:

a. Also(also)
b. Besides(besides)
c. However(however)
d. Nevertheless(nevertheless)
e. Nor(nor)
f. Then(then)
g. Whereas(whereas)
h. For(for) example
i. By(by) contrast
j. As(as) a result

41. _____denotation refers to the most basic, explicit definition of a word, connotation refers to the feelings that a particular word arouses.

42. Small cars conserve energy. They are inconvenient and uncomfortable on long trips, _____, because of their limited passenger and trunk space.

43. Many older people not only have unavoidable health problems but also financial difficulties:_____, they often feel unsafe, useless, and alone.

44. The divorce rate is high._____, there are many single-parent families.

45. Edwin Land started the Polaroid Corporation in 1937. _____, in 1948, he invented the Instamatic camera.

46. In Europe, churches and other religious buildings were filled with paintings that depicted people and stories from the Bible._____, images of humans and animals are seldom found in Islamic art.

47. American college students are interested in politics and impatient for social change, so together they demonstrate against war and work to solve social problems._____, when they have to get jobs, they give up most of their political activities, and nowadays they don't travel much, either.

48. According to some studies, Americans' standard of living might decrease because half of the service jobs pay low wages._____, three out of five new jobs between 1979 and 1985 paid less than $7,000 a year.

49. Having a credit card enables you to carry very little cash, a consideration in big cities where people think about security. Buying on credit_____makes it possilbe to spread the payments over a period of time.

50. We know dinosaurs principally by their skeletons, from which we measure their heights and lengths. But this information does not tell us the weight that these skeletons, particularly their limbs, had to support. _____do the measurements of length and height help us make comparisons between dinosaurs of different shapes.

V. Arrange the following sets of sentences to make them coherent paragraphs. (Write the numbers.) (20%)

A. (1) In the early 1900s, few cancer patients had any hope of longterm survival.
   (2) The gain from one in four to one in three represents about 58,000 lives saved each year.
   (3) Progress is gradually being made in the fight against cancer.
   (4) In the 1930s, less than one in five cancer victims lived more than five years.
   (5) In the 1950s, the ratio was one in four. Now the radio in one in three.

B. (1) Although scientists have experimented with different methods of prediction, from observing animal behavior to measuring radio signals from quasars, they have not proven successful.
   (2) Earthquakes are the most destructive natural disasters known to man, in terms of the millions of deaths and billions of dollars in property loss that they cause.
   (3) Despite these heavy losses, scientists are still unable to predict earthquakes.
   (4) This paper will review the history of the science of earthquake prediction, then discuss each of the methods in more detail, and finally present data indicating the success-failure ratios of each method.

C. (1) Infidelity is just a symptom of trouble.
   (2) It is a symbolic complaint, a weapon of revenge, as well as an unraveler of closeness.
   (3) Most often extramarital sex destroys a marriage because it allows an artificial split between the good and the bad--the good is projected on the new partner and the bad is dumped on the head of the old.
   (4) Dishonesty, hiding and cheating create walls between men and women.

D. (1) Responsibility could easily deteriorate into domination and possessiveness, were it not for respect.
(2) Respect means the concern that the other person
should grow and unfold as he is.
(3) Respect, thus, implies the absence of exploitation.
(4) Respect is not fear and awe; it denotes, in accordance with the root of the word (respicere=to look at),
to see a person as he is, to be aware of his unique
individuality.

E. (1) Over the decades, the nebular hypothesis has been
greatly refined and modified, but the basic concept
remains.
(2) They proposed a nebular hypothesis of the solar
system's origin.
(3) It shapes current thinking on how and where planets
form and, therefore, how one might go about searching
for them.
(4) The current view of the origin of the solar system
has its roots in concepts developed by Immanuel Kant
and Pierre Simon Laplace late in the 18th century.

51. What is the first sentence of paragraph A?

52. What is the first sentence of paragraph B?

53. What is the first sentence of paragraph C?

54. What is the first sentence of paragraph D?

55. What is the first sentence of paragraph E?

請找出以上各段的第 1 句（請寫數字）。

56. What is the sentence order of paragraph A?

57. What is the sentence order of paragraph B?

58. What is the sentence order of paragraph C?

59. What is the sentence order of paragraph D?

60. What is the sentence order of paragraph E?

請排出以上各段的順序，如 23154 或 1423 等。

國立交通大學八十一學年度
碩士班研究生入學考試英文試題詳解

I. 字彙：40%

1. (**o**)　status〔'stetəs〕*n*. 地位

2. (**b**)　addicted〔ə'dıktıd〕*adj*. 沈迷的；上癮的
　　　 * drug〔drʌg〕*n*. 毒品；藥物

3. (**c**)　adequate〔'ædəkwıt〕*adj*. 適當的

4. (**s**)　versatility〔,vɝsə'tılətı〕*n*. 用途廣泛

5. (**j**)　enhance〔ın'hæns〕*v*. 增強；提高
　　　 * competitiveness〔kəm'pɛtətıvnıs〕*n*. 競爭力

6. (**t**)　susceptible〔sə'sɛptəbḷ〕*adj*. 可能的；容許的

7. (**k**)　hemisphere〔'hɛməs,fır〕*n*. 半球

8. (**q**)　vulnerable〔'vʌlnərəbḷ〕*adj*. 易受傷的
　　　 * ***heart attack*** 心臟病發作　　ulcer〔'ʌlsɚ〕*n*. 潰瘍

9. (**e**)　chaos〔'ke,ɑs〕*n*. 混亂
　　　 * blackout〔'blæk,aʊt〕*n*. 停電

10. (**a**)　accommodate〔ə'kɑmə,det〕*v*. 容納

11. (**h**)　defiance〔dı'faıəns〕*v*. 反抗
　　　 * curfew〔'kɝfju〕*n*. 宵禁

12. (**i**)　enforce〔ın'fors〕*v*. 實施
　　　 * regulation〔,rɛgjə'leʃən〕*n*. 規定

13. (**l**)　illiterate〔ı'lıtərıt〕*adj*. 文盲的

14. (**g**)　counterpart〔'kaʊntɚ,pɑrt〕*n*. 互相對應的人或物

15. (n)　promote〔prə'mot〕v. 促進

16. (d)　alternative〔ɔl't3nətɪv〕n. 選擇
　　　　　* offset〔'ɔf,sɛt〕v. 抵消；補償
　　　　　　deficit〔'dɛfəsɪt〕n. 赤字　　　tax〔tæks〕n. 稅

17. (f)　compromise〔'kɑmprə,maɪz〕v. 和解；妥協

18. (m)　perspective〔pə'spɛktɪv〕n. 整體觀點
　　　　　* pastor〔'pæstə〕n. 牧師

19. (r)　therapist〔'θɛrəpɪst〕n. 醫師；治療學家

20. (p)　stereotype〔'stɛrɪə,taɪp〕n. 刻板印象

Ⅱ. 字彙選擇：10 %

21. (**A**)　aspect〔'æspɛkt〕n. (問題的某一)觀點；方面
　　　　　(B) respect〔rɪ'spɛkt〕n. 方面(aspect 通常是指「考慮某件事物之一個觀點」，而 respect 則用於不特定之事物)。
　　　　　* unfathomable〔ʌn'fæðəməbḷ〕adj. 深不可測的

22. (**A**)　illusion〔ɪ'ljuʒən〕n. 幻想
　　　　　(B) allusion〔ə'luʒən〕n. 暗指；引喻

23. (**B**)　impact〔'ɪmpækt〕n. 衝擊
　　　　　(A) compact〔'kɑmpækt〕n. 合同；小型汽車

24. (**A**)　implement〔'ɪmpləmənt〕v. 實施
　　　　　(B) epidemic〔,ɛpə'dɛmɪk〕n. 傳染病
　　　　　* complement〔'kɑmpləmənt〕v. 補充

25. (**A**)　innovative〔'ɪnə,vetɪv〕adj. 革新的
　　　　　(B) disabled〔dɪs'ebḷd〕adj. 殘廢的
　　　　　* renovative〔'rɛnə,vetɪv〕adj. 修補的

26. (**B**)　ensure〔ɪn'ʃur〕v. 確保(可直接接 that 子句)
　　　　　(B) assure〔ə'ʃur〕v. (向某人)擔保(須先接名詞或代名詞為受詞，才可接 that 子句。)
　　　　　* law-abiding adj. 守法的

27.（ B ）　resources〔 rɪ'sorsɪz 〕 *n. pl.* 資源
　　　　　(A) source〔 sors 〕 *n.* 來源

28.（ B ）　ethnic〔'ɛθnɪk 〕 *adj.* 種族的；民族的
　　　　　(A) ethic〔'ɛθɪk 〕 *n.* 倫理；道德規範
　　　　　＊ Hispanic〔 hɪs'pænɪk 〕 *n.* 西班牙裔居民
　　　　　　minority〔 maɪ'nɔrətɪ 〕 *n.* 少數民族

29.（ B ）　segregation〔ˌsɛgrɪ'geʃən 〕 *n.* 隔離
　　　　　(A) congregation〔ˌkɑngrɪ'geʃən 〕 *n.* 集會

30.（ A ）　access〔'æksɛs 〕 *n.* 使用～的權利
　　　　　(B) assess〔 ə'sɛs 〕 *v.* 核定
　　　　　＊ install〔 ɪn'stɔl 〕 *v.* 安裝

Ⅲ. 用字選擇：10 ％

31.（ c ）　affluent〔'æfluənt 〕 *adj.* 富裕的

32.（ i ）　benign〔 bɪ'naɪn 〕 *adj.* 良性的
　　　　　tumor〔'tjumɚ 〕 *n.* 腫瘤

33.（ d ）　controversial〔ˌkɑntrə'vɝʃəl 〕 *adj.* 引起爭論的
　　　　　issue〔'ɪʃʊ 〕 *n.* 問題；論點

34.（ h ）　eloquent〔'ɛləkwənt 〕 *adj.* 雄辯的

35.（ g ）　flexible〔'flɛksəbḷ 〕 *adj.* 有彈性的

36.（ b ）　hereditary〔 hə'rɛdəˌtɛrɪ 〕 *adj.* 遺傳性的

37.（ e ）　hierarchical〔ˌhaɪə'rɑrkɪkḷ 〕 *adj.* 階制制度的

38.（ f ）　hypnotic〔 hɪp'nɑtɪk 〕 *adj.* 催眠的

39.（ j ）　superfluous〔 sʊ'pɝfluəs 〕 *adj.* 不必要的；多餘的

40.（ a ）　urban〔'ɝbən 〕 *adj.* 都市的

Ⅳ. 連接詞：20％

41.(g)　whereas *conj.* 反之；在另一方面
　　　　　* denotation〔‚dino'teʃən〕*n.* 原意
　　　　　　explicit〔ɪk'splɪsɪt〕*adj.* 明確的
　　　　　　connotation〔‚kɑnə'teʃən〕*n.* 言外之意

42.(c)　however *prep.* 然而
　　　　　* conserve〔kən'sɝv〕*v.* 節省；保存
　　　　　　trunk〔trʌŋk〕*n.* 行李箱

43.(b)　besides *conj.* 此外

44.(j)　as a result　因此
　　　　　* divorce〔dɪ'vors〕*n.* 離婚

45.(f)　then *prep.* 然後；接著

46.(i)　by contrast　相反地
　　　　　* depict〔dɪ'pɪkt〕*v.* 描繪

47.(d)　nevertheless *conj.* 儘管如此
　　　　　* demonstrate〔'dɛmən‚stret〕*v.* 示威

48.(h)　for example　例如
　　　　　* wage〔wedʒ〕*n.* 工資

49.(a)　also *conj.* 也
　　　　　* security〔sɪ'kjʊrətɪ〕*n.* 安全
　　　　　　payment〔'pemənt〕*n.* 付款額

50.(e)　nor *conj.* 也不…
　　　　　* dinosaur〔'daɪnə‚sɔr〕*n.* 恐龍
　　　　　　principally〔'prɪnsəpl̩ɪ〕*adv.* 主要地
　　　　　　skeleton〔'skɛlətən〕*n.* 骨架
　　　　　　limbs〔lɪmbz〕*n.pl.* 四肢

V. 重組：20 %

A. (*3 / 452*) (3)人們努力對抗癌症，已逐漸有進展。

　　(1)在二十世紀早期，癌症病人幾乎很少有長期存活的希望。

　　(4)到了一九三○年代，有少於五分之一的癌症患者可以活過五年。

　　(5)到了一九五○年代，比例則爲四分之一。現在的比例爲三分之一。

　　(2)從四分之一到三分之一的比例，顯示每年約有五萬八千條生命被救活。

B. (*23 / 4*) (2)由地震所造成的數百萬人死亡與好幾億的財產損失看來，地震是人類所知，最具破壞性的天然災害。

　　(3)儘管地震造成的損失如此慘重，科學家們仍無法預測地震。

　　(1)雖然科學家已實驗過各種不同的預測方法，從觀察動物的行爲到測量類星體所發出的無線電訊號，但都未能成功。

　　(4)這份報告是回顧預測地震的科學史，更詳盡地探討每一種方法，最後再指出每種方法成功與失敗的比例。

　　＊ quasar〔'kwesɑr〕*n.* 類星體

C. (*43 / 2*) (4)不誠實、隱瞞和欺騙，在男女之間築起了一道牆。

　　(3)通常婚外情會破壞婚姻，因爲它使人在好壞之間，加以不自然的劃分，好的方面都被投射在新的伴侶身上，壞的方面則落在舊伴侶的頭上。

　　(1)不貞只是麻煩的徵兆。

　　(2)它也是種象徵性的抱怨、報復的工具，以及親密關係的破壞者。

　　＊ infidelity〔ˌɪnfə'dɛlətɪ〕*n.* 不貞

　　unraveler〔ʌn'rævl̩ə〕*n.* 解開之物

　　dump〔dʌmp〕*v.* 傾倒

D.（*24I3*）　(2)尊敬意謂著對他人的關心，認爲應該讓他人成長，開展自我。

(4)尊敬並非害怕或敬畏；根據 respect 的字根來看，它意謂著看見人的本質，並察覺其獨立之人格。

(1)責任若沒有了尊敬，很容易變成支配及佔有。

(3)因此，尊敬就意味著不去剝削別人。

* deteriorate〔dɪˈtɪrɪəret〕*v*. 變質；惡化
  domination〔ˌdɑməˈneʃən〕*n*. 支配
  unfold〔ʌnˈfold〕*v*. 開展
  exploitation〔ˌɪksplɔɪˈteʃən〕*n*. 剝削；利用

E.（*423I*）　(4)目前對於太陽系起源的看法，是源於十八世紀後期康德和拉普利斯所發展出來的概念。

(2)他們提出太陽系起源之星雲假說。

(3)這套假說形成現今對於行星如何形成以及形成的地點，因而指出要尋找這些行星，要如何進行的方法。

(1)數十年來，星雲假說已被大幅修改，但基本的概念仍然存在。

* nebular〔ˈnɛbjələ˞〕*adj*. 星雲的
  hypothesis〔haɪˈpɑθəˌsɪs〕*n*. 假說
  current〔ˈkɝənt〕*adj*. 目前的

國立中山大學八十一學年度
碩士班研究生入學考試英文試題

I. Vocabulary: 20%

Complete the sentences with a proper word from the list below.

afford, charge, denigrate, dismiss, dismay, distinguish, elaborate, forgive, inquire, interrupt, recognize, revise, sabotage, scatter

1. I'm not rich and can't＿＿＿＿a new car every year.

2. Some people have so little conscience that they can't ＿＿＿＿between right and wrong.

3. They don't seem to enforce the fines against littering here. Garbage is＿＿＿＿ed all along the highway.

4. We were having an interesting conversation when my mother＿＿＿＿ed us to say that dinner was ready.

5. Jim's face was a picture of＿＿＿＿when he realized he'd left his bags in the bus station.

6. A pen like this usually costs $10, but they only＿＿＿＿ed me $8 for it.

7. We had a quarrel, I know. But let's just＿＿＿＿and forget.

8. A human being is not an animal, and we should not＿＿＿＿ him.

9. Just tell us the facts and don't＿＿＿＿on them.

10. I hadn't seen Peter for ten years, and when we met he had changed so much that I hardly＿＿＿＿ed him.

II. Idioms: 20%

Fill in the blanks with a proper preposition or adverbial particle.

Example: The room smells _of_ paint.

1. He could not account＿＿＿＿his foolish mistake.

2. I cannot agree_____such a proposal.

3. Her parents disapprove_____her staying out late at night.

4. He left_____the grounds of ill health.

5. History furnishes us with a case_____point.

6. He is not so much a scholar_____a writer.

7. We must be prepared_____inflation.

8. I talked them_____doing business with us.

9. I cannot distinguish one twin_____the other.

10. You must think it_____before you make a decision.

III. Correcting Sentences: 20%

In each of the following sentences there is a word or phrase which needs to be corrected. Identify the error and rewrite the sentence in a correct form.

Example: Fruit is more cheaper than vegetables.
Corrected sentence: Fruit is cheaper than vegetables.

1. Mary is leaving Taiwan and many of her friends came to see her off at the airport.

2. I felt very boring after a long day's work, so I watched TV in the evening.

3. Because she was too young, so she couldn't enter the beauty contest.

4. The child approaches learning as problem-solving has an advantage.

5. The vanilla vine sends out tiny rootlets by which the vine attaches itself to trees.

6. We were told this morning that Mr. Chen was dead of a heart attack last night.

7. When his alarm went off this morning, he shut it off, rolled over, and slept for more twenty minutes.

8. When I walked into my office, I caught a thief look through my desk drawer.

9. Since Mary is a diligent student, I expect her passing the test.

10. I didn't do well on the test because I didn't study for it last night. I should study last night.

IV. Cloze Test: 20%

Fill in the blanks with any appropriate word to complete the paragraph.

The Effect of Television Violence on Children

Parents and teachers are worried about the effect of television violence on children. Many children___1___television for several hours every day, and even___2___they are watching children's programs,___3___may still be confronted with___4___of violence and terror.___5___this constant exposure to violence encourages children to act___6___violently themselves is not certain.___7___has been a general increase in violence in society in recent years,___8___experts have not been able to trace this trend directly to television. Yet, they___9___out that the situation is dangerous because TV teaches children at an early age to accept violence ___10___a natural part of life.

V. Reading Comprehension: 20%

Read the articles given and answer the questions after them.

An allergy is an extreme response by the body to a foreign substance. The foreign substance, called an antigen, causes a defensive chemical reaction when it enters the body the first time. If the antigen enters the body again, an allergic reaction occurs.

The body produces antibodies (special molecules) to fight and destroy foreign substances. When we get sick, the foreign substance might be a virus or a bacterium. Our bodies produce antibodies to fight the virus or bacterium, and eventually we get well. During an allergic reaction, too, our bodies produce antibodies to fight the foreign substance. But instead of attacking the antigen, the antibodies attack the body itself. Scientists do not understand why this happens.

An antigen can be almost any substance that is foreign to the body. It is not necessarily a toxic substance: It can be food or plants. These natural substances can become toxic if a person has an allergic reaction to them. We can breathe antigens (dust, pollens, molds); we can ingest antigens (food, drugs and medicines that we take orally); antigens can be injected (drugs, vaccines); and antigens can come into contact with our skin (chemicals, certain plants).

Probably the most common allergies are asthma and hay fever. Scientists do not know what causes asthma, but its symptoms are well known: wheezing, coughing, and difficulty in breathing. Asthma attacks can occur very suddenly, perhaps in response to physical or emotional stress. Hay fever is an allergic reaction to antigens in the air. Its symptoms are sneezing, scratchy, watery eyes, and runny nose. Some people get hay fever only at certain times of the year. Pollens from plants and trees cause this kind of hay fever. Other people get hay fever at any time of the year. These people might be allergic to dust, molds, or animals (especially cats and dogs). Allergies to foods are not as common as hay fever in adults, but many children have food allergies.

Why do some people have allergies and others do not? Some kinds of allergies seem to be hereditary--they run in families. Others appear at one time of life and disappear at another. Unfortunately, we do not have specific answers to our questions. Scientists hope someday to understand the cause of allergies. Only then can they find a cure.

1. What is an antigen? It is a
   (A) toxic substance existing in the body.
   (B) chemical reaction produced by the body.
   (C) substance that causes allergic reactions.

2. Which of the following statements best summarizes the
   main idea in the second paragraph?
   (A) Antibodies are produced to fight substances foreign
       to the body.
   (B) Antibodies cause allergic reactions.
   (C) Antibodies attack not only antigens but also the body
       itself.

3. People may get hay fever
   (A) when they breathe antigens.
   (B) when they are under emotional stress.
   (C) when their skin comes into contact with antigens.

4. According to the article, which of the following state-
   ments is not true?
   (A) Food allergies are not as common in adults as in
       children.
   (B) People get hay fever only at certain times of the
       year.
   (C) A virus or a bacterium will cause the production of
       antibodies.
   (D) Toxic substances can cause allergic reactions.

5. The main topic of this article is:
   (A) how antigens enter our body.
   (B) how allergies happen.
   (C) a future cure for allergies.
   (D) symptoms of common allergies.

   One of the most difficult problems in many divorces is
determining custody of the children. Parents should know
their legal rights and responsibilities when deciding who
will take care of the children. However, this is not easy,
since there have been many changes in custody arrangements
through the years. A hundred years ago in the United States,
the father always received custody. Later, custody was most
often given to the mother, because the mother was considered
the more important caregiver. At the present time, while

custody is still usually awarded to the mother, more and more fathers are asking for and receiving custody.

The judges in a court look at each parent's personality and caregiving ability in order to determine who can best take care of the children. Usually, custody arrangements can be worked out in a friendly way, but sometimes there are bitter battles over custody and even the kidnapping of a child by the parent who wasn't awarded custody. Too often these battles do great harm to the children the court is trying to protect, so courts and family counseling services have begun to use mediation to help families make the best decision for the children.

6. The main purpose of the first paragraph is to
   (A) explain parents' legal rights concerning child custody.
   (B) describe custody arrangements of the last century.
   (C) explain how difficult it is to determine custody of the children.
   (D) state the principles of child custody.

7. What does the article say about child custody at the present time?
   (A) The father usually receives custody.
   (B) The mother is considered the more important caregiver.
   (C) Custody time is shared by parents.
   (D) It depends on the judge.

8. According to the article, which of the following statements is not true?
   (A) More and more fathers think that they can take good care of the children.
   (B) At the present time, the mother may be denied custody.
   (C) A bitter fight in the court for custody is unavoidable.
   (D) It is not easy for parents to know their legal rights and responsibilities concerning child custody.

9. In the context of the passage, mediation means
   (A) agreement.   (B) consultation.
   (C) intervention.   (D) court decision.

10. Which of the following factors is not important in the
    judge's decision regarding child custody?
    (A) parent's personality
    (B) parent's caregiving ability
    (C) family counseling
    (D) previous arrangements by the court

國立中山大學八十一學年度
碩士班研究生入學考試英文試題詳解

I. 文意字彙: 20％

1. *afford* 〔ə'fɔrd〕 *v.* 買得起；負擔得起

2. *distinguish* 〔dɪs'tɪŋgwɪʃ〕 *v.* 分辨
   * conscience 〔'kɑnʃəns〕 *n.* 良心

3. *scattered* scatter 〔'skætɚ〕 *v.* 散落四方
   * enforce 〔ɪn'fors〕 *v.* 實施；履行　　fine 〔faɪn〕 *n.* 罰鍰
   litter 〔'lɪtɚ〕 *v.* 丟垃圾

4. *interrupted* interrupt 〔,ɪntɚ'rʌpt〕 *v.* 打斷

5. *dismay* 〔dɪs'me〕 *n.* 驚慌；沮喪

6. *charged* charge 〔tʃɑrdʒ〕 *v.* 索價；收費

7. *forgive* 〔fɔr'gɪv〕 *v.* 寬恕；原諒
   * quarrel 〔'kwɑrəl〕 *n.* 吵架

8. *denigrate* 〔'dɛnə,gret〕 *v.* 毀壞名譽

9. *elaborate* 〔ɪ'lebə,ret〕 *v.* 詳述

10. *recognized* recognize 〔'rɛkəg,naɪz〕 *v.* 認出

II. 慣用語: 20％

1. *for*　　*account for* 說明；解釋

2. *with*　*agree with* 同意

3. *of*　　*disapprove of* ～ 不贊成～

4. *on*　　*on the grounds of* ～ 由於～

5. *in*　　*a case in point* 一個適合的例子

6. *as*　　*not so much A as B* 與其說是A，不如說是B

7. *for*　　*be prepared for ~* 為～作準備
　　　　　* inflation〔ɪnˈfleʃən〕*n.* 通貨膨脹

8. *into*　　*talk sb. into* + V-ing　說服某人～

9. *from*　*distinguish A from B* 分辨A與B

10. *over*　*think over* 仔細考慮

Ⅲ. 改正下列句子：20％

1. Mary is leaving Taiwan and many of *her* friends *will come* to see her off at the airport.

2. I felt very *bored* after a long day's work, so I watched TV in the evening.

3. Because she was too young, she couldn't enter the beauty contest.

4. The child *who* approaches learning as problem-solving has an advantage.

5. The vanilla vine sends out tiny rootlets *with* which the vine attaches itself to trees.
　　* vanilla〔vəˈnɪlə〕*n.* 香草　　vine〔vaɪn〕*n.* 蔓；藤
　　rootlet〔ˈrutlɛt, ˈrutlɪt〕*n.* 幼根
　　attach〔əˈtætʃ〕*v.* 附著

6. We were told this morning that Mr. Chen *died* of a heart attack last night.

7. When his alarm went off this morning, he shut it off, rolled over, and slept for *another* twenty minutes.

8. When I walked into my office, I caught a thief *looking* through my desk drawer.

9. Since Mary is a diligent student, I expect her ***to pass*** the test.

10. I didn't do well on the test because I didn't study for it last night. I should ***have studied*** last night.

Ⅳ. 填充：20%

1. ***watch***　*watch television*　看電視

2. ***when***　依句意，須填when 當～時候。

3. ***they***　空格應填一主詞，依句意，填 they 代替 children。

4. ***those***　爲了避免重覆，用 those 代替前面出現過的複數名詞 programs 。

5. ***Whether***　whether 引導名詞子句，作句子的主詞。

6. ***more***　*act more violently* 行爲較粗暴

7. ***There***　there ＋ be 動詞，表「有；存在」。

8. ***but***　依句意，填 but 「但是」。

9. ***point***　*point out* 指出

10. ***as***　*accept* A *as* B　認爲 A 是 B

V. 閱讀測驗：20%

【譯文】

　　過敏是人體對異物所產生的極端反應。這種異物，被稱之爲抗原，當它第一次進入人體時，會使人體產生防禦性的化學反應。如果該抗原再度進入人體，人體就會產生過敏的反應。

　　人體會產生抗體（即特殊的分子）來抵抗或消滅異物。當我們生病時，異物可能是病毒或細菌，最後我們還是會康復。過敏的反應產生時，人體也會製造抗體來對付這些異物。但這些抗體並沒有消除抗原，相反地，它會侵襲人體本身。科學家們還無法了解爲什麼會如此。

　　幾乎所有異於人體的物質都可能成爲抗原。但抗原未必就是毒性物質：它可能是食物或植物。如果人體對這些天然物質過敏，那它們就可能變得具有毒性。我們可能會吸進一些抗原（如灰塵、花粉、黴菌）；我們可能會吃下一些抗原（如食物或口服的藥物）；抗原也可能經由注射進入人體（如藥物、疫苗）；而抗原也可能與皮膚有所接觸（如化學藥品、某些植物）。

　　可能最常見的過敏症是氣喘與花粉熱。科學家們並不知道導致氣喘的眞正原因爲何，但氣喘的症狀是衆所皆知的：哮喘、咳嗽、以及呼吸困難。氣喘隨時都可能發生，也許是因爲生理或情緒方面的壓力而產生的反應。花粉熱是對於空氣中抗原所產生的反應。其症狀是打噴嚏、發癢、流淚、以及流鼻水。有些人只有在每年的某些時候才會得花粉熱。植物和樹的花粉導致了這種花粉熱。有些人則每年的任何時候，都有可能得花粉熱。這些人可能對灰塵、黴菌、或動物（特別是貓和狗）過敏。成人對食物過敏的情況不像花粉熱那麼普遍，但許多兒童卻會對食物過敏。

　　爲什麼有些人會有過敏的現象，而有些人卻不會呢？有些過敏似乎是遺傳性的——過敏的現象在家人之間非常普遍。有些人在一生中的某段時期會過敏，但其他時期則不會。不幸的是，對於這些問題，我們並沒有明確的答案。科學家們希望，將來有一天能夠了解導致過敏的原因。唯有知道原因，才能找出治療的方法。

【答案】

1. (C)	2. (A)	3. (A)	4. (B)	5. (B)

【註】

allergy〔ˈælədʒɪ〕*n.* 過敏症　antigen〔ˈæntədʒən, -dʒɪn〕*n.* 抗原
defensive〔dɪˈfɛnsɪv〕*adj.* 防禦性的　antibody〔ˈæntɪˌbɑdɪ〕*n.* 抗體
molecule〔ˈmɑləˌkjul〕*n.* 分子　virus〔ˈvaɪrəs〕*n.* 病毒
bacterium〔bækˈtɪrɪəm〕*n.* 細菌　toxic〔ˈtɑksɪk〕*adj.* 有毒的
pollen〔ˈpɑlən〕*n.* 花粉　mold〔mold〕*n.* 黴菌
ingest〔ɪnˈdʒɛst〕*v.* 嚥下；攝取　orally〔ˈorəlɪ, ˈɔrəlɪ〕*adj.* 口服地
inject〔ɪnˈdʒɛkt〕*v.* 注射　vaccine〔ˈvæksin, -sɪn〕*n.* 疫苗
asthma〔ˈæsmə, ˈæzmə〕*n.* 氣喘　symptom〔ˈsɪmptəm〕*n.* 症狀
hay fever 花粉熱　wheeze〔hwiz〕*v.* 哮喘
scratchy〔ˈskrætʃɪ〕*n.* 發癢　runny〔ˈrʌnɪ〕*adj.* 流鼻涕的
hereditary〔həˈrɛdəˌtɛrɪ〕*adj.* 遺傳的　cure〔kjʊr〕*n.* 治療方法

【譯文】

　　在許多離婚事件中，最難處理的就是決定孩子的監護權問題。當決定要由誰來照顧孩子時，父母應該要知道自己合法的權利與責任。然而，事情卻沒那麼簡單，因為好幾年以來，監護權的安排方式已有許多的改變。美國在一百年前，監護權總是由父親獲得。後來，監護權常常判給母親，因為一般都認為母親在照顧孩子這方面，扮演的角色要重要得多。現在，由於監護權通常仍然由母親取得，越來越多的父親也會要求並取得監護權。

　　為了要判定父母二人哪一位能使孩子獲得最好的照顧，法院中的法官通常會注意父母的人格，以及照顧孩子的能力。通常監護權的安排會以友好的方式順利完成，但是有時也會有激烈爭奪監護權的情形，甚至有無法獲得監護權的父親或母親綁架自己的小孩。通常這些爭執會對法院極力要保護的孩子造成莫大的傷害。所以法院和家庭諮詢服務機構便開始使用「調解」的方式來做出對孩子最好的決定。

【答案】

6. (C)	7. (D)	8. (C)	9. (C)	10. (D)

【註】

'divorce〔dəˈvors, -ˈvɔrs〕*n*. 離婚　　custody〔ˈkʌstədɪ〕*n*. 監護權
caregiver *n*. 照顧者　　award〔əˈwɔrd〕*v*. 授與
court〔kort, kɔrt〕*n*. 法院　　bitter〔ˈbɪtɚ〕*adj*. 劇烈的
battle〔ˈbætḷ〕*n*. 鬥爭；戰鬥　　kidnap〔ˈkɪdnæp〕*v*. 綁架
do harm to～ 對～有害　　counsel〔ˈkaʊnsḷ〕*v*. 諮詢
mediation〔ˌmidɪˈeʃən〕*n*. 調解

國立成功大學八十一學年度
碩士班研究生入學考試英文試題

I. Read each passage carefully and then answer the questions about it. In each question, select, on the basis of the passage, from among the four choices marked A, B, C, and D, the one which best answers the question. (20%)

Louis XV died when Marie Antoinette was nineteen, and the Dauphin became Louis XVI. He and his Queen were too young and inexperienced to reign successfully. The very persons who should have been the Queen's advisers, her husband's aunts, the Princesses Adelaide, Victoria, Sophia, and Louisa, were jealous and fond of scandal. Marie Antoinette found that if she had been ruled by ceremony when she was Dauphiness, she was bound fast by it now. There was a rule for everything she did, and when she broke the most trifling, the Comtesse de Noailles, chief lady-in-waiting, was sure to inform her. "On that occasion," the Comtesse would say, "Your Majesty ought to have bowed in such a manner, on this occasion in another way. Your Majesty smiled when it was not seemly, nodded when a curtsy was needed."

The Queen found these constant rebukes almost more than she could bear. One day a donkey on which she was riding threw her. Her companions ran forward in alarm, but the Queen lay laughing on the grass. "Run quickly," she exclaimed, "and ask Madame Etiquette how the Queen of France ought to behave when thrown by a donkey."

1. Marie Antoinette's attitude toward court ceremony was one of
   (A) annoyance.　　　　　　(B) resignation.
   (C) curiosity.　　　　　　(D) fear.

2. The companions were alarmed because they feared that the
Queen
(A) had broken a rule.　　　(B) had hurt herself.
(C) was angry with them.　　(D) was laughing at them.

3. The passage suggests that the title "Dauphin" was given
to
(A) any young French prince.
(B) the French king.
(C) the French queen.
(D) the heir to the French throne.

4. In making her request in the last two lines of the
passage, Marie Antoinette's intention was to
(A) find out what she should do.
(B) flatter the Comtesse.
(C) make a joke at the expense of the Comtesse.
(D) make her companions look ridiculous in the eyes of
the Comtesse.

5. Madame Etiquette was
(A) Princess Adelaide.　　　(B) Comtesse de Noailles.
(C) Princess Louisa.　　　　(D) Princess Victoria.

6. "Fast" in line 8 most nearly means
(A) cruelly.　　　　　　　　(B) rapidly.
(C) ahead of time.　　　　　(D) tightly.

7. "Seemly" in line 14 most nearly means
(A) agreeable.　　　　　　　(B) proper.
(C) courteous.　　　　　　　(D) necessary.

　　"It's so stupid at home," she greeted me, "and Miss
Minnie is so absurd. She talks such nonsense about its being
necessary for the day to be aired before I come out. Aired!
On a Sunday morning when I don't practise, I must do something. So I told Papa last night I must come out. Besides,
it's the brightest part of the day. Don't you think so?"

　　I ventured a bold flight and said (not without stammer-
ing) that it was very bright to me then, though it had been
very dark a moment before.

"Do you mean a compliment?" exclaimed Alice, "Or has the weather really changed?"

8. Alice indicates that Miss Minnie
   (A) does not want her to take walks alone.
   (B) does not want her to go out early in the morning.
   (C) is offended by her disobedience.
   (D) thinks she should be practising.

9. It seems that the writer has
   (A) never met Alice before.
   (B) tried to avoid meeting Alice.
   (C) just begun the conversation with Alice.
   (D) been talking with Alice for a long time.

10. When the writer says that he "ventured a bold flight," he means that he
    (A) made an impolite remark.
    (B) disagreed with Alice.
    (C) dared to say something nice to Alice.
    (D) used big words.

II. Here are ten common words frequently misspelled. Select the lettered item which looks right to you. (10%)

1. (A) occurrance   (B) occurrence   (C) occurance
2. (A) ecstasy   (B) ecstacy   (C) extacy
3. (A) drunkeness   (B) drunkenness   (C) drunkedness
4. (A) embarassing   (B) embarrassing   (C) embarrasing
5. (A) irresistible   (B) irresistable   (C) irrisistible
6. (A) supersede   (B) supercede   (C) superceed
7. (A) disappoint   (B) dissapoint   (C) dissappoint
8. (A) occassional   (B) occasional   (C) occasionel
9. (A) indispensable   (B) indispensible   (C) indespensible
10. (A) perseverance   (B) perseverence   (C) perserverance

III. Write two words that are synonymous with the given words. (10%)

   Example: beautiful   lovely, pretty
            strong   rugged, powerful

1. short   2. defects (noun)

3. desire (noun)
4. true
5. luminous
6. suitable
7. doubtful
8. vulgar
9. admiration
10. very

IV. Translate the following into English, and vice versa. (20%)

1. 新年團聚是中國家庭的傳統。

2. 一頓豐盛的早餐，對於營養的好壞，可能比午晚餐更加重要。

3. 心理學家認為，流行使用暴力，都是電影和電視搞出來的。

4. The Fair Trade Law is the realization of an ideal. In principle, we are all against the things that the law aims to eliminate: monopoly, deception, and all other forces created in business that attempt to manipulate our lives in favor of exessive profits.

5. Nowadays, "public opinion" has turned into such a magic phrase that it seems that virtually every proposal has to be justified on the basis of whatever might be perceived as the will or wish of the citizenry.

V. In the following passage, there are words underlined and marked with A, B, C, and D. Identify the words that should be corrected or rewritten, and write down on your answer sheet the letters of the underlined words you have chosen. (20%)

My first week in America was one of the most interesting <u>week</u> I have ever lived through. I <u>was assign</u> to a
      A   B
<u>nearby</u> school where I found that I <u>wasn't only</u> non-English-
C   D
speaking student. Unfortunately, none of my new classmates
spoke my native <u>language</u>; however, I <u>began make</u> progress in
       E   F
English immediately. After school every <u>days</u>, a friend took
             G
me <u>sightseeing</u>. The shopping centers were very impressive,
  H
and the number of movies and theaters <u>was</u> overwhelming.
            I

There was also a few things that disappointed me. One of
　　 J
them were the subway which seemed to be the worse in the
　　 K　　　　　　　　　　　　　　　　　　　　　　 L
world. Other very disturbing thing was the poor condition
　　　　　 M
of many neighborhoods. I didn't expect to see so many of
　　　　　　　　　　　　　　　　　　 N
them in such bad shape.
　　　　　 O

VI. Combine the sentences below into a paragraph that con-
　　 tains several coordinating connectives. (20%)

1. I sat down in the chair.

2. I pretended to read a book.

3. I kept watching Petey.

4. I watched him out of the corner of my eye.

5. He was a torn man.

6. First he looked at the coat.

7. He had the expression of a waif.

8. The waif was at a bakery window.

9. He turned away.

10. He set his jaw.

11. The setting was resolute.

12. He looked back at the coat.

13. He had even more longing in his face.

14. He turned away.

15. He had not so much resolution this time.

16. Back and forth his head swiveled.

17. Desire waxed.

18. Resolution waned.

19. Finally he didn't turn away at all.

20. He just stood there.

21. He stared at the coat.

22. He stared with mad lust.

Suggestion: The sentences above describe a man caught in a
　　　　　　 quandary, a perplexing state of uncertainty,
　　　　　　 wherein he vacillates between desire and reso-
　　　　　　 lution.

國立成功大學八十一學年度
碩士班研究生入學考試英文試題詳解

I. 閱讀測驗：20％

A.

【譯文】

　　法國國王路易十六去世時，瑪麗・安朵奈特年僅十九歲，當時的皇太子就即位為路易十六。當時國王和王后二人都十分年輕而無經驗，無法將國家治理得很好。那些國王的姑媽們——安德列公主、維多利亞公主、蘇菲亞公主以及露易莎公主，她們身為皇后的顧問，但卻善妒，而且對醜聞有興趣。瑪麗・安朵奈特覺得，如果說她在身為太子妃的時候，是受禮儀的規範的話，那麼她現在就可說是正被這些繁文縟節綁得死死的。她做的每一件事，都有規則必須遵守，而且如果她違反了最微不足道的規則時，那位主要的服侍她的宮女——來自諾亞里斯的伯爵夫人，一定會如此對她說——「在那種情況上，皇后陛下，您應該這樣鞠躬，而在這種情況下，是採用另一種方式鞠躬。皇后陛下您在不適當的時機微笑，在應屈膝行禮時卻只是點點頭而已。」

　　皇后覺得這種經常性的指責已經超過她能忍受的限度。有一天她從驢子背上摔了下來。她的隨從們十分驚慌地跑向前去，而皇后卻躺在草地上哈哈大笑。「快跑，」她說道，「去問那位掌管禮儀的女士，當法國皇后從驢子背上摔下來的時候，她該怎麼辦。」

【答案】

1.（A）　2.（B）　3.（D）　4.（C）　5.（B）　6.（D）　7.（B）

【註】

dauphin〔'dɔfɪn〕*n*. 法國皇太子　　　　reign〔ren〕*v*. 統治

trifling〔'traɪflɪŋ〕*adj*. 微不足道的　　seemly〔'simlɪ〕*adj*. 恰當的

curtsy〔'kɜtsɪ〕*n*. 屈膝禮　　　　　　rebuke〔rɪ'bjuk〕*v*. 譴責

exclaim〔ɪk'sklem〕*v*. 呼喊　　　　　etiquette〔'ɛtɪkɛt〕*n*. 禮儀

B.

【譯文】

　　「在家眞無聊，」她迎接我時如此說道。「而且密妮小姐眞是太荒謬了。她說這樣的日子我該在出去之前先讓房間通風一下。通風！在星期天早上我通常不需要做事，我一定得想想辦法。所以我昨晚就告訴爸爸我要出去。而且這是一天之中最晴朗的時刻，你不覺得嗎？」

　　我便大膽地對她說（還是免不了有點結巴）我的確覺得天氣十分晴朗，儘管一會兒之前，天氣十分地陰暗。

　　「你這算是恭維嗎？」艾莉絲如此喊道，「還是天氣眞的變了？」

【答案】

　　8.（ B ）　　　9.（ C ）　　　10.（ C ）

【註】

absurd〔əb'sɝd〕*adj.* 荒謬的　　air〔ɛr〕*v.* 通風
venture〔'vɛntʃɚ〕*v.* 大膽；冒險　　flight〔flaɪt〕*n.*（思想）奔放
stammer〔'stæmɚ〕*v.* 結結巴巴地說
compliment〔'kɑmpləmənt〕*n.* 恭維

Ⅱ. 選出正確的字：10％

1.（ B ）occurrence〔ə'kɝəns〕*n.* 事件

2.（ A ）ecstasy〔'ɛkstəsɪ〕*n.* 狂喜

3.（ B ）drunkenness〔'drʌŋkənɪs〕*n.* 醉態

4.（ B ）embarrassing〔ɪm'bærəsɪŋ〕*adj.* 令人困窘的

5.（ A ）irresistible〔ɪrɪ'zɪstəbḷ〕*adj.* 不能抵抗的

6.（ A ）supersede〔ˌsupɚ'sid〕*v.* 取代

7.（ A ）disappoint〔ˌdɪsə'pɔɪnt〕*v.* 使失望

8.（ B ）occasional〔ə'keʒənḷ〕*adj.* 偶然的

9.（ A ）indispensable〔ˌɪndɪ'spɛnsəbḷ〕*adj.* 不可缺少的

10.（ A ）perseverance〔ˌpɝsə'vɪrəns〕*n.* 堅忍

Ⅲ. 同義字：10 ％

1. short → brief, insufficient
2. defects → shortcomings, flaws
3. desire → longing, lust
4. true → real, faithful
5. luminous → shining, radiant
6. suitable → proper, fitting
7. doubtful → uncertain, incredulous
8. vulgar → impolite, coarse
9. admiration → commendation, praise
10. very → fairly, quite

Ⅳ. 翻譯：20 ％

1. Getting together during the New Year is a tradition for Chinese families.

2. An abundant breakfast is, nutritionally, probably more important than lunch and dinner.

3. Psychologists believe that the prevalence of violence stems from cinemas and television.

4. 公平交易法實現了一個理想。原則上，該法所要遏止的事，也是我們所反對的，如壟斷、詐欺，以及其他企圖操縱我們生活，以換取暴力的商業勢力。

5. 現在「輿論」已經成為一個神奇的詞彙，好像每個提議都必須被認為是全體市民的意志或希望才能被認可。

V. 改錯：20％

【答案】

（A）（B）（D）（F）（G）（J）（K）（L）（M）

（A） *week → weeks*　　one of ＋複數名詞，表「～其中之一」。

（B） *was assign → was assigned*

（D） *wasn't only → wasn't the only*

（F） *began make → began making*

（G） *days → day*

（J） *There was → There were*

（K） *were → was*

（L） *the worse → the worst*

（M） *Other → The other*

VI. 重組：20％

　　Sitting down in the chair and, pretending to read a book, I kept watching Petey out of the corner of my eye.　He was a torn man. First he looked at the coat with the expression of a waif at the bakery window.　Then he turned away and set his jaw resolutely. But he looked back at the coat with even more longing in his face. He turned away, but he had not so much resolution this time. Back and forth his head swiveled ; desire waxed and resolution waned. Finally he didn't turn away at all.　He just stood there, staring at the coat with mad lust.

國立中興大學八十一學年度
碩士班研究生入學考試英文試題

I. Vocabulary: 10%

To each question, choose <u>one</u> answer, (A), (B), (C), or (D) that best completes the sentence.

Example: No evil can_____a good man.
(A) harm　　(B) hate　　(C) hide　　(D) hire
Answer : (A)

1. The crisis of liberal education is an intellectual crisis of the greatest_____.
(A) magnetism　　　　　　(B) magnitude
(C) maximum　　　　　　 (D) magnificence

2. European observers sometimes classify him as a_____ curiosity, neither fully American nor satisfactorily European.
(A) hybrid　　　　　　　　(B) hysterical
(C) hypocritical　　　　　(D) hygienic

3. His religious belief is not_____with reason.
(A) inconceivable　　　　(B) incomparable
(C) incomplete　　　　　　(D) incompatible

4. In all criminal_____a man has a right to demand the cause and nature of his accusation.
(A) persecutions　　　　　(B) prohibitions
(C) prosecutions　　　　　(D) propositions

5. Arsenic is a_____drug.
(A) toxic　　　　　　　　　(B) typical
(C) tropical　　　　　　　 (D) topical

6. The soil in which the plants are grown must be_____in order to have a big crop.
(A) futile　　　　　　　　　(B) fertile
(C) fervent　　　　　　　　(D) firm

7. Viruses are very small_____.
(A) mechanics　　　　　　(B) organisms
(C) organics　　　　　　　(D) materials

8. The question of immortality is traditionally_____as a
   question about the soul or the spirit of man.
   (A) formalized   (B) formulated
   (C) formed   (D) fornicated

9. For many reasons, the_____from war to peace is
   extremely difficult.
   (A) tradition   (B) transmission
   (C) transaction   (D) transition

10. More and more teachers_____to teach basic, general, or
    introductory courses, which, however, are what the
    undergraduates need most.
    (A) decline   (B) incline
    (C) intend   (D) declaim

II. English Structure and Writing Ability. 30%

A. On the answer sheet, put down under the number of each
   question the parenthesized capital letter that precedes
   the expression that best completes the sentence.

   Example: He is a good boy, and_____pleases his father.
          (A) it   (B) that   (C) so   (D) which
   Answer : (B)

1. Warren,_____on the staff of the local hospital.
   (A) an excellent surgeon, is
   (B) being an excellent surgeon
   (C) is an excellent surgeon, he is
   (D) he is an excellent surgeon

2. Newly enacted antipollution laws have presented
   scientists with challenges which_____.
   (A) are being met as technological advances permit
   (B) technologically are being met by advances
   (C) advance as technology permits overcoming it
   (D) are permitted by technological advances to be
        overcome

3. Xenon has a number of applications,_____may be
   mentioned its use in flash lamps for high-speed
   photography.
   (A) among which
   (B) which
   (C) and which
   (D) each of which

4. It is considered that the moon contains all the elements found on earth, including_____.
   (A) those required to generate nuclear energy
   (B) they that are necessary for the generating of nuclear energy.
   (C) elements for generating of nuclear energy
   (D) those are required for the generation of nuclear energy

5. Having been served lunch,_____.
   (A) the problem was discussed by the members of the committee
   (B) the committee members discussed the problem
   (C) it was discussed by the committee members the problem
   (D) a discussion of the problem was made by the members of the committee

6. John's score on the test is the highest in the class; _____.
   (A) he should study last night
   (B) he should have studied last night
   (C) he must have studied last night
   (D) he must had to study last night

7. _____, people and objects are presented in a flat, often angular, abstract manner in Jacob Lawrence's paintings.
   (A) Always able to recognize
   (B) The ability to recognize always
   (C) While always recognizable
   (D) Always can be recognized

B. To each question, choose the <u>one</u> of the underlined expressions that is grammatically incorrect and put down the capital letter beneath it under the number of the corresponding question on the answer sheet.

Example: Between <u>you</u> and <u>I</u>, I <u>know</u> nothing <u>about</u> it.
　　　　　　　A　　　B　　　C　　　　　　D
Answer : B

8. It was the <u>last train</u> from London to <u>a Midland town</u>, a
　　　　　　　A　　　　　　　　　　　　B

<u>stopping train</u>, one of those trains which <u>gives</u> you an
　　C　　　　　　　　　　　　　　　　　　　D

understanding of eternity.

9. Anthropologists <u>have noted</u> that man has flourished <u>for</u>
   A
   a surprising long time <u>with no increase in</u> the size of
   B   C
   <u>his brain</u>.
   D

10. Columbus Day <u>is celebrated</u> <u>on</u> the <u>twelve</u> of October
    A   B   C
    because on that day in 1492, Christopher Columbus first
    landed in <u>the Americas</u>.
    D

11. By the time <u>the sun rose</u> the following morning, <u>we</u>
    A
    <u>restored</u> all 83 bottles to their original condition, but
    B
    <u>we did not have time</u> <u>to recondition</u> the jugs.
    C   D

12. They considered <u>it</u> a thing <u>of importance</u> that the
    A   B
    meeting <u>postpone</u> for a week <u>or so</u>.
    C   D

13. Purchasing power <u>has</u> not kept pace <u>to</u> inflation and,
    A   B
    <u>consequently</u>, real income <u>has declined</u>.
    C   D

14. The personnel director conveys the feeling <u>that he is</u>
    A
    <u>a person</u> to whom employees can <u>turn to</u> when they face
    B   C
    problems <u>on the job</u>.
    D

15. What we know about nomadic life comes <u>not so much</u> from
    A
    the writings of historians, Myrda <u>explained</u>, <u>as from</u>
    B   C
    the songs and speeches of the people <u>itself</u>.
    D

III. Reading comprehension: 30%

Read the following passages carefully, choose the one best answer to each question, and put down the capital letter of the answer under the corresponding number of the question on the answer sheet.

A.

Criminals were once considered sinners who chose to offend against the laws of God and man. They were severely punished for their crimes. Modern criminologists regard society itself as in large part responsible for the crimes committed against it. Poverty, poor living conditions, and inadequate education are all causes of crime. Crime is fundamentally the result of society's failure to provide a decent life for all the people. It is especially common in times when values are changing, as after a war, or in countries where people with different backgrounds and values are thrown together, as in the United States. Crimes, generally speaking, are fewer in countries where there is a settled way of life and a traditional respect for law.

1. This passage deals with
   (A) criminals.
   (B) society.
   (C) the laws of God and man.
   (D) the reasons for crime.

2. The main idea of this passage is that
   (A) criminals are sinners.
   (B) crime is common when values are changing.
   (C) crime is the result of poverty.
   (D) society is largely responsible for crime.

3. According to the passage, which is not a cause of crime?
   (A) slums   (B) poverty
   (C) wickedness   (D) ethnic mixing

4. To prevent crime, the author implies that society should
   (A) provide stiffer penalties for criminals.
   (B) provide a decent way of life for everyone.
   (C) segregate the poor.
   (D) give broader powers to the police.

B.

During the summer session there will be a revised schedule of services for the university community. Specific changes for intercampus bus services and cafeteria, summer hours for the infirmary and recreational and athletic facilities will be posted on the bulletin board outside of the cafeteria. Weekly movie and concert schedules, which are in the process of being arranged, will be posted each Wednesday outside of the cafeteria.

Intercampus buses will leave the main hall every hour on the half hour and make all of the regular stops on their route around the campus. The cafeteria will serve breakfast, lunch, and early dinner from 7 a.m. to 7 p.m. during the week and from noon to 7 p.m. on weekends. The library will maintain regular hours during the week, but shorter hours on Saturdays and Sundays. Weekend hours are from noon to 7 p.m.

All students who want to use the library borrowing services and the recreational, athletic, and entertainment facilities must have a valid summer identification card. This announcement will also appear in the next issue of the student newspaper.

5. Which of the following is the main purpose of this announcement?
   (A) To tell campus personnel of the new library services.
   (B) To announce the new movies on campus this summer.
   (C) To notify university people of important schedule changes.
   (D) To remind students to validate their identification cards.

6. Which of the following facilities are listed in this announcement, for specific schedule revisions?
   (A) Athletic and recreational.
   (B) Food and transportation.
   (C) Bookstore and post office.
   (D) Medical and audio-visual.

7. Times for movies and concerts are not listed in this
   announcement because _____
   (A) a film or concert occurs every Wednesday at 7 p.m.
   (B) the full list would be too long.
   (C) films and concerts cannot be announced publicly.
   (D) the full list is not ready yet.

8. According to the announcement, a valid identifica-
   tion card is required to_____
   (A) ride on intercampus buses.
   (B) read announcements in the cafeteria.
   (C) make use of the infirmary.
   (D) check books out of the library.

9. The main purpose of this announcement is to help
   members of the university community to_____
   (A) make better use of intercampus buses.
   (B) secure faster service in the cafeteria.
   (C) make more effective use of campus facilities.
   (D) obtain extensions on overdue library books.

C.

　　Criticism of research lays a significant foundation for
future investigative work, but when students begin their own
projects, they are likely to find that the standards of
validity in field work are considerably more rigorous than
standards for most library research. When students are faced
with the concrete problem of proof by field demonstration,
they usually discover that many of the "important relationships" they may have criticized other researchers for
failing to demonstrate are very elusive indeed. They will
find, if they submit an outline or questionnaire to their
classmates for criticism, that other students make comments
similar to some they themselves may have made in discussing
previously published research. For example, student researchers are likely to begin with a general question but
find themselves forced to narrow its focus. They may learn
that questions whose meanings seem perfectly obvious to them
are not clearly understood by others, or that questions
which seemed entirely objective to them appear to be highly

biased to someone else. They usually find that the formulation of good research questions is a much more subtle and frustrating task than is generally believed by those who have not actually attempted it.

10. What does the author think about trying to find weaknesses in other people's research?
(A) It should only be attempted by experienced researchers.
(B) It may cause researchers to avoid publishing good work.
(C) It is currently being done to excess.
(D) It can be useful in planning future research.

11. According to the passage, what is one major criticism students often make of published research?
(A) The research has not been written in an interesting way.
(B) The research has been done in unimportant fields.
(C) The researchers did not adequately establish the relationships involved.
(D) The researchers failed to provide an appropriate summary.

12. According to the passage, how do students in class often react to another student's research?
(A) They react the way they do to any other research.
(B) They are especially critical of the quality of the research.
(C) They offer unusually good suggestions for improving the work.
(D) They show a lot of sympathy for the student researcher.

13. According to the passage, what do student researchers often learn when they discuss their work in class?
(A) Other students rarely have objective comments about it.
(B) Other students do not believe the researchers did the work themselves.
(C) Some students feel that the conclusions are too obvious.
(D) Some students do not understand the meaning of the researchers' questions.

14. According to the passage, student researchers may have
    to change their research projects because
    (A) their budgets are too high.
    (B) their original questions are too broad.
    (C) their teachers do not give adequate advice.
    (D) their time is very limited.

15. What does the author conclude about preparing suitable
    questions for a research project?
    (A) It is more difficult than the student researcher may
        realize.
    (B) The researcher should get help from other people.
    (C) The questions should be brief so that they will be
        understood.
    (D) It is important to follow formulas closely.

IV. Composition: 30%

    Write a well-organized and sufficiently-developed
    composition on the topic "The Way to Happiness."

國立中興大學八十一學年度
碩士班研究生入學考試英文試題詳解

I. 字彙：10％

1.（ B ）(A) magnetism〔'mægnə,tızəm〕*n.* 磁性
   (B) ***magnitude***〔'mægnə,tjud〕*n.* 重大
   (C) maximum〔'mæksəməm〕*n.* 最大量
   (D) magnificence〔mæg'nıfəsn̩s〕*n.* 華麗
   crisis〔'kraısıs〕*n.* 危機　　***liberal education*** 通才教育

2.（ A ）(A) ***hybrid***〔'haıbrıd〕*n.,adj.* 雜種的
   (B) hysterical〔hıs'tɛrık!〕*adj.* 歇斯底里的
   (C) hypocritical〔,hıpə'krıtık!〕*adj.* 僞善的
   (D) hygienic〔,haıdʒı'ɛnık〕*adj.* 衞生學的
   curiosity〔kjʊrı'asətı〕*n.* 稀奇的人或物

3.（ D ）(A) inconceivable〔,ınkən'sivəb!〕*adj.* 想像不到的
   (B) incomparable〔ın'kampərəb!〕*adj.* 無與倫比的
   (C) incomplete〔,ınkəm'plit〕*adj.* 不完全的
   (D) ***incompatible***〔ınkəm'pætəb!〕*adj.* 不能相容的；矛盾的

4.（ C ）(A) persecution〔,pɝsı'kjuʃən〕*n.* 宗教迫害
   (B) prohibition〔,proə'bıʃən〕*n.* 禁止
   (C) ***prosecution***〔,prası'kjuʃən〕*n.* 告發；起訴
   (D) proposition〔,prapə'zıʃən〕*n.* 建議
   criminal〔'krımən!〕*adj.* 犯罪的　　nature〔'netʃɚ〕*n.* 性質
   accusation〔,ækjə'zeʃən〕*n.* 控告；罪名

5.（ A ）(A) ***toxic***〔'taksık〕*adj.* 有毒的
   (B) typical〔'tıpık!〕*adj.* 典型的
   (C) tropical〔'trapık!〕*adj.* 熱帶的
   (D) topical〔'tapık!〕*adj.* 話題的
   arsenic〔ar'sɛnık〕*n.* 砷

6. (**B**) (A) futile〔'fjutl̩〕*adj.* 無用的
    (B) ***fertile***〔'fɝtl̩〕*adj.* 肥沃的
    (C) fervent〔'fɝvənt〕*adj.* 熱烈的
    (D) firm〔fɝm〕*adj.* 穩固的

7. (**B**) (A) mechanic〔mə'kænɪk〕*n.* 技工
    (B) ***organism***〔'ɔrgən,ɪzəm〕*n.* 有機體
    (C) organic〔ɔr'gænɪk〕*n.* 有機物
    (D) material〔mə'tɪrɪəl〕*n.* 原料
     virus〔'vaɪrəs〕*n.* 病毒

8. (**B**) (A) formalize〔'fɔrml̩,aɪz〕*v.* 形式化
    (B) ***formulate***〔'fɔrmjə,let〕*v.* 有系統地陳述；明確地表達
    (D) fornicate〔'fɔrnə,ket〕*v.*（未婚男女間）私通
     immortality〔,ɪmɔr'tælətɪ〕*n.* 不朽

9. (**D**) (B) transmission〔træns'mɪʃən〕*n.* 傳送；傳導
    (C) transaction〔træns'ækʃən〕*n.* 交易
    (D) ***transition***〔træn'zɪʃən〕*n.* 轉換；轉移
     extremely〔ɪk'strimlɪ〕*adv.* 極度地

10. (**A**) (A) ***decline***〔dɪ'klaɪn〕*v.* 拒絕；婉絕
    (B) incline〔ɪn'klaɪn〕*v.* 傾向
    (C) intend〔ɪn'tɛnd〕*v.* 意欲；想
    (D) declaim〔dɪ'klem〕*v.* 叱責
     undergraduate〔,ʌndɚ'grædʒuɪt〕*n.* 大學生

Ⅱ. 文法與修辭：30％

(1) 文法：

1. (**A**) an excellent surgeon 是 Warren 的同位語。

2. (**A**) 本句意思是：「新制定的污染防治法使得科學家面臨一些挑戰，而這些挑戰只要在技術進步許可下，都可以被克服。」依句意和文法，只有(A)正確。

3.（ **A** ）「氙氣有許多用途，其中之一是可用在高速攝影的閃光燈上。」依句意，是許多用途的一種，故須先加介系詞 among，再加上關係代名詞 which。

4.（ **A** ） include 之後只能加名詞，不可加子句，所以(B)(D)不合。(C)的 elements 一字，已在句子的前面出現過，所以必須用 those 來代替，以避免重複，故選(A)。

5.（ **B** ）獨立的分詞構句，其前後主詞須一致，故選(B) the committee members 作 Having been served lunch 意義上的主詞。

6.（ **C** ）推測過去的事情要用「must have + pp.」「一定～」。

7.（ **C** ）while 做「當～的時候」解時，其所引導的子句之主詞，若與主句之主詞相同，往往省略其主詞及 Be 動詞。(A)(B)(D)都不含連接詞、關係代名詞或獨立的分詞構句，因此不可和後面的主句連接。

(2) 挑錯：

8.（ **D** ） *gives → give* 先行詞 trains 為一複數名詞，故須用複數動詞。

9.（ **B** ） *surprising → surprisingly* 修飾形容詞 long，須用副詞。

10.（ **C** ） *twelve → twelfth* the twelfth「（某月的）十二日」。

11.（ **B** ） *restored → had restored* restore 的動作發生在日出之前，故用過去完成式。

12.（ **C** ） *postpone → be postponed* meeting 是「被」延後，故用被動語態（should）be postponed。

13.（ **B** ） *to → with* keep pace with～ 與～步調一致

14.（ **C** ） *turn to → turn* 不定冠詞 a 用於表示其後的名詞在語意上是非特定的；而本題中的 person 是「員工們在面臨工作上的問題時可以求助的人」，也就是 the personnel director，其語意特定，故須改用定冠詞 the。

15.（ **D** ） *itself → themselves* 因本題中的 people 並不是一個民族，只是一群遊牧的人，故 people 為一複數名詞，反身代名詞須改為 themselves。

Ⅲ. 閱讀測驗：30 ％

Part A

【譯文】

　　罪犯一度被認為是違反神和人律法的罪人。他們皆因其所犯的罪，遭到嚴厲的懲罰。現代犯罪學者認為社會本身必須為反社會的罪行負大部分的責任。貧窮、低劣的生活條件，以及教育不足都是犯罪的起因。基本上犯罪是社會無法供給所有人民良好生活的結果。在社會價值變動的時代，例如戰後，或是在一些國家，聚集著不同背景和價值觀的人民，例如美國，這種情形就更為普遍。大體而言，在生活安定以及在傳統上尊重法律的國家，犯罪情形比較少。

　　　　【答案】

　　1.（ D ）　　　2.（ D ）　　　3.（ C ）　　　4.（ B ）

【註】

criminal〔'krɪmənḷ〕*n.* 罪犯　　　sinner〔'sɪnɚ〕*n.* 罪人
offend〔ə'fɛnd〕*v.* 違反；冒犯　　severely〔sə'vɪrlɪ〕*adv.* 嚴厲地
criminologist〔,krɪmə'nɑlədʒɪst〕*n.* 犯罪學家
inadequate〔ɪn'ædəkwɪt〕*adj.* 不足的　decent〔'disṇt〕*adj.* 體面的；合宜的
slums〔slʌm〕*n.* 貧民窟　　wickedness〔'wɪkɪdnɪs〕*n.* 邪惡；罪孽
ethnic〔'ɛθnɪk〕*adj.* 人種的；民族的　stiff〔stɪf〕*adj.* 強硬的
penalty〔'pɛnḷtɪ〕*n.* 刑罰；懲罰　segregate〔'sɛgrɪ,get〕*v.* 隔離；分離

Part B

【譯文】

　　在下學期本大學校區的各項服務的時間將會有所更動。校際公車服務、餐館、醫務室夏季診療時間、以及休閒和運動設施等特定變更項目會張貼在餐廳外的布告欄上。正在安排中的每週影片以及音樂會節目表，每週三會張貼在餐廳外面。

　　校際公車在每個鐘頭的三十分時，會從大禮堂開出，並在校園的各個站牌，作例行的停留。平常每天早上七點到下午七點，以及週末的中午到下午七點，餐廳會提供早餐、午餐和較早的晚餐。圖書館平常會定期開放，但在週六和週日開放時間較短。週末從中午開放到下午七點。

所有想要使用圖書館借書服務，及休閒、運動和娛樂設施的學生，必須持有一張有效的暑期證明。這項公佈的內容也會刊載在下一期的學生報紙上。

【答案】

5.（ C ）　　6.（ B ）　　7.（ D ）　　8.（ D ）　　9.（ C ）

【註】

session〔'sɛʃən〕n. 學期　infirmary〔ɪn'fɝmərɪ〕n. 醫院；醫務室
facility〔fə'sɪlətɪ〕n. 設施　***bulletin board*** 佈告欄
every hour on the half hour 每個鐘頭的三十分時
valid〔'vælɪd〕adj. 有效的；正確的
announcement〔ə'naʊnsmənt〕n. 宣佈；公告
issue〔'ɪʃʊ〕n.（報紙、刊物的）一期
personnel〔,pɝsṇ'ɛl〕n. 人事；人員　notify〔'notə,faɪ〕v. 通知
extension〔ɪk'stɛnʃən〕n. 續借　overdue〔'ovɚ'dju〕adj. 過期的

Part C
【譯文】

研究批評對未來的調查性工作，奠定了重要的基礎，但是當學生們開始著手自己的研究計畫時，很多可能會發現實地調查中正確性的標準，比起大部分在圖書館裏所做研究的標準，要嚴格得多了。當學生們在調查過程中，面對需要證據的具體問題時常會發現，許多他們用來批評其他研究者，認爲他們無法證明的「重要關聯」，事實上是很難以界定的。如果他們提出一項大綱或是問卷，請他們的同學來批評，他們會發現其他學生所做的批評，和他們自己從前在討論別人先前發表的研究時，所做的一些批評很像。例如，研究的學生很可能用涵蓋面較廣的問題開始做研究，但卻發現自己不得不縮小範圍。他們可能會察覺到有些對他們而言，意思十分明白清楚的問題，別人卻無法清楚地瞭解；或者有些在他們看來，是完全客觀的問題，在其他人看來卻是極爲偏頗的。他們常發現，要定出好的研究問題，是一件比那些未曾實際嘗試過的人所想的，要更難以捉摸，更令人深感挫折的工作。

【答案】

10. (D)　11. (C)　12. (A)　13. (D)　14. (B)　15. (A)

【註】

investigative〔ɪnˈvɛstə,getɪv〕*adj.* 調查的

project〔ˈprɑdʒɛkt〕*n.* 研究計畫　validity〔vəˈlɪdətɪ〕*n.* 正確性；妥當性

field work 實地調查　rigorous〔ˈrɪgərəs〕*adj.* 嚴格的；嚴密的

be faced with ～（使人）面對～　demonstrate〔ˈdɛmən,stret〕*v.* 證明

elusive〔ɪˈlusɪv〕*adj.* 無法捉摸的；難以界定的

submit〔səbˈmɪt〕*v.* 提出　comment〔ˈkɑmɛnt〕*n.* 意見；批評

biased〔ˈbaɪəst〕*adj.* 偏頗的；存有偏見的

attempt〔əˈtɛmpt〕*n.,v.* 企圖；嘗試　excess〔ɪkˈsɛs〕*n.* 過度

adequately〔ˈædəkwɪtlɪ〕*adv.* 適當地；足夠地

involve〔ɪnˈvɑlv〕*v.* 包含；牽涉　budget〔ˈbʌdʒɪt〕*n.* 預算

Ⅵ. 作文：30%

The Way to Happiness

　　Many people have spent their whole lives contemplating " the way to happiness " and many books have been written on the subject.　Indeed happiness is hard to obtain for many people and what constitutes happiness is different for everyone.　For me, however, I think the most important thing is to find a good husband.　I think it is also important to have an interesting and challenging job in which I could help people in some way.　I also believe that " everything must be taken in moderation "; I have seen many people drink and smoke too much, and I think many people in Taiwan work too hard.　It is also important to eat right and keep your body in good shape.

　　I believe that in order to be happy, you have to know what really makes you happy; you have to set goals (such as " I want a more interesting job ") and then you must try your best to reach those goals.

私立淡江大學八十一學年度
碩士班研究生入學考試英文試題

I. Vocabulary:

Each of the following sentences has a word or phrase underlined. Below each sentence are four other words or phrases. Choose the letter of the word or phrase that keeps the meaning of the original sentence.

1. Your story <u>intrigues</u> me.
   (A) shocks (B) bores
   (C) confuses (D) interests

2. It was a <u>crucial</u> decision.
   (A) very important (B) difficult
   (C) unpopular (D) special

3. His looks have changed <u>considerably</u>.
   (A) unnecessarily (B) thoughtlessly
   (C) probably (D) a lot

4. I need to <u>go over</u> this.
   (A) look again at (B) replace
   (C) renovate (D) remove

5. I can't <u>figure this out</u>.
   (A) use this (B) understand this
   (C) draw this (D) measure this

6. You must be <u>elated</u> by the news.
   (A) upset (B) surprised
   (C) made happy (D) confused

7. It was too late to <u>rescue</u> the animal.
   (A) punish (B) feed
   (C) reward (D) save

8. Your work has improved <u>immensely</u>.
   (A) a little (B) very little
   (C) somewhat (D) a lot

9. Can these bottles be <u>recycled</u>?
   (A) used again　　　　　　(B) transported
   (C) included　　　　　　　(D) duplicated

10. Would you mind making a <u>duplicate</u> of this for me?
    (A) structure　　　　　　(B) issue
    (C) payoff　　　　　　　 (D) copy

11. A lot of people are <u>boycotting</u> that store.
    (A) going to　　　　　　 (B) staying away from
    (C) shopping　　　　　　 (D) talking about

12. Fifty percent of the applicants were <u>admitted</u> to the
    program.
    (A) transported　　　　　(B) reinstated
    (C) allowed to enter　　 (D) taken

13. That's a <u>unique</u> idea.
    (A) funny　　　　　　　　(B) uncommon
    (C) impossible　　　　　 (D) enormous

14. This course is <u>mandatory</u>.
    (A) easy　　　　　　　　 (B) required
    (C) enjoyable　　　　　　(D) unnecessary

15. The professor commented that his writing lacked
    <u>profundity</u>.
    (A) shallowness　　　　　(B) dullness
    (C) deep meaning　　　　 (D) proof

16. This is an <u>anthology</u> of writings by a famous scholar.
    (A) collection　　　　　 (B) principle
    (C) philosophy　　　　　 (D) example

17. He attempts to <u>integrate</u> these dimensions within an
    Asian context.
    (A) interpret　　　　　　(B) exclude
    (C) combine　　　　　　　(D) introduce

18. His voice deserves to be heard, his message <u>pondered</u>.
    (A) condensed　　　　　　(B) considered
    (C) wondered　　　　　　 (D) thought over carefully

19. She gave him the <u>cue</u> to stand up.
    (A) signal　　　　　　　 (B) answer
    (C) routine　　　　　　　(D) rule

20. The national <u>decennial</u> census has been more than a
    simple headcount.
    (A) every twenty years   (B) every ten years
    (C) annual   (D) decisive

II. Grammar:

In each of the following sentences, one of the four
underlined parts is wrong. Choose the letter of the
wrong part. One point each.

21. <u>Last week</u> John <u>got on</u> the bus and went to his <u>sister</u> new
       A   B   C

    apartment to visit <u>her</u>.
                  D

22. If you want <u>to stay</u> later, I <u>come</u> back <u>to pick</u> you <u>up</u>.
               A   B   C   D

23. If you <u>don't</u> listen <u>careful</u>, you might not <u>hear</u> <u>the date</u>
          A   B   C   D

    of the exam.

24. My brother and sister <u>have been living</u> with my uncle
                             A

    <u>since</u> December <u>because</u> my parents <u>were</u> on a trip.
      B   C   D

25. My <u>brother's</u> restaurant <u>has become</u> very popular since it
          A   B

    <u>has opened</u> three months <u>ago</u>.
      C   D

26. How <u>would</u> you feel if a good friend stopped <u>speaking</u>
        A   B

    or <u>writing</u> to <u>yourself</u>?
        C   D

27. <u>By the time</u> my brother got here, we <u>had</u> already decided
       A   B

    <u>going</u> out <u>for</u> dinner.
      C   D

28. If you work <u>steady</u>, you <u>will finish</u> this before the bell
              A   B

    <u>rings</u> and you <u>have to</u> leave.
      C   D

29. One of <u>mine</u> friends <u>has</u> the same name <u>as</u> an actor <u>who</u> is
    A   B   C   D

  very popular today.

30. One of my <u>sister's</u> lives on Pond Street, <u>which</u> is the
      A   B

  <u>last</u> street <u>after</u> the library.
   C   D

31. We <u>have been</u> talking for several hours <u>when</u> she suddenly
   A   B

  told <u>me</u> that she was <u>going</u> to get married.
   C   D

32. My brother <u>bought</u> a computer last year <u>so</u> he <u>did</u>
      A   B   C

  his work more <u>efficiently</u> now.
        D

33. She <u>gained</u> so <u>many</u> weight while she was <u>on</u> vacation that
   A   B   C

  she had to go <u>on</u> a strict diet.
      D

34. If she <u>hadn't spent</u> so much money <u>at</u> the beginning of
    A   B

  the trip, she wouldn't have <u>run out</u> of money before she
            C

  <u>gets</u> home.
  D

35. They wanted <u>to expand</u> the restaurant <u>so as</u> they <u>could</u>
      A   B   C

  <u>serve</u> more people.
  D

36. <u>Because of</u> the class was <u>cancelled</u>, <u>no one</u> had to get up
   A   B   C   D

  early.

37. Sharon <u>had decided</u> to stay <u>for</u> an extra week <u>because</u> the
    A   B   C

  weather in California <u>is</u> beautiful now.
         D

38. I asked him <u>to get</u> me a video, <u>that</u> he <u>had seen</u> and
           A   B C   D
    enjoyed.

39. If you buy a car in order <u>as</u> to get to school, how <u>are</u>
     A
    you going to <u>be able</u> to pay for the gasoline?
                 D

40. You should <u>have</u> told me that you <u>are</u> going to throw <u>out</u>
                A   B   C
    all of the old furniture <u>that</u> was upstairs.
                         D

41. If you <u>are</u> interested <u>to go</u> to the beach, <u>I'm planning</u>
           A   B   C
    to drive there <u>as soon as</u> I have finished my work.
                  D

42. I hope to <u>take</u> a trip at the end of the month<u>,</u> but I'm
             A   B
    not sure <u>that</u> I <u>would have</u> enough money.
             C   D

43. <u>Since</u> I got this computer, I <u>haven't had</u> much time to
     A   B
    use <u>them</u>, but I hope <u>to have</u> more time next month.
        C   D

44. I wish <u>I knew</u> that you were thinking <u>of</u> <u>buying</u> a house
            A   B C
    <u>that</u> is so far away.
     D

45. I was <u>very</u> surprised <u>when</u> Maria asked <u>that</u> I wanted <u>to</u>
          A   B   C
    <u>borrow</u> her new car.
     D

46. <u>By</u> next year, we <u>will have finished</u> <u>building</u> our new
     A   B   C
    house and <u>pay</u> for it.
            D

47. If you had told me that your car was for sale, I might
    $\qquad$ A $\qquad$ B $\qquad$ C
    buy it.
    D

48. She told me to call Mr. Martin, whom is the president of
    $\qquad$ C $\qquad$ B
    the company, because he is in charge of hiring.
    $\qquad$ C $\qquad$ D

49. He had worked for a major accounting firm for almost
    $\qquad$ A $\qquad$ B $\qquad$ C
    fifteen years when the company is sold.
    $\qquad$ D

50. If you are interested in the profession of law, but you
    $\qquad$ A
    do not want to spend so many years in school, you might
    $\qquad$ B $\qquad$ C
    consider to become a legal assistant.
    $\qquad$ D

III. Reading Comprehension: 20%

Read the following passages and answer the questions. Choose the letter of the correct answer.

In 1990, revolution broke out in Katmandu, the capital of Nepal. It was a tense time for Julia Chang Bloch, who had just arrived in the country. As the new U.S. ambassador to Nepal, Bloch was responsible for the safety of the nearly 2000 Americans in the country. She did her job competently, and Nepal's new prime minister, K.P. Bhattarai, later described her as a "very impressive person." Julia Chang Bloch was just 48 years old when she became ambassador to Nepal. For someone who had come to the United States as a refugee, this was a remarkable achievement.

Born in China in 1943, Julia Chang lived with her family in the city of Chang Chih-hsing. Her father, who had studied law in the United States, spoke fluent English. In Chang Chih-hsing, he was the head of the customs office,

which was an important government position. When the Communists took over in 1949, however, the Chang family left
for Hong Kong. From there they got visas to enter the United
States.

Although her father spoke English fluently, Julia Chang
had never studied the language. When she entered school in
the United States, she could not speak English at all. Her
father helped her to learn the language and within a year,
she had won a speaking contest--in English. More honors
followed. After graduating from the University of California
at Berkeley, she worked for the Peace Corps in Southeast
Asia. Later, she worked at Harvard's Institute of Politics
and the Agency for International Development (AID). By the
time she left her job with the Agency for International
Development, she had risen to head its Asia and Near East
Bureau. She had also earned a reputation for being an
extremely hard worker. Her reputation for getting a job
done, as well as her varied background, made her an excellent candiate for the position as ambassador.

51. The revolution in Nepal started
    (A) shortly after Bloch arrived in the country.
    (B) just before Bloch arrived in the country.
    (C) when Bloch arrived in the country.
    (D) because Bloch went there.

52. In the first paragraph, the word "remarkable" probably
    means
    (A) funny.
    (B) scary.
    (C) unusual.
    (D) common.

53. The purpose of the second paragraph is to
    (A) tell us about Bloch's experiences in Nepal.
    (B) explain how she became an ambassador.
    (C) describe Bloch's education.
    (D) tell us about Bloch's background.

54. When did Bloch's father study law?
    (A) Before he went to the United States.
    (B) While he was working at the customs office.
    (C) After 1949.
    (D) While he was in the United States.

55. Which of these statements is true about Julia Chang
    Bloch's career?
    (A) She joined the Peace Corps before graduating from
        the University of California.
    (B) For a time, she was the head of AID's Asia and Near
        East bureau.
    (C) She has always worked for the same organization.
    (D) All of her jobs have been in the United States.

    If you had lived several hundred years ago, you
wouldn't have worn shoes. Instead, you would have worn
schewis or shooys. Over the years, the English word shoe has
has been spelled in at least seventeen different ways. The
earliest Anglo-Saxon word was sceo which means to cover.
This eventually became schewis in the plural and later
shooys. Today, of course, we call them shoes. And the
spelling of the word shoes isn't the only thing that has
changed. Shoe styles have gone through some extraordinary
transformations, too.

    Perhaps one of the most dangerous shoe styles was the
fourteenth century English crakow. The crakow was a shoe
with a very long toe. Every year the tip of this popular
shoe got a little bit longer. In fact, the crakow got so
long that King Edward III finally enacted a law prohibit-
ing shoes that extended more than two inches beyond the
human toe. The law must not have been popular. By the early
1400s, people could be seen wearing shoes with tips of
eighteen inches. They could also be seen routinely tripping
over the ends of their very long shoes.

    In the 1500s, a German shoe called the pump became
popular in Europe. This shoe was a type of loose slipper

with a low heel. Its name may have come from the sound that
the shoe made on a wooden floor--plump, plump, plump.

High-heeled shoes were popular in sixteenth-century
France. Unlike today, however, these shoes were first worn
by men. The King of France, Louis XIV, may have started this
fad. Because he was short, he added a few inches to the
heels of his shoes so that he would appear taller. Eager to
be in style, the men and women at court hurried to copy him.
This, of course, forced the King to increase the height of
his own shoes.

If high heels and pointed toes are popular today, you
can be almost certain that they won't be popular tomorrow.
Shoe styles seem to change faster than you can wear out your
old shoes. Who knows what will be in style tomorrow. Let's
just hope that it is not the crakow.

56. What is the main topic of this passage?
(A) How the spelling of the word shoes has changed.
(B) How shoe styles have changed.
(C) Why the crakow was dangerous.
(D) What people were in the past.

57. In the first paragraph, the word transformations
probably means
(A) spellings.   (B) ways.
(C) uses.   (D) changes.

58. Which statement is true according to the reading
passage?
(A) The crakow was an unpopular type of shoe.
(B) People stopped wearing the crakow because of King
Edward's law.
(C) The crakow got longer after King Edward enacted his
law.
(D) The crakow was popular in the 1600s.

59. From the reading, which statement is true about the
pump?
(A) It didn't have a high heel.
(B) It was similar to the crakow.
(C) It was not very comfortable.
(D) It was popular for many years.

60. Which of the following questions is not answered in the passage?
    (A) When were high-heeled shoes popular in France?
    (B) How did the pump get its name?
    (C) Why did people stop wearing the crakow?
    (D) Why did Louis XIV wear high-heeled shoes?

IV. Composition: 30%

Write a composition in English in of less than 200 words on "Traffic in Taipei". Your composition must contain an introductory paragraph, two or three discussion paragraphs, and a concluding paragraph.

私立淡江大學八十一學年度
碩士班研究生入學考試英文試題詳解

I. 字彙：20％

1. (**D**)　intrigue〔ɪn'trig〕*v.* 使感興趣
    (A) shock〔ʃɑk〕*v.* 使震驚

2. (**A**)　crucial〔'kruʃəl,'kruɪʃəl〕*adj.* 極重要的

3. (**D**)　considerably〔kən'sɪdərəblɪ〕*adv.* 相當地；非常

4. (**A**)　go over　溫習
    (A) ***look again at*** 再看一次　　(B) replace *v.* 取代
    (C) renovate〔'rɛnə,vet〕*v.* 革新
    (D) remove〔rɪ'muv〕*v.* 移開

5. (**B**)　figure out　理解

6. (**C**)　elate〔ɪ'let, i-〕*v.* 使興高采烈
    (A) upset〔'ʌpsɛt〕*v.* 使難過

7. (**D**)　rescue〔'rɛskjʊ〕*v.* 解救
    (C) reward〔rɪ'wɔrd〕*v.* 報酬

8. (**D**)　immensely〔ɪ'mɛnslɪ〕*adv.* 極大地；非常
    (C) somewhat〔'sʌmhwət〕*adv.* 稍微

9. (**A**)　recycle〔rɪ'saɪkl̩〕*v.* 再利用
    (B) transport〔træns'port,-'pɔrt〕*v.* 運輸
    (D) duplicate〔'djupləkɪt,-,ket〕*v.* 複製

10. (**D**)　duplicate〔'djupləkɪt, -,ket〕*n.* 複製品
    (B) issue〔'ɪʃʊ,'ɪʃjʊ〕*n.* 發行
    (C) payoff〔'pe,ɔf〕*n.* 清還
    (D) ***copy***〔kɑpɪ〕*n.* 複製品

11. (**B**) boycott〔'bɔɪ,kɑt〕*v.* 聯合抵制

12. (**C**) admit〔əd'mɪt〕*v.* 允許進入
    (B) reinstate〔,rɪɪn'stet〕*v.* 恢復；復職
    applicant〔'æpləkənt〕*n.* 申請人

13. (**B**) unique〔ju'nik〕*adj.* 獨一無二的
    (B) *uncommon*〔ʌn'kɑmən〕*adj.* 罕有的
    (D) enormous〔ɪ'nɔrməs〕*adj.* 極大的

14. (**B**) mandatory〔'mændə,tɛrɪ〕*adj.* 強制性的；命令的
    (B) *required*〔rɪ'kwaɪrd〕*adj.* 命令的

15. (**C**) profundity〔prə'fʌndətɪ〕*n.* 深度
    (A) shallowness〔'ʃælonɪs〕*n.* 淺薄
    (B) dullness〔'dʌlnɪs〕*n.* 單調乏味

16. (**A**) anthology〔æn'θɑlədʒɪ〕*n.* 詩集；文選
    (A) *collection*〔kə'lɛkʃən〕*n.* 收集
    writings〔'raɪtɪŋz〕*n.pl.* 著述；作品
    lack〔læk〕*v.* 缺少

17. (**C**) integrate〔'ɪntə,gret〕*v.* 使完全；整合
    (A) interpret〔ɪn'tɝprɪt〕*v.* 解釋
    (C) combine（kəm'baɪn）*v.* 結合
    dimension〔də'mɛnʃən〕*n.* 要素；特質
    context〔'kɑntɛst〕*n.* 上下文

18. (**D**) ponder〔'pɑndɚ〕*v.* 考慮；沈思
    (A) condense〔kən'dɛns〕*v.* 濃縮
    (C) wonder〔'wʌndɚ〕*v.* 驚歎；想知道

19. (**A**) cue〔kju〕*n.* 信號；暗示
    (C) routine〔ru'tin〕*n.* 慣例；例行公事

20. (B)　decennial 〔dɪˈsɛnɪəl〕 *adj.* 十年一度的
　　　(C) annual 〔ˈænjʊəl〕 *adj.* 一年一次的
　　　(D) decisive 〔dɪˈsaɪsɪv〕 *adj.* 決定性的
　　　　census 〔ˈsɛnsəs〕 *n.* 人口調查　headcount *n.* 清點人數

Ⅱ. 改錯：30％

21. (C)　*sister → sister's*

22. (B)　*come → will come*

23. (B)　*careful → carefully*　修飾動詞 listen, 應用副詞, 故將 careful
　　　改為 carefully 。

24. (D)　*were → are*　由現在完成進行式：「have been ＋V-ing」可
　　　知，哥哥和妹妹現在仍然和叔叔同住，故其父母現在仍在旅行途
　　　中，故將 were 改為 are 。

25. (C)　*has opened → opened*　連接詞 since 通常和過去式連用，所以
　　　動詞應用過去簡單式。

26. (D)　*yourself → you*

27. (C)　*going → to go*　decide ＋ to V. 決定要～

28. (A)　*steady → steadily*　修飾動詞 work, 須用副詞, 故將 steady
　　　改為 steadily 。

29. (A)　*mine → my*　my ＋名詞＝mine, 由於空格後為名詞 friends,
　　　故將 mine 改為 my 。

30. (A)　*sister's → sisters*　one of ＋複數名詞　…的其中之一

31. (A)　*have been → had been*　兩個動作發生在過去，先發生的用過
　　　去完成式。

32. (C)　*did → does*　依句意，動詞應用現在式，故將 did 改為 does 。

33. (B)　*many → much*　由於 weight 是不可數名詞，故應用 much 修飾。

34. (**D**)　*gets → got*　「If＋S＋had＋過去分詞，…would have＋過去分詞」表與過去事實相反的假設，故動詞時態應用過去簡單式，故將 gets 改為 got 。

35. (**B**)　*so as → so that*　由於空格後為一子句，故應改為 so that「以便～」引導子句。

36. (**A**)　*Because of → Because*　because of＋名詞，because＋子句，而空格後有主詞、有動詞，顯然是一子句，故改為 because 。

37. (**A**)　*had decided → has decided*　依句意，應用現在完成式，故將 had decided 改為 has decided 。

38. (**B**)　將逗點去掉。

39. (**B**)　*as* 去掉
　　　　　　in order to 為了要～

40. (**B**)　*are → were*　「should have＋p.p.」表「過去應做而未做」，依句意為過去式，故須將 are 改成 were 。

41. (**B**)　*to go → in going*
　　　　　　be interested in～ 對～感興趣

42. (**D**)　*would have → will have*　敘述未來可能之事實，用未來式。

43. (**C**)　*them → it*　由於 computer 為單數名詞，故 them 須改為 it 。

44. (**A**)　*knew → had known*　與過去事實相反的假設，主要子句應用 had＋過去分詞。

45. (**C**)　*that → if*　依句意，that 應改為 if（是否）。

46. (**D**)　*pay → paying*　and 為對等連接詞，所以兩個動詞時態須一致，故 pay 應改為 paying 。

47. (**D**)　*buy → have bought*　與過去事實相反的假設，其公式為：If…had＋過去分詞…（should, would, could, might）＋have＋過去分詞。故 buy 應改為 have bought 。

48. (B) *whom → who*　whom 爲受格，不能當子句中的主詞，故應改爲 who。

49. (D) *is sold →was sold*　依句意，應用過去式，故 is sold 須改爲 was sold。

50. (D) *to become → becoming*　consider ＋V-ing　考慮~

Ⅲ. 閱讀測驗：20％

【譯文】

　　一九九〇年時，尼泊爾首都加德滿都爆發了一場革命。對於剛到尼泊爾的茱莉亞而言，這時期是相當緊張的時刻。身爲新上任的美國駐尼泊爾大使，茱莉亞必須對當地近二千人的美國人的安全負責。她工作十分稱職，而尼泊爾的新首相巴特瑞，事後曾描述她「是位令人難忘的人」。茱莉亞出任美國駐尼泊爾大使時，年僅四十八歲。對於一位流亡尼泊爾的美國人而言，是項了不起的成就。

　　茱莉亞於一九四三年出生於中國，和家人一起住在 Chang Chih-hsing 市。她的父親曾在美國研讀法律，所以英語十分流利。在 Chang Chih-hsing 市，她父親是海關的一位主管，在當時那算時十分重要的職位。而當中共於一九四九年竊據大陸之後，他們就舉家遷往香港。在香港獲得美國簽證之後，便前往美國。

　　儘管茱莉亞的父親英文說得十分流利，但她卻從未學過英文。當她上美國學校時，英文一句也不會說。她的父親幫助她學英文，而在一年之內，她就在演講比賽中獲勝——是英語演講比賽。接著她獲得越來越多的榮耀。當她自柏克萊加州大學畢業之後，她任職於東南亞和平工作團。後來她又替哈佛的政治學會以及國際發展機構工作。當她辭去在國際發展機構的工作時，便升任該機構在亞洲及近東分部的負責人。她更因爲工作十分努力而廣爲人知。她達成工作的聲譽，以及其多樣的背景，都是使她能成爲大使職位的優秀候選人。

【答案】

51. (A)　　52. (C)　　53. (D)　　54. (D)　　55. (B)

【註】

revolution〔,rɛvəˈluʃən〕*n*. 革命　tense〔tɛns〕*adj*. 緊張的
ambassador〔æmˈbæsədə〕*n*. 大使
competently〔ˈkɑmpətəntlɪ〕*adv*. 勝任地
remarkable〔rɪˈmɑrkəbḷ〕*adj*. 顯著的　customs〔ˈkʌstəmz〕*n*. 海關
visa〔ˈvizə〕*n*. 簽證　bureau〔ˈbjʊro〕*n*. 局；處
reputation〔,rɛpjəˈteʃən〕*n*. 名聲
candidate〔ˈkændə,det,ˈkændədɪt〕*n*. 候選人

【譯文】

　　如果你是生於幾百年之前，你就會沒穿過鞋子，而是穿「shewis」或是「shooys」。歷年來，英文字「shoe」的拼法，至少有十七種。最早的盎格魯‧撒克遜單字是「sceo」，意思是「覆蓋」。後來複數變成「schewis」，然後再變成「shooys」。當然，現在我們稱之為「shoes」。而改變的不只是該字的拼法而已。鞋子的款式也經歷了一些不尋常的轉變。

　　也許十四世紀英國的「crakow」就是鞋子最危險的款式之一。這種鞋的腳尖部份很長。而且每年這種十分受歡迎的鞋，鞋尖都會增長一些。事實上，由於此鞋的鞋尖過長，以致於愛德華三世最後終於頒佈一項法令，禁止鞋尖長度超過人類腳趾二英寸以上。這項法令一定不是非常盛行。在一四○○年代初期，還可看見人們穿著鞋尖十八英寸長的鞋子，而且還常常會因為鞋子過長而跌倒。

　　在一五○○年代，有種叫「pump」的德國鞋在歐洲十分盛行。這是種低跟、寬鬆的拖鞋。它的名字可能是來自於鞋子在木板上發出「啪啦、啪啦、啪啦」的聲音而來。

　　十六世紀時高跟鞋在法國十分流行。然而和今天不同的是先穿高跟鞋的是男人。法國國王路易十四可能是這種流行的起始人。由於他身材矮小，所以在鞋子下加上了數英寸的高跟，這樣看起來會高一點。為了要能夠趕上流行，宮廷中的男女便很快地摹仿國王的穿著。如此一來，當然國王便不得不加高他鞋跟的高度了。

　　如果高跟和尖頭的鞋現在很流行，那麼你就幾乎可以確定它們明天就退流行了。鞋子的款式改變得很快，在你鞋子還沒穿壞之前就變了。誰知道明天又會流行什麼樣的款式，讓我們共同來祈禱不要是「crakow」吧。

【答案】

56.(B)	57.(D)	58.(C)	59.(A)	60.(C)

【註】

extraordinary 〔,ɛkstə'ɔrdn̩,ɛrɪ〕 *adj*. 不尋常的
transformation 〔,trænsfə'meʃən〕 *n*. 變形
prohibit 〔prə'hɪbɪt〕 *v*. 禁止　routinely 〔ru'tinlɪ〕 *adv*. 例行地
trip 〔trɪp〕 *v*. 以輕快的步伐行走　　loose 〔lus〕 *adj*. 寬鬆的
slipper 〔'slɪpɚ〕 *n*. 拖鞋　　heel 〔hil〕 *n*. 跟
fad 〔fæd〕 *n*. 一時的流行　　*in style* 流行

Ⅳ. 作文：30%

　　Taipei traffic is bad now, but I think it will soon get much better. Once the MRT is finished, and new freeways are built, the situation will improve immensely. I really think that the MRT will work very well since the land area of Taipei city is so small. In addition, the government will probably think of many other ways to ease the traffic problem; for example, the government might create more jobs in other cities in order to get some people to move out of Taipei. Also I think more people would walk to school and to work if the air was cleaner and the sidewalks were more pleasant. In order to do this the government could make new laws to reduce pollution and the sidewalks could be cleared if there were more underground parking garages.

　　Of course there are numerous other things that could be done as well. But in the meantime we must all be patient; soon Taipei's traffic will run smoothly.

私立逢甲大學八十一學年度
碩士班研究生入學考試英文試題

I. Vocabulary: 20%

Fill each blank with an appropriate word.

1. One of the_____that most pained and angered South
   Africans over many years was the ban on their participa-
   tion in international Cricket and Rugby games.
   (A) actions   (B) sanctions
   (C) saints   (D) motives

2. Hoping to become the first to break the trash habit,
   Germany_____tough new packaging rules.
   (A) exposes   (B) imports
   (C) imposes   (D) exports

3. In a passionate speech to the jury, the prosecuting
   attorney demanded a "guilty"_____.
   (A) exposes   (B) version
   (C) diction   (D) verdict

4. One of the most chilling aspects of last year's_____
   attempt in the Soviet Union is that--for 76 hours--the
   top-secret nuclear release codes were in the hands of
   men denounced as "adventurists" by Gorbachev.
   (A) coupon   (B) corps
   (C) corpse   (D) coup

5. Local media organizations rely heavily on the services of
   foreign news agencies for world news_____.
   (A) average   (B) storage
   (C) coverage   (D) passage

6. He wrote an_____letter to the director of the research
   center.
   (A) enthusiastic   (B) impatient
   (C) ultimate   (D) annual

7. It is my_____to speak on behalf of all the staff
   members and welcome you to our company.
   (A) originality   (B) privilege
   (C) reinforcement   (D) average

8. The＿＿＿between the two different ways of living is
most important to bear in mind.
(A) attitude (B) altitude
(C) contrast (D) protest

9. Transport systems were not＿＿＿to deliver the supplies
to remote areas.
(A) adequate (B) potential
(C) formidable (D) proportional

10. You need to learn to resist the＿＿＿to buy many things
that are on sale.
(A) comprehension (B) contempt
(C) temptation (D) apprehension

II. Grammar & Structure: 20%
A. Choose the incorrect one from the four underlined parts.

1. The mountain climbers were lost in the snow, and nearly
　　　　　　　　　　　　　　　　A　　　　B　　　　　　　　　　　C

freeze to death.
D

2. It is said that the regime has been successful to reform
　　　A　　　B　　　　　　　　　　　C　　　　　　　　　　D
the society.

3. Sitting on the airplane and watching the clouds pass
　　　　　　　　　　　　　　　　　　　　　　　　　　　　A

beneath me. I let my thoughts wandering to the new
　　　　　　　　　　　　　　　　　　B

experiences that were in store for me during the next
　　　　　　　　C　　　D

two years of living abroad.

4. A desire to know more about the different sides of a

question and a craving to understand something of the
　　　　　　　A　　　　　　　　　　　　　　　B

opinions of other peoples and other times make the
　　　　　　　　　　　　　　　　　　　　　　　　C

educating man.
D

5. There cling in my memory a story once told me by my
        A   B   C   D
   science teacher.

B. Choose the correct expression from the four sentences.

6. (A) My visit to Tokyo was a good possibility for me to
       learn Japanese.
   (B) My visit to Tokyo gave me a good opportunity to learn
       Japanese.
   (C) It was a good opportunity for me to visit Tokyo to
       learn Japanese.
   (D) It was my good opportunity to visit Tokyo for my
       learning Japanese.

7. (A) Nowadays we hear a lot about pollution and its
       results on our health.
   (B) Nowadays we hear a lot of about pollution and the
       results from our health.
   (C) Nowadays we hear a lot of about pollution and its
       effects on our health.
   (D) Nowadays we hear much about pollution and their
       effects in our health.

8. (A) The medias, such as radio and television, tell us
       what is happening in the world.
   (B) The medias, such as radio and television, can tell
       us what is happened in the world.
   (C) The media, such as radio and television, tell us what
       is happening in the world.
   (D) The media, such as radio and television, tell us what
       is happened in the world.

9. (A) Pat always enjoyed studying science in high school,
       therefore, she decided to major in biology in
       college.
   (B) Pat always enjoyed studying science in high school;
       therefore, she decided to major in biology in
       college.
   (C) Pat always enjoyed studying science in high school,
       therefore; she decided to major in biology in
       college.
   (D) Pat always enjoyed studying science in high school;
       therefore; she decided to major in biology in
       college.

10. (A) We hired a professional photographer to take
       pictures of everyone that participated in our wedding.
    (B) We hired a professional photographer taking
       pictures of everyone that participate in our wedding.
    (C) We hired a professional photographer take pictures
       of everyone that participated in our weeding.
    (D) We hired a professional photographer take pictures
       of everyone that participate our wedding.

III. Reading comprehension: 20%

A.
  Every time we open a magazine or newspaper, we find
advertisements for various products. Every time we drive
down a street, we see advertisements on billboards--the huge
signs next to roads and highways. Every time we turn on a
TV or radio, we find commercials for cars, toothpaste,
washing machines, house paint, hair color, jeans, and dozens
of other products. In the modern world, there is no escape
from advertising; it is everywhere.

  More than just a part of modern business, advertising
is vital to successful business; i.e., it is of the greatest
importance. Why is advertising so essential to people who
manufacture and sell products? The main reason is competition; there are many, many companies which are producing
items very similar to one another, and each company needs to
succeed in order to stay in business. Advertising gives
consumers information about a new product and allows them to
compare the quality and price of several similar items
before they choose which to buy.

  However, some modern advertising doesn't give any
information at all about the product except its name.
Imagine a TV commercial for jeans. There are several teen-
agers sitting on a stairway; they are talking about the
problems of growing up. There is no mention at all of the
product--jeans--until the very end of the commercial, when
the name of the manufacturer simply appears on the TV

screen. Imagine a magazine ad for a certain brand of coffee.
A man and woman are sitting on a sofa. They look happy,
friendly, and relaxed. The woman has a cup of coffee in her
hand, but the magazine reader might not even notice it. The
name of the coffee company appears in the corner of the ad,
but, again, there is no information about the product.

How can this advertising be successful if it doesn't
include information about the products? The answer is psychology; advertisers know that people often choose products
for emotional reasons, not for rational ones. Therefore, the
goal of many advertising programs is simply to make consumers feel good about themselves or to make them believe
that they will be happier people if they buy the products in
the ads. For example, a cigarette advertisement that shows a
very strong, masculine cowboy might catch the interest of a
man who would like to see himself as strong and masculine,
too. Although this man doesn't even realize it, he associates the cigarette with his idea of the person he would like
to be; i.e., he feels that he will be strong and masculine
if he smokes that brand of cigarette. This is irrational, of
course. Advertisers use their knowledge of human irration-
ality when they plan ads and commercials.

Some people say, "Advertising doesn't influence me. I
make my own decisions. I don't follow ads and commercials."
However, most of us cannot escape the influence of advertising at least some of the time; it influences us even when
we don't realize it. If you don't believe this, go into your
bedroom closet, bathroom, and kitchen. Look at the products
that you have bought recently. Is every product really
necessary in your life? Can you remember why you chose
certain brands? The answers might surprise you!

1. What is the main idea of the reading selection?
   (A) It's important to have information about a product before you buy it.
   (B) Advertising is everywhere.
   (C) Advertising is more important in modern business than it was in the past because of competition.
   (D) Most people are under the influence of advertising when they buy products, but their choices are not always rational.

2. What's the main factor of a successful advertisement if it does not give any information at all about the product except its name?
   (A) Age.   (B) Psychology.
   (C) Profession.   (D) Actors in the ads.

3. What statement about advertising is not true?
   (A) Advertisers use their knowledge of human irration-ality when they plan ads and commercials.
   (B) In the modern world, there is no escape from advertising.
   (C) Most of us can escape the influence of advertising at least some of the time.
   (D) It is a part of modern business.

4. Why is advertising so essential to manufacturers and sellers?
   (A) Because the market is too competitive.
   (B) Because it is included in the budget.
   (C) Because people like to see advertising.
   (D) Because it is a common way of doing business.

5. Which is not the possible goal of advertising?
   (A) To provide information about a new product.
   (B) To simply make consumers feel good about themselves.
   (C) To help consumers see what products are bad.
   (D) To make consumers believe that they will be happier people if they buy the products in the ads.

B.
   The justification for a university is that it preserves the connection between knowledge and the zest of life, by uniting the young and the old in the imaginative considera-tion of learning. The university imparts information, but it imparts it imaginatively. At least, this is the function which it should perform for society. A university which

fails in this respect has no reason for existence. This
atmosphere of excitement, arising from imaginative consideration, transforms knowledge. A fact is no longer a burden on
the memory: it is energizing as the poet of our dreams, and
as the architect of our purposes.

Imagination is not to be divorced from the facts: it is
a way of illuminating the facts. It works by eliciting the
general principles which apply to the facts, as they exist,
and then by an intellectual survey of alternative possibilities which are consistent with those principles. It enables
men to construct an intellectual vision of a new world, and
it preserves the zest of life by the suggestion of satisfying purposes.

Youth is imaginative, and if the imagination be
strengthened by discipline, this energy of imagination can
in great measure be preserved through life. The tragedy of
the world is that those who are imaginative have but slight
experience, and those who are experienced have feeble
imaginations. Fools act on imagination without knowledge;
pedants act on knowledge without imagination. The task of
a university is to weld together imagination and experience.

1. The main theme of the passage is:
   (A) The importance of imagination to the young.
   (B) The interaction of imagination and experience.
   (C) The role of imagination in our lives.
   (D) The function of universities.

2. According to the passage, the justification of a
   university is:
   (A) It imparts knowledge to imaginative people.
   (B) It combines imagination with knowledge and
       experience.
   (C) It creates an atmosphere of excitement based on
       imagination.
   (D) It presents facts and experience to young and
       old.

3. What does the author say about youth?
   (A) It has great measure of strength.
   (B) It needs to be disciplined.
   (C) It is imaginative but needs knowledge and experience.
   (D) It has the energy of disciple.

4. Which sentence in the third paragraph expresses the main idea?
   (A) Sentence one.   (B) Sentence two.
   (C) Sentence three.   (D) Sentence four.

5. The word "discipline" in the passage above mainly means:
   (A) instruction and exercise designed to train.
   (B) punishment inflicted by way of correction.
   (C) a particular area of study.
   (D) the study of human behavior.

VI. Translate the following sentences into English. 20%

1. 隨著工商的發達，噪音已成為都市中一個嚴重的問題。

2. 根據多項研究發現，噪音會對健康造成許多不良的影響。

3. 由於環保已成為大衆十分關切的問題，因而民衆也較重視過量噪音的危害。

4. 唯有更多民衆來正視這個問題，吾人始能享有一個更寧靜健康的環境。

V. Composition: 20%

TV violence has become a controversial issue recently. What is your opinion about TV violence? (100-150 words)

私立逢甲大學八十一學年度
碩士班研究生入學考試英文試題詳解

I. 字彙：20％

1.（ **B** ）(A) action〔'ækʃən〕*n.* 行爲　(B) **sanction**〔'sæŋkʃən〕*n.* 制裁
   (C) saint〔sent〕*n.* 聖人　　(D) motive〔'motɪv〕*n.* 動機
   ban〔bæn〕*n.* 禁止　　cricket〔'krɪkɪt〕*n.* 板球
   Rugby〔'rʌgbɪ〕*n.* 橄欖球

2.（ **C** ）(A) expose〔ɪk'spoz〕*v.* 暴露
   (B) import〔ɪm'port, -'pɔrt〕*v.* 輸入
   (C) **impose**〔ɪm'poz〕*v.* 強制施行
   (D) export〔ɪks'port, 'ɛksport〕*v.* 輸出

3.（ **D** ）(A) verity〔'vɛrətɪ〕*n.* 眞實
   (B) version〔'vɝʒən, 'vɝʃən〕*n.* 譯本
   (C) diction〔'dɪkʃən〕*n.* 用字；措辭
   (D) **verdict**〔'vɝdɪkt〕*n.* 判決
   passionate〔'pæʃənɪt〕*adj.* 熱情的
   jury〔'dʒʊrɪ〕*n.* 陪審團　**prosecuting attorney** 檢察官

4.（ **D** ）(A) coupon〔'kupɑn〕*n.* 優待券　(B) corps〔kor〕*n.* 兵團
   (C) corpse〔kɔrps〕*n.* 屍體
   (D) **coup**〔ku〕*n.* 突然而有效的一擊
   chilling〔'tʃɪlɪŋ〕*adj.* 令人心寒的
   denounce〔dɪ'naʊns〕*v.* 當衆指責

5.（ **C** ）(A) average〔'ævərɪdʒ〕*n.* 平均數
   (B) storage〔'storɪdʒ〕*n.* 貯藏
   (C) **coverage**〔'kʌvərɪdʒ, 'kʌvrɪdʒ〕*n.* 報導
   (D) passage〔'pæsɪdʒ〕*n.* 通道

6. (**A**) (A) ***enthusiastic*** 〔 ɪn,θjuzɪ'æstɪk 〕 *adj.* 熱誠的
   (B) impatient 〔ɪm'peʃənt〕 *adj.* 沒耐心的
   (C) ultimate 〔'ʌltəmɪt〕 *adj.* 最終的
   (D) annual 〔'ænjʊəl〕 *adj.* 一年一次的

7. (**B**) (A) originality 〔ə,rɪdʒə'nælətɪ〕 *n.* 獨創力
   (B) ***privilege*** 〔'prɪvḷɪdʒ〕 *n.* 榮幸
   (C) reinforcement 〔,riɪn'forsmənt〕 *v.* 加強
   (D) average 〔'ævərɪdʒ〕 *adj.* 平均的
   on behalf of ～ 代表～　staff 〔stæf〕 *n.* 全體人員

8. (**C**) (A) attitude 〔'ætə,tjud〕 *n.* 態度
   (B) altitude 〔'æltə,tjud〕 *n.* 高度
   (C) ***contrast*** 〔'kɑntræst〕 *n.* 明顯的差異；對比
   (D) protest 〔'protɛst〕 *n.* 抗議
   bear in mind 牢記在心

9. (**A**) (A) ***adequate*** 〔'ædəkwɪt〕 *adj.* 足夠的
   (B) potential 〔pə'tɛnʃəl〕 *adj.* 潛在的
   (C) formidable 〔'fɔrmɪdəbḷ〕 *adj.* 難以克服的
   (D) proportional 〔pro'pɔrʃənḷ〕 *adj.* 成比例的
   remote 〔rɪ'mot〕 *adj.* 偏遠的

10. (**C**) (A) comprehension 〔,kɑmprɪ'hɛnʃən〕 *n.* 理解力
    (B) contempt 〔kən'tɛmpt〕 *n.* 輕視
    (C) ***temptation*** 〔tɛmp'teʃən〕 *n.* 誘惑
    (D) apprehension 〔,æprɪ'hɛnʃən〕 *n.* 憂慮；恐懼

Ⅱ. 文法與結構：20%

Part A 改錯

1. (**D**) *freeze → **frozen*** 　依句意，「被凍死」應用被動語態，故將 freeze 改為 frozen。

2. (**D**) *to reform → **in reforming*** 　be successful in＋V-ing 成功地～

3. (**B**) *wandering* → *wander*　let 為使役動詞，加受詞之後，須接原形動詞表主動，故 wandering 須改為 wander。

4. (**D**) *the educating* → *the educated*　依句意，應是「受過教育的」人，現在分詞 educating 應改為過去分詞 educated。

5. (**B**) *cling* → *clings*　副詞 there 放句首，句子須倒裝。由於主詞為 a story，故動詞 cling 須改為單數動詞 clings。

Part B：選出正確的句子

6. (**B**) (A) good possibility 應改為 good opportunity。
(C) to visit Tokyo 與 to learn Japanese 之間須有連接詞 and。
(D) for me 應置於 good opportunity 之後。

7. (**C**) (A) results → effects
(B) a lot of → a lot；the results from → the effects on
(D) their effects in → its effects on

8. (**C**) (A) medias → media
(B) medias → media；happened → happening
(D) happened → happening

9. (**B**) 副詞 therefore 放在句中時，其前面須有分號（；），後面須有逗點隔開。

10. (**A**) (B) taking → to take；participate → participated
(C) weeding → wedding　(D) participate → participated

Ⅲ. 閱讀測驗：20%

A.
【譯文】

　　每次我們翻開報紙或雜誌，就會發現裏面有各種商品的廣告。每當我們開車上街，也會看見告示板——那些在馬路或公路旁的巨大告示——上的廣告。每次當我們打開電視或收音機，就會看見或聽見汽車、牙膏、洗衣機、油漆、染髮劑、牛仔褲和其他許多商品的商業廣告。在現代的世界中，我們都避不開廣告；廣告是無所不在的。

廣告不僅僅是現代商業的一部分，它還是使商業成功的重要因素；也就是說，廣告非常地重要。爲什麼廣告對買賣商品的人而言，是不可或缺的呢？主要的原因就在於競爭；有許多公司所生產的商品都十分類似，而每家公司都必須要成功，才能在商場上生存下去。廣告使消費者能夠獲得關於新產品的資訊，並且可以讓他們在選擇要購買的商品時，能夠比較幾種類似產品的品質與價格。

然而有些現代的廣告除了商品的名稱之外，並沒有提供任何的資料。想像一下一則電視上的牛仔褲廣告：有幾個青少年坐在樓梯上；他們正在談論成長的問題。直到廣告最後，才提到產品——牛仔褲，而且也只是讓廠商的名稱出現在電視螢幕上。再想像一下一則雜誌上某種廠牌的咖啡：有一男一女坐在沙發上，看起來很快樂、友善，也很輕鬆。那女子手上端了一杯咖啡，但是雜誌的讀者可能根本就沒注意到那杯咖啡。那家咖啡廠商的名字出現在廣告的一角，但是，還是一樣，並沒有提供任何關於這項產品的資訊。

如果廣告裏沒有提到關於這項商品的任何資訊，這項廣告又怎麼會成功呢？答案就是心理學。廣告商知道人們選擇商品，常是訴諸感情，而非理性。因此，許多廣告計劃的目標，就是要讓消費者對自己覺得很滿意，或者是讓消費者相信，只要買了廣告中的商品，他們就會變得比較快樂。例如，在一則香煙廣告中，一位強壯、有男子氣概的牛仔，可能會吸引男人的興趣，因爲他們也想和那位牛仔一樣強壯、一樣有男子氣概。這些男人們可能不知道，自己把這種香煙，和他理想中的自己聯想在一起；也就是說，他們覺得如果自己抽了那種牌子的香煙，自己會變得強壯而有男子氣概。當然，這種現象是國內外皆然。當廣告商們製作廣告時，他們就會運用自己對於人的這種不理性態度的知識。

有些人說：「廣告影響不了我。我會自己做決定。我不會聽從廣告上所說的。」然而我們大多數的人，至少有些時候都逃離不了廣告的影響；我們甚至會不知不覺地就受到廣告的影響。如果你不相信，就進去你的洗手間、浴室和厨房看一看那些你最近買的產品。每一項產品眞的是你生活上所必需的嗎？你還記不記得你爲什麼要選那種廠牌的商品？答案可能會使你大吃一驚！

【答案】

1.（D）　　2.（B）　　3.（C）　　4.（A）　　5.（C）

【註】

　billboard〔'bɪl,bord〕*n.* 告示牌

　commercial〔kə'mɜˈʃəl〕*n.*（廣播或電視上的）廣告

　masculine〔'mæskjəlɪn〕*adj.* 有男子氣概的

　irrationality〔ɪ,ræʃə'nælətɪ〕*n.* 無理性

B.

【譯文】

　　大學存在的理由就是它能以想像的學術方面的考量，結合年輕的和年老的，成功地維繫了知識與對生命的熱愛之間的關係。大學能傳授知識，但是以想像的方式來傳授。至少，這是大學對於社會所能產生的功能。如果大學不能做到這一點，那它就沒有理由存在。這種使人振奮的氣氛，是來自於想像上的考量，它能使知識有所轉變。事實對記憶力而言，不再是種負擔：它能像我們夢想中的詩人、我們目的的建築師般地生動。

　　想像力不該和事實完全分離：它是種闡釋事實的方式。想像力的作用就是引出應用於事實上的通則，而且對於與那些規則一致的多種可能性，加以理智地考量。想像力也可以使人對於新的世界有明智的看法，而且藉著提供令人滿意的目標，使人保持對生命的熱忱。

　　年輕是十分富有想像力的，而且如果能夠藉著訓練再強化想像力，那麼它的大部份力量將能持續終生。這世界的悲劇就在於想像力豐富的人，缺乏經驗，而那些經驗豐富的人，卻沒什麼想像力，愚笨的人只以想像力來行事，而毫無知識；賣弄學問的人是以知識為行為準則，但卻沒有任何的想像力。大學的任務就是要將想像力與經驗結合在一起。

【答案】

1.（ D ）　　2.（ B ）　　3.（ C ）　　4.（ D ）　　5.（ C ）

【註】

　justification〔,dʒʌstəfə'keʃən〕*n.* 理由　　zest〔zɛst〕*n.* 熱情

　impart〔ɪm'pɑrt〕*v.* 傳授(知識)　　divorce〔də'vors〕*v.* 分離

　illuminate〔ɪ'lumə,net〕*v.* 說明　　elicit〔ɪ'lɪsɪt〕*v.* 引出

　alternative〔ɔl'tɜnətɪv〕*adj.* 選擇性的　　*in great measure* 大部份

　feeble〔'fibl〕*adj.* 微弱的　　pedant〔'pɛdənt〕*n.* 賣弄學問的人；腐儒

　weld〔wɛld〕*v.* 結合

Ⅳ. 中譯英： 20％

1. With the booming of industry and commerce, noise pollution has become a serious problem in the city.

2. Research has shown that noise has many evil influences on health.

3. Since environmental protection has become a public concern, the public are putting more emphasis on the danger of excessive noise.

4. We can enjoy a quieter and healthier environment only after more people concern themselves with this problem.

Ⅴ. 作文： 20％

TV Violence

Most people complain that the quality of TV programming is far too low, and many people would also say that there is too much mindless violence on TV. Unfortunately, big cable TV companies have decided they have a captive audience and that the people will watch almost anything.

However, in many countries, such as America, the recent deregulation of the cable TV industry has allowed many new TV companies to come into being. Many of these companies provide a higher level of programming and have forced old, established networks to in turn improve the quality of their programming.

I believe that governments should treat TV as an educational medium. They should insist on a certain quality standard for TV programs. In this way most violence and especially senseless violence would thereby be eliminated.

私立海洋大學八十一學年度
碩士班研究生入學考試英文試題

I. Choose the word closest in meaning to the word in the left-hand column. 20%

1. exaggerate　　(A) describe　　　(B) overstate
　　　　　　　　(C) expatiate　　　(D) explain

2. combine　　　(A) join　　　　　(B) cooperate
　　　　　　　　(C) imitate　　　　(D) resist

3. nonplused　　(A) displeased　　(B) diminished
　　　　　　　　(C) dumbfounded　(D) blocked

4. recluse　　　(A) convict　　　　(B) candidate
　　　　　　　　(C) hermit　　　　(D) reject

5. covert　　　(A) hidden　　　　(B) complete
　　　　　　　　(C) new believer　(D) open

6. alienate　　(A) improve　　　(B) estrange
　　　　　　　　(C) adopt　　　　(D) confiscate

7. compel　　　(A) persuade　　　(B) force
　　　　　　　　(C) control　　　　(D) collect

8. mammoth　　(A) old　　　　　(B) excellent
　　　　　　　　(C) dinosaur　　　(D) huge

9. collapse　　(A) assemble　　　(B) fall apart
　　　　　　　　(C) revive　　　　(D) plot together

10. puerile　　(A) sterile　　　　(B) infantile
　　　　　　　　(C) mobile　　　　(D) fertile

II. Read and answer the following questions
A. (15%)

　　While no one knows what causes Alzheimer's violent assault on the brain, there is little question that defective genes are at work in triggering some forms of it. Chromosome 21, one of the 23 gene packages present in all human cells, may play a central role in unraveling the

mystery. People with Down's syndrome, a congenital form of
mental retardation brought on when a fetus receives an extra
copy of chromosome 21, invariably develop lesions in their
brains identical with those seen in Alzheimer's.

1. This paragraph argues that an important factor in
   Alzheimer's is
   (A) infection   (B) heredity
   (C) contagion   (D) environment

2. Down's syndrome
   (A) develops from Alzheimer's.
   (B) causes Alzheimer's.
   (C) is comparable to Alzheimer's.
   (D) is unrelated to Alzheimer's.

3. The trouble seems to come from
   (A) a flaw in chromosome.
   (B) not enough chromosome 21.
   (C) the wrong kind of chromosome 21.
   (D) flaws in other chromosomes.

4. Alzheimer's causes
   (A) psychological disorders.
   (B) brain tumors.
   (C) other kinds of brain damage.
   (D) a deep coma.

B. (15%)

The evils of urban society also first made themselves
felt in this age. Absentee landlords and tenancy problems in
Chinese agriculture were common Widespread pauperism also
appeared among the city proletariat. Private charity agencies
came into being in the late T'ang, performing such services
as caring for orphans and indigent old people or burying dead
paupers. These institutions were nationalized and greatly
extended in the early twelfth century. The Sung army was the
chief means of taking care of the unemployed, but the
government also provided work relief and special granaries
for the support of the poor.

1. According to this paragraph, the development of cities led to
   (A) good results.　　　　(B) bad results.
   (C) population increase.　(D) greater prosperity.

2. Problems were caused for farmers because
   (A) there was not enough land.
   (B) the land was not productive enough.
   (C) farmers did not own their own land.
   (D) taxes were too high.

3. According to this paragraph government aid to the poor in the twelfth century were
   (A) extensive.
   (B) late and inadequate.
   (C) provided by private agencies only.
   (D) rejected as a part of government policy.

4. A pauper is most likely
   (A) a farm animal.　　　(B) a government person.
   (C) a poor person.　　　(D) a person native to the city.

III. Composition: 50%

1. A Bombing Event

2. Crime

Note: 1. The topics of the composition above you may choose one to write within 100 words.

　　　2. The following words and phrases may be used in your composition:

criminal	robbery	burglary
policeman	the mentally ill	murderer
kidnap	terrorist	violence
juvenile	morality	detonate
ransom	arms	gun
firearms	commit	home-made
black-mail	plant	blast
injure	vengeance	extortionist
McDonald's restaurant		explosive device

註：兩題選一，以一百字寫作爲限 。
　　所提供的單字片語可用在文章裡 ，也可作參考不用 。

私立海洋大學八十一學年度
碩士班研究生入學考試英文試題詳解

I. 字彙：20％

1. (B) exaggerate〔ɪgˈzædʒəˌret〕*v.* 誇大
   (A) describe〔dɪˈskraɪb〕*v.* 描述
   (B) ***overstate***〔ˈovəˈstet〕*v.* 誇張
   (C) expatiate〔ɛksˈpetrɪˌet〕*v.* 放逐
   (D) explain〔ɪksˈplen〕*v.* 解釋

2. (A) combine〔kəmˈbaɪn〕*v.* 使結合
   (A) ***join***〔dʒɔɪn〕*v.* 聯合　　(B) cooperate〔koˈɑpəˌret〕*v.* 合作
   (C) imitate〔ˈɪməˌtet〕*v.* 模仿　(D) resist〔rɪˈzɪst〕*v.* 抵抗

3. (C) nonplused〔nɑnˈplʌst〕*adj.* 困惑的
   (A) displeased〔dɪsˈplizd〕*adj.* 不高興的
   (B) diminished〔dəˈmɪnɪʃt〕*adj.* 縮小的
   (C) ***dumbfounded***〔ˌdʌmˈfaʊnd〕*adj.*（因不解）而啞口無言的
   (D) blocked〔blɑkt〕*adj.* 受到阻礙的

4. (C) recluse〔rɪˈklus〕*n.* 隱士
   (A) convict〔kənˈvɪkt〕*n.* 罪犯
   (B) candidate〔ˈkændədɪt〕*n.* 候選人
   (C) ***hermit***〔ˈhɝmɪt〕*n.* 隱士
   (D) reject〔rɪˈdʒɛkt〕*v.* 拒絕

5. (A) covert〔ˈkʌvɚt〕*adj.* 隱密的
   (A) ***hidden***〔ˈhɪdn̩〕*adj.* 秘密的
   (B) complete〔kəmˈplit〕*adj.* 完整的
   (C) new believer 新的信教者
   (D) open〔ˈopn̩〕*adj.* 開放的

6. (**B**)　alienate〔'eljə,net〕*v.* 使疏遠
　　　(A) improve〔ɪm'pruv〕*v.* 改善
　　　(B) ***estrange***〔ə'strendʒ〕*v.* 使疏遠
　　　(C) adopt〔ə'dɑpt〕*v.* 領養；採用
　　　(D) confiscate〔'kɑnfɪs,ket〕*v.* 沒收

7. (**B**)　compel〔kəm'pɛl〕*v.* 強迫
　　　(A) persuade〔pɚ'swed〕*v.* 說服　(B) ***force***〔fors〕*v.* 強迫
　　　(C) control〔kən'trol〕*v.* 控制　(D) collect〔kə'lɛkt〕*v.* 收集

8. (**D**)　mammoth〔'mæməθ〕*adj.* 巨大的
　　　(A) old〔old〕*adj.* 老的
　　　(B) excellent〔'ɛkslənt〕*adj.* 優秀的
　　　(C) dinosaur〔'daɪnəsɔr〕*n.* 恐龍
　　　(D) ***huge***〔hjudʒ〕*adj.* 巨大的

9. (**B**)　collapse〔kə'læps〕*v.* 倒塌
　　　(A) assemble〔ə'sɛmbḷ〕*v.* 組合　(B) ***fall apart*** 倒塌
　　　(C) revive〔rɪ'vaɪv〕*v.* 復活　(D) plot together 共同密謀

10. (**B**)　puerile〔'pjuə,rɪl〕*adj.* 孩子的
　　　(A) sterile〔'stɛrəl〕*adj.* 貧瘠的
　　　(B) ***infantile***〔'ɪnfən,taɪl〕*adj.* 孩子似的
　　　(C) mobile〔'mobɪl〕*adj.* 流動的
　　　(D) fertile〔'fɝtḷ〕*adj.* 肥沃的

Ⅱ. 閱讀測驗：

A.
【譯文】
　　雖然沒有人知道是什麼導致Alzheimer 的腦部受到嚴重損害，但一定是某些不完美的基因所導致的。人體的細胞裏有二十三對染色體，其中第二十一對可能可以解開這個謎。患有唐氏症這種先天智障的人，在胎兒時就多了另一對第二十一對染色體，所以頭腦才會因而受到損害，就像在Alzheimer 腦部的情形一樣。

> **【答案】**
>
> 1.（ B ）　　2.（ C ）　　3.（ A ）　　4.（ C ）

【註】

assault〔ə'sɔlt〕*v.* 襲擊　　defective〔dɪ'fɛktɪv〕*adj.* 有缺點的

gene〔dʒin〕*n.* 基因　　trigger〔'trɪgɚ〕*v.* 引起

chromosome〔'kromə,som〕*n.* 染色體

package〔'pækɪdʒ〕*n.* 全部之物　　cell〔sɛl〕*n.* 細胞

unravel〔ʌn'rævl̩〕*v.* 解開　　Down's syndrome 唐氏症

congenital〔kən'dʒɛnətl̩〕*adj.* 先天性的

mental retardation 智障　　fetus〔'fitəs〕*n.* 胎兒

invariable〔ɪn'vɛrɪəbl̩〕*adj.* 一定的　　lesion〔'liʒən〕*n.* 損害

B.

【譯文】

　　都會社區的壞處首度在這時代裏顯現出來。地主和租賃問題在中國文化中是很常見的。都市的無產階級間，出現了廣泛的貧窮。私人慈善機構出現於晚唐。提供的服務包括照顧孤兒和貧苦的老人，以及埋葬死亡的窮人。這些機構在十二世紀初期才國家化，並大量地擴充。宋朝的軍隊就是照顧失業者最主要的方式，但是政府仍然提供了失業救濟金和特別的穀倉給窮人。

> **【答案】**
>
> 1.（ B ）　　2.（ C ）　　3.（ A ）　　4.（ C ）

【註】

urban〔'ɝbən〕*adj.* 都市的　　***absentee landlord*** 不居於產權所在地的地主

tenancy〔'tɛnənsɪ〕*n.* 租借　　widespread〔'waɪd'sprɛd〕*adj.* 普及的

pauperism〔'pɔpərɪzm〕*n.* 貧民

proletariat〔,prolə'tɛrɪət〕*adj.* 無產階級的

charity〔'tʃɛrətɪ〕*n.* 慈善　　orphan〔'ɔrfn̩〕*n.* 孤兒

indigent〔'ɪndədʒənt〕*adj.* 窮困的　　pauper〔'pɔpɚ〕*n.* 窮人

work relief 失業救濟金　　granary〔'grænərɪ〕*n.* 穀倉

Ⅲ. 作文：50％

Crime

Almost all crimes are directly related to economics. In countries or areas where good jobs are plentiful such as modern Japan, Taiwan or the U.S. of the 1950s, the crime rate is quite low. In the U.S. today, however, good jobs are much harder to find and the crime rate is much higher, and huge slums filled with various " undesirables " exist in nearly every large American city.

Poverty results in broken families, in frustration and violence, in depression and drug use and so on. Most criminals end up resorting to crime mainly because they don't believe they have much of a future.

In order to solve the problem, governments must work in tandem with prominent people in society in order to create opportunity for everyone, and everyone must be made to feel that they are an important part of society.

心得筆記欄

國立台灣大學七十九學年度
碩士班研究生入學考試英文試題

Choose the <u>BEST</u> answer. Put a cross--"X"--in the appropriate box on the answer sheet to indicate your choice. Make certain you have read the whole passage before attempting any answer.

Example: Karen was so angry when she came home that I had to _____ her by agreeing with everything she said in order to pacify her.
　　　　(A) humor　　(B) indulge　　(C) pamper　　(D) spoil

Answer :　　A　　B　　C　　D
　　　　　　X　　☐　　☐　　☐

I.

　　Whether we like it or not, we have already entered rough seas, and the storm signals are up. Under such conditions, there is only one place for the Captain, and ___1___ is the bridge.

1. (A) that　　　(B) which　　(C) for that　(D) of which

II.

　　Every child spends the first years of life learning social skills, first through play and ___2___ others, and later at school. Gradually, he or she learns how to move about, talk and ___3___ to other people.

2. (A) imitating (B) imitated (C) imitate　　(D) to imitate
3. (A) close　　(B) yield　　(C) getting　　(D) relate

III.

--I'm surprised that the men agreed so easily.
--Men will agree to anything so long as they think it was their own idea. All we have to do now is keep a careful eye on them to ___4___ they don't make any mistakes.

--How can they make mistakes?

--Oh, believe me, my dear, if a man gets a wrong notion into his head, he can ruin everything. And wrong notions are very difficult to ___5___ .

4. (A) watch   (B) see   (C) be safe   (D) be definite

5. (A) stay   (B) shift   (C) comply   (D) vanish

IV.

    "No, no, it's not fair to say I disapprove. I'm ___6___ , perhaps. But, anyway, ___7___ I say is likely to make any difference, is it? I mean, you've made your mind up already, haven't you? It's just that, well, I'd always thought it would turn ___8___ differently. We've always had a particular way of life, done certain things, ___9___ in certain circles. No, I don't disapprove. I don't really know him, anyway. So how can I disapprove? But what about Billy? You've told him, I suppose? You know, I'd always ___10___ expected it would be Billy. It seemed so natural. So suitable ..."

6. (A) disgraced   (B) disavowed
    (C) disappointed   (D) disparaged

7. (A) much   (B) the less   (C) nothing   (D) everything

8. (A) up   (B) out   (C) in   (D) off

9. (A) motioned   (B) moved   (C) formed   (D) drawn

10. (A) somehow   (B) somewhat
    (C) somewhere   (D) some day

V.

    Now and again I have had horrible dreams but not enough of them to make me lose my delight in dreams. As a child I could never understand why grown-ups ___11___ dreaming so calmly when they could make such a fuss about any holiday. This still puzzles me. I am mystified by people who say they never dream and appear to have no interest in the ___12___ . It is much more astonishing than if they said they never went out for a walk. Most people do not seem to

accept dreaming as part of their lives. They appear to see
it as an irritating ___13___ habit, like sneezing or yawning.
I have never understood this.

11. (A) took　　　(B) make　　　(C) saw　　　(D) woke up
12. (A) object　　　　　　　(B) subject
    (C) objective　　　　　　(D) subjective
13. (A) fatal　　(B) deliberate　(C) convivial　(D) little

VI.

　　"Thought," says Pascal, "makes the greatness of man.
The universe can destroy an individual by ___14___ breath; but
even if the entire force of the universe were employed to
destroy a single man, the man "would still be more noble
than that which destroys him, since he is aware of his own
death and of the advantage which the universe has ___15___
him: of all this the universe knows nothing." This awareness
of himself and of the universe is no doubt what chiefly distinguishes man from all other ___16___ of life.

14. (A) an only　　　　　　(B) a resuscitating
    (C) a mere　　　　　　 (D) an endangered
15. (A) provided　(B) supplied　(C) upon　(D) over
16. (A) modes　　(B) models　　(C) shapes　(D) forms

VII.

　　One of the greatest television successes of the 1970s
was Roots, the ___17___ story of a young American called Kunta
Kinte who traced his history back through two centuries
to a village in West Africa where his forebearers had been
taken into slavery. Social, economic and ethnic ___18___
vanished as huge audiences identified with the young man's
need to reach back through time and find his origins. The
story struck ___19___ with an apparently universal uncertainty about where we come from. The desire to remove that uncertainty is very strong indeed: it is what the great the-

ologian Paul Tillich ___20___ to as "the ultimate concern".

17. (A) fictional   (B) legendary
    (C) figurative   (D) fabricated

18. (A) values   (B) barriers
    (C) obstructions   (D) fronts

19. (A) a cry   (B) a deception
    (C) a chord   (D) an apprehension

20. (A) referred   (B) resorted
    (C) subjected   (D) proposed

VIII.

    My first impression was that the stranger's eyes were
of an unusually light blue. They ___21___ mine for several
blank seconds, vacant, unmistakably scared. Startled and
innocently naughty, they half reminded me of an incident I
couldn't quite ___22___ ; something which had happened a long
time ago, to do with the school classroom. They were the
eyes of a schoolboy surprised in the ___23___ of breaking one
of the rules. Not that I had caught him, apparently, at
anything except his own thoughts: perhaps he imagined I
could ___24___ them. At any rate, he seemed not to have heard
or seen me cross the compartment from my corner to his own,
for he started violently ___25___ the sound of my voice; so
violently, indeed, that his nervous recoil hit me like a re-
percussion. Instinctively I took a ___26___ backwards.

21. (A) stroke   (B) met
    (C) glanced at   (D) looked on

22. (A) endure   (B) stir up   (C) place   (D) experience

23. (A) activity   (B) acting   (C) action   (D) act

24. (A) freeze   (B) twist   (C) read   (D) vaporize

25. (A) on   (B) at   (C) to   (D) with

26. (A) hand   (B) foot   (C) pace   (D) stride

IX.

    People usually think of stress as something the world
___27___ on them. Worry and hassle are blamed for all kinds

of ___28___ , from asthma to headaches, from high blood pressure to stomach ulcers. And we often blame other people for making us feel bad: when we call someone a "pain in the ___29___ ", we are describing the physical and psychological effect they have on us.

Although it is ___30___ to regard stress as some nasty germ attacking us from outside, the truth is that we are largely responsible for what stress ___31___ to our bodies. Once we make ourselves aware of how our bodies respond to worry, fear, anger and fatigue (all of which are forms of stress), we can start ___32___ to relax.

27. (A) inflicts　　　　　(B) conflicts
　　(C) affects　　　　　(D) effects
28. (A) ailments　　　　 (B) remedies
　　(C) sicknesses　　　 (D) deformities
29. (A) neck　　(B) heart　　(C) head　　　　(D) hand
30. (A) tempting　　　　 (B) useless
　　(C) worthy　　　　　(D) satisfying
31. (A) means　(B) does　　(C) bears　　　　(D) influences
32. (A) to have to learn　(B) having learned
　　(C) to be learned　　 (D) learning

X.

　　The country was weary and worried. Eagles and lions would have been out of place, almost laughable: no one wanted to ___33___ or to roar. There was no ___34___ for experiment and adventures, for bold imaginative leadership, for greatness. The country muddled along. If there were survivors of the war generation, or post-war young men fit to speak a different language, the stage was not ___35___ for them; their appeal would have sounded false and hollow, and the words would have died ___36___ .

33. (A) sail　(B) loom　　　(C) soar　　　　(D) glide
34. (A) say　　(B) rush　　　(C) opening　　 (D) call
35. (A) cast　(B) set　　　　(C) performed　 (D) done

36. (A) in all their glory   (B) on their lips
    (C) triumphant   (D) a protracted death

XI.

If we look at history, it is hardly surprising that
parents, educators, and other moral   37   of our own day
should be greatly worried about the damage television is
   38   to all of us, and particularly to our children.
Moralists, by nature, have always had a tendency to worry
about and   39   the newest dominant form of popular entertainment. In Plato's ideal state, all imaginative literature was to be banned because of the bad influence it 40
exercised, although this same literature has been admired
ever since its creation as one of the proudest achievements
of man.

Any form of mass entertainment is viewed with considerable   41   until it has been around for some time. It usually becomes accepted once people realize that life goes on
in the same   42   way as before. Then a newer entertainment
medium becomes the   43   of the same concerns. When I was
a child, all kinds of evil influences were   44   to the
movies; today these are blamed on television. When I was a
young man, the comics were   45   because they were said to
incite the innocents to violence.

Even then, however, it was acknowledged that children
were not all that innocent. It was known that they   46
angry, violent, destructive, and even sexual fantasies that
are far from innocent. Today as well, those who   47   the
impact of television on children ought to truly understand
what children are all about ....

New forms of entertainment are particularly   48   to
adults who had no chance to enjoy them in childhood. Most
parents who are young enough to have thoroughly enjoyed

watching television in their childhood worry even less about its __49__ effects. They know that their own youthful hours watching television did not prevent them from getting edu-cated or from living useful lives. If they feel __50__, it is about using television as a baby-sitter for their own children.

37. (A) observers　　　　　　(B) forerunners
　　(C) overseers　　　　　　(D) pathfinders

38. (A) playing　(B) taking　(C) making　(D) doing

39. (A) pop up　(B) prop up　(C) uphold　(D) decry

40. (A) supposedly　　　　　　(B) is supposingly
　　(C) has supposed　　　　　(D) supposes

41. (A) census　　　　　　　　(B) consensus
　　(C) suspicion　　　　　　(D) conscience

42. (A) conformist　　　　　　(B) confounded
　　(C) haphazard　　　　　　(D) hell-raising

43. (A) mark　(B) aim　(C) focus　(D) prism

44. (A) blamed　(B) betrayed　(C) given　(D) ascribed

45. (A) upheld　　　　　　　　(B) denounced
　　(C) published　　　　　　(D) circulated

46. (A) grew　　　　　　　　　(B) sought
　　(C) tended to be　　　　　(D) harbor

47. (A) rate　(B) evaluate　(C) estimate　(D) determine

48. (A) prone　　　　　　　　(B) popular
　　(C) suspect　　　　　　　(D) accommodated

49. (A) detrimental　　　　　(B) extrinsic
　　(C) exhilarating　　　　　(D) propitious

50. (A) uneasy　　　　　　　　(B) flustered
　　(C) frustrated　　　　　　(D) worked up

國立台灣大學七十九學年度
碩士班研究生入學考試英文試題詳解

I.

【譯文】

　　不管我們喜不喜歡，我們已經進入洶湧的海洋，而暴風雨的信號也已升起。在這種情況下，艦長只可能待在一個地方，那就是艦橋。

【註】　bridge〔brɪdʒ〕*n*. 艦橋（橫架於兩舷間之高座，為艦長發號施令之所在）

1.（**A**）　此處需要一個代名詞以取代前面的 one place，故選(A) that。

II.

【譯文】

　　每個小孩生命的頭幾年，都花在學習社交技巧上面；首先是透過遊戲及模仿他人，後來則是在學校裏學到。漸漸地，他或她就學會了如何行動、說話、以及和其他人保持良好的關係。

【註】　*move about*　"動來動去"

2.（**A**）　and 連接兩個字詞作介詞 through 的受詞，故此處應選動名詞(A) imitating。

3.（**D**）　*relate to* ～　"和～保持良好的關係"
　　　　(A) close（關閉），(B) yield（屈服），句意不合。(C) getting 文法錯誤。

III.

【譯文】

　　——這些人這麼容易就同意了，真令我吃驚。
　　——只要是跟他們自己想法相同的事，人們都會同意的。我們現在所要做的，就是小心看著他們，別讓他們犯錯。
　　——他們怎麼可能犯錯？

——哦，親愛的，相信我！如果一個人的腦子裏有了錯誤的觀念，他就會毀了一切。而錯誤的觀念是很難革除的。

4.（ **B** ）　*see* **＋** *that* 子句　　" 留意～ "

5.（ **B** ）　根據句意，此處應選(B) shift〔ʃɪft〕*v.* 除去
　　　　　　(A) stay 停留　　(C) comply 順從　　(D) vanish 消失

Ⅳ.

【譯文】

　　「不，不，說我不贊成並不公平，或許是失望吧！不過，無論如何，不管我說什麼也不會造成任何改變，對吧？我是說，你已經下定決心了，對不對？嗯，就這樣了。我原來一直認為結果會有所不同。我們總是以一種特殊的方式生活、做特定的事情、在特定的圈子裏活動。不，我並不是不贊成。反正，我不太認識他。所以，我怎麼反對呢？但是比利呢？我想，你已經告訴他了吧？你知道，不知怎麼地，我一直就認為會是比利。這似乎是那麼自然、那麼合適……」

6.（ **C** ）　根據句意，應選(C) disappointed（失望的）。
　　　　　　(A) disgrace〔dɪsˈgres〕*v.* 玷辱
　　　　　　(B) disavow〔ˌdɪsəˈvaʊəl〕*v.* 否認
　　　　　　(D) disparage〔dɪˈspærɪdʒ〕*v.* 輕視

7.（ **C** ）　由本句句尾的附加問句（ is it？）可知，此處應選表否定之主詞
　　　　　　(C) nothing。

8.（ **B** ）　*turn out* " 結果變成 "
　　　　　　(A) turn up " 出現 "　　　　　　(C) turn in " 告密；進入 "

9.（ **B** ）　根據句意，應選(B) moved（活動）。

10.（ **A** ）　*somehow* 不知怎麼搞地
　　　　　　(B) somewhat 有點　　　　　　(C) somewhere 某處
　　　　　　(D) some day （未來）有一天

V.

【譯文】

　　我時常會做惡夢，但是次數並不會多到令我失去對夢的喜愛。小時候，我總是不了解，爲什麼大人把做夢看得那麼不在乎，但是對假日卻小題大做。這件事到現在仍然令我困惑。至於那些說他們從不做夢，而對這個話題顯得漠不關心的人，我總是難以理解。這比他們說從來沒出去散過步，還要令人吃驚。大部分的人都不把做夢當成生命的一部分。他們似乎只把它當成一個惱人的小習慣，像打噴嚏或打呵欠一樣。這一點，我一直無法了解。

【註】 ***now and again*** "時常"

　　　　make a fuss about *sth.* "對某事小題大做"

11.(**A**) 根據句意，應選(A) took（認爲）。

12.(**B**) (A) object 物體；目標　　　　(B) ***subject*** 話題；問題

　　　　　(C) objective 客觀的　　　　　(D) subjective 主觀的

13.(**D**) 根據句意，應選(D) little（小的；不重要的）。

　　　　　(A) fatal〔'fetḷ〕*adj.* 致命的

　　　　　(B) deliberate〔dɪ'lɪbərɪt〕*adj.* 有意的

　　　　　(C) convivial〔kən'vɪvɪəl〕*adj.* 歡樂的

VI.

【譯文】

　　巴斯噶說：「思想成就了人類的偉大。」宇宙萬物不費吹灰之力就可以摧毀個人。但是，即使宇宙動用一切的力量來摧毀一個人，這個人「還是比他的毀滅者高尚，因爲他能意識到自己的死亡，以及宇宙凌駕在他之上的優勢：對於這些事，宇宙萬物一無所知。」無疑地，這種對於自己以及宇宙的認知，就是人類和其他所有生命形式之間最大的不同。

【註】 Pascal〔'pæskḷ,（法)pɑs'kal〕*n.* 巴斯噶（ 1623-1662，法國哲學、數學及物理學家）

　　　　distinguish A from B "區別 A 和 B"

14.(**C**)　根據句意，應選(C) mere（僅僅），其他選項均不合句意。

    (A) only 當形容詞，表「唯一的」。

    (B) resuscitating〔rɪ'sʌsə,tetɪŋ〕*adj.* 令人復甦的

    (D) endangered〔ɪn'dendʒəd, ɛn-〕*adj.* 瀕臨絕種的

15.(**D**)　根據句意，此處指「凌駕在他之上的」優勢，故選(D) over。

16.(**D**)　(A) mode　模式　　　　　　(B) model　模型

    (C) shape　形狀　　　　　　　(D) *form*　形式

Ⅶ.

【譯文】

    一九七○年代最成功的電視節目之一就是「根」。這是一個小說改編的故事，敍述一個名叫康塔‧金特的美國年輕人，上溯他自己的家族歷史長達兩個世紀之久，一直追尋到西非，他的祖先被俘成為奴隸的一個小村落。隨著廣大的觀眾認同這個年輕人的渴求，回溯時光、找尋根源，社會、經濟以及種族的隔閡都消失了。這個故事藉著顯然是普遍存在的一種不確定性——我們是從哪裏來的——引起了人們的共鳴。想要去除這種不確定性的欲望實在是非常強烈：這也就是偉大的神學家保羅‧提里赫所謂的「終極關懷」。

【註】

    ethnic〔'ɛθnɪk〕*adj.* 種族的

    Paul Tillich 保羅‧提里赫（1886-1965，美國神學及哲學家）

    theologian〔,θiə'lodʒən, -dʒɪən〕*n.* 神學家

    ultimate〔'ʌltəmɪt〕*adj.* 終極的；最後的

17.(**A**)　*fictional*〔'fɪkʃənḷ〕*adj.* 小說的

    (B) legendary〔'lɛdʒənd, ɛrɪ〕*adj.* 傳奇的

    (C) figurative〔'fɪgjərətɪv〕*adj.* 比喻的

    (D) fabricated〔'fæbrɪ,ketɪd〕*adj.* 捏造的

18.(**B**)　根據句意，應選(B) barriers（障礙；界線）。(C) obstruction 作可數名詞，指具體的「障礙物」，在此處不合。(A) values（價值觀），(D) fronts（態度；正面），均不合句意。

19.(**C**)　chord〔kɔrd〕*n*. 和絃　　***strike a chord*** "引起共鳴"
　　　　(B) deception〔dɪ'sɛpʃən〕*n*. 欺騙
　　　　(D) apprehension〔,æprɪ'hɛnʃən〕*n*. 恐懼

20.(**A**)　***refer to ～ as*** … "稱呼～爲…"
　　　　(B) resort to "訴諸；依靠"　　(C) subject to "服從於"
　　　　(D) propose to sb. "向某人提議；向某人求婚"

Ⅷ.

【譯文】

　　我的第一印象是，這個陌生人的眼睛是一種不尋常的淡藍色。這雙眼睛毫無表情地盯著我的眼睛看了幾秒鐘，既空洞，又毫無疑問地流露出害怕。這雙受驚嚇，而帶著無邪的頑皮的眼睛，幾乎讓我想起一件我不太記得的事情；一件很久以前發生的事，跟學校教室有關的。那是一個小學生因破壞校規而感到吃驚時的眼睛。很顯然，我並不是抓到他在做什麼事，而是抓到了他的思想：或許他以爲我可以看穿他的想法。無論如何，他似乎沒聽見或看見我穿越小房間，從我這個角落走向他那個角落，因爲我的聲音使他猛然嚇了一跳。他的驚嚇眞的是非常猛烈，因此他緊張地退縮了一下，而造成了我的的連帶反應：我本能地也後退了一步。

【註】

　　compartment〔kəm'pɑrtmənt〕*n*. （火車、船艙中的）小房間
　　recoil〔rɪ'kɔɪl〕*n*. 退縮
　　repercussion〔,ripɚ'kʌʃən〕*n*. 回響

21.(**B**)　met 在此處指「（眼、耳等的）接觸」。因句中提到 for several seconds,故不能選 (C) glanced at （瞥見）。(A) stroke （敲擊）, (D) looked on （觀望），句意均不合。

22.(**C**)　place 在此指「認出」（= *identify*）。(A) endure （忍耐）, (B) stir up （慫恿）, (D) experience （經歷），均不合句意。

23.(**D**)　***in the act of V-ing*** "在從事～之際"

24.(**C**)　根據句意，應選 (C) read （看穿）。
　　　　(D) vaporize〔'vepə,raɪz〕*v*. 蒸發

25.(B)　***start at sth.***　" 被某事嚇一跳 "

26.(C)　pace 一步　　　(D) stride 闊步

Ⅸ.

【譯文】

　　人們通常認為壓力是外界所施加在他們身上的。所有的小病痛，從氣喘到頭痛，從高血壓到胃潰瘍，都被歸咎於擔憂和爭吵。而且我們經常怪別人使我們不舒服：當我們說某人是個「頭痛人物」時，我們所指的就是他對我們造成的身體及心理上的影響。

　　雖然我們很容易把壓力看成某種難纏的細菌，從外界襲擊我們，但事實上，壓力對我們的身體所造成的影響，我們自己要負大部分的責任。一旦我們讓自己意識到身體對擔憂、恐懼、憤怒和疲勞（這些都是壓力的不同形式）會如何反應，我們就能夠開始學習放鬆了。

【註】　hassle〔ˈhæsḷ〕*n.* 爭吵
　　　asthma〔ˈæsmə, ˈæzmə〕*n.* 氣喘　　　ulcer〔ˈʌlsɚ〕*n.* 潰瘍
　　　nasty〔ˈnæstɪ〕*adj.* 難纏的

27.(A)　inflict〔ɪnˈflɪkt〕*v.* 施加
　　　(B) conflict（衝突）通常和 with 連用。(C) affect（影響），(D) effect（引起），均為及物動詞，不接介詞而直接接受詞。

28.(A)　ailment〔ˈelmənt〕*n.* 疾病（輕微或慢性的）
　　　(B) remedy（藥物），(D) deformity（畸形的人或物），均不合句意。(C) sickness（疾病）不使用複數形。

29.(A)　***a pain in the neck***　〔俚〕" 極難對付的人或事 "

30.(A)　tempting〔ˈtɛmptɪŋ〕*adj.* 誘惑人的
　　　(B) useless（無用的），(C) worthy（有價值的），(D) satisfying（令人滿意的），均不合句意。

31.(B)　根據句意，應選(B) does（做）。

32.(D)　***start ＋ V-ing***　" 開始做～ "

X.

【譯文】

　　這個國家的人民既疲憊憊又憂慮。老鷹和獅子都沒有了立足之地，這幾乎是很可笑的：沒有人想展翅高飛或放聲大吼。完全沒有需要去實驗、冒險、大膽地想像領導權、或做大事。整個國家都在敷衍了事。假如戰爭那一代的人還有存活者，或有持不同看法的戰後年輕人，也不會有為他們而搭的舞台。他們的訴求聽起來會是虛假而空洞的，而他們的話在說出來以前，就會被吞回去。

【註】
　　muddle along "敷衍"

　　speak a different language "想法不同"

33. (C) 由 or 所連接的另一個不定詞 to roar（獅子等的吼叫）可知，此處乃是繼續使用本句句首之兩種動物（ eagles and lions ）來做為象徵，故本題應選適合鷹的動作(C) soar（高飛）。(A) sail（航行），(B) loom（隱約出現），(D) glide（滑行）。

34. (D) (A) say 發言權　　　　　　(B) rush 匆忙
　　　　 (C) opening 空隙　　　　　 (D) *call* 需要；理由

35. (B) *set a stage* "搭設舞台"
　　　　 (A) cast 丟　　　　　　　 (C) perform 表演

36. (B) 根據句意，應選(B) on their lips（在他們唇邊）。
　　　　 (D) protracted〔pro'træktɪd〕*adj.* 延長的

XI.

【譯文】

　　如果我們回顧歷史，再來看看現在的父母、教育家、以及道德監督者竟然如此憂心電視對我們，尤其是我們的小孩所造成的傷害，就不會感到驚訝了。道德家天生就有一種傾向，會對於大眾娛樂中最新、最佔優勢的形式，產生疑慮，並加以譴責。在柏拉圖的理想國中，由於想像的文學或許會產生不良影響，所以必須被禁；雖然這些文學作品從創作之初就被認為是人類最值得驕傲的成就之一，而一直受到讚賞。

任何形式的大眾娛樂從出現開始，總有一段時間會受到相當大的質疑。一旦人們了解，生活仍然和以前一樣地隨意，通常就會開始接受它。然後，另一種更新的娛樂媒介又會成為這種關切的焦點。在我小的時候，所有不良的影響都歸咎於電影；現在，卻又都怪在電視頭上。我年輕時，連環漫畫被認為會煽動單純的人走向暴力，因此受到公然抨擊。

然而，就算在當時，人們也已承認，小孩並不是那麼天真無邪的。人們知道，小孩有憤怒、暴烈、毀滅、甚至是性方面的幻想，而這些都是一點也不天真的。在現今也一樣，那些評價電視對兒童有什麼影響的人，應該真正去了解兒童到底是怎麼一回事。

在兒童時代沒有機會享受新娛樂形式的成人，對這些娛樂形式特別感到懷疑。而年紀較輕，在小時候曾經完全享受過看電視樂趣的父母之中，則有大部分不太擔心電視會造成有害的結果。他們知道，他們年輕時花在看電視的時光，並沒有阻礙他們受教育，或成為有用的人。如果他們感到不安，那是因為他們把電視當作小孩保姆的緣故。

【註】　dominant〔ˈdɑmənənt〕 *adj.* 優勢的；支配的
exercise〔ˈɛksəˌsaɪz〕 *v.* 產生（影響）
comics〔ˈkɑmɪks〕 *n.pl.* 連環漫畫（= *comic strips* ）
incite〔ɪnˈsaɪt〕 *v.* 煽動

37. (**C**)　(A) observer 觀察者　　　　(B) forerunner〔ˈforˌrʌnə〕 *n.* 先驅
(C) ***overseer***〔ˈovəˌsiə , ˌovəˈsɪr〕 *n.* 監督者
(D) pathfinder〔ˈpæθˌfaɪndə , ˈpɑθ-〕 *n.* 拓荒者

38. (**D**)　造成傷害（ damage ）用動詞 do 。

39. (**D**)　(A) pop up " 突然出現 "　　　(B) prop up " 倚靠；支撐 "
(C) uphold〔ʌpˈhold〕 *v.* 支持　(D) ***decry***〔dɪˈkraɪ〕 *v.* 譴責

40. (**A**)　根據句意，此處應選(A) supposedly 來修飾動詞 exercised 。
supposedly〔səˈpozɪdlɪ〕 *adv.* 或許

41. (**C**)　(A) census〔ˈsɛnsəs〕 *n.* 人口普查
(B) consensus〔kənˈsɛnsəs〕 *n.* （意見）一致
(C) ***suspicion***〔səˈspɪʃən〕 *n.* 懷疑
(D) conscience〔ˈkɑnʃəns〕 *n.* 良心

42. (**C**) (A) conformist〔kən'fɔrmɪst〕*adj*. 因襲的
　　　　　　(B) confounded〔kən'faʊndɪd〕*adj*. 困惑的
　　　　　　(C) **haphazard**〔,hæp'hæzəd〕*adj*. 隨便的
　　　　　　(D) hell-raising〔'hɛl,rezɪŋ〕*adj*.〔俗〕大吵大鬧的

43. (**C**) 根據句意，應選(C) focus（焦點）。
　　　　　　(A) mark 記號　　(B) aim 目標　　(C) prism〔'prɪzəm〕*n*. 三稜鏡

44. (**D**) ascribe〔ə'skraɪb〕*v*. 歸因於
　　　　　　A be ascribed to B "把A歸因於B"
　　　　　　(A)用法應為 *be blamed on* "歸咎於"。(B) betray（背叛），(C)
　　　　　　give（給予），均不合句意。

45. (**B**) (A) upheld〔ʌp'hɛld〕*v*. 支持（*uphold* 之 p.p.）
　　　　　　(B) **denounce**〔dɪ'naʊns〕*v*. 公開抨擊
　　　　　　(C) publish 出版
　　　　　　(D) circulate〔'sɝkjə,let〕*v*. 流通

46. (**D**) harbor〔'hɑrbɚ〕*v*. 心懷（惡意等）
　　　　　　(A) grew（生長），(B) sought（尋找），(C) tended to be ～（有
　　　　　　成為～的傾向），均不合句意。

47. (**B**) (A) rate 估價
　　　　　　(B) **evaluate**〔ɪ'væljʊ,et〕*v*. 評價
　　　　　　(C) estimate 估計（價錢）　　　　(D) determine 決定

48. (**C**) (A) prone〔pron〕*adj*. 易於～的　　(B) popular 受歡迎的
　　　　　　(C) **suspect**〔'sʌspɛkt〕*adj*. 可疑的
　　　　　　(D) accomodate〔ə'kɑmə,det〕*v*. 容納

49. (**A**) **detrimental**〔,dɛtrə'mɛntḷ〕*adj*. 有害的
　　　　　　(B) extrinsic〔ɛk'strɪnsɪk〕*adj*. 外在的
　　　　　　(C) exhilarating〔ɪg'zɪlə,retɪŋ,ɛg-〕*adj*. 令人歡喜的
　　　　　　(D) propitious〔prə'pɪʃəs〕*adj*. 順遂的

50. (**A**) **uneasy** 不安的　　(B) flustered〔'flʌstəd〕*adj*. 慌亂的
　　　　　　(C) frustrated 沮喪的　　(D) worked up "漸漸興奮的"

國立台灣師範大學七十九學年度
碩士班研究生入學考試英文試題

I. Choose the most appropriate word to complete each of the following sentences. 20 %

1. To _____ means to cut into small bits with a knife.
   (A) chop   (B) wrap
   (C) dump   (D) broil

2. The driver pushes the _____ in his car to make a loud warning noise.
   (A) sear   (B) shift
   (C) horn   (D) bonnet

3. The _____ youngster was afraid to ask for a second helping of pie.
   (A) handsome   (B) happy
   (C) versatile   (D) timid

4. By spending as little as possible, the _____ old woman was able to live on the little money she had.
   (A) thrifty   (B) lonely
   (C) cheerful   (D) lovely

5. My neighbors play loud, sharp, unpleasant music. I can't stand it when the music _____ from their windows.
   (A) yells   (B) howls
   (C) blares   (D) flares

6. To go on a(n) _____ means to take a short pleasure trip.
   (A) tour   (B) embargo
   (C) outing   (D) vacation

7. The paragraph was so wordy that he was able to _____ it and express the same idea in half as many words.
   (A) expand   (B) economize
   (C) condense   (D) alternate

8. When people comment that she is successful, and she says that it's just because she had good luck, she's being _____.
   (A) fortunate   (B) inconsiderate
   (C) friendly   (D) modest

9. The long-distance runner was _____ when he learned
that he had set a new record.
(A) dejected   (B) elated
(C) exhausted   (D) consulted

10. Despite all hardships, Mary _____ in her efforts to
complete college education.
(A) relaxed   (B) failed
(C) persisted   (D) faltered

II. Choose the best answer for each blank in the following passage.
20％

How important is your appearance? Although everyone
wants to be ___1___, are beautiful people always happier people? For example, ___2___ must be a problem to be a really
beautiful woman, because some men may be more interested in
looking at you than ___3___ to you. They think of you as a
picture ___4___ a person. ___5___ are also some people who think
that women who are exceptionally pretty and men who are
___6___ handsome must be stupid. They believe that only ___7___
people can be intelligent.

On the other hand, no one wants to be really ugly, and
have a face ___8___ even his or her own mother doesn't want
to look at; and no one wants to be ___9___ either--that is to
be neither attractive nor unattractive, and have a face that
is easily ___10___.

1. (A) rich   (B) long-lived
   (C) good-looking   (D) successful

2. (A) she   (B) they   (C) you   (D) it

3. (A) talk   (B) talking   (C) to talk   (D) talked

4. (A) rather than   (B) as well as
   (C) less than   (D) as much as

5. (A) Those   (B) They   (C) Then   (D) There

6. (A) particularly   (B) pickingly
   (C) mentally   (D) knowingly

7. (A) cheerful   (B) unattractive
   (C) depressed   (D) uncouth

8. (A) that   (B) than
   (C) if   (D) while

9. (A) straight   (B) plain
   (C) composed   (D) unpleasant

10. (A) remembered   (B) immemorable
    (C) recalled   (D) forgotten

III. Choose the best answer for each blank in the following two dialogues. 20 %

(A)

Clerk: Good evening, sir. Can I help you?

David: Yes. __1__

Clerk: Do you have a reservation, sir?

David: Yes.

Clerk: __2__

David: Lin, David Lin.

Clerk: Oh, yes, __3__. A single room for two nights, is that correct?

Dvaid: Yes, that's right.

Clerk: OK, Mr. Lin. Please fill out this__4__.

David: All right. Here you are. __5__

Clerk: One o'clock in the afternoon. But if you can't leave that early, you may check your luggage at the check-room.

1. (A) I'd like to cash a check.
   (B) I'd like to check in.
   (C) I'd like to live in the hotel.
   (D) I'd like to make a reservation.

2. (A) What's your reservation for?
   (B) Do you have any identification?
   (C) What's your name, please?
   (D) How long do you plan to stay?

3. (A) here we are
   (B) here it is
   (C) there you are
   (D) you are right

4. (A) registration form   (B) application form
    (C) identification form   (D) deposit slip

5. (A) What time is it?
    (B) When can I check in?
    (C) What time are you leaving?
    (D) What's the check-out time?

(B)

John: __6__

Jack: I play volleyball and table tennis. Sometimes I go skiing, too. __7__

John: I was the soccer ace on my high school team.

Jack: Great! What position did you play?

John: __8__

Jack: Did you have lots of fans?

John: Yes, quite a few.

Jack: __9__

John: My father talked me into going to college.

Jack: __10__

John: No. I'm sort of an amateur now. I feel happier because I don't have to worry whether I live up to the expectations of the coach and the fans.

6. (A) Do you play table tennis?
    (B) How often do you go skiing?
    (C) Why do you like sports?
    (D) What sports do you like to play?

7. (A) How about you?
    (B) Do you play table tennis, too?
    (C) Have you ever played volleyball?
    (D) What do you do?

8. (A) I played very good positions.
    (B) I was the goal keeper.
    (C) I scored six points every game.
    (D) I positioned myself behind the coach.

9. (A) Why didn't you become a pro?
    (B) Why did you play that position?
    (C) What does your father do?
    (D) Did your fans like the position you played?

10. (A) Do you still like soccer now?
    (B) Do you enjoy your college life?
    (C) Do you regret your choice?
    (D) Do you talk to your father now?

IV. Reading Comprehension　20%

(A)

Woman: I'm sorry, but you are on the library check list.

Man　: What does that mean?

Woman: It means you owe money or something to the library,
and you won't be permitted to register for classes
until the problem is taken care of.

Man　: You're kidding! This is the last day of registration.
How am I supposed to take care of it and get back in
time to finish registering?

Woman: Well, you still have the rest of the afternoon. I
suggest you go over to the library right away.

Man　: Can't I go through registration now and take care of
the problem at the library later?

Woman: No, I'm afraid I'll have to have a check-list-release
card from the library before I can let you proceed
any further with registration.

Man　: Isn't there anyone I can talk to about going through
registration without the release card?

Woman: There's a representative of the admissions office
at that table over there; you might try speaking to
him, but I don't think it will do any good.

Man　: I'll try anything to get out of walking all the way
over to the library.

Woman: I really think you should go to the library first.
They're the only ones that can help you. I'm sure
it's not anything that can't be taken care of in
just a few minutes. This happens all the time.

Man　: Maybe you are right.

1. This conversation most likely takes place around
   (A) 11:00 a.m.   (B) 10:00 a.m.
   (C) 1:00 p.m.   (D) 5:00 p.m.

2. What can't the man do?
   (A) Go to the library.
   (B) Get a check-list-release card.
   (C) Go through registration.
   (D) Pay the money.

3. How does the man feel?
   (A) Infirm.   (B) Gratified.
   (C) Frustrated.   (D) Elated.

4. The woman thinks that the man should
   (A) go through registration then pay the bill.
   (B) register for classes before going to the library.
   (C) talk to the admissions representative.
   (D) go to the library and obtain a check-list-release
       card.

5. Which of the following is probably true?
   (A) The woman will help the man through registration.
   (B) The man owes money to the library.
   (C) The man has finished registration, but doesn't have
       enough money to pay for his classes.
   (D) The man has to talk to the admissions officer.

6. The library is most likely
   (A) closed today.
   (B) a little far from registration.
   (C) a few minutes walk from registration.
   (D) supposed to take care of this problem before regis-
       tration.

(B)

　　　There are approximately 6,000 tribes in Africa today.
The people of each tribe speak the same language and have
the same customs and traditions. They are expected to protect each other from unfriendly outsiders. They have an
elected or hereditary chief who may be assisted by a tribal
council. When the colonial powers divided Africa, they
disregarded tribal groupings. Boundaries drawn to suit the
convenience of the Europeans were usually retained when the
new nations of Africa were established after World War II.
Some tribes were split among several nations. Some smaller

tribes gained control over segments of much larger groups.
It was impossible to reestablish national states on single
tribes or even related tribes. The problem which faces African leaders today is how to combine tribalism with nationalism. Long-standing tribal traditions must blend with the
needs of the entire nation. Tribalism and nationalism should
be used to reinforce each other, rather than to pull in different directions.

7. The boundaries of modern African countries
   (A) follow geographical features, like rivers and
       mountains.
   (B) are based on tribal relationships.
   (C) were reset by the United Nations.
   (D) were made by non-Africans.

8. Tribalism is based on
   (A) democratic selection.
   (B) rules and regulations made in the past.
   (C) European explorations.
   (D) national laws and regulations.

9. Tribalism and nationalism come into conflict when
   (A) there is too much poverty in the country.
   (B) laws are based on tribal custom and national needs.
   (C) members of a tribe are ruled by an outsider.
   (D) national leaders disregard tribal customs.

10. A major task for present-day leaders of African coun-
    tries is to
    (A) combine customs and traditions with national needs.
    (B) establish tribal customs.
    (C) reset boundaries.
    (D) identify tribes.

Write a short composition on the following topic. 20 %

   Second-hand Smoke

國立台灣師範大學七十九學年度
碩士班研究生入學考試英文試題詳解

Ⅰ. 請選出下列各題最適當的答案。20％

1.（**A**） *chop*〔tʃɑp〕*v.* 砍 　　 (B) wrap〔ræp〕*v.* 包
　　　(C) dump〔dʌmp〕*v.* 傾倒　 (D) broil〔brɔɪl〕*v.* 烤

2.（**C**） *horn*〔hɔrn〕*n.* 喇叭 　 (A) sear〔sɪr〕*n.* 烙印
　　　(B) shift〔ʃɪft〕*n.* 變換 　　(D) bonnet〔'bɑnɪt〕*n.* (婦孺用)軟帽

3.（**D**） *timid*〔'tɪmɪd〕*adj.* 膽小的
　　　(C) versatile〔'vɝsətɪl, -taɪl〕*adj.* 多才多藝的
　　　＊ helping〔'hɛlpɪŋ〕*n.* 一份（食物）

4.（**A**） *thrifty*〔'θrɪftɪ〕*adj.* 節儉的

5.（**C**） *blare*〔blɛr, blær〕*v.* (喇叭般的)鳴響
　　　(B) howl〔haʊl〕*v.* （犬、狼等）嗥叫
　　　(D) flare〔flɛr〕*v.* 閃耀

6.（**C**） *outing*〔'aʊtɪŋ〕*n.* 遠足
　　　(B) embargo〔ɪm'bɑrgo〕*n.* 禁運

7.（**C**） *condense*〔kən'dɛns〕*v.* 使簡潔
　　　(A) expand〔ɪk'spænd〕*v.* 擴張
　　　(B) economize〔ɪ'kɑnə,maɪz, i-〕*v.* 節約
　　　(D) alternate〔'ɔltɚ,net, 'æltɚ,net〕*v.* 交替

8.（**D**） *modest*〔'mɑdɪst〕*adj.* 謙虛的
　　　(B) inconsiderate〔,ɪnkən'sɪdərɪt〕*adj.* 不體貼的
　　　＊ comment〔'kɑmɛnt〕*v.* 談論

9. (**B**) *elated* 〔ɪˈletɪd〕 *adj.* 興高采烈的
    (A) dejected 〔dɪˈdʒɛktɪd〕 *adj.* 沮喪的
    (C) exhausted 〔ɪgˈzɔstɪd, ɛg-〕 *adj.* 疲憊的
    (D) consult 〔kənˈsʌlt〕 *v.* 請教

10. (**C**) *persist* 〔pɚˈzɪst, -ˈsɪst〕 *v.* 堅持
    (A) relax 〔rɪˈlæks〕 *v.* 放鬆　(D) falter 〔ˈfɔltɚ〕 *v.* 畏怯；動搖

Ⅱ. 請選出下列空格最適當的答案。20 %

1. (**C**) *good-looking* 〔ˈgʊdˈlʊkɪŋ〕 *adj.* 漂亮的
    (B) long-lived 〔ˈlɔŋˈlaɪvd, ˈlɑŋ-, -lɪvd〕 *adj.* 長壽的

2. (**D**) 本句之真正主詞為不定詞片語 to be … woman，故選 *it* 作形式主詞。

3. (**B**) than 為表比較之連接詞，在此連接兩個動名詞(前一個為 looking)，故選 *talking*。

4. (**A**) 根據句意，此處應用 *rather than*。A *rather than* B 與其是 B，不如是 A。

5. (**D**) *there* + *be* 動詞… "有…"

6. (**A**) *particularly* 〔pɚˈtɪkjələlɪ, pɑr-〕 *adv.* 特別地
    (B) pickingly 挑剔地　(C) mentally 心理地　(D) knowingly 故意地

7. (**B**) *unattractive* 〔ˌʌnəˈtræktɪv〕 *adj.* 無吸引力的
    (A) cheerful 快樂的　(C) depressed 憂鬱的
    (D) uncouth 〔ʌnˈkuθ〕 *adj.* 笨拙的

8. (**A**) 關係代名詞 *that* 引導形容詞子句，修飾先行詞 a face；在子句中，*that* 又作 look at 之受詞。

9. (**B**) 根據後半句的解釋，此處應選 *plain* (平常的；不美的)。(A) straight (直的)，(C) composed (安靜的)，(D) unpleasant (令人不快的)，均不合句意。

10. (D) *forgotten* 被忘的　(B) immemorable〔ɪˈmɛmərəbl〕*adj.* 不值得紀念的
　　　(C) recall 想起

Ⅲ. 在下列兩段對話中，請選出空格最適當的答案。20％
（A）

【答案】

1. (B)　　2. (C)　　3. (B)　　4. (A)　　5. (D)

【註】

reservation〔͵rɛzəˈveʃən〕*n.* 預訂　　*fill out* "填好"

check〔tʃɛk〕*v.* 暫存　　checkroom〔ˈtʃɛk͵rum, -͵rʊm〕*n.* 衣帽間

1. (B) *check in* "(旅館)住宿登記"

2. (B) identification〔aɪ͵dɛntəfəˈkeʃən〕*n.* 證件

4. (A) *registration form* "登記表"　　(B) *application form* "申請表"
　(D) *deposit slip* "存款單"

5. (D) check-out〔ˈtʃɛk͵aʊt〕*n.* (旅館)退房

（B）

【答案】

6. (D)　　7. (A)　　8. (B)　　9. (A)　　10. (C)

【註】

volleyball〔ˈvɑlɪ͵bɔl〕*n.* 排球　　ace〔es〕*n.* 傑出的人才

talk sb. into sth. "說服某人做某事"

amateur〔ˈæmə͵tʃʊr, -͵tʊr〕*n.* 業餘者

live up to～ "依(某種標準)生活"

expectation〔͵ɛkspɛkˈteʃən〕*n.* 期望

8. (B) *goal keeper* "守門員"　　(C) score〔skor, skɔr〕*v.* 獲得(分數)

9. (A) pro〔pro〕*n.* 職業選手(= *professional*)

Ⅳ. 閱讀測驗：20 ％

（A）

【答案】

1.（ C ）　　2.（ C ）　　3.（ C ）　　4.（ D ）　　5.（ B ）　　6.（ B ）

【譯文】

女士：很抱歉，你的名字出現在圖書館的核對清單上。

男士：這是什麼意思？

女士：這表示你欠圖書館錢，或其他東西。在這個問題解決之前，你不能夠註冊選課。

男士：妳是在開玩笑吧！今天是註冊的最後一天。我怎麼能去解決這個問題，然後及時趕回來辦完註冊？

女士：嗯，下午還有剩餘時間啊！我建議你立刻就到圖書館去。

男士：我不能先辦完註冊，然後再去解決圖書館的問題嗎？

女士：恐怕不行。在讓你繼續辦理註冊手續之前，我必須先拿到一張圖書館的卡片，證明你已經不在核對清單上。

男士：如果我沒有那張卡片，但是想完成註冊的手續，有沒有人可以談一談？

女士：那邊那張桌子有一位入學許可處的代表，你可以和他說說看。不過，我認為這是沒有用的。

男士：我要盡力設法避免大老遠走到圖書館去。

女士：我真的認為你應該先到圖書館去。唯一能幫你忙的人都在那裏。我相信只是個小問題，在幾分鐘之內就可以解決。這種事總是不斷發生的。

男士：或許妳說的沒錯。

【註】

check list "核對清單"　　***go through*** "做完"

release〔rɪˈlis〕*n.* 免除　　admission〔ədˈmɪʃən〕*n.* 入學（許可）

3. (A) infirm〔ɪnˈfɝm〕*adj.* 虛弱的

(B) gratified〔ˈɡrætəˌfaɪd〕*adj.* 滿足的

（B）

【答案】

7.（ D ）　　　　8.（ B ）　　　　9.（ D ）　　　　10.（ A ）

【譯文】

　　現今在非洲大約有六千個部落。同一個部落的人都講同一種語言，並且擁有相同的習俗和傳統。他們有責任互相保護，以抵禦不友善的外族人。他們有一位經由選舉產生或世襲的酋長，還可能有一個部落會議來輔助他。當那些殖民大國瓜分非洲時，他們把部落的分類置之度外。而第二次世界大戰後，非洲新國家成立之時，為了遷就歐洲人的方便而畫的疆界通常也都被保留了下來。有的部落被好幾個國家瓜分了。有些較小的部落，卻控制了其他較大部族團體中的小部分。想要根據單一部落，甚至是有相互關係的部落，來重新建立國家，是不可能的事。今天，非洲領袖們所面對的問題是：如何把部落意識和國家意識結合在一起。歷時久遠的部落傳統，必須跟整個國家的需要相溶合。部落意識和國家意識應該用來加強彼此的力量，而不該是雙頭馬車。

【註】

hereditary〔hə'rɛdə‚tɛrɪ〕*adj*. 世襲的
council〔'kaʊnsḷ〕*n*. 會議　　colonial〔kə'lonɪəl〕*adj*. 殖民（地）的
segment〔'sɛgmənt〕*n*. 部分
tribalism〔'traɪbḷɪzm̩〕*n*. 部落意識（對自己部落之忠誠）

7. (C) *United Nations* " 聯合國 "

作文：20 ％

Second-hand Smoke

Ever since the anti-smoking campaign in Taiwan got going, many people have become more aware of their right to clean and healthful living. It is, *in fact*, now even socially acceptable to ask someone to refrain from smoking in the presence of other people. *Occasionally*, though, you still encounter rude people who, despite signs that explicitly prohibit smoking within certain premises, continue to indulge in such a thoughtless and insidious activity. What is even more infuriating is to be curtly asked to mind your own business.

I really don't have any quarrel with people who want to puff themselves to death, but to endanger innocent and unwilling victims with their cloud of obnoxious and poisonous fumes is truly unforgivable and irresponsible. These indiscriminate smoke belchers have absolutely no right to choke the rest of the population to death with them. *For something so basic and all-important*, the air we breathe can not and should never be the sole possession of just an unscrupulous few.

國立政治大學七十九學年度
碩士班研究生入學考試英文試題

I. Vocabulary：

In each of the following 15 sentences, there is a word underlined. Below each sentence are four other words, marked (A), (B), (C), and (D). You are to choose the one that best keeps the meaning of the original sentence if it is substituted for the underlined word. Choose the best answer and write its corresponding letter on the answer sheet. (30%)

Example: When a liquid boils, it becomes a gas.
　　　　(A) vapor　(B) danger　(C) fuel　(D) bubble

The correct answer is A.

1. The sales manager is noted for his business acumen.
　(A) shrewdness　　　　　(B) foible
　(C) folly　　　　　　　(D) acme

2. The two countries have arrived at a bilateral agreement.
　(A) an unequal　　　　　(B) an equitable
　(C) a two-sided　　　　(D) a partial

3. The impoverished family could not withstand another cataclysm.
　(A) boon　　　　　　　(B) disaster
　(C) mortality　　　　　(D) malady

4. If you continue to work in that desultory way, you will never finish anything.
　(A) prudent　　　　　　(B) alert
　(C) aimless　　　　　　(D) dauntless

5. Many a poet has lamented the ephemeral joys of youth.
　(A) transient　　　　　(B) spiritual
　(C) material　　　　　　(D) abiding

6. Do you think love is a fallacy?
　(A) truism　　　　　　(B) certainty
　(C) blessing　　　　　(D) delusion

7. Gluttony was once regarded as one of the seven deadly sins.
　(A) Arrogance　　　　　(B) Overeating
　(C) Sloth　　　　　　　(D) Wrath

8. The steep stairs look <u>hazardous</u>.
   (A) perilous　　　　　　(B) propitious
   (C) peculiar　　　　　　(D) punctual

9. The magician's <u>ingenious</u> escape bewildered the young
   audience.
   (A) clever　　　　　　(B) clumsy
   (C) exquisite　　　　　(D) shameful

10. Jack appears very <u>modest</u> despite his lofty ambitions.
    (A) cruel　　　　　　(B) ruthless
    (C) humble　　　　　(D) noble

11. Some employees tend to bother the supervisor with <u>petty</u>
    matters.
    (A) significant　　　　(B) trivial
    (C) stupendous　　　　(D) magnanimous

12. Most students will muster up all their <u>stamina</u> to pre-
    pare for the final examination.
    (A) frailty　　　　　　(B) time
    (C) vitality　　　　　(D) impediment

13. The police made <u>a thorough</u> investigation into the case
    of murder.
    (A) a slipshod　　　　(B) a relentless
    (C) an exhaustive　　　(D) an imperfect

14. The prince thought that his mother had remarried with
    <u>undue</u> haste.
    (A) discreet　　　　　(B) excessive
    (C) perennial　　　　(D) unmistakable

15. The guards ought to be <u>vigilant</u> at all times.
    (A) watchful　　　　　(B) industrious
    (C) oblivious　　　　(D) ubiquitous

II. Grammar : 30%

In the following 15 sentences, each has four underlined
words or phrases marked (A), (B), (C), and (D). Choose
the one underlined that is <u>grammatically incorrect</u> and
write the corresponding letter on the answer sheet.

Example: College is, <u>for</u> many, <u>an</u> once-in-a-lifetime
　　　　　　　　A　　　　　B
　　　　chance to discover our <u>civilization's</u> greatest
　　　　　　　　　　　　　　　　　C
　　　　achievements and <u>lasting</u> visions.
　　　　　　　　　　　　D

The answer is <u>B</u>.

1. Man has gradually freed <u>himself</u> from <u>many</u> environmental
   A   B
   imperatives, <u>includes</u> some of the temporal <u>rhythms</u> of
   C   D
   nature.

2. It is <u>safe</u> to have <u>a</u> whole people respectably enlightened
   A   B
   than <u>a few</u> in a high state of science and <u>the many</u> in
   C   D
   ignorance.

3. Computers began to <u>alter the way</u> payments and transac-
   A
   tions <u>were made</u> in the travel field, the <u>brokerage trade</u>,
   B   C
   real estate, and <u>banker</u>.
   D

4. The car accident <u>happened</u> yesterday was <u>due to</u> the
   A   B
   <u>drivers'</u> <u>recklessness</u>.
   C   D

5. Many students go every year to <u>universities</u> in Europe,
   A
   and <u>still</u> more to America, <u>to learn</u> science or <u>economi-</u>
   B   C   D
   <u>cal</u> or law or political theory.

6. We now understand that language is not <u>stationary</u>, that
   A
   it is in a state of <u>continuous</u> development, and that
   B
   standards which may hold <u>good</u> for one century are not
   C
   necessarily <u>apply</u> to another.
   D

7. The art of life is <u>to focus</u> on difficulties and <u>deal</u>
   A   B
   <u>with</u> them <u>as possible as</u> one can, without making psy-
   C

chological problems <u>out of</u> them that then lead to night-
D

mares.

8. Today, hardly <u>there is</u> an industry that does not make
A

   use of the results of atomic physics, and the influence

   <u>these</u> have had on the political structure of the world
B

   though <u>their</u> application to atomic <u>weaponry</u> is well
C　　　　　　　　　　　　D

   known.

9. For <u>over</u> 25 years, the calm, <u>determined</u> dignity of im-
A　　　　　　　　　　B

   prisoned Nelson Mandela has provided almost mythic in-

   spiration for black South Africans <u>struggled</u> against
C

   <u>white-imposed</u> apartheid.
D

10. Tom, my good colleague, told me that I could rest

    <u>assured</u> that he <u>would</u> give me <u>fully</u> support of the plan
A　　　　　　B　　　　　　C

    I <u>had advanced</u>.
D

11. It is <u>almost</u> a definition of <u>a</u> gentleman <u>saying</u> he is
A　　　　　　　　　　B　　　　　　　C

    one who never inflicts pain <u>on</u> others.
D

12. To let others <u>to determine</u> whether we shall be rude or
A

    gracious, elated or depressed, <u>is to</u> relinquish <u>control</u>
B　　　　　　　　C

    over our own personalities, <u>which</u> is ultimately all we
D

    possess.

13. The necessary <u>qualities</u> <u>for</u> political life--guile,
A　　　　　B

ruthlessness, and garrulity--he learned <u>by</u> <u>careful</u>
                                         C   D

studying his father's life.

14. It is <u>absolutely</u> essential that the patient <u>takes</u> one of
          A   B

<u>her</u> pills <u>every</u> four hours.
C   D

15. The storm <u>began worrying</u> the passengers, but the cap-
              A

tain's confidence and cheerful <u>laugh</u> <u>helped dispel</u> their
                               B   C

<u>misgivens</u>.
D

III. Reading Comprehension : 30%

Based on what is stated or implied in the following
passages, choose the one best answer, (A), (B), (C), or
(D), to each question and write its corresponding letter
on the answer sheet.

Example:

   In 1955 Martin Luther King, Jr., gained national
recognition for his nonviolent methods used in a bus
boycott in Montgomery. This peaceful boycott, under Dr.
King's guidance, changed the law which required black
people to ride in the backs of buses. After this success, Dr. King used his nonviolent tactics in efforts to
change other discriminatory laws.

1. According to the passage, as a consequence of his
   protest in 1955, Dr. King became
   (A) peaceful in his tactics.
   (B) famous throughout his country.
   (C) frustrated in his efforts.
   (D) successful in the transportation business.
   The passage says King "gained national recognition."
   Therefore, you should choose (B).

2. Dr. King continued his nonviolent methods because
   (A) they were legal in Montgomery.
   (B) they were effective.
   (C) most people were incapable of violence.
   (D) most people believed he would receive the Nobel
       Peace Prize.

The last sentence ("After this success...") says the tactics were successful, that is, effective. Therefore, you should choose (B).

(i) Questions 1-6

Although the great Eastern religions of Asia admonish people to live in harmony with nature, the reality, whether in the push for economic growth or the quagmire of poverty, has often been quite different. Alarmed by pollution-caused diseases, such as mercury poisoning, which first surfaced in the late 1950s and '60s, Japanese have banded together to halt construction of new airports, nuclear power plants and even golf courses, as they begin to weigh economic development against the quality of their lives. Over the past decade, environmental activism has gained enormous momentum. One housewives' cooperative owns organic dairies and manufactures soap from recycled cooking oil.

The quality of life has also become a pressing issue in Hong Kong, where thousands of small, polluting factories occupy high-rises, and sewage from the most densely packed population on the planet is dumped, generally untreated, into the harbor. "We can't take it anymore," says Barbara Kakee-Pyne, who helped found the Lamma Island Conservation Society. "We can't live in it." Some groups are going far beyond simple cleanup campaigns. Hong Kong's Green Power, for example, which includes a number of Buddhist, Catholic and Protestant clergy, seeks to bridge the gap between East and West in a kind of spiritual ecology. "We are interested not just in pollution control," says founder Simon Chau, "but in a holistic approach, an entire cultural change, a green life and green thinking. We promote women's rights, animal rights, vegetarianism, spiritualism, bicycling and the sorts of things that contribute to green consciousness."

1. According to the author, Asians have been traditionally
   taught to
   (A) boost economic growth.
   (B) live in harmony with nature.
   (C) live in poverty.
   (D) fight against diseases.

2. In the late 1950s and '60s, Japanese began to
   (A) build nuclear power plants and golf courses.
   (B) halt economic development.
   (C) develop organic dairies.
   (D) become conscious of pollution-caused diseases.

3. Many multistory apartments in Hong Kong are
   (A) sparsely populated.
   (B) filled with small factories.
   (C) plagued with mercury poisoning.
   (D) manufacturing soap from recycled cooking oil.

4. Japan over the past ten years has
   (A) made futile effort in the fight against pollution.
   (B) packed more new airports on earth.
   (C) campaigned against poverty successfully.
   (D) made great strides in the movement to control
       pollution.

5. Aside from pollution control, an entire cultural change
   is advocated by
   (A) Hong Kong's Green Power.
   (B) Japan's housewives.
   (C) all the Asian nations.
   (D) environmental activists in both Japan and Hong Kong.

6. It can be inferred that
   (A) quality of life will be ignored in the future.
   (B) the earth will eventually be doomed.
   (C) green consciousness is on the rise.
   (D) economic development will be continued at all costs.

(ii) Questions 7-15

Once a name has been tainted by infamy, it is difficult
to cleanse. Over the past year, the words Tiananmen Square
and Beijing have become almost reflexive antecedents to
"massacre" and "crackdown." Trying to erase the stains, the
hard-liners who are running China have turned to national
pride to mask tragedy. In the hope that it can rechannel
the concerns of foreigners and its own citizens, the Chinese

government is rushing ahead with preparations for the quad-
rennial Asian Games, which are scheduled to begin in Beijing
on Sept. 22. The regime has been portraying the Games as
a stepping-stone toward winning the right to host the Olympics in the year 2000--and further recognition of China's
progress toward modernization.

The capital has thrown itself into preparations with all
the fervor of a Great Leap Forward. In an area that will be
part of the athletes' village, students, workers and soldiers
are sweeping the ground and digging ditches. Schoolchildren
wearing yellow baseball caps and vests designating them as
official volunteers are wielding brooms and shovels in nearly
completed stadiums. Soldiers are planting pine trees in front
of hotels. Some 40,000 laborers are working around the clock
to finish or refurbish 33 stadiums as well as high-rise
apartments, hotels, a conference hall and a press center.
Says Wan Siquan, secretary-general of the Asian Games'
organizing committee: "If China can host the Olympics in the
year 2000, we will only need to build a new stadium and expand
the Games village."

Yet no less a figure than Premier Li Peng has voiced
concern about China's ability to get through the 16 days of
the eleventh Asian Games. Though he is on record as saying
that success will inspire the Chinese people and demonstrate
that the country is not near collapse, as some in the West
suggest, he has admitted that if Beijing had a choice, it
might like to skip the Games because of economic difficulties.

7. The words Tiananmen Square and Beijing have had an
   implication of
   (A) notoriety.　　　　　　(B) prosperity.
   (C) inspiration.　　　　　(D) modernization.

8. How long will the Asian Games last?
   (A) Less than a week.　　(B) 16 days.
   (C) 33 days.　　　　　　 (D) 11 days.

9. Those running China believe that the Asian Games will
   (A) harm national pride.
   (B) unmask national tragedy.
   (C) contribute to erasing national infamy.
   (D) increase national wealth.

10. The Asian sports extravaganza is held once in
    (A) 4 years.　　　　　　　　(B) 6 years.
    (C) 8 years.　　　　　　　　(D) 10 years.

11. Preparations in Beijing have
    (A) received lukewarm welcome.
    (B) been in full swing.
    (C) hit a snag.
    (D) come to a halt.

12. Who is not mentioned in the preparation for the
    forthcoming Games?
    (A) Schoolchildren.　　　　(B) Merchants.
    (C) Soldiers.　　　　　　　(D) Workers.

13. Wan Siquan, secretary-general of the Games' organizing
    committee, is looking forward to
    (A) refurbishing the stadiums.
    (B) planting pine trees.
    (C) working around the clock.
    (D) hosting the Olympics in the year 2000.

14. Important figures like Li Peng have shown concern about
    (A) the country's near collapse.
    (B) the burden China must shoulder for the Olympics.
    (C) the nation's ability to host the Asian Games.
    (D) whether the Chinese people will support the regime.

15. To put on the scheduled sports spectacle, the Beijing
    regime
    (A) is sure of success.
    (B) plans to skip the Games.
    (C) seems worried about space crunch.
    (D) faces financial difficulties.

IV. Translate the following sentences into Chinese. 10％

1. The enemy soldiers were killed to a man.

2. As parents, the Changs hold that ethical education
   cannot be over-emphasized when it comes to raising
   children.

3. Mary often says she could not care less if she were to
   be laid off.

4. The seamy side of Taiwan's money game has been a rise in crime, particularly robbery and extortion of the well-to-do.

5. It doesn't take much to make the foreman angry.

國立政治大學七十九學年度
碩士班研究生入學考試英文試題詳解

I. 字彙：30％

1.（**A**）**shrewdness**〔ˈʃrudnɪs〕 n. 精明
   (B) foible〔ˈfɔɪbḷ〕 n. 弱點　　(C) folly〔ˈfɑlɪ〕 n. 愚笨
   (D) acme〔ˈækmɪ，ˈækmi〕 n. 頂點
   ＊ acumen〔əˈkjumɪn，‐mən〕 n. 敏銳

2.（**C**）**two‐sided**〔ˈtuˈsaɪdɪd〕 adj. 兩方面的
   (B) equitable〔ˈɛkwɪtəbḷ〕 adj. 公平的
   (D) partial〔ˈpɑrʃəl〕 adj. 偏袒的
   ＊ bilateral〔baɪˈlætərəl〕 adj. 雙方的

3.（**B**）**disaster**〔dɪzˈæstɚ〕 n. 災禍
   (A) boon〔bun〕 n. 恩賜　　(C) mortality〔mɔrˈtælətɪ〕 n. 必死之命運
   (D) malady〔ˈmælədɪ〕 n. 疾病
   ＊ impoverished〔ɪmˈpɑvərɪʃt〕 adj. 極窮的
      cataclysm〔ˈkætəˌklɪzəm〕 n.（政治、社會的）劇變

4.（**C**）**aimless**〔ˈemlɪs〕 adj. 無目的的
   (A) prudent〔ˈprudn̩t〕 adj. 謹慎的
   (B) alert〔əˈlɝt〕 adj. 警覺的
   (D) dauntless〔ˈdɔntlɪs，ˈdɑnt‐〕 adj. 勇敢的
   ＊ desultory〔ˈdɛsḷˌtorɪ，‐tɔrɪ〕 adj. 散漫的

5.（**A**）**transient**〔ˈtrænʃənt〕 adj. 短暫的
   (D) abiding〔əˈbaɪdɪŋ〕 adj. 永久的
   ＊ lament〔ləˈmɛnt〕 v. 悲嘆
      ephemeral〔əˈfɛmərəl〕 adj. 瞬息的

6.（ D ）*delusion*〔dɪˋluʒən, -ˋlɪuʒən〕*n.* 謬見；妄想
　　(A)　truism〔ˋtruɪzəm〕*n.* 公認的眞理
　　* fallacy〔ˋfæləsɪ〕*n.* 謬誤

7.（ B ）*overeating*〔ˋovɚˋitɪŋ〕*n.* 過量的吃
　　(A) arrogance〔ˋærəgəns〕*n.* 傲慢
　　(C) sloth〔sloθ, slɔθ〕*n.* 怠惰　　(D) wrath〔ræθ, rɑθ〕*n.* 憤怒
　　* gluttony〔ˋglʌtn̩ɪ〕*n.* 暴食

8.（ A ）*perilous*〔ˋpɛrələs〕*adj.* 危險的
　　(B) propitious〔prəˋpɪʃəs〕*adj.* 順遂的
　　(D) punctual〔ˋpʌŋktʃʊəl〕*adj.* 守時的
　　* hazardous〔ˋhæzɚdəs〕*adj.* 危險的

9.（ A ）*clever*〔ˋklɛvɚ〕*adj.* 巧妙的；聰明的
　　(B) clumsy〔ˋklʌmzɪ〕*adj.* 笨拙的
　　(C) exquisite〔ˋɛkskwɪzɪt, ɪkˋs-〕*adj.* 精美的
　　* ingenious〔ɪnˋdʒinjəs〕*adj.* 巧妙的
　　　bewilder〔bɪˋwɪldɚ〕*v.* 使迷惑

10.（ C ）*humble*〔ˋhʌmbl̩〕*adj.* 謙遜的
　　(B) ruthless〔ˋruθlɪs〕*adj.* 殘忍的
　　* lofty〔ˋlɔftɪ, ˋlɑftɪ〕*adj.* 高超的

11.（ B ）*trivial*〔ˋtrɪvɪəl〕*adj.* 瑣屑的
　　(C) stupendous〔stjuˋpɛndəs〕*adj.* 驚人的
　　(D) magnanimous〔mægˋnænəməs〕*adj.* 寬大的
　　* petty〔ˋpɛtɪ〕*adj.* 瑣屑的

12.（ C ）*vitality*〔vaɪˋtælətɪ〕*n.* 活力
　　(A) frailty〔ˋfreltɪ〕*n.* 脆弱
　　(D) impediment〔ɪmˋpɛdəmənt〕*n.* 阻礙
　　* muster〔ˋmʌstɚ〕*v.* 聚集　　stamina〔ˋstæmənə〕*n.* 體力

13.(C) *exhaustive*〔 ɪgˋzɔstɪv 〕 *adj.* 徹底的
　　　(A) slipshod〔 ˋslɪpˌʃɑd 〕 *adj.* 隨便的
　　　(B) relentless〔 rɪˋlɛntlɪs 〕 *adj.* 殘酷的

14.(B) *excessive*〔 ɪkˋsɛsɪv 〕 *adj.* 過度的
　　　(A) discreet〔 dɪˋskrit 〕 *adj.* 小心的
　　　(C) perennial〔 pəˋrɛnɪəl 〕 *adj.* 永久的
　　　＊ undue〔 ʌnˋdju 〕 *adj.* 不適當的

15.(A) *watchful*〔 ˋwɑtʃfəl 〕 *adj.* 留心的
　　　(B) industrious〔 ɪnˋdʌstrɪəs 〕 *adj.* 勤勉的
　　　(C) oblivious〔 əˋblɪvɪəs 〕 *adj.* 健忘的
　　　(D) ubiquitous〔 juˋbɪkwətəs 〕 *adj.* 無所不在的

Ⅱ. 文法：30％

1.(C) *includes → including* （由補述用法的關代子句 which includes some…nature 簡化而成的分詞構句，補充說明 imperatives。）
　　　＊ imperative〔 ɪmˋpɛrətɪv 〕 *n.* 規則　　rhythm〔ˋrɪðəm〕 *n.* 節奏

2.(A) *safe → safer* （由表比較的連接詞 than 可知，此處應用比較級。）
　　　＊ enlighten〔 ɪnˋlaɪtṇ 〕 *v.* 敎化；啓蒙

3.(D) *banker → banking* （此處提到的，是幾種行業，而不是從事這些行業的人。）
　　　＊ banking〔ˋbæŋkɪŋ〕 *n.* 銀行業
　　　　 transaction〔 trænsˋækʃən, trænzˋækʃən〕 *n.* 交易
　　　　 brokerage〔ˋbrokərɪdʒ, ˋbrokrɪdʒ〕 *n.* 仲介業
　　　　 real estate “ 不動產；房地產 ”

4.(A) *happened → which happened* （此處爲形容詞子句修飾 accident；子句中缺主詞，故應補上關係代名詞 which 。）
　　　＊ *due to* “ 由於 ”　　recklessness〔ˋrɛklɪsnɪs〕 *n.* 魯莽

5. (**D**) *economical* → **economics** （ or 為對等連接詞，在此連接四門學科。）
   * economics 〔 ˌikə'namıks，ˌɛk- 〕 *n.* 經濟學

6. (**D**) *apply* → **applicable** （ 在 that standards … another 子句中已有 be 動詞 are，不可再用動詞 apply，故將其改為形容詞。）
   * applicable 〔 'æplıkəbḷ 〕 *adj.* 適合的
     stationary 〔 'steʃənˌɛrı 〕 *adj.* 固定的　***hold good*** " 有效 "

7. (**C**) *as possible as* → **as best as** （ deal with 表「處理」，根據句 意，不可用 possible 修飾。）

8. (**A**) *there is* → **is there** （ hardly 表「幾乎不」，為否定詞，置於 句首時，主詞與 be 動詞或助動詞須倒裝。）
   * weaponry 〔 'wɛpənrı 〕 *n.* 武器（集合稱）

9. (**C**) *struggled* → **struggling** （ 此處分詞片語所修飾之 black South Africans 為主動，故應用現在分詞。）
   * impose 〔 ım'poz 〕 *v.* 強制
     apartheid 〔 ə'parthet，-haıt 〕 *n.* 種族隔離政策
     white-imposed apartheid " 白人強制推行的種族隔離政策 "

10. (**C**) *fully* → **full** （ 修飾名詞須用形容詞。）

11. (**C**) *saying* → **to say** (*that*) （ It 為虛主詞，而 to say…others 才是真正 主詞。）
    * inflict 〔 ın'flıkt 〕 *v.* 施加

12. (**A**) *to determine* → **determine** （ let 為使役動詞，其後若接主動動 作，應用原形動詞：let ＋O. ＋原形 V.）
    * relinquish 〔 rı'lıŋkwıʃ 〕 *v.* 放棄　ultimately 〔 'ʌltəmıtlı 〕 *adv.* 最終

13. (**D**) *careful* → **carefully** （ studying 在此處為動名詞，有動詞的性 質，應用副詞修飾。）
    * guile 〔 gaıl 〕 *n.* 狡猾　garrulity 〔 gə'rulətı 〕 *n.* 饒舌

14.(B) *takes* → *take* （It is essential ＋ that ＋ S. ＋（should）＋原形
　　　　 V.，此爲說話者認爲「應該如此」時所用的句型。）

15.(D) *misgivens*（無此字）→ *misgivings*
　　　　 ＊ misgiving〔mɪs'gɪvɪŋ〕*n.* 疑懼　　dispel〔dɪ'spɛl〕*v.* 驅除

Ⅲ. 閱讀測驗：30％

（i）1－6題

【答案】

　　1.(B)　　2.(D)　　3.(B)　　4.(D)　　5.(A)　　6.(C)

【譯文】

　　　雖然東亞的大宗教都告誡人們要和自然和諧共存，但是，無論是因爲
經濟成長的壓力、或難以擺脫的貧困，實際情況和這項告誡總是有相當大
的差異。在一九五〇年代末期和六〇年代，諸如水銀中毒之類，由污染而
引發的疾病，首度出現。日本人在驚嚇之餘，開始在經濟發展和生活品質
之間權衡輕重，於是便團結起來阻止新機場、核能發電廠，甚至高爾夫球
場的興建。在過去十年之間，積極的環境運動已經造成了很大的勢力。一
家由家庭主婦組成的合作社，擁有不使用化學肥料的天然酪農場，並從回
收再利用的烹飪油中製造肥皂。

　　　生活品質在香港也已經成爲迫切的問題。在那兒，數以千計製造污染
的小工廠佔據著高樓大廈，而這些全球密度最高的人口所製造的污水，通
常都未經處理，就被排放到港口裡。曾經協助「拉馬島保存協會」創立的
芭芭拉·卡奇一潘恩說：「我們再也不能忍受了。我們無法住在這裏。」
有些團體所做的事，已經遠超過簡單的清掃活動。例如，香港的「綠色勢
力」，其中成員包括佛教、天主教和基督教的神職人員；他們正尋求以一
種宗教上的生態學，爲東西雙方之間的隔閡搭一座橋樑。創辦人卓賽門說：
「我們感興趣的，不只是污染的控制而已；對於全盤著眼的方法、完全的
文化改變、綠色生活以及綠色思想，我們也有興趣。我們提倡女權、動物
權、素食主義、唯心論、騎自行車、以及對綠色意識有貢獻的事物。」

【註】

admonish〔əd'mɑnɪʃ〕v. 告誡

quagmire〔'kwæg,maɪr, 'kwɑg-〕n. 難以擺脫之困境

mercury〔'mɝkjərɪ〕n. 水銀　　 band〔bænd〕v. 團結

activism〔'æktəvɪzəm〕n. 行動主義；積極精神

momentum〔mo'mɛntəm〕n. 勢；動力

cooperative〔ko'ɑpə,retɪv〕n. 合作社

organic〔ɔr'gænɪk〕adj. 只用有機肥料的（不用化學肥料的）

dairy〔'dɛrɪ〕n. 酪農場　　 recycle〔ri'saɪkl̩〕v. 再生利用

high-rise〔'haɪ'raɪz〕n. 高層建築

sewage〔'sjuɪdʒ, 'su-〕n.（下水道之）污水；污物（＝ sewerage ）

ecology〔ɪ'kɑlədʒɪ〕n. 生態學　　 holistic〔ho'lɪstɪk〕adj. 全盤的

vegetarianism〔,vɛdʒə'tɛrɪənɪzəm〕n. 素食主義

spiritualism〔'spɪrɪtʃʊəl,ɪzəm〕n.〔哲〕唯心論

1. (A) boost〔bust〕v.〔俚〕吹捧

3. (C) plague〔pleg〕v. 折磨

5. *aside from* "除了"　　 advocate〔'ædvə,ket〕v. 提倡

6. (B) doomed〔dumd〕adj. 註定死亡或衰敗的

(D) *at all costs* "不計任何代價"

(ii) 7－15 題

【答案】

7.(**A**)	8.(**B**)	9.(**C**)	10.(**A**)	11.(**B**)
12.(**B**)	13.(**D**)	14.(**C**)	15.(**D**)	

【譯文】

　　一個名字一旦沾染了惡評，就很難洗刷了。在過去一年來，「天安門廣場」和「北京」這幾個字幾乎會立刻令人想到「大屠殺」以及「嚴格懲治」。為了想要抹去污點，中國當權的強硬派已經轉而使用國家尊嚴來掩飾這樁悲劇。四年一度的亞洲運動會預定九月二十二日在北京開幕，而中國政府正如

火如荼地進行準備工作，希望能藉此再次獲得外國人士及本國人民的關心。中國政府一直把亞運描述成贏得西元兩千年奧運主辦權—— 以及各國進一步承認中國在現代化方面的進展—— 的踏腳石。

首都北京已經帶著「大躍進」的所有熱忱，完全地投入了亞運的準備工作。在一個即將成爲部分選手村的地區，學生、工人和軍人正在掃地、挖水溝。小學生穿戴著表示自願擔任公務的黃色棒球帽及背心，正在接近完工的運動場中揮動著掃帚和鏟子。軍人在飯店前面種植松樹。約有四萬名工人，一天二十四小時不斷地在落成或整修三十三座運動場、高層公寓、飯店、一座會議廳以及一個新聞中心。亞運籌備委員會秘書長萬西寬（譯音）說：「如果中國能夠主辦兩千年的奧運，我們將只需要再蓋一座新的體育館，並擴大選手村就可以了。」

然而，至少要像總理李鵬這樣的人物，才會對於中國是否有能力渡過爲期十六天的第十一屆亞運，提出關切。雖然他公開表示，亞運的成功將會激勵中國人，並展現出中國並沒有瀕臨崩潰；但是，正如某些西方人士所言，他也曾經承認，假如北京有選擇的餘地，那麼由於經濟上的困難，他們可能會願意不辦亞運。

【註】

infamy〔ˈɪnfəmɪ〕*n.* 惡評　　reflexive〔rɪˈflɛksɪv〕*adj.* 反射的

antecedent〔ˌæntəˈsidn̩t〕*n.*〔文〕先行詞

massacre〔ˈmæsəkɚ〕*n.* 大屠殺

crackdown〔ˈkræk͵daʊn〕*n.* 嚴厲懲罰

hard-liner〔ˈhɑrdˈlaɪnɚ〕*n.* 強硬者　　rechannel〔riˈtʃænl̩〕*v.* 再注入

quadrennial〔kwɑdˈrɛnɪəl, -njəl〕*adj.* 每四年一次的

Asian Games "亞洲運動會"（= *Asiad*）

host〔host〕*v.* 主辦　　fervor〔ˈfɝvɚ〕*n.* 熱心

stadium〔ˈstedɪəm〕*n.*（有多層看台的露天）運動場

around the clock "整天地"　　refurbish〔riˈfɝbɪʃ〕*v.* 整修

no less than "至少"　　***on record*** "公開發表地"

7. (A) notoriety〔͵notəˈraɪətɪ〕*n.* 惡名

10. extravaganza〔ɪk͵strævəˈgænzə, ɛk-〕*n.* 盛事

11. (A) lukewarm〔ˈlukˈwɔrm,ˈlɪuk-〕*adj.* 冷淡的

　　(B) *in full swing* "全力進行中"

14. (B) shoulder〔ˈʃoldɚ〕*v.* 負擔

15. (C) crunch〔krʌntʃ〕*n.* 危機

Ⅳ. 英譯中：10％

1. 敵軍被殺得一個不剩。

2. 身為父母，張氏夫婦認為養育小孩時，倫理教育再重要不過了。

3. 瑪麗常說，假如被解雇，她一點也不在乎。
　　* *lay off* "〔美〕暫時解雇"

4. 台灣金錢遊戲的黑暗面在於犯罪增加，特別是搶劫以及勒索有錢人。
　　* *the seamy side* "（社會的）黑暗面
　　extortion〔ɪkˈstɔrʃən,ɛk-〕*n.* 勒索
　　well-to-do〔ˈwɛltəˈdu〕*adj.* 富裕的

5. 要激怒工頭，不是什麼難事。
　　* foreman〔ˈformən,ˈfɔr-〕*n.* 工頭

◀◀ 心得筆記欄 ▶▶

研究所全眞英文試題 —— 政治大學㈠

I. Translate the following into Chinese. 25%

It was the barking of two young police dogs taking a natural, unsentimental interest in an individual in distress which first called my attention to what I still think of as "my" bat, though I am sure nothing in nature prepared him to believe that I would assume any responsibility for his welfare. At first, I did not know what he was because a fish out of water looks no less inexplicable than a bat in it. The enormous wings attached to this tiny mouse's body had helped, no doubt, to keep him afloat, but they were preposterously unmanageable in a dense, resistant medium. The little hooks on his arms by means of which he climbs clumsily on a rough surface were useless on the vertical tiled sides of the pool. When I lifted him out with a flat wire net, he lay inertly sprawled, his strange body so disorganized as to have lost all functional significance, like a wrecked airplane on a mountainside which does not look as though it had ever been able to take to the air.

II. Translate the following into English. 25%

有時候，在遠處海邊緩緩前進的一隻帆船，也成爲我遐想的目的物。這個世間的小玩意是多麼有趣，看它那麼匆匆地又要去加入芸芸衆生！它是人類發明中的一個何等光榮的成就，它曾戰勝了狂風巨浪；它曾溝通天涯海角；它曾把南方一切豐饒的產物傾倒在北方的荒蕪的地區裏；它曾把知識的光芒和文明生活的福澤散佈各地；它曾把散居在各方的人們 —— 大自然似乎有意築成一種不能超越的障礙來分隔的人們 —— 連繫在一起。

III. Write a composition of about 350 words on the following topic. 50%

The Importance of Moral Courage

☆ 研究所全眞英文試題詳解——政大(一)

Ⅰ. 將下文翻譯成中文：25％

　　是兩條年輕警犬以自然、不帶傷感的興趣，對一個遭難者所發出的吠叫聲，首先引起我對仍被視爲「我的」蝙蝠的注意，但是我確信，根本沒有理由使它相信，我會對它的幸福負起任何責任。起先，我不知道它是什麼東西，因爲一條出水的魚，看起來和掉到水裡的一隻蝙蝠同樣不可思議。附著在這個小老鼠身體上的大翅膀，無疑地曾經幫助它持續漂浮，但是這些翅膀在濃密、有阻力的環境中，却反常地礙手礙脚。他手臂上那些藉以笨拙地爬上粗糙表面的小鈎，在水池鋪磁磚的垂直面却派不上用場。當我用一個平的鐵絲網把它撈出來時，它遲鈍地手脚張開躺著，它奇形怪狀的軀體扭曲得所有機能都喪失了功用，就像一架撞上山腰發生空難的飛機，看起來不像曾經會飛似的。

　　inexplicable〔ɪn'ɛksplɪkəbḷ〕*adj*. 不能理解的
　　preposterously〔prɪ'pɑstərəslɪ〕*adv*. 反常地
　　medium〔'midɪəm〕*n*. 媒體；媒介物
　　clumsily〔'klʌmzɪlɪ〕*adv*. 笨拙地；醜陋地
　　vertical〔'vɝtɪkḷ〕*adj*. 垂直的
　　inertly〔ɪn'ɝtlɪ〕*adv*. 不活潑地；遲鈍地
　　sprawl〔sprɔl〕*v*. 手足展開仰臥
　　wrecked〔rɛkt〕*adj*. 破毀的　mountainside〔'mauntn̩,saɪd〕*n*. 山腹
　　take to the air " 從事飛行；當飛行員 "

Ⅱ. 將下文翻譯成英文：25％

　　Sometimes I daydream about a sailboat slowly moving forward by a faraway coast. How fascinating the worldly little plaything is! Look how it hurries to rejoin the living world. It is one of the prideworthy achievements amongst human inventions. It has conquered howling winds and tremendous waves, connecting with all corners of the world. It has transported all the bounteous products from the South to the barren North, spread all over the world the brightness of knowledge and the welfare of civilized life and has brought people dispersed all over the world—whom nature seems to have purposefully separated by creating an insurmountable obstacle—closer together.

Ⅲ. 依下列標題寫一篇大約三百五十個字的作文。

The Importance of Moral Courage

It is particularly important to have moral courage if we hope to build a better world in the future. *In these modern times*, people tend to ignore traditional values. *However*, things won't be so bad as long as we retain at least one of those virtues — moral courage.

Before continuing on this subject, let me define what I mean by the term "moral courage". *In my view*, moral courage is the courage to correct someone else's behavior, even when this runs against the stream of popular sentiment. It is easy to correct our juniors — a mother admonishing a child for sneaking a cookie, *for example*, but it really takes moral courage to correct our seniors or a stranger.

In order to have a harmonious society we all ought to follow public laws and regulations. When someone violates these laws, we should summon up our moral courage to correct their behavior. If we don't assume this responsibility, more and more people will stop obeying the rules in order to benefit themselves. *Eventually*, this will escalate into disregard for the rights of others. *In the end*, this pattern of behavior will result in a lawless society. *Of course* no one wants this to happen. *But*, in order to avoid it, we need to emphasize to all members of society the importance of moral courage.

Since moral courage seems to be so vital, how then can we cultivate it? As moral courage is something desirable in all of us, it would seem natural to begin by examining ourselves for correct behavior. This means asking ourselves difficult questions such as, "Do

I always follow the law, even when no one else is watching?"or,"Does my behavior set the kind of example that I would want others to emulate?" and, " Do I stop short of seeking my benefits at the expense of others' rights?" *Obviously*, we cannot wish for a harmonious society unless we seek positive answers to these questions. How and when should we begin such a pattern of correct behavior? Any day is the right day. No special occasions are needed, nor do we have to stand about waiting for some event to trigger our response. There are plenty of occasions in everyday life for us to exhibit the virtue of moral courage. I've made my decision—won't you join me?

研究所全眞英文試題 —— 政治大學(二)

I. Composition : 50%

Instruction:

1. Write at least 250 words on the topic. You will lose credit if your paper is shorter.
2. Be sure your handwriting is legible.
3. You will be graded on how well you communicate your ideas, not on the ideas themselves.
4. You may make any corrections you wish in the body of the composition. You will not be graded on the appearance of your paper.

Topic: If I Were a Diplomat

II. Translation : 30%

Translate the following passages into English.

近代醫學對於保護一個兒童的身體健康已經做得很多，但是如何確保他有同樣健康的心理却做得很少。儘管美國是以兒童爲中心的社會，然而受心理困擾的兒童數目高得驚人。雖然主旨以告訴父母們如何培育快樂的，極能適應環境的靑少年的暢銷書很多，但是很多的美國靑年的心理健康都太不如意。太多的靑年學生心理上有毛病，而他們的父母却未察覺此種眞象。

III. Sentence Improvement : 20%

Improve the following sentences.

下列各句，在引述、修飾語、對稱結構或句構的前後一貫等方面各有瑕疵，請予以修改不必抄題，將修改後的句子按序寫在試卷上？

1. Speech lessons gave me self-confidence when speaking to a group or when I had to interview a job applicant.
2. Be a good citizen, and you should make your country proud of you.
3. When David was talking to Robert, he was very angry.

4. Diana told her parents when her brother went abroad for advanced study she would go abroad too.

5. I read an article about table manners at the library in a magazine.

6. In talking with my boss, he told me that Henry would replace me as sales manager.

7. The selection committee asked the applicant if he had three years' experience in teaching English and could he teach French too.

8. Although she is fond of poetry, she has never written one herself.

9. While walking across the street, a city bus almost knocked him down.

10. Mr. Johnson was respected by his acquaintances, won the admiration of his friends, and his employees loved him.

☆ 研究所全眞英文試題詳解 —— 政大(二)

Ⅰ. 作文：50％

If I Were a Diplomat

When I was young I dreamed of one day becoming an ambassador. I desired this because I wanted to travel the world.When I grew up I learned that it is not easy to be an ambassador and that a responsible diplomat shouldn't and doesn't travel all the time. *Moreover*, hard work and absolute courage are needed to be a successful diplomat. If I really want to fulfill my dream, I should begin by identifying the characteristics of a successful diplomat.

First of all, I would have to master diplomatic protocol and proper etiquette for all social situations. I would also need a sense of humor. To aid in cultivating mutual friendships with my counterparts, I would also be wise to learn to play sports such as tennis and golf.

Second, I would require a thorough background in political geography, a basic requirement for duty in the foreign service.One must understand the current political situations of other nations, particularly those of neighboring States and the superpowers, whose activities could have profound effects on us. An excellent diplomat is familiar with the history, culture, people, and national interests of the receiving State. The more thorough the background preparation, the better the diplomat can both recognize opportunities to improve relations and identify areas of contention between the countries.

Last but not least, I would have to be loyal to my own nation. A diplomat is not merely a national salesman or lobbyist, but a government agent as well. He does what his government tells him to do and reports back valuable intelligence. His career is filled with challenges and temptations, but still, he cannot betray his country.

A good diplomat, **such as** Wellington Koo, contributes enormously to his country. **Conversely**, an ineffective diplomat can ruin a nation's reputation, or worse. If I am fortunate enough to be appointed as a diplomat for the Republic of China, you know I'll do my best for my country!

II. 翻譯:(30%)

將下文翻譯成英文。

Contemporary medicine has done much to protect children's physical health, but little to ensure the same quality of mental health. Al*though* American society is *youth-oriented*, the number of children suffering from mental problems is surprisingly large. Though there are many best sellers that are meant to teach parents how to bring up happy and *well-adapted children*, the psychological condition of many American youths is *very unhealthy*. There are too many young students with psychological disorders, while their parents *remain unaware of this situation.*

III. 修改下列句子:20%

1. Speech lessons gave me self-confidence when I spoke to a group or had to interview a job applicant.

2. Be a good citizen, and make your country proud of you.

3. David was very angry when he talked to Robert.

4. Diana told her parents that when her brother went abroad for advanced study she would also go abroad.

5. I read an article about table manners in a magazine at the library.

6. During a conversation with my boss, I was told that Henry would replace me as sales manager.

7. The selection committee asked the applicant if he had had three years' experience in teaching English and if he could also teach French.

8. Although she is fond of poetry, she has never written a poem herself.

9. While he was walking across the street, a city bus almost knocked him down.

10. Mr. Johnson was respected by his acquaintances, loved by his employees, and admired by his friends.

研究所全眞英文試題——政治大學⑤

I. Composition : 50％

Instructions:

1. Write on the topic given below. If you write about something else, you will not receive a grade.

2. Write at least 200 words. You will lose credit if your paper is shorter.

3. You will be graded on how well you communicate your ideas, not on the ideas themselves.

Topic: Describe the kind of person who would be a good university professor.

II. Translate the following into Chinese. 25％

1.　　Chinese painting is unique in the world's art, for it is inseparably linked to poetry. Together they have contributed to the enrichment of our civilization. To those of us whose ears are attuned, Chinese painting communicates with a quiet voice and speaks with inexhaustible wisdom. And because Chinese painting is pre-eminently that of poetic moods and inspiration, it is highly literary, possesses a quality of profound harmony and has a gift of transcending tranquility which gives it singular appeal. 15%

2.　　Active happiness—not mere satisfaction or contentment—often comes suddenly, like an April shower or the unfolding of a bud. Then you discover what kind of wisdom has accompanied it. The grass is greener, bird songs are sweeter. The shortcomings of your friends are more understandable and more forgivable. Happiness is like a pair of eyeglasses correcting your spiritual vision. 10%

III. Translate the following into English. 25％

在一個非西方觀察者的眼中，當前西方最令人震驚的現象，就是勇氣的淪喪。不論就整體或個體來看，西方世界都已失去了它的道德勇氣。這種現象普遍存在於每一個國家，政黨與政府，聯合國當然更不在話下。尤其在各國統治階層及高級知識分子中更為顯著，使人感覺到似乎整個社會都已失去了勇氣。當然，具有勇氣的人仍然很多，可是他們對大眾生活却無決定性的影響力。

☆ 研究所全眞英文試題詳解 —— 政大(三)

I. 作文：50%

Qualities of a Good University Professor

A good university professor should be professionally knowledgeable, capable of leading others, and highly communicative. A good professor must possess a wealth of professional knowledge, both in formal classroom training as well as in its practical applications. *After all*, if professors don't have much to teach, what can their students learn?

Second, a good professor is an effective leader. He must be able to excite students' interest in the subject and stimulate them to learn through self-study. A good professor demands the students' best efforts to master the subject, yet he must also exhibit the patience necessary to ensure comprehension of the material. A good professor needs to set a moral and professional example of desirable behavior for students to emulate. *Further*, he must be able not only to answer all of the students' questions but, *more importantly*, to encourage students to find answers on their own. Learning lies not only in answers to questions but also in the attempts at finding them.

Finally, a good professor is a good communicator, skilled in all aspects of teaching techniques, with a single focus of improving comprehension of the subject material.

In summary, the three qualities of excellent professional knowledge, effective leadership capabilities, and good communication skills distinguish the good university professor.

II.將下文翻譯成中文：25％

1. 中國畫因為與詩牢不可分地結合，而在世界藝壇上獨樹一幟。二者對豐富我們的文化有同樣的貢獻。對我們之中那些喜歡悅耳之音的人而言，中國畫傳達出一種寧靜的聲音，講述著無窮的智慧。也因為中國畫明顯的詩意及靈感，故而具有高度的文學性、深奧和諧的特質及脫俗寧靜的意境，就是這種寧靜賦予中國畫奇特的吸引力。

2. 發自內心的快樂——沒有更稱心如意或滿足的快樂了——常常像四月的陣雨或蓓蕾的綻放一般，驟然而至。然後你發現有某種智慧伴隨而來。草變得更綠，鳥兒的歌聲更悅耳，你的朋友的缺點更可以理解與寬恕。快樂就像一幅眼鏡一樣，矯正了你心靈的視野。

inseparably〔ɪn'sɛpərəblɪ〕*adv*.不能分離地

attune〔ə'tjun〕*v*.使調和

preeminently〔prɪ'ɛmənəntlɪ〕*adv*.卓越地；顯著地

inspiration〔,ɪnspə'reʃən〕*n*.靈感

transcending〔træn'sɛndɪŋ〕*adj*.超然的；優越的

tranquility〔træn'kwɪlətɪ〕*n*.寧靜　appeal〔ə'pil〕*n*.吸引力

III.將下文翻譯成英文：25％

　　To a non-Western observer's view, presently the most surprising phenomenon in the West is the disappearance of courage. The West, whether from the macro-societal view or that of the individual, has lost its moral courage. This phenomenon generally exists in every nation, political party and government, not to mention the United Nations. It is especially manifest among the ruling hierarchies and higher intellectuals of every country from whom *we are made to feel* that the whole of society has lost courage. Of course, there are still many people with courage, but they have no decisive influence over the lives of the public.

▓▓ 研究所全眞英文試題——政治大學㈣ ▓▓

Ⅰ. Write at least 200 words on the following topic. 40%

The Danger of Extravagant Tastes and Habits

Ⅱ. Translate the following into Chinese. 20%

What the world stands so much in need of at the present time, and what it will continue to need if it is to endure and increase in happiness, is more of the maternal spirit and less of the masculine. We need more persons who will love and less who will hate, and we need to understand how we can produce them; for if we don't try to understand how we may do so we shall continue to flounder in the morass of misunderstanding which frustrated love creates. For frustrated love, the frustration of the tendencies to love with which the infant is born, constitutes hostility. Hatred is love frustrated. This is what too many men suffer from and an insufficient number of women recognize, or at least too many women behave as if they didn't recognize it. What most women have learned to recognize is that the much-bruited superiority of the male isn't all that it's cracked up to be. The male doesn't seem to be as wise and as steady as they were taught to believe. But there appears to be a conspiracy of silence on this subject. Perhaps women feel that men ought to be maintained in the illusion of their superiority because it might not be good for them or the world to learn the truth.

Ⅲ. Translate the following into English. 20%

我小的時候也喜愛這樣的小湖，和夏日炎炎的日子。太陽和夏日依舊，只是那小孩和小湖已今非昔比。因爲小孩已長大成人，不再有很多時光可以閒散。而昔日的小湖也被一座大城市所併吞。他往日捕捉鷺鷥的沼澤地帶，如今已是到處是高樓的社區。往日飄浮著百合的水灣，如今已是佈滿船隻的港口。總之，童年所喜愛的一切已蕩然無存，殘留的只是成人腦海中的回憶。

IV. Reading Comprehension :

Choose only one answer for each problem. 20%

(A)

Only 30 at the time of his death, Tristan Corbiere had been an eccentric and very maladjusted man: he was the son of a sea captain who had also written sea stories and he had had an excellent education, but he chose for himself the life of an outlaw. In Paris, he slept all day and spent the nights in the cafes or at his verses. He had a half-harsh, half-tender fellow feeling for the exile from conventional society, which, when he was at home in his native Brittany, caused him to flee the house of his family and seek the company of the customs-house men and sailors—living skeleton and invalid as he was, performing prodigies of courage and endurance in the navigation of a little cutter which he sailed by preference in the worst possible weather. He made a pose of his unsociability and of what he considered his physical ugliness, at the same time that he undoubtedly suffered over them. Melancholy, with a feverishly active mind, full of groanings and practical jokes, he used to amuse himself by going about in convict's clothes and by firing guns and revolvers out the window in protest against the singing of the village choir.

1. Corbiere often fled his home because
   (A) he had to hide from the law.
   (B) his family exiled him.
   (C) his family wouldn't let him sail his boat.
   (D) it was too conventional.

2. Which of the following was NOT one of Corbiere's attributes?
   (A) eccentricity   (B) melancholy
   (C) mild manner   (D) poor health

3. How did Corbiere feel about his physical appearance?
   (A) He was unhappy about it.
   (B) He ignored it.
   (C) He tried to disguise it.
   (D) He was proud of it.

4. The passage states that Tristan's father
   (A) wrote sea stories.
   (B) was maladjusted.
   (C) was an outlaw.
   (D) had an excellent education.

5. Corbiere visited the customs-house men and sailors because
   (A) he liked to visit the sick and invalid.
   (B) they were the only ones who accepted him.
   (C) they were good story material.
   (D) he felt sympathetic towards them.

(B)

   It was perfectly clear to me what I ought to do. I ought to walk up to within, say, twenty-five yards of the elephant and test his behavior. If he charged, I could shoot; if he took no notice of me, it would be safe to leave him until the mahout came back. But also I knew that I was going to do no such thing. I was a poor shot with a rifle and the ground was soft mud into which one would sink at every step. If the elephant charged and I missed him, I should have about as much chance as a toad under a steam-roller. But even then I was not thinking particularly of my own skin, only of the watchful faces behind me. For at that moment, with the crowd watching me, I was not afraid in the ordinary sense, as I would have been if I had been alone. An Englishman mustn't be frightened in front of "natives"; and so, in general he isn't frightened. The sole thought in my mind was that if anything went wrong these two thousand Burmans would see me pursued, caught, trampled on and reduced to a grinning corpse like that Indian up the hill. And if that happened it was quite probable that some of them would laugh. That would never do. There was only one alternative. I shoved the cartridges into the magazine and lay down on the road to get a better aim.

6. The author was probably
   (A) an Englishman.   (B) a Burman.
   (C) an Indian.   (D) a "native".

7. The author didn't feel afraid of the elephant because
   (A) he was a very good shot.
   (B) he was occupied with other fears.
   (C) the Burmans would help him.
   (D) the mahout was coming back.

8. Who does the author compare to a toad?
   (A) The elephant.   (B) Himself.
   (C) The mahout.   (D) The Indian.

9. Who was killed by the elephant?
   (A) A mahout.   (B) A hunter.
   (C) An Indian.   (D) A Burman.

10. In the passage the author finally
    (A) decides to shoot the elephant.
    (B) misses the elephant.
    (C) shoots the elephant.
    (D) tests the elephant.

☆ 研究所全眞英文試題詳解——政大㈣

Ⅰ. 依下列標題寫一篇二百個字以上的短文：40 ％

The Danger of Extravagant Tastes and Habits

The dangers resulting from extravagance in personal tastes and habits seem very obvious. There would seem to be no need to belabor the results of extravagance in bad habits *such as* cigarette smoking or the taking of illicit drugs, both of which have been proven to cause internal bodily damage. We are constantly confronted with one research study after another outlining these dangers. *But* how about the extravagance of the so-called "good" habits and tastes?

Good tastes and habits may also result in dangers if they are carried to extremes. *For example*, medical science generally accepts that the injection of a small amount of alcohol may improve the body's circulatory system and reduce the stresses of daily living, *yet* consuming large quantities of alcohol over a period of time can cause great damage to the internal organs and central nervous system. Okay, that's an acceptable example but here is another that may not be so clear. Suppose you like to go jogging — this is a good, healthy physical exercise, right? *Well*, medical science is discovering all types of "new" leg and ankle injuries as a result of a person's daily jogging over long distances. This same pattern of extremes could be carried out in watching movies, listening to music, watching sports, or eating. What would you be like as a result of extravagance in these "harmless" habits?

My suggestion is to never do anything to extravagance and not let your tastes and habits control your life. The results of such extravagance may not be immediate but might be tragic.

II. 將下文翻譯成中文：20％

　　如果這世界要持續下去，並增進幸福，那麼目前所急需的，而且將會持續需要的是更多的母性慈愛，及較少的陽剛性。我們需要更多有愛心的人，較少心懷恨意的人，並且必須了解如何才能製造出更多有愛心的人；對此，我們並未嘗試去了解可以怎麼做，所以我們會繼續在受挫的愛引起的誤解所造成的困境中掙扎。因為受挫的愛，嬰兒時期與生俱來的愛人傾向受到挫折，而形成敵意。恨就是愛受到挫折的結果。這是太多男人遭受過的痛苦，而女人多半並未體認到，或者至少太多女人表現得好像她們並未有此體認。大部分女人已經學會去體認的是，男性極富散播性的優越感，並不全是人們所讚揚的那樣。男性似乎不如人們教她們相信的那麼聰明、穩健。但就這個主題來說，似乎有一種緘默的協定。或許女人覺得男人應該被維持在他們優越感的幻覺中，因為對他們或世界來說，知道實情可能不太好。

　　　maternal〔mə'tɚnl̩〕*adj.* 母親的

　　　masculine〔'mæskjəlɪn〕*adj.* 男性的；陽性的

　　　flounder〔'flaʊndɚ〕*v.* 掙扎　morass〔mo'ræs〕*n.* 困境

　　　constitute〔'kɑnstə,tjut〕*v.* 構成；組成

　　　hostility〔hɑs'tɪlətɪ〕*n.* 敵意

　　　insufficient〔,ɪnsə'fɪʃənt〕*adj.* 不充足的

　　　bruit〔brut〕*v.* 傳布；謠傳

　　　crack up（to be）　"（誇大地）讚揚"

　　　conspiracy〔kən'spɪrəsɪ〕*n.* 陰謀

III. 將下文翻譯成英文：20％

　　I was also fond of such a little lake and sunny summer days when I was a child. The sun and summer stand as they are, but the child and the little lake are not what they were. This is because the child has grown up and has no more time to idle away, while the lake of the past has been swallowed up by a big city. The swamp where he caught egrets before is now a community with tall buildings everywhere. The bay where lilies floated before is now a harbor filled with ships. To sum up, what I was fond of in my childhood has all disappeared, and all that remains is only the memories of a grown-up man.

Ⅳ. 閱讀測驗：每一題都是單選題。20％

(A)

【答案】

1. (D)　　2. (C)　　3. (A)　　4. (A)　　5. (B)

【註】

eccentric〔ɪkˈsɛntrɪk〕*adj.* 古怪的

maladjusted〔ˌmæləˈdʒʌstɪd〕*adj.* 不適應的

outlaw〔ˈaʊtˌlɔ〕*n.* 被放逐者

harsh〔hɑrʃ〕*adj.* 嚴厲的；苛刻的

fellow feeling "同情；同感" exile〔ˈɛgzaɪl〕*v.* 放逐；流外

skeleton〔ˈskɛlətn̩〕*n.* 輪廓　invalid〔ˈɪnvəlɪd〕*n.* 病弱者

prodigy〔ˈprɑdədʒɪ〕*n.* 可驚的事物　cutter〔ˈkʌtɚ〕*n.* 快艇

pose〔poz〕*n.* 姿勢　melancholy〔ˈmɛlənˌkɑlɪ〕*n.* 憂鬱

practical joke "惡作劇"　convict〔ˈkɑnvɪkt〕*n.* 罪犯

revolver〔rɪˈvɑlvɚ〕*n.* 連發手鎗；左輪

protest〔prəˈtɛst〕*v.* 抗議；反對

(B)

【答案】

6. (A)　　7. (B)　　8. (B)　　9. (C)　　10. (A)

【註】

charge〔tʃɑrdʒ〕*v.* 攻擊

mahout〔məˈhaʊt〕*n.*（印度及東印度群島之）象奴；馭象者

steam-roller〔ˈstim,rolɚ〕*adj.* 如壓路機的

sole〔sol〕*adj.* 唯一的；僅有的　Burman〔ˈbɝmən〕*n.* 緬甸人

trample〔ˈtræmpl̩〕*v.* 踐踏；蹂躪　corpse〔kɔrps〕*n.* 屍體

shove〔ʃʌv〕*v.* 推擠；撞　cartridge〔ˈkɑrtrɪdʒ〕*n.* 子彈；槍彈

magazine〔ˌmægəˈzin〕*n.* 彈夾

研究所全真英文試題——政治大學(五)

Ⅰ. 詞彙：10%

說明：下面1～5題，各附五個答案，每題都有一個字劃有橫線，請選出一個最符合劃線的意義的答案。

1. During final examination week we needed all the physical <u>stamina</u> and mental sharpness we could muster up to sur— vive.
   (A) ability　　　　　　　(B) endurance
   (C) suffering　　　　　(D) intelligence
   (E) snack

2. A mature person will not regard prayer as a means of getting out of a <u>predicament</u>.
   (A) a dilemma　　　　　(B) a failure
   (C) an enigma　　　　　(D) an extension
   (E) a burden

3. <u>Millennia</u> have passed since the Pyramids were built.
   (A) Hundreds of years　(B) Several centuries
   (C) Thousands of years　(D) Millions of decades
   (E) Scores of months

4. Other channels through which English is <u>inundating</u> all lands include radio and television, motion pictures and recordings of popular songs.
   (A) evading　　　　　　(B) engraving
   (C) curbing　　　　　　(D) parching
   (E) flooding

5. The meat looked red and <u>succulent</u> when it was taken from the oven.
   (A) juicy　　　　　　　(B) neat
   (C) sticky　　　　　　　(D) dehydrated
   (E) supple

Ⅱ. 閱讀能力：20%

(A)

　　One of the most disappointing aspects of computers today is that so few people have access to them. Even those who do are usually responsible for getting a particular job done and have no access to computers for personal use.

One United States electronics distributor hopes to change this situation with a home computer system that will sell for approximately six hundred dollars. The HC 30 will be a basic system with many of the characteristics of the larger computers. Once the customer is familiar with the standard program, he can purchase options that expand the machine's capabilities.

6. According to the passage, the makers of the HC 30 expect to sell their product to
   (A) larger companies.   (B) high-income people.
   (C) the general public.   (D) scientists and engineers.

7. According to the passage, people who ordinarily use computers use them
   (A) as part of their professional work.
   (B) to solve personal problems.
   (C) to determine the cost of a project.
   (D) as an aid in making decisions.

8. According to the passage, the HC 30 has
   (A) optional equipment.   (B) disappointing aspects.
   (C) limited access to information.
   (D) familiar programs.

9. The machine that is being described throughout the passage is one that
   (A) has little similarity to other computers.
   (B) will be available soon.
   (C) is available only in the United States.
   (D) has been used as a toy.

10. How does the HC 30 probably compare with other computers?
    (A) It is cheaper.   (B) It is larger.
    (C) It is more complex.   (D) It is more versatile.

(B)

One phase of the business cycle is the expansion phase. This phase is a two-fold one, including recovery and prosperity. During the recovery period there is an ever-growing expansion of existing facilities, and new facilities for production are created. More businesses are created and

older ones expanded. Improvements of various kinds are made.
There is an ever increasing optimism about the future of
economic growth. Much capital is invested in machinery or
"heavy" industry. More labor is employed. More raw materials
are required. As one part of the economy develops, other
parts are affected. For example, a great expansion in automobiles results in an expansion of the steel, glass, and
rubber industries. Roads are required; thus the cement and
machinery industries are stimulated. Demand for labor and
materials results in greater prosperity for workers and
suppliers of raw materials, including farmers. This increases purchasing power and the volume of goods bought and
sold. Thus prosperity is diffused among the various segments
of the population. This prosperity period may continue to
rise and rise without an apparent end. However, a time comes
when this phase reaches a peak and stops spiralling upwards.
This is the end of the expansion phase.

11. We may assume that in the next paragraph the writer will
discuss
(A) union demands.　　(B) the status of the farmer.
(C) the higher cost of living.
(D) the recession period.

12. The title below that best expresses the ideas of this
passage is
(A) The Business Cycle　(B) The Recovery Stage
(C) Attaining Prosperity
(D) The Period of Good Times

13. Prosperity in one industry
(A) reflects itself in many other industries.
(B) will end abruptly.
(C) will spiral upwards.
(D) will help all segments of society except the farmers.

14. Which of the following industries will probably be a
good indicator of a period of expansion?
(A) Foodstuffs　　　(B) Cosmetics
(C) Machine tools　　(D) Farming

15. During the period of prosperity, people regard the future
(A) bearishly.　　　(B) in a confident manner.
(C) opportunely.　　(D) indifferently.

III. 文章作法：10％

　　說明：以下這段共省略了五處的起頭、銜接或轉折語。請在文後所
　　　　　列的每處四種用語中選擇最適合前後文意的一種。

　　　　　　16 , the members of one culture will interpret
the "national characteristics" of another group in terms of
their own values. __17__ , the inhabitants of a South Pacific island may be considered "lazy" by citizens of some
industrialized nations. __18__ , it may be that the island-
ers place a great value on social relationships __19__
little value on "productivity." The negative connotation of
the label "lazy" is __20__ unjustified from the point of
view of the island culture.

16. (A) In short   (B) To begin with
　　(C) Frequently   (D) Moreover

17. (A) For example   (B) First of all
　　(C) In any event   (D) Of course

18. (A) On the other hand (B) Above all
　　(C) Consequently   (D) On the one hand

19. (A) however   (B) or
　　(C) unless   (D) but

20. (A) now   (B) thus
　　(C) also   (D) furthermore

IV. 中譯英：15％

　　中共的一架民航機，載着一百零五人，於五月五日下午二時降落在漢城
附近的一處軍用機場，投奔自由。這一事件，再一次的顯示了大陸同胞對於
中共暴政的唾棄；再一次顯示了大陸同胞對於自由的嚮往，也再一次的向全
世界宣告：中華民國是大陸十億人民希望之所在。

V. 英譯中：15％（每題3分）

　　說明：下段文字劃底線部份根據上下文譯成中文

　　There are three kinds of book owners.The first has all

the standard sets and best sellers——unread, untouched.
21.
(This deluded individual owns wood pulp and ink, not books.)
22.

The second has a great many books——a few of them read
through, most of them dipped into, but all of them as
23.
clean and shiny as the day they were bought. (This person
is restrained by a false respect for their physical appearance.) The third has a few books or many——every one of
24.
them dog-eared and dilapidated, marked and scribbled in
from front to back. (This man owns books.)
25.

VI. 作文：以200字爲度，請勿過少或過多。30％

題目：Duty First! Pleasure Second!

研究所全真英文試題詳解——政大㈤

I. 詞彙：10%

【答案】

1. (B)　　2. (A)　　3. (C)　　4. (E)　　5. (A)

【註】

1. 在期末考週期間，我們需要一切能夠振作的體力和靈敏的心智，以求生存。　**stamina**〔ˈstæmənə〕 *n.* 耐力；體力
   muster〔ˈmʌstɚ〕 *v.* 鼓起；振作　　(E) snack〔snæk〕 *n.* 點心

2. 一個成熟的人不會把祈禱視為脫離困境的方法。
   get out of "避免；放棄"　　**predicament**〔prɪˈdɪkəmənt〕 *n.* 困境
   (A) dilemma〔dəˈlɛmə〕 *n.* 左右為難的狀況
   (C) enigma〔ɪˈnɪgmə〕 *n.* 謎

3. 自從埃及金字塔建造迄今已過了幾千年。
   millennia〔məˈlɛnɪə〕 *n.* (*pl.* of millennium) 幾千年
   the Pyramid〔ˈpɪrəmɪd〕埃及金字塔

4. 英文正經由其他途徑氾濫於各地，包括收音機和電視、電影和錄音的流行歌曲。
   channel〔ˈtʃænl〕 *n.* 途徑；頻道
   inundate〔ˈɪnʌnˌdet〕 *v.* 氾濫；使充滿
   (A) evade〔ɪˈved〕 *v.* 逃避　　(B) engrave〔ɪnˈgrev〕 *v.* 雕刻；銘記
   (C) curb〔kɝb〕 *v.* 抑制；勒(馬)
   (D) parch〔pɑrtʃ〕 *v.* 烘；炒

5. 這塊肉剛出爐時，看起來紅潤多汁。
   succulent〔ˈsʌkjələnt〕 *adj.* 多汁的
   (C) sticky〔ˈstɪkɪ〕 *adj.* 黏的
   (D) dehydrated〔diˈhaɪdretɪd〕 *adj.* 脫乾的
   (E) supple〔ˈsʌpl̩〕 *adj.* 柔軟的

Ⅱ. 閱讀能力：20％

(A)

　　6.(C)　　7.(A)　　8.(A)　　9.(B)　　10.(A)

【註】

have access to " 能使用；能接近 "

electronics〔ɪˌlɛkˈtrɑnɪks〕*n.* 電子學

option〔ˈɑpʃən〕*n.* 選擇權

capability〔ˌkepəˈbɪlətɪ〕*n.*（常用 *pl.*）可發展之能力

versatile〔ˈvɝsətɪl〕*adj.* 可作多種用途的

(B)

　　11.(D)　　12.(A)　　13.(A)　　14.(C)　　15.(B)

【註】

phase〔fez〕*n.* 局面；階段　　cycle〔ˈsaɪkl̩〕*n.* 循環；周期

two-fold " 雙重（倍）"　　optimism〔ˈɑptəˌmɪzəm〕*n.* 樂觀

result in " 導致 "　　cement〔səˈmɛnt〕*n.* 水泥

stimulate〔ˈstɪmjəˌlet〕*v.* 激勵；刺激

diffuse〔dɪˈfjuz〕*v.* 擴散；傳布

segment〔ˈsɛgmənt〕*n.* 部分；片斷　　peak〔pik〕*n.* 頂點；尖端

spiral〔ˈspaɪrəl〕*adj.* 螺旋形的；盤旋的

recession〔rɪˈsɛʃən〕*n.* 退卻；商業暫時衰落的現象

indicator〔ˈɪndəˌketə〕*n.* 指示者（器）

cosmetic〔kɑzˈmɛtɪk〕*n.* 化粧品

bearish〔ˈbɛrɪʃ〕*adj.* 粗暴的；下跌的

opportunely〔ˌɑpəˈtjunlɪ〕*adv.* 相反地；相對地

Ⅲ. 文章作法：10%

【答案】

16.（ C ）　　17.（ A ）　　18.（ A ）　　19.（ D ）　　20.（ B ）

【註】

in terms of "以…之觀點（方式）"　　inhabitant〔ɪnˈhæbətənt〕*n*. 居民
negative〔ˈnɛɡətɪv〕*adj*. 負的
connotation〔͵kɑnəˈteʃən〕*n*. 涵義；暗示　　label〔ˈlebḷ〕*n*. 標籤

中譯英：15%

A communist Chinese civil airplane with 105 passengers aboard landed at a military airport near Seoul at 2 p.m. on May 5, seeking political asylum. This incident once more manifests that our compatriots on the mainland spurn Chinese communists' tyrannical regime, and are earnestly eager for freedom. Again, it signifies to the world that the Republic of China is the hope of one billion people on the mainland.

Ⅴ. 英譯中：15%

21. 第一種人擁有各種成套的標準本及暢銷書——沒讀過，也沒翻過。
　　* best　seller "暢銷書"

22. 這種自欺欺人者擁有的只是木質紙漿和墨水，而不是書。
　　* delude〔dɪˈlud〕*v*. 欺騙　　wood pulp *n*.（製紙原料）木質紙漿

23. 有些書徹底讀過了，大部分則瀏覽過而已。
　　* *dip into* "瀏覽"

24. 這種人因為對書本外表錯誤的尊敬，而抑制自己去碰書。

25. 每一本書從第一頁到最後一頁都摺過角、破損、作過記號、塗寫過。
　　dog-ear〔ˈdɔɡ͵ɪr〕*v*. 將書頁摺起角
　　dilapidate〔dəˈlæpə͵det〕*v*. 變破　　scribble〔ˈskrɪbḷ〕*v*. 塗鴉；亂寫

Ⅵ. 作文：以200字為度，請勿過少或過多。30%

Duty First! Pleasure Second!

Hearing or seeing the word "duty" raises in us many different mental images. *For some members of society* "duty" means duty to the country typified by service in the armed forces. To others among us "duty" refers to our obligations as members of a free society, *such as* paying taxes or voting in an election. Then there are the duties of employer and employee towards each other. These are often spelled out in contracts or labor agreements, in clauses such as "a day's work for a day's wages" or "a safe working environment." *Also*, we have clearly defined duties toward our parents and other family members. *Further*, there are duties, broad in scope and definition, as members of a society of men. *Perhaps* this type is best illustrated by the "Golden Rule" in the West, and the Confucian adage to "behave towards others as we would have them behave towards us." Of greatest importance is the very personal duty to ourselves : protect our health and increase our knowledge. Without accomplishing this, the fulfillment of all other duties is not possible.

Some would portray "duty" and "pleasure" as opposites, but this is simply not so. Many members of society derive great pleasure in performing some, if not all, of their duties. *Nor* should "duty" be thought of as "good" and "pleasure" regarded as somehow "bad". We all need and rightfully deserve pleasure in our lives, but not pleasure achieved through neglect of our duties.

研究所全眞英文試題——政治大學㈥

I. 詞彙（ 10％）

下列左邊有 10 個字，右邊有 15 條解釋，請找出每字的正確解釋，將代
表該解釋的大寫字母填入試卷內。注意：解釋共 15 條。其中 5 條是沒
有用的。

1. segregation	A. predominance
2. triviality	B. catastrophic
3. pugnacious	C. quick to judge and understand
4. preponderance	D. similar
5. menial	E. pettiness
6. perspicacious	F. succor
7. jocund	G. servile
8. dissipation	H. severe vexation
9. parochial	I. amusement
10. callous	J. separation
	K. limited; narrow
	L. unfeeling
	M. gay
	N. exploitation
	O. quarrelsome

II. 閱讀能力（ 20％）

請仿照下列格式在試卷紙上作答。如每題答案均寫Ａ、Ｂ、Ｃ或Ｄ同一
答案，則全部以零分計算。

(A)

In the long run a government will always encroach upon
freedom to the extent to which it has the power to do so;
this is almost a natural law of politics, since, whatever
the intentions of the men who exercise political power, the
sheer momentum of government leads to a constant pressure
upon the liberties of the citizen. But in many countries

society has responded by throwing up its own defenses in the shape of social classes or organized corporations which, enjoying economic power and popular support, have been able to set limits to the scope of action of the executive.

Such, for example, in England was the origin of all our liberties—won from government by the stand first of the feudal nobility, then of churches and political parties, and latterly of trade unions, commercial organizations, and the societies for promoting various causes. Even in European lands which were arbitrarily ruled, the powers of the monarchy, though absolute in theory, were in their exercise checked in a similar fashion. Indeed the fascist dictatorships of today are the first truly tyrannical governments which western Europe has known for centuries, and they have been rendered possible only because on coming to power they destroyed all forms of social organization which were in any way rivals to the state.

11. The main idea of this paragraph is best expressed as
    (A) limited powers of monarchies
    (B) functions of trade unions
    (C) ruthless ways of dictators
    (D) safeguards of individual liberty

12. The writer maintains that there is a natural tendency for governments to
    (A) become more democratic
    (B) become fascist
    (C) assume more power
    (D) increase individual liberties

13. Monarchy was first checked in England by the
    (A) trade unions   (B) church
    (C) people   (D) nobles

14. Fascist dictatorships differ from monarchies of recent times in
    (A) getting things done by sheer momentum
    (B) promoting various causes
    (C) destroying people's organizations
    (D) exerting constant pressure on liberties

B.
    Two months before the birth of her cubs, through some

miracle of hormone-dictated behavior, the mother polar bear begins to dig a maternity den. The den usually consists of a room deep inside a snowbank, with a narrow downslope entryway. Some dens have two or even three rooms, with breathing holes to control the temperature. Eskimos have long told of how bears plug the holes with snow to save heat during the coldest periods, a fact corroborated by zookeepers. It is reported that the dens may actually be forty degrees warmer than the outside air.

During much of the two months, the mother bear sleeps, and although her heart rate, respiration, and metabolism drop considerably, her sleep is not hibernation. Her temperature stays constant and, unlike true hibernators who need several days to awaken, the mother polar bear can spring into action almost instantly. In December or January her cubs are born--blind, hairless, a pound and a half in weight, more fetus than young animal. From this moment on, few mothers in nature are so devoted to their young.

15. According to the passage, the mother polar bear digs a maternity den
   (A) when she needs a new home
   (B) about sixty days before giving birth to her cubs
   (C) just prior to the birth of her cubs
   (D) in order to find shelter from the cold

16. According to the passage, how does the mother polar bear conserve heat in the maternity den?
   (A) By filling the breathing holes with snow
   (B) By building more than one room
   (C) By building a downslope entryway
   (D) By sleeping more and breathing less

17. It can be inferred from the passage that a pregnant polar bear differs from certain other animals in that she
   (A) hibernates differently
   (B) does not truly hibernate
   (C) hibernates mainly during December and January
   (D) does not hibernate if her metabolism drops

18. According to the passage, which of the following is true
    of hibernating animals?
    (A) They do not awaken suddenly from hibernation.
    (B) They tend to be more active in the spring.
    (C) They can awaken and return to sleep instantly.
    (D) Their heart rate and metabolism do not drop.

19. According to the passage, new-born polar bears differ
    from most other young animals in that they are
    (A) heavier   (B) less healthy
    (C) hairier   (D) less developed

20. According to the passage, which of the following is true
    of mother polar bears?
    (A) Their temperature fluctuates.
    (B) They are very active.
    (C) They care for their young better than most animal
        mothers do.
    (D) There are very few of them in zoos.

III. 文章作法（ 10％ ）

    以下這段共省略了五處的起頭，銜接或轉折語。請在文後所列的每處
    四種用語中選擇最適合前後文意的一種，並將答案（A、B、C 或 D ）
    寫在試卷紙上。

    ____21____, there is, in China, a great eagerness to ac-
quire Western learning, not simply in order to acquire national strength and be able to resist Western aggression, but
because a very large number of people consider learning a
good thing in itself. It is traditional in China to place a
high value on knowledge, ____22____ in the old days the knowledge
sought was only of the classical literature. ____23____ it is
generally realized that Western knowledge is more useful.

    ____24____, many students go every year to universities in
Europe, and still more to America, to learn science or economics or law or political theory. These men, when they return to China, mostly become teachers or civil servants or
journalists or politicians. They are rapidly modernizing the
Chinese outlook, ____25____ in the educated classes.

21. (A) In short   (B) To begin with
    (C) No doubt   (D) Moreover

22. (A) however   (B) or
    (C) and   (D) but

23. (A) Nowadays   (B) Furthermore
    (C) For this reason   (D) Namely

24. (A) In addition   (B) Above
    (C) As a result   (D) On the one hand

25. (A) especially   (B) for example
    (C) in any event   (D) consequently

IV. 英譯中（15%）

下段文字劃底線部份，根據上下文譯成中文。

I dislike the contemporary Western advertising business. It has made a fine art out of taking advantage of
human silliness. It rams unwanted material goods down sur-
feited throats when two-thirds of all human beings now alive
are in desperate need of the bare necessities of life. This
is an ugly aspect of the affluent society; and, if I am told
that advertising is the price of affluence, I reply without
hesitation that affluence has been bought too dear. Another
item in the price of affluence is the standardization of
mass-produced goods and services. This is, in itself, a de-
plorable impoverishment of the material side of human culture, and it brings spiritual standardization with it, which
is still worse.

中譯英（15%）請把下列三句，譯成英文。

29. 觀光業（tourism），一般視之為「無煙囪的工業」，因其可以賺取外滙，
有些國家藉發展觀光業，來增加收入。

30. 多年來，我國觀光業有長足發展，以去年為例，國外觀光客多達一百四十
五萬人，國人出國觀光者也近百萬。

31. 在觀光業開展上，除了天然風景，歷史古蹟維護外，交通旅館各項服務也
須努力改善。

作文（30%）根據下列題目，至少寫200字。

No Pain, NO Gain

☆ 研究所全眞英文試題詳解──政大(六)

Ⅰ. 詞彙：10%

1. (**J**) segregation〔ˌsɛgrɪˈgeʃən〕 *n*. 隔離；分開
   separation〔ˌsɛpəˈreʃən〕 *n*. 隔離

2. (**E**) triviality〔ˌtrɪvɪˈælətɪ〕 *n*. 瑣事　　**pettiness**〔ˈpɛtɪnɪs〕 *n*. 小事

3. (**O**) pugnacious〔pʌgˈneʃəs〕 *adj*. 好戰的；好鬥的
   quarrelsome〔ˈkwɔrəlsəm〕 *adj*. 愛爭吵的

4. (**A**) preponderance〔prɪˈpɑndrəns〕 *n*. 優勢
   predominance〔prɪˈdɑmənəns〕 *n*. 優越

5. (**G**) menial〔ˈminɪəl〕 *adj*. 傭人的；卑賤的
   servile〔ˈsɝvɪl〕 *adj*. 卑躬的

6. (**C**) perspicacious〔ˌpɝspɪˈkeʃəs〕 *adj*. 敏於判斷與了解的；聰敏的

7. (**M**) jocund〔ˈdʒɑkənd〕 *adj*. 歡樂的　　gay〔ˈge〕 *adj*. 歡樂的

8. (**I**) dissipation〔ˌdɪsəˈpeʃən〕 *n*. 娛樂
   hilarious〔həˈlɛrɪəs〕 *adj*. 高興的
   amusement〔əˈmjuzmənt〕 *n*. 娛樂

9. (**K**) parochial〔pəˈrokɪəl〕 *adj*. 褊狹的（原意：教區的）

10. (**L**) callous〔ˈkæləs〕 *adj*. 無情的　　unfeeling〔ʌnˈfiliŋ〕 *adj*. 無情的

Ⅱ. 閱讀能力：20%

A.

【答案】
> 11. (**D**)　　12. (**C**)　　13. (**D**)　　14. (**C**)

【註】　***in the long run*** " 最後地；終極地 "
　　　encroach upon " 侵犯 "　　***to the extent*** " 至此程度 "
　　　sheer〔ʃɪr〕 *adj*. 全然的；絕對的
　　　momentum〔moˈmɛntəm〕 *n*. 動量；衝力
　　　the executive " 執政者 "　　feudal〔ˈfjudḷ〕 *adj*. 封建的

arbitrarily〔'ɑrbə,trɛrəlɪ〕 *adv.* 專制地；獨斷地

monarchy〔'mɑnəkɪ〕 *n.* 君主政權

fascist dictatorships "法西斯式獨裁政權"

tyrannical〔taɪ'rænɪkl̩〕 *adj.* 暴政的；暴君的

B.

【答案】

15. (**B**)　　16. (**A**)　　17. (**B**)　　18. (**A**)　　19. (**D**)　　20. (**B**)

【註】

cub〔kʌb〕 *n.* 幼獸　　hormon-dictated 受荷爾蒙控制的

maternity den 產穴；母熊生產用的洞穴　　snowbank 雪丘

corroborate〔kə'rɑbə,ret〕 *v.* 確證；進一步證實

metabolism〔mə'tæblɪzəm〕 *n.* 新陳代謝

hibernation〔,haɪbə'neʃən〕 *n.* 冬眠　　fetus〔'fitəs〕 *n.* 胚胎

Ⅲ. 文章作法：10％

【註】

aggression〔ə'grɛʃən〕 *n.* 侵略

place a high value on "重視"

21. (**B**) *to begin with* "首先"

　　(A) 總而言之　　(C) 無疑地　　(D) 此外

22. (**D**) 此處缺少連接詞，因前後子句句意相對，故用 but。

　　(A) however 前面要用句點或分號。

23. (**A**) nowadays〔'naʊədez〕 *adv.* 現今

　　(B) 而且　　(C) 因為這個緣故　　(D) 即是

24. (**C**) *as a result* 結果；因此

　　(A) 此外　　(B) 在…之上　　(D) 另一方面來說

25. (**A**) especially "特別是"

　　(B) 例如　　(C) 無論如何　　(D) 結果

Ⅳ. 英譯中：15%

26. 當三分之二人類迫切需要基本的生活必需品時，它卻將多餘的物質產品塞進飽足的喉嚨。

27. 這是當今富裕社會醜陋的一面，如果有人告訴我廣告是富裕的代價，我會毫不猶豫的回答：富裕賣得太貴了。

28. 其本身就是可悲的人類物質文化貧瘠的表現；加上它又帶來精神上的一元化，使情形更加惡化。

Ⅴ. 中譯英：15%

29. Tourism is generally regarded as a "chimneyless industry"; because it earns foreign exchange, some countries increase revenue by developing their tourism.

30. For many years, our tourism has expanded significantly. For example, the number of foreign tourists amounted to 1.45 million people last year, and the number of our people touring abroad came close to 1 million.

31. In the development of the tourism industry, aside from preserving our natural scenery and historic relics, we must also endeavor to improve such services as transportation and accommodation facilities.

Ⅵ. 作文：30%

No Pain, No Gain

Those who sow with tears must reap with laughter. It you want the Lord to fill your cup till it runneth over, you must do your best in all endeavors. *In other words*, the way to success is not as smooth as you might imagine. *It goes without saying that* idling away your time will only build your tomb.

Our victory over Japan was due to the sacrifices of millions of our countrymen. If they had been afraid of death, had wanted to live comfortably and had given in to the enemy, what would have become of us? *In a word*, there is no manna from heaven, and as the proverb says "There are no gains without pains". Observe accomplished men. Theirs are stories of struggles and bitterness, but the fruits of their industry are sweet. *On account of this*, we find anyone can succeed if he devotes himself to accomplishing his goals. *Further*, the more you give, the more you get. A proverb says, "Practice makes perfect".

Every drop of rain falling on your head will change into a pearl, but every minute you waste disappears forever. *In conclusion*, there is no substitute for hard work in achieving your goals.

研究所全眞英文試題 —— 政治大學(七)

I. 英翻中

1. The natural Chinese attitude is one of tolerance and friendliness, showing courtesy and expecting it in return. If the Chinese chose, they could be the most powerful nation in the world. But they only desire freedom, not domination. It is not improbable that other nations may compel them to fight for their freedom, and if so, they may lose their virtue and acquire a taste for empire.

2. Moscow has imposed its will on Eastern Europe and Afghanistan and peddled its arms and political influence over five continents. But it has yet to prove that communism works. Its economic program has failed to bring prosperity to the Soviet people or to Moscow's satellites.

3. I dislike the contemporary advertising business. It has made a fine art out of taking advantage of human silliness. It rams unwanted material goods down over-fed throats when two-thirds of all human beings now alive are in desperate need of the bare necessities of life.

II. Read the following passages and then select the best answer to each of the questions. 30%

(A)

Some may not realize that fog is simply a cloud that touches the ground. Like any cloud, it is composed of tiny droplets of water, or in rare cases, of ice crystals that form an ice fog. Ice fogs usually occur only in extremely cold climates. Because water droplets are so tiny, they don't solidify until the air temperature is far below freezing, generally thirty degrees below zero centigrade or lower. The droplets of fogs are nearly spherical. The transparency of fog depends mainly on the concentration of droplets---the more droplets, the denser the fog is. Since water is 800 times denser than air, investigators were puzzled for a long time as to why the water particles in fog didn't simply fall to the ground, making the fog disappear. It turns out that droplets do fall at a predictable rate; but in fog-creating conditions, they are either supported by rising air currents, or continually replaced by new droplets condensing from the water vapour in the air.

1. What is the main topic of the passage?
   (A) The shapes of water droplets.
   (B) The formation of rain clouds.
   (C) The spread of air currents.
   (D) The characteristics of fog.

2. According to the passage, how are fog and clouds related?
   (A) The both form in large spherical masses.
   (B) They are both made of tiny water droplets.
   (C) They are both common only in cold climates.
   (D) They both change shape when temperatures vary.

3. What is the main factor that determines the transparency of fog?
   (A) The density of the water droplets in the air.
   (B) The size of the water droplets.
   (C) The temperature of the water droplets.
   (D) The purity of the water vapor.

4. What used to puzzle investigators about fog?
   (A) Why fog freezes at low temperatures.
   (B) How very small droplets can form.
   (C) Why the density of fog varies.
   (D) How water droplets stay suspended in air.

(B)

Rhythm in literature is a more or less regular occurrence of certain elements of writing: a word, a phrase, an idea, a pause, a sound, or a grammatical construction. We are also accustomed to this recurrence in the alternate heavy and light beats in music. Our love for rhythm seems to be innate: witness the responses of a small child to lively music. Children love to beat on toy drums or empty boxes. They stamp their feet and chant nursery rhymes or nonsense syllables, not unlike primitive dancers. As children grow older, they are taught to restrain their responses to rhythm, but our love of rhythm remains. We live in rhythms; in fact we are governed by rhythms.

Physiologically, we are rhythmical. We must eat, sleep, breathe, and play regularly to maintain good health. Emotionally we are rhythmical, too, for psychologists say that all of us feel alternate periods of relative depression and exhilaration. Intellectually we are also rhythmical, for we must have periods of relaxation following periods of concentration. It naturally follows then that rhythm, a fundamental aspect of our lives, must be a part of any good literary work----whether poetry or prose.

5. What is the main idea of the passage?
   (A) Rhythmic patterns in literature are helpful to physicians and psychologists.
   (B) Rhythmic patterns in literature are among the natural manifestations of rhythm in all facets of life.
   (C) Rhythm tends to be more accentuated in music than in poetry.
   (D) Rhythm tends to be more regular in literature than in other facets of life.

6. According to the passage, what is rhythm?
   (A) A regular occurrence of an action or response
   (B) A special kind of music
   (C) A kind of emotional disorder
   (D) A stage in the development of young children

7. According to the passage, an adult's reaction to rhythm in music would probably be
   (A) uninhibited
   (B) indifferent
   (C) restrained
   (D) responsible

8. It can be inferred from the passage that conscious thought plays the most significant part in creating
   (A) physiological rhythms   (B) emotional rhythms
   (C) psychological rhythms   (D) literary rhythms

9. According to the passage, which of the following pairs of activities best illustrates intellectual rhythm?
   (A) Studying a science book and then studying a psychology book
   (B) Learning a poem and then taking a nap
   (C) Playing ball at the beach and then going swimming
   (D) Solving a math problem and then solving a chemistry problem

10. What would the next paragraph probably discuss?
    (A) How to write poetry
    (B) How to understand rhythm in music
    (C) The kinds of rhythm found in good literature
    (D) The importance of rhythm in planning our lives

(C)

Criticism of research lays a significant foundation for future investigative work, but when students begin their own projects, they are likely to find that the standards of validity in field work are considerably more rigorous than the standards for most library research. When students are faced with the concrete problem of proof by field demonstration, they usually discover that many of the "important relationships" they may have criticized other researchers for failing to demonstrate are very elusive indeed. They will find, if they submit an outline or questionnaire to their classmates for criticism, that other students make comments similar to some they themselves may have made in discussing previously published research. For example, student researchers are likely to begin with a general question but find themselves forced to narrow its focus. They may learn that questions whose meanings seem perfectly obvious to them are not clearly understood by others, or that questions which seemed entirely objective to them appear to be highly biased to someone else. They usually find that the formulation of good research questions is a much more subtle and frustrating task than is generally believed by those who have not actually attempted it.

11. What does the author think about trying to find weaknesses in other people's research?
    (A) It should only be attempted by experienced researchers.
    (B) It may cause researchers to avoid publishing good works.
    (C) It is currently being done to excess.
    (D) It can be useful in planning future research.

12. According to the passage, what is one major criticism students often make of published research?
    (A) The research has not been written in an interesting way.
    (B) The research has been done in unimportant fields.
    (C) The researchers did not adequately establish the relationships involved.
    (D) The researchers failed to provide an appropriate summary.

13. According to the passage, how do students in class often react to another student's research?
    (A) They react the way they do to any other research.
    (B) They are especially critical of the quality of the research.
    (C) They offer unusually good suggestions for improving the work.
    (D) They show a lot of sympathy for the student researcher.

14. According to the passage, student researchers may have to change their research projects because
    (A) their budgets are too high
    (B) their original questions are too broad
    (C) their teachers do not give adequate advice
    (D) their time is very limited

15. What does the author conclude about preparing suitable questions for a research project?
    (A) It is more difficult than the student researcher may realize.
    (B) The researcher should get help from other people.
    (C) The questions should be brief so that they will be understood.
    (D) It is important to follow formulas closely.

III. Composition. 40%

Write a composition of approximately 150 to 200 words, discussing the following aspects about street vendors (people selling things in the street) and roadside food stands.

(1) Why do they gain popularity?

(2) What are some of the problems they create?

(3) What is the best solution to these problems?

☆ 研究所全眞英文試題詳解 —— 政大㈦

I. 英翻中：

1. 中國人的天性是忍讓與友善，不但對人彬彬有禮，同時也希望他人答之以禮。假如中國人願意選擇的話，他們會是世界上最強盛的國家。但是他們渴望僅自由而不喜支配他人。其他國家是可以強迫他們爲自由而戰，這並非不可能。果眞如此，中國人將失去他們的美德，並一嚐身爲大帝國的滋味。

2. 莫斯科控制了東歐與阿富汗，並將其武力與政治的影響擴及五大洲。但是莫斯科仍未能證明共產主義行得通。其經濟計劃並無法替蘇聯人民與其附庸國家帶來繁榮。

3. 我厭惡現代的廣告業。它利用人類的愚昧來創作藝術。當世上三分之二的人口極需最基本的生活必需品時，它卻向已過分饜飽的人們強灌不必要的物品。

II. 閱讀能力：

A.

【註】　droplet〔'drɑplɪt〕n. 水滴　　spherical〔'sfɛrəkl〕adj. 球形的
transparency〔træns'pɛrəns〕n. 透明
condense〔kən'dɛns〕v. 液化

1.（ D ）本段主題爲何？
　　(A)水滴的形狀　　　　　　　(B)雨雲的形成
　　(C)氣流的分布　　　　　　　(D)霧的特性

2.（ B ）依據本段，霧與雲有何相關？
　　(A)兩者都形成大球體　　　　(B)兩者均由小水滴組成
　　(C)兩者通常只出現在氣候寒冷時
　　(D)當溫度改變時，兩者都會變形

3.（**A**）決定霧的透明度的主要因素爲何？

(A) 空氣中水滴的密度　　　(B) 水滴的大小

(C) 水滴的溫度　　　(D) 水蒸氣的純度

4.（**D**）過去一直困擾霧研究者的是什麼？

(A) 爲何霧在低溫會結冰　　　(B) 水滴能變得多小

(C) 爲何霧有不同的密度　　　(D) 爲何水滴會懸浮在空中

B.

【註】　recurrence〔rɪ'kɝəns〕*n*. 重視

alternate〔'ɔltənɪt〕*adj*. 輪流的；交替的

innate〔ɪn'net〕*adj*. 天生的　　　chant〔tʃænt〕*v*. 唱

nursery rhyme 兒歌

physiologically〔ˌfɪzɪə'lɑdʒɪkl̩ɪ〕*adv*. 生理學上地

depression〔dɪ'prɛʃən〕*n*. 情緒低落；沮喪

exhilaration〔ɪgˌzɪlə'reʃən〕*n*. 興奮

5.（**B**）本文主題爲何？

(A) 文學的節奏模式對醫生及心理學家有用處。

(B) 文學中的節奏型式，是生活中四處可見的節奏的一種自然表現。

(C) 音樂比詩更強調節奏的重要。

(D) 文學中的節奏比生活其他方面的節奏更有規律。

6.（**A**）根據本文，節奏就是

(A) 一個動作或反應規律的出現　(B) 一種特別的音樂

(C) 一種情緒異常　　　(D) 兒童成長過程的一個階段

7.（**C**）依據本文，成人對音樂中節奏的反應可能會是

(A) 不受拘束的　　　(B) 無動於衷的

(C) 受約束的　　　(D) 有反應的

8.（**D**）從文中可推知,自覺性的思考在創造下列何者時擔任了重要角色？

(A) 生理節奏　　　(B) 情緒節奏

(C) 心理節奏　　　(D) 文學節奏

9.（ B ）依據本文，下列何組活動最能說明思想節奏？
　　　　(A)先讀科學書再讀一本心理學的書
　　　　(B)讀一首詩，然後小睡一下
　　　　(C)在海灘玩球，然後下水游泳
　　　　(D)解一道數學題，再解一道化學題

10.（ C ）本文下一段可能討論什麼問題？
　　　　(A)如何寫詩　　　　　　　　(B)如何了解音樂的節奏
　　　　(C)好的文學作品中的節奏種類
　　　　(D)節奏對我們生活計畫的重要

C.

【註】　　investigative〔ɪnˋvɛstəˏgetɪv〕*adj.* 調查的
　　　　validity〔vəˋlɪdətɪ〕*n.* 有效性
　　　　rigorous〔ˋrɪgərəs〕*adj.* 嚴格的
　　　　elusive〔ɪˋlusɪv〕*adj.* 薄弱的；規避的
　　　　questionnaire〔ˏkwɛstʃənˋɛr〕*n.* 問卷

11.（ D ）作者對於挑別人研究中的錯處看法如何？
　　　　(A)只有有經驗的研究者才該這麼做。
　　　　(B)它會造成研究者避免發表好作品的情形。
　　　　(C)現在有太多人這樣做了。
　　　　(D)它有助於訂定未來研究計劃。

12.（ C ）根據本文，學生對已發表的研究經常的評論以什麼為主？
　　　　(A)研究報告寫得不夠生動有趣。
　　　　(B)研究的對象都不夠重要。
　　　　(C)研究者沒有完全建立研究對象間的關係。
　　　　(D)研究者沒有提出合適的綱要。

13.（ **A** ）根據本文，在課堂上，學生對其他學生的研究反應如何？
　　　(A) 就像他們對其他研究的反應一樣。
　　　(B) 他們對研究的品質特別挑剔。
　　　(C) 他們常提出改進研究的好建議。
　　　(D) 他們對同學的研究相當客氣。

14.（ **B** ）根據本文，學生研究員改變他們的研究目標是因為
　　　(A) 他們的預算太高了。　　　(B) 他們原來的問題範圍太廣了。
　　　(C) 老師未給予適度指導。　　　(D) 時間太有限。

15.（ **A** ）作者對如何準備適當的研究題目結論為何？
　　　(A) 這要比學生研究所所想像的難。
　　　(B) 研究者應尋求他人的幫助。
　　　(C) 問題應簡短，以便於了解。
　　　(D) 重要的是謹遵公式來定題目。

Ⅱ. 作文：

Street Vendors

　　Walk along the streets of Taipei, day or night, and you'll find street vendors and roadside food stands. Why do they remain so popular when we have modern department stores and supermarkets? I think the most obvious reason is their accessibility. On one's way to go shopping or to see a movie, the novelties sold by street vendors charm his eyes. *In addition*, the savory aromas coming from the food stands call to his stomach. How can one resist such temptations? *Furthermore*, Their goods are usually cheaper than those in supermarkets so everyone can afford them.

　　However, they really create problems. The streets are so jammed with vendors that vehicles can hardly pass. Shoppers busy at bargaining also risk being knocked down. *In addition*, they generate noise pollution, and both sellers and buyers leave the streets littered with refuse.

　　The best solution to this situation goes back to solving the unemployment problem. *But* the problem is not so simple. While most people would prefer a fixed job, others will not forsake vending as a livelihood. Government authorities should build a special district for them to do business. Only when practical alternatives are available, should the police issue citations to vendors.

研究所全眞英文試題——文化大學㈠

I. Write out the difference between the words in each group.

1. conscious
   conscientious

2. nominee
   candidate

3. statesman
   politician

4. speech
   oration

II. Choose the word or phrase nearest in meaning to the key word. then make a sentence for each key word.

1. unabashed--(A) ruthless (B) incessant(C) bewildered
   (D) not embarrassed

2. eradicate--(A) to nurture (B) halt (C) exclude
   (D)destroy

3. bigoted--(A) ignorant (B) selfish (C) generous
   (D) intolerant

4. probity--(A) immorality (B) smugness (C) confidence
   (D) integrity.

III. What is the opposite word(antonym) of the following words.

1. separate 2. hate 3. dishonest 4. war   5. destroy
6. careless 7. late 8. selfish   9. noisy 10. evil

IV. Correct the error in each of the following sentences?

1. I through the ball to my friend.

2. Can you weight for me at the theatre?

3. Give me a peace of that cake, please.

4. We had beef stake for dinner.

5. His voice was horse from shouting.

V. Write 5 sentences using each of the following words.

1. home 2. family 3. friend 4. nation 5. religion

☆ 研究所全眞英文試題詳解——文化㈠

Ⅰ. 寫出下列每一組字的區別。（選4組）

1. "**Conscious**" means aware (knowing things because one is using the bodily senses and mental powers) or realized by oneself, while "**conscientious**" means guided by one's sense of duty or done carefully and honestly.

2. "**Nominee**" means a person who is nominated for 〔to〕 an office or appointment, while "**candidate**" means a person who wishes, or who is put forward by others, to take an office, honor, prize or position.

3. "**Statesman**" is a person who plays an important part in the management of State affairs, or an impartial political leader. In addition to the meaning of a person actively taking part in politics, or much interested in politics; "**politician**" may also carry a negative meaning, referring to a person who follows politics as a career, regardless of principle, and often for personal gain.

4. "**Speech**" is just a talk or an address given in public, while "**oration**" means a formal speech made on a public occasion.

Ⅱ. 選出意思與關鍵字最接近的字或片語，然後用關鍵字造句。

1. (D) **unabashed** 〔͵ʌnə'bæʃt〕 *adj*. 不因害羞而侷促不安的
   The little boy is **unabashed** when meeting strangers.

2. (D) **eradicate** 〔ɪ'rædɪ͵ket〕 *v*. 根除
   It is the business of the police to prevent, detect, and **eradicate** crime.

3. (D) **bigoted** ['bɪgətɪd] *adj.* 固執己見的

If you weren't so **bigoted**, you'd let other people be as they are.

4. (D) **probity** ['prɑbətɪ] *n.* 剛直；廉潔

Mr. Collins is a man of **probity**.

Ⅲ. 寫出反義字。

1. separate → **unite** or **combine**　　2. hate → **love** or **cherish**

3. dishonest → **honest**　　4. war → **peace**

5. destroy→**construct** or **establish**　6. careless → **careful**

7. late → **early**　　8. selfish→**selfless** or **unselfish**

9. noisy →**quiet** or **silent**　　10. evil → **virtuous** or **good**

Ⅳ. 改正下列各句的錯誤

1. *through* → **threw**　　2. *weight* →**wait**

3. *peace* → **piece**　　4. *stake* → **steak**

5. *horse* → **hoarse**

Ⅴ. 用下列每個字造五個句子。

1. He looks forward to seeing the old **home** again.

2. Almost every **family** in the village has a man in the army.

3. He made **friends** with whomever he could.

4. Russians are a **nation**, but not a single race.

5. Christianity, Islam, and Buddhism are three great **religions** of the world.

研究所全眞英文試題 —— 文化大學(二)

I. Fill the following blanks with appropriate words. 20％

1. The plane has just taken ＿＿＿＿＿（起飛）.

2. She has turned ＿＿＿＿＿（拒絕）their request.

3. I'll look you ＿＿＿＿＿（探望）when I visit New York.

4. Let's make ＿＿＿＿＿（和解）.

5. Our car broke ＿＿＿＿＿（拋錨）on the road.

6. I'll back you ＿＿＿＿＿in this matter.（支持）

7. What's holding ＿＿＿＿＿（阻塞）the traffic?

8. Keep ＿＿＿＿＿the grass!（離開此地）

9. It took me a long time to get ＿＿＿＿＿（痊癒）my cold.

10. The meeting has been called ＿＿＿＿＿（取銷）.

II. Translate the following into English. 20％

1. 有志竟成 。

2. 有朋自遠方來 ,不亦悅乎 ?

3. 溫故知新 。

4. 不患人之不己知 ,患不知人也 。

III. Write a composition in English on either of the following subjects. 60％

1. Free China Today

2. My College Days

★ 研究所全眞英文試題詳解──文化(二)

Ⅰ. 填空：填入適當的字詞。20%

1. off   2. down   3. up   4. up   5. down   6. up   7. up

8. off   9. over   10. off

Ⅱ. 中翻英：20%

1. Where there is a will there is a way.

2. Isn't it a pleasure when there is a friend coming from far away〔afar〕?

3. Reviewing old lessons, one learns something new from them.

4. Don't worry if others don't understand you, but do worry if you don't understand them.

Ⅲ. 英文作文：60%

My College Days

I did not learn to lead an enjoyable and independent life until I became a college student. ***During the four years in college***, I was provided the opportunity not only to increase my knowledge as much as possible, but also to go through many helpful and useful experiences.

In college, I majored in English, and the program was very tough. I will never forget how I racked my brains for papers and compositions, or how I struggled with those metaphysical and romantic poets. ***However***, hard work is always a worthwhile endeavor. ***At the end of the strict training***, I found I had made considerable progress in English and was well prepared for advanced studies.

In addition to my studies, I took part in many activities in college. Through extracurricular activities, I learned to deal with things under different circumstances and, what was even more important, to get along with others. *Also*, by participating in various activities, I had the chance to get acquainted with other students who shared common interests with me. These activities in college broadened my mind; *furthermore*, they made my college days one of the most colorful and memorable periods in my life.

研究所全眞英文試題——文化大學㈢

I. Fill the following blanks with appropriate words. 20%

1. _____ he should do such a thing is quite beyond my expectation.

2. _____ you have confidence in yourself, do not try to take the risk.

3. I wondered _____ she was going to a party in such a nice dress.

4. Make hay while the sun shines, _____ you will lose the big prize.

5. Ugly _____ she looks, all the classmates are eager to make friends with her.

6. He is a liar. I never believe_____ he says.

7. _____ drives a car should have got a license.

8. _____ often he does it, he always makes a mistake.

9. I solved as many of the problems _____ I could.

10. _____ the Third World War will break out is everybody's guess.

II. Underline, in each of the following parentheses, the word which you believe is grammatically preferable. 20%

1. There is something going on between Judy and (him, he).

2. Jack as well as Allan (is, are) having lunch with us today.

3. It was (I, me) you were talking about, wasn't it?

4. He is one of those men who (has, have) no consideration for others.

5. Neither the television nor the radios (works, work).

6. John, together with James and William, (was, were) late.

7. The teacher accompanied by some 20 students (was, were) visiting the college that morning.

8. If World War II had not happened, the present world situation (would be, would have been) quite different.

9. John told his mother yesterday that he (has, had) quitted his job a month ago.

10. When the summer sale (ended, had ended), the store closed.

III. Revise the following sentences. 20%

1. My father often advised me to practice the adage that honesty was the best policy.

2. In the book it says that English is as difficult to learn as French.

3. I can't hardly believe what he told me.

4. We are looking forward to see you again soon.

5. The teacher said that each one of the students should sign their name on the paper.

6. John asked Paul what he had done wrong.

7. In Taiwan the summer is as warm as Kwangtung.

8. Henry is as old, if not older than, Paul.

9. A person ought to ask questions when confused.

10. When only a small boy, my father took me with him to Shanghai.

IV. Answer the following questions briefly. 20%

1. What is your purpose in seeking admission to a graduate school?

2. What do you know about the Chinese Communists?

V. Translate the following sentences into English. 20%

1. 今日能爲之事，勿待明日爲之。

2. 讀書愈多，見識愈廣。

3. 君君，臣臣，父父，子子。

4. 生之者衆，食之者寡，則財恒足矣。

★ 研究所全眞英文試題詳解──文化㈢

I. 填空：填入適當的字詞。20%

【答案】

1. That 2. Unless 3. whether〔if〕 4. or 5. as
6. what 7. Whoever 8. However 9. as 10. That

【註】

1. that 引導名詞子句作動詞 is 的主詞。

3. wonder＋wh. 子句 "想知道"

4. *Make hay while the sun shines.* 把握時機。〔諺〕

5. ugly *as* she looks ＝ though she looks ugly

6. what（＝all that）用在前面沒有先行詞的場合。

8. 複合關係副詞 however（＝no matter how）修飾 often。

II. 將下列括弧內你認為較合乎文法的字下面劃線：20%

【答案】

1. him 2. is 3. me 4. have 5. work 6. was
7. was 8. would be 9. had 10. ended

【註】

1. 用 him 做介系詞 between 的受詞。

2. A *as well as* B 做主詞時，動詞須與 A 一致。

3. me 作子句內介系詞 about 的受詞。

4. who 的先行詞為 those men, 故用複數動詞。

5. *neither* A *nor* B 做主詞時，動詞與最接近的主詞一致。

6. A *together with* B 做主詞時，動詞與 A 一致。

7. 主詞爲 the teacher，分詞片語 accompanied by some 20 students 作形容詞用，修飾 the teacher。

8. If 子句用過去完成式，表示與過去事實相反，但主要子句表示與現在事實相反，故用過去式。

9. quit 的動作比 tell 先，故主要子句用過去式動詞 told，名詞子句的動詞應該用過去完成式。

10. 兩個動作無明顯先後之分，故 end 與 close 一樣用過去式。

Ⅲ. 改正下列各句：20%

1. My father often advised me to practice the adage that *honesty is* the best policy.

   * 名詞子句說的是真理、格言或不變的事實，一律用現在式。

2. *The book says* that English is as difficult to learn as French.

3. I *can hardly* believe what he told me.

   * 本身即否定副詞，hardly 不必再加 not。

4. We are looking forward to *seeing* you again soon.

5. The teacher said that each one of the students should sign *his* name on the paper.

6. John asked Paul what *Paul* had done wrong.

   * he 如不改，造成混淆，句意不明。

7. The summer *in Taiwan* is as *warm* as *that in Kwangtung*.

8. Henry is as old as *Paul*, *if not older*.

9. A person ought to ask questions *when he is confused*.

10. When *I was* only a small boy, my father took me with him to Shanghai.

Ⅳ. 簡要回答下列問題：20%

1. Aside from the obvious goal of improving myself through further study, I also wish to bring honor to my family and

assist my country in any way that I can. I believe that given the opportunity to expand my knowledge and capabilities through attending graduate school, I can attain all of these goals.

2. The Chinese communists are familiar to us all as the self-seeking totalitarian occupiers of the Republic of China's rightful domain, the Chinese mainland. They suppress our countrymen there, disallowing the expression and development that all human beings desire and deserve, and simultaneously spread untruths about the R.O.C. to our mainland compatriots, attempting to negate with empty words and slogans the success — both economic and political — of the people of Free China.

Ⅴ. 中翻英: 20 %

1. Don't put off until tomorrow what you can do today.

2. The more one reads, the greater one's knowledge becomes.

3. Everyone should act according to his duty.

4. If there are many people producing and few people consuming, then wealth must be sufficient.

研究所全眞英文試題——文化大學(四)

I. Correct the following sentences. 20%

1. He kept me to wait.
2. Had I seen him, I would tell him.
3. Each day and each hour bring its duty.
4. I intended to have been present.
5. He wears a worrying look.
6. I hope you will excuse me leaving early.
7. What kind of a flower is it?
8. My uncle asked my brother and myself to dinner.
9. This is the only one of his poems that are worth reading.
10. These are good rules to live.

II. Fill in the blanks with appropriate prepositions. 20%

1. He thinks better _____ it now.
2. It goes _____ his heart to see so much misery.
3. The goat subsists _____ the coarsest of food.
4. Newly acquired freedom is sometimes liable _____ abuse.
5. He advised us to desist _____ that attempt.
6. He has proved his case _____ my satisfaction.
7. I have no time to waste _____ trifles.
8. These oranges are sold _____ the dozen.
9. It is difficult to swim _____ the stream of ready-made opinions.
10. It is no use crying _____ spilt milk.

III. Fill the blanks with conjunctions. 20%

1. You will not succeed _____ you work harder.
2. I waited _____ the train arrived.
3. He fled _____ he should be killed.
4. He asked _____ he might have a holiday.
5. Answer the first question _____ you proceed further.
6. _____ he slay me, yet will I trust him.
7. Hurry up _____ else you will be late.

8. Many things have happened _____ I left school.
9. _____ the shower was over, the sun shone again.
10. I would rather suffer _____ that you should want.

IV. **Make sentences with the following phrases. 20%**

1. by virtue of
2. with a view to
3. in consequence of
4. at the expense of
5. on condition that

V. **Translate the following into Chinese. 20%**

What really divides the Chinese people today is not the Taiwan Strait but the two totally different systems— the benevolent Three Principles of the People and tyrannical Communism. During these same 31 years, we have carried out the Three Principles of the People in this bastion of national revival, furthered Chinese culture, vigorously implemented constitutional government and generated economic prosperity characterized by an affluent and happy life for every individual and every family. We have established the pattern for a harmonious, open and progressive society suitable for the Chinese people and consistent with their cultural tradition. We have opened up a road of hope for the Chinese and pointed the way to a promising future for China.

研究所全眞英文試題詳解 —— 文化㈣

Ⅰ. 改正下列句子：20%

1. He kept me *waiting*.

2. Had I seen him, I would *have told* him.

3. Each day and each hour *brings* its duty.

4. I intended to *be* present.

5. He wears a *worried* look.

6. I hope you will excuse *my* leaving early.

7. What kind of *flower* is it?

8. My uncle asked my brother and *me* to dinner.

9. This is the only one of his poems that *is* worth reading.

10. These are the good rules *to live by*.

Ⅱ. 填入適當的介系詞：20%

【答案】

1. of	2. to	3. on	4. to	5. from	6. to
7. on	8. by	9. against	10. over		

【註】

1. *think better of* "改變～的念頭"

2. *go to one's heart* "使受感動；使傷心"

3. *subsist on* "以～爲生"　　coarse〔kɔrs〕*adj.* 粗糙的

4. *be liable to* "易患；易於"　　abuse〔əˈbjuz〕*v.* 濫用

5. desist〔dɪˈzɪst〕*v.* 停止(與 from 連用)；休想

6. *to one's satisfaction* "使某人滿意"

9. *swim against the stream* "背道而馳；在不利的情況下奮鬥"

10. *cry over* "慟哭"

Ⅲ. 填入適當的連接詞：20％

1. unless   2. until〔till〕   3. as if   4. if   5. before
6. Though   7. or   since   8. since   9. After   10. than

Ⅳ. 用下列片語造句：20％

1. **by virtue of** " 由於；憑藉著 "
He was promoted **by virtue of** his ability.

2. **with a view to** " 爲了～的目的；期望（獲得）"
We have established the institute **with a view to** disseminating scientific knowledge.

3. **in consequence of** " 由於；因～的結果 "
In consequence of his bad conduct he was dismissed.

4. **at the expense of** " 以～爲代價；犧牲 "
He became a brilliant scholar, but only at the expense of his health.

5. **on condition that** " 只有在～條件下；倘若 "
You can go swimming *on condition that* you don't go too far from the river bank.

Ⅴ. 英翻中：20％

今日眞正阻隔在中國人之間的，不是台灣海峽，而是兩種完全不同的制度── 仁民愛物的三民主義和專制的共產主義。同樣在這三十一年期間，我們在此復興基地實行三民主義，推行中華文化，大力實施憲政，而創造經濟繁榮，其特徵可以由每個個人和家庭富裕、快樂的生活顯示出來。我們已經建立起適合中國人，而且與中國文化傳統一致的祥和、開放、進取的社會模式。我們已爲中國人打開一條希望之路，指出中國未來前途光明之道。

* benevolent〔bə'nɛvələnt〕*adj.* 仁愛的；慈善的
bastion〔'bæstʃən〕*n.* 基地；堡壘   revival〔rɪ'vaɪvl̩〕*n.* 回復；再興
implement〔'ɪmplə,mɛnt〕*v.* 實現；完成
generate〔'dʒɛnə,ret〕*v.* 產生；創造
affluent〔'æfluənt〕*adj.* 富裕的

研究所全眞英文試題 —— 文化大學(五)

I. VOCABULARY: 20%

part I

Read each sentence and the three words or phrases below it. Choose the one that has about the same meaning as the underlined words in the sentence.

1. When my mother sews, she likes to have her scissors <u>near at hand.</u>
   (A) in her hand (B) within easy reach (C) to cut with

2. <u>Without a moment's hesitation</u>, Larry decided to take the path to the right.
   (A) without caring　(B) without trying to stop
   (C) without stopping for a second

3. Mom and I stopped to <u>pass the time</u> with our mailman, Mr. Taylor.
   (A) mail a clock　(B) let him walk around us
   (C) visit a while

4. My uncle said the incident <u>called to mind</u> an earlier escapade of mine.
   (A) made him obey (B) made him remember (C) made him forget

5. The boat was <u>barely making headway</u> against the high waves and strong winds.
   (A) ahead of schedule　(B) almost at a standstill
   (C) making good time

6. My advisor assured me that he would accept my explanation <u>without a doubt</u>.
   (A) with certainty (B) with honesty (C) with interest

7. Just as the ball game was ready to start, it began to rain <u>cats and dogs</u>.
   (A) very hard (B) pet animals (C) in a light drizzle

8. After the convention, leftover posters were <u>a dime a dozen</u>.
   (A) inexpensive (B) scarce (C) plentiful

9. In a very short time, Jack <u>turned out</u> a well-written story.
(A) banished forever (B) scribbled (C) produced

10. The firemen hoped the prairie fire would not <u>break out</u> in some other place later.
(A) collapse (B) start suddenly (C) come apart

Part Ⅱ

From the four choices given, you should choose the one word or phrase which could be substituted for the underlined word without changing the meaning of the sentence.

11. The old woman is too <u>feeble</u> to cross the street without her nephew's help.
(A) tired (B) weak (C) timid (D) blind

12. It is impossible for a parent to <u>shield</u> his children from every danger.
(A) protect (B) conserve (C) relieve (D) free

13. He was such a <u>shrewd</u> businessman that he never lost money in any transaction.
(A) fortunate (B) clever (C) wealthy (D) well-liked

14. There was no <u>trace</u> of poison in the coffee the chemist analyzed.
(A) indication (B) taste (C) color (D) smell

15. One <u>symptom</u> of the disease is high fever.
(A) symbol (B) sign (C) cause (D) pain

16. There is no <u>alternative</u>; the president must approve the bill if congress passes it.
(A) chance of agreement (B) help (C) other choice
(D) mistake

17. The boy felt <u>disgraced</u> because he knew that he had been wrong to steal.
(A) ashamed (B) worried (C) tempted (D) phony

18. The world leaders had a <u>chat</u> early this morning at United Nations headquarters.
(A) friendly, unimportant talk (B) disagreement
(C) serious discussion (D) high-level conference

19. The criminal <u>insinuated</u> that he had been roughly
    treated by the arresting officer.
    (A) suggested indirectly   (B) denied positively
    (C) argued convincingly   (D) stated flatly

20. Those who live by the sword will <u>perish</u> by the sword.

    (A) breathe   (B) survive   (C) die   (D) win

II. READING COMPREHENSION : 30%

part I

Read each paragraph and the three sentences below it. Choose
the sentence that best tells the main idea of the paragraph.

1. Iron is a plentiful metal and is one of the most useful
   materials on earth. A surgeon's knife, steel beams in a
   building, and even the wire in a spiral notebook may
   be made of iron. Another quality of iron is its ability
   to be magnetized. Its many uses make iron valuable in
   numerous ways.
   (A) Iron is a useful metal. (B) Iron is very plentiful.
   (C) Steel beams are made of iron.

2. Casey leaned out of the cab window and looked back toward
   the caboose for the brakeman's signal. Then he checked
   his watch again. People depended upon the freight getting
   into the station on time. Other men helped him, but it
   was Casey's responsibility as engineer to see that his
   train arrived when it was due.
   (A) A train is easy to run. (B) Freight is due on time.
   (C) Casey's watch had stopped.

3. It is important to protect every kind of animal wildlife.
   In areas where mountain lions and coyotes are no longer
   found, herds of deer have grown too large for the food
   supply. Thus many deer starve. By allowing seemingly
   harmful animals to live, a better balance of nature can
   be maintained.
   (A) Nature's balance is best. (B) Some animals starve
   easily. (C) Coyotes are extinct.

4. In cold weather, people can put on warmer clothing and
   stay indoors more. Wild animals must find other ways to
   survive. Some leave for a warmer climate, while others
   crawl into a cave and sleep until spring arrives. Many
   grow heavier coats of fur. Animals seem well equipped to
   survive even under conditions of extreme cold.
   (A) Animals suffer from cold (B) People stay inside in
   winter. (C) Animals survive winter differently.

5. In 1986 , people around the world will look for the
return of a very special comet. Since it was first
observed in 240 B.C., Halley's comet has been seen
about every seventy-five years. It is not the only
comet seen; but because of its brightness and regular
appearance, it has always been of great interest.
(A) Comets are seen every night.
(B) Halley's comet is special.
(C) Only one comet is important.

part Ⅱ

Choose the answer whose meaning is closest to that of the
given sentence.

6. Cancer cells multiply faster and spread more rapidly
than normal cells do.
(A) Normal cells, which multiply more rapidly than
cancer cells, spread more slowly.
(B) Cancer cells, which multiply faster than normal
cells, also spread faster.
(C) Cancer cells spread more slowly, although they
multiply more rapidly, than normal cells.
(D) Because normal cells spread more slowly, they also
multiply more slowly than cancer cells.

7. More is known of conditions on Mars than of conditions
on Pluto.
(A) Conditions on Pluto are better known than condi-
tions on Mars.
(B) Neither conditions on Mars nor the conditions on
Pluto are well known.
(C) We know less about conditions on Mars than about
conditions on Pluto.
(D) Conditions on Pluto are less well known than condi-
tions on Mars.

8. In dense woods where little sunlight penetrates, one is
likely to find just about as much moss on the south
side as on the north side of a tree trunk.
(A) When little sunlight comes through the thick forest,
the south and the north side of a tree trunk have about
the same amount of moss.
(B) When bright sunlight comes through the dense woods,
the moss on the north side of the tree trunk is thicker
than that on the south side.
(C) When not much sunlight penetrates the thick woods,
the moss on the south side of the tree trunk is thicker
than that on the north side.
(D) When a great deal of sunlight penetrates the thick
forest, very little moss grows on either the south or
the north side of the tree trunk.

9. Lava from some volcanoes flows for a long distance; lava from others solidifies quite quickly, resulting in a mass of jagged blocks.
(A) All volcanoes produce lava which sometimes flows for a long distance and sometimes solidifies rapidly.
(B) Lavas from some volcanoes become solid very rapidly, producing rough blocks, while lava from other volcanoes flows for long distances.
(C) Volcanic lava may flow quickly or slowly, become solid, or stay liquid.
(D) Some volcanoes produce two types of lava, quick-flowing lava, and quickly solidifying lava.

10. Zoysia grass, which is good in southern areas, may be very poor in cooler areas where it turns green too late in spring and goes brown too early in the fall.
(A) Zoysia grass gets brown early in the fall and turns green early in spring in cooler areas.
(B) Zoysia grass turns green later in southern areas than it does in cooler areas.
(C) Zoysia grass is good in southern areas, because it turns green late in spring and does not turn brown in fall.
(D) Zoysia grass is good in southern areas, but is not recommended for cooler areas.

Part Ⅲ

Choose the best answer to each question from the choices given.

(一) Poland today is faced with technical difficulties caused by disparity between the output of coal (which is nevertheless great) and the rapid progress of industry.

11. Poland's production of coal is _____ .
(A) less than before industrial expansion
(B) very limited   (C) relatively large
(D) hampered by industrial problems

12. Industry in Poland is _____ .
(A) at a standstill   (B) undergoing rapid growth
(C) declining
(D) having problems because of a scarcity of manpower

13. In Poland, coal _____ .
(A) is probably the major industrial fuel
(B) is responsible for the rapid progress of industry   (C) is produced only in industrial areas
(D) is produced only in areas far distant from industrial centers

(二) The Mediterranean climate is little suited to stock-breeding; only sheep and goats can make use of the extensive grazing land with its meager rainfall.

14. The Mediterranean climate is described as
    (A) humid (B) dry (C) extremely cold
    (D) generally moderate, but with heavy rainfall

15. The Mediterranean area is _____ .
    (A) good for raising all varieties of animals
    (B) poor for raising animals
    (C) suitable for some animals, but not for sheep and goats
    (D) well suited to breeding animals

16. According to this sentence animal grazing land in the Mediterranean are
    (A) severely limited in size.
    (B) very steep and rocky.
    (C) large, but not very good for grazing
    (D) large, but very swampy.

(三) At the battle of Gettysburg, General George G. Meade, who succeeded General Hooker as commander of the Army of the Potomac, threw back Lee's attacks and hurt the Confederate army badly. Meade had fought a skillful defensive battle, but he was satisfied with his victory as it was. He was content to see Lee leave his front, and his principal concern was to "herd" Lee back over the Potomac. Like other Federal generals, he lacked the killer instinct, which all the great battle captains have had, to finish off the enemy. After the engagement he issued a congratulatory order to his troops in which he praised them for having driven the enemy from "our soil". After all, this was a civil war! When Lincoln read the order, he exclaimed in anguish, "My God! Is that all?"

17. The battle of Gettysburg _____ .
    (A) was won by the Confederate army
    (B) was won by Hooker
    (C) was won by the Federal army
    (D) was won by Lee

18. George G. Meade did not _____ .
    (A) hurt the Confederate army
    (B) fight a good defensive battle
    (C) force Lee to retreat
    (D) completely destroy the enemy

19. When Lincoln heard of Meade's order, he _____ .
    (A) was delighted　(B) congratulated the troops
    (C) was dismayed　(D) prayed

20. The implication of the paragraph is that _____ .
    (A) Meade was totally incompetent
    (B) Meade was ruthless
    (C) Meade should have "finished off" the enemy
    (D) Meade was well-loved by his men

III. CORRECT ALL OF THE FOLLOWING MISTAKES. 20%

Example: Her is a Girl. (1)(2)　(1) Her → She
　　　　　　　　　　　　　　(2) Girl → girl

If I Were a English Teacher (1)

I is glad to be a teacher, (2) particular a English teacher. (3)(4) So if I were a English teacher, (5) I would made every student use English in life. (6) Because English is a language, so how to speak, how to write, and how to use English are the most important point. (7) But how can we learn how to use English in life?

I have an opinions about how my would teach. (8)(9) First, I will order students to write a diary. No matter what I correct their diary or not, (10)(11)(12) The motto "practice make perfect" is alway right. (13)(14) Otherwise students will be out of practice at writing. Second, to speak is very important. Every students can speaks on the platform in classroom and pass along his or her opinion. (15)(16)(17) I thinked this way may help students to using English in right way. (18)(19)(20)

IV. ENGLISH COMPOSITION : 30%

ATTENTION! Write about 100 words, but no more than 150. You will be graded on your ability to use a variety of verb tenses, prepositions, the definite and indefinite articles, dependent clauses and complex sentences.

TOPIC: MY WAY OF LIFE

☆ 研究所全眞英文試題詳解——文化(ɪɪ)

Ⅰ. 字彙：

PART Ⅰ. 選出與句中劃線的字同意者：

【答案】

1.（ B ）	2.（ C ）	3.（ C ）	4.（ B ）	5.（ B ）
6.（ A ）	7.（ A ）	8.（ A ）	9.（ C ）	10.（ B ）

【註】

1.（*near*）*at hand* "在近處；在手頭上"

3. *pass the time of day*（with）"（與）互相寒喧；問候"

4. *call to mind* "想起"

5. barely〔'bɛrlɪ〕*adv.* 幾乎不
   make headway "（船）航行；（事務的）進展"

6. *without a doubt* ＝ no doubt "無疑地；必定"

7. *rain cats and dogs* "下傾盆大雨"　(C) drizzle〔'drɪzl̩〕*n.* 細雨

8. *a dime a dozen* "多得不稀罕；不值錢"
   leftover〔'lɛft,ovɚ〕*adj.* 殘餘的　poster〔'postɚ〕*n.* 海報

9. *turn out* "生產；製造"　(A) banish〔'bænɪʃ〕*v.* 驅逐
   (B) scribble〔'skrɪbl̩〕*v.* 亂寫；潦草書寫

10. prairie〔'prɛrɪ〕*n.* 大草原
    break out "（火災、戰爭等）突然發生"
    (A) collapse〔kə'læps〕*v.* 倒塌

PART Ⅱ. 選出一個適合劃線的字，且不改變句意者：

【答案】

11.(B)	12.(A)	13.(B)	14.(A)	15.(B)
16.(C)	17.(A)	18.(A)	19.(A)	20.(C)

【註】

11. feeble〔'fibḷ〕*adj*. 衰弱的

12. shield〔ʃild〕*v*. 防禦；保護　(B) conserve〔kən'sɜv〕*v*. 保存；保全

13. shrewd〔ʃrud〕*adj*. 精明的；惡毒的
 transaction〔træns'ækʃən〕*n*. 處理；執行

14. trace〔tres〕*n*. 蹤跡　analyze〔'ænə,laɪz〕*v*. 分析
 (A) indication〔,ɪndə'keʃən〕*n*. 指示

15. symptom〔'sɪmptəm〕*n*. 徵候；徵兆

16. alternative〔ɔl'tɜnətɪv〕*n*. 二者擇一
 congress〔'kɑŋgrəs〕*n*. 國家立法的機關

17. disgraced〔dɪs'grest〕*adj*. 丟臉的
 (D) phony〔'fonɪ〕*adj*. 假的；僞造的

18. chat〔tʃæt〕*n*. 閒談　United Nations headquarters 聯合國總部

19. insinuate〔ɪn'sɪnjʊ,et〕*v*. 暗示；暗指
 (C) convincingly〔kən'vɪnsɪŋlɪ〕*adv*. 令人心服地

20. perish〔'pɛrɪʃ〕*v*. 死；毀滅

Ⅱ. 閱讀測驗：30％

PART Ⅰ. 閱讀下文，選出最能表達各篇文章主要意思的句子：

【答案】

1.（A）　　2.（B）　　3.（A）　　4.（C）　　5.（B）

【註】

1. surgeon〔'sɝdʒən〕*n.* 外科醫生
   spiral〔'spaɪrəl〕*adj.* 螺旋形的；盤旋的
   magnetize〔'mægnə,taɪz〕*v.* 使磁化

2. cab〔kæd〕*n.* 火車頭之遮蓋部（司機與司爐所坐處）
   caboose〔kə'bus〕*n.* 載貨火車之守車（通常為最後的車廂）
   brakeman〔'brekmən〕*n.* 火車上控制煞車者

3. coyote〔'kaɪot ; kaɪ'ot〕*n.*（北美大草原之）土狼
   seemingly〔'simɪŋlɪ〕*adv.* 表面上地
   (C) extinct〔ɪk'stɪŋkt〕*adj.* 滅種的

4. crawl〔krɔl〕*v.* 爬行　　fur〔fɝ〕*n.* 獸皮的軟毛；毛皮

5. comet〔'kɑmɪt〕*n.* 彗星

PART Ⅱ. 選出與下列句子意思最接近的答案：

【答案】

6.（B）　　7.（D）　　8.（A）　　9.（B）　　10.（D）

【註】

6. 癌細胞繁殖、蔓延得比正常細胞快。
   multiply〔'mʌltə,plaɪ〕*v.* 繁殖

7. 人們對火星的情況比對冥王星的情況了解得多。
   Mars〔mɑrz〕*n.* 火星　　Pluto〔'pluto〕*n.* 冥王星

8. 在濃密的樹林裡，日光不易穿透，人們可能會發現樹幹南邊和北邊的苔蘚剛好一樣多。

penetrate〔'pɛnə,tret〕v. 穿入；透過

9. 有些火山的岩漿流得很遠，其他的則很快就凝固，產生大量鋸齒狀的巨岩。

lava〔'lævə；'lɑvə〕n.（火山所流出的）熔岩；岩漿

solidify〔sə'lɪdə,faɪ〕v. 凝固　　*result in*　"導致"

jagged〔'dʒægɪd〕*adj.* 有鋸齒形的邊的

block〔blɑk〕n.〔地質〕火山口所噴出的巨岩

10. 左伊細亞草原在南部地區是很優良的，在溫帶地區春天時太晚才變綠，秋天時又太早變黃，可能會非常貧瘠。

PART Ⅲ. 選出最好的一個答案：

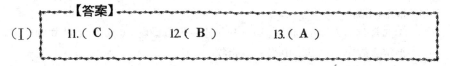

【答案】

(Ⅰ)　11.(**C**)　　12.(**B**)　　13.(**A**)

【註】

今天的波蘭正面對煤礦產量（儘管很大）和工業快速進步不一致所引起的科技困難。

disparity〔dɪs'pærətɪ〕n. 不一致；懸殊

11. 波蘭的煤產量＿＿＿＿＿＿。

(A)比工業擴張以前少　(B)非常有限　(C)相當大　(D)受工業問題所阻礙

hamper〔'hæmpɚ〕v. 妨礙；阻礙

12. 波蘭的工業＿＿＿＿＿＿。

(A)處於停頓狀態　(B)快速成長　(C)衰弱　(D)因爲主要動力不足而產生困難

standstill〔'stænd,stɪl〕n. 停頓

13. 在波蘭，煤＿＿＿＿＿＿。

(A) 或許是主要的工業燃料　(B)對工業快速進步負有責任　(C)只有工業地區才生產　(D)只有在離工業中心很遠的地區才生產

（Ⅱ）　　14.（ **B** ）　　　15.（ **B** ）　　　16.（ **C** ）

【註】

地中海的氣候—點也不適合畜牧；只有綿羊和山羊可以利用這種疏耕的放牧地和貧乏的雨量。

Mediterranean〔‚mɛdətə'reniən〕 *adj.* 地中海的
stockbreeding〔'stɑk‚bridɪŋ〕 *n.* 畜牧（業） *grazing land* 放牧地
meager〔'migɚ〕 *adj.* 貧乏的；不足的
extensive〔ɪk'stɛnsɪv〕 *adj.*〔農〕疏耕的

14. 地中海的氣候被描述為＿＿＿＿＿＿。
    (A)潮濕　(B)乾燥　(C)極端寒冷　(D)普遍溫和，但有很多雨量

15. 地中海地區＿＿＿＿＿＿。
    (A)適合飼養各種不同的動物　(B)不適合飼養動物　(C)適合某些動物，但不適合綿羊和山羊　(D)很適合畜牧

16. 依據這個句子，在地中海地區飼養動物的放牧地＿＿＿＿＿＿。
    (A)範圍上受到嚴格的限制　(B)非常陡峭多岩石　(C)大，但不很適合放牧
    (D)大，但非常濕而鬆軟
    graze〔grez〕 *v.* 放牧　　swampy〔'swɑmpɪ〕 *adj.* 濕而鬆軟的

（Ⅲ）　17.（ **C** ）　　18.（ **D** ）　　19.（ **C** ）　　20.（ **C** ）

【註】

在蓋茨堡戰場上，喬治・G・米德將軍使李將軍的攻擊延遲，而把南軍打得慘敗，他是繼胡克爾將軍之後，成為波多馬克軍隊的指揮官。米德打了一場技巧的防禦戰，但是他對勝利的現狀感到很滿意。他滿意地看李離開前線，而首要的顧慮則是把李領囘波多馬克。就像其他聯邦的將軍一樣，他缺乏所有大戰役領袖具備的殺手的直覺，把敵軍殺光。在交戰之後，他向軍隊發布一道恭賀的命令，其中他讚揚他們把敵軍驅逐出「我們的土地」。

畢竟，這是內戰啊！當林肯讀到這條命令，他苦惱地叫道：「天啊，就是這樣嗎？」

Gettysburg〔ˈgɛtɪz,bɝg〕n. 蓋茨堡（美國賓州南部的歷史名鎮，南北戰爭時北軍擊敗南軍之處。）

throw back "使延遲"

Confederate〔kənˈfɛdərɪt〕n. adj. 南部同盟（的）

as it is（was）"照原狀、現狀"（放在句尾時）

herd〔hɝd〕v. 領一群人至某地

17. 蓋茨堡戰役_____。
　　(A)是南軍贏　(B)胡克爾贏　(C)聯邦軍隊贏　(D)李贏

18. 喬治・G・米德將軍並沒有_____。
　　(A)傷到南軍　(B)打一場漂亮的防禦戰　(C)迫李徹退　(D)完全殺毀敵軍

19. 當林肯得知米德的命令時，他_____。
　　(A)很高興　(B)恭賀軍隊　(C)很驚慌　(D)祈禱
　　dismay〔dɪsˈme〕v. 驚慌；不安

20. 本文的含意是_____。
　　(A)米德完全無能　(B)米德很冷酷　(C)米德應該把敵軍殺光　(D)米德很受人們愛戴
　　incompetent〔ɪnˈkɑmpətənt〕adj. 無能的
　　ruthless〔ˈruθlɪs〕adj. 冷酷的

Ⅲ. 改正下列所有的錯誤：20％

(1) a → **an**　　(2) is → **would be**　(3) particular → **particularly**

(4) a → **an**　　(5) a → **an**　　(6) made → **make**

(7) point → **points**　　(8) an → **some**

(9) my → **I**　　(10) will → **would**

(11) No → **no**　　(12) No matter what → **whether**

(13) make → **makes**　　(14) alway → **always**

(15) students → **student**　　(16) speaks → **speak**

(17) classroom → **the classroom**　　(18) thinked → **think**

(19) using → **use**　　(20) right way → **the right way**

Ⅳ. 英文作文：30％

My Way of Life

To me, the Bohemian way of life is anticipated but never carried out. *In novels* the protagonists often lead a life of great intensity, experiencing violent ups and downs throughout their flamboyant careers. I also like to pursue adventure rather than live conservatively. The concept of "Golden Means" is deeply appreciated by me.

I like freedom. *But* I know pure freedom is almost impossible. Who can be totally free from the influences of others' ideas and actions? *Therefore*, I accept the limitations of human beings.

I love leisure. *Only in leisure* can I enjoy books, music, fine arts, and those great creations of the geniuses. *Only in leisure* am I blessed with what Wordsworth called "natural piety. Reading and meditation especially afford me great pleasure. I hope my life will go thus on, without swerving too far.

I may be green in my judgments, yet I would like to manage my own life.

研究所全眞英文試題 ——— 淡江大學

EXAMINATION IN ENGLISH FOR ALL APPLICANTS TO THE GRADUATE SCHOOL

General Directions: 1. Write all your answers on your answer sheets—Questions. 1-90 on appropriate blanks and your composition on page seven (the last page). 2. You can have only one answer to all questions numbered from 1 to 90. Your choice of more than two answers for one question will result in your losing point for that question.

I. Vocabulary: Choose the word that best fits the given sentence. 20%

1. Spark plugs (A. ignite; B. illuminate; C. ignore; D. illustrate) in the automobile engine.

2. After driving a bus all day, Norris liked to be a (A. pediatrician; B. pedestrian; C.pedagogue; D.peddler) and take a long, casual walk in the evening.

3. I was there as a witness to (A. vivify; B.vex; C.testify D. tax) against the bus driver.

4. Pop was uneasy about taking the (A. detour; B. deport; C. depose; D. detract) in this strange town.

5. When a husband prospers in his business, his (A.spondee; B. squire; C. spouse; D. squid) benefits also.

6. Industry sources said that Japanese automobile makers planned to expand (A. domestic; B. dominical; C.dormant; D. doltish) sales as their exports were expected to be hard hit by the yen's rise.

7. In the light of its relatively high accident rate in recent months, CAL should make (A. token; B. disastrous; C. excessive; D. drastic) changes in aircraft maintenance policies.

8. Air is a mixture of about 20% (A. oxide; B. oxhide; C. oxyacid; D. oxygen) and 79% nitrogen, with small amounts of rare gases, but the proportions vary a little from one place to another.

9. It was a dome, pierced by forty windows, which seemed not to rest upon a solid foundation, but to cover the place beneath as though it was (A.suspensed; B.swabbled; C. suspended; D. swashed) from heaven by a golden chain.

10. The firemen's (A. valence; B. vale; C. valor; D.valance) in rushing into the flaming house saved the occupants from a horrid fate.

11. Hazards in mineral mining can be avoided or reduced by adequate (A. veneration; B. retaliation; C. ventilation; D. incrimination).

12. The economic development has brought wealth and (A. affray; B. afflux; C. affliction; D. affluence) to our society.

13. A (A. depreciation; B. devastation; C. detonation; D. detraction) of the New Taiwan dollar will prove to be beneficial to our international trade.

14. Gadhafi intensified his (A. terrorist; B. terroristic; C. terrorialistic; D. teristic) war, sending his agents around the world to maim or murder innocents.

15. Interest in the project was (A.contaminated; B.condoled; C. condensed; D. contagious), and soon all opposition to the project collapsed.

16. Julia's handwriting is beautiful and (A. edible; B. legible; C. eligible; D. legislative).

17. The value-added tax system can do away with the double taxation and reduce tax (A. exit; B. evasion; C. evaporation; D. evacuation).

18. Juvenile offenders are not (A. exemplified; B.examined; C. exempt; D. exhaled) from punishment.

19. Danny's anger (A. submitted; B.subsidized; C.subsided; D. subscribed) when the culprit apologized.

20. Dr. Anderson (A. expatiated; B.expedited; C.expatriated; D. extracted) my tooth in an amateur fashion.

II. Grammar and Rhetoric: Choose the one best element out of the four provided to complete the sentence. 20%

21. People come in all types. When I was younger, (A. in fact; B. since; C. however; D. otherwise), my classmates and I thought that they came in only two types-- those that were good-looking and those that were not.

22. To the left of the entrance is an old oak dresser that once (A. belonged; B. had belonged; C. has belonged; D. belongs) to my grand mother. It is one of my most cherished possessions.

23. The Wilderness Society is one of the groups (A. who's; B. whose; C. that; D. which) purpose is to preserve the few sites of uninhabited land left.

24. On Earth Day, 1970, many cities staged demonstrations that were both dramatic and (A. something very out of ordinary; B. a thing quite to incite people; C.extraordinary; D. every thing very much exceptional).

25. Although it is very hot by the lake, from which a river flows through mountains, (A. it; B. they; C.the weather; D. the water) looks inviting.

26. Carson's "The Sea Around Us" is (A. famous and; B. as famous as; C. the same famous as; D. equally famous as) her" Silent Spring."

27. Occasionally, it seems necessary to ask what (A. the purpose of life is; B. for what is the purpose of life; C. what is about living purpose; D. what is life purpose?).

28. (A. Believing; B. To believe; C. The belief; D. It is believed) that the formation of the sun, the planets, and other stars began with the condensation of an interstellar gas cloud.

29. It has been almost a year since the restaurant (A. made its door public; B. made the public welcome; C. opened its door to the public; D invited the public to its doors).

30. Altruism is not merely a matter of being helpful; it is helpfulness (A. at the cost to; B. with the cost to; C. costly; D. what costs).

31. Anyone (A. interesting in; B. interested to; C. interested in; D. interesting in) receiving information about the organization should write to the secretary.

32. No one could have imagined how much damage the flood (A. would do to the city; B. was on the city; C.washed over the city; D. took to the city).

33. Mary wanted to leave the hospital even (A. she was hardly able walking; B. though hardly able walking; C. hardly able to walk; D. though she was hardly able to walk).

34. An analysis of the election results proves (A. that a majority of voters exist who are liberals; B. the existence of a majority of liberal voters; C. the voting liberals are the existing majority; D. that a majority of liberals who vote exist).

35. (A. Although a; B. That a; C. A; D. Because) beaver can make a tree fall wherever he wants it to is untrue.

36. (A. The rate of evaporation which; B. It is the rate of evaporation; C. While the rate of evaporation; D. The rate of evaporation) decreases as the moisture content of the air increases and approaches saturation.

37. I stopped in front of the building and (A. my things left in back, got out of the car; B. with my things left in the back, got out of the car; C. got out of the car, leaving my things in the back; D. without my things, which I left in the back, got out of the car.

38. One should read books on ecology (A. to learn; B. for the sake of learning; C. will learn; D. so that he shall learn) about the threats to his environment.

39. (A. The; B. With the; C. While the; D. It was during the) advent of the First World War, the United States became the dominant force in the motion-picture industry.

40. Continuing its Earth Week observance, (A. the Today show interviewed Dr. Chang; B. Dr. Chang was interviewed; C. the Today show director was interviewed; D. the program was interviewed).

III. Written Expression: Each problem consists of a sentence in which four words or phrases are underlined. The four underlined parts of the sentence are (A), (B), (C), and (D). You are to identify the one underlined word or phrase that should be corrected or rewritten.

41. Cooking utensils should be chosen for their utility and
         A   B   C
    ease of care the same as their attractive appearance.
               D

42. The standards on which the metric system are based have
        A   B   C
    been found to be slightly inaccurate.
      D

43. One of Mark Twain's most startling and sarcastic work
                A   B   C
    is "Letters from the Earth."
     D

44. Sodium is the six most abundant element in the earth's
         A   B   C   D
    crust.

45. O'Hare Airport in Chicago handles more freight and mail
                   A   B
    than any another airport in the United States.
     C   D

46. With a history of more than four thousand years ago the
             A   B
    drum is one of the oldest and most widely used musical
                         C   D
    instruments.

47. Dacron sails are <u>lighter and stronger</u> than cotton sails
    　　　　　　　　　　　　　A
    <u>and</u> they dry <u>more quicker</u> <u>than</u> cotton sails.
    　B　　　　　　　C　　　　　D

48. Many <u>retired people</u> now <u>find</u> satisfaction by <u>working</u>
    　　　　　A　　　　　　　　B　　　　　　　　　　C
    <u>hardly</u> for the good of <u>their communities</u>.
    　　　　　　　　　　　　　　　D

49. Abraham Lincoln <u>delivered</u> his famous <u>Gettysburg Address</u>
    　　　　　　　　　A　　　　　　　　　　B
    <u>at dedication</u> of a national cemetery <u>in</u> Gettysburg in
    　　C　　　　　　　　　　　　　　　　D
    1863.

50. The student <u>made</u> his <u>homework</u> <u>quickly</u> so that he could
    　　　　　　A　　　　　B　　　　　C
    <u>play</u> football before bedtime.
    　D

51. The adult mosquito usually lives for <u>about</u> thirty days,
    　　　　　　　　　　　　　　　　　　　　A
    <u>although</u> the life span <u>varied</u> widely with the tempera-
    　B　　　　　　　　　　　　C
    ture, humidity, and <u>other</u> factors of the environment.
    　　　　　　　　　　　D

52. The <u>amount</u> of <u>endangered</u> species <u>increases</u> every year
    　　　A　　　　　B　　　　　　　　C
    <u>as</u> natural habitats disappear.
    　D

53. One of the really important <u>thing that matters</u> <u>to</u> the
    　　　　　　　　　　　　　　　　A　　　　　　　B
    children is <u>how soon</u> they can <u>go fishing</u> with their
    　　　　　　　C　　　　　　　　　　D
    father.

54. At the same time, a <u>growing</u> human population <u>has forced</u>
    　　　　　　　　　　　A　　　　　　　　　　　　B
    all African elephants back into once remote parks, <u>when</u>
    　　　　　　　　　　　　　　　　　　　　　　　　　C
    elephant density has in many cases <u>exceeded</u> the natural
    　　　　　　　　　　　　　　　　　D
    food supply.

55. <u>Only after</u> he had acquired considerable <u>facility</u> <u>in</u>
    　A　　　　　　　　　　　　　　　　　B
    speaking <u>he began</u> to learn to read and to write.
    　C　　　D

56. The domestic self-sufficiency <u>which is</u> so characteristic
<u>to</u> the American suburbs <u>is not nearly</u> so common <u>in other</u>
sections.
   - A: which is
   - B: to
   - C: is not nearly
   - D: in other

57. <u>After writing</u> novels unsuccessfully <u>for several years,</u>
the novelist was not certain <u>that</u> he should quit <u>or</u>
continue with his art.
   - A: After writing
   - B: for several years
   - C: that
   - D: or

58. The librarian insists that John <u>will take</u> no more <u>books</u>
from the library before he <u>returns</u> all the books he has
<u>borrowed</u>.
   - A: will take
   - B: books
   - C: returns
   - D: borrowed

59. In the production of prunes, the fruit <u>is gathered</u>,
dipped in a lye solution <u>to prevent fermentation</u>, and
then <u>they dry them</u> in the sun <u>or</u> in large ovens.
   - A: is gathered
   - B: to prevent fermentation
   - C: they dry them
   - D: or

60. <u>Because</u> his limited resources Robert knew he <u>had to</u>
choose between <u>buying</u> a winter coat <u>and spending</u> a week
at the seashore.
   - A: Because
   - B: had to
   - C: buying
   - D: and spending

IV. Each of the following readings is followed by several
questions. Choose the most appropriate answer to the
question and give your answer on the answer sheet.

It is strange how much time we spend studying the
events of the past, and how little preparation we make
for the future. It is true, of course, that we often
think about the future but most of these thoughts are
rather casual and fleeting. They hardly compare with the
systematic study of history which is found in most
schools. The educational theory is that after having
studied the past we shall be better able to anticipate
the future. The truth is, however, that too often we
leave the future to look after itself--or view it with
ill-disguised apprehension. The result is that we are
sometimes badly prepared for it when it arrives.

In the early days of the 1939-45 war, the British
Government decided that all the people should have
identity cards. In due course, every Briton was given a
numbered identity card which showed his name and address
but which did not include a photograph or thumbprint.

These cards were made of quite thick paper but were easily torn. They were issued free and no protective cover was given with them. This was a nuisance because each person was supposed to carry his identity card with him at all times, and the constant use soon damaged the card. Very quickly the average citizen looked round for some convenient wallet or plastic cover in which to carry his card.

He did not have to look very far. Almost before the cards were issued, hawkers were offering a variety of wallets for sale; leather, cloth and plastic covers appeared in the streets and shops overnight. For many weeks brisk business was done. Somebody had looked ahead--and made a small fortune as a result. A few shrewd men had realized that people would need covers for their identity cards and had started to manufacture them even before the cards were issued. The risk was small; the profit was large.

We can find many similar examples of this in history. The moral is always the same: the man who looks forward makes a profit; the man who looks backward stands still or makes a loss.

61. The main idea of the article is that (A. we should not study events of the past at the expense of making preparation for the future; B. only after we study the past carefully and systematically can we have a firm grasp of the future; C. it is sad to see the study of history neglected by the general public; D. the study of history should be casual and fleeting while the study of the future ought to be systematic).

62. We are sometimes badly prepared for the future because we (A. consider it only casually, thinking that it will take care of itself; B. view it with optimism and fortitude; C. try to confront it with lessons from the past; D. deal with it with insight and bravery).

63. The author uses the example of the identity card to tell us that (A. identity cards are important in modern society; B. an identity card should have a photograph and thumb-print of the bearer; C. each identity card should be protected by a cover; D. looking into the future is often beneficial).

64. By saying "the man who looks backward stands still," the author means that (A. We cannot hope to achieve progress only by reflecting on the past; B. The man who thinks only of the present will be shortsighted; C. The man who looks to the future will fall behind others; D. The man will become backward if he stands still).

65. Wallet makers made huge profit by (A. making a systematic study of history; B. learning the secret of the identity cards before they were issued; C. foreseeing that many people would need to protect their identity cards from damage, D. investing their small fortunes in buying stocks of war weapons).

The convention of Western art that often appears to be lacking in traditional Chinese landscape painting is the use of scientific perspective, that is, the principle that as objects recede in space they diminish in size. Instead, the idea of receding space is conveyed by arranging the near and far elements on different levels of the composition, moving from the bottom for the nearest objects to the top for the most distant objects, without necessarily diminishing the proportionate size of the distant objects. Thus a mountain in the background may be rendered in height as through it were being seen from a closer viewer, as long as its position extends to the top portion of the composition. A lake in the middle ground may reach as high toward sky at the top of the composition as the artist feels is necessary to convey its expanse, without regard to a conventional horizon line.

In this use of sectioned space on the flat surface of the paper, Chinese painting opens up endless vistas of soaring mountain ranges, plummeting waterfalls, verdant forests and meandering streams, where the observer is invited to wander rather than to note a specific point of view. Consistent with the underlying concepts of landscape painting, man's vulnerable and transitory position in nature's immensity is expressed by depicting human forms, dwellings, bridges, and boats as relatively small elements of the picture. The minuteness of human activity, in contrast to the grandeur of high mountains and cascading waterfalls, is said to contribute to perspective, as does the shrouding of mountains in vaporous clouds and mist.

66. By means of scientific perspective, Western painters render objects in their paintings to appear diminishing in size from (A. the bottom up to the top; B. the nearest to the farthest; C. the left to the right; D. the center to the four sides).

67. In Chinese paintings an object in the farthest background may be rendered as though it were seen from (A. the nearest place beneath the object; B. a place over the object; C. a place behind the object; D. its front).

68. The use of sectioned space tells us that Chinese land-
    scape paintings are (A. inferior to Western paintings
    for lack of scientific perspective; B. rendered from a
    fixed point of view; C. rendered from various points of
    view and therefore look ridiculous; D. are rendered
    from many changing viewpoints).

69. Chinese artists depict human forms as relatively small
    elements in a landscape painting, for they (A. think man
    is weak, tiny, and transitory in comparison with nature;
    B. look down upon man's position on earth; C. think man
    cannot be happy without nature; C. think that man can
    always control nature, however small he may be).

Radar is an electronic device that is used for the
detection and location of objects. It operates by transmit-
ting a particular type of wave-form, a pulse-modulated sine
wave for example, and detects the nature of the echo signal.
Radar is used to extend the capability of man's senses for
observing his environment, especially the sense of vision.
The value of radar lies not in being a substitute for the
eye, but in doing what the eye cannot do. Radar cannot
resolve detail as well as the eye, nor is it yet capable of
recognizing the "color" of objects to the degree of sophis-
tication of which the eye is capable. However, radar can be
designed to see through those conditions impervious to
normal human vision, such as darkness, haze, fog, rain, and
snow. In addition, radar has the advantage of being able to
measure the distance or range to the object. This is probably its most important attribute.

70. This passage tells a lot about radar, but it does not
    discuss (A. its limitations; B. its advantages; C. its
    future in military operations; D. its comparison with
    human vision).

71. According to the author, human vision (A. cannot recog-
    nize colors sometimes; B. cannot see beyond phenomena;
    C. suffers from optical illusions; D. cannot measure
    the distance of a faraway object correctly).

72. Which of the statements below is correct? (A. Radar can
    analyze differences among objects B. Radar can acceler
    ate the speed of a flying object. C. Radar can locate
    a distant object. D. Radar can evaluate a military
    operation).

73. The author thinks that (A. we should not trust our eyes
    so much as we trust radar; B. we should trust our eyes
    more than we trust radar; C. Radar and our eyes are
    equally functional in all situations; D. Radar and eyes
    can compensate for each other's weaknesses).

Laboratory fertilization, though, is just a first and indispensable step toward greater threats against mankind, the most formidable of which is cloning. It should not be necessary to reiterate the arguments against such an attack on human individuality, sexuality, and identity. The ability to make unlimited copies of any human reduces the uniqueness and sanctity of the individual. Apart from all the psychological complications of having an exact replica as a parent or child, the social benefits of this practice redound chiefly to the technocratic state. The state would have to decide which genotypes were most worthy of reproduction. This power is too great to invest in any human authority. It is power not merely over the immediate arrangements of human life but also over all future generations.

74. The purpose of this passage is (A. to encourage further experiment on laboratory fertilization; B. to argue in favor of laboratory fertilization; C. to attack the practice as unnecessary, dehumanizing, and generally harmful to present and future human existence; D. to show the necessity of maximizing the efficiency and reasonableness in the practice).

75. The author's viewpoint on this subject is essentially that of (A. a technologist; B. a moralist; C. an ecologist; D. a humanist).

76. The author argues that the power to decide which genotypes are most worthy of reproduction should be (A. given to technologists; B. taken away by an honest dictator; C. divided equally among government authorities; D. held by no human beings).

It does no good to fault Egypt or Malta or Greece for the death of 60 passengers in the storming of Egypt Air Flight 648. The responsibility for the carnage falls squarely on the terrorists. But to recognize that brings us no closer to understanding the mystery behind this chilling episode: Why did they do it? · · ·

What can be said in the wake of this butchery is that airport security is still insufficient and that all civilized nations, not just Egypt, need more effective countermeasures against aerial piracy. Greece insists that all bags and passengers were rigorously checked under a new procedure instituted at the Athens airport. It may well be that the weapons were already hidden on the aircraft, which came from Cairo. The obvious need is to check the planes before passengers board them.

There is a natural tendency at times of such cruelty to seek comfort in generalizations. Never negotiate, some say, forgetting that even Israel has in some circumstances found it wise to negotiate. Simplism plays into the hands of terrorism. All terrorist acts are unique, and few fixed rules can guide governments.

When at last resort governments use violence against terrorists, all need to improve their techniques to minimize casualties. Debating whether Egypt's commandos had to be called in is a matter of hindsight; evaluating their performance is preparation for the next time. Such operations should transcend concerns of national sovereignty. Foresight argues for a pooling of skills to provide the best help when terrorists strike with such hatred.

77. The author indicates that the terrorists' weapons might have been (A. hidden in the bags of some passengers; B. taken to the aircraft before the plane left Cairo; C. carried to the aircraft by Greek pilots; D. carried to the aircraft when the plane stopped over in Malta).

78. The author thinks that (A. it is necessary to debate the need of Egypt's storming the airplane; B. it is not necessary to evaluate the operations of the commandos; C. it does no good to cry over the death of 60 passengers ; D. a pooling of skills is necessary to counteract future terrorism).

79. Simplism plays into the hands of terrorism, for (A. terrorists are simple-hearted; B. terrorists can be pacified; C. terrorists can be coerced into inaction; D. terrorists' acts are not predictable).

80. Which of the statements below is correct? (A. The author does not think it wise to negotiate with aerial pirates; B. He presses Egypt and Greece to retaliate against the aerial piracies; C. He urges terrorists and Greece to avoid confrontations; D. He urges all the governments concerned to be more cooperative in fighting against aerial piracies).

V. Translation: The following questions consist of sentences followed by their translations (either into English or Chinese, as the case may be). Choose a letter that represents the best translation and write your choice on the answer sheet. 10%

81. 他當選主席了。
    A. He was selecting as the Chairman.
    B. He was pickled as Chairman.
    C. He was being selected the Chairman.
    D. He was elected Chairman.

82. He isn't likely to come.
    A. 他不想來。
    B. 他不喜歡來。
    C. 他可能不會來了。
    D. 他來了會不高興。

83. Many can bear adversity, but few contempt.
    A. 很多人能忍受逆境，但有些人輕蔑它。
    B. 人多了就能抵抗逆境，人少了就得承受輕蔑。
    C. 有些人能忍受各種的逆境，却只能忍受少許的輕蔑。
    D. 很多人能忍受逆境，但是很少人能忍受輕蔑。

84. 眞是沒想到會在這兒遇見你。
    A. I never expect to meet you here.
    B. I didn't expect to meet you here.
    C. I don't expect to meet you here.
    D. I won't expect to meet you here.

85. 我哥哥去年和珍妮結婚了。
    A. My brother married with Jane last year.
    B. My brother married Jane last year.
    C. My brother was married with Jane last year.
    D. My brother had marriage with Jane last year.

86. Tom will finish his homework in no time.
    A. 湯姆沒有時間做他的功課。
    B. 湯姆剛剛做完他的功課。
    C. 湯姆永遠不可能做完他的功課。
    D. 湯姆馬上就會做完他的功課。

87. Nothing less than that will satisfy him.
    A. 至少要那樣才能滿足他。
    B. 沒有任何東西能滿足他。
    C. 比那樣少一些就能滿足他。
    D. 就算沒有給他任何東西,他也滿足了。

88. 昨夜他喝太多而醉倒了。
    A. He had too many liquor last night.
    B. He had one cup too many last night.
    C. He drank too many wines and fell last night.
    D. He had had too many cups last night.

89. He was the last man I wanted to sit next to.

    A. 他是唯一我想坐在一起的人。B. 他是我最不想坐在一起的人。

    C. 他是最後一位我想坐在一起的人。

    D. 自從他死後，我再也不想和別人坐在一起了。

90. She looked me in the eyes.

    A. 她用眼睛看我。   B. 她盯著我看。

    C. 她的眼睛看起來像我。   D. 她只看著我的眼睛。

VI. Composition: Choose to do either (A) or (B) and write neatly on page 7 (i.e, the back cover, which is the last page). You may use the back of your question sheets for your draft. Write clearly and only on the lines. Do only one; if you do both, you will be graded on only your first one. 10%

(A) Write a brief paragraph in which you give two reasons for or against the construction of a fourth nuclear power plant in Taiwan. (If you cannot say yes or no on this subject, you may choose to do the next one on a young girl in love.)

    I support   effective solution
    I am opposed to   for... reasons
    with our technology   at the expense of
    meet the demand of   radiation contamination
    risk the danger   economic growth
    waste disposal   environmental pollution
    no other choice (or alternative)

(B) If you were Ann Landers, how would you give a brief answer to the young woman "In Dante's Inferno"? Read the following letter carefully before you write your letter. The following phrases are given to prompt your thinking. If you can use them effectively, you may gain some extra points, but you do not have to use them. If you do use any of them, however, underline them clearly as they appear in your writing.

    do not live in hell   devote (yourself) to
    go through the ordeal(or test)
    the end of the world   for a better tomorrow
    get involved in   will live through
    campus activities   blame...for...
    in the meantime   when the year is over
    will be better able to

☆ 研究所全真英文試題詳解——淡大

I. 字彙：20%

1. (**A**) **ignite** 〔 ɪg'naɪt 〕 v. 發火；著火

(B) illuminate 〔 ɪ'l(j)umə,net 〕 v. 照亮

(C) ignore 〔 ɪg'nor 〕 v. 忽視

(D) illustrate 〔 'ɪləstret , ɪ'lʌstret 〕 v. 舉例說明

spark plug "（內燃機的）火星塞"

2. (**B**) **pedestrian** 〔 pə'dɛstrɪən 〕 n. 行人

(A) pediatrician 〔 ,pidɪə'trɪʃən 〕 n. 小兒科醫生

(C) pedagogue 〔 'pɛdə,gɑg 〕 n. 教師（常含蔑視之意）

(D) peddler 〔 'pɛdlə 〕 n. 小販

3. (**C**) **testify** 〔 'tɛstə,faɪ 〕 v. 作證

(A) vivify 〔 'vɪvə,faɪ 〕 v. 使生動

(B) vex 〔 vɛks 〕 v. 使煩惱   (D) tax 〔 tæks 〕 v. 課以稅

4. (**A**) **detour** 〔 'ditʊr , dɪ'tʊr 〕 n. 繞道；改道

(B) deport 〔 dɪ'port 〕 v. 驅逐出境   (C) depose 〔 dɪ'poz 〕 v. 免職

(D) detract 〔 dɪ'trækt 〕 v. 減損；轉移

5. (**C**) **spouse** 〔 spauz 〕 n. 配偶

(A) spondee 〔 'spɑndi 〕 n. 〔詩〕揚揚格

(B) squire 〔 skwaɪr 〕 n. 鄉紳   (D) squid 〔 'skwɪd 〕 n. 烏賊；魷魚

6. (**A**) **domestic** 〔 də'mɛstɪk 〕 adj. 國內的；家務的

(B) dominical 〔 də'mɪnɪkḷ 〕 adj. 基督的；主的

(C) dormant 〔 'dɔrmənt 〕 adj. 睡眠狀態的

(D) doltish 〔 'dotɪʃ 〕 adj. 笨重的

7. (**D**) *drastic* 〔'dræstɪk〕 *adj.* 徹底的

    (A) token〔'tokən〕 *n.* 象徵

    (B) disastrous〔dɪz'æstrəs〕 *adj.* 招致不幸的

8. (**D**) *oxygen*〔'ɑkəsədʒən〕 *n.* 氧

    (A) oxide〔'ɑksaɪd〕 *n.* 氧化物

    (B) oxhide〔'ɑks,haɪd〕 *n.* 牛皮

    (C) oxyacid〔,ɑksɪ'æsɪd〕 *n.* 含氧酸

9. (**C**) *suspend*〔sə'spɛnd〕 *v.* 使懸浮（與 from 連用）

    (A) suspense〔sə'spɛns〕 *n.* 不確定狀況

    (B) swabble 無此字   (D) swash〔swɑʃ〕 *v.* 澎湃

        dome〔dom〕 *n.* 圓頂

10. (**C**) *valor*〔'vælɚ〕 *n.* 勇氣

    (A) valence〔'veləns〕 *n.* 原子價   (B) vale〔'veli〕 *n.* 分別

    (D) valance〔'væləns〕 *n.* 短帷幔

11. (**C**) *ventilation*〔,vɛntḷ'eʃən〕 *n.* 通風

    (A) veneration〔,vɛnə'reʃən〕 *n.* 欽佩

    (B) retaliation〔rɪ,tælɪ'eʃən〕 *n.* 報復

    (D) incrimination〔ɪn,krɪmə'neʃən〕 *n.* 控告

12. (**D**) *affluence*〔'æfluəns〕 *n.* 富裕

    (A) affray〔ə'fre〕 *n.* 滋擾   (B) afflux〔'æflʌks〕 *n.* 滙集

    (C) affliction〔ə'fɪkʃən〕 *n.* 痛苦

13. (**A**) *depreciation*〔dɪ,priʃɪ'eʃən〕 *n.* 貶值

    (B) devastation〔,dɛvəs'teʃən〕 *n.* 毀壞

    (C) detonation〔,dɛtə'neʃən〕 *n.* 爆炸

    (D) detraction〔dɪ'trækʃən〕 *n.* 誹謗

14. (**B**) **terroristic**〔,tɛrəˈrɪstɪk〕 *adj.* 恐怖主義的

    (A) terrorist〔ˈtɛrərɪst〕 *n.* 恐怖主義者

    (C) terrorialistic 無此字   (D) teristic 無此字

    Gadhafi "格達費"   maim〔mem〕 *v.* 使殘廢

15. (**D**) **contagious**〔kənˈtedʒəs〕 *adj.* 蔓延的；易感染的

    (A) contaminated〔kənˈtæmə,netɪd〕 *adj.* 被污染的

    (B) condoled〔kənˈdold〕 *adj.* 被同情的

    (C) condensed〔kənˈdɛnst〕 *adj.* 濃縮的

16. (**B**) **legible**〔ˈlɛdʒəbḷ〕 *adj.* 清楚的

    (A) edible〔ˈɛdəbḷ〕 *adj.* 可食的

    (C) eligible〔ˈɛlɪdʒəbḷ〕 *adj.* 合格的

    (D) legislative〔ˈlɛdʒɪs,letɪv〕 *adj.* 立法的

17. (**B**) **evasion**〔ɪˈveʒən〕 *n.* 逃避

    (C) evaporation〔ɪ,væpəˈreʃən〕 *n.* 蒸發

    (D) evacuation〔ɪ,vækjʊˈeʃən〕 *n.* 撤退

    do away with "免除"   tax evasion "逃稅"

18. (**C**) **exempt**〔ɪgˈzɛmpt〕 *v.* 使免除

    (A) exemplify〔ɪgˈzɛmplə,faɪ〕 *v.* 例證

    (D) exhale〔ɪgˈzel〕 *v.* 呼氣

    juvenile offender "少年犯"

19. (**C**) **subside**〔səbˈsaɪd〕 *v.* 平息

    (A) submit〔səbˈmɪt〕 *v.* 屈服

    (B) subsidize〔ˈsʌbsə,daɪz〕 *v.* 收買；津貼

    (D) subscribe〔səbˈskraɪb〕 *v.* 同意

    culprit〔ˈkʌlprɪt〕 *n.* 被告

20. (**D**) **extract** 〔 ɪkˈstrækt 〕 v. 拔取

　　(A) expatiate 〔 ɪkˈspeʃɪˌet 〕 v. 鋪陳

　　(B) expedite 〔 ˈɛkspɪˌdaɪt 〕 v. 速辦

　　(C) expatriate 〔 ɛksˈpetrɪˌet 〕 v. 放逐

Ⅱ. 文法與修辭

21. (**C**) **however**（然而；不過）在此當副詞性的連接詞用，與逗點並用，可置於句中或句尾。

　　(A) in fact（事實上），(B) since（從那時起），(D) otherwise（在其他方面），都不合句意。

22. (**A**) once "曾經"，指過去的事，用簡單過去式 belonged。

　　oak 〔 ok 〕 n. 橡樹　　dresser 〔 ˈdrɛsɚ 〕 n. 化妝臺

　　cherished 〔 ˈtʃɛrɪʃt 〕 adj. 珍愛的

　　possession 〔 pəˈzɛʃən 〕 n. 所有物（常用複數）

23. (**B**) 關係代名詞的所有格 whose，在此引導形容詞子句,修飾 groups，並在子句中修飾 purpose。

　　(A) who's , (C) that , (D) which 雖是關代，但無所有格的功用。

　　preserve 〔 prɪˈzɝv 〕 v. 保護　　site 〔 saɪt 〕 n. 位置；場所

24. (**C**) **extraordinary** 〔 ɪkˈstrɔrdn̩ˌɛrɪ , ˌɛkstrəˈɔr- 〕 adj. 特別的

　　both … and ～是對等連接詞，其所連接的字詞的文法作用應相同。因為 dramatic 是形容詞，故只能選 (C)。

　　stage 〔 stedʒ 〕 v. 上演

　　demonstration 〔 ˌdɛmənˈstreʃən 〕 n. 示威運動

　　dramatic 〔 drəˈmætɪk 〕 adj. 如戲劇的　　incite 〔 ɪnˈsaɪt 〕 v. 鼓動

25. (**A**) **it** 在此代替 Although it is … mountains 整個子句，以避免重覆。第一個 it 是指天氣。from which … mountains 則是補述用法的形容詞子句，補充說明 the lake。

　　inviting 〔 ɪnˈvaɪtɪŋ 〕 adj. 引人入勝的

26.(**B**) *as … as* ～（和～一樣…）
(C) the same 是形容詞，不可修飾 famous。

27.(**A**) *what the purpose of life is* 是間接問句，作 ask 的受詞，其
句中主詞和動詞的排列順序與敘述句相同。
occasionally〔əˈkeʒənḷɪ〕 *adv.* 有時

28.(**D**) *It is believed that* …（大家相信…）中，It 是指後面的 that
子句，用被動語態是為了作客觀的說明。
formation〔fɔrˈmeʃən〕 *n.* 構成；形成
planet〔ˈplænɪt〕 *n.* 行星
interstellar〔ˌɪntəˈstɛlə〕 *adj.* 星際的

29.(**C**) *open one's door to* "迎接"
the public "民衆；大衆"

30.(　) 本題無答案。(A)和(B)都缺少受詞；(C)昂貴的；犧牲很大的，不
合句意；(D)為名詞子句不合文法。

31.(**C**) *interested in* … 是由形容詞子句 that is interested in … 簡
化而來的分詞片語，修飾 Anyone。
organization〔ˌɔrgənəˈzeʃən, -aɪˈze-〕 *n.* 組織

32.(**A**) *do damage to* "使…受到損害"

33.(**D**) even though（即使）引導副詞子句修飾 leave，表讓步。且 *be
able to ＋ V*，不可用 *be able ＋ V-ing*。

34.(**B**) liberal 作名詞時，常表示「自由黨員」；作形容詞是「自由主
義的」，故選 liberal voters「自由主義的選民」較恰當。

35.(**B**) That 引導一個名詞子句，作句子的主詞。
beaver〔ˈbivə〕 *n.* 海狸；海獺

36. (**D**)　The rate of evaporation 作此句之主詞。
　　　　　　　evaporation〔ɪ'væpə'reʃən〕*n.* 蒸發
　　　　　　　saturation〔,sætʃə'reʃən〕*n.* 飽和

37. (**C**)　stopped in front of the building, got out of the car 和
　　　　　　　leaving my things in the back 的主詞都是 I，其中 leav-
　　　　　　　ing … back 是分詞構句，意思等於 and left … back。

38. (**A**)　to learn about … environment 是表目的的副詞片語，修飾
　　　　　　　read。(A) for the sake of 表原因，在此不合句意。
　　　　　　　ecology〔ɪ'kɑlədʒɪ〕*n.* 生態學

39. (**B**)　***with*** the advent … war（隨著第一次世界大戰的來臨）
　　　　　　　advent〔'ædvɛnt〕*n.* 來臨

40. (**A**)　前面的分詞構句意義上主詞是 the Today show，所以主要子句
　　　　　　　要以 the Today show 作主詞。

Ⅲ. 挑錯題

41. (**D**)　*the same as* → ***as well as***　　as well as " 和 " 連接 their
　　　　　　　utility … care 與 their attractive appearance，作 for 的受
　　　　　　　詞。the same as 是 " 與…同類的 " 不合句意。

42. (**C**)　*are based* → ***is based***　　主詞是 the metric system, 故用單
　　　　　　　數動詞。

43. (**C**)　*work* → ***works***　　one of 的後面要接可數複數名詞。

44. (**B**)　*six* → ***sixth***　　第六應用序數 the sixth。

45. (**D**)　*any another* → ***any other***

46. (**B**)　*years ago* → ***years***

47. (**C**)　*more quicker* → ***more quickly***　　修飾動詞 dry 應用副詞 quickly,
　　　　　　　比較級是 more quickly。

48. (**C**) *working hardly* → **working hard**   hard 本身是副詞，hardly 則指「幾乎不～」。

49. (**C**) *at dedication* → **in dedication**

50. (**A**) *made* → **did**   做功課要用動詞 do。

51. (**C**) *varied* → **varies**   此句陳述事實，故用現在式。

52. (**A**) *amount* → **number**   species 是可數名詞，要用 number 表示，不可用 amount。

53. (**A**) *thing that matters* → **things that matter**   one of 之後須接可數複數名詞。

54. (**C**) *when* → **where**   先行詞是 parks，故用關係副詞 where。

55. (**D**) *he began* → **did he begin**   以 only 為句首的句子，其主要子句須倒裝。

56. (**B**) *to* → **of**   be characteristic of "具有～特性的"。

57. (**C**) *that* → **whether**   whether … or ～ "是…抑或～"。

58. (**A**) *will take* → **should take**   insist 之後須接假設用法的子句：that … should + V…，其中 should 可省略。

59. (**C**) *they dry them* → **dried**   and 連接三個動詞；gathered，dipped, dried 共用前面的 is。

60. (**A**) *Because* → **Because of**   because of 接名詞，because 接子句，his limited resources 是名詞片語，故應用 because of。

Ⅳ. 閱讀測驗

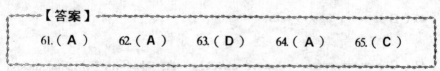

【答案】

61. (**A**)   62. (**A**)   63. (**D**)   64. (**A**)   65. (**C**)

【註】

anticipate〔æn'tɪsə,pet〕v. 預期

apprehension〔,æprɪ'hɛnʃən〕n. 明瞭；了解

in due course "終於；在適當的時候"

nuisance〔'njusn̩s〕n. 討厭的人或物

hawker〔'hɔkɚ〕n. 沿街叫賣的小販

brisk〔brɪsk〕adj. 興隆的；迅速的　　shrewd〔ʃrud〕adj. 精明的

【答案】

66.（ **B** ）　　67.（ **A** ）　　68.（ **D** ）　　69.（ **A** ）

【註】

landscape painting "山水畫"

perspective〔pɚ'spɛktɪv〕n. 透視　　recede〔rɪ'sid〕v. 縮小

vista〔'vɪstə〕n. 回想；展望　　soaring〔'sorɪŋ〕adj. 遠大的

plummeting〔'plʌmɪtɪŋ〕adj. 垂直落下的

verdant〔'vɝdn̩t〕adj. 青翠的

meandering〔mɪ'ændɚɪŋ〕adj. 蜿蜒而流的

vulnerable〔'vʌlnərəbl̩〕adj. 脆弱的

transitory〔'trænsə,torɪ〕adj. 短暫的

immensity〔ɪ'mɛnsətɪ〕n. 無際　　depict〔dɪ'pɪkt〕v. 描寫

minuteness〔mə'njutnɪs〕n. 細微　　grandeur.〔'grændʒɚ〕n. 偉大

cascading〔kæs'kedɪŋ〕adj. 像瀑布般落下的

shrouding〔'ʃraʊdɪŋ〕adj. 隱藏的

【答案】

70.（ **C** ）　　71.（ **D** ）　　72.（ **C** ）　　73.（ **D** ）

【註】

detection〔dɪ'tɛkʃən〕n. 偵察　　sine〔saɪn〕n. 正弦

substitute〔'sʌbstə,tjut〕 *n.* 代替物　　resolve〔rɪ'zɑlv〕 *v.* 分辨
sophistication〔sə,fɪstɪ'keʃən〕 *n.* 不純之混合物
impervious〔ɪm'pɜvɪəs〕 *adj.* 不能透過的
attribute〔'ætrə,bjut〕 *n.* 性質；屬性

【答案】

74.（ C ）　　　75.（ D ）　　　76.（ D ）

【註】

fertilization〔,fɜtlə'zeʃən〕 *n.* 受精作用
indispensable〔,ɪndɪs'pɛnsəbḷ〕 *adj.* 不可避免的
cloning〔'klonɪŋ〕 *n.* 由無性生殖之繁殖
reiterate〔ri'ɪtə,ret〕 *v.* 重述　　sanctity〔'sæŋktətɪ〕 *n.* 神聖
replica〔'rɛplɪkə〕 *n.* 複製　　redound〔rɪ'daʊnd〕 *v.* 有助於
technocratic〔tɛknə'krætɪk〕 *adj.* 主張技術專家政治的
genotype〔'dʒɛno,taɪp〕 *n.* 遺傳型；因子型

【答案】

77.（ B ）　　78.（ D ）　　79.（ D ）　　80.（ D ）

【註】

carnage〔'kɑrnɪdʒ〕 *n.* 大屠殺；殘殺
in the wake of "跟隨；隨…之後"
countermeasure〔'kaʊntə,mɛʒə〕 *n.* 對策
rigorously〔'rɪgərəslɪ〕 *adv.* 嚴密地
negotiate〔nɪ'goʃɪ,et〕 *v.* 談判；磋商
resort〔rɪ'zɔrt〕 *n.* 手段　　commando〔kə'mando〕 *n.* 突擊
hindsight〔'haɪnd,saɪt〕 *n.* 後見之明
pooling〔'pulɪŋ〕 *n.* 聯營；共同合作

V. 翻譯

81. (**D**) (A) 應作 He was selected as the Chairman.
　　(B) pickle 作「醃菜、肉」解，句意不對。
　　(C) 同(A)。
　　(D) elect 作「選舉」解，Chairman 是補語。

82. (**C**) *be likely to＋V* "可能…"

83. (**D**) few 指「很少」，contempt 是名詞，作「輕蔑」解，故原句
　　即指 Many can bear adversity, but few can bear contempt。

84. (**B**) never 強調「從沒有；眞是沒有」，較合句意。

85. (**B**) marry 作「與…結婚」解，是及物動詞，不須接介詞，故A與
　　B結婚是A marry B，而marriage 是名詞，指結婚狀態或婚禮。

86. (**D**) *in no time* "立卽；馬上"

87. (**A**) less than that 是形容詞片語，修飾 nothing，作「比那個少」
　　解，故全句是說「比那個少的東西沒有一樣能滿足他」，卽「至
　　少要那樣才能滿足他」。

88. (**B**) *have one cup too many* "喝醉酒"

89. (**B**) *the last* "最不願…的"

90. (**B**) *look sb. in the eyes* "盯著某人"

VI. 作文

　　I am opposed to the construction of a fourth nuclear power
plant in Taiwan for two reasons. ***The first reason concerns*** the
disposal of nuclear waste. Nuclear energy can be transformed
into electricity, but the waste of nuclear fusion and fission is
hard to dispose of. We already have three nuclear power plants
here, and the problem of waste disposal is really a headache for

the authorities concerned. ***Unlike garbage***, nuclear waste, with its harmful reaction, will cause serious pollution and even ecocide if not properly disposed of. ***Furthermore***, Taiwan is too small an island to find more places for waste disposal. ***Therefore***, we shouldn't construct another nuclear power plant, at the expense of our health, for further economic growth, which can be achieved through other channels.

The second reason is that a nuclear power plant itself is dangerous. Take the Soviet nuclear power plant in Chernobyl for example. Its nuclear reactor exploded only recently, and resulted in thousands of deaths. The radiation it radiated influenced almost the whole of the Northern Hemisphere, and the side effects caused by the radiation will last for around forty years.

We can, therefore, see how terrible a nuclear power plant is if anything goes wrong with it！Building a nuclear power plant is just like installing explosives around us. ***So*** despite the guarantees given by those "experts," we cannot run the risk of losing our lives and endangering our descendants. ***For these two reasons***, I object to the construction of a fourth nuclear power plant in Taiwan.

　　基於兩個理由，我反對在台灣建立核四廠。第一個理由是關於核子廢料的處理。核能可以轉換成電，但是原子核融合和分裂的廢料很難處理。我們在此地已有了三個核能發電廠，而核能廢料的問題確實令有關當局頭痛。核能廢料不同於垃圾，而具有有害的反應。它會引起嚴重的污染，假如處理不當，甚至會破壞生態。再者，在台灣這麼一個小島，已無法再找更多的場所來處理廢料。所以我們不該為了進一步的經濟成長，犧牲我們的健康再建造一個核能發電廠，經濟成長是可以透過其他管道來達成的。

　　第二個理由是，核能發電廠本身就是很危險的。拿蘇聯的徹諾堡發電廠做例子吧！這個核子反應爐最近爆炸，導致數千人死亡。它所放射出來的輻射線幾乎影響了整個北半球，而且輻射線的副作用會持續約四十年之久。

　　所以我們可以知道萬一出了一點差錯，核能電廠會是多可怕！建造核能發電廠就像在我們四周安置炸彈。儘管有「專家」保證，我們也不能冒喪失生命和危害子孫的風險。基於這兩個理由，我反對在台灣建核四廠。

附 錄▶研究所英文準備要點

●Graduate

研究所翻譯
拿分要訣

1
翻譯的原則

東、西方語言結構、習慣用法迥然不同，使得中英對譯成為一項吃力的工作。譯者不但要精通英文，對於母語——中文更不能稍有疏忽。須記得，翻譯的最高境界就是絲毫看不出另一種語言痕跡，純粹、道地的中文或英文，亦即「儘可能按照中（英）文的習慣，忠實表達原文的意義」。

所以有人訂出「信、雅、達」三個標準。也有人將其改為「忠實、通順、美」或者「形似、意似、神似」的，說法雖然不同，主張卻是一樣。

以下摘錄學者專家所提出的「翻譯要點」，作為翻譯者的參考，應有很大的助益。

(1) 翻譯切不可不守紀律、沒有尺寸或亂添亂減。（雙關語、俏皮話等的確不可翻者例外）

(2) 切不可譯字，要譯意、譯情、譯氣勢、譯作者用心處。

(3) 切不可抱定一個英文字只有一個中文解釋的觀念，定要勤查字典。

(4) 翻譯不可僅參考一兩本英漢字典，多查幾本好的英文字典才是上策。

(5) 譯完的文稿必須再逐字逐句校過，切不可以為已經十全十美。

(6) 不懂的題材，不可輕易動手翻譯，一定要詢問專家或查過百科全書。

(7) 沒有絕對把握的中文成語不要亂用。

2 中翻英、英翻中的方法

(1) 省譯法：

翻譯貴在簡潔。中文和英文由於在文法結構上時有差異，因此無論英譯中或中譯英都無法逐字對譯。有時，在英文中是必要的字詞，在中文裏必需省略；有時中文裏不可缺的部份，譯成英文卻又變成贅言。因此，懂得如何省略；能用最少的字眼表達出原句的全義，是翻譯的一大原則。

大致而言，英文中的代名詞、冠詞、連接詞和介系詞譯成中文常可省略；而在中文中重覆使用的單字或片語，譯成英文卻可因前後語法相同而加以省略。以下舉例說明：（括弧中的字詞表示省略）

例 1. She covered **her** face with **her** hand as if to protect **her** eyes.
　　她用（她的）手蒙著（她的）臉，好像要保護（她的）眼睛。

例 2. **The** earth is round.
　　（這）地球是圓的。

例 3. Five minutes more, **and** all would be over.
　　再過五分鐘，（而）一切都將結束。

例 4. Smoking is prohibited **in** the classroom.
　　（在）教室裏禁止抽煙。

例 5. **It** is never too late to mend.
　　改過永不嫌遲。

例 6. 我屬於你，你屬於我。
　　I belong to you, and you (belong) to me.

(2) 增譯法：

就如同常常要注意「省略」的技巧一樣，翻譯時也要經常注意譯文是否有語意不全的情況產生。如此一來，「增譯」的工夫就不可或缺了。增譯有兩個目的：**第一**是爲求譯文合乎文法而必須添加字詞；**第二**是爲讓讀者能夠充分了解原文的意思而添加的詞語。當然，譯者絕不可憑一己之猜測、或隨興之所至地任意增譯，否則不但不能使譯文增色，反而很可能會扭曲原文的意義。這樣不但對原著者不公平，對譯文讀者也會產生誤導。以下舉例說明：（畫底線的字表示需要增譯的部份。）

例 1. I am looking forward to the holidays.

我在<u>等待</u>假期的到來。

例 2. 恐怕要下雨了。

<u>I am</u> afraid <u>it is</u> going to rain.

例 3. Courage in excess becomes foolhardiness, affection weakness, thrift avarice.

勇敢過度，即成蠻勇；感情<u>過度</u>，<u>即成</u>溺愛；節儉過度，<u>即成</u>貪婪。

例 4. 子曰：「學而時習之，不亦樂亦？」

The master said, "How pleasant it is to learn and practice constantly <u>what one has learned</u>."

(3) 轉譯法：

英文句子中，除非有 and, but, or 等對等連接詞來連接動詞，否則一定只有一個本動詞。而中文裏卻可以把幾個動詞連綴在一起而不需任何連接詞，例如：我 " 要 " " 去 " " 釣魚 "。寫成英文變成：I want to go fishing. 只有 " want " 一字為本動詞， "to go" 為不定詞， " fishing" 則為動名詞。由此可見，中英翻譯是不可能逐字對譯的。原文的名詞翻成譯文有時會變成動詞、形容詞或副詞；形容詞可能需要翻成副詞；而形容詞或分詞也有時會譯成名詞。以下舉例說明：

例 1. His *drawings* of children are exceptionally good.

他畫小孩畫得特別好。

例 2. They made *careful observation* on the way.

他們一路仔細觀察。

例 3. 有才幹的人往往很謙虛。

A man *of talent* is usually very modest.

例 4. 他覺得這個問題<u>難以</u>解決。

He found ***difficulty*** in solving this problem.

例 5. All the ***wounded*** were sent to the hospital right away.

所有<u>傷者</u>立即被送入醫院。

例 6. He walked ***round*** the house.

他 <u>繞屋</u>而行。

(4) 倒譯法：

倒譯法的產生是由於中英文的字詞順序（word order）不同而來的。字詞順序相異，甚或相反，是中英文最大的不同點之一。例如英文的副詞大部份都擺在句尾，而中文卻擺在句首；英文限定用法的形容詞子句放在所修飾名詞的後面，翻成中文則要搬到名詞之前；中文地址是由國、省、市，一直寫到幾號幾樓，英文卻是完全相反等等…。諸如此類，如果翻譯不小心，就會翻出一些滑稽，甚至不知所云的句子來。因此，注意兩國文字中不同的字詞順序，也是中英翻譯中的一大課題。以下舉例說明：

例 1. He drinks half a bottle of wine ***with each of his meals***.

他<u>每餐</u>都喝半瓶酒。

例 2. The Chinese-English dictionary ***that I bought yesterday*** is very useful for composition.

<u>我昨天買的</u>那本漢英字典對作文很有用處。

例 3. I shall leave ***her*** a note.

我要留個便條<u>給她</u>。

例 4. 我們<u>每天</u>在<u>教室裏用功讀書</u>。

　　　(1)　　(2)　　　(3)

We ***study hard in the classroom every day***.

　　　(3)　　　　　(2)　　　　　(1)

例 5. ***What do you mean*** by reading my letters without my permission?

你未經我同意就看我的信，<u>究竟是什麼意思</u>?

(5) 改譯法：

　　改譯法的目的在於使譯文通暢易讀，而不致於生硬彆扭，因此也是翻譯中一項不可缺的技巧。舉例而言，英文中被動語態 (passive voice) 佔了不少的份量，而在中文裏卻較少使用。又如原文中肯定句到了譯文可能需要改為否定句，而原來的否定句卻又可能非譯成肯定句不可了。如英文中 "too … to …" 的句型就是個極佳的範例：" She is *too* short *to* reach the box on the shelf." 要譯成「她太矮了，以致於拿不到架子上的盒子」；相反地，" She is *too* beautiful *not to* be noticed." 卻要譯成「她太美麗了，所以一定會受矚目。」以下再舉數例：

例1. I *had my hair cut* yesterday.

　　　我昨天去<u>剪頭髮</u>了。

例2. *It is unbearable for him* to work ten hours a day.

　　　<u>他受不了</u>一天工作十小時。

例3. We did *not* go home *till* midnight.

　　　我們<u>直到午夜才</u>回家。

例4. *Machinery* has made the products of factories very much cheaper than formerly.

　　　<u>由於機器的緣故</u>，工廠產品比以前便宜了許多。

3
英文長句的譯法

　　和英文比起來，中文是非常簡潔的文字。因此，一個英文長句翻成中文，可能會變成好幾句，或是必需多用幾個標點符號。尤其十九世紀以前的英文中，數十個字的句子比比皆是；譯到這些長句時，一定要將句子完全融會貫通，再從適當的地方加以斷句，這樣才能使譯文流暢易懂。以下舉五種長句的譯法爲例。

(1) 在關係子句處斷開

例1.　The reader of this celebrated treatise may admire the sleuthhound-like sagacity and tenacity with **which** the writer follows the devious tracks of his adversaries.

　　讀這篇著名論述的人都會欽佩作者警犬一般的精明與堅毅。就是憑著這些特質，他才能追踪敵人曲折的路徑。（在關係代名詞處切斷。）

(2) 在副詞處斷開：

例2.　This phenomenon is generally existing in every nation, political party and government, including the United Nations, **especially** manifestly in the ruling groups and intellectuals of each state.

　　這種現象普遍存在於每個國家、政黨及政府，包括聯合國在內。在各國統治階層及知識份子中尤爲顯著。

(3) 在動詞處斷開：

例3.　Simpson, in his agitation at the discovery that the stock of half-penny stamps was also exhausted, **dropped** his letter face downwards on the pavement, from **where** he retrieved it with the addition of a large blot of mud.

　　由於發現連半便士的郵票存貨也都已用罄，辛普森激動不已。於是他把信封面朝下地掉在人行道上。等他再撿起來時，信封上已多了一大塊爛泥。（第一個斷句在動詞處；第二個斷句則在關係副詞處，屬於前文所提的第一類斷句法。）

⑷ 在名詞或名詞子句處斷開：

例4. This play is the most titanic of the tragedies, *a huge* , shattering almost superhuman play *whose* very shapelessness is part of its strength.

這齣劇是所有悲劇中最磅礴的。此劇規模宏大，震撼人心，且超乎尋常。它鬆散的結構也正是造成其氣勢的部分原因。（第一個斷句處在兩個名詞之間；第二個斷句則在關係代名詞處，亦屬於第一類的斷句法。）

例5. He indicated to me that he would not want to stay too long in Singapore as he was in his mid-forties *and that* his purpose of remaining in this university was because he could find the time to do his own research.

他對我說，因為他已經四十五、六歲了，所以不想在新加坡待太久。他又說，他留在這個大學的目的，在於他可以找到時間做自己的研究。（斷句處在兩個名詞子句之間。）

⑸ 在連接詞處斷開：

例6. *King Lear* is as unreasoning as a storm, but with all a storm's strength and magnificence, *and* if Shakespeare had written nothing but *King Lear*, he would still rank as one of the world's greatest playwrights.

「李爾王」這部悲劇就如暴雨般地無理性，但也充滿了暴風雨般的氣勢和宏偉。即便莎士比亞除了「李爾王」以外什麼都沒寫，他仍會被列為世界上最偉大的劇作家之一。

4
翻譯實例練習

(1)中譯英：

1. 他因在這次戰役中的功績而被提升爲上校．

Because of his meritorious service in the battle he was promoted *the colonel*．（誤）

Because of his meritorious service in the battle he was promoted **colonel** 〔 **to the rank of colonel** 〕．（正）

2. 只要我們堅持工作，我們一定會贏得勝利．

So long as we keep on working we *must* win in the end.（誤）

So long as we keep on working we **will surely** win in the end．（正）

So long as we keep on working we **are sure to** win in the end．（正）

3. 新房子和舊房子式樣不同．

The style of the new building is different from the old building．（誤）

The style of the new building is different from **that of** the old building．（正）

＊本句在比較兩棟房子的式樣。第一句所比的却是" the style of the new building"和" the old building "，所以不通。第二句中的 that爲代名詞，指的就是 the style 。

4. 中國人爲了反對日本侵略者，堅持抗戰八年．

Chinese people resisted eight years for **opposing to** the Japanese aggressor．（誤）

The Chinese people resisted eight years *in opposition to* the Japanese agressor．（正）

5. 我們雖然遭受嚴重的自然災害，但一定能克服困難．

Though we *are suffered from* serious natural calamities,we

are sure to overcome all difficulties. （誤）

Though we *suffer from* serious natural calamities, we are sure to overcome all difficulties. （正）

6. 這新建的水庫的儲水量是那個舊的水庫的十倍。

This new-constructed reservoir holds *10 times water as much as* the old one. （誤）

This *newly*-constructed reservoir holds *10 times as much water as* the old one. （正）

7. 我們對計畫作了一些修改，目的在於改進工作。

We made some changes to our plan with a view to *improve* our work. （誤）

We made some changes in our plan with a view to *improving* our work. （正）

8. 這部新出版的小說已經售完，他大失所望。

To his great disappointment *that* every copy of this newly-published novel has been sold out. （誤）

To his great disappointment, every copy of this newly-published novel has been sold out. （正）

＊第一句中缺獨立之主要字句，文法不對。

9. 醫生將給他動手術。

The doctor will make an operation *to him*. （誤）

The doctor will perform an operation *on him*. （正）

10. 在美國黑人遭到歧視。

In America African-Americans *are discriminated*. （誤）

In America African-Americans *are discriminated against*. （正）

11. 外國代表在發言中，盛讚中國球員參加比賽所表現的友誼態度。

In the foreign delegates' speeches they paid great tribute to the friendly attitude shown by the Chinese sportsmen at the sports meeting. （誤）

In their speeches the foreign delegates paid great tribute to the friendly attitude shown by the Chinese sportsmen at the sports meeting. （正）

* 第一句中，代名詞 " they " 為主詞，但在前後文中，看不出所指為何，因此與中文文意不符。

12. 抗日戰爭是在1937年爆發的．

The Anti-Japanese War *was broken out* in 1937 . （誤）

The Anti-Japanese War *broke out* in 1937 . （正）

13. 中國人民已經擺脫帝國主義的壓迫．

The Chinese people *have broken away* from imperialist op-pression. （誤）

The Chinese people *have been broken away* from imperialist oppression. （正）

14. 他變得很多，我幾乎認不得他．

He has changed so much that I *almost cannot* recognize him.
（誤）

He has changed so much that I can *hardly* 〔 *scarcely* 〕 rec-ognize him. （正）

* almost 應放在 can 之後，但 can almost not 不如 can hardly 〔scarcely〕常用。

15. 這幅水彩畫比那幅油畫更吸引觀衆．

This painting in watercolor has a stronger appeal for the visitors than that one in *oil* . （誤）

This painting in watercolor has a stronger appeal for the visitors than that one in *oils* (= oil paints). （正）

16. 這座大樓是李先生設計的，不是張先生設計的．

This building was designed by Mr. Li *instead of* Mr. Chang.
（誤）

This building was designed by Mr. Li, *not by* Mr. Chang.
（正）

17. 他甚至還以為自己是一個偉大的科學家.

He even went so far as to *think himself as* a great scientist.
（誤）

He even went so far as to **think himself** a great scientist.
（正）

18. 你以為哪一本小說最有趣？

Do you think which novel is the most interesting？（誤）
Which novel do you think is the most interesting？（正）
＊ do you think是插入語，應置於疑問詞which novel 之後。

19. 他就職不久，就著手對他的部門作一系列的改革.

Right after he *took his office*, he started a series of reforms in his department.（誤）
Right after he **took office**, he started a series of reforms in his department.（正）

20. 該新政府窮於應付人民愈來愈強烈的不滿情緒.

New government has a hard time contending to the growing dissatisfaction of *their* people.（誤）
The new government has a hard time contending with the growing dissatisfaction of *its* people.（正）

21. 我們不可隨地吐痰.

We must not spit *everywhere*.（誤）
We must not spit **anywhere**.（正）

＊第一句之意為“We may spit somewhere.”因此意義有誤。一般而言，“some ”或“every ”之類的字眼用於肯定直述句，“any ”則用於否定及疑問句。

22. 我們大家都不感到累，因為我們是輪流值班的.

None of us felt tired, as we *took a turn* at keeping watch.
（誤）

None of us felt tired, as we ***took turns*** at keeping watch.
（正）

23. 沒有週密的調查研究，我們不能作出任何結論．

We cannot ***make*** any conclusion without careful investigation.
（誤）

We cannot ***come*** to any conclusion without careful investigation. （正）

24. 所有出席的人都批評他不應該這樣魯莽．

All present criticized him ***that he should not act so rashly.***
（誤）

All present criticized him ***for his rashness***. （正）

* " criticize"之後不可接名詞子句，要用 criticize ～ for…的形式。

25. 約翰容易感冒．

John is ***easy*** to catch cold. （誤）

John catches cold ***easily***. （正）

John is ***liable*** to colds 〔 to catch cold 〕. （正）

John is ***subject*** to colds. （正）

26. 他問我出了什麼事．

He asked what was wrong with me ? （誤）

He asked me, " What's wrong with you " ? （誤）

He asked what was wrong with me. （正）

* 此句之主要子句並非問句，受詞子句才是問句，因此第一句中問號要改成句點。此外，英文的標點用法中，逗點、句點、問號、驚嘆號等要放在引號之內，故第二句之標點錯誤。

27. 不論武裝干涉或戰爭威脅，都不能使他們屈服．

No matter armed intervention ***or*** threat of war can cow them into submission. （誤）

Neither armed intervention ***nor*** threat of war can cow them into submission. （正）

28. 你願意和我在公園中蹓躂一會兒嗎？

Do you *mind to take* a stroll in the park with me？（誤）

Do you *care to take* a stroll in the park with me？（正）

Do you *care for* a stroll in the park with me？（正）

29. 這孩子痛改前非，他的父母非常高興.

The boy has turned *to* a new leaf and his parents are very *pleasant*.（誤）

The boy has turned *over* a new leaf and his parents are very *pleased*.（正）

30. 在這場友誼比賽中，我們能戰勝二班.

We can *win* Class Two in the friendly match.（誤）

We can *win over* Class Two in the friendly match.（誤）

We can *win* the friendly match *with* Class Two.（正）

　＊“win”當不及物動詞是「贏」、「勝利」之意；當及物動詞則是「打勝」（比賽、戰爭等）。「打敗某人」不可用“win someone”而要用“beat someone”或“defeat someone”。

31. 會議在進行時，任何人都不得入內.

Anyone is *not* admitted while the meeting is in progress.

（誤）

No one is admitted while the meeting is in progress.（正）

(2)英譯中：

1. He lives what he teaches.

他以教書爲生。（誤）

他以身作則。（正）

2. I am going to take a leaf out of your book to devote myself to studying.

我要從你書上撕下一頁專心唸。（誤）

我要以你爲榜樣專心唸書。（正）

3. Many can bear adversity, but few contempt.

很多人能夠忍受逆境，但是很少人瞧不起它。（誤）

很多人不能忍受逆境，有少數人瞧不起它。（誤）

很多人能忍受逆境，但是很少人能忍受輕蔑。（正）

＊本句爲省略句，完整的句子爲：Many people can bear adversity, but few people can bear contempt.

4. Homekeeping youth have ever homely wits.

守在家裏的青年總有家常的機智。（誤）

足不出國門的年輕人，常是心智平庸的。（正）

老是待在國內的年輕人，總是頭腦呆板的。（正）

5. That incident made his hair stand on end.

那件事使他栽了跟斗。（誤）

那件事使他怒髮衝冠。（誤）

那件事使他毛骨悚然。（正）

6. I never persuaded him to do it.

我從未勸過他做那種事。（誤）

我勸他做這件事，總是勸不成功。（正）

＊ " persuade " 爲「說服」、「勸成」之意。若是「勸」，則應用 " try to persuade " 或 " advise " 。

7. Time hangs heavy on his hands.

他忙得不可開交。（誤）

時間慢得使他難以度過。（正）

8. I helped tide you over the difficulty but it laid you under no obligation.

我幫你渡過難關，但你沒有義務。（誤）

我幫你戰勝困難，但沒留下義務讓你完成。（誤）

我幫助你渡過難關，但你不必感激我。（正）

9. This will go a long way in overcoming the difficulty.
　　在克服困難上要走很遠的路。（誤）
　　這在突破難關時是很有幫助的。（正）
　　* go a long〔 good 〕way　"有幫助"

10. Better not be at all than not be noble.
　　與其不能高尚，不如完全不要。（誤）
　　與其忍辱偷生，不如光榮而死。（正）
　　寧爲玉碎，不爲瓦全。（正）

11. The orders are not followed to the letter.
　　命令未照函示進行。（誤）
　　命令未徹底遵循。（正）

12. Dr. Chen and my father are on a first name basis.
　　陳博士和我父親都是在第一名的基礎上。（誤）
　　陳博士和我父親在原則上都有第一名的希望。（誤）
　　陳博士和我父親很熟，都直呼名字。（正）
　　* on a first name basis　"（關係很熟）直呼名字"

13. They are on speaking terms with each other.
　　他們正在談判條約。（誤）
　　他們只是見面打招呼的交情。（正）
　　* terms爲「交情」、「關係」之意，永遠爲複數形。be on good
　　〔 bad 〕terms with…的意思爲「與……要好（不要好）」。

14. Let us be happy and live within our means.
　　讓我們高高興興的並以我們自己的方式生活。（誤）
　　讓我們高高興興的以我們自己的方法做事。（誤）
　　讓我們快快樂樂過著量入爲出的生活。（正）

15. It is the man behind the gun that tells.
　　話說的是在大砲後面的人。（誤）
　　勝敗在人而不在武器。（正）

　　* 此處的 tell 是「命中」、「奏功」之意。

16. You must have your head screwed on the right way.

　　你必須埋首苦讀。（誤）

　　你必須通達事理。（正）

17. He must needs talk to her when she does not care to talk.

　　不管她願意與否，他始終纏住她談個不停。（誤）

　　他偏偏在她不高興時同她談話。（正）

18. Most people have a daily fight to keep the wolf from the door.

　　許多人每天都在奮鬥，以免引狼入室。（誤）

　　許多人每天都在與飢餓奮鬥。（正）

　　* wolf 象徵飢餓。

19. With country people time is of no moment.

　　跟鄉下人在一塊玩，時間並不重要。（誤）

　　鄉下人不重視時間。（正）

　　* with country people 是「在鄉下人眼中」。此處 moment 為「重要」之意（＝ importance ）。

20. He is a sad apology for a teacher.

　　他傷心地向老師道歉。（誤）

　　他當教員只是濫竽充數。（正）

　　* *be a sad* 〔 sorry 〕 *apology for*… “是……的勉強替代物”

21. All my advice falls flat on him.

　　我的忠言使他平地跌倒。（誤）

　　他失敗之後才想起我的忠告。（誤）

　　他把我的忠言當作耳邊風。（正）

22. The student is in high favor with his teacher.

　　學生非常喜歡這老師。（誤）

　　老師很寵愛這學生。（正）

23. He may be drowned for all I care.

   不顧我怎樣當心，他或許仍然會溺死的。(誤)

   他也許會溺死，但不關我的事。(正)

   * for all I care 意爲「不關我的事」、「我不管」。

24. It is not to be had for love or money.

   愛情與金錢不可兼得。(誤)

   無論出任何代價也得不到它。(正)

25. Those students absented themselves from the sitting for Wednesday's examination.

   爲了星期三的考試，這些學生從座位上開溜了。(誤)

   星期三的考試，這些學生缺考。(正)

   * *sit (down) for an exam* " 參加考試"。

26. If he had never done much good in the world he had never
   done much harm.

   假如他沒有在世界上做過很多好事，那是因爲他沒有做過太多傷天
   理的事。(誤)

   他旣不行善，又不行惡。(誤)

   他在世上固然沒做過太多善事，但他也沒有做過什麼惡事。(正)

27. He is a bookkeeper.

   他是書店老板。(誤)

   他是書局編輯。(誤)

   他是一名記賬員。(正)

28. He is a mad-doctor.

   他是個瘋醫生。(誤)

   這醫生發脾氣了。(誤)

   他是精神病醫師。(正)

29. I wish peace could be saved at the eleventh hour.

   我希望在第十一點鐘和平可以得救。(誤)

我希望在最後五分鐘可以挽囘和平 。（ 正 ）

30. I have no say in this matter, so I can't put in a word for him.
　　對於此事我是沒有話說的 ，所以就不向他提及了 。（ 誤 ）
　　我無權過問此事 ，故無法爲他美言幾句 。（ 正 ）
　　* *have no say in* " 無權過問 "　*put in a word for* …" 爲…
　　…美言 "

31. It is a wise man that never makes mistakes.
　　聰明人從來不做錯事 。（ 誤 ）
　　智者千慮必有一失 。（ 正 ）

32. I would rather have his room than his company.
　　我寧肯要他的房間 ，不要他的公司 。（ 誤 ）
　　我寧願他不在此 。（ 正 ）
　　* room 在此爲「空間」之意 ；his room 也就是「他不在」 。com-
　　pany 指「陪伴」 。

心得筆記欄

II

●Graduate

研究所英作文
拿分技巧

1. 培養英作文能力的方法

(1) **增加字彙與成語**：這兩者是一篇文章最小的單位，沒有豐富的單字，則難以下筆；沒有足夠的成語，就會使文章單調軟弱。所以充足的字彙與成語，是您揮灑自如的第一要件。

(2) **加強文法實力**：文法觀念清楚，寫起文章才能無後顧之憂。而且文法基礎穩固，才談得上修辭。

(3) **多讀多寫**：這是寫好文章亘古不變的鐵則，讀得越多和寫得越多，越能靈活運用。（請參閱 pp. 80～99 的範文）

(4) **活用基本句型**：句型是文章的骨架，因此句型使用恰當，是寫好文章的一大重點。如能靈活運用五大句型，必定能寫出像樣的文章。

(5) **熟背萬用句型及轉承語**（pp. 75～79）：這點能夠協助您快速活用句型，並將文章順暢地連貫起來，避免單調乏味。

英作文寫作要領

(1)**抓住題目的重心**——有些人寫文章洋洋灑灑一大篇，句子都正確無誤，只可惜內容散漫，層次不分，容易造成偏離主題。所以必須句句皆與主題息息相關，緊緊相扣，才能寫出好文章。

(2)**單複句混合使用**——太多單句會顯得單調、缺乏韻律感；太多複句則易造成混雜難懂。適當的輪用單句和複句，有助於語氣的承接和轉折。

(3)**善用「起承轉合」**——一篇文章或一個段落都應遵循起承轉合的順序：一開始先陳述一個較廣泛的主題，這就是「起」（開頭）；接著將細節一一詳述，這是「承」（承接）；如果遇到相對的語氣或比較時，就用「轉」（轉折）；最後，總結前面所有的陳述，而下結論，這就是「合」（綜合或總結）。這樣的文章才能上下一貫，緊緊相連。

(4)**寫完通盤檢查**——拼字、漏字、標點、單複數…等是最常發生錯誤的項目。所以最好預留幾分鐘修改時間，迅速檢查一遍，並加以修正，才能避免無畏的犧牲。

3. 英作文「起承轉合」萬用語句

　　英文作文和中文作文一樣，在語氣上有「**起、承、轉、合**」之分。一般寫英作文可分為四段，每段的開頭由表示「**起、承、轉、合**」的字詞來引導。引言段表示「起」；第一個推展段表示「承」；第二個推展段表示「轉」；結論段表示「合」。

(1) **用於文章的「起承轉合」萬用語句：**

① **常用於引言段開頭的字詞：**

A proverb says: " … "　有句諺語說：「…」

As the proverb says …　如諺語所說…

Generally speaking, …　一般說來，…

It goes without saying that …　不用說…

It is (quite) clear that …… because ……　很明顯地……因為…

It is often said that …　常常有人說…

Many people often ask this question: " … ? "

　　許多人常常問這個問題：「…？」

② **常用於第一個推展段開頭的字詞：**

Everybody knows that …　每個人都知道…

It can be easily proved that …　那是很容易證明…

It is true that …　…是真實的

No one can deny that …　誰也不能否認…

One thing which is equally important to the above mentioned

　is …　跟上述同樣重要的一項是…

The chief reason why …… is that …　為什麼…的主要原因是…

We must recognize that …　我們必須承認…

There is no doubt that …　無疑地…

I am of the opinion that …　我認為…

This can be expressed as follows:　可分為下列數點：

To take … for an example, …　以…為例，…

Therefore, we should realize that…　因此我們應該瞭解…

We have reason to believe that …　我們有理由相信…

(Now that) we know that … （既然）我們知道…

What is more serious is that … 更嚴重的是…

③ **常用於第二個推展段開頭的字詞**（語氣與第一個推展段不同或相反）：

Another special consideration in this case is that …

  對這個問題的另一考慮是…

Besides, we should not neglect that …

  除此之外，我們更不能忽視…

But it is a pity that … 但是很可惜…

But the problem is not so simple. Therefore, …

  然而問題並非如此簡單。因此，…

However, … 然而；無論如何…

Others may find this to be true, but I do not. I believe

  that … 在別人看來可能是對的,但我個人並不認為如此,我認為…

On the other hand, … 另一方面，…

Perhaps you'll question why … 也許你會問為什麼…

There is a certain amount of truth in this, but we still have

  a problem with regard to …

  這在大體上是對的，不過對於…我們還有一點問題。

Though we are in basic agreement with …

  雖然基本上我們同意…

What seems to be the trouble is … 似乎困難是在…

Yet differences will be found, that's why I feel that …

  然而其中仍有不同的地方，這也是我為什麼認為…

So long as you regard this as reasonable, you may …

  只要你認為合理，你可以…

④ **常用於結論段的字詞：**

 From this point of view, … 從這個觀點來看，…

 In a word, … 總而言之，…

 In conclusion, … 總之，…

 On account of this we can find that … 由此我們可以知道…

 The result is dependent on … 結果視…而定

Therefore, these findings reveal the following information：
　這些發現顯示下列消息：

Thus, this is the reason why we must …
　因此，這就是我們為什麼必須…

To sum up, …　總而言之，…

⑵ **用於段落的「起承轉合」萬用語句**：

　　「一個段落就像一篇迷你文章」，因此**一個段落中語氣的起、承、轉、合等的變化，大致上與一篇文章相似**。開頭常用主旨句和表示「首先」、「第一」的字詞引導；再以「接下來」、「其次」表示承接；遇到語氣轉折時用「可是」、「然而」；結尾通常用「最後」、「因此」、「總而言之」等引導結尾句表示「合」。下面是常用於段落中「起、承、轉、合」的字詞，這些字詞多用於連接句子，但有些也可用於連接段落，我們已在上一章做了詳細的說明。

① **有關「起」的常用字詞**：用來引導主旨句或跟在主旨句的後面，引導第一個推展句。

at present 現在；當今　　　in the first place 首先；第一
currently 現在；最近
it goes without saying that …　不用說…
first 首先；第一　　　　　lately 最近
first of all 首先　　　　　now 現在；目前
firstly 首先　　　　　　　presently 現在；此刻
generally speaking 一般說來　recently 最近
in the beginning 起初（的一段時間）
to begin with 首先；第一

② **有關「承」的常用字詞**：用來承接主旨句或第一個推展句。

after a few days 幾天之後　incidentally 順便一提
after a while 過了一會兒　　indeed 的確
also 並且；又　　　　　　meanwhile 於此時；此際
at any rate 無論如何　　　moreover 而且；此外

at the same time 同時（用在「轉」時作「可是」解）

no doubt 無疑地

besides（this）此外　　　　　obviously 明顯地

by this time 此時　　　　　　of course 當然

certainly 無疑地；確然地　　　particularly 特別地

consequently 因此；結果　　　second 第二；第二點

for example 例如　　　　　　secondly 第二

for instance 例如　　　　　　similarly 同樣地

for this purpose 為了這個目的　so 所以

from now on 從現在開始　　　soon 不久

furthermore 而且；此外　　　still 仍然

in addition 此外　　　　　　then 然後

in addition to … 除…之外　　third 第三；第三點

in fact 事實上　　　　　　　thirdly 第三

in other words 換句話說　　　truly 事實上；真實地

in particular 特別（地）　　　unlike … 不像…；和…不同

in the same manner 同樣地　　what is more 而且；此外

③ **有關「轉」的常用字詞**：用來表示不同或相反的語氣。

after all　畢竟　　　　　　in the same way 同樣地

all the same 雖然；但是　　　likewise 同樣地

anyway 無論如何　　　　　　luckily 幸運地

at the same time 同時；可是　nevertheless 不過；雖然如此

but 但是　　　　　　　　　no doubt 無疑地

by this time 此時　　　　　notwithstanding … 雖然

conversely 相反地　　　　　on the contrary 相反地

despite … 儘管…；雖然…　　on the other hand 另一方面

especially … 特別地…　　　otherwise 否則

fortunately 幸運地　　　　　perhaps … 或許…

however 然而；無論如何　　　unfortunately 不幸地

in other words 換句話說　　　unlike … 不像…；和…不同

in particular 特別地　　　　whereas … 然而

in spite of … 儘管…；雖然　yet 仍；然而；但是

④ **有關「合」的常用字詞：**用來引導結尾句或最後一個推展句，表示段落的結束。

above all 最重要的是	hence 因此
accordingly 於是	in brief 簡言之
as a consequence 因此	in conclusion 最後；總之
as a result 結果	in short 簡言之
as has been noted 如前所述及	in sum 總之；簡言之
as I have said 如我所述	in summary 摘要之
at last 最後	on the whole 就全體而論；整個看來
at length 最後；終於	therefore 因此
by and large 一般說來	thus 因此
briefly 簡單扼要地	to speak frankly 坦白地說
by doing so 藉此	to sum up 總言之
consequently 因此	to summarize 摘要之
eventually 最後	
finally 最後	

5. 研究所英作文實例 (1)

Why I Want to Attend Graduate School

我爲何想唸研究所

I would like to attend graduate school because I take great pleasure in studying and because I know there are many areas of academic research that are waiting to be explored. Although I have just spent four years at college, I have only just begun to scratch the surface of the field in which I took my major — linguistics.

我之所以想唸研究所，是因爲自己對唸書有莫大興趣，我知道學海無涯，學術領域中有許多待探索的知識。雖然我剛唸完四年大學，就我主修的語言學而言，只是開始它最表面的研究罷了。

From my college education, I have learned how to form my own opinions, think independently and how to analyze a complex situation. Being a student of linguistics, I have iearned how to search for linguistic truth. I am no longer satisfied with just attending lectures and I hope I can work by myself to further my knowledge of linguistic problems. *I strongly believe that* graduate school can provide me with a proper environment in which I am able to engage in my studies.

從大學教育中，我學會了獨立思考、判斷以及分析複雜問題的方法。身爲語言學的學生，我已學會如何尋求語言學的眞相。單單聽課已無法滿足我，而我希望能靠自己的研究增進語言學方面的知識。我深信研究所能給我一個投身研究工作的適當環境。

I do not, *of course*, merely desire to be a specialist. Should I become a graduate student, I will set aside some time to read books that are concerned with various aspects of life and different fields of learning. Graduate school is the place which will enable me to live the kind of life that I have always wanted to live, and so that is why I want to attend it.

當然，我並不只希望成爲一個語言專家。如果我能成爲研究生，我會抽空閱覽關於人生百態及各方面知識的書籍。研究所是一個能使我過自己一直想過的生活的地方。這就是我想唸研究所的原因。

linguistics〔lɪŋ′gwɪstɪks〕*n.* 語言學
further〔′fɜðɚ〕*v.* 促進；增進
specialist〔′spɛʃəlɪst〕*n.* 專家

研究所英作文實例 ⑵

Cultivating Good Reading Habits

培養良好的讀書習慣

In order to gain more knowledge, it is very important to be able to read effectively. Cultivating reading habits will enhance our ability to read and understand more, and by doing so we will be encouraged to read even more books.

爲了獲得更多的知識，如何才能有效地閱讀是非常重要的。培養良好的讀書習慣，會提高我們閱讀和理解的能力，這樣我們將會受到激勵去讀更多的書。

On the whole, it is very important to know what types of books we should read. *By and large*, we should read good literature as well as books of a professional nature. This should provide the mind with a stimulus for ideas as well as a well-rounded field of knowledge. While an occasional popular novel can provide a diversion, it should not constitute the major part of the literary diet. *Otherwise*, the mind will be constrained. Nor should professional reading matter be limited to a narrow specialty. *Rather*, reading professional

大致上來說，了解我們應該閱讀那些類型的書是十分重要的。大體而言，我們應該閱讀上乘的文學作品以及專業知識的書籍。這樣可以激發內心的靈感，以及提供各方面兼備的知識。雖然偶爾看點通俗小說可以提供娛樂，然而不足以構成文學大餐的主要角色。否則，心智的發展就會受到束縛。專業性的閱讀也不該限制於狹隘的專門研究。的確，閱讀專業性的體材，包括相關的

materials in related fields may provide just the right perspective for
solving a problem in one's area of
special interest. We should also ensure
that we have a quiet, well-lit place to
read in, and that we position the reading materials at least twelve inches
from the eyes in order to avoid strain.

領域，可能僅僅在個人特殊的興趣範圍提供解決問題的正確看法。同時我們要確信自己在一個安靜，光線良好的地方讀書，並且將書本置於離眼至少十二英吋的地方，以避免眼睛過度疲勞。

To summarize, good reading habits
will help to ensure our mental processes
remain at their peak. Not only will
we learn more about the world around
us, we will also learn more about ourselves.

總而言之，良好的閱讀習慣會幫助我們確使心智發展維持高峯狀態。我們不但會多了解周遭的世界，而且也會多了解自己。

enhance〔ɪnˈhæns〕*vt.* 提高
on the whole = by and large 大體而言
professional〔prəˈfɛʃənl〕*a.* 專業的
diversion〔dəˈvɝʒən, daɪ-, -ʃən〕*n.* 娛樂
stimulus〔ˈstɪmjələs〕*n.* 刺激
constrain〔kənˈstren〕*v.* 受束縛
constitute〔ˈkɑnstə,tjut〕*vt.* 構成

研究所英作文實例 (3)

The Choice of Companions

擇　友

It is often said that a man is known by the company he keeps. *Obviously*, it is very important to take great care when choosing friends.

常聽人說：觀其友可知其人。顯然地，謹愼擇友是十分重要的。

Good friends are always kind and polite, and willing to help in times of need. An oft-quoted proverb says, " A friend in need is a friend indeed. " A true friend then stands by you when it is not popular to do so. Truly good friends are patient with, and accept, our shortcomings, and of course, trustworthy enough to share our innermost secrets with. Having good friends is especially important for students because our school years are the period in our lives when we learn about social relationships outside the family.

好的朋友總是心地善良而溫和有禮，並且樂於患難相助。有句常被引用的俗語說得好，「患難見眞情。」一個眞實的朋友會在不利的情況下支持你。眞正地好朋友總是容忍並且接納彼此的缺點，當然也值得信賴來分享我們心田深處的秘密。結交好朋友對學生來說特別重要。因爲我們的學生時代是我們一生中學習家庭以外的社交關係的重要階段。

Bad friends, *however*, should be avoided at all costs. Such so-called

壞朋友無論如何得避得遠遠的。這種所謂的朋友會

friends will flatter you to your face, but *at the same time* gossip about you behind your back. *Moreover*, when you are in crisis, they will leave you as rats depart a sinking ship. What is more, such " fair weather friends " will deny even knowing you！

當面奉承你，同時在你的背後中傷你。再說，當你遇到困難時，他們會離你而去有如樹倒猢猻散。而且，這種「見風轉舵的朋友」甚至矢口否認有你這個朋友！

In summary, a true friend is not easy to find, and, once found, should be nurtured as one would a rare plant, for they have the ability to lift you above your limitations.

總而言之，一個眞心的朋友可遇不可求，可是一旦找到了，應該像培育珍奇花木般地珍惜，因爲他們有能力提昇你的境界。

at all cost 無論作多大的犧牲
flatter〔ˈflætɚ〕*vt.* 奉承
gossip〔ˈgɑsəp〕*v.* 說閒話
crisis〔ˈkraɪsɪs〕*n.* 危機
nurture〔ˈnɝtʃɚ〕*v.* 養育

學習出版，天天進步

研究所英作文實例 (4)

The Advantages and Disadvantages of Modern Civilization

現代文明的利與弊

Undoubtedly, modern civilization benefits us a lot, yet it still leads us to destruction. What on earth are the advantages and disadvantages of modern civilization?

毫無疑問地，現代文明使我們受益良多，可是它依然帶領著我們走向毀滅。究竟現代文明的利與弊何在呢？

Modern civilization brings to us convenience, progress, prosperity and comfort. Modern aircraft transport us from our homes to the other side of the world in a matter of hours. Advanced medicine releases us from the threat of disease and death. Numerous inventions help us out in many ways, and enable us to live more comfortably than was ever possible before. Modern civilization develops the domain of human knowledge and gives us a greater degree of self-realization.

現代文明帶給我們便利，進步，繁榮與舒適。現今的飛機將我們從家鄉運送到世界的另一端在短短幾個小時之內。進步的醫學將我們從疾病和死亡中拯救出來。無可數計的發明在各方面爲我們解決困難，使我們能夠過著前人所無法享受的舒適生活。現代文明拓展了人類知識的領域而且帶給我們更大的自我實現的能力。

Nevertheless, it is accompanied by a lot of negative forces—doubt, anxiety, pollution, *and worst of all*, human de-

然而，隨著文明而來的是許多負面的效果——疑慮、憂懼、污染，最糟的是人類

generation. Modernized transport increases the speed of transportation,
but the pace causes anxiety. The
aggressive spirit of modern civilization leads to suspicion and distrust.
Many inventions bring about the pollution of our environment as well as
of the human mind. We have lost our
souls and have fallen victims to the
forces of materialism.

的沈淪。現代運輸工具加快
了運輸的步調，但同時導致
了焦慮。現代文明的積進精
神反帶來了懷疑和不信任。
許多發明帶來的是環境和人
類心靈的污染。我們的靈魂
已迷失且成為唯物主義的犧
牲品。

Every coin has two sides. *It
goes without saying that* both advantages and disadvantages exist in
our modern civilization. What is most
important is the way in which we
use it. How can we take control of
it instead of being dominated by it ?

硬幣都有正反兩面。因
此現代文明之利弊兼具是自
不待說的。而最重要的是我
們如何去應用它，如何控制
它而不致於反被支配。

convenience [kən'vinjəns] *n.* 方便；適合
prosperity [pras'pɛrətɪ] *n.* 繁榮
degeneration [dɪ,dʒɛnə'reʃən] *n.* 退化；墮落

研究所英作文實例 (5)

| The Influence of Modern Communication | 現代傳播通訊的影響 |

The only way to exchange messages in the old days was to talk to others face to face, or to write a letter to others. Those ways of communicating took a lot of time and effort. However, time is money today, and that's the reason why modern communication is highly developed and has rapidly advanced.

從前人們交換訊息的唯一方法，就是走向對方面對面溝通，或是寫封信給對方。這些溝通訊息的方法似乎是時間及精力的一種耗費。然而到了今天，由於時間就是金錢，現代通訊因而高度發展且迅速進步。

Based on the human ear, men have invented the telephone and radio, which can transmit sounds over long distances without impairing quality. *Therefore*, people can frequently keep in touch, while still separated by a long distance. *Besides*, in a state of emergency, *for example*, if there is a fire, we can save lives before it is too late by calling 119.

由耳朵，人類產生構思而發明了電話和收音機，來傳送長途的聲音而不損音質。因此，人們即使相隔甚遠，也能常常保持連繫。此外，在緊急的情況下，例如火災發生時，我們能及時打119求援以挽救生命。

Based on the human eye, we have television and computers which, unlike

由眼睛，我們發明了電視和電腦。不同於電話及收

the telephone and radio, can deliver news and knowledge in the form of an image. *Of these*, the computer has become the most popular modern invention in the world because it can provide us with up-to-date information to help us buy food , read newspapers, work and study, and so on. *Thus*, we can stay at home in comfort and let the computer solve all our problems.

音機的是，它們能藉著影像傳送新聞及知識。而其中，電腦又是世界上最受歡迎的發明，因為它能提供我們最新的消息，在購物、閱報、工作與讀書等方面協助我們。因而，我們只要舒舒服服地待在家裏，電腦就能替我們解決所有的問題。

To sum up, the influence of modern communication is great and significant. *Due to modern technology* , people can hear and see what they want to know more easily and in a shorter time as well as keep pace with the rapid changes in society.

　總而言之，現代通訊的影響深遠且廣泛。人們能在更短的時間內更容易地聽到或看到他們想知道的，且得以與社會急遽的改變同步，當歸功於現代科技。

communication 〔kə͵mjunə'keʃən〕 *n*. 傳播；通訊
impair 〔ɪm'pɛr〕 *v*. 損害
information 〔͵ɪnfɚ'meʃən〕 *n*. 消息；知識

研究所英作文實例 (6)

Science and Literature　　　　　科 學 與 文 學

　　At first sight, science and literature seem poles apart, because the
former is logical and full of order,
while the latter is flexible and full
of feeling. *However*, on closer examination, we find in both of them
the gradual progress made by human
beings. Although their functions differ,
they do not contradict each other but
can develop alongside each other.

　　Science can help men discover all
truths and phenomena by means of
analyzing or synthesizing matters in
disarray. *By putting science into practice*, the secrets of man and the
universe are easily unravelled and, *moreover*, it can lead people to live a more
convenient life. *In the same way*, literature can enrich our imagination and
enable us to cultivate a better tem-
perament and thus can influence man's
mind and heart. Literature, like med-

　　乍看之下，科學和文學
似是差得天南地北，因為科
學重邏輯和秩序，而文學則
自由而感性。然而如果細想，
我們會發現它們都是人類進
步的痕跡。雖然目的不同，
但不致相互抵觸，反倒能相
輔相成。

　　科學能幫助人類在雜亂
無章的事物中，藉著分析、
綜合等方法，發掘種種事實
和現象。把科學付諸實際生
活，則能輕易地解開人類和
宇宙的奧祕，甚至能使人過
著更舒適便利的生活。同樣
地，把文學溶入生活，則能
豐富我們的想像，陶冶我們
的性情，進而影響我們的心
智。當人們進入文學的世界
時，就像吃藥一般，文學讓

icine, can help people forget their
unhappiness and troubles as they take
refuge in a good book.

人忘卻一切的煩憂。

In general, the function of scient
is direct and conspicuous, while that of
literature function is indirect and obscure.
Unfortunately, *near-sighted* people
often abandon literature to pursue science. This kind of prejudice does harm
to human welfare. Science is like the
body, and literature is like the soul
and neither of them can be gotten rid
of. *In fact*, science fiction enlarges the
field of science, and, *at the same time*,
helps us to study literature's structure
and development. *Accordingly*, let us
regard science and literature as equally
important as we build a harmonious and
advanced world.

一般而言，科學的功能
直接而顯著，而文學的功能
卻間接而隱晦。不幸的是，
一些短視近利的人常棄文學
而就科學。這種偏見實破壞
了人類的福祉，因爲若把科
學比爲身體，則文學就是靈
魂，兩者的關係是密不可分
的。不但如此，科學小說反
而擴大了科學的領域，且同
時幫助我們探討文學結構和
發展。因此，我們應賦予科
學和文學以平等的重視，來
創造一個和諧進步的世界。

disarray 〔,dɪsə're〕 *n.* 雜亂；無秩序
unravel 〔ʌn'rævl̩〕 *v.* 解開
conspicuous 〔kəns'pikjuəs〕 *adj.* 顯而易見的

研究所英作文實例 (7)

The Responsibilities of an Intellectual

A farmer has to sow and plow so as to reap. *Similarly*, a worker has to sweat and labor to earn his living and a merchant calculates his profit and loss to make ends meet. They all play an important role in society, making it a more comfortable and enjoyable place to be in. What, then, can an intellectual do to reciprocate for all of these acts? As he doesn't have to sow, to sweat, or to maintain accounts, he makes contact with the abstract more than with the practical, and with theory more than with reality.

Therefore, deep in his mind, he still cherishes an ideal which has not yet been polluted by money, power, or greed. This is the most precious thing he possesses, the thing which he can use to benefit society. There is no

一個知識分子的責任

農夫必須播種、耕耘，才有收獲。同樣地，工人必得辛勤工作以維持生計，而商人估量盈虧以平衡收支。這些人都扮演著極重要的角色，他們使我們的社會成為一個更適合居住的安身之所。然而，身為一個知識分子，該如何來回饋眾生呢？知識分子既不須耕田，也不須作苦工，甚或為錢疲於奔命。他接觸的事物抽象多於實際，理論多於現實。

也正因如此，在內心深處他仍懷著一份未被金錢、權利或貪婪所玷污的理想。這就是他所有最珍貴的東西，以此他得以改善這個社會。毋庸置疑地，知識若不被清

doubt, *of course*, that knowledge could be abused if not employed by a man of purity. If knowledge is correctly transformed into reality, it would surely benefit human beings.

心的人所用，則知識可能被濫用。而知識如果能正確地用於實際的事物上，它就必定能造福人群。

An intellectual has also been endowed with the reponsibility to reclaim society from vice. Though he doesn't seem to have any money, his words are of the same value, and carry the same power that a president might have. *Therefore*, just like a soldier stands in front in a war, an intellectual stands in front in society, ready to immerse himself in the world to resist evil and empower the weak.

知識分子負有匡正時局的責任。雖然他看似貧困，但他的言語字字珠璣，其力量更不遜於一個總統。因此，就如同兵士站在戰爭的前線一樣，知識分子站在社會的第一線上，時時準備投身於大眾，做隱惡揚善、濟弱扶傾的先鋒。

calculte〔ˈkælkjə,let〕*v.* 計算；估算
reciprocate〔rɪˈsɪprə,ket〕*v.* 回報；報答
reclaim〔rɪˈklem〕*v.* 糾正；匡正

研究所英作文實例 (8)

We Are the World

四 海 一 家

When God first created the world, many thousands of years ago, it was full of compassion, peace, and love. *At that time* there were luxurious lands and people had pure minds. *But then* man was tempted to sin and vice overcame virtue. *Today* we no longer live in Eden; we've lost it forever.

千萬年前，神初創天地時，世界尚充滿同情、和平和愛。那時土地生產豐碩，人類心靈滌淨。直到人受引誘而犯罪，邪惡勝正。於是今日的我們再尋不回昔日的伊甸園，而求遠失去那段純潔的時光了。

Even in absolute darkness there still can be light and warmth so long as there burns a little candle. A candle burns to lighten the world. It never asks for anything but always seeks to give. If we're all candles, darkness will surely be driven out. It is our duty as well as our right to shine as bright lights in the darkness. " There lives no beast but knows a touch of pity." Being able to sacrifice makes us noble and unbending.

然而，在全然的黑暗之中，只要一根小小的蠟燭還在燃燒，就會有光和熱。它燃燒自己來照亮整個世界，它從不要求報酬，只是不斷地付出。如果我們都能成為世上的蠟燭，就定能驅走黑暗。這不僅是我們的責任，更是我們的權利。「就是禽獸也還有一絲憐憫之心。」由於人能犧牲小我，他就比野獸更尊貴而剛毅不屈。

Thus , while we ourselves are

因此，當我們自身受到

suffering from pain and sorrows, let us believe that we are not alone. *Somewhere in the world*, there are people who need care and love more than we do. *So* let us refresh ourselves and be ready to give, —— not just of our material possessions but equally of ourselves. When we do so, we are truly saving our own lives！

痛苦憂愁的煎熬時，我們要知道自己並不孤單，在世界的某處，還有比我們更需要關懷與愛心的人。讓我們振作起來，隨時準備付出——不僅在物質上我們付出，更在精神上奉獻自我。而當我們如此犧牲自己時，我們實已完成了自我的救贖！

compassion〔kəmˊpæʃən〕*n*. 憐憫；同情
absolute〔ˊæbsə‚lut〕*adj*. 純粹的；完全的
sacrifice〔ˊsækrə‚faɪs〕*v*. 犧牲；獻身

研究所英作文實例 (9)

Reading Newspapers

閱 讀 報 紙

Reading newspapers is a way of informing ourselves of what is happening in the world. Since this is a world in which everything changes and progresses at an incredible speed, one can't keep up with the times without reading a newspaper everyday. Such daily habits will enrich our understanding and knowledge of life and the world.

Generally speaking, a newspaper is divided into many sections. The first page usually consists of the news about political or economic decisions made by the government or international events. *Next* comes the editional page featuring one or two editorials which present views concerning matters of political, economic or social importance. Other pages are devoted to sports news, social news, features, advertisements and essays.

閱報是使我們獲悉世界時事的一種途徑。由於今日的世界每天以令人難以置信的速度，不斷改變和進步，所以不每天閱報的人，便跟不上時代潮流。養成每天閱報的習慣，可以增廣見聞並擴大我們的心胸。

一般而言，一份報紙通常分成許多版面。第一版包括政治新聞、政府的經濟決策或國際事件。接下來的第二版，是以一兩則有關政經或社會新聞的社論為其特色。其餘各版則涵蓋各樣新聞，體育新聞、社會新聞、演藝界特稿、專欄、漫畫、甚至廣告、小品文，無所不包。

The headlines in a newspaper immediately give us the highlights of things which are of great importance. We can read the headlines first and then decide whether to go into greater detail or not. Some people read only the headlines, and some people go through every story and even the classified advertising. ***Perhaps***, for some people, at least, reading a newspaper helps to pass the time away. No matter what our purpose in reading a newspaper is, newspaper-reading has become a necessary part of modern life. No one in this day and age wants to be behind the times.

　　新聞的標題可直接突出其重點。所以我們可先讀標題，再決定是否詳閱內容。有的人習慣只讀標題，有的人無所不看，包括分類廣告在內。也許對某些人而言，閱讀報紙至少是打發時間的一種方法吧。而無論我們閱報的動機目的何在，它已是今日生活中不可或缺的部分。這個時代的人，大都不想落伍吧。

editorial 〔͵ɛdə'torɪəl〕 *adj*. 編輯的 *n*. 社論
feature 〔'fitʃɚ〕 *n*. 演藝特寫、專欄或漫畫
highlight 〔'haɪ͵laɪt〕 *n*. 最精采、顯著的部分

研究所英作文實例 ⑽

To Learn from Failure

從失敗中記取教訓

Ever since I was a small child, I have been taught not to fail, but rather to be a winner in everything. ***However,*** I gradually found out that it was impossible to succeed in everything. The fear of failure haunted me day and night, I was too accustomed to success to know how to accept failure.

自童年起，大人就教我不可失敗，無論什麼事都要以勝利者的姿態出現。然而，漸漸地我發覺永遠要做贏家是不可能的。害怕遭受失敗的恐懼如鬼魅般教我日夜不安。對於成功我早已習以為常，反而不知如何接受失敗了。

" I'm not better, I'm just different." I have spent some twenty years slowly realizing that I am not a god, but just an ordinary man, who is bound to fail at some time or another. This revelation releases me from all the fears that used to fetter my mind. The past twenty years of my life may have been years of failure, but they have not been years spent in vain. ***Now*** I know how to face failure and, ***moreover,*** I have at the same time discovered how to learn from failure and thus gain most valuable experience.

「人的價值不在於他比別人優秀，而在於他獨特的存在。」活了這二十年的歲月，我終於領悟這個道理，清楚自己並不是神，而只是一個再平凡不過，時時會犯錯的人。這個啟示終將我從禁錮心靈已久的恐懼中釋放出來。過去的廿年也許是一種失敗，但這段歲月並非徒然。它使我終於學會面對失敗，更重要的是，我同時學會了從失敗中記取教訓，從而獲得最寶貴的經驗。

Learning from our present failures is the best way of avoiding failures in the future. It is impossible to fail all the time if we learn from our past failures. *Therefore*, the way to be successful in our lives is to learn from our failures and to make every achievement the beginning of another step forward.

從眼前的失敗記取教訓，是避免將來失敗的最好方法。能從過去失敗的經驗中虛心學習，就不會永遠失敗。因此，以失敗爲前車之鑑，且莫忘百尺竿頭更進一步，當是通向成功的大道！

haunt〔 hɔnt 〕v. 縈繞於心
fetter〔 ˊfɛtɚ 〕v. 束縛；限制
revelation〔 ˏrɛvlˊeʃən 〕n. 啓示

新一代英語教科書・領先全世界

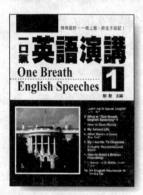  

學習語言以口說為主・是全世界的趨勢

|||||||||||||||| ●學習出版公司門市部 ●|||||||||||||||||

台北地區：台北市許昌街 10 號 2 樓 TEL：(02)2331-4060・2331-9209
台中地區：台中市綠川東街 32 號 8 樓 23 室
TEL：(04)2223-2838

||||||||||||||||||||||||||||||||||||||||||||||||||||

研究所英文試題詳解②

主　　編／謝　靜　芳
發 行 所／學習出版有限公司　　　　☎ (02) 2704-5525
郵 撥 帳 號／0512727-2 學習出版社帳戶
登 記 證／局版台業 2179 號
印 刷 所／裕強彩色印刷有限公司
台 北 門 市／台北市許昌街 10 號 2 F　　☎ (02) 2331-4060・2331-9209
台 中 門 市／台中市綠川東街 32 號 8 F 23 室　　☎ (04) 2223-2838
台灣總經銷／紅螞蟻圖書有限公司　　☎ (02) 2795-3656
美國總經銷／Evergreen Book Store　　☎ (818) 2813622
本公司網址　www.learnbook.com.tw
電 子 郵 件　learnbook@learnbook.com.tw

售價：新台幣四百八十元正

2005 年 1 月 1 日一版二刷

ISBN 957-519-620-1　　　　　　　　　　　　版權所有・翻印必究